MW00984567

WRITERS REPUBLIC

Odyssey of a Phoenix

DOWN IN FLAMES

By
Jed Morgan

WRITERS REPUBLIC L.L.C.
515 Summit Ave. Unit R1
Union City, NJ 07087, USA

Website: *www.writersrepublic.com*
Hotline: *1-877-656-6838*
Email: *info@writersrepublic.com*

Ordering Information:
Quantity sales. Special discounts are available on quantity purchases by corporations, associations, and others. For details, contact the publisher at the address above.

Library of Congress Control Number: 2021909023
ISBN-13:   978-1-63728-505-3   [Paperback Edition]
                  978-1-63728-534-3   [Hardback Edition]
                  978-1-63728-506-0   [Digital Edition]

Rev. date: 05/19/2021

Dedicated to

the many Airmen who have taken their own lives,

failed by the country they defend.

TABLE OF CONTENTS

PROLOGUE XI

PART 1: THE AEGIS 1

    CHAPTER 1: COLD STEEL...3
    CHAPTER 2: DEATH OF A HERO...8
    CHAPTER 3: THOSE LEFT BEHIND..11
    CHAPTER 4: THE ENDLESS HOWLING..17
    CHAPTER 5: BIRDS OF A FEATHER 20
    CHAPTER 6: LEGACY 28

PART 2: APOLLO 37

    CHAPTER 7: NOT WORTH THE HURT...39
    CHAPTER 8: INQUISITIONS PAST 44
    CHAPTER 9: GAY FOR PAY 49
    CHAPTER 10: FIRST STEPS 56
    CHAPTER 11: RUBBLE OF AN OLD LIFE...62
    CHAPTER 12: FAMILY LEADS 67
    CHAPTER 13: GODS OF PREJUDICE 70
    CHAPTER 14: LOVE'S SHADOW...79
    CHAPTER 15: A WITCH'S DESIRE 84
    CHAPTER 16: TO BE OR NOT TO BE 91
    CHAPTER 17: MEAGER FAITH 94
    CHAPTER 18: TEARS OF A FATHER...98

PART 3: HERMES...101

    CHAPTER 19: NOT MADE FOR BLISS 103
    CHAPTER 20: BROODING LIES...105
    CHAPTER 21: SOCIALLY AWKWARD 108
    CHAPTER 22: DRUNK PERSONA...112
    CHAPTER 23: PRAYERS ANSWERED 117
    CHAPTER 24: BURN!...123
    CHAPTER 25: DYING LIGHT 125
    CHAPTER 26: ROAD TRUTHS 128
    CHAPTER 27: GOD OF TRAVELERS 131
    CHAPTER 28: FOR THOSE WE'VE LOVED 134
    CHAPTER 29: TORTURE FOR THE GOOD..138
    CHAPTER 30: BLURRED HISTORY 144

PART 4: DIONYSUS...151

    CHAPTER 31: ANCIENT NEEDS 153
    CHAPTER 32: DAYDREAMS..156
    CHAPTER 33: MY FAIR LADY 159
    CHAPTER 34: BEING POSH 162
    CHAPTER 35: CHANGING PARTS 168
    CHAPTER 36: MODERN DYSPHORIA 173
    CHAPTER 37: HIDDEN SON 176

CHAPTER 38: VEILED CONFUSION 179
CHAPTER 39: RUNNING OF THE BULLS 182
CHAPTER 40: TRIBAL SCHOLAR 187
CHAPTER 41: MOUNT NYSA 191
CHAPTER 42: DRAGONSLAYER 197

PART 5: HEPHAESTUS 205

CHAPTER 43: LIQUID COURAGE 207
CHAPTER 44: PHANTOM OF THE WICKED.......................................210
CHAPTER 45: LITTLE ORPHAN TY 214
CHAPTER 46: FACING THE SHADOW 217
CHAPTER 47: ANGEL ON OUR SHOULDER 225
CHAPTER 48: STRIKING STEEL 230
CHAPTER 49: ANOTHER ROUND 235
CHAPTER 50: REPRESSED LOVE 240
CHAPTER 51: MUTUALLY ASSURED ENDS.....................................246
CHAPTER 52: WAR GAMES 250
CHAPTER 53: WORLD WAR III 256
CHAPTER 54: AMONG US 261

PART 6: HERA 265

CHAPTER 55: THE WAY, TRUTH, AND LIFE 267
CHAPTER 56: SKELETONS OF BELIEF 272
CHAPTER 57: MOTHERHOOD 277
CHAPTER 58: THE IMPOSSIBLE CHILD...282
CHAPTER 59: INTO THAT GOOD NIGHT 285
CHAPTER 60: DARK DISEASE 289

PART 7: ARES 293

CHAPTER 61: STRANDED..295
CHAPTER 62: INNER NELLY 298
CHAPTER 63: SEEN HORNS 303
CHAPTER 64: VOID WITHIN 307
CHAPTER 65: SELF ODYSSEY...311
CHAPTER 66: TEMPTED NORMAL 316
CHAPTER 67: CRUSADE...319
CHAPTER 68: RAINING MORTARS..322
CHAPTER 69: SELF OR FUTURE 328
CHAPTER 70: SWORD OF A HUN 332
CHAPTER 71: MASTER SMITH 335
CHAPTER 72: TO BE 300 339

PART 8: APHRODITE 345

CHAPTER 73: ANCESTRY..347
CHAPTER 74: BE NOT BLIND...350
CHAPTER 75: WEBS OF REGRET 353
CHAPTER 76: SCARRED BEAUTY 357
CHAPTER 77: LOVE AND HATE...362
CHAPTER 78: DENIED CRAVING 369

PART 9: HESTIA 375

    Chapter 79: Clara 377

    Chapter 80: Robbed Hell 384

    Chapter 81: Family Ties 387

    Chapter 82: Consequences of Lust 393

    Chapter 83: Hearth Fire 396

    Chapter 84: Rabid Titan 401

PART 10: DEMETER 409

    Chapter 85: Love Betrays 411

    Chapter 86: Denied Forgiveness 415

    Chapter 87: Rat in the House 419

    Chapter 88: Precious Dove 421

    Chapter 89: Truth Will Out 424

    Chapter 90: Matricide 439

PART 11: ARTEMIS 443

    Chapter 91: Ignorance was Bliss 445

    Chapter 92: Falling for Her 448

    Chapter 93: Second Start 452

    Chapter 94: Marias River 455

    Chapter 95: Starlight 461

    Chapter 96: Eitr 466

PART 12: POSEIDON 471

    Chapter 97: A Father's Love 473

    Chapter 98: Embraced Passion 476

    Chapter 99: Playing Detective 480

    Chapter 100: Land Shark 483

    Chapter 101: Blood of a Dolphin 489

    Chapter 102: Strength of Belief 493

PART 13: ZEUS 497

    Chapter 103: Foreign Delights 499

    Chapter 104: Twilight Choice 504

    Chapter 105: The King of Wall Street 507

    Chapter 106: Living 510

    Chapter 107: Eat, Drink, and be Merry 515

    Chapter 108: The Bolt 521

    Chapter 109: First to Love the Same 524

    Chapter 110: Guiltless Murder 528

    Chapter 111: Misconstrued 532

    Chapter 112: Securing Fate 539

    Chapter 113: Pain vs. Hate 543

    Chapter 114: A Needed Lie 547

PART 14: HADES..**551**

Chapter 115: Making Gods Fear 553

Chapter 116: Impossible Mission 558

Chapter 117: Childlike Wants 561

Chapter 118: The Land Below 565

Chapter 119: Gargantuan...569

Chapter 120: We Believe 572

PART 15: ATHENA **581**

Chapter 121: Unforgiving Sam 583

Chapter 122: Council of Fire 587

Chapter 123: Mortal Nights...592

Chapter 124: Mother of Maidenhood 595

Chapter 125: The Price of Heroism 598

Chapter 126: Still Victim 604

Chapter 127: Deals Made.. 606

Chapter 128: Messiah Lost 610

Chapter 129: Engines of War 613

Chapter 130: The Siege of Olympus 616

Chapter 131: The Final Yard 626

Chapter 132: Down in Flames 629

EPILOGUE **633**

PROLOGUE

Selena Wilhelm, world-famous tennis champion, renowned philanthropist, beloved celebrity, and the lonely Greek goddess Nike. The fallen goddess of victory nurses a beer in a dilapidated Irish pub in downtown Boston, alone and ignored by all there save one drunk with a taste for lonely women. The drunk slides into the barstool next to Selena, her smile broadening when she recognizes Selena; she gushes, "Holy shit. It's you, isn't it?"

Selena doesn't even turn to acknowledge the drunk, replying, "You must be thinking of someone else."

"I don't think so. You're Selena Wilhelm, the tennis champion."

Selena's body tenses ever so slightly before she mutters, "I'm no champion."

"That's right. You lost to Hilary Carnegie today, didn't you?"

Selena tightens her jaw and takes a swig of beer to calm herself, muttering, "Your tact is astounding." She downs the rest of her beer and orders another.

The drunk looks up and down Selena's body, biting her lip and taking in all her beautiful curves. "I'm Karmen, and you look like you need some cheering up. Why don't you come back to my place, and I'll fuck those perfect tits off you?"

"I'm not interested."

Karmen slides off her stool, grabs Selena's arm, and commands, "I think you are."

Selena reaches over and grips Karmen's wrist with lightning speed, twisting it at an awkward angle to pop it, making her scream. Selena shoves her to the stained floor and turns back to her beer, taking a sip as if nothing has happened. "Fuck off."

Karmen struggles to her feet, retreating to her friends. The bartender pulls out a shot glass, filling it for Selena. She objects, "I didn't order that."

"It's on the house. That bastard is a pain in my ass. I've already had to drag her off 2 girls tonight. I thought I'd have to do the same for you, but you can handle yourself."

"Why haven't you thrown her out?"

"She's the boss's daughter. I could lose my job if I mess with her."

"That must suck."

"She's actually a good kid when she's not drinking, but her fiancée just died." The bartender sighs, grabbing a rag to wipe down the counter, adding, "She's been in here every night since."

Karmen and a group of her friends walk up behind Selena; a barrel of a man towering over the others taps her on the shoulder, which she ignores. He growls, "I think you owe my friend an apology."

"Is she too much of a cunt to ask for herself?"

"The fuck you just say?"

Selena finishes her drink, stands, and turns to Karmen and her friends, repeating, "I said, is she too much of a cunt to ask for her own fucking apology?"

"Fuck, you."

The drunk takes a swing at Selena, which she easily sidesteps. The bartender just leans back with a rag and a glass to watch the fight unfold. Selena is soon standing over the unconscious bodies of Karmen and her friends. "Holy shit," the bartender whispers, impressed.

"Fuck lot of good you were," Selena fires back with a glare.

"You had it under control."

She picks up her bag, pays her bill, and heads toward the door, saying, "Feel free to jump in next time."

Once she's stormed out, he stares down at his comatose customers. A moan comes from under the bar, drawing his attention to the real bartender bound and gagged. The imposter draws a knife and throws it down to impale the floor, inches from the bartender's face, offering him freedom if he can just reach it. Quickly untying his apron and hanging it up, the mysterious enigma follows Selena.

***

Barely surviving her drive home, Selena unlocks her home door and walks in, turning on the lights. She grabs a beer from the fridge, unseeing of the imposter standing in the shadows behind her.

"It's a nice place you've got, Nike," the imposter whispers.

Selena doesn't even flinch, replying, "Glad you let yourself in, Atlas." She never looks at the intruder; she just shuffles through her kitchen to make herself a sandwich.

Atlas hefts his mighty ax, explaining, "This is the key to unlock any door."

"Timorian send you?"

The name 'Timorian' hangs in the air like something forbidden. Atlas tenses slightly, condemning, "He really doesn't like to be called that."

Selena scoffs slightly under her breath, muttering, "Forgive me if I don't adhere to my executioner's every whim."

"Oh, I'll be filling that role today."

Selena freezes, turning to look at Atlas for the first time, surprise in her eyes. "Really? I thought he liked to do these sorts of things himself. Make sure the job is done."

"He has been a little preoccupied the last few years."

"He finally meet his lady love?"

He smiles slightly, amused at how accurate Selena's guess is. "In a manner of speaking."

Selena takes a large bite from her sandwich and finishes her beer before turning back to Atlas, noting, "Gotta go some time. I can't always win."

"No, you can't."

Atlas swings the butt of his ax up into Selena's chin, knocking her out cold. He stares down at her still form, sadness filling his eyes at the senseless and pointless violence required of him. Sighing, he kneels to bind her still form.

A loud ringing builds, filling the room and making Atlas's hair stand on end. He turns to stare out a window into the night sky. Somethings changed. He can feel it. There's godly power in the world again. An age-old war is about to begin anew.

Part 1:

THE ÆGIS

CHAPTER 1: COLD STEEL

<u>Arien</u>

Cold! I'm just so cold. An icy wave of fear floods through me, making me shiver, despite the warm Arizona breeze blowing through my window. Frostbite traces through my chest, emanating from the cold steel of the 9mm Glock cradled in my hands. The Glock which will end all my pain; end the cold. My eyes drift up to the slow, methodical spinning of the ceiling fan, briefly losing myself in its entrancing rotations.

I shake my head, turning to stare into my reflection in the mirror mounted on my unassuming shit-brown wall. A solitary string out of place catches my attention on my otherwise immaculate Air Force dress blues. Staring at it for a moment, I reach up to remove it; after I adjust my tie, I take a deep breath, a single tear leaking out of the corner of my eye. I'm afraid, so afraid, but my resolve is firm. I know this is what I need to finally find peace, or perhaps to find merely pure emptiness. There's no other way on the gods' green Earth for me to be happy. I've tried everything I could to get over my demons. No amount of pills, talking, or distractions have ever been able to calm the screaming in my head, the ice in my heart, or the delusional fantasies of endless torture. I'm alone without hope of recourse other than the cold steel in my hand.

After slowly sitting down on my couch, I pull out my phone and start a voice recording, saying, "My name is . . ." I shudder, my emotions overwhelming me, forcing me to pause. Taking a breath to slow my heartbeat, I continue, "My name is Arien Vlahos, previously known as Samael Mathus. And this is my suicide note. Molly, I, ah . . ."

Again, I stop to take a moment, smiling sadly and wiping a few tears away from my eyes. My thoughts wander as I try to come up with the right words to say, the right goodbye. The words that will show my pain, grief, and love; that will make people understand. But I soon realize that no words will ever do justice to the pure agony that is my tortured existence. Nothing will compare to how I truly feel, to what I truly am. "Oh, you already know."

My hands shaking violently, I slowly lower my phone and raise the tool of my redemption, the Glock. With one hand, I reach up to gently grip the owl pendant around my neck, while with the other, I turn off the Glock's safety.

I hold the pendant tight while I press the gun's barrel into my temple. This is it. There's no going back as soon as I squeeze just a little; all my agony will be finished. I can finally rest. All my muscles tighten, preparing to pull the trigger.

The shaking of my hand increases the longer I push off the end; soon, it's too violent to hold the gun steady. I readjust the Glock and shove the barrel deep into my mouth to stabilize it. Tears flow freely down my cheeks, I begin to squeeze.

I CAN'T DO IT!

With a cry of agony, I drop the Glock onto the coffee table in front of me. I cradle myself, the sobs overwhelming me. Anger and disappointment fill me with regret and disdain for my weakness.

Trying to calm myself by slowly rocking back-and-forth, I'm interrupted by the sound of the front door opening. Charlie and Susan walk in, smiling and glowing with young love. Charlie turns her smiling eyes to me, saying, "Yo. What's up?" Her eyes darken, seeing my tears and the loaded Glock before me. "Oh, my god." She hurries over to envelop me in her warm embrace; I let everything go and hold her tight.

"I couldn't do it. I tried. I want to so much, but I just can't do it. Why can't I do it?" I sob.

Charlie strokes my hair, cooing softly, "It's alright. I'm here."

Susan walks up behind Charlie, rubbing her back and whispering, "I'll give you guys some space. Call me later, OK?"

With a smile and a nod, Charlie replies, "OK." They kiss briefly, and Susan discreetly leaves. Charlie holds me tight as I continue to sob.

***

My shudders slowly subside, apathy setting in. Charlie pulls back from our embrace, smiles down at me, and asks, "Are you feeling better, Sam?"

"Arien. My name is Arien," I whisper.

Her face becomes strained, guilt filling her eyes. "Right. Sorry, I forgot."

I nod in understanding, leaning back to wipe my eyes clean of tears and affirm, "I'm alright, now."

"I'm going to make you some tea," she soothes, standing and expertly unloading the Glock, taking it to the kitchen. I sit on the couch, utterly empty of feeling or thought while Charlie boils water for tea. When she thinks I'm not paying attention, she pulls out her phone and calls Susan, gushing, "Hey, babe."

A quiet screeching sound fills the air coming from Charlie. I pretend not to hear it, trying to see what she's doing from the corner of my eye. She's carving into a strange metal sheet with an ancient-looking nail.

4

Carving the whole while, she whispers, "With Arien in the condition he's in, I don't think I should come over tonight. . . Thanks, honey. I'll see you in the morning."

Guilt floods through me, followed by the realization of what today is. I choose this day to kill myself because it was my birthday, fitting poetry to wrap up my life, but I'd forgotten that this day was also Susan and Charlie's anniversary. Just another social blunder to add to the reasons why I should end it. I never try to be this inconsiderate, but I always am. How can Charlie care for me at all after everything I've done to her? "You can't cancel your anniversary on my account," I contend.

Charlie hangs up her phone and turns to me with feigned acceptance, replying, "It's really no problem."

"I'll be fine. Take all the weapons and sharp objects if it'll make you feel better."

Hesitating, she stares down at the sheet of metal she's still trying to hide from me. Eventually, she concedes, "If it weren't my anniversary, I'd never even consider it." She lets out a pent-up breath, giving in, "Fine, but promise me you'll call Molly."

I smile softly in thanks, surprised and a little hurt she agreed, but ultimately happy that I wasn't imposing. "Promise."

"I'll be in my room, just grabbing a few things." As she leaves, she tries to hide the metal sheet without me seeing it. Once she's gone, I stand and get the tablet from its hiding spot. Ancient runes have been carved into its surface, with the final symbol being drawn in blood. No matter how hard I try, I can't turn away from the tablet. There's something about it that I can't explain. Something otherworldly. Something impossible.

Faint whispers fill my head, seemingly promising wisdom and power if I can just hear them. I should be afraid, but I'm not. The tablet comforts me and makes me smile ever so slightly.

Slowly and with great effort, I put the tablet back where I'd found it, shaking my head. I stumble to the bathroom, stripping naked and stepping into the shower. Every time I'm nude, I try not to look, but the jagged scars on my wrists call to me, no longer covered by the long-sleeved shirts they force me to wear. Leaning against the shower wall, I raise my arms to stare at and massage the scars, the ancient ghost of suicide attempts long since failed.

My vision darkens, my focus zeroing down at the scars. Memories of my childhood wash over me, giving me the chills and making my hair stand on end. The lights in the room flicker violently and the shadows grow.

A single drop of blood falls through the air to splash into the pool of water around my feet. I stare at the blood in shock, concerned about its source. Afraid to look, I slowly turn my gaze to my chest.

Several massive lacerations crisscross my chest, all pouring blood.

My phone buzzes, breaking me free of my trance. My breaths ragged and forced, I stare around; all blood, wounds, and shadows are gone. I rub my face with water to clear my head before peaking around the shower curtain to stare at my phone. Molly's face flashes as the caller ID.

I know I should answer it; Molly is the only family I have left, the only family that cares at least. I shouldn't let her go, let our relationship slip, but I'm not ready to talk to anyone right now, even my cousin.

Shaking my head, I turn back to the shower, leaving it unanswered.

To distract myself, I turn to the thing that causes me the most happiness and the most pain. I reach down and grip my altogether average penis, starting to stroke it slowly. Warmth fills my body, forcing me to become more and more erect, pulling a soft moan out of me, and helping me forget my problems. I shudder, and spray my seed across the shower walls, the euphoria fading, leaving only the thought that no woman will ever do that for me.

I am alone.

Anger and self-loathing fill me; I scream and release my rage, slamming my fist into the wall. Tears stream down my face and are washed away by the water cascading down my body. I sniff slightly, turning off the water.

Once dry, I get dressed and walk to my room. I kneel in front of my altar to Athena, the only place that I feel safe. Though my faith is not firm, it makes me want to try to be better. It can't be false if I just try. Lighting all the candles on the altar while holding the owl pendant around my neck, I stare at Athena's portrait behind the altar. When everything is prepared, I wash my head and hands with khernips before opening the Orphic Hymns to recite a prayer to Athena:

"Only-Begotten, noble race of Zeus, blessed and fierce, who joy'st in caves to rove:

O, warlike Pallas, whose illustrious kind, ineffable and effable we find:

Magnanimous and fam'd, the rocky height, and groves, and shady mountains thee delight:

In arms rejoicing, who with Furies dire and wild, the souls of mortals dost inspire.

Gymnastic virgin of terrific mind, dire Gorgons bane, unmarried, blessed, kind:

Mother of arts, imperious; understood, rage to the wicked, wisdom to the good:

Female and male, the arts of war are thine, fanatic, much-form'd dragoness, divine:

O'er the Phlegrean giants rous'd to ire, thy coursers driving, with destruction dire.

Sprung from the head of Zeus, of splendid mien, purger of evils, all-victorious queen.

Hear me, O goddess, when to thee I pray, with supplicating voice both night and day,

And in my latest hour, peace and health, propitious times, and necessary wealth,

And, ever present, be thy vot'ries aid, O, much implor'd, art's parent, blue eyed maid."

A single tear escapes my eye and rolls down my cheek to splash gently into the pages of the Orphic Hymns.

"You know, sometimes I wonder why I do this," I confess. "You're not real. There's no such thing as God or gods. It's our way of finding meaning in a hopeless existence. It's my way of finding meaning. Maybe I'm just compensating for my childhood, but maybe not. I left home to find meaning. I joined the military to find hope. But I'm just as lost and confused as I was when I left my parents. They may not have been the problem. Maybe there's just something wrong with me." I lean forward against the altar, my emotions swelling and a few more tears dropping out. "I just need to know who I am. I need to believe I'm special." Shaking my head in defeat, I wipe my eyes and pull out a wine canister, pouring a shot. "To all the gods on high, I humbly give this offering."

I pour the shot of wine into a stone basin on the altar, take a deep breath, and start to meditate.

I twitch and grimace, an itch developing on my chest where I had seen the phantom lacerations in the shower. Scratching to get rid of it does nothing. I try to ignore it and return to my meditation, but the itch doesn't subside, it grows. It soon becomes unbearable, so I let out a sigh and lean forward to blow out the candles.

A tortured scream is ripped from my throat.

I collapse to the ground, writhing in agony. Convulsing violently, my eyes glow with a godly light. The carpet around me bursts into flames; I start to float up off the ground.

The fire spreads across the room, and I'm pulled higher, stretched spread-eagled. My skin crackles, catching fire. All sound fades, leaving me only able to let out a silent scream. All the light in the room is sucked toward me before it blasts outward in a massive explosion.

CHAPTER 2: DEATH OF A HERO

Arien

A wall of bitter cold air slams into me; I appear in the sky, high above a snow-covered peak. Letting out a small scream, I crash down into a snowbank, wearing only my owl pendant. My body convulses, not from the cold but from the heat. My hands are on fire. No amount of snow can quench the flames; the heat melts the snow too fast to cool me.

"Who are you?"

I turn to stare at the strange man standing in the snow behind me, a massive battleax in hand. My voice shaking with confusion and fear, I ask, "What?"

The man gives me a curious look, repeating, "Who are you? A human shouldn't have been able to do what you just did."

'Human?' Am I not human? I stare at my flaming hands for a moment, consumed by a feeling akin to hopeful horror at the thought, but an excuse that simple could never explain or excuse the pain of my past. I look back up at the man and affirm, "I'm human."

"No, I don't think you are. At least not entirely. I can sense the power inside you, it's somehow familiar." His face is lost in thought, seemingly remembering the person my supposed power reminds him of. Shaking his head to dispel the memory, he continues, "Who are you?"

"I don't know."

"You might be a demigod."

My heart skips a beat. A demigod? But that would mean one of my parents was a god, that the gods were real. Could my hidden source of solace be founded in truth? "What are you talking about?" I ask, still utterly confused.

"Who are your parents, child?"

Anger fills me at the memory of my parents, dispelling the brief hope that I'd felt. I bite my lip and clench my now flameless fist to release my anger, whispering, "I have no parents. None that cared, at least."

"An orphan, then? Pity. I would have liked to have killed a god. No matter. I'll have to settle for you." Terror drowns all other emotion as the man grows taller, his clothes and ax growing with him. He towers over me at a height of at least 25 feet. The gods may not be real, but magic is, for I have never seen anything like this before.

This Titan among men speaks to me, his voice echoing down from his lofty height, "Your death will not be meaningless, if that's a comfort. It will herald the dawning of a new age for humanity. One where hunger, pain, and loss will be extinct. Take comfort in that if you can."

Hefting his ax, he swings downward at my cowering form. My natural survival instincts overtake me, making me roll to the side with surprising speed. I pull myself to my feet, stumbling back to avoid a second swing. Fear being the strongest instinct, it forces me to slowly retreat from the looming Titan, his eyes empty of desire or pleasure at the task before him. I trip over a stone protruding from the snow and fall back.

He presses his advantage, rushing forward to deliver the killing blow, but again I manage to roll free in time. As I clamber to my feet, the Titan attempts to sweep them out from under me; I jump back and cower beside a large boulder.

He grins slightly, not a smile of joy or victory, one of disappointment and pain, but not directed at me. He whispers, "If you see my daughter where you're going, tell her I love her."

How could a creature, a monster, like this have a daughter? I stare up at my executioner, for the first time, unwilling to accept my death. I roll one more time to avoid the ax's blade; it bounces and sparks harmlessly against the boulder while I back up to a safe distance.

Turning to me, respect in his eyes, he affirms, "You've got heart, kid. I'm not going to enjoy this, but my war must go on until every vestige of the gods has been eradicated. Only then can I, and everyone I love, have peace."

The Titan turns to the boulder beside him and hefts it high above his head; my body is frozen with fear and shock. No thoughts crossing my mind, I slowly watch the boulder flung toward me. It crashes into me, crushing every bone in my body and sending me flying backward off a cliff edge. I plummet down to the ground far below, where I'm skewered on rows of jagged stone. I lay in a dazed trance, my nerves too overwhelmed to transmit the pain. I faintly notice the Titan leap down from the cliff above to land beside my mangled body. My mind's too far gone to care that he lifts the bloodstained boulder again.

I retreat further into myself with every repeated blow of the boulder against my face until there is nothing but darkness.

<u>Atlas</u>

'The ends justify the means.' These age-old words of tyrants and heroes have comforted me in days of yore, but they have done little more than salt the wounds of my guilt these past centuries. Such is the same now as I stand above the body of my latest victim. A mere boy cursed with godly power, doomed to die for what he is, just like the apple of mine eye. I stare down at the pulpy mess of the boy's crushed skull, seeing only the face of my daughter fair.

Stumbling back in fraught distress, my vision clears till tis only the boy's mangled body there upon the ground. The dolphin pendant hanging upon my chest calls to me. I wrap my fist round the sign of my daughter, almost hearing her voice, telling me to honor a fallen foe, an act I have bestowed on none for millennia. With a nod, I commit to honor this boy of unknown heritage, commending, "You fought well. I am honored to have vanquished you."

***

In the tradition of the warriors of ancient Sparta, I construct a funeral pyre to honor the passing of a worthy foe with a warrior's soul. I have covered the nakedness of the fallen with the clothes off mine own back, leaving nothing to brace myself against the biting cold. Only one more thing is required, I take a single silver coin and place it beneath the boy's tongue. In doing this, I hope he might find passage with Charon cross the River Styx, somehow foil my poachers hunting the dead, and find peace in a life hereafter.

There, all is prepared; I reach down to lift a burning torch from the snowy ground. Walking to the pyre, I lean down to light it, sending the soul of the mortal on his journey to the Underworld or to Utopia.

Stepping back, I watch the flames engulf the boy as I begin my Hymn to Thanatos for the boy's safe passage:

"Hear me, O Thanatos, whose empire unconfin'd, extends to mortal tribes of ev'ry kind.
On thee, the portion of our time depends, whose absence lengthens life, whose presence ends.
Thy sleep perpetual bursts the vivid folds, by which the soul, attracting body holds:
Common to all of ev'ry sex and age, for nought escapes thy all-destructive rage;
Not youth itself thy clemency can gain, vig'rous and strong, by thee untimely slain.
In thee, the end of nature's works is known, in thee, all judgment is absolv'd alone:
No suppliant arts thy dreadful rage controul, no vows revoke the purpose of thy soul;
O blessed pow'r regard my ardent pray'r, and human life to age abundant spare."

The boy's corpse twitches slightly, melting into ash. The flames start to die down, leaving only a smoldering mound. Honor has been appeased.

I bow to the ash in farewell and vanish.

CHAPTER 3: THOSE LEFT BEHIND

Charlie

It's all my fault. Everything would have been different; would have been better if I'd never left Arien alone. He wouldn't be dead, and I'd never have seen . . .

The memory is too painful to even recall. I wipe away a tear and look back at a beautiful young woman, dressed in black, carrying an urn down a row of people toward an open grave. I stare around at the gathered crowd, angry that so few had shown, and fewer still seemed to care that my best friend was gone. The only one who mourned his loss with tears as fierce as mine was the woman carrying the urn herself. Arien had always said his cousin Molly was the only family he had left; this grieving woman must be her.

When Molly gets to the grave, she places the urn in an open casket and steps back to let a priest of the Temple of God's Time close the lid. The priest turns around to the crowd, pompous disingenuousness oozes from him as he begins his eulogy, "Samael Mathus was not a happy man. He was burdened in ways many of us cannot understand. To lose a brother in such a way must give us all pause.

"We all have demons lurking within us. We must all look within to see if those demons have chance to see the light of our souls to darken our hearts and lead us astray. Let us all turn to our loved ones and the Lord for strength that we too do not stumble as our brother Samael has. To be led by the evil one to take one's own life is not a sin easily forgiven but let us pray that God has mercy on his soul, and he has finally found peace in the life to come."

The priest opens his Bible to a bookmarked passage, reading, *"Come to me, all you who are weary and burdened, and I will give you rest. Take my yoke upon you and learn from me, for I am gentle and humble in heart, and you will find rest for your souls. For my yoke is easy and my burden is light."*

Tears flow freely from Molly's cheeks, and the priest nods at some nearby men to begin lowering the coffin into the greedy earth.

***

Molly is standing alone, staring at the open grave, when I get the sudden urge to comfort her, asking, "You're Molly, right? Arien's cousin."

She turns and looks me up and down, wiping her tearstained eyes and replying, "Arien? Right. That's what he liked to be called. Yes, I'm Molly."

"I'm Charlie, his, ah . . ." What was I to him? We never said. Now I'll never get to ask. "I'm his roommate."

Molly's eyes soften, and she smiles. "Charlie? He talked about you a lot. You weren't in the Air Force with him, right?"

"No, we were just roommates."

"I was worried about him when he got stationed so far away, but I was glad to hear he had you." Sighing and turning back to the grave, Molly continues, "I always hated funerals. Not because of the death; death always comes, and it merely means a new chapter. But funerals, they're far more insidious."

"How do you mean?" I ask with raised brow.

"At funerals, we're all fake or broken. Either way, the world sees the type of person you really are; they see if you can feel. They can hear the wailings of a broken soul, or see the tears of a false griever. None are safe from a funeral's piercing gaze." Turning to glance back at me, she continues, "What are you? Fake or broken?"

In a moment of vulnerable confession, I reveal, "I don't know, and that scares me more than anything. I feel inhuman for not feeling enough pain, for feeling enough broken."

Grasping my hand, Molly squeezes it to comfort me, consoling, "That you feel guilt, means you're broken, just like me. Now, look." She turns me to overlook the gathered crowd mingling around the grave, asking, "Who is fake? And who is broken?"

My vision clears; I suddenly see what she means. I can see who is wailing inside, fighting for every breath past the clump of grief in their gut. There are so few of them. A mere handful compared to the heartless or distant bastards here out of obligation. Tears truly welling in my eyes, reacting to the grief flooding me, I say, "I see."

"Sucks, doesn't it? Seeing people for who they are. Funeral's reveal secrets best left hidden." She returns to staring at the hungry earth, waiting for all of us to be swallowed up.

The true extent of her grief now apparent to me, I attempt to comfort her, but the deep well of sadness and regret in Molly's eyes gives me pause. Kind words are not my strength, they always come out coarse and disingenuous, but I have to try. "You know, he always talked about you too. He always said that you were his emotional grounding. He called you the only family he had left. You were the only reason he got through his childhood."

Molly nods at me with what appears to be genuine gratitude; her eyes go distant, thinking of Arien's final moments. "Were you there when it happened?"

I look down in shame, remembering the part I played in Arien's demise. "No. I should have been, but I wasn't there for him. There was nothing left when I got there."

Fresh tears glisten down Molly's cheeks, and she mumbles, "That's a horrible way to kill yourself. You ever hear about anyone else doing it that way?"

My skin grows hot as I seem to see the flames engulfing Arien, then engulfing me. "Never. I don't know why he did it like that."

"All we can do is have faith that he found happiness in the end. I think God would understand after everything he went through."

Before I can respond, we're interrupted by the most beautiful woman that I've ever seen. I recognize her from the photos Arien had shown me. Her name is Anna Whitney, and she's the love that got away. Bottled perfection, as Arien put it. Anna walks up to Molly and hugs her tightly, stroking her back and whispering into her ear, "I'm so sorry for your loss."

"Thank you."

Anna pulls back to stare into Molly's tear-filled eyes, asking, "How have you been doing?"

Molly looks away, unable to meet Anna's gaze, replying, "As good as can be expected."

Anna nods, surprisingly little sadness in her own eyes. "Of course. If you need anything, let me know."

"I will, thank you."

Anna smiles at Molly before walking over to talk to the other funeral guests. I turn to Molly, needing to confirm my suspicions about the young woman's identity. "Who was that?"

Staring after Anna, she affirms, "Anna. The girl Sam . . . Arien was in love with. She was never looking for anything with him, so I'm surprised that she drove all the way from Amber to be here." Molly sighs, seeing Anna walk up to talk to a couple funeral guests. "She's talking to Arien's parents now. She's one of the only people I know that can't see them for what they are."

My anger swells, drowning out my grief; I turn to watch Anna with Ephraim and Dinah Mathus. My voice is calm and cool, concealing the raging fire burning inside of me, "Those are his parents?"

Molly smirks slightly, concealing her own anger. "Not what you were expecting?"

"I half expected horns."

"I always leaned more toward cloven hoofs."

The anger inside of me dissipates, and I turn to smile at Molly, amused by her joke. "Smart. Harder to verify. Leaves more to the imagination."

Atlas

All these people are here to mourn the loss of someone I robbed them of. My presence would incur all of their wraths if they'd known how the events of the boy's death had truly transpired. But my presence is not by mine own design.

My uncle Hyperion and I are concealed beneath an oak a safe distance from the gathered mourners, intent on discovering the source of the boy's power. Being a prideful Titan with far less power than he supposed, my uncle tried to take charge over me despite my place as leader being decreed by Lord Kronos himself. He doesn't even deem to turn to me as he says, "Do you have any idea why he was so special?"

I ignore his dishonor, replying, "None. If those are his parents, I was wrong about him being a demigod."

A strange feeling draws my attention to two young women hugging briefly. Magic oozes from one, a witch for sure. The witch turns from the other woman to look at the boy's parents, fire blazing in her eyes. The boy's Father leans down to whisper something in his wife's ear, making her giggle softly. This lack of mourning seems to snap something inside of the witch, boiling her blood. She storms over to the boy's parents, clearly intent on recompense for the slight against their son.

Charlie

My mind is not my own, rage fueling my actions, pushing me toward the parents of the man I loved. "Mr. and Mrs. Mathus?!"

They turn to me, judgment burning in their eyes; Dinah asks, "Yes? What is it? Is dinner ready?"

Racial assumption aside, the mere look in their eyes is enough to make me lose all control. I hiss, "My name's Charlie. Arien's roommate."

Dinah's lip curls in unrestrained disgust, her words biting, "Ah, the little brown girl who led our son astray, the famous lesbian Wiccan. Tell me, was it you who convinced *Samael* to turn heathen and change his name?"

"Was it you that drove Arien into the depression that led to his suicide? Was it you who drove him to join the Air Force at 18 just to get the hell away from you?"

Ephraim steps forward to the defense of his wife, his eyes cutting daggers at me. "I don't appreciate how you're talking to my wife. We were the best parents Samael could have asked for.

He's lucky we didn't cast him out when we saw the darkness that festered inside of him, given to him by the devil. We had no hand in putting it there. We only did our best to root it out."

I smile to contain my anger and to stop myself from punching this smug man in his self-righteous face, condemning, "I heard in detail how you *rooted* it out. Sounded a little sadistic, to me."

Dinah steps around Ephraim, nodding up at him that she can handle me. "We only did what the Lord commanded."

"Did the Lord command you to drive all the way from Oklahoma to a funeral for a kid you disowned just so you could parade around like you're good parents?"

Righteous indignation filling Ephraim, he steps forward to sneer down at me, inches from my face, whispering, "We came to our kid's funeral. How is that not being good parents?"

I smile again, not to contain my anger but to condemn Ephraim and show him that he can't intimidate me. "Because you did it for yourselves and what other people will think of you. The gracious saints who forgave their estranged son to send him on his way into the next life. You hated him. You don't disown your children for a reason small enough to be forgiven this easily."

"We disowned him because he shirked his responsibilities as a member of the Temple of God's Time and fled here. You must have seen the darkness inside of him. The shadows behind his eyes. You don't see those in a righteous soul."

"He had the purest heart of anyone I've ever met. He was good despite the horrors he went through. He held onto the belief that people were good, no matter what. That they deserved to be happy. But he never felt like *he* deserved it because you told him over and over that he didn't deserve to live. To be happy. To have a life of his own." I finally lose all control and scream into Ephraim's face, "It's your fucking fault that he killed himself. He lit himself on fire because of you."

Molly hears my screaming and runs over to calm me just as I take a swing at Ephraim. She catches the blow and struggles to drag me away, thrashing and screaming, tears filling my eyes.

Dinah is holding Ephraim back with more success than Molly. She grabs his chin and turns him to look into her eyes, commanding, "Calm down, Ephraim. You're the patriarch. You need to act like it. You can't let the mewlings of every depraved quim rile you up into unbecoming outbursts of conviction. She shall get her just deserts for her sins but in God's time."

Ephraim nods, slowly calming. "Of course, my love."

Molly finally manages to drag me away from those monsters when I suddenly stop fighting her. The pendant charm around my neck is humming softly. Molly stares at the humming pendant in utter confusion, asking, "What is that?"

I reach up to grab the pendant, turning to look at a large oak at the cemetery's edge, but there's nothing there. I stare at the tree in confusion for a moment, muttering, "I don't know."

There's been magic here, something dark and ancient.

CHAPTER 4: THE ENDLESS HOWLING

Arien

Nothing! There's nothing for all eternity, endless, infinite emptiness expanding outward through a borderless, solidness universe. My eyes slowly open onto this nothingness. I moan softly and sit up, my hands pressing into the black obsidian ground. Rubbing my eyes does nothing to dispel this impossible emptiness before me. Am I dead? I rub my hands over my body to confirm its solidness. If I'm not dead, where am I?

In the distance, I can just make out the huddled form of a man sitting on the ground, also alone in this primordial place. I get to my feet and trek through this endless world toward the man. As I walk, I marvel at how I can see anything with the complete absence of light; my eyes seemingly adjusted to see in this place of eternal night.

The huddled man is rocking himself back-and-forth to the cadence of his own quiet ramblings, "Don't let chaos in. Chaos is us, for us, above us. Not safe. Must find the fire. Fire burn chaos. Chaos flee. Leave me alone. White-hot. White-hot knife. Cut and dice and slash and burn and kill. Must kill. Must eat. Must fight to stop her. Stop the pain. Brittnie die. Brittnie live. We cannot live. Utopia is coming for us all. Not safe. The endless howling. The howling in my head. Stop the howling. Fire burn bright. Silence the howling. Of fire and night born and from whence he came. Killing of primordial fear. Fear we all share. Dispel the empty."

These strange words strike a chord inside me. I've heard them before; I know them. They're somehow meant for me. I shake off my reverie, reaching out to touch the man's shoulder, asking, "Are you alright?"

The Empty-Man whirls and grabs my arm, pulling me down to his eye level, stammering, "Don't trust her. She kill. She bite. She end. Must protect the boy. Boy can stop her. You shall not harm the boy. Promise me, you won't hurt the boy." He squeezes his hand tighter, causing me to wince.

"Alright, I promise."

The Empty-Man reaches up with both hands to grab my head; a wave of darkness passes from him into me, making my vision darken. The Empty-Man vanishes; fog forms around me and solidifies into what look like the Empty-Man's memories.

***

I am suddenly standing in a shadowy version of the Temple of God's Time. A black shockwave blasts outward from the front altar and envelopes the collected disciples. The darkness is sucked into the disciples' eyes, turning them black. Feral bloodlust overtaking them, they start to tear each other apart. I watch in horror, unable to do anything as the bodies begin to pile up.

The fog reforms into a teenage girl's bedroom.

A beautiful teenage girl with raven black hair is sitting on her bed doing homework when she looks up and out the window to see the Empty-Man staring at her from across the street. The voice of the girl's Mother echoes up from downstairs, saying, "Brittnie, you're late for Bible study."

Brittnie doesn't turn away from the Empty-Man, yelling back, "Coming, ma."

To my surprised horror, I avert my eyes; the fog reforms into the Empty-Man and Brittnie having sex on the bed.

The fog shifts into a basement of horrors, a serial killer's wet dream, with chains hanging from the ceiling and bloody torture devices strewn about.

Brittnie is chained, her arms daggling from the ceiling, screaming. A fireball swirls around her; the shadows deepen, and she lets out her final breath.

The fog dissipates and reforms into an insane asylum.

A man with hate in his soul is torturing the bound Empty-Man with a giant Scythe, commanding, "Tell me about her?"

The Empty-Man screams as the torturer slashes two deep lacerations across his chest. A dark aura leaks out from the wounds before dissipating.

When all the Empty-Man can do is chatter nonsense, the torturer turns to the cell wall where there are thousands of daily tally marks. He makes another mark on the wall and turns back to the Empty-Man, hissing, "Forever is ahead."

The torturer walks out, and the fog dissipates completely, returning me to the endless darkness.

***

I swoon slightly, coming to. To my horror, the Empty-Man's hands are still cupping my cheeks. I pull back in pain and confusion, stammering, "What was that? What did it mean?"

"Leave. You must leave. Not safe. Leave." The Empty-Man stands and starts screaming, "Leave. Boy is in danger. Save the boy. Leave." His voice grates at my soul, flooding me with fear and despair. I huddle up in pain, the Empty-Man's voice echoing inside my skull and from every direction as if the air itself is screaming, "Leave!"

A black shockwave blasts out of the Empty-Man and sends me flying back.

***

I can't breathe! I choke and spit, clawing my way up and out of a mound of ash. Bending over, I cough violently onto the mossy ground. Once my coughing subsides, I look around to see that I'm naked, wearing only my owl pendant, in a mountainous forest.

Ice shoots through my heart at the sound of faint sniffing coming from behind me. The sound is too loud and deep to be anything other than a grizzly bear contemplating me as its next meal.

With inhuman speed, I twist around and snap the bear's neck with my bare hands; it collapses to the ground without a sound. I scramble to my feet and stare down at the corpse, shocked and horrified at what I'd just done. It's impossible, no human could have done that.

I stare down at my hands, wondering what I am.

My gaze shifts from my nakedness back to the bear, my memories of hunting coming back to me.

I know what I have to do.

CHAPTER 5: BIRDS OF A FEATHER

<u>Arien</u>

Smoke! There's smoke nearby. I sniff the air tentatively, tracking my source of rescue. I try not to run as I trek through the woods; the smoke grows closer. I step from a line of trees onto a road; across the street is what appears to be a lumberjack bar. I smile, tears welling in my eyes. I'm safe, finally.

Taking a deep breath to calm myself, I cross the street toward the bar. A soft screeching draws my attention to the bar's roof, where an owl is gracefully perched. Odd, it's full daylight. What's an owl doing out here?

I shrug off my curiosity, stepping into the bar.

The casual noises of the bar, clinking glasses, soft conversation, and the shuffle of cards all stop; the bar's occupants turn to stare at me standing in the doorway. My self-conscious nature reasserting itself, I realize how strange I look with my bearskin clothes, full beard, and body covered in blood and dirt. My eyes averted in shame, I shuffle to the bar to order, "You got Irish stout?"

The bartender twitches nervously, stammering, "What? Yes, we have it." I ignore the bartender's skittish nature, noticing his accent. Am I in Canada? He adds, "That'd be 5.50, sir."

I become uncomfortable, suddenly realizing I have no money, confessing, "You see, the thing is I don't have any money. I'd be happy to trade or work for it."

"I'm sorry, sir. But you'll have to pay cash or scoot."

"I'm sure we can work something out."

The voice of a stranger echoes from the open doorway, saying, "I'll pay for his drink." I turn to stare up and down the generous man walking toward the bar. The man appears to be in his early thirties; he's short, unassuming, and oddly plain in every way. Even his receding hairline does nothing to make him any more distinguishable. He is literally the most uninteresting man I've ever laid my eyes on. As he speaks again, I notice his strange accent, Eastern European perhaps. "I'll have what he's having," he continues. "And we'll take it over there. Maybe add a side of fries." The man points at the corner table; smiling up at me, he walks over to it, just expecting me to follow.

Shaking my head, I concede to the man and follow him. Warily, I sit down across from him as the bartender brings us our drinks. Nodding in thanks to the bartender, he turns to me and explains, "The name's Otus. Otus Sowa. Pleasure to meet you." Otus reaches across the table to shake my hand.

"Arien Vlahos."

"Vlahos? That's an interesting name. Greek, right?"

I raise an eyebrow, surprised that he recognized my name; no one has before. "That's right."

"So, what brings you to this backwoods bar, Arien?"

Otus's true intentions become clear to me, widening my eyes. I chuckle nervously, muttering, "Otus, though I appreciate your interest, I'm don't really swing for that team."

The ruckus laughter echoing from Otus surprises me; his response seems diametrically opposed to his unassuming nature. "No, that's not what this is about. Though I do occasionally swing for that team, my interest is strictly professional."

We're interrupted by two scantily clad women walking up and starting to dance for us; one coos, "You boys look like you need a little distraction. Jasmine and I will take care of you."

I'm too tired to resist, knowing full well what is about to happen. Jasmine crawls onto my lap and starts to grind. As soon as she does, her eyes go distant; she stands up, walking to Otus to help her friend entertain him. Every woman who's ever touched me has done the same, I've merely gotten used to how revolting I am to them.

With a pitied smile, Otus consoles, "It's alright, Sam. I'm sure this has happened to you before."

My heart stops at the sound of my old name. Tensing with fear and anger, I draw the bear-bone-knife I'd fashioned from the bear's jawbone, hissing, "What'd you call me?"

"You've been very slow."

I pause, looking at Otus in surprise and loosening the grip on my knife. "How's that?"

"Look around at all the people here." I raise an eyebrow, obeying; he explains, "You see the chains on the bartender's feet and the scars on his back. The scars that these two lovely women share. But most importantly, look at everyone else in here. What does everyone else have?"

My heart stops for a second time, shock flooding through me. It's impossible. "They only have one eye."

Otus smiles, "Good."

My mind races, contemplating the meaning of this discovery. I ask, "Are they Cyclopes?"

"No, I'd say they're even worse. They're Arimaspi, an ancient tribe of one-eyed men; I don't really know why they're one-eyed, though. In ancient days, they were in a constant war with griffins until they eventually learned to train them. Timorian granted them immortality if they joined him. Now they're guarding something."

This cluster-fuck of information breaks my brain. It's too much. "What the hell are you talking about? Who's Timorian?"

"Why do you think you were drawn here when you changed? The Aegis is buried in the mountain; it's too heavily defended for them to retrieve, so they're guarding it."

I slowly stand, staring at Otus in utter confusion. Giving in to the irrational part of my brain and my fear, I contend, "I don't know what you're talking about, but I want no part of it." I lied; I want everything he's saying to be true. I want a chance to be a part of something extraordinary, but I'm never that lucky. It's better I leave now before I get hurt when it turns out to be false.

I turn to go but all the Arimaspi stand and stare at me. My hand tenses on the handle of my knife as I contemplate my options. With trepidation, I slowly sit back down. The Arimaspi all mirror my actions and proceed to ignore me again. The lights start to flicker, and the shadows grow, the tension building.

Otus looks up at the lights with surprise, explaining, "They're not going to let you leave."

Turning to Otus, anger fills me, making my vision darken. "Who are you? How do you know what's going on?"

"I'm a friend. That's all you need know for now. We'll need to fight our way out of here before we get into the pleasantries."

Releasing some of my tension, I turn to survey the opposing Arimaspi. A calm confidence has overwhelmed me from an unknown place. My normal fear and trepidation are gone. "13 against 2? Not much of a fair fight."

"Not to mention the griffins."

"If they're real, we'll have to deal with them later."

Otus pushes Jasmine and the other woman away while I wave over the bartender, requesting, "Another round, please. And could you add a couple burgers? Thanks." The bartender nods and turns to leave, but I grab his arm and pull him back, adding, "When it starts, stay down behind the bar." He looks at me in horror and nods. I pull the bartender's pen out of his apron and let him go. Turning to Otus, I ask, "Have you ever been in a fight before?"

"Have you?"

"Once, and I got killed."

"That doesn't inspire a lot of confidence."

"To be fair, he was 25 feet tall and bashed my head in with a boulder." I pause, shocked at my own capacity to quip in a situation like this. It almost feels as if I'm merely channeling another personality, someone else's. A better, stronger person. Maybe it's just who I wish I was bleeding through.

Otus turns to me with incredulity, gaping, "What?"

"Don't worry, I'll try not to die again."

Scoffing slightly, he mumbles, "It's me I'm more worried about."

I smile at Otus, in a way unlike me at all. "Then don't die."

"I'll see what I can do."

The lights flicker violently again; Otus looks up at them with curiosity and not fear, again noting, "A little ominous, isn't it?"

Glancing up at the lights, I return my attention to the Arimaspi, asking, "Ready?"

"Fuck, no."

I grin and leap at the nearest Arimaspi, stabbing the bartender's pen into her single eye. The Arimaspi screams and falls to the ground, clutching her eye. Otus sits back and watches me draw my bear-bone-knife to attack the other Arimaspi.

All hell breaks loose as I struggle against my many opponents. The bartender is cowering in fear behind the bar when I throw an Arimaspi over it next to him. He starts vomiting when he sees the assortment of blood and guts hanging off the Arimaspi's corpse.

My eyes have gone black, and a fierce anger and bloodlust has overwhelmed me. The Arimaspi rush me with weapons drawn, but my berserker rage drowns out any pain of injury. I throw them back one-by-one. None have a chance to stand against me as I cut, and slice, and tear through them. My mind is detached from my body, merely watching at the bloodbath that I incur.

I tear an Arimaspi's head clean off with my bare hands, blood spraying up and covering my face. Dropping the top half of the Arimaspi's head, I turn to the last one.

Tearing an ax out of the Arimaspi's hands, I reach up to choke him, pushing him against the wall and lifting him so I can stare directly into his eyes, his light starts to fade. His faint voice squeaks, and he struggles to speak through my iron grip, whispering, "Please, have mercy."

An insane grin cracks my face; my gaze lowers to watch the tip of my knife resting on the Arimaspi's collarbone. I slowly trace the tip of the blade along his sternum, pressing slightly into his gut, my grin never relenting. I whisper with a quiet intensity and a sick pleasure, "You weren't going to have mercy on me."

I open the Arimaspi up from throat to navel; organs spill out and thud against me; the warm blood washes over me, cleansing me and fulfilling my bloodlust. My grip slackens, slowly letting the body slide to the floor.

My heavy breathing turns ragged, my eye color lightens, clearing my vision, and the lights return to normal.

Otus stands and starts clapping exuberantly, cheering, "Well, done. You really showed it to them."

I turn to Otus, my rage returning, blackening my gaze and darkening the lights again. The color leaves Otus's cheeks, fear overwhelming him. With a feral grunt, I rush at him, grabbing his throat, shoving him up the wall, and resting the tip of my knife against his collarbone like my last victim. My voice is dark and strained as I try to fight my need to kill, to taste blood. I hiss, "Fuck lot of good you were."

"You had it under control."

"Shut the fuck up. Now, I'm not interested in this world. This fantasy that only ends in blood. I don't want to kill. I'm not going to help you with anything. I just want to go back to my old life." My vision clears, and the lights return to normal while I wrestle back control. "Stay away from me."

I let Otus drop to the floor and turn to see the carnage I had caused. What type of monster could do all of this? The worst part was that I had enjoyed it. My primal, carnal side had reveled in the pure ecstasy of violence. A tear leaks out of my eye, and I rush to the door to escape what I've done.

"Your old life's gone," he calls after me.

I pause in the doorway, turning to see Otus massaging his throat. I whisper, "What?"

"They all think you're dead. Molly, Charlie, even Anna, and your parents. They all went to your funeral. They think you gave up. That you lit yourself on fire just to escape your memories. You don't really want to go back. You never wanted that life. The choice has already been made for you. You can finally leave it behind you. You don't have to go back."

All my old self-hatred rears its head as I drop my knife and walk back to Otus, crying, "You think you know so much, but you don't understand. I've always known there was something wrong with me, now I have proof." I motion to the bodies around the room, adding, "Anyone's who's capable of all this, doesn't deserve to live. You're right that I never wanted that life and that I wanted to leave it behind. They're better off without me. But am I better off without them? You start putting people in danger simply because of what you are, then you'll understand."

Otus smiles in sympathy, confessing, "I do understand."

I smile to hold back the rage that swells inside of me. No one can possibly understand what I'm going through, what I am. The dam breaks, flooding me with madness; I punch Otus in the face. I hold him against the wall so I can hit him over and over again until he collapses. Letting him fall, I start kicking him repeatedly as he screams.

Stumbling back in horror and tripping on one of the Arimaspi corpses, I sob at the sight of all the blood covering my hands. Otus struggles to sit up while I try to wipe my hands clean. I cry out and crawl back from Otus's comforting touch, shouting, "Stay away from me."

I struggle to my feet and grab my knife, running outside.

ROAR!

Freezing, my self-loathing and regret forgotten at the sound of a screeching roar coming from the sky, I look up. A massive griffin lands in front of the bar, just as majestic and beautiful as the myths and art claimed. "Shit."

My fear again dictates my actions as I turn to rush back inside, but the door is shut and locked before I can. "Otus, let me in. There's a fucking griffin out here."

When he doesn't respond, I turn back to the griffin, in awe and fear at this magnificent beast. It preens and licks its claws like a cat, waiting for me to act. I whisper, "Oh, god."

The griffin ruffles its feather, extending its right leg to bow at me. I stare at it in confusion and bow back awkwardly. While off balance, the griffin leaps at me. I let out a scream as I'm picked up and flown high into the air.

I'm taken higher and higher, my heart races, my mind struggling to find an escape. The other me takes over again, squashing my fears and taking action.

Drawing my knife, I manage to stab the griffin in the chest. It screeches in annoyance, heading back down to the ground. Once we land, it tosses me against the bar wall. I moan and roll to my feet, only to find that my previous blow hadn't even drawn blood from the griffin. It just pissed it off. "You got to be shitting me," I mutter.

The griffin spins to swing its barbed tail; I jump over it and roll in closer to the griffin. It swipes at me with its wing, sending me flying back again. Blood fills my mouth; I spit it out, and I get back up. The griffin pounces and pins me to the ground with its clawed feet, its beak dripping with saliva as it slowly lowers toward my throat.

Out of nowhere, an owl flies up and starts pecking at the griffin's eyes. Roaring, it pulls back, releasing me. I get to my feet and rush in.

Instinct controlling me again, I grab the griffin's wing and roll across its back, using my full weight to snap the wing around its body. The griffin cries out in pain, the bone in its wing breaking. It whips its tail around into me, sending me to crash into the back of a pickup truck.

My vision warps and shifts as I struggle to pull myself up. I rub my head to clear it when I see a chainsaw in the truck with me. I smile, an idea coming to me.

As I power up the saw, Otus walks out of the bar, waving his arms at the griffin and shouting, "Yo, Horus. Why don't you pick on a bird your own size?"

With the griffin distracted by Otus, I walk up to it and chop its head off with the chainsaw, blood spraying everywhere, drenching me.

Otus stares at my blood-covered form with awe. I give him a confused look, asking, "Horus?"

"It was a joke. You know, the Egyptian god."

"Hilarious." I shake my head in exasperation. My body squeaks and squelches from all the blood as I lower the saw to the ground. A hose beside the house catches my attention, so I walk over to it to wash myself. No emotions are left, leaving me empty and blank-faced, devoid of all motivation.

Otus walks up behind me, asking, "Do you see, now? You're here because you were drawn to the Aegis. It's your destiny to claim it and restore the world to its former glory."

Ignoring him, not caring what he has to say, I return to the bar and lock myself in, leaving him outside to talk through the door, "You don't know what it's like, always living on the run. Being afraid that Timorian's forces will find you. I lost everything, just trying to survive. We all have. Everyone who's different and didn't want to become monsters. We're tired of running. We need you to help us end it, one way or another."

I step out of the bar with clean clothes fresh off an Arimaspi corpse and with a beer in hand. Walking toward the nearest truck, still without emotions left to care, I mutter, "You're barking up the wrong tree."

"I'm actually quite good with trees."

I stop for a moment, finally mustering up an emotion, confusion as I stare at Otus. "It's a metaphor, dude."

"I know."

Shaking my head, dismissing my confusion, I continue to the truck, noting, "You're a little weird."

"It's hard to keep up with how much language changes after living for as long as I have."

"You can't be more than thirty."

Otus smiles slightly as if he's an old woman taking a compliment on her youthful complexion. "I'm a little older than that." I open the truck door and start looking for keys while Otus pensively asks, "Are you going to help us?"

"You don't want me anywhere near you or anything like this. I just break stuff."

"There's something special inside of you."

Normally a compliment or statement like that would have made me awkward and self-conscious, but not this time. This time I mutter, "Don't you think I would have noticed if I was anything more than a disease?"

"I'm serious. There's a power, or a divinity if you will, inside of you that can get this all started. You're just the vessel."

I smile to myself, realizing that my self-conscious response would have been deserved. "So, I'm not special, just something I have is? You sound like my ex."

"You don't have an ex."

An instant of anger flashes through me before my apathy regains control. I find the keys in the cupholder, climb in, shut the door, and start the truck. Turning to look down at Otus through the open window, I warn, "Stay away from me. You'll be better off."

"Where will you go?"

"Maybe find a cliff to drive off, or cure world hunger. One or the other. Toodaloo."

I drive off, leaving Otus alone.

CHAPTER 6: LEGACY

Atlas

I try not to show my disgust at my own actions as I circle the unconscious Selena dangling from the asylum's ceiling by golden ropes. Her eyes slowly open; she moans and shakes her head to clear her bleary vision, groggily muttering, "Atlas?"

Presenting my calm and confidant demeanor, I reply, "How are you feeling?"

"Why didn't you just kill me?"

"Because it is unwise to risk our greatest weapon for every minor deity."

I smile softly, hefting the Scythe. She shakes her head and spits into my face, hissing, "It's that important to you that I stay dead?"

"No. I need your soul to break a particular blood curse. You'll be added to an ever-growing communion of deities inside this weapon. I will soon have enough to do it. Your death will mean the salvation of all humanity past and present. So, you are not dying in vain."

Selena grimaces and tenses her muscles. "How do you sleep at night?"

Glancing down, I grab the dolphin pendant around my neck, mumbling, "I slumber deep with dreams of the perfect island, and the possibilities stolen there. What will you dream of?" Grunting, I swing the Scythe to impale Selena in the chest. She shudders, falling still. A white gold light passes from the corpse into the Scythe; the rest of the body turns into starlight and floats up through the ceiling. I stare up at the starlight returning to the vast chaos of space.

Arien

The night closes in, enveloping my truck in darkness. I flick on the headlights, trying to carve a way through the chaos. Shapes seem to float in the shadows, visions of the Empty-Man's horrors. I see piles of bodies from the Temple of God's Time, Brittnie's death, and the Empty-Man tortured; all these visions dance before me out of the shadows.

While distracted by these faint sights, an owl crashes into the windshield. I slam on the brakes, sending the owl rolling off the truck and down the street. As it rolls, it morphs into Otus. I stare in shock; he comes to a stop and doesn't move.

Otus was the owl who saved my life from the griffin; he's been watching me.

I get out of the truck and hurry to his side, rolling him to face me to see the extent of his injuries. Otus has broken several ribs, but I think he'll be alright.

"Not the landing I was hoping for, but I had to get your attention," he explains.

"That was you earlier, with the griffin? You saved my life."

"Just doing my job."

I have to make a decision now on whether or not I trust him. There's been endless proof of magic, endless proof of everything he's said, but I'm afraid. Afraid of it still being a lie, of me not being good enough, and despite all this, still not being special to myself or anyone. "Your job? What are you? How did you end up like this?" I ask.

"After the battle of Pompeii against Timorian, I gave the injured Athena shelter. She agreed to grant any wish I had in return. I asked to serve her forever. She turned me into a shapeshifter, and I've served her ever since. But now, she is you. You are Athena, in every way that counts. The divinity inside of you is Athena's godly spirit. Her power, her grace, and her heritage."

My heart stops in hope; I hadn't dared to believe it was the Greek gods that were real, despite what the Titan and Otus had said. "Athena?" I whisper. "The Greek gods are real?"

"As real as death."

Joyful tears swell in my eyes, a happiness unbeknownst to me flooding through my chest, warming the permanent ice. "Why didn't you tell me it was them?"

Otus gives me a strange look, clearly surprised at the strength of my reaction. He says, "I thought you knew."

"So, I haven't been wasting my life, after all. I have a purpose."

"You're basically a god. You weren't a waste."

I let out a short bark of laughter, experiencing happiness and hope for the first time in a long time. A single tear drops off my cheek and lands on Otus's exposed skin. His skin starts to glow with a fiery light. We both stare at the light spreading, healing Otus's wounds as it goes.

He sits up and checks that all his injuries are completely healed. Dumbfounded, I reach out to trace his now unbroken ribs, muttering, "What just happened?"

"You proved that you're capable of doing good."

"How?"

Staring into my eyes as if he's looking for something, he exclaims, "You're a phoenix."

The word echoes in my head, somehow I know it's true, but it also fills me with fear. "A phoenix? Aren't they firebird things?"

"That's impossible. Phoenixes are extinct."

I need a moment to process all this, so I sigh, "I need another drink before I hear anymore. Can you stand?"

"I think so."

Pulling him to his feet, I help him to the truck.

***

I check the bar's backroom for Arimaspi or the slaves, pour two beers, and sit across the bar from Otus, saying, "The bartender and the girls skipped town."

"Good. It looked like they had it pretty rough."

I down my whole beer and refill it, asking, "Alright, start from the beginning. Who's Timorian?"

"Jesus Christ."

Laughing nervously, not sure what to think, I mutter, "Very funny. But seriously. Who is he?"

"I am serious, at least partially," he affirms. "Timorian is the merged soul of Jesus and the Titan Kronos. Kronos created Christianity to steal humanity's belief from the gods to strengthen himself." I can do nothing except shake my head in incredulity as Otus continues, "Are you familiar with Kronos and the first Titan war?" He rolls a small owl figurine between his fingers while I lean back to listen to his story, "In the days before mankind walked the earth, the great Mother Gaia laid to rest and gave dominion of the earth to her 12 children: The Titans. Foremost among the Titans was Kronos, lord of time. Kronos Fathered what he called the golden age, but this era was still fraught with its own troubles.

"Having been prophesied that a child born from him would lead to his destruction, Kronos began to devour his children at birth to ensure his reign. Kronos's wife, Rhea, began to plot against her husband to get back her beloved children. With the help of her youngest son, Zeus, whom she had replaced at birth, she arranged for her husband to spew forth her other children. With his siblings behind him, Zeus led an army to defeat his villainous Father.

"With Kronos vanquished, the gods deliberated on the punishment worthy of a child eater. They decided to turn his own Scythe against him, to cut him into a thousand pieces and throw his remains into the depth of Tartarus, the primordial god of the deep places beneath the earth. There he waited for thousands of years and saw the rise of man from when they first came blinking into the sun. With the development of man, his escape became clear. As man's minds elevated, they began to affect the world around them. Their belief in divinity gave the gods heightened abilities and a farther reach. If Kronos could take that belief and channel it into himself, he stood a chance of reclaiming his throne on high. Kronos chose from the hordes of men a champion to begin his reclamation of power.

"Kronos spoke in Abram of Canaan's ear and told him that he was the one true God, and he needed a prophet to deliver his will to mankind. Abram became Abraham and led astray more and more of humanity until, generations later, Moses arose to lead the now mighty people of Israel. Kronos whispered to Moses and told him many stories about the birth of the universe and the rise of mankind. Kronos made himself into a god and a devil to create a theology capable of competing with the Greek religion in the hearts of men. From then on, Kronos continued to draw strength from their belief in an attempt to create a new body to pass his consciousness into.

"Once his strength was sufficient, Kronos traveled through Tartarus and forced him to impregnate Gaea, using Kronos's life essence. Kronos then stole the child and impregnated a young mortal girl named Mary with it. When the child was born, Kronos named him Timorian or Jesus. Kronos raised him to be the messiah and used him to create his masterpiece, Christianity. After Jesus's resurrection, Kronos possessed him to lead the war against the gods. Even with the combined forces of all the gods' religions, Greek, Roman, Norse, and Egyptian, they were unable to hold back the might of Christianity. The battle of Pompeii was the first major conflict of the war between Timorian and the gods. After that day, the gods knew they'd lost. There was no withstanding Timorian and Christianity."

My brain feels as if it's melted from the sheer mass of information dumped onto me. I pour myself a shot of something stronger to get through Otus's history lesson.

He continues, "Things were tough after the battle of Pompeii. The gods went into hiding, and Timorian started killing magical creatures to ensure humanity didn't believe in magic and kept worshiping him. Atlas retrieved Kronos's Scythe from the gods and dipped it in the blood of eternity, so it could actually kill gods and Titans and return their essences to the primordial chaos. No weapon ever created had ever had that power. The Olympians were forced to go into deeper hiding. The only way to do that was to tear out their divinities and become mostly mortal. They scattered, leaving their divinities hidden around the world. The final moves are being made to set up the resolution."

The sheer scale of this history leaves me feeling smaller and more insignificant than even I was accustomed to. "Where do I come in?" I ask timidly.

"On May 3rd, 1999, an F5 tornado hit Oklahoma City. It passed over the olive grove where I was guarding Athena's divinity. The winds managed to jostle it free and send it to Amber. Where I assume it found its way to you, for some reason. You then became the vessel of her power. In theory, you now have all her power and abilities."

"So, what am I supposed to do?"

"Give us all an honorable death."

I give Otus a curious look, realizing that he doesn't believe that there is any hope in this war. "What?"

"Nothing's changed. There's no hope of beating Timorian, but the gods and all the rest of us are tired. We're ready to die, but we want to die trying one last time. With the Aegis, Athena's ancient shield, you have a chance to restore all the gods to their divinities and lead the final battle against Timorian."

There really is no hope, hope that I might be anything more than I am, a waste. I can't even help save the world. "Why should I fight if there's no hope? I haven't been on the run forever," I mumble.

"Yes, you have," he affirms. I stare at Otus in resentment before turning away in shame. He continues, "That's what you are. A runaway. You ran from your parents. You ran from me when I showed you a bigger world. You joined the military to run away as fast as you could from everything you'd ever known. Even those who loved you. You ran from Molly, the only family you have left. You've been running your whole life from something. Whether it be a painful past, love, hate, or even insanity. You've always run. I'm giving you the ultimate chance to run away. To escape. You've been suicidal your whole life, but you were never able to pull the trigger. You could never kill yourself. But the path I'm putting you on will. You want to die? I'm offering you a chance at a life worth living and a death worth dying. Suicide by heroism."

Death, the thing that gods and men cannot share, is the one thing that they want to unite us, to motivate me. Are my motives not so different than the gods themselves? Am I not so different? I turn away, a single tear leaking out of the corner of my eye. My gaze falls upon the carnage I had caused, still strewn about the bar floor. The pain and suffering I'd inflicted the moment I chose to walk through that door. "I'm not a hero," I confess. "I'm just a coward too afraid to live." I'm forced to pause, my emotions overwhelming me until I make my decision, adding, "I'll do it, but only if you promise me something. If by some miracle we win and I survive, I want you to find a way to kill me. Promise me that."

Otus hesitates for a moment, nodding, "I promise."

A firm resolve takes root in me as I ask, "What do I need to do?"

"Follow me."

We both finish our drinks, and Otus leads me out into the night.

***

Otus is leading me through the trees to a lonely cabin built into the hillside. I look up and down the unassuming structure, noting, "What now? Is it just in there?"

"Athena praises intellect above all else. The way to her greatest weapon will require a certain practical display of the seeker's cleverness."

I still don't understand, but I say, "Alright."

"There's a riddle above the door. Solve it, and it will open for you."

"Aren't you coming?"

"No, there are certain tests that I would not survive. You'll need to do this alone."

"Whatever." Despite my confusion, I step forward to inspect the inscription above the door, reading aloud, "*I am chaos. The great empty void. I draw the breath from your lungs. I freeze the heart in your chest. I am everything. I am nothing. All see me, but none can touch me. I am over all, and through all, and in all. I am.*"

I turn to stare at Otus, asking, "Seriously? It couldn't be the 4 feet, 2 feet, 3 feet, one?"

"It couldn't be too easy."

"It's not too hard. From just, *the great empty void* I'd say the answer is outer space."

We both wait, expecting the door to open. After waiting for a moment, I ask, "Is something supposed to happen?"

"I don't know. Maybe you need to say the answer in Greek."

"OK. What's it in Greek?"

"Xáos."

I nod and walk closer to the door, shouting with a commanding voice, "Xáos." Nothing happens. I turn back to Otus, exacerbated. "Now what?"

"I don't know."

"Fuck this." I shoulder my way through the door and step into the unassuming cabin. Old cobwebbed covered furniture fills the room, nothing extraordinary or interesting.

Otus shouts from outside, unwilling to come inside for some reason. "Anything?"

"There's nothing here. Nothing magical, at least." An old bookshelf at the back of the cabin catches my attention. I walk to it and start looking through the books. "There's a great library here, though. Dickens, Shakespeare, Thoreau, and Verne." I stop suddenly and stare at the last book on the row. "Verne's: From the Earth to the Moon."

"So?"

"It's the only one about space." I reach up and try to pull it off the shelf, but it's stuck. Smiling, I trace my finger down the binding. "Xáos."

The book starts to glow. The glowing spreads to the other books and the bookshelf until it burns them away to reveal the entrance to a secret tunnel.

"Leave your knife." I turn to see Otus standing in the doorway.

"What?"

"Athena may be the goddess of war, but she doesn't revel in it. She'll have made this a peaceful test of the mind."

"Fine." I toss my knife to Otus, heading down into the tunnel.

Otus

I should feel guilty for lying to the boy, but it's what I needed to do. It's what she demanded of me. In my two thousand years of service, she's never led me astray. I didn't lie when I said I was tired of running, but I don't want to die. Until this war is won, I can never see my family again. To that end, I will tell this boy any lies I must.

The owl figurine in my pocket calls to me as it does whenever I'm alone. I pull it out just to rub its worn surface. A long time ago, my friend Michelangelo had offered to restore it for me, but I could not bear for it to change in any way from when I'd given it to my daughter.

Tears fill my eyes as they always do as I rub the owl. Eve wouldn't approve of me mourning after her for so long, but I was never going to be able to let her go. The image and smell of her burnt flesh was never going to leave me or stop haunting my dreams.

No cause, no matter how right, can justify the burning of their opposition. Fear of the unknown is a powerful thing, it's been the downfall of many empires, and that's all it ever can do, destroy. No one is guilty of the sins of another, regardless of any shared beliefs. No just cause can long survive the bloodlust of fanatics. My family's killers and I agreed in principle, but practice was another matter. There are villains and heroes on both sides of every conflict in history. Their death is proof of that. I can never let myself forget that or lose my resolve.

A noise in the woods makes me turn. When the source does not reveal itself, I go to investigate.

A screeching fills the sky as the brush rustles around me. Suddenly, I'm surrounded by a horde of Arimaspi and a griffin. "Fuck."

Arien

The rough stone walls of the tunnel strangely comfort me. A solid piece of nature that I understand, that can ground me in this tumultuous time. The tunnel opens up into a massive cavern reaching high into the belly of the mountain. The cavern floor is riddled with dozens of statues set as a warning. At the far end is a pedestal with the severed head of a snake-haired woman upon it, the head of Medusa.

I gasp in horror at the sight. "Shit." I try to turn away or close my eyes, knowing the fate that will befall me if I don't.

Suddenly, I relax. If I'm not dead yet, I may yet survive. The snakes of Medusa's head rise up and start hissing at me. I tentatively start walking past the statues of fallen heroes and villains toward Medusa's pedestal. The only answer to explain my survival is Athena's divinity inside of me, which is some comfort. I continue around the pedestal and into another tunnel.

This tunnel doesn't go for long before it opens up onto a massive cliff falling off into a bottomless pit. I pick up a nearby stone and throw it off the edge to test the depth. The hole is too deep to hear the rock land. A small shrine to Athena on the side of the tunnel mouth catches my attention. A prayer doesn't seem amiss at this moment. I sigh and kneel to pray.

A low voice starts to echo through the tunnel, just too quiet to make out. I look down and inspect the small altar that protrudes from the base of the shrine. My eyes widen, an idea coming to me.

A sacrifice is needed.

I check the pockets of my stolen clothes and find a pack of cigarettes and a lighter. I return to the cavern to retrieve Medusa's head, bringing it to the shrine. After placing the head on the altar, I light the shrine's candles and lift an urn of oil left there for me. I pour the oil out over Medusa's head and ignite it with the lighter.

"Oh, great goddess Athena. Please grant unto me a way forward that I may complete this task in your honor." Medusa's head burns away to ash, leaving behind a small steel box alone upon the altar. I carefully pick it up and open it. There is only a small strip of parchment inside with a single word upon it, 'Zephyrus.'

Smiling, I turn to kneel before the open chasm and recite the Orphic Hymn to the god of the west wind, Zephyrus:

"Sea-born, aerial, blowing from the west, sweet gales, who give to weary'd labour rest:
Vernal and grassy, and of gentle found, to ships delightful, thro' the sea profound;
For these, impell'd by you with gentle force, pursue with prosp'rous Fate their destin'd course.
With blameless gales regard my suppliant pray'r, Zephyrs unseen, light-wing'd, and form'd from
air."

Wind begins to howl up from the base of the cliff. I smile, standing and jumping off.

Down and down I fall. I feel no fear as I go deeper into the mountain. The wind rushes up and gently carries me to the base of the chasm.

After checking my balance, I look up to see a golden light coming from ahead. I walk slowly toward the light. The light fades to reveal a majestic spear and shield. The shield has the face of Medusa carved into the metal and is called the Aegis.

I smile, finally accepting my destiny.

Otus

I'm dragged by my captors into their camp and bound with golden rope that prevents me from shapeshifting.

An Arimaspi bends down to stare into my eyes, his breath rank with an eternity of barbarity. "Who are you?"

"Nobody."

My Odyssey reference stops the Arimaspi, dumbfounding him. "You must be someone."

"It's an Odyssey reference. You know, telling a one-eyed guy that you're Nobody?" The Arimaspi still only gives me a blank expression. I shrug and say, "So uncivilized."

A scream echoes from the forest.

Everyone whirls in that direction. Flames burst to life in the distance as more Arimaspi scream. I smile, knowing what's coming for them. "Nobody's coming to get you."

The Arimaspi turns his fear-filled gaze on me. "I thought you were Nobody."

"I lied. I'm just the damsel. He's Nobody."

Arien slowly walks into camp. The Arimaspi scream and charge. Arien and his new weapons tear through the Arimaspi as he fights his way toward me. An Arimaspi pulls out a horn and blows, sending a low-pitched bellow throughout the forest. Several griffins soon fall from the sky and land between us.

Arien manages to keep the griffins at a distance as he starts circling them to get around to me. I roll to a fallen Arimaspi, using her knife to cut my bonds. I stand and pull a torch from the campfire and throw it at a tent near the griffins. The griffins roar and retreat from the flames, giving us a chance to turn and flee into the woods. The Arimaspi camp burns behind us as we disappear into the night.

Part 2:

APOLLO

CHAPTER 7: NOT WORTH THE HURT

<u>Arien</u>

Fog swirls in the endless darkness, morphing into Molly huddled on the ground, crying. I'm standing above her; she looks up at me with fear. "What are you?"

My body is not my own; my eyes are black as I smile and crouch to cup her cheek in my hand. She rubs against my hand for comfort, trying to let go of her fear. The pounding of blood in my head pushes my true self deeper; I lean forward to kiss her forehead. She looks up at me, her fear finally gone.

I stab her repeatedly in the stomach. She screams as her eyes begin to melt and run out of her head. She lets out her final breath before I step back and freeze as I realize what I've done.

Looking down at my blood-covered hands, I sob as a haunting laughter echoes through the darkness. A faint shape walks out of the fog toward me, it's Otus. My sobs increase as I back away from Molly's corpse, my voice cracks with fear and shame as I try to defend myself. "I didn't mean to. It was an accident."

Otus's face is set in stone as he stabs me in the gut. I gasp before falling to the ground, screaming as Otus continues to stab me over and over again. The blood pools around me and mixes with the watery obsidian of the ground, turning it into red stone.

Otus stops and stares into my eyes, smiling. "Not worth the hurt."

Otus slits my throat.

***

I wake up in a cold sweat, breathing hard, haunted by the horrors of my dreams in the empty darkness. Otus sits up on the couch, rubbing his eyes to bring them into focus. "You alright?"

I shake my head to clear it, replying, "Fine." Otus goes back to sleep as I stare at the wall in silence, unable to return to sleep, afraid of what I might see.

***

I didn't get any more sleep last night after my nightmare, but a little extra coffee and I managed to drive us to a local fast-food-joint without incident. We've ordered and are waiting outside while we brainstorm our path forward. "Where are we headed, Otus?"

Otus pulls out his phone and starts a video before handing it to me. "Here."

I recoil in shock at the extremely graphic gay porn on the phone. "What, the fuck, man? A little warning next time. Please. Why are you showing this to me?"

"I was watching this the other day, and I recognized an old friend."

"Those your old coworkers while you were paying your way through college?"

"No, they work in LA. This was in Miami."

Otus's life story gets more and more confusing the longer I get to know him, and his grasp on modern humor and idioms is startlingly lacking. "It's so hard to joke with you."

"That was a joke?"

I roll my eyes, unwilling to explain further. "Never mind. Who'd you recognize?"

Otus pauses the video on a close-up of one of the Porn Stars. "This is Dick Van Hugo in the porno: Who's your Daddy?"

"Charming."

"His real name is Apollo."

I raise an eyebrow in surprise. "That's Apollo? The dude with a dick in his mouth? How can you tell?"

"I've seen him do that before. We had . . . an encounter in 16th Century England. At the time, he went by William Shakespeare."

Charlie and I used to read Shakespeare plays together, pouring over them like the nerds we were. Funny how I was reading the work of a god that whole time. It's fitting really, the words were too powerful for a normal human to write. "Apollo was Shakespeare, and you did him?"

Otus gets defensive; clearly, history had not always been kind to him. "Yeah. Something wrong with that?"

"No, I'm just surprised a guy like you could bag a guy like him."

Otus smiles slightly, taking the joke. "I'll have you know, I am a very charming and sophisticated gentleman."

"Clearly."

Before we can continue our banter, a fast-food worker brings over our food. "Thank god. I'm starving." I take a bite but pause when I notice the worker staring at the Aegis' exposed face next to me. Glancing around, I see that everyone is doing the same. The face of the Aegis has a strange effect on people. It draws fundamental fears to the forefront of your mind; a single tear leaks out of the worker's eye.

Quickly, I take off my jacket and throw it over the Aegis, concealing the face. The worker shakes her head to clear it before turning back to me. "Will you guys be needing anything else?"

"No, we're good. Thank you."

The worker nods, turns, and walks back inside. I smile faintly after her before turning to the mountain of food in front of me.

Otus stares at me as I devour an entire burger. "You get enough food?"

I look up at Otus with a mouth full of food, embarrassed. "I don't know why, but I'm always hungry nowadays."

"You've got an active god inside of you. That burns a lot of calories."

"That's probably the best thing to come out of all of this." I swallow another burger before wiping my mouth and taking a drink. "So, Apollo's in Miami. Is that where we're headed?"

"For a start." Otus continues to talk, but his words fade away as I see two missionaries from the Temple of God's Time. So many horrific memories flood through me, my worst moments brought back to life. My vision darkens as I hear the screams from my nightmares, the cries of the Temple of God's Time's mass suicide. My eyes turn black as my anger and fear deepen.

Otus snaps to get my attention. "Arien, what's wrong?"

My eyes return to their normal blueness as I turn my hateful gaze onto Otus. "Do you ever shut up?"

Otus recoils in pained surprise. "What?"

Violent shivers rack through me, so I grab my jacket from off the Aegis and put it back on.

"Are you alright?"

"All you do is talk and talk. But you never do anything. You're a lazy disgrace of a person."

Otus's body tenses, reacting to my venomous words. "What, the hell, is wrong with you?" Otus notices that several people are staring at the Aegis again. "Arien, can you just cover the Aegis with something? People are starting to stare again."

I feel no regard for anything but my rage, dismissing the stares. "Why does it matter? It shows them their deepest fears and regrets. It shows them who they really are. Why should we take that away from them?"

"Arien, cover it up. We can't afford to be noticed."

"Noticed? Why not? What's the point of having all this power if I don't use it? I could be a god. A superhero. People need to see me. They need someone to believe in. Why not me?" A pounding noise rings through my ears, making me wince. "The world is on the verge of chaos. I'm the only one that can help."

"Not like this."

A horse scream is torn from my lips as I draw my knife and pin Otus's wrist to the table with it. Everyone around gasps and stares at us. Otus looks up in horror into my now blackened eyes. The crowd starts pulling out their phones and recording the scene. My gaze is drawn up to see the missionaries get on their bikes and leave. Their departure releases some of the tension in me, clearing my eyes. "Shut up, Otus."

After I pull the knife out of the table and stand, Otus turns to the crowd to show them his torn sleeve. "It's alright, everyone. We're just practicing for a play."

"Everyone can go fuck themselves. It's not a fucking play." When no one moves, I growl and turn to lift the Aegis. "Get, the fuck, out of here."

The image of the Aegis being wielded sends fear into everyone's hearts, making them scatter.

Otus stands and quickly covers the Aegis. "What are you doing?" I shove the Aegis into his arms, all my emotions swallowed back into my void. "I need more food."

I go inside the fast-food-joint, leaving Otus to stare after me.

Inside, I get in line to order. I glance up at the TV above the counter to watch a 'Friends' re-run. The tension in my body slowly relaxes as I smile and start laughing softly. The person in front of me finishes, so I step forward to order. My gaze is continually drawn to the TV as I struggle to focus long enough to order. The fast-food worker turns to look up at the TV as well. She smiles and asks, "You a big 'Friends' fan?"

I smile, remembering the long nights at Tech School spent alone re-watching 'Friends' over and over. "The biggest. This is the one where Rachel and Ross nearly get back together. Well, one of the times at least."

"With Ross's bald ex-girlfriend."

I laugh a little as I remember. "That's right."

"You may be a big fan, but you're not as big of a fan as my parents."

My smile widens, enjoying our playful, flirtatious banter. "Really?"

"They named me Rachel."

I lean forward against the counter, trying my best to seem cool. "Ah, the hot one. I can see why."

"There's more to Rachel than that." Rachel smiles, not truly offended.

"Of course. She's got to be crazy to love someone like Ross."

"Ross is sweet."

"He tries."

We just smile at each other for a moment before someone behind me coughs to get our attention. Rachel shakes her head to clear it and lifts her notepad, asking, "Right. What can I get for you, sir?"

My smile saddens as I reply, "Just a cheeseburger meal to go. Thanks."

Rachel nods, "That'll be 8.50, sir."

I quickly pay and take my receipt, which has a phone number written on the back. Rachel winks at me and notes, "If Ross ever wants to see if something can work with Rachel, he can just call her."

Smiling, I reply, "I think he definitely will."

"He'd better."

I step out of line just as Otus rushes through the door and toward me. His voice cracks with excitement, crying, "I hope you got your shit together because I found the porn studio. It's called Humping Harry's."

Rachel overhears the comment and recoils a little in disgust at the mention of a 'porn studio.' She walks into the backroom as I turn to glare at Otus. "Say it a little louder next time."

Otus looks down, embarrassed. "Sorry."

I grab my food from a different worker, mumbling, "Let's get out of here.

CHAPTER 8: INQUISITIONS PAST

Rachel is alone in the fast-food-joint cleaning up after closing. She looks up at the TV to watch 'Friends' for a second before shaking her head and changing the channel. She returns to cleaning as she listens to Robin Smulders delivering the nightly news. "Though the authenticity of these accusations have not been verified, it doesn't look good for the Hanks family. Moving on to more local news, the following video taken this morning at a mom-and-pop fast-food-joint outside of Buffalo has taken the internet by storm."

Rachel looks up at the TV in surprise to see a video of Arien terrorizing the people outside the fast-food-joint with the Aegis. "Witnesses say that the design on the shield quote; 'stirred something inside of them. A primordial fear.' Though no charges are being pressed, the police would still like to bring this man and his companion in for questioning. The rapid rise in the popularity of this video has experts baffled. All anyone can say is that it has a strange effect on them. Something that can't be fully described. Something almost mythical."

A crashing noise echoes from behind the door to the back; Rachel turns to stare at the door. She slowly walks forward, slightly terrified. She tentatively pushes the door open to see a pile of trays that had fallen to the ground. "The fuck?" Rachel shakes her head and quickly picks them up and puts them back on the counter. Rachel returns to the TV and changes the channel back to 'Friends.'

The lights start flickering violently; Rachel screams as electricity shoots down from a light, striking the floor.

A shadowy person rises from the electricity burnt floor, becoming an incorporeal man.

Rachel screams again as the shadow jumps her and slits her throat. Blood splashes up onto the TV and streaks down over the crying 'Friends' faces.

Rachel's now limp body is dragged behind the counter by the Eidolon ghost of ancient Procrustes, 'the Stretcher,' slain by great Theseus on his journey to Athens. Procrustes lays down inside the already cold body before shakily standing up, using the counter for support. Rachel lifts her hands to stare at them before licking her lips. She massages her breasts, her eyes widening as she reaches a single hand down the front of her pants, making her smile broadly. When Rachel speaks, her voice is deeper and distorted as if she's underwater. "Oh, that's nice. I haven't felt a nice pussy since Jack the Ripper."

The sound of the TV draws her attention away from masturbation; she grabs the remote and changes the station back to the news where Robin is still staring at the video of the Aegis, lost in a trance. "This image is just somehow irresistible."

Rachel stares closely at the video trying to make out Arien's face. "Who are you?" Rachel gets out her phone and dials a number.

Atlas answers, "Hello."

"It was here."

"That is impossible."

"This body has memories of it. She relived her Mother's suicide when she saw it."

"Who was carrying it?"

"A boy."

Rage fills Atlas's voice at the mention of a 'boy.' He says, "A mere boy could not have defeated the Arimaspi to get to the Aegis."

"He had a friend. A much older man. A man not at home in this time."

The rage in his voice is replaced by hopeful curiosity as he asks, "Could it be a god?"

"This human had eyes only for the boy."

"Find them and bring me the Aegis, or your life shall not be restored when Utopia descends."

"I am to serve."

Atlas hangs up, leaving the line dead. Rachel opens her phone and searches for 'Humping Harry's,' remembering when Otus had let it slip as their destination. Rachel hisses, seeing Apollo pole dancing on the studio's home page. She rummages through her pockets until she finds a set of car keys; she smiles smugly, her way forward clear.

Arien

Miami, the sweaty, swampy, deceivingly beauteous armpit of America. I struggle to breathe through the humidity as Otus and I walk into the Humping Harry's Studio to escape it.

The rather unassuming lobby of Humping Harry's studios doesn't seem like a place that you'd find a god. It seems more like where celebrities catch STDs. But I've decided I need to trust Otus . . . for now.

Otus and I try to sneak past the security desk only to be intercepted by a portly security guard. "Can I help you?"

I pretend to shake with excitement, exclaiming, "Yes, we're here to see Dick Van Hugo. We're big fans of his."

"Fans aren't allowed past the lobby to protect the artists' privacy."

"Artists?"

"It's what they like to be called."

"Are you sure there's nothing you can do? Dick has just been part of some of our most intimate moments." I grab Otus's hand and pull him close to sell it. "I knew this idiot was the one for me when he agreed to reenact Dick's scene from 'Who's Your Daddy' on our last anniversary."

"I'm sorry. Employees only."

"Thank you for your time. Sorry to bother you."

Otus and I turn, heading for the door. Once we get outside and around the corner of the studio, I turn to Otus. He shrugs and asks, "What are we going to do now?"

"I think it's time I use some of my COMM skills to hack them."

"You were a hacker?"

"More or less."

"I've got a laptop you can use, but I'll need to clean it up first."

I raise an eyebrow, surprised. "Why?"

"There's a lot of . . . well, porn on it. Like a lot. I'm fairly sure I have like a thousand of those virus things."

My stomach churns at the idea of so many viruses and the mistreatment of a computer. "You've got issues, man."

Otus signs, scratching his head before saying, "You have no idea."

Otus

The gentle humming and buzz of the coffee shop soothes my fragile psyché as Arien works on my computer, trying to break into the studio's servers. A barista silently delivers our coffee before giving us privacy. Once we're alone, I ask, "What are you doing?"

He doesn't even look up as he responds, "I'm breaking into the studio's intranet server to access the potential client database. I'm going to create a fake portfolio for myself and get hired as one of the new artists."

"Why don't you just access Apollo's personal records and get his address?"

"It's stored on an offline database, I'd have to be onsite to access it either way, and this way I'll be able to get an invitation to see Apollo. He probably has some security of his own. Besides, this is more fun."

I shake my head in incredulity, remembering my porn star days to be far less glamourous. "What kinda porn star is he?"

"The kind with houses in three American cities and two European ones."

"So, how are you going to pretend that you're like him? Won't you need a demo reel or photos or something?"

"I am very good at Photoshop and DeepFake."

I smile slightly at the absurdity of the plan. "So, you're faking that you're a gay porn star to get hired and meet Apollo on the set of a porno?"

Arien misses the tone of my voice, continuing to type furiously. "Basically. I'm saying that I've moved from LA to Miami and need to get signed on with a new agency. Humping Harry's doubles as an agency. I'm even drafting fake character references from my old one."

"I had no idea you could do stuff like this."

Arien's voice comes off as passive-aggressive and slightly worried as notes, "There's a lot you don't know about me."

I stare at Arien for a moment, saddened by this little boy who craves meaning but will never find it. "I'm starting to see that."

Arien clears his throat and shakes his head, finally looking up from the laptop. "What about you? Tell me about yourself. What was it like living for 2 thousand years?"

I stiffen suddenly, my mind filling with memories of a life gone. "Not really much to say. It's hard to remember a lot of things after all this time." My eyes go distant as I smile a little, remembering the good times. "There was this girl, once."

"Really? Tell me about her."

"Her name was Cassia. I met her when I was 16 on the road to Rome. I was moving there from Sparta because I wanted to be a sculptor, and Sparta isn't exactly known for its art. My cart slipped on the edge of a ravine and was being pulled in. My horse was only just keeping it from falling in. That's when she showed up. Her eyes were the color of pure gold, and her hair shone in the sun like an autumn's breeze. She helped pull out my cart with her horse.

"She was traveling with a group of Christian missionaries to Naples. She asked if I wanted to join her caravan for the rest of the journey. I accepted, and we spent every moment together for the next two weeks. We fell in love, and I asked her to marry me. I gave up my dreams of being a sculptor to move with her to Naples. It was hard at first being of two different faiths, but we eventually learned to respect each other's beliefs and learn to love each other, no matter what.

"We had a daughter together. Her name was Eve. She was so beautiful. She had her Mother's eyes. For Eve's third birthday, we took her to the market to let her pick out any toy that she wanted. She chose a silver owl figurine." I slowly pull the dilapidated owl figurine from my pocket.

"It cost a month's wage, but it was worth it for the look in her eyes. She named it Little Eve. That was the last time I saw her smile. A group of Roman puritans rode into the market and started herding everyone together, hunting for Christians. A local priest was with them. He told them who was Christian and who was not. They dragged my wife and daughter into the square and burned them at the stake. I've never felt so helpless as I did that day. I tried to get them to kill me too, but the priest told them I was Greek, so they refused. There weren't enough non-Christians in the world, and they had to preserve everyone that they found."

Arien's eyes are filled with pity; he confesses, "That's horrible. Christianity shouldn't be a death sentence, despite its creator."

"That's the day I learned that every religion has monsters and heroes. But I stopped believing that there was a higher power. It was just me, alone in the world. For a long time, I wanted to die just like you. Even now, I sometimes regret not doing it. I found purpose again in serving Athena after she fell out of the sky into my house. She gave my life meaning again. Gave me hope. When she asked if I had any wish she could fulfill, I considered asking to join my family, but I knew they'd never understand the man that I had become. The darkness I had let fester. So, I asked her to let me serve her until I was a man who could look them in the eye and know I deserved them. I've been alone for 2 thousand years because I don't think I can ever become that man. But I'm always trying. And isn't that the whole point?"

Arien seems to look at me with newfound respect in his eyes. I wipe the tears rolling down my cheeks, changing the subject, "Anyway, how's it coming?"

Arien sighs softly, slowly turning the laptop to show me. He explains, "I am now Jeffery Harden. Gay porn star from LA. I still need time to finish the photos and videos, but I've created my identity and inputted it into their system. I just need to call the agent and set up an appointment now."

"Great. I'm just going to run to the loo real fast." I get up and quickly walk to the back, embarrassed and ashamed that I'd opened myself like that.

CHAPTER 9: GAY FOR PAY

A security guard whistles as he locks up Humping Harry's for the night. Locking the front door, he turns off the main lights and returns to his desk. Rachel is suddenly standing just inside the front door. She lilts sweetly, "Excuse me?"

The guard turns in surprise before looking down at the keys in his hands in confusion. Rachel notices and explains, "The door was unlocked. Is this Humping Harry's Studios?"

"Yes, but we're closed, so you'll have to come back tomorrow."

Rachel walks up to the guard's desk while playing with her jacket's zipper. "I have an audition. They told me 10:30."

"Sorry, they must have meant a.m. because we're closed."

"Maybe I can just audition with you." Rachel unzips the front of her jacket to reveal her bare breasts. The guard gulps violently before sitting down to hide his boner. Rachel smiles, "You like what you see?"

"Uh-huh."

"Do you think I'd be a good fit?"

The guard shakes his head to clear it before standing. "We have people like you coming in all the time. You'll have to verify your appointment and come back while we're open."

"But I don't like not getting what I want."

The guard scoffs slightly, "Get used to it. It's being an adult."

"But what about little William?"

The guard stares at Rachel in shock and slight horror. "William?"

Rachel smiles, menacingly. "I always get what I want, no matter what. So, how's little Willy gonna feel when he wakes up and doesn't have a Father?"

The guard draws his baton. "Are you threatening me?"

"Just stating facts. Though, I don't think little Willy will be all that disappointed after you walked out on him because you didn't love Mommy."

The guard tenses. "I didn't walk out on him. We have shared custody."

Rachel cocks her head to the side at an awkward angle and puffs out her bare chest as Willy's voice comes out of her mouth, "Daddy, why'd you leave me? Do you not love me?"

Stumbling back in fear, the guard stares at Rachel with unrestrained terror. "Who are you?"

In her ghostly muted voice, Rachel says, "Anyone I want." She reaches up and slits the guard's throat with her nails; he clutches his throat before falling to his knees. Rachel reaches down and grabs his security badge before pushing him to the floor. Sitting at the guard's desk, she uses his card to sign into his computer.

When she's prompted for a password, Rachel turns to the dying man and asks, "Password? Hey, what's your password?" The guard just gurgles up some blood. "William1? Should have guessed that."

Rachel signs in and smiles when she sees that the guard's wallpaper is of Emma Watson posing sexily. "Emma Watson, huh? You've got the right idea. I haven't really enjoyed a good murder in a while." She turns and rolls her chair closer to the guard before lifting up one of her legs onto the desk. "Can you turn this way a little? I like to look my victims in the eyes when I do this."

The guard doesn't move as his life is finally starting to fade away.

"I said turn." Rachel snaps her fingers and the guard rolls over to face her. "That's better." Rachel reaches down and dips her hand in the guard's blood before sticking it down the front of her pants. She moans softly as she starts to pleasure herself. Her hand moves faster and faster until she screams softly.

"Love a good pussy."

Rachel wipes her hand and re-buttons her pants before turning back to the computer. She opens the employee database and searches for 'Dick Van Hugo.' She smiles as his address pops up.

Otus

Music hums over the surround sound, giving off a distinctly hospital lobby vibe. Arien and I walk to the front desk as the secretary answers her ringing phone. "Humping Harry's Studios, Courtney Greene's office. This is Annie speaking. How may I help you?" Annie takes out a pen and starts to write down what she's hearing. "OK, just let me write this down. The new venue is at 221B Privet Drive in Hill Valley. That's just like half a mile down the beach, right?

"Perfect. Thanks, Ronnie. I'll see you later. Bye."

Annie hangs up and turns to us; she pauses as she looks up and down Arien's frankly absurd outfit, an amalgamation of classic Michael Jackson and Pennywise. "How can I help you?"

I try not to laugh or smile as Arien speaks, his character a country valley girl and gangster hybrid, strange as it sounds. "Yeah, man. I'm here for like my audition and stuff. Gotta beat the meat, girrrrrrl."

Annie's eyes fill with incredulity as she tries to process Arien's persona. "Excuse me?"

I step forward, ready to play my part of grounded lawyer to offset Arien's off-putting demeanor. "I'm sorry. My name's Daniel Kaffee. This is my client Jeffery Harden. We have an appointment with Mrs. Greene for 9:30."

Annie glances between Arien and I, clearly confused about our relationship. She eventually turns to me, choosing the spokesman. "What type of client is he to you?"

"I'm his legal counsel."

"Most artists don't bring legal counsel to auditions."

"Jeff is a special case. Highly talented, but needing a little extra attention." I motion for Annie to look at Arien, who has just got his fingers stuck in a decorative Chinese finger trap from Anne's desk.

"I see. Please have a seat and Mrs. Greene will be right with you."

"Thank you." I turn to Arien, who is still struggling to free his fingers. "Come on, Jeff."

Arien pretends to pout, glaring at his fingers. "I'm stuck."

"Give it here." I struggle to get Arien free, wondering if he's truly stuck or acting. His fingers are eventually freed. I give Annie an awkward smile and herd Arien over to a line of chairs, sitting him down next to a stranger.

Sighing, I lean back and run my fingers through my hair; this is proving to be more challenging than I'd thought.

The stranger catches Arien's attention; I look over to see a fit man with greying-black hair and a book in hand. Arien leans over the stranger's shoulder to look at the book. "Whatcha reading? How to bone 101?" Arien lets out an awkward laugh before softly punching the stranger's shoulder for effect.

The man recoils slightly in mild disgust, condemning, "No, it's Plato's Republic."

"Woah. You're like brainy and stuff? What are you doing here?"

"I enjoy the work and it pays well. Gotta fund my doctorate somehow."

Arien snorts comically. "You're gonna be a doctor. That's funny. Hey, your stage name could be Dr. Cock." Arien lets out his ridiculous laugh again.

"Despite what you seem to believe, most porn stars are just regular people with regular lives. By your adolescent ideas of us, it's clear you've never done this before."

"True, I ain't been doing this long, but porn stars ain't normal. We are above average. We special. A special kinda horny." Arien thrusts his hips forward.

The stranger sneers at Arien with un-abashed dislike. "You're a disgrace to this industry. It's people like you that give us a bad name."

Annie stands up from her desk and grabs her bag before turning to the stranger. "You ready, Mike."

Mike nods and answers, "Coming." He stands, grabbing his stuff before walking to Annie and kissing her.

Annie pulls back and turns to me. "She's ready for you. You can go right in. I'll be back from my breakfast break soon if you need anything." Annie and Mike walk out hand-in-hand as Arien and I head into the inner office.

Courtney Greene stands up to greet us as we walk in. "It's a pleasure to meet you both. I'm Mrs. Greene. I'll be conducting your interview and audition today."

We shake hands and I explain, "I'm Daniel Kaffee and this is my client, Jeffery Harden."

"Yes, Annie told me about your unique situation. Please, have a seat." Everyone sits down as Courtney pulls up Arien's portfolio on her computer. "I see you started out as a stripper before joining with the Asinine agency. What type of work did you do for them?"

Arien shrugs and wipes his nose, trying to be cool and aloof. "Ah, yeah. I did, like, mostly butt stuff with them, yeah. They were like so cool. They really let me take the spotlight and show my big dick off."

Courtney's eyes widen a little in exacerbation before shaking her head and turning to me. "What was Jeffery's primary genre?"

"His trademark was threesomes reenacting scenes from film and television. His big audience were nerds with fantasies of Black Widow and Scarlet Witch going at it with Hawkeye, for example."

"There's not a big market out here for nerd driven films. The closeted stepbrother category is what's really popular right now. He doesn't have a lot of gay films listed here. Is he open to doing them?"

"Jeff is down for whatever."

"You have a lot of great material. I'll just need a practical demonstration from Jeff and if it's satisfactory, we can move forward with the hiring process."

"Great. What would you like him to do?"

Courtney stands and motions for us to follow her to the small studio in her office corner. "My approach is somewhat unique. I believe if a performer can seduce an inanimate object and make it look sexy, then they can make anything look sexy." Courtney motions for Arien to stand in front of the camera next to a small desk.

My eyes widen as I struggle to restrain my laughter, realizing what Arien's going to have to do.

Courtney waits for Arien to walk to the desk, explaining, "Seduce the desk and fuck its brain's out."

Arien stares at the desk in confusion, his performance forgotten. "There's no hole."

"Just hump under the countertop, or something. You're not doing anything for real, it's just for appearance's sake. Figure something out. Make it a distinctly you performance."

Arien shakes his head, accepting his fate. "Alright."

I move to stand behind the camera, relishing in the absurdity of the scene as I take out my phone to record as well, knowing this footage will be priceless someday.

Courtney motions for Arien to begin.

Arien turns to the desk and gushes, "Hey, baby. Have you been wicked?" He sexily strokes his fingers along the edge and moans softly. "You're so soft." Sliding the very tips of his fingers under the edge of the countertop, he adds, "So wet." Arien takes off his shirt before sliding down to his knees. "You're so goddamn beautiful." With a tentative kiss on the lip of the desk, he reaches up and traces a single finger over the curves of the edge. He sticks out his tongue and licks the desk's soft lips. "Ah, yeah. You like that, baby. You dirty slut. Take it."

Arien sticks three fingers under the edge and starts sliding them in and out, faster and faster, as he continues to lick the lip. He starts to moan encouragement as his fingers continue to go faster and faster. Stopping suddenly, he stands and pulls down his pants. Courtney gasps as she sees his cock.

Arien bends down and starts humping below the edge of the desk. He reaches his hand around and slaps its side. "Fuck, yeah. Take that big cock."

Courtney is entranced by Arien's graceful seduction of a hunch of wood. Arien slows as he pretends to climax before dressing.

Arien turns to Courtney, his character of Jeff back in place. "That there was great. You've a fucking sexy desk. Barely knew that it wasn't a woman."

Courtney shakes her head at Arien's stupidity before leading us back to her desk. "You definitely qualify to continue the process of getting hired. To start with, I always hire performers on a contract basis until their worth is proven. We have an orgy shoot on the beach tomorrow at noon. When Annie gets back, she can help fill out all the paperwork for the contract. For contractors, we pay $35 by the hour. We'll do a few jobs together, then I'll consider making you a full-time member of the Humping Harry's family. Is that acceptable?"

I reach out to shake Courtney's hand. "Yes, very acceptable. You've given me far more than I'd hoped for. Thank you for your time."

Arien shakes Courtney's hand, noting, "That there is a great desk, you have."

She smiles awkwardly. "Thank you."

I drag Arien out of the office as Courtney stares after us.

Arien

Shame fills me and occasionally forces me to stop and re-live the fucking of the desk. I'm not ashamed that I did it, I'm ashamed that it's the most I've ever done, the closest to a woman's touch. After another fit of embarrassment, I shake my head to clear it before carrying a stack of pizzas into our hotel room. Otus and I start eating and I note, "Gotta carb up for my big performance tomorrow."

Otus turns to me in surprise. "You're not actually going to film the orgy."

I pretend to smile, trying to play myself off as a player. "What do you mean? I could use some good sex."

Otus grins broadly with a trace of sadness. "You're not going to be able to go through with it."

My heart stops, wondering if he knows my shame, my deepest secret. "Of course, I will. It's just sex."

"It's not going to be up to you."

"What are you talking about?"

"Nothing."

My phone buzzes, changing the subject. "It's Annie. She just sent over the address for the venue tomorrow. She says to make sure that I show the text to you because it's a little complicated."

"That's all due to that ridiculous performance of yours."

"Had to have an excuse for you to come too."

"You know I'm posting that video online as soon as this is all over, right?"

I shake my head, praying that he never will. "You'd have to figure out how to use a computer first."

"I know how to use one."

"Just for porn. I saw your computer, remember?"

Otus stiffens up as he gets defensive; obviously, his addiction is a touchy subject. "It gets rough after being alone for 2 thousand years."

The sharp turn that our conversation had just made surprises me. The fake smile I've been forcing fades as I remember Otus's story. "Sorry."

Otus grunts as he contains his annoyance. "Whatever. Just remember, tomorrow we're just getting on set to talk to Apollo. Nothing else. Got it?"

"I got it."

Otus nods and turns back to eating his food.

CHAPTER 10: FIRST STEPS

Two intimidating bouncers filter guests into a party raging in an ornate penthouse. Rachel joins a group and tries to slip in unnoticed, but a bouncer grabs her and pulls her aside. "Who are you?"

Rachel's voice high and lilting, she says, "Oh, hi. I'm here as a guest of Dick's. We met on the pier last week. It was so magical. He told me about this party and said I just needed to ask for him and I could get in."

The bouncer sneers slightly, relishing in his perceived power. "Dick's been in Barcelona for the last month. Only got back in yesterday. So, get on out of here." The bouncer gently pushes Rachel back toward the door. "A little advice, next time you try sneaking into a celebrity's party, wear something a lot nicer. You look like a diner worker."

Rachel cocks her head to the side, her sorority girl demeanor gone. "I didn't want to get blood on my nice clothes."

"What?"

Rachel draws a pistol and shoots the bouncer in the face. Everyone screams and dives for cover as she turns and fires at the other bouncer. Rachel continues shooting until all the guests outside of the penthouse are dead and strewn around the hallway.

Rachel stares down at her gun in awe. "I really wish that I had one of these back in the day." Rachel drops her empty gun before walking into the still raging party.

Rachel stops in surprise, not only because the music is so loud that no one had heard the gunfire, but also because this isn't a party, it's an orgy.

A naked woman walks up to Rachel and looks her over. "Whatcha doing, baby? You're wearing too many clothes."

"Maybe I need some help taking them off."

"I'll see what I can do." The woman briefly kisses Rachel before kneeling down and unbuttoning her pants. Rachel runs her fingers through the woman's hair as she goes down on her. A man walks up and kisses Rachel before kneeling down behind the woman and thrusting into her from behind.

Rachel slowly starts to moan louder and louder as she presses the woman's face into her. She screams and finishes before stabbing the woman in the back of the head. The woman's body goes limb causing the man the fall back in horror. Rachel re-button's her pants as the man starts screaming, completely unnoticed.

Rachel's eyes are drawn to the fireplace, where a set of katanas are mounted on the wall. She smiles sinisterly.

***

Newbie cop Mark Gibbs walks down the sidewalk with 2 coffees in hand toward his patrol car, where his senior partner Jamal Jordan waits.

A group of political protesters march past Mark with signs held high calling for gun control. As Mark walks through the group, all chanting and cheering stops as they stare at him.

A protester sneers and whispers, "Pig!"

Mark ignores the whispered abuse being thrown his way and continues on towards his car.

The protesters become more confidant as one shouts, "Protect, serve, and murder us."

Mark accidentally bumps into a young and beautiful black woman named Clara Williams as he gets through the protesters. The whole group becomes silent, staring at Mark.

Clara steps back and holds her hands up, genuine fear in her voice. "Don't shoot me. It was an accident."

Mark's eyes filling with fear and confusion, he stammers, "I'm not . . . I'm sorry, it was my fault."

A protester screams, "Police brutality. Racial targeting."

The protesters all take up the cry and surround Mark, their yelling getting louder and louder. Mark tries to shout over the noise and explain the misunderstanding, but when he is ignored, he reaches back and hovers his hand over his taser. "Please step back and let me through."

"You can't kill us all."

Jamal gets out of his car and rushes to help his partner. "Step away from him."

The protesters suddenly get quiet when they see Jamal, surprised that he is also African American.

Whispers float through the air, saying things like, "Traitor!" and, "Uncle Tom."

Jamal carefully makes his way through the mob to Mark's side. "You OK?"

"Fine."

Jamal turns back to the crowd. "Nothing's happened here that can't be forgotten. Best keep it that way and keep moving."

"Did you just threaten us?"

"Not yet. Let's end this peacefully."

"Pigs get killed all the time."

Jamal's jaw clenches, remembering his fallen brothers and sisters. "More than anyone cares to notice. We're trained to protect ourselves and others. If you do this, we'll win, but it will look very bad for us and people will get hurt when no one needs to. You can stop this."

A shout and a war cry ring out. "Death to pigs."

A white man grabs Mark from behind and punches him in the face. Jamal draws his baton and hits the man in the stomach before pushing him back. The protesters all surge forward as Mark and Jamal barely manage to keep them back.

Jamal has had enough, so he draws his gun. "Stand down."

The group scatters, leaving only the man who struck Mark on the ground and Clara hiding in a nearby alley.

Jamal turns to Mark. "You good?"

"Yeah, I'm good."

"Hell of a first day."

"Tell me about it."

Jamal looks down at the moaning white man. "Help me with him?"

"Yes, sir."

Jamal and Mark handcuff the man and put him in the back of their patrol car before Mark asks, "Why do they hate us so much? We never did anything to them."

Jamal sighs and leans against the patrol car. "Remember the 2020 protests? A lot of bad cops made everyone believe that we're all sadistic monsters like them."

"They even hated you. I thought they hated cops because of racism."

"Some of the do, and maybe rightly so, but it's not always about racism. Some people pervert a just cause to support their own violent tendencies."

Clara carefully steps out of the alley and walks toward Mark. Jamal tenses and motions for Mark to turn around.

Clara puts her hands back in the air. "I'm not here to fight. I just want to talk."

Jamal relaxes and motions for Clara to put her hands down. She approaches and concedes, "I'm sorry about what happened. I know it was an accident, and I overreacted."

"What's someone like you doing with people like them?"

Clara looks away, not entirely proud. "It's how my parents raised me. All white folks and cops are bad, especially after 2020." Clara turns to Mark. "But you're not. I guess no one chooses what their Fathers do."

Mark smiles sadly, full of innocence soon to be spoiled. "I just wanna help."

Clara nods slightly. "Maybe things have gotten a little better since George Floyd, especially if you both are the new norm."

Jamal looks down at Clara with a shared understanding. "Maybe."

Clara nods at both of them, turning to walk away.

The sound of glass breaking comes from the penthouse of the apartment building far above. Mark looks up to see several bodies falling, crashing down towards them. He steps forward and pushes Clara out of the way just as a body slams down. Mark is hit and flattened into the pavement.

Jamal rushes to Mark's prone form and checks for vitals as he hears Mark whisper, "I just wanted to help."

When Mark stops breathing, Jamal turns on his radio. "This is Officer Jordan. Requesting backup and medical personnel to Clinton Apartments on Jefferson way. Officer Gibbs is down. Multiple casualties. They've been stabbed and thrown from the top floor. I'm proceeding up to investigate."

Jamal stands and turns off his radio before drawing his gun and proceeding into the building.

***

Rachel cleans off her katanas as she oversees the horde of bodies she had just dismembered. A slight breeze coming from the broken window ruffles her hair as sparks fly from the broken speakers. "The Japanese knew what they were doing when they designed katanas."

A naked man moans and moves slightly despite the gaping hole in his chest.

Rachel smiles, impressed. "Oh, you're a tough guy, aren't you?" Rachel walks to the man and lifts him up by his hair. "You know, you look like a guy I used to know from Troezen. Or was it Athens?" She stares to the side as she tries to remember. "His name was Theseus, I think. Sly little bastard killed me to prove himself heroic. Bunch of bullshit, considering how he ended up." Rachel returns her gaze to the man and smiles. "I was known as 'The Stretcher' back then. Maybe I should bring back some of my old techniques." She leers menacingly at the man. "Where's Apollo?"

The man's eyes are filled with fear and panic, his voice trembling with pain. "Who?"

Rachel rolls her eyes in exacerbation. "Dick."

"I don't know. He's not here."

"Too bad. I may have let you live." Rachel presses the edge of her sword against the man's throat.

"Wow, I know where he's going to be. It's . . . ah."

Growing impatient, Rachel commands, "Speak."

"221B Privet Drive in Hill Valley on the beach, I think. There's a shoot going on there."

A smile cracks Rachel's face. "Finally, a man of character."

Jamal bursts through the door, gun raised; he stares in horror at the bodies littered about.

Rachel turns, standing, and biting her lip in excitement. "A lawman. How nice."

Jamal turns his gaze back to Rachel before cocking his pistol. She raises her hands in mock surrender, gushing, "Ooh, with a gun too. Finally, someone who has a chance of stopping me."

"Stand down. I'm with Miami PD. You will cease and desist."

In the bedroom, a nude Rose Piper crawls out from her hiding place under the bed toward the closet as Jamal starts yelling louder in the next room. "Step away from that man."

"What are you gonna do? Too many laws stop you from pulling that trigger. What can you do?"

Rose opens the closet door to reveal a large gun safe. She carefully enters the code to unlock it before choosing a shotgun. Walking to the built-in bedroom bar, she opens another safe hidden beneath it, pulling out ammo for her shotgun.

Jamal's voice trembles as his stares at the blood-soaked Rachel. "I am authorized to shoot you in defense of myself or hostages, if necessary."

"What if there aren't any hostages?"

"What?"

Rachel slits her hostage's throat before throwing the body at Jamal with incredible force. Jamal is thrown back against the wall and trapped beneath the man's body.

Rachel sneers in perverse pleasure. "What now?"

Jamal struggles out from beneath the body, only to smile slightly as he sees Rose gearing up to shoot Rachel. "You shouldn't have stood so close to the window."

With the faintest sign of fear and confusion, Rachel mumbles, "What?"

Rose steps round the corner and fires both barrels of her shotgun into Rachel's gut. Rachel is thrown back and out the window.

Rose huffs slightly as she stares after Rachel. "Welcome to Florida, bitch."

Jamal checks that the man is dead before rushing to the window and looking down. There's a massive dent in the roof of his patrol car but no body. Jamal stares in horror as several police cars pull up and rush the building. He sighs as he sees that Clara is still knelt over Mark's crushed body.

CHAPTER 11: RUBBLE OF AN OLD LIFE

<u>**Arien**</u>

I tremble with fear, anticipation, and shame as Otus and I walk toward the gated beach in our swimsuits. Otus turns to me and asks, "Are you ready for this?"

My voice quavers, "Fuck, no." I wonder if Otus knows my secret. It seemed like he hinted at it last night, but I can't be sure. Can my shame be seen?

A security guard stops us at the beach gate. "Can I help you?"

I breathe in deep, taking on my Jeffrey Harden persona. "Yeah, course, my man. Of course. I'm like, with the Humping Harry's crew. Name's Jeffery Harden. The one and only."

The guard flips through his list of names on a clipboard. "Jeffery Harden? Yes. You're here. Can I see some ID?"

"Course, my man." I pretend to check his pockets, kicking myself for not making a fake ID. "Ah, fuck. I left my wallet in my jeans."

"I can't let you in without verifying your identity."

Otus sees Annie walking by and starts waving at her. "Annie, over here."

Annie walks over, smiling. "It's alright, Kyle. They're with us.

"Alright. Go on through."

Annie leads us through the gate and down to the beach where they're setting up for the orgy. "You guys can just hang out for now. I'll come and get you when we're ready for you."

Annie walks away as we start looking around for Apollo. "You see him?"

Otus shakes his head slowly. "No. He's the star. He'll probably be the last one to show up."

Several hot and scantily clad women saunter over to us. "Hey, handsome. You going to be fucking us today?"

I gulp slowly, trying not to show my intimidation as the woman starts to trace her fingers over my bare chest. Otus smiles at me, stroking the woman fawning over him.

"That's the hope," I mutter with feigned confidence.

"Well, I hope you wreck my cunt and fuck my brains out." The woman reaches down and grabs my dick tightly. I gasp as the woman's eyes go distant; she lets go before turning and walking away.

Otus kisses his woman before sending her on her way. "That's happened before, hasn't it?"

Pain fills my head, pressing into my eyes. "Every time I've almost been with a woman. It's as if they can't see or even remember me."

"You're a virgin?"

It's not a question, but I turn away in shame and nod slightly anyway. "I act tough but, honestly, it's one of the reasons that I tried to kill myself. I always thought it was because I was ugly but now . . ."

"You're an idiot."

I turn back to Otus, shocked, and hurt. "Thanks for that. Way to hit me while I'm down."

"I was trying to tell you yesterday. You're a maiden goddess."

"What?"

"You have the divinity of Athena inside of you. Anytime you get close to having sex, the divinity will intervene to maintain its purity."

I rub my chin, processing this information, hoping it's true, hoping for an excuse that means I'm not repulsive. "I guess I won't be filming this orgy."

"No."

An almost magical song starts wafting across the beach. Otus and I both turn to see Apollo slowly walking across the beach toward the set. Time seems to slow as he winks and points at one of the many people staring at him. Several jaws drop as this magical movie moment continues.

The spell is suddenly broken as Apollo turns to walk under his private pavilion.

Otus drools, "He's like a Marvel Chris."

"I just became a little gay."

"Join the club, man."

Annie climbs onto an apple box and shouts, "Alright, everyone. We'll be starting soon. Dick just needs to get warmed up, then we'll get started. Get to your starting positions."

Apollo starts doing a short workout routine in-between his lawn chairs as Otus says, "Let's go talk to him."

We start heading toward Apollo's pavilion but Annie steps in front of us. "Alright, Jeffery. You're going to be working mainly with Saint Mary today." Annie turns to point at a pair of girls making out. "She's the one over there making out with the redhead. We want you to start with doggy style, but feel free to shake things up as you go along. Switch partners or whatever. You will be expected to do some gay stuff, just so you know. We'll start as soon as Dick's ready. Just ask Mary where she wants to start and go from there. OK? Any questions?"

Otus steps forward to answer. "No, I think we're good."

"Great. Good luck."

Annie moves on to another group of models as we continue on toward Apollo. Apollo is standing behind a chair, getting a blowjob from Mike; he lifts his champagne glass off Mike's head to salute us with it. "Hey, how are you guys?"

Otus raises an eyebrow, clearly hoping Apollo remembers him "Good."

"You guys new? I don't think we've met. I'm Dick Van Hugo." Apollo reaches over Mike's head to shake both our hands.

"It's good to see you, Will."

Apollo's grin disappears as he looks closer at Otus. "Otus?"

Smiling sadly, Otus notes, "Long time."

Apollo swats Mike away and zips up his pants. "Give me a second." He turns and yells at everyone inside his pavilion. "Everybody out. I need some time alone with these two." Everyone, begrudgingly, leaves as Apollo motions for us to sit down. "How'd you find me?"

"You have a memorable face."

Tensing, Apollo turns to glare at me. "I like my life, and I don't want any demigods screwing it up."

"I'm not a demigod."

"Then, who are you?"

"Can't you tell?"

Apollo looks deep into my eyes before leaning back in shock. "Athena?"

A soft scream in the distance makes us all turn. A group of people are gathering around the gate and crying. Apollo looks back at me, ignoring the crowd. "So, why are you here?"

Otus leans forward, "One last effort to kill Timorian."

Apollo grins and shakes his head at our perceived stupidity. "How?"

I suddenly realize that Apollo doesn't want his old life back, he doesn't want things to change. I hadn't prepared to convince him otherwise, so I simply say, "By making you all gods again."

Otus clearly knows what Apollo desires because he declares, "Songs will be sung about you. People will remember you again. They'll worship you. You'll be more famous than ever if you just help us."

Apollo smiles and starts to speak but is interrupted by Annie running over and trying to talk between the sobs racking her. "Dick, they're dead. They're all dead."

Apollo stands and holds Annie tightly. "Slow down, Annie. Who's dead?"

"Everyone at your house last night. They're all dead."

The color drains from Apollo's face as he pulls back to look into Annie's eyes. "What happened?"

"Some crazy woman."

"What?"

"She killed them all."

Apollo breathes deep and bites his lip, trying to control his emotions. "How many people were there?"

"They don't know yet. They're still cleaning up all the bodies."

Annie's sobs get stronger, so Apollo pulls her back into a hug. "What about Rose?"

"I don't know."

"It's gonna be alright."

"How can you know that? Any one of us could have been there. Any of us could be dead now. If you hadn't come over last night, I don't know what I would have done."

"We're OK. We're safe." Apollo glares at Otus and I before leading Annie over to the outdoor bar and getting her a drink. Once Annie is good, Apollo storms back over to us. "You brought monsters here."

I shake my head, not knowing what to do. "We couldn't have."

A scream from the gate makes us all turn. A woman is at the gate standing over the security guard's corpse. Everyone screams and scatters as the woman starts walking toward Apollo's pavilion.

My eyes widen as I recognize her. "Rachel?"

Apollo growls, "She's possessed by an Eidolon."

Otus's body tensing, he mutters, "Fuck."

Apollo turns and glares at me. "Because of you, she's killed my friends. My life's over. Now, I'm going to kill her."

Horrified, I say, "No, Rachel's a good person."

"That's not Rachel anymore. My divinity is in Phoenix in my first folio. There's a witch, Medea, guarding it. You'll need a witch's help to get it. Bring my divinity back and I'll fight. Can't fuck forever."

Apollo starts walking toward Rachel across the beach, leaving Otus and I to turn and run.

Apollo

I stand now in the rubble of my old life, it crumbles even as I watch. The fair child with the spirit of a monster inside slowly saunters toward me, killing indiscriminately as she goes. All I can do is put on a brave and disarming smile, asking, "You here for the orgy? I'm afraid we're fully booked, but I'm sure I could give you a private show."

The Eidolon's deep and distorted voice echoes across the beach, like a drum calling me to war, calling me back to my old life. "Are you Apollo?

"The one and only. Singer of songs and fucker of all. Part-time dancer too."

"You stand accused of godhood and are sentenced to death in the name of Kronos, lord of all."

"So formal. You'll make a girl blush."

The child's hand is raised, lifting a gleaming knife, droplets of blood drip off the blade, each standing in judgment of me, blaming me for the part I played in spilling them.

The blade slashes through the air toward my exposed throat, I side-step, grabbing my assailant's wrist and twisting it behind her back. "Oh, nice ass."

The girl's head crashes back into my chin, forcing me to loosen my grip. She spins around to cut at my side.

Hordes of police cars pull up to the beach; a tall, intimidating officer with death in his eyes leads the charge toward our raging bodies. He refrains even from a shout of warning before drawing his pistol and firing round after round into Rachel.

The Eidolon turns and stares as she takes bullet after bullet. She fights for every step toward the officer before he grabs an automatic rifle from a nearby SWAT officer and starts unloading fresh rounds into her.

I stare slack-jawed and dumbfounded as Rachel stumbles back and collapses. The officer stops firing long enough to walk up to Rachel's corpse before firing several more rounds into her exposed skull.

The SWAT officer rushes up and takes the gun from the officer. "Holy shit," he whispers in shock. He handcuffs Jamal, declaring, "Officer Jamal Jordan. I have no choice but to put you under arrest."

Jamal doesn't fight his arrest as he glares at Rachel's mangled corpse. "Careful, she doesn't die easily."

The SWAT officer drags Jamal away. I stare down at the girl, feeling a pang of regret at her fate before turning to follow the officers.

An officer screams in surprise as Rachel struggles to her feet and turns to run into the ocean. The SWAT officer dragging Jamal away stares in horror as loads of policemen rush in after her.

Jamal's jaw clenches as he says, "Told you. You wanna take these off?" The SWAT officer takes off the handcuffs before running to join the chase. Jamal turns to speak to me but pauses when I am nowhere to be found.

CHAPTER 12: FAMILY LEADS

<u>Arien</u>

Otus opens the hotel room door and carries a pile of library books to the corner desk. He stops and sighs when he sees me downing a bottle of vodka on the bed. "Come on, man. That's not going to help."

"It's worth a shot."

Otus sits down in a chair next to the bed. "It's not your fault."

"On what planet have you been living on for the last 2 thousand years? Of course, it's my fault. They were following us, and they found Rachel. I literally put people in danger by just being near them. What fucking good am I to humanity if I keep getting people killed. I couldn't kill myself outright and now other people are dying. What's the goddamn point? OK? So, go suck a dick and fuck off." Tears stream down my cheeks as I take another large swig of vodka.

"If there's one thing that I've learned in 2 thousand years is that people die. Some that should and some that shouldn't. That's never going to change. So, either blow your fucking brains out or grow a pair and keep moving. You'll never forget her or any of the others left in your wake, but how many more dead will there be if you don't try. You'll never know, but at least you will have tried to make a goddamn difference." Otus stands up and walks to the desk. I stare after him, surprised at the passion in his voice. "If you're sober enough, come help me find out how to bag a witch. Get your mind off of it."

I nearly take another sip of vodka but decide not to, stoppering the bottle and standing to help Otus. Picking up a book and starting leafing through it, I stop and moan, "We're never going to find anything in here."

"You got a better idea?" he replies. I shake my head, turning back to the book, so he adds, "Then, try to boogie down and enjoy this." I look back at Otus, confused by his old-timey idiom. He just shakes his head and mutters, "Oh, shut up."

I smile slightly, momentarily forgetting my depression before turning back to the book. "What do we know about this Medea? Why is she guarding the divinity? Isn't she the witch from the story of Perseus?"

"Jason, actually. She was his wife and after he left her, she murdered her children and went on the run. Rumor has it that she ended up in England in the 16th century where she got caught up in the North Berwick witch trials. She was only saved by a renowned playwright named William

Shakespeare, or Apollo as we know him. She swore that day on the river Styx to repay the debt. It's believed that Apollo left her soon after because he saw the darkness inside, but, obviously, he asked her to guard his divinity, instead."

"And we need a witch to what? Garner her trust?"

"As far as I can tell, yes?"

"Which type of witches are we talking about? Harry Potter or the Conjuring?"

"Neither. More like Supernatural."

Impressed by Otus's pop-culture knowledge, I ask, "You can't get a catchphrase from the last century right, but you watch Supernatural."

"What? I'm a sucker for a good gay love story."

I raise an eyebrow, "There's no gay love story."

"Oh, believe me, Destiel is a thing."

Laughing softly, I concede, "You've got a point." I shake my head to refocus, adding, "So, witches with hex bags and the like."

"Yeah, well, no. Papyri scrolls, and curse tablets were their tools of choice."

"Curse tablets?"

"Yeah, old sheets of metal with curses carved into them. In recent years, witches have found if you use the correct wording, the curses can be for good things like, if Cesar goes into battle, his enemies will be cursed with his survival."

I look down and bite my lip, sadness overwhelming me as I remember that I've seen a curse tablet before. "Or, if the man who fears life tries to take is own, he will be cursed with a long, happy life."

"Possibly."

Sighing, I say, "I think I know someone."

"Who?"

"My old roommate, Charlie Bills."

"She still live at your old place?"

"Considering I exploded the last time I was there, I don't think so."

"Do you have any way of contacting her?"

"I don't have her number memorized, but I know someone who probably has it."

"Who?"

"My cousin Molly."

Otus shakes his head violently. "No, absolutely not."

"Why not? They would have met at my funeral and they'd have liked each other. I'm sure they switched numbers. We can just swing by Amber on the way to Phoenix."

"No way. You have to stay dead. If the military finds out you're alive, they'll hunt you for being AWOL. And if the Titans ever find out who you are, they can try to find you through your family. It's better that they think you're dead."

I shrug, knowing Otus is right but unable to imagine a future without Molly. "Molly is all the family I have left. I need to see her."

"Does anyone else know Charlie? Girlfriend? Boyfriend? Family? You're risking everything on your cousin maybe switching phone numbers with her at your funeral. It's a pretty slim chance."

"Maybe, but I do need to see Molly, either way."

Otus lets out an exacerbated sigh. "I don't suppose that I can stop you."

"She's my family. I can't let her think I'm dead."

Family means more to Otus than anything, so he understands my desire. Shaking his head and throwing his hands in defeat, he concedes, "Fine, but I don't like this."

"Not much to like, these days."

CHAPTER 13: GODS OF PREJUDICE

Rachel crawls out of the surf and drags herself up onto the sand under the cover of darkness; she takes a moment to breathe, her breath rattling the mangled mess of her face. A shadowy figure leans over her, blocking out the starlight. Rachel recoils in fear, but the figure just stares down at her, breathing hard.

Tears of fear filling Rachel's eyes, she cries, "There was nothing I could do. There were too many of them."

The figure leans back into the light, it's Atlas. "Mortals did this?"

"They had help. A god was with them."

"Who?"

Rachel smiles as she realizes her life is spared.

***

Apollo walks into his apartment building's lobby, a brisk pep in his step and a fearful look in his eyes. He waves at Margery, who's sitting behind the front desk. "Hey, Margery. How're the kids?"

"Fucking terrible."

Apollo smiles as he presses the button for the elevator. "Yeah, better you than me."

As the elevator closes, a noise draws Margery toward the backdoor. She gingerly reaches out and opens the door.

A scream is torn from her throat as a tremendous force crashes into her.

Up in the penthouse, Apollo cuts through the police tape to get in. He stops and looks around at all the bloodstains and broken furniture. He lets out a sigh of regret before walking back into his bedroom and starting to pack a bag.

Once he's packed, he returns to the lobby, a dead look in his eyes. He adjusts the bag on his shoulder before walking to the front desk and ringing the bell. Apollo waits for a second before leaning to look behind the desk; he can just see a pair of feet dangling beneath an office chair. "Margery, is that you? I need my car pulled around." The woman in the chair doesn't move. "Margery?"

Apollo grabs the back of the chair and spins it around to face him. He screams when he sees Rachel's face, still gaping with bullet holes, staring back at him.

"Aren't I a pretty lady?"

Apollo stumbles back as Rachel stands and starts walking around the desk toward him. He falters as he backs into a giant form behind him. He slowly turns and stares up into Atlas's eyes.

Apollo breathes heavily to calms himself, noting, "Long-time no see."

Atlas punches Apollo in the chest and sends him flying through the front desk. Apollo moans as he struggles to get up before freezing when he sees Margery's mangled corpse hidden beneath the desk.

Apollo spits out blood before looking up at Atlas and Rachel. "How'd you find me? You can't have known that I'd come back."

"Your friend Rose. You shouldn't trust people as much as you trust her."

Grief flashing in Apollo's eyes, he asks, "Rose is dead?"

"Yes, and be glad of that. You wouldn't have been able to withstand the sight of the horrors that Procrustes inflicted on her."

Rachel licks her lips as a tear leaks out of the corner of Apollo's eye.

A strange sadness flickers briefly across Atlas's face, not at home within his hard demeanor. "She was a dryad, yes? Pity. There are so few dryads left."

"If Timorian wants me dead, just do it. Stop dragging it out."

Atlas reaches down and picks up Apollo by the front of his shirt. "No, the man of songs has one last song to sing."

Arien

My heartbeat echoes loudly, loud enough I'm sure the whole world can hear. I stare at the diner's back door with trepidation, almost hoping no one will come out, hoping that I won't need to face her.

Every nerve in my body is on edge being in this town. The air itself seems hostile to me, reminding me of my old life, the person I used to be. Amber is not a town of milk and honey and happy memories for me. It's a dark place of torture and depression. I shouldn't have come back.

The door opens, and Molly steps out. I wait in the shadows, holding my breath and preparing myself. She locks the door behind her for the night before leaning against the wall to collect herself. She seems to be struggling with something before she sighs and shakes her head. "Ah, crap." She removes a grate in the diner wall before pulling out a cigarette box and lighting one up. She gives it a single long puff before starting to visibly relax.

I tense and step out of the shadows. "Still smoking, huh?"

Molly turns and stares at me in shock. "Sam?"

I smile slightly, for the first time happy in this town. "Hey, Molly." I give Molly a sober smile as tears start streaming down her face. "I missed you."

***

As the sun's rays start to peek above the horizon through the diner windows marking the end of a long night, I carefully watch Molly as she processes my story. She rubs her face before reaching across the table to refill her coffee. "Who are you anymore?"

A pang of sadness rings in my heart. Have I changed that much? "What do you mean?"

Molly lets a sigh of exacerbation, waving her hand for emphasis. "I mean, that all can't be true. It's too messed up. It's hard enough to believe that your obsession with Hellenism drove you to join the military, turning from God and becoming pagan, but now you expect me to believe that the Greek gods are real, and that you have one living inside of you, and that an evil ancient Titan created Christianity to destroy the world. Which, by the way, means my entire life has been meaningless. Then you tell me you're on a 'quest' to restore the gods to their glory and lead a war to save mankind from Jesus."

"We're not actually pagan. We don't like that term." Molly gives me a venomous stare, so I add, "Yeah, but the rest is pretty much accurate."

"Alright, then tell me this. If evil Jesus has control of everything, why is he letting everyone discredit Christianity like they've been doing?"

"I don't know. I don't have all the answers."

"Well, you should if you're trying to convert me, or whatever."

"I'm not trying to convert you. I'm just trying to tell you where I've been."

A ruckus and a crash come from the kitchen. Molly and I turn to see Otus standing just inside the door with an awkward grin on his face. "Sorry about that, but the motorcycle was giving me cramps."

I shake my head; trying not to sound condescending, I ask, "You waited all night on the bike?"

"Well, no. Not all night. I got hungry and caught a few mice."

Molly's lip curls in disgust. "You eat mice?"

"He's an owl."

Moly turns to me, dumbfounded. "What?"

Otus starts staring about frantically, looking for something. "Can I use your bathroom? I turned human too soon, and mice don't sit well in a human stomach."

Shaking her head, Molly puts aside her confusion for a moment. "Sure, it's just round the corner."

"This corner?"

After letting Otus search around like a blind man for a moment, I get up, sigh and exclaim, "For God's sake," leading him to the bathroom. Once he's in, I turn and smile at Molly. "Sorry about him. He's like an eccentric old uncle who doesn't understand idioms. I asked for Gandalf got Michael Scott."

"He's not that old."

"He's just shy of 2 thousand."

Molly scoffs slightly. "Sure, he is." She stands and picks up the empty coffee pot, carrying it into the back room.

I watch her walk by before going to the window to stare out at the town bathed in morning's first light. "You know, I can't believe that I'm back here. I fought so hard to leave this place. To escape. And I'm right back where I started. I'm definitely not ready to be back. I can feel all those same feelings coming back. The fear, anxiety, and pain. There's so much pain for me here. All the memories come flooding back."

I hear Molly's footsteps across the floor before I feel her hand upon my shoulder. "Maybe you shouldn't have come."

"You're worth it. You're the only family I have left. You're the only reason I got through my childhood. I owed you this much."

Molly leans against me in gratitude, staring out at the slumbering beast of Amber, waiting for the smallest reason to lash out. "I'm glad you're alive. I know I never said it, but I am."

My body tenses, rejecting that anyone could care for me. "You'd be the first. I . . . ah." I freeze, my self-loathing replaced with deep shame as I see Anna across the street opening up the post office. I grunt and shake my head, trying to play off as casual. Nodding in Anna's direction, I ask, "How's Anna?"

"She went to your funeral, you know."

My surprise makes me turn. "In Phoenix?"

"Yeah."

I turn back to stare at Anna, lost in my memories. Was I wrong about her? "I didn't know she cared that much."

"I think she cared a whole lot more than you ever thought." A car pulls up in front of the diner; Molly twitches and pulls back. "We should go. They'll be opening up soon."

***

From atop a fence, Molly and I watch horses prancing merrily in a field, lost in blissful ignorance. Molly smiles slightly and asks, "You and Anna, huh?"

My jaw clenches, remembering when Anna and I had last sat upon this very fence and the pain that memory holds. "Yeah, well. I don't know if that's ever gonna change. Doesn't matter that she broke my heart." I stop and sigh as the sound of a train at the edge of the field drowns my voice out. Once it's passed, I note, "I definitely wasn't ready to be back here. In this town . . . with these memories."

Sympathy fills Molly's eyes as she glances at me. "You're a good man . . . Arien."

I smile and nod at Molly, thanking her for using my new name for the first time. Pausing, I stare down at my hands, lost in thought. "Molly?"

"Yeah?"

"Have you ever heard of anyone named Brittnie in relation to me?"

"I don't think so. Why?"

"I've been having these visions lately, about a lot of different things, but this Brittnie seems to be at the center of them. I can't tell if she's part of my future or my past. I feel like I should know her. Every time I see her something stirs inside of me. . . She feels like a memory."

"Who do you think she is?"

"I don't know." I stare emptily at the ground for a moment, adding, "Remember how I don't have memories of anything before I was 7, and I remember not having them back then?"

A flicker of tension in Molly briefly catches my attention before disappearing. "Yeah."

"My parents said I ran away. Maybe Brittnie's the one who took me in when I did."

"Maybe."

My eyes wander, deep in contemplation, but I stiffen as I see Rachel standing amidst the horses, just staring at us. "Molly, you need to run."

"Why?" Molly follows my gaze and flinches when she sees Rachel. "Who is she?"

I slide off the fence and take a few steps towards Rachel. "A victim of my depression. Go find Otus and tell him Rachel's here."

"But . . ."

"Go!" I yell with authority. "I've got this."

Rachel walks forward, getting close enough that Molly can see the gaping bullet holes riddling her face and body. She stares in horror at Rachel's deformed face before gagging a little. "Oh, my god."

I heft a nearby pitchfork before walking out to meet Rachel. Molly is rooted to the spot in fear as Rachel and I stop a few paces from each other. Guilt filling me, I exclaim, "Rachel."

Rachel speaks but with the garbled voice of the ghost possessing her. "Name's Procrustes."

"How'd you find us?"

"A quest to Phoenix for godhood, and you stop for sentiment along the way. You're dumber than Atlas gave you credit." I tense at the name of 'Atlas.' "Ah, yes. We know who you are and what you're doing. Your little buddy Apollo sang like a canary. Light a fire under someone and anyone will find their voice. Even now, he's singing of gods and heroes and the lies they tell themselves about how they have a chance to withstand the onslaught that we have prepared for them. Utopia cannot be stopped by anyone."

"Ah, suck a dick."

Rachel smiles as I charge; she ducks under my first blow and spins to slash at the back of my knees. I bring the pitchfork back to block the blow with surprising speed.

I glance up to see Molly still there, staring at us. "Molly, run!"

Rachel smiles at Molly, shoving me back. Molly runs toward the road as I stab Rachel in the back to get her attention. Rachel turns back to me and smiles through her deformed face before reaching around her back and pulling out the pitchfork. I stumble back and trip over a branch, falling to the ground.

Rachel steps forward and admires the blood dripping off the points of the pitchfork. "When Atlas found out that you were still alive, he told me tales of your strength and abilities, but I am, frankly, disappointed." She lets a few drops of blood drip onto her fingers before licking them off. "He said that you came back from the dead. I'll just have to be more thorough."

Rachel raises the pitchfork to deliver the killing blow.

My eyes go black and I scream, sending a dark shockwave shooting out of my upraised hand. Rachel is thrown back as I slowly stand, eyes dancing with fire and night. She cowers as I pick up her discarded blade and start walking toward her. Stopping, I stare down at Rachel's emaciated form, all humanity gone from us both.

Rachel pleads in her human voice, "Please don't hurt me. I didn't mean to kill anyone. I was just following orders. I just wanted to get into Utopia."

Ignoring her petition, I raise the blade for my killing blow. I suddenly stumble back, my hand pressed against my head.

***

I am alone, standing in the endless darkness. Fog swirls up and forms into the fast-food-joint. My memory of Rachel plays as it had happened. Her smile lights up the room, 'Friends' brightening her.

"You a big 'Friends' fan?"

I smile, tears filling my eyes at the star my actions robbed this world of. "The biggest."

Rachel turns to look back at the TV. "This is the one where Rachel and Ross get back together, one of the times at least, with Ross's bald ex-girlfriend."

I laugh a little as I remember. "That's right. . . And the one with her essay that was too long for Ross to see all the details. To see the hurt they'd caused each other."

"I guess. . . You may be a big fan, but you're not as big of a fan as my parents."

I bite my lip, struggling to hold back my tears. "Yeah, why's that?"

"They named me Rachel."

Sniffing, I say, "Ah, the hot one. I can see why."

"There's more to Rachel than that." Rachel smiles, not truly offended.

"So much more. I'm just sorry I didn't get a chance to see it before I got you killed."

"That's sweet."

"I try."

We just smile at each other for a moment, my eyes lost in guilt. Rachel turns back to her register and rings me up. "That'll be 8.50, sir." I quickly pay and take my receipt, which has her phone number written on the back. Rachel winks at me, noting, "If Ross ever wants to see if something can work with Rachel, he can just call her."

I try and fail to smile, whispering, "I think he definitely will."

"He'd better."

***

Back in the pasture standing above the cowering Rachel, my eyes return to their natural blueness as she stares up at me.

Taking a deep breath, I say, "I can't kill you. Not as long as there's a way to save Rachel."

Rachel's eyes fill with hope as she rambles. "Yeah, she's here. She's safe. Keep me alive and she won't get hurt."

Molly and Otus come running up as I start tying Rachel up with some nearby bailing twine.

Otus stares at what I'm doing in shock. "What the hell happened? What are you doing?"

My voice empty of emotions, I explain, "Giving Rachel a break."

"Fuck, man. What are you thinking? She'll kill you first chance she gets. I've been around long enough to know that you can't trust anyone who allies themselves with the Titans."

"We can exorcise her."

"This isn't 'The Case Against Satan.' That's not how it works."

I turn to Otus in confusion. "Case against what?"

"Never mind, just exorcisms aren't a thing. That's Christian lore. Besides, any damage the body takes while possessed is permanent. We 'exorcise' her and those bullet holes in her face kill her instantly. It's too late."

"There's got to be something we can do for her."

"Kill the bastard and give her justice."

Molly steps forward, "No one's killing anyone on my family's property."

"She's a thing. You have to know that. Just look at her fucking face. Nothing human could survive that many gunshots and still smile."

"You're right, I know that there are things that I can't explain, but God says that murder is to be abhorred."

"There's no fucking god. It's just Timorian."

"I'd appreciate it if you didn't say things like that in front of me. There will be no atrocities committed on my property as long as I am here."

Otus throws his hands in defeat. "What are we supposed to do then? Can't let her go. Can't kill her. What, then?"

I stand and stare across the pasture at the railroad. "This is a railroad town."

"What?"

"We can put her on a train. She could end up anywhere."

"Then she comes back with an army and kill us all."

Molly nods slightly. "I'm with Arien."

Otus tenses and grunts. "No, you don't get a vote. You're new."

Turning to Otus, I declare, "There's no other choice."

Otus lets out an exacerbated sigh before reaching up to rub his chin. "Your morality is gonna get us killed."

"Maybe, but it's the only thing that separates us from them."

"I won't be responsible for what happens if we let her live."

"You won't be."

***

Otus and I load the bound and gagged Rachel onto the halted train while Molly watches. I slide the door shut and step back as the train starts to build up speed again.

"What now?" Molly asks, trying her best to maintain herself despite how many times her world has been rocked today.

"We keep going."

"You remember Charlie's new address?"

"Yeah, thanks for that." I turn and look down into Molly's eyes. "At least we get a proper goodbye this time."

"I'm glad you're back. I missed you."

"I know."

Molly pulls me in for a hug as Otus walks back to the motorcycle. Molly sighs, her breath warming my neck. "How long are you gonna be gone this time?"

"I don't know. Could be a long time. I have at least 12 gods to restore."

"I still don't know if I believe in gods and Titans, but I believe in monsters now. And you're the man who fights the monsters to keep us safe. I believe in you, if nothing else."

I pull back from the hug and look back down at Molly. "I'm gonna miss you."

"You know where to find me."

"Goodbye."

"Bye."

I let go and walk back to Otus and our motorcycle before mounting it.

Otus stares at me; sympathy filling his voice, he notes, "You know, we could stay. We've waited 2 thousand years. What's a few more days?"

I don't even consider it. "No, can't delay the inevitable."

"You mean your death, don't you?"

Ignoring Otus's remark, I start the motorcycle and drive away. Otus shakes his head and sighs before transforming into an owl, flying after me.

As I turn down the main road through the center of town, Anna steps out of the post office and freezes when she sees me driving by. I bite my lip, hoping she doesn't recognize me. She stares after me in confusion as I disappear over a hill.

CHAPTER 14: LOVE'S SHADOW

Night closes in, darkening the streets and alleys of Miami, prophesying as a brooding omen of death. A homeless man pushes a shopping cart down an alley, stopping to pick up a discarded earring and admire it. He pockets the earring before continuing to rummage through the garbage piled in the alley.

A dress shoe reflecting the streetlamp's incandescent light catches the man's attention; he reaches out to pick it up. With a tug and a pull, the man tears the shoe out from under the mountain of trash only to see a ghostly foot in its place.

Horrified, the man stumbles back.

Once he's recovered from the shock, the homeless man moves the garbage off the body to free Apollo's mutilated corpse.

Arien

I raise my hand to knock, but I hold back for a second, unable to open this wound. After a soft cough from Otus, I press on. We wait in awkward silence until the door opens and Charlie steps out. My heart stops; we never knew why, but Charlie and I always had a connection unexplainable, too complicated to call love, something eternal.

Charlie stares at me in shock, tears filling her eyes as she mumbles, "Arien?"

I smile slightly, holding back my own tears. "Hey, Charlie."

I brace myself for a slap, but Charlie just smiles and hugs me through her tears. "I knew you were a tough son of a bitch to kill, but I didn't know even you couldn't get the job done."

A short burst of humorless laughter is torn from my throat. "That's not funny."

"I missed you. I really did." Charlie pulls back just to stare at me as if to ensure that I'm real. "You look like shit. What happened?"

"We need your help."

"We?" Charlie raises an eyebrow before turning to look at Otus.

Otus waves a little and says, "Hey. My name's Otus. I'm part owl."

"Uh, OK." Charlie stares at Otus with mild dislike before turning back to me. "Come on in." Charlie motions for us to come inside the house; she clears some clothes off the couch and throws them in a box, so we have room to sit. "Sorry about the mess. I'm just changing some things around."

"It's fine." Otus and I sit awkwardly on the couch.

Charlie sits across from us and smiles in embarrassment. "So, what do you need my help for?"

"We need you to talk to another witch."

Charlie stiffens and gets flustered as she tries to deflect. "I'm not a witch. I don't know what you're talking about."

"I found the curse tablet before the fire started."

Charlie grunts and rubs her knees nervously. "What's a curse tablet?"

I give her a knowing look. "Charlie. I know."

Sighing, she resigns herself. "It was supposed to help with your emotional state and stop you from trying to kill yourself. Didn't work out, did it?"

"I didn't try to kill myself."

"What?"

***

Charlie swallows a long gulp of whiskey straight from the bottle, taking it all in. "Fuck." She pulls out a glass and starts making a cocktail. "Just give me a minute."

I nod, knowing how hard it is to accept the journey that lies ahead. Glancing around, I raise an eyebrow, surprised by all the boxes cluttered around the room. "Are you moving out, Charlie?"

Charlie visibly tenses more, contending, "What makes you say that? I could be moving in."

"I've been dead for weeks. You would have moved in by now if you were going to."

Charlie lets out a sigh of resignation. "I never moved in. I'm just taking all the stuff I kept here. Susan and I broke up."

Sadness fills me; if Susan and Charlie couldn't make it, nobody can. "I'm sorry."

"It's my own fault. Who wants to date someone like me?" I give her a pained expression as she takes a sip of her drink. Charlie's face hardens before she walks back over to the couch and sits down. "I'll help you, but only if I get to stick around afterward."

Otus lets out a bark of laughter. "What? You join us?"

"Deal."

Otus turns to stare at me in shock. "You can't be serious. She's a witch. Witches can't be trusted."

Charlie glares at Otus, venom in her words. "Shut up before I pluck you." Otus gulps in intimidation as Charlie turns back to me. "Now, how do we find Medea?"

"We don't know."

Nodding, deep in thought, Charlie mutters, "Maybe I can help with that. Shakespeare's plays have become a fundamental part of our culture for centuries. Because of that, the first folio will be a massive nexus of psychic energy. People pouring their emotions, thoughts, and beliefs into the stories. I can track a psychic connection like that."

I smile, glad to be back with Charlie. "What do you need from us?"

"Nothing. Just stay back." Charlie stands and starts rummaging through her stuff, finding a wooden box with ancient writing carved into the sides. She sits down in the center of the floor, opening the box and digging through the contents. She names the items under her breath as she takes them out of the box. "Rose perfume, feather of an ibis, linen cloth, and Coptic eye-paint."

Otus stiffens in confusion. "Hold on. Coptic? You're no witch. Coptic is Egyptian, idgit. Not Greek. It's not going to work."

With another venomous glare, Charlie contends, "Roman, Norse, Hindu, *and* Egyptian religions all originate from Hellenic origins, so some of their magic works. Now, shut up and let me work." Otus is taken aback by Charlie's intensity. She ignores his response, turning back to her box and pulling out a jar of flies and a papyri scroll. She lets a single fly out, catching it with lightning-fast reflexes. She crushes it before mixing it with the Coptic face-paint.

Charlie moves everything from the floor in front of her, closing her eyes and starting to meditate while humming a mantra to clear her mind.

My body tingles, fundamentally rejecting what I'm seeing, trained from birth by my parents to abhor all things non-temple oriented. I struggle to overcome my programming to flee or attack.

Once she's calm, Charlie scoops out a hand full of Coptic face-paint and smears it over her eyes. She rubs the excess paint into her hands before gently lifting the ibis feather and dipping it in the rose perfume. She lays the feather to rest at the linen cloth's end and rolls it up like a parchment. Lifting the bundle and holding it up with outstretched arms, she opens her eyes.

Charlie's right eye stares forward as her left drifts to the side until the pupil fully disappears. "MOUN EIPSOS EU PHTHA NOUTHI THEI SEMI NOUEI NEITHI CHRECHREO SININORPS MOUCH OROOU ENTHERINI EOB MOUNIACH NESOI MOUNESOCH MOUNEI ENIME CHREMOU RENENE SON SNEI OS MOUCHOROOU ENTHERINI ANOK SOS ERMIACHO ENTEUMOUTOICHNE CHREMOU TBSAS PNETE KYPHOCH EMM IEBOCHNES TCHNEB PHIMOU CHNOU NYOICHOOIM SEOUNEUMOI INONRI." Charlie gasps as a ghostly image of a third eye appears in the center of her forehead. "Valley of the sun. It's too bright." She screams as the third eye disappears.

I rush forward as Charlie drops the scroll and goes limp. "Charlie, you OK?"

Charlie slowly sits up and shakes her head to clear it. "Yeah, I'm good."

Staring down with worry, Otus asks, "You find it?"

Charlie shakes her head in disappointment. "Medea knows what's she's doing. It's shielded, but I can get you in the ballpark. It's here, like you said. When I saw the city, there was a massive black spot where I couldn't see anything. It's got to be in there. That area is protected against any magical discernment."

"Where is it?"

"Paradise Valley."

Otus turns as he thinks. "That's still a massive area to cover. How are we going to narrow it down?"

"Charlie, if we get you within that area, could you find it?"

Charlie rubs her head, pushing back a headache before grunting. "On the inside of the shielded area? Maybe, but it will take a while for me cover all that ground."

Smiling, Otus exclaims, "I have an idea. Do you have a map of town?"

"Sure." Charlie stands, grabs her laptop, and brings up a map of Paradise Valley.

"There. Phoenix Mountain Reserve. Does that stretch of houses bordering the reserve fall within the shielded area?"

"Yeah, pretty near the center, actually."

"It's the only part of town that's partly secluded because of the mountainous backdrop. Comfort and privacy."

Charlie looks at Otus with a newfound respect. "Not bad." The sound of the garage door opening draws our attention from the map. "Susan's home. Can you guys wait for me in the car? I need to talk to her."

"Sure. We'll be outside," I say, leading Otus out to give Charlie some privacy.

Charlie

Dread fills me for the conversation ahead; I don't think I'm strong enough. I clean up my witchcraft materials just as Susan walks in. My heart stops; despite everything, she's still the most beautiful woman I've ever seen.

We awkwardly stare at each other, neither wanting to be the first to speak. Susan eventually sighs and mutters, "Hey."

"Hey." One small word but charged with so much meaning, so much pain.

"Who were those guys?"

"Just some friends helping me with my stuff."

"Oh. . . You still living back in with your Mom?"

"Yeah." The awkwardness intensifies as we both search for something to say. "I have to go, but the movers will be here in a couple hours to take my stuff to the storage locker."

"OK."

I walk to the door and open it; I hear Susan almost whisper behind me. "I'm sorry." I pause and turn back to her for a moment. Tears fill her eyes as I do the hardest thing I've ever down, leave without saying a word.

CHAPTER 15: A WITCH'S DESIRE

<u>Charlie</u>

Trepidation and suspense ripple off Arien and Otus in waves as they watch me recast the divination spell. My third eye opens, revealing our path ahead. "It's on the mountain itself on its own. The road is hidden next to the third house on the left. Look for a red mailbox." Arien nods, starting the car, and driving down the road until I catch a glimpse of the red mailbox. "Turn in here." Arien follows what looks like a driveway as it loops behind a house. The road continues up the hill until ending at a massive iron gate. "We'll need to walk from here. No knowing what protective spells Medea has in place."

I get out and lead the way up the hill toward the gate where we can just make out the Victorian mansion hidden behind the trees. A strange tingling tickles at the fringes of my mind, forcing me to slow and shake my head. Turning, I notice that Arien and Otus are no longer following me; they're just standing with confused expressions. "Come on, guys."

"I don't want to."

"What?"

"We should leave. There's nothing here."

The dots connect in my mind, from the tingling to their behavior. It's a spell to dissuade visitors, a variation of an apotropaic spell protecting the house, making anyone approaching have an immense desire to leave. My natural immunity to magic must be the only thing allowing me to resist as well as I am. It's going to be tremendously challenging to proceed.

I walk to Arien and Otus, grabbing their hands and dragging them toward the house. "Come on."

With immense effort, I get us all to the gate; I shake it only to discover that it's locked. "Dammit. I hate this spell." Opening my satchel and pulling out a jar of myrrh with a ram's umbilical cord floating in it, I prepare the spell. I gingerly extract the pungent cord from the myrrh, wrapping it around the gate's lock. "Anoíxte gia ména, anoíxte gia ména, boulóni pórtas na anoíxei, na anoíxei, pórta vída, giatí eímai o Ermís o megálos, 'akchephreneosou phirigx,' gios tou Día kai Maia. Thélo na fýgei o ágios Tyfón. Amésos, amésos grígora, grígora." I push the gate and it swings open.

After repacking my gear, I grab the wandering Arien and Otus and lead them back up the road and through the gate.

The spell intensifies, too strong for even me to fully resist. My feet drag and my vision blurs as I struggle forward. The pressure in my mind telling me to flee overwhelms me, forcing me to stop and lean against a tree. Collapsing, I release my grip on Otus and Arien, who immediately turn and start heading back.

I blink slowly to clear my vision when I notice the statue of a bearded satyr with a giant penis by the front door of the house, an ash tree towering over it. A way forward becomes clear to me; closing my eyes, I begin to sing. "Nymphs, who from Ocean's stream derive your birth, who dwell in liquid caverns of the earth. Nurses of Dionysus secret-coursing pow'r, who fruits sustain, and nourish ev'ry flow'r: Earthly, rejoicing, who in meadows dwell, and caves and dens, whose depths extend to hell: Holy, oblique, who swiftly soar thro' air, fountains and dews, and mazy streams your care: Seen and unseen, who joy with wand'rings wide and gentle course, thro' flow'ry vales to glide.

"With Pan exulting on the mountains height, loud-founding, mad, whom rocks and woods delight: Nymphs od'rous, rob'd in white, whose streams exhale the breeze refreshing, and the balmy gale; With goats and pastures pleas'd, and beasts of prey, nurses of fruits, unconscious of decay: in cold rejoicing, and to cattle kind, sportive thro' ocean wand'ring unconfin'd. Nysian, fanatic Nymphs, whom oaks delight, lovers of Spring, Pæonian virgins bright. With Dionysus, and with Demeter, hear my pray'r. And to mankind abundant favour bear; propitious listen to your suppliant's voice, come, and benignant in these rites rejoice; give plenteous seasons, and sufficient wealth, and pour; in lasting streams, continued health."

My body tightens as I press on. "Prosféro ton teleftaío spóro ton Chamadryádon os prosforá voítheias."

The ash tree beside the statue shimmers, releasing a beautiful nude nymph from within its ashen bark. The nymph flips her hair back to expose her perfectly formed breasts and supple skin. I stare at the nymph's naked form with lust, transfixed by her beauty. She waves at me, so I gingerly wave back, still fighting hard against the apotropaic spell.

The nymph walks to the satyr statue and stares at its enormous penis with disgust before reaching up and pushing it over. The statue falls to the ground and shatters.

Arien, Otus, and I are released from the spell, falling to the ground, no longer fighting to move forward.

Arien approaches and asks, "What was that?"

"The penis was creating the apotropaic spell telling us to leave. I made a deal with a Nymph to break it."

"What deal?"

We all turn as the nymph approaches; she stops in front of me and stares into my eyes. I reach into my satchel and pull out a large acorn, handing it to the nymph. The nymph smiles at me, leaning in for a kiss. She steps back, smiles again, and fades away into a whirlwind of leaves that floats back to the ash tree, disappearing.

A smile cracks my lips for a moment before I turn back to the others.

"What did you give her?"

"One of the last seeds of a Hamadryad. Everything magical is going extinct these days. Something like that is very precious."

"How'd you know she was there?"

"Some nymphs can be called to any tree with the right song. They're powerful enough to bypass most magical barrier. I made a deal with her for the seed if she broke the statue and let us in."

Otus looks down in embarrassment, conceding, "I was wrong about you. You're handy to have around." I take his words as a compliment, nodding at him in thanks.

Arien hefts the Aegis and rolls his spear arm. "Let's go."

We step through the partially open door into the enormous decorative entryway, staring around in awe at the pristine house, our mission all but forgotten.

"Does my house please you?" We all look up the curving staircase to a balcony on the second floor where Medea is looking down at us. "It's ever so nice to meet you. Please, make yourselves at home. I've been expecting you." Medea turns and starts to slowly walk down the staircase.

Arien gulps, trying to keep on track. "You were expecting us?"

"Of course. No one may enter my grounds without my knowledge. Perks of being a witch." She reaches the bottom of the stairs and greets each of us with a kiss. "Welcome. Help yourselves to refreshments." Medea motions to an alcohol trolley at the side of the room.

Arien twitches violently, his eyes glazed over. We all turn to him in surprise, only to see his massive erection. I raise an eyebrow in surprise, not in judgment, because I'm sure I'd be having a similar problem if I had the equipment.

"I'd invite you in to sit, but I imagine our business will be short. Please." Medea again motions to the trolley, so Arien puts down his spear and the Aegis before following Otus to the trolley. I am hesitant but soon join them.

"Thank you for your hospitality."

"It's my pleasure."

Otus flinches just like Arien had, now with an erect boner as well. I turn from Otus and try to diffuse the sexual tension by asking, "Would you like something?"

"No, thank you. I only just had dinner where I enjoyed a glass of fine 1943 Chateau Cheval Blanc."

Once everyone has a drink, Medea smiles and snaps her fingers. The air is sucked from my lungs, blurring my vision; Medea and I are on the ground, our naked bodies entwined in beautiful harmony. She gently rubs her perfectly shaven clit against mine, forcing moans of passion to be torn from my throat, leading to a full scream.

As my scream fades, my vision clears, and I am again standing, fully clothed, next to the trolley. Everyone is staring at me; my cheek flush red as I scramble. "It's just a really great cosmo." I take another sip to cover my embarrassment.

I suddenly realize that Arien and Otus both must have seen similar visions leading to their erections.

Medea smiles knowingly. "Indeed. Only the best for my guests."

Arien shakes his head, trying to focus us, but our minds still wander, not our own. "Should we get down to business?"

"Yes, of course. I assume you are here for the divinity."

"Apollo sent us to retrieve it for him."

"While I appreciate your enthusiasm, you do not meet the requirements for my releasing of the divinity to you. If Apollo had indeed sent you, he would have ensured that you met the instructions he set for me. But as seeing that you don't, I must assume that you have malicious intent and must, therefore, destroy you."

"Come again?"

"You really shouldn't accept unsolicited drinks from strangers. Did your Mothers teach you nothing?"

Horror fills us as we stare down at our drinks. Arien tries to speak but starts choking. Soon all three of us are on our knees, gagging.

"It's a variation of the potion used by Circe on Odysseus and his men."

Through my choking, I manage to whisper, "Circe?"

"Yes, I assume you know the story."

I fight hard against the spell taking over me, dragging myself toward my discarded bag. Before I can find the cure, my hands turn to hooves.

I turn in time to see Otus grab his butt as a pigtail pushes its way out of his pants and starts curling behind him.

Soon, we're all pigs crawling out of our clothes. Struggling to maintain my rational mind, I tip over and squeal as I fall and cannot get up. Medea crouches down and starts stroking my snout.

"Shush. It's alright. You'll have a good life. I'll keep you for breeding. You will live to a ripe old age and pass away surrounded by generations of your offspring."

Forcing myself to act calm, I convince Medea to leave me be as she herds the others toward the back door. Once I'm alone, I carefully roll to my feet and walk on my unstable hooves toward my bag. Using my snout, I rifle through it until I find my bundle of moly herb.

I swallow the herb whole, starting my transformation back into human. Laying naked on the floor, I breathe heavily, exhausted from the ordeal. The sound of clapping slowly makes me raise my head to see Medea standing in the doorway.

Medea picks up my satchel and searches through it. "I'm impressed. Moly herb, huh? You, obviously, are very well educated. And what's this?" From a small front pocket of the satchel, Medea pulls out a curse tablet. "Is this a curse tablet?" Medea looks inside the bag and smiles. "A tablet that opens a portal to your laboratory. Ingenious. Experimental and dangerous. But ingenious. Where's your lab? Looks like a storage locker, yes? I'm impressed, and I rarely am. You're very powerful for a first-life witch."

I struggle to sit up, using my hands to maintain my modesty. "What now? You gonna turn me back into a pig?"

Medea crouches down, reaching up to stroke my cheek. "No, I don't think I will. I didn't realize that you were a witch. I assumed that you were too young, but I was wrong. Swear to me on the river Styx that you come from Apollo and only intend to deliver his divinity to him."

"What?"

"Just do it."

"I swear. We were telling the truth."

Medea smiles and sighs before helping me to my feet. "I apologize for all that. I had to be sure." Her eyes wander up and down my nude form. "You are beautiful." She looks up and stares into my eyes. "You know, Apollo hates witches. We live in the dark. He is the sun. Only a witch swearing on the river Styx that she's from Apollo can release me from my promise to protect the divinity." Her gaze lowers again to my breast as she bites her lip. "Apollo also included a little something for fun. Only my orgasm brought about by said witch can break the spell binding me to his service and allow me to release the divinity."

I stare at Medea in shock. "What? No way. I'm not having sex with you." Medea smiles and simply reaches down to pull one of her supple breasts out of the top of her dress. Despite myself, I look down at the nipple and gulp, trying to restrain myself. "Don't get me wrong, you are very, very beautiful and I would love to sleep with you, but I have principles. I can't just sleep with someone I just met."

Medea reaches up and undoes the top of her dress, letting it fall down around her ankles, leaving her naked. I let out a hoarse laugh and shiver as Medea starts stroking my shoulders.

"You like that?"

"We really shouldn't be doing this. We should get the guys and turn them back. Can't imagine being stuck in such a tight environment." I finally give in and kiss Medea passionately, her tongue dancing against mine.

Medea pulls back and licks from my chin to the tip of my nose. "You taste so good."

We kiss again.

I kiss down from her lips to her neck and her large breast. Giving the nipple a tentative lick, I swallow the breast, trying to suck in as much of it as I can. Medea tilts her head back and moans before reaching down to finger herself.

Pulling back, I look up and Medea. "You ready for that?"

"God, yes."

I smile before kissing Medea in a line from a nipple to her inner thigh. "Tell me you want it."

"Shut up."

She grabs a fistful of my hair and pushes my face into her lustrous pussy. I massage her firm butt as my tongue trances her lushes lips, the taste of sweet perfume running down my face.

Medea digs her fingers into my hair, her moaning gets louder. "Get up here." She pulls me up for a kiss, licking the wetness off my face.

We both reach down and gently run our fingers against each other's clits before pressing in, while trying to maintain the kiss. The kiss breaks as we start moaning into each other's open mouths.

Pain suddenly shoots through my tender flesh. "Ow, too much."

"Sorry, it's been a while."

"It's fine."

"Come here."

I giggle as Medea pulls my legs up to straddle her hips. She carries me into the sitting room and gently sits me down on the couch. Medea pulls back, kneeling in front of me, tracing a single fingertip down my supple chest. "Relax."

I grin, inviting Medea to continue. She licks her way down from my nipple to exposed flesh, sensitive to every touch. She lifts my knees over her shoulders and drives in, sending fire coursing through my veins. I run my fingers through Medea's hair as my pleasure builds.

After countless minutes of pure ecstasy, Medea comes up for air. She leans against me briefly before spinning me to lie flat. Mounting me, she braces her hands against her hips and thrust into me, kissing my face and neck the whole while.

Medea's hips drive up and down faster and faster to the rhythm of my screams. When my cries grow too loud, Medea stops and places a finger over my lips. "Shush. Not so loud. The boys may be enjoying this too much."

"OK."

"Here, let's give your mouth something to do."

Medea spins atop me; we start grinding into each other's faces with renewed vigor.

The couch is too small, so we both accidentally roll-off, ending with me lying atop Medea.

We laugh uncontrollably before continuing to pleasure each other.

The racks of my pleasure soon become too strong for me to continue licking Medea, so I lean back and start riding her face, rotating slowly. Ignoring all restraints, I scream uncontrollably, climaxing.

I go limp as my climax fades. Medea slides out from under me, sitting up and kissing me.

"Your turn. Turn around."

Medea smiles and turns around. I push her down onto all fours, kneeling up behind and bracing my hand in between us. I thrust in doggy style.

Medea's breast bounce and swing as I thrust faster and faster. Medea starts screaming louder and louder until a bright light flares up and explode out of her as a shockwave, expanding through the house and out into the world.

CHAPTER 16: TO BE OR NOT TO BE

Charlie

Ragged breaths rattle my chest, sending pleasure throughout my body. I lie still next to Medea's nude form, just enjoying our closeness. Medea gets to her feet and pulls her hair behind her ear, walking toward the library. "I'll get the book."

I slowly get to my feet as well; gathering my clothes, I return to the entryway and dress. Medea walks in, fully dressed, carrying a first folio of William Shakespeare. I stare at it in unabashed awe. "This is it?"

"Indeed."

"Wow. I always loved Shakespeare."

"Let me guess, 'Much Ado About Nothing' was your favorite?"

Smiling, I raise a flirtatious eyebrow at Medea. "Yeah, it was. How'd you know?"

"Lucky guess." She hands me the book, tension throughout her body, seemingly lost without this symbol of her purpose.

"Thank you. What about the boys?"

"Are you sure you want them back? I could keep them for you."

"Thank you, but yes. I'll need them back. They're my best friends."

"As you wish." Medea reaches down and picks up Arien and Otus's clothes before walking out back.

I stare down at the first folio, stroking its spine with restrained reverence. Flipping through the ancient pages, I stop at Hamlet Act 3, scene 1, to read. "To be, or not to be, that is the question." Turning, I look up with sad eyes at Arien as he walks in with Otus and Medea.

Arien looks down at the book and smiles. "Is that it?"

"Yeah, Shakespeare's first folio."

"What'd it cost?"

I ignore the question and change the subject. "How do you guys feel?"

"Like curling up in some mud."

Medea steps around the boys to stand next to me. "That will eventually pass. You may exhibit some animal-like tendencies for the next few days, but that is just the last vestiges of the potion wearing off."

Otus shakes his head to clear it, muttering, "Well, if that just doesn't make you want to flash the hash."

Arien turns to Otus, his lip curled in disgust and embarrassment. "Come on, man. We talked about this. From this century."

Medea ignores them and turns back to me. "Your friends fully restored as agreed."

"Thank you for everything."

"It was my pleasure."

"What are you going to do now?"

With a lady-like sigh, Medea's gaze drifts to a window. "I don't know. Over 4 hundred years working for the same man and I'd never thought there would be an afterward. It's almost exhilarating, not knowing. Not having a path. I imagine I'll take it one day at a time, just like everyone else."

"Good luck." We hug and kiss briefly.

"Thank you."

"If you ever need anything, give us a call."

"I will."

Arien picks up his spear and the Aegis before letting me lead the way out the front door. Once out, Arien and Otus continue down the driveway toward the gate, but I stop to turn and wave at Medea standing in the doorway.

A scream is torn from my throat as Medea is impaled through the chest from behind. She spits up blood before collapsing, revealing a young girl with a bullet-ridden face standing behind her.

Arien and Otus turn and run back, weapons drawn. Arien cries, "Rachel?"

I rush forward, ignoring the danger to cradle Medea's convulsing body as her life slips away.

Rachel grins down at Arien and condemns, "Never let an enemy live. Mercy gets people killed."

The ground shakes as a towering Titan walks out of the trees. "Arien Vlahos, the man of mysteries. Stand down. I have no wish to kill you or your friends." The Titan seemingly shows his sincerity by shrinking down to human size. "See."

Jaw clenched, Arien screams back, "You can't kill Medea and just expect us to be cool."

"I am sorry about Medea. She could have been a powerful ally and her history suggested that she might have been willing. But Procrustes can be overzealous." Rachel smiles through her broken jaw down at me, cradling Medea's now empty corpse. "I regret killing you the last time we met. You are, obviously, far more special than I could have ever perceived."

I brush at the tears cascading down my face, blurring my vision. Determination and anger fill me, forcing my limbs to action as I stand and walk the others. Clasping Otus's hand tight, I nod for him to grasp Arien's as well.

The Titan raises his eyebrow when he sees all three of us holding hands. "What's this?"

My grief and anger fuel my words as I cry, "You can go straight to hell, you titanic asshole. We were here to retrieve a god's divinity. A divinity that wants to be reunited with its master. And gods can teleport. And maybe, just maybe, I can siphon off enough energy to do this."

The Titan's eyes widen as realization of my plan fills them. "No, stop." He leaps toward me just as we vanish.

CHAPTER 17: MEAGER FAITH

<u>**Arien**</u>

With a flash of bright light, Otus, Charlie, and I go from Medea's mansion to a darkly lit morgue in parts unknown; beside us, an operating table with a mutilated corpse displayed.

Charlie groans and stumbles against a table, clutching her burning hand. I rush to her side, grasping her shoulders to keep her upright. "Charlie, what's wrong?"

"I touched a god's divinity. I just got burned a little."

Otus reaches out and inspects her hand. "It's not that bad. A first-degree burn, I'd say."

I raise an eyebrow at Otus. "How do you know that?"

"2 thousand years of living, I got hurt sometimes. Served to have some first-aid knowledge."

"I'm fine." Charlie straightens up and stares down at the corpse. "Are we in the right place? The divinity should have taken us to Apollo."

I look down at Apollo's corpse with sadness in my eyes. "It did." Collapsing into a nearby chair, I clench my jaw, defeated. "It's over. This whole dumb quest is over before it even got started."

Otus bows his head in respect. "The porn industry has lost one of its best sons."

I clench my fist, restraining the anger and hopelessness that floods through me. "What, the fuck, is wrong with you, Otus? A god is fucking dead. What's the goddamn point to the world if you can't even believe or trust in gods? We live our meaningless lives with meaningless people in pursuit of an unobtainable goal only to die and find that it was all for nothing. There's no higher power to rely on. There's no higher plan. It's just us. Us against everything in the world. It's not a fight worth fighting. There's no victory in anything, not even survival. We all end up right here on a slab with our innards dissected."

"We can win happiness in the next life. I think Apollo's at peace."

"There's no peace in death. Just, hopefully, forgetting. Now, I may never know what that feels like. We don't know how my powers work. Without a quest to ensure my death, I may live forever. Never seeing an end to the day-to-day monotony."

A tear leaks out of the corner of my eye as Charlie kneels down in front of me and grabs my knees, ignoring her burnt hand. "You're right, or nearly so. Our lives may seem meaningless, but the people around us aren't. We still have each other. The three of us against the world. If we lose that, then we are lost."

"I'm not strong enough."

"It's not about strength. It's about hope. As long as we're still together, there's hope. We can do anything if there's hope."

"How do we move on? There's no resurrecting him."

"Maybe there is."

A faint flutter of hope warms my chest for a moment. "What?"

"Gods don't have souls like humans do. But their divinities serve a similar role for them. Which means, this body can survive without a *soul*. If we can heal the body, he may come back because we don't have to retrieve his soul from the Underworld."

"How?"

"Who happens to be known for his medical skills in Greek mythology?"

My eyes widen in understanding. Standing, I walk to Apollo. "Apollo."

"I might be able to siphon off some of his healing powers from his divinity like I did for getting here. It's all psychic energy that I can transfer. Once his body is healed, it can go home."

Otus finally interjects, "It's too dangerous. You burned your hand just telling the divinity to return home. But you'd be actively using Apollo's power. Absorbing it. It might kill you."

"No, it won't. I can do it."

Losing Charlie is unacceptable, so I volunteer. "I'll do it."

"I won't pander to your death wish. You don't know the first thing about magic. It might kill you, but you'd never heal him."

I sigh in resignation. "You're sure it won't kill you?"

"I'm sure."

"Do it."

Charlie smiles and turns to Apollo before pulling out the first folio from her bag. She grimaces as she psychs herself up. "This is gonna hurt." She closes her eyes and places her hand on the first folio. The book glows with a bright white light; Charlie's veins start to pop out and turn white, crawling up from her hand to her head. She opens her eyes and screams as they burn white-hot. Dropping the book and stepping closer to Apollo, she reaches out to touch his shoulder.

There's a flash of white; Charlie stumbles back and falls to the ground, covered in burns. "Charlie!" I scream, rushing to her side. Cradling her sizzling body, I let the tears flow freely. "Oh, my god, Charlie. I should never have let you do it."

Charlie coughs through her burnt lips. "You couldn't have stopped me."

"I know."

A noise makes me turn; Apollo wraps the privacy towel around his waist and stands before bending down to pick up the first folio. The book glows bright white.

We are forced to avert our eyes as Apollo is engulfed in a pillar of white fire. He's lifted off the ground and spread-eagled in the center of the burning pillar. The fire and light fades, leaving Apollo standing on the ground, unharmed.

Apollo rolls his neck and cracks it a little. "Oh, that feels so good."

With a hoarse whisper, awed by a true god before me, I whisper, "Apollo?"

"For the first time in 2 thousand years, yes." Apollo looks down at Charlie's burnt form. "Is this your witch?"

"Yes, and she's dying for you."

Apollo crouches down in front of Charlie and reaches out to stroke her cheek. "What's your name?"

"Charlie."

"Charlie, it's no secret that I dislike witches, but if you are a staple of your kind, I may have been mistaken. You are a credit to all witches, humanity, and your friends." Apollo places his palm against Charlie's forehead. A bright white light engulfs her. When it disappears, Charlie is healed. Apollo smiles before grabbing the first folio and handing it to Charlie. "I sense you have a love for my literary work. This is yours. If it ever helped you or meant something to you, then my life will not have been for naught."

Through now perfect rosy lips, Charlie replies, "Thank you."

Apollo stands and steps back as Otus and I help Charlie to her feet. "This is the first scene of the final act to a play that has taken millions of years to unfold. And it will not be myself and my family taking the stage at this last hour. It will be the three of you, Clara, and Adonis against the marching of Utopia coming for us all."

The name 'Clara' twinges at something inside of me. "Clara?"

"She is the woman who will make you into the man you must needs be to defend against the chaos of the future. You shall be meeting her soon."

Otus bites his lip, saying, "What are you going to do?"

Apollo smiles down at Otus. "Otus, my old friend. I go to prepare the hosts of Olympus for the final chapter." Apollo turns back to me. "When the time comes, you will have an army to lead against the Titans."

Horror floods through me at the prospect of all that weight upon my shoulders. "I can't lead."

"If not you, then who?" I lower my head in shame. "The next god in need of restoration is Hermes. I tried to keep in contact with him over the years. Last I heard, he was working for

ChatDen. That is all the aid I can give you for now. If you need my assistance, sacrifice to me and I will hear you." Apollo disappears in a flash of light.

I snort derisively, trying to off play the stakes of the journey ahead. "Quite the showman."

Otus stares longingly after Apollo. "He always had the flare for the dramatic."

"What now?"

Charlie steps forward, grasping my hand tight. "We need to go. Atlas must know this is where we'd go."

CHAPTER 18: TEARS OF A FATHER

<u>Atlas</u>

White-hot anger floods through my veins, controlling my actions, crushing everything in reach. I stop my rampage to stare at the ruins of the morgue around me, my chest heaving hard.

Procrustes cowers in the corner, hoping my rage does not turn upon him.

I grab a surgical bowl, sit on the ground, and place it on the floor in front of me. From a bag on my belt, I pull out a candle. I place the candle on the ground behind the bowl before lighting it. "To all the souls of those who've gone, I humbly give this offering." Taking 5 urns from my bag, I slowly pour a libation out from each into the bowl. Libations of milk, honey, mellow wine, water, and then of barley. My voice cracking, I begin a prayer to Thanatos:

> "Hear me, O Thanatos, whose empire unconfined, extends to mortal tribes of ev'ry kind. On
> thee, the portion of our time depends, whose absence lengthens life, whose presence ends.
> Thy sleep perpetual bursts the vivid folds, by which the soul, attracting body holds:
> common to all of ev'ry sex and age, for nought escapes thy all-destructive rage; Not
> youth itself thy clemency can gain, vig'rous and strong, by thee untimely slain. In
> thee, the end of nature's works is known, in thee, all judgment is absolv'd alone: No
> suppliant arts thy dreadful rage control, no vows revoke the purpose of thy soul; O
> blessed power regard my ardent prayer, and human life to age abundant spare."

I place my dolphin pendant in the bowl before reaching into my bag and pulling out a squirming rat. "Aa emptokom basym, protect me." I take out a knife and slash open the rat, letting its blood pour into the bowl to mix with the other ingredients. Putting aside the rat and knife, I raise my hands and close my eyes. "Eláte, psychí tou agapiménou kai chaménou mou."

I open my eyes, waiting for something to happen. Nothing does. A tear leaks out of the corner of my eye. I whisper quietly, hoping it reaches through the veil like my spell cannot. "I'm sorry, Calypso. I'll find a way to bring you back."

Procrustes tentatively slinks from his corner. "Sir, you can't reach her. The gates are closed."

"You got past them."

"I got out before the gates were sealed. I know you miss her, but you'll see her again when Utopia rises."

"If I can't get her here, can I get someone to her?"

"With foreknowledge, a single soul might slip past Thanatos's blood seal."

"Thank you. Tell Calypso, her Father loves her and he's doing everything he can to bring her back. Utopia awaits her."

"What?"

I stand, grabbing Procrustes by the throat and lifting him off the ground. He squirms and fights as a fire begins to burn beneath his skin. Procrustes screams, his eyes exploding into flames; the Eidolon possessing the girl is expelled. The Eidolon morphs into a pink mist that is sucked into the nearest light bulb.

The girl's body is turned to ash as tears flow freely down my cheeks.

Part 3:

HERMES

CHAPTER 19: NOT MADE FOR BLISS

<u>Arien</u>

A baby's cries echo through the endless darkness, suddenly cutting off. The fog clears before my mind's eye; Brittnie is crawling her way through the darkness toward the sound, leaving a trail of blood and dragging a still-attached umbilical cord behind her. Tears stream freely down her cheeks as she struggles against death to reach her child. "I'm coming, Julian. I'm not going to leave you."

Brittnie digs her fingernails into the obsidian ground to get a grip, her hands come away bloody, but she still pushes on. A baby's muffled screams can be heard coming from ahead. "Julian."

A cloaked woman slowly is revealed from the surrounding fog as Brittnie crawls closer. Brittnie stops when she sees the woman. "Hello. Can you help me?" The woman turns and raises a finger to shush Brittnie. With a sharp inhale, Brittnie's heart stops; her baby is struggling in the woman's arms. "Julian. What are you doing to him?"

The woman smiles, turning back to the infant, checking that all of its airways are blocked by her hand.

"You're gonna kill him."

"The boy must die."

Brittnie tries to struggle to her feet, but she trips on her umbilical cord and falls hard. "Please, stop."

The baby's struggles slowly stop; it slips out of the woman's arms to the cold hard ground. Brittnie screams in anguish, looking down to see both the baby's corpse and the Empty-Man's body lying upon the ground.

"Not made for bliss." The woman smiles before disappearing.

Brittnie crawls to her baby and cradles it as her sobs increase. The Empty-Man's corpse suddenly blinks and gasps. He rolls over to stare at Brittnie's huddle form. The fog rushes in surrounding the Empty-Man to obscure the Mother and her child.

The fog recedes to reveal the insane asylum.

The Empty-Man is strapped down to an operating table, a Titan I instinctually know is Iapetus, smiling down at him. Iapetus uses the Scythe to castrate the Empty-Man, who screams and struggles against the golden ropes that bind him.

"Seed planted in the dark." Iapetus licks the gaping hole that was the Empty-Man's genitalia as if performing oral sex. "Tastes like pussy."

The Empty-Man turns and looks to the side as the fog rushes up around him, reforming into the Temple of God's Time.

I finally see my body and can move; I'm standing in a shadowy version of the Temple of God's Time in the mists of dozens of people murdering each other. I scream and huddle on the ground with my hands on my head to close off from the horrors around me. Insanity worming deep inside me.

I slowly open my eyes and look up after the fighting dies off.

Screaming again, I stumble back; Medea and Rachel are both mounted on massive crosses behind the altar.

Tears slip free as I notice another body resting on the altar itself. I get to my feet and tentatively walk across the blood-soaked carpet to see who the body is. I gag violently; my own face is staring back at me with dead eyes.

"What are you?" I turn to see a terrified Molly standing in the aisle of pews. "You kill everything you touch."

"No, I didn't do this."

Molly points at the crosses behind me. "Ask them if they believe you."

I turn back and shudder; more of my friends are being crucified. Charlie, Otus, Anna, Medea, and Rachel are all mounted on crosses. Their empty eyes stare down at me in judgment.

My heart heavy with guilt, I turn to defend myself, but Molly is gone, mounted on a cross of her own.

I look back to my friends and grunt as the Empty-Man stabs me in the heart.

"You didn't protect the boy."

CHAPTER 20: BROODING LIES

Otus

Arien wakes up in a cold sweat, breathing hard. Taking a moment to calm down, he tries to return to sleep, thinking that he didn't wake anyone. I stare at him with sadness, knowing how painful the journey ahead will be for him and that the horrors of his past will not be easily overcome.

***

My bird-like gaze watches Arien closely as he types on his laptop with one-hand and eats breakfast with the other. I sigh softly to brace myself before saying, "How'd you sleep?"

"Fine."

Filled up on lies, I reach over and close his laptop, forcing him to look at me. "We need to talk about this. You're having nightmares."

Arien gives me a flustered look. "What? No, I'm not."

"Arien, I saw you last night."

He sighs in resignation. "It's not that big of a deal. I've always had nightmares."

"What about?"

"Recently, the people I've let down. Medea's death is my fault. I let Rachel go when I should have killed her."

"Yes, you should have. Your mercy was a mistake."

"Loads of help you are."

"But you've learned from it. You need to move on and never do it again."

Arien goes to speak but pauses when he sees Charlie walk into the dining hall and up to the food line. She waves at us before turning away.

Arien tries to conceal the guilt on his face, unsuccessfully.

With mild horror, I realize what he plans to do. "Oh, no. You can't be thinking of telling her."

"We need to be honest with each other on a mission like this. If we don't have trust, it could destroy everything."

"It'll only make things worse for both of you. She liked Medea, but she's OK. If you tell her, that could all change."

"But she's blaming herself for what happened."

"What you have to say won't change that."

We both stop talking as Charlie sits down next to us. "Hey, what are you guys talking about?"

I speak quickly to stop Arien from responding. "Finding Hermes." I give Arien a meaningful look, enforcing his silence.

"You find anything?"

Arien sighs, opening back up his laptop. "I've downloaded an algorithm and re-purposed it to search ChatDen profiles for any users that claim to work for ChatDen and share any similarities with Hermes myths. The problem is, that's a shit-ton of people and we have no idea where Hermes lives."

"Any way to narrow it down?"

"Well, people post too much these days about their personal lives, so there's an astronomical amount of data to sort through. Even with the algorithm, it'll take days."

"Is there any faster way?"

Arien gives us a thin, strained smile. "Maybe, but it's not going to be easy."

"Shocker."

"I need access to the employees' data without the endless fluff that ChatDen provides. I need a refined pool of information with only the fundamental data about these people."

"The company records?"

"Exactly."

All this computer jargon confuses me, but I think I've managed to figure it out, so I say, "So, you're just going to hack in, get what you need, and Bob's your uncle."

Arien gives me a withering look. "No, actually. There's no public data and the company keeps their records on an intranet server only transmitted between hubs using asymmetric cryptography with an AES 256, SHA-1 public key system."

Charlie tenses, worried and confused. "Is that bad? That sounds bad."

"I can't hack it. It's military-grade security."

"Then, what are we going to do?"

"I'll leave my algorithm going on the ChatDen profiles in case my plan doesn't work. But I think we can get in to access those records on ChatDen's server."

"How?"

"Their data transmission may be top of the line, but their onsite security isn't. They contract out security for their Miami hub to the Ganon Protection Firm. I've managed to intercept the security footage being transmitted back to their firm. They're basically emailing it over WI-FI, so it wasn't too difficult to access." Arien turns his laptop to show us. "Otus can monitor the security cam footage as overwatch from the hotel as Charlie and I break into an office with high enough clearance to code in a back door for me into the records."

Charlie shakes her head, impressed. "Wow. When'd you have time to do all this?"

"I couldn't sleep last night." I give Arien a knowing look before he says, "Anyway, what do you guys think?" He tries to smile, deflecting the looks Charlie and I are giving him.

CHAPTER 21: SOCIALLY AWKWARD

Charlie

My hands shake slightly, from fear or excitement, I can't tell. Otus's voice echoes from my earpiece, saying, "Charlie, calm down. You look really fidgety."

"I'm sorry, but I've never broken into a multi-billion-dollar company before."

Arien reaches down to squeeze my hand before saying, "It's alright, just relax. Our plan's going to work." I nod in response, stepping out from behind a decorative pillar to approach the front desk of ChatDen International.

As we approach the security guard, I stop and start riffling through my bag. 'Dammit, I forgot my ID in the car."

"It's alright, honey. I can go get it."

"No, it's fine." I sneak a glance at the guard's name badge, memorizing the name before saying, "Just wait here with Kevin and I'll be right back."

"OK, baby. Hurry."

"I will."

I turn, walking back toward the door as Arien approaches Kevin and says, "Hey, how's it going? Women, right?" He smiles to distract Kevin so I can duck behind the pillar. "Can't live with them, can't live without them. Am I right?"

"I guess," Kevin replies.

I pull a seashell and a vial of blood from my bag; drawing Kevin's name on the seashell with the blood, I whisper, "I adjure you, shell, by bitter Necessity, and by those who have been placed in charge of the Punishments, LAIU LAKIO LAKIMOU MOUKILA KIIAMOU IOR MOUOK MOUDRA MAXTHA MOUSATHA: attract him, Kevin, whom woman bore. Do not be stubborn, but attract him, OUCH OUCH CHAUNA MOUCHLIMALCHA MANTOR MOURKANA MOULITHA MALTHALI MOUI EIEI YYY AIE YOO GI AEI AEI AOA AOA AOA IAO OAI OAI AIO OM IOA OAI, attract him, Kevin. As the moon waxes in Aries or in Taurus."

I attach the shell to a string and tie it around my wrist as a bracelet. Putting the rest of my gear back in my bag, I return to the front desk just in time to hear Arien say, ". . . That's when Charlie fell to the floor, completely naked and covered in bees. It's a miracle that she wasn't stung." Arien waits for the laughter that should have followed the punchline of his story, but Kevin just stares up at him.

I grab Arien's arm and squeeze it tightly. "Honey, I thought that we'd agreed to never speak about that again."

"What, it's a distracting story."

I give Arien a concerned look before turning to Kevin, seductively placing my hand on his. "Hey, Kevin. I seem to have left my card at home. Is there any way we can work something out?"

"I don't think so, ma'am." Kevin pulls his hand back, leaving me dumbfounded. "Those are the rules. You need an ID to get past the checkpoint."

"I understand that, but . . ." My eyes wander down, the corner of a gay porn magazine poking out of a drawer catches my eye. Smiling, I understand why the love charm isn't working. "Perhaps my husband can clear things up." I slip off the seashell bracelet and give it to Arien.

Arien looks down at it in surprise, understanding slowly dawning. "Yes, maybe we can. Just check my VIP ID." Arien pulls out a driver's license and hands it to Kevin, their hands briefly touching.

Kevin's eyes glaze over as he looks at the ID; he smiles up at Arien with unabashed affection. "You seem to be a very important man."

"In some circles."

"You're so big and strong. I imagine that men and women throw themselves down before you because of your brilliance."

"It's been known to happen."

Kevin stands and starts stroking Arien's cheek. "I'd take you right here and now. I'd show you the time of your life."

"That sounds wonderful, but the boss is expecting us. You know, me being so important and all. So, do you think you can let us through?"

"Of course. Anything for you, my love." Kevin walks to the turnstile and scans his ID, unlocking it for Arien and me.

"Thanks, dear." we walk through the turnstile and toward the elevator. Arien turns and smiles awkwardly at Kevin, saying, "I'll be back to get that time of my life and stuff, I guess."

"I'll be waiting."

Arien nods as the elevator doors close.

As soon as the doors are secure, I take the bracelet back and smash it underfoot. "If we'd left it and you didn't get with him, he'd have started humping anything near him. It's not that pretty to watch."

The elevator dings as we reach our destined floor.

Arien

The elevator doors open onto heaven on earth. The air itself seems to ring with nerd love, computer code floating across the breeze, breathing life into all our fantasies. No collared shirts in sight, only comic book, Doctor Who, and Star Wars shirts, pure fashion.

"Are those beanbags?"

"And a cereal bar." I smile broadly, ignoring Charlie's upraised lip.

"This place is . . ."

"Awesome."

". . . nice. Wait, you like this?" Charlie turns to stare at me in disbelief.

"What? I'm a nerd at heart. This place is dope as hell."

Charlie shakes her head in confusion before re-focusing on the task at hand. "Whatever. Which office do you think is the boss's?" She starts looking at the nameplates by office doors. "Is that a Spider-Man nameplate?"

"Really. Let me see." I step forward, an almost childlike excitement taking over me. "You're right. Looks like the Tobey Maguire era. Good choice."

"Can you focus?"

"Right, sorry."

"How can we tell these offices apart? They all look the same."

Otus surprises us, his voice again echoing in our earpieces. "There's only one man not wearing a comic-book shirt. He's in the office around the corner from the gaming room."

My heart skips a beat as I say, "There's a gaming room?"

Charlie rolls her eyes, saying, "Thanks, Otus."

Charlie leads the way down the hallway toward the boss's office. I slow as we pass the game room, tempted to abandon the mission and join in the Smash tournament, but Charlie grabs my arm, dragging me along.

A nerd rounds the corner ahead of us, nearly bumping into Charlie. "Hey, sorry about that. How are you guys?"

I step forward to shake his hand before saying, "Good, and you?"

In a perfect British accent, the nerd says, "Molto bene!" We both smile and laugh at the reference. Charlie stares at us, unimpressed.

I turn to her, worried. "Do you get it? It was the 10th Doctor's catchphrase. One of them, at least." Charlie glares at me, making me grunt and scratch my ear. "No?"

The nerd raises an eyebrow at Charlie before turning back to me. "Anyway, so are you guys new? I haven't seen you around before."

"No, yeah. We're new. Just came up from HR. We're rearing to go."

"Great to have you. Are you guys front-end or back-end? It's just I'm the team lead for back-end and would be your boss."

"No, we're both front-end. I did a stint as a graphic designer, so I really enjoy the visually creative options of engineering front-end designs with PHP and C++."

"That's cool. I know the team lead for front-end and could introduce you if you're looking for her."

"We were actually told to see the project lead first to check-in."

"Of course. His office is the second on your left. We've got a meeting in ten, so you won't have long to talk. Good luck."

"Thank you." We start to walk away, but the nerd stops us.

"Hey, so we have a weekly Doctor Who party after work on Mondays. Would you be interested?"

My smile cracks wider than ever as I say, "Yeah, allons-y." He giggles at my Doctor Who reference before I continue, "We'd love to. That sounds awesome. Which season are . . .?" A sharp elbow to my side from Charlie makes me grunt softly. "Yeah, not this week. We're very busy, but maybe next week."

"OK, I'll see you guys around."

Charlie gives him a fake smile, saying, "Yeah, see ya." Once he's walked away, Charlie turns back to me. "How do you fit in so well here?"

"They're techie nerds like me."

"Being a nerd is fine, these guys are just too happy for me."

"They're not, though. Why do you think they have so many after-work activities?"

Charlie nods in understanding. "So, what now?"

"He said they have a meeting in ten. We wait till then, and break into the boss's office."

CHAPTER 22: DRUNK PERSONA

Charlie

With a gag and a grimace, I return my ram's umbilical cord to my bag before opening the freshly unlocked door. "Have I told you how much I hate that spell?"

Arien smiles slightly in pity before hurrying to the boss's computer, taking out a CD, putting it in the computer, and getting to work. "We don't have much time."

"You need anything from me?"

"Just keep an eye out. Thanks."

I nod, allowing my eyes to wander; they catch on a bookshelf covered with action figures and Lego sets. "Whoa, this guy's a big nerd." Picking up a Power Ranger toy, I stare at it, my mind flooded with memories of a similar toy. Susan had one above her headboard that I'd knock over whenever I used a strap-on on her.

My whole-body tenses remember the pain and the piece of my heart I'd left behind in that bedroom. Turning away to wipe away my tears, I freeze when I look through the office window across the hall and into a conference room full of people. I gasp and hurry out of the window's path, hoping that no one had seen me.

Arien looks up from the computer and cocks his head. "What is it?"

"There's a big-ass window into the hallway. What kinda boss has a window into the building? Not out, but in."

"They're just friendly people. They like to feel connected."

"Well, it's gross."

Arien looks up at me in surprise. "What's wrong with you? What do you have against nerds today? You've known me for years and never had a problem with me being a nerd."

Sighing, I run my fingers through my hair, unwilling to talk about it. "It's nothing."

"No, it's something."

I sigh again, conceding. "It's Susan, OK. She was a big nerd, now all these people are just reminding me of her. Between that and what happened with Medea, I don't know. I'm just kinda messed up."

Arien's gaze fills with sympathy as he reaches out to grasp my hand. "I'm sorry."

Smiling, I shake my head and lean down to look at the computer. "So, how's it going?"

After an awkward pause, Arien says, "I've managed to get into the computer's internal command prompt by booting off a windows 10 CD. I just created an admin account for myself, so once it restarts, I should be able to get in."

"How long will it take to create the backdoor?"

Holding up a USB with an antenna on it, Arien says, "I just need to authorize this device to access the sharedrive and connect it to the WI-FI, then we're good."

"Doesn't sound too bad."

Arien signs into his newly created Admin account before grimacing. "Fuck."

"What is it?"

"These bastards don't have WI-FI."

"What?"

"These people call themselves nerds, but they don't even have WI-FI. The higher-ups must take security more seriously than the average programmer."

"So, what do we do?"

Arien pockets the USB, saying, "Well, we can't use this without WI-FI, and I can't break their encryption to make a backdoor through their network. We'll have to try and download the whole database."

A short bark of laughter is torn from me. "What? No, that's impossible. Especially with the time we have."

"Do you have a better idea? We don't have time to search each profile now. We have to get the data back to my computer."

I stare down at the database on the computer, thinking. "Maybe we can narrow it down, though."

"What?"

Reaching into my bag, I pull out my backup plan, a curse tablet USB, and plug it into the computer. "I didn't trust your algorithm to find what we needed, so I made this."

"Is that a USB curse tablet?"

"Yeah."

Arien grabs me and violently kisses my forehead. "You're brilliant, Charlie. Truly."

I grin, channeling confidence that I don't feel. "I know." Suddenly, an oddly named folder appears on the desktop. "There. Any employees with a remotely strange history or a connection with the Greek mythology relating to Hermes. Arien opens the folder. In horror, I say, "Dammit. There's still 500 profiles."

"Not bad. Now it's my turn."

Arien plugs in his own USB. "You've narrowed it down enough for my algorithm to search through quickly. I even added a little facial recognition to match with any ancient statues of Hermes."

"Smart."

Taking out an external hard drive, Arien starts the download. "Any matches will automatically be downloaded onto this, so all we have to do now is wait."

We sit in awkward silence for several minutes; I twiddle my thumbs, lost in my own mind, dreaming of the happy days with Susan, but every memory leads to our anniversary, and where it all ended. Sighing and hoping to distract myself, I start riffling through the desk drawers.

"What are you doing?" Arien says.

"It always pays to look through someone's desk." A smile cracks my lips upon finding a distraction. I pull a whiskey bottle out of the drawer to show Arien. "Looks like you were right about them not being too happy."

"I don't know, Charlie. Maybe we shouldn't. We're working."

Otus's voice crackles over the wire. "Yeah, definitely don't. You could get caught."

Taking out both of our earpieces, I say. "Oh, shut up, Hedwig."

"Charlie!"

"Come on. I can't stay in this nerd heaven a second longer without getting wasted or slitting my wrists." I extend the bottle to Arien. "Your choice." Arien gives me a sad look before sighing and taking the bottle. "There you go." He takes a big swig and grimaces. "That's the spirit."

"That's awful."

Laughing softly, I take the bottle and drink as well.

We pass the bottle back-and-forth until we are well and truly wasted. Arien opens an employee's file and bursts out laughing before showing me. "This chick's name is Sarah Doctor Smith."

I burst out laughing too. "I don't even know why that's funny."

We both clutch our stomachs as our laughter increases, and Arien says, "Sarah Jane Smith was the 4th Doctor's first companion in classic Who. Her parents must have been uber-nerds." The nonsensical laughing gets louder. "And she's from Aberdeen too." Arien's phone starts ringing violently. "Hello."

I can barely make out Otus's voice wafting from the phone like a lilting breeze in summer's air. "You idiots. The meeting's over. The boss is coming back."

"Wow, man. It's all good. The download's done."

"Then get out of there."

"Right."

A churning in my stomach overwhelms me; I turn and heave my guts into the wastebasket. After clearing my stomach's contents, I moan and turn to Arien, wiping my mouth. "I think I had too much."

"They must have been something else in that whiskey."

Arien grabs the bottle and blinks, trying to focus on the label. "Oh, my god. This is one of those scotches from Colorado where they put weed in with it."

"So, we're high and drunk?" I laugh hysterically before having to vomit again.

"Dude, that's so cool. Maybe we shouldn't have finished the bottle though."

"You're right, man."

I hear a noise behind me, but my body is stuck by the basket, immobilized by the fear of vomiting again.

The boss must be standing in the doorway because he says, "What, on earth, is going on here?"

Arien giggles and says, "Uh-oh, busted."

"You want to explain what you're doing in my office?"

I fight my weak stomach to stand and lean against Arien as he says, "Super-secret spy stuff."

I gasp, nudging Arien, and saying, "Hey, shush."

The boss's lip curls, his anger burning us. "Are you drunk?"

"Drunk and high. Or is it high and drunk? We're highly drunk. Drunkenly high."

"I will be taking corporate action against the two of you for this. What are your supervisors' names?"

Arien stares at the ceiling, thinking. "Ah, Emma."

I jump in with my boss's name. "And Hermione." Arien and I laugh at our Harry Potter references.

"I do not find this funny at all. I will see you both fired for this."

Arien's voice suddenly becomes cold, focused. "No, you won't."

"And why not?"

"Because this is yours." Arien hands the boss the whiskey bottle. "If you don't want anyone to know you keep this stashed in your desk, you'll forget we were ever here. Like, poof and we're gone."

I wave my hands in the air. "Like magic."

"Yeah, like we're witches or something."

The boss grimaces as he accepts his fate. "Fine. Just leave and stay out of my way."

"Wait, that actually worked?"

Shaking my head in awe, I say, "I can't believe that worked."

The boss sighs, ushering us out of his office. "Just go." We stumble out of the office and toward the elevator.

Otus

I cannot remember a generation more irresponsible or destructive as Arien and Charlie's. They stumble into the hotel room, my glare following them, condemning them. "What the hell was that guys?"

Charlie giggles softly. "Just a little fun, Bubo."

"Did you get the files?"

"Yeah, got 'em here." Arien hands me an external hard drive. "Chill, man."

Sighing in relief, I say, "Alright, I'll go through them while you two sober up." Arien wobbles to the window and starts to dreamily watch cars go by as I sit down, plug in the hard drive, and start sifting through the profiles. "How many are on here?"

"50ish. Charlie did this really smart thing and narrowed them down for me. She's really smart. Did you know that?"

I ignore Arien's question, focusing on the files. Charlie sits down next to me, her breath hot and blowing into my ear, her fingers twirling my hair. "Charlie, what are you doing?"

"You're such a big handsome man. Did I ever tell you?"

I turn to face Charlie, saying. "Sweetie, you're a lesbian. If I let you go any further, you're going to be very mad at me later. And I do not care to have a witch as powerful as you out to get me. I like not getting castrated by a devastating STD brought about by a curse tablet. Okie dokie?"

She reaches up to stroke my cheek. "Oh, sugar. That doesn't sound like me."

Charlie turns and vomits into a wastebasket as I sigh and look up in prayer, "Daughters of darkling Nyx, much-nam'd, draw near infinite Fates, and listen to my pray'r. Why, the hell, am I destined to save the world with these idgits?" I shake my head, returning to work.

CHAPTER 23: PRAYERS ANSWERED

The screams of dozens of maniacs echo through the halls of the insane asylum. The Litai prayer spirits struggle against their golden bonds that have them dangling horizontally from the ceiling. These ghostly old women shiver and shake as they hear every prayer being spoken on earth echoing through their heads.

The Titan Koios is sitting beneath the Litai with his hand resting on one of their foreheads. Otus's prayer echoes through the Litai and into Koios's head.

"Daughters of darkling Nyx, much-nam'd, draw near infinite Fates, and listen to my pray'r. Why, the hell, am I destined to save the world with these idgits?"

Koios smiles as he traces the prayer back to its source. "Where are you?" Darkness fills the room as Koios projects his thoughts into a physical image that he alone can see. Out of the darkness, a ghostly vision of Arien's Miami hotel room can be seen with Otus praying in a loop. "Daughters of darkling Nyx, much-nam'd, draw near infinite Fates, and listen to my pray'r. Why, the hell, am I destined to save the world with these idgits?"

Koios's smile widens as he lets the image fade. "Thanks, bird-man." He stands and leaves the cell, walking to Iapetus's chamber.

Iapetus is meditating on the floor in the center of the room, ignoring Koios standing in the doorway. "Sir?"

Iapetus sighs but doesn't move or open his eyes. "What is it?"

"Sorry to bother you, sir. I know you're busy, but I'm looking for Atlas. I found Arien."

Iapetus stands and turns to Koios. "My son has been called lunar-side to speak with Kronos, himself. Apparently, our lord is not satisfied with his efforts to capture this Arien."

"Will you go, then?"

"I am far too busy with my search. Primordial gods are not easy to find. I still have not been forgiven for losing him the first time, though it was not my mistake. I cannot delay my search for anything."

"Of course not, sir."

"We cannot leave the Litai's unattended, so you must contact Hyperion. His D.C. operation can survive without him long enough to deal with these children."

"Yes, sir. Should we send him the Scythe, as well?"

Iapetus looks down at the Scythe leaning against the wall. "No need to risk our only god-killer for such a diminutive task."

"Of course."

"You may leave."

Koios bows and leaves Iapetus to return to his meditation.

Otus

My eyes widen in hope as they trace through a file, a smile cracks my lips. "I think I found him." Arien and Charlie just moan from their places on the bed. I shake my head and continue on. "Herman Schou, a resident of LA with a history of mischief. He hasn't appeared to have aged in 15 years of working for ChatDen. He even kinda looks like the old statues. And Herman and Hermes sound alike."

Arien moans, "Great."

I stand and start packing our gear. "Alright, guys. We need to go."

Charlie appears to cry as she says, "No, not now."

"Yes, now. We left the bike and your car in Phoenix, so we need to find transportation, which will take a while."

Struggling, I force them both to their feet and toward the door. "Come on." I freeze, noticing the sun's morning rays spill in through the window. "What, the hell?"

"What's wrong?"

"It's sunrise."

"So?"

"It's 8 o'clock pm and that's east."

"That's weird."

"You think?"

Charlie's eyes widen as she finally understands. "We need to get out of here."

"Yeah."

Charlie reaches into her bag and pulls out a potion. Drinking it, she is immediately sober. She hands it to Arien just as a bright flash of sunlight illuminates the room. We cover our eyes as a Titan appears by the window.

He smiles as the sunlight fades. "Hello, there."

I leap for the door but stumble back as the doorknob melts off.

"Please, don't."

I turn to face the Titan. "You're Hyperion."

"Yes, very good. Now, kneel."

"What?"

We all grimace as our skin burns, forcing us to kneel. Once we've knelt, the burning subsides.

"That's better. It's always polite to kneel before your superiors."

Arien says, "What makes you our superior?"

Charlie and I both elbow the still drunk Arien.

"No, please. It's a good question. I am your superior because I have been there since the birth of humanity, guiding you into a better, brighter future. A future where 'all that is solid melts into air, all that is holy is profaned, and man is at last compelled to face with sober senses, his real conditions of life, and his relations with his kind.' That is why."

Charlie disregards self-preservation to say, "At what cost? Our free will?"

"Free will has done nothing for humanity but perpetuate their violent tendencies and their desire to be better than everyone else at the expense of all. In the world I strive to create, there will be no racism, sexism, prejudice, or creeds. Humanity will finally have equality."

I follow Charlie's lead to say. "But not equality with you. Just sounds like more of the same."

"Titans will forever stand above humanity and act as their guides and rulers. Humanity has proven untrustworthy with your own fate. We must be better than you to make you better than you are. Your weakness is what has led you to the brink of destroying yourselves. We may have influenced much in recent years, but all we did was give the world a little push off the cliff you were already teetering on. Despite that, we are not allowed to force large change regularly. Humanity has to give up their desire for free will voluntarily before we can make a Utopia for all mankind. As such, we would have achieved Utopia decades ago if it were not for America believing in free will to the degree it does."

I look away in defeat, my eye focusing on Arien's owl pendant dangling from his neck. I smile as an idea comes to me.

"None the less, you shall all still reap the benefits of Utopia after I kill you. Take comfort in that."

I lean over and whisper in Charlie's ear. "The power of prayer." She smiles in response.

We start mumbling a prayer to Athena under our breath as Hyperion kneels in front of Arien. "What makes you so important? I couldn't sense anything special about your parents, but there's something fundamentally different about you. The only explanation that I can think of is, those aren't your parents." Arien is coherent enough to be shocked by this revelation. Hyperion grabs Arien's chin and stares into his eyes. "Both your parents must be very special. There's fire and night roaring against each other inside of you."

Hyperion's eyes widen in surprise. "With a glimmer of godly power. You have a divinity inside of you. Faint but growing." Hyperion stands and steps back. "No matter. Two birds with one stone, as they say. It seems a shame that you will still receive your reward after how disappointing of an adversary you have been, but all our children are loved."

I stop mumbling to say, "I disagree. You'll find us worthy adversaries."

"And why is that?"

"Because humanity is power. Humanity united gives those we believe in strength."

"I already know this. That's why we destroyed any belief in gods or magic."

"But even one human has the power to give strength and hope. The prayer of one lost and tired soul managed to unlock the power of a god inside of him and give his life meaning. Imagine what the prayers of two can do."

Charlie and I stand, chanting in unison:

"Only-Begotten, noble race of Zeus, blessed and fierce, who joy'st in caves to rove:

O, warlike Pallas, whose illustrious kind, ineffable and effable we find:"

Hyperion stares at us in confusion. "What are you doing?" Arien starts to glow with a godly light leaving him completely sober.

"Magnanimous and fam'd, the rocky height, and groves, and shady mountains thee delight:

In arms rejoicing, who with Furies dire and wild, the souls of mortals dost inspire."

Hyperion stares at Arien in horror. "No." He lifts his hand, and a spear of pure sunlight appears in it. He throws the beam at Charlie and I in an attempt to silence us. A golden aura appears around us, emanating from Arien and protecting us from Hyperion's blast.

"Gymnastic virgin of terrific mind, dire Gorgons bane, unmarried, blessed, kind:

Mother of arts, imperious; understood, rage to the wicked, wisdom to the good:

Female and male, the arts of war are thine, fanatic, much-form'd dragoness, divine:"

Arien glows brighter as he's lifted off the ground and spread-eagled. Hyperion fires a continuous beam of light at Arien, his fear growing.

"O'er the Phlegrean giants rous'd to ire, thy coursers driving, with destruction dire.

Sprung from the head of Zeus, of splendid mien, purger of evils, all-victorious queen.

Hear me, O goddess, when to thee I pray, with supplicating voice both night and day,

And in my latest hour, peace and health, propitious times, and necessary wealth,

And, ever present, be thy vot'ries aid, O, much implor'd, art's parent, blue eyed maid."

As we finish the hymn, we cover our eyes from Arien's bright light. The Aegis and Athena's spear fly into his hands as the light fades, and he is put back on the ground.

Hyperion blasts Arien with a wave of sunlight. Arien throws up the Aegis to block as he slowly advances.

Hyperion stares at the face of the Aegis before turning away and shaking his head. While Hyperion is distracted by whatever memory the Aegis is making him relive, Arien spins out from in front of the beam and stabs down at Hyperion's foot with his spear.

Hyperion screams as the spear cripples me. Turning, he jumps out the open window.

Charlie rushes to the window to verify that Hyperion is gone while Arien stumbles against the wall.

I hurry to Arien as he collapses, and the room catches fire. "We've gotta go. This place is gonna burn."

"Right. Let's go."

Charlie

My frantic breathing rattles my chest; I try to slow it, controlling my fear, the image of a murderous Titan still seared into my mind. Arien hobbles along with Otus's help across the lobby. Otus turns to me and says, "Charlie, we need a car, now."

"How do I get one?"

"Use your seashell."

I scan around the lobby for a guiltless victim of grand theft auto. My gaze settles on a classic country-valley girl speaking to the receptionist. The woman screams and stamps her foot, clearly vexed by the hotel not waiting on her hand-and-foot. "I mean, like, come on, dude. I'm, like, insta famous. I'm a celebrity and I expect to be treated like it."

The receptionist's face constricts, forcing a kind demeanor as she says, "I'm sorry, ma'am. But I can't take your car to pick up your dry cleaning. I could get fired."

"But I'm Becki Carson, @babeliciousbecki. I'm a celebrity."

"We're just a small B&B, we aren't prepared for high-profile guests."

"I'm gonna go all over Insta and I'm gonna tell everyone that you suck. I have, like, 225 thousand followers, so you're gonna lose a lot of business because you treated me so terribly."

"I'm sorry, ma'am. But I don't have a choice."

"Uh, you're awful. Why are you so mean to me? Am I not pretty, or something?"

"What? No, you're pretty, but rules are rules."

With my target selected, I pull out a seashell and a vial of blood; drawing Becki's name on the shell, I whisper, "I adjure you, shell, by bitter Necessity, and by those who have been placed in charge of the Punishments, LAIU LAKIO LAKIMOU MOUKILA KIIAMOU IOR MOUOK

MOUDRA MAXTHA MOUSATHA: attract her, Becki, whom woman bore. Do not be stubborn, but attract her, OUCH OUCH CHAUNA MOUCHLIMALCHA MANTOR MOURKANA MOULITHA MALTHALI MOUI EIEI YYY AIE YOO GI AEI AEI AOA AOA AOA IAO OAI OAI AIO OM IOA OAI, attract her, Becki. As the moon waxes in Aries or in Taurus."

Attaching the shell to a string, I tie it around my wrist as a bracelet. After returning the rest of my gear to my bag, I walk to Becki and the receptionist, saying, "Excuse me, ma'am."

Becki turns to look me up and down, her lip curling in judgment. "What is it?" I reach out to shake her hand. As soon as we touch, her eyes widen, and her cheeks blush. "Oh, hello."

I smile, reaching up to stroke her cheek. "Hi, I can pick up your dry cleaning for you."

"Oh, yeah. That'd be great. Here, take my car." Becki hands me her car keys.

"Great, I'll have it back to you right away."

I turn to leave, but Becki reaches out and grabs my arm. "Bring it up to my room and I'll pay you well." She winks seductively.

"OK, thanks. Bye." I hurry over to where Otus and Arien are leaning against a wall. "I got it. Let's go." Using the key's beeper, I find Becki's car before helping Otus slide Arien into the backseat.

I pause to look around the dirty cesspit of a car, my stomach curdling. "Aw, this is fucking disgusting. For an Insta model, she's a slob."

"Just get in."

Otus and I climb in before I start the car and pull out of the parking lot, driving away. As we pass the hotel door, I notice Becki going to town, humping a lamppost while several people stare. Despite myself, I crack a smile as I throw the seashell into a bush, dooming Becki to hump until she finishes. "Ain't karma a bitch?"

I continue on, driving off into the sunset.

CHAPTER 24: BURN!

Arien

My eyes slowly open into darkness; I'm lying on the cold obsidian ground of the endless darkness. Tears flood down my cheeks as I struggle to my feet and scream, "What do you want from me? Tell me."

I clutch my head, blood pouring from every orifice. Falling to my knees, a pounding starts to shake the darkness, the Empty-Man's voice echoing through my head, saying, "Burn, burn, burn!"

"No!"

"Flee the empty."

The blood is suddenly gone; I turn to see a bloody Brittnie standing in front of me. "Who are you?"

"You let my son die."

I respond, instinctual horror and regret filling me. "No, it wasn't my fault."

"You killed him."

"No."

"My son had a pure soul and you corrupted him."

"I don't know who you are."

Tears stream down Brittnie's blood-stained cheeks. "What do you call a Mother who's lost a child? Why is there no word for that? Orphans have no parents. But I have no child. What are you? An orphan or a childless Father?"

"I don't know."

"You're an orphan without your child."

"I'm not an orphan."

"Then why'd you let my beautiful son die? You let the dark in." Brittnie punches me in the face. I spin from the impact, the fog swirling around me, forming into a ghostly version of my childhood home.

I'm hit again, blurring my vision. I struggle to see, just making out Dad's face before he hits me again. My body aches more than it should; I realize that I'm seven-years-old again, lost in the memory.

As Dad continues to beat on me, Mom reads the Bible in the corner. "My son, despise not the chastening of the Lord; neither be weary of his correction: For whom the Lord loveth he correcteth; even as a Father the son in whom he delighteth." Mom closes the Bible and looks up at me, Dad still beating me. "We must punish you for the darkness within you and root out your evil before it has chance to spread."

Dad lets up his assault long enough for me to say, "I'm not evil."

Dad's teeth grind together, taking my response as talking back. "We are your parents, and you will adhere to our diagnosis of your prevalence for sin."

"I didn't do anything."

Mom smiles sadly, disappointed. "It's what you are, not what you've done. You're a thing. We have tried so hard to purge your nature imbued in you at birth, but you have repeatedly refused to become the Samael that you need to be. The warrior for the Temple of God's Time."

Dad leans close, his threatening breath upon my cheek. "Unless you begin to show your devotion toward imitating our perfection, we will be forced to enact the final sacrifice to our Lord of time. Only your belief can save you."

Tears stream down my bloody cheeks as I beg for mercy, "I believe."

"Then you will never speak to Molly again."

"Why?"

Dad tightens his fist to strike again, but Mom steps forward and says, "That girl has secrets. She may be one of us, but she's not with us. She believes we should passively love everyone for being children of God, but our God is a vengeful God. A God who does not forgive sin as easily as she believes He does."

"I can't. She's my best friend."

"You're not allowed to have friends. You are a member of the Temple of God's Time. Our purpose is to fulfill the Lord's will at any cost. Personal connection will only prevent us from achieving that goal."

"I'm sorry."

Mom sighs before nodding at Dad. He smiles sinisterly, saying, "Then you give us no choice." He swings, striking again.

Mom watches sadly as Dad hits me again and again. "You will learn, eventually."

I curl up into a fetal ball to protect myself.

When I look up, the fog has cleared into the endless darkness, and I'm alone. The Empty-Man's voice echoes through the darkness again, "Forever is ahead."

I curl back up, letting the tears overwhelm me.

CHAPTER 25: DYING LIGHT

Morning rays filtered through the shaded windows onto a paradoxically picturesque 1950s hospital room, the idea of a depressing slow death repressed by flowers and smiles.

Nancy Hall was dying in a hospital bed while nurses did all they could to make her comfortable. Nancy grasped at a passing nurse and stared up into her eyes. "My husband, Herman, is he coming?"

"I don't know, ma'am."

"He must be. He's such a good man. He'd never leave me alone. Not now."

"I'm sure he is, ma'am."

"I ever tell you how I met Herman?"

"Yes, ma'am. Several times."

"I was coming home from church with my parents when I saw him. He was so handsome and pure. He was helping an elderly woman cross the street and was having trouble carrying her bags and supporting her, so I ran to help. He smiled at me in thanks, and that's when I knew that this was the type of man that I wanted to spend the rest of my life with. He was just so special. I have often thought about how much chance went into the two of us meeting exactly in that way. My life would have been so different if the pastor had ended his sermon a minute sooner, or if that woman had decided to stay home that day, or I hadn't been brave enough to help. God really knew what he was doing that day."

The wayward god of travelers finally settled with a home where to lay his head, smiled from the door where he'd been listening for a while. Hermes stepped forward, a bundle of flowers in hand. "Now, now, Nancy. I don't think this lovely nurse wants to hear this story again."

"Herman, is that you?"

"Yes, my love. You need to stop bothering this young lady."

"I was only making friendly conversation."

The nurse smiled, nodding at Hermes. "It's alright, sir."

Hermes waved his hand at the nurse to reassure her. "No need to humor her, miss."

"Yes, sir." The nurse finished her responsibilities before walking to Hermes to speak privately.

"How is she doing?"

"The doctor says there's nothing we can do."

"Are you certain?"

"I'm sorry, sir."

"How long does she have?"

"She might make it until morning, if she's lucky."

Hermes turned to stare longingly at his dying wife, lost in her own world. "So soon."

"You should say your goodbyes, sir. We cannot be certain when we'll lose her."

"Thank you."

"Yes, sir."

The nurse nodded, walking out, leaving Hermes to go to his wife's bedside and give her the bouquet of flowers. "For you, my dear."

"Ah, Herman. They're beautiful. You shouldn't have."

"I wanted to do something nice for you." Hermes kissed Nancy on the forehead before sitting next to the bed.

"I, honestly, don't see what all the fuss is about. I feel well enough to get up and return home. I could even get dinner on the table for you on time. Would you like that?"

"Not this time, Nance. When we get you home, I'm cooking."

Nancy laughed a little. "I'll definitely end up dying if you cook." Hermes sadly smiled at Nancy's joke. "I'm sorry. That was in poor taste."

He grabbed her hand to comfort her. "No, it's alright."

Nancy sighed and stared into Hermes's eyes. "Did you ever think this is how it would end for us?"

Tears threatened at the corners of Hermes's eyes as he said, "Don't talk like that. It's not ending here."

"I see how the nurses look at me. There's no cause for hope. I'm already losing myself. Forgetting things and making a fool of myself."

"No one thinks you a fool."

"Be realistic, Herman. This is how it was always going to end. I would never admit it to myself and I never would have guessed that this day would come this soon, but there was never going to be another ending to our story. At the end of the day, you're you and I'm me. You being who you are, I'd wither away and die at some point and you'd always look the same."

Hermes sighed and shook his head, a single tear leaking out. "2 thousand years of running and I never allowed myself to fall in love, but I couldn't help myself with you, Nancy. I knew I was going to get my heart broken, but I didn't care. You're everything to me."

Nancy smiled, her eyes going distant as she shook her head to clear them. "Herman? When did you get here?"

Hermes sighed and wiped his eyes, reaching up to move a lock of hair out of Nancy's face. "Just now."

"Is Lucy coming? I'd like to see her too."

Hermes tensed up and turned away, grief overwhelming him. "Lucy's gone, Nance."

"Gone? Gone where?"

"You miscarried 6 months ago. Don't you remember?"

The memory of losing her child overcame Nancy. "Oh, yes. I remember."

Hermes smiled to put on a brave face as Nancy turned to stare out the window.

CHAPTER 26: ROAD TRUTHS

<u>**Arien**</u>

Countless hours pass stilled curled up alone in the endless darkness, voices pounding through my head. The voices of the Empty-Man, screaming, "Forever is ahead;" Dad's cold voice saying, "Only your belief can save you;" Brittnie whispering, "You killed him;" a woman cackling, "The boy must die;" and Iapetus saying, "Seed planted in the dark."

My body seizes as the voices start to echo.

***

I slowly blink, the sun blinding me. The vision clears to see a mountainous pile of garbage, green with mold. Struggling to sit up, a glance around to see Charlie driving us through an empty desert, and Otus staring at me with worry.

Otus says, "Hey, how are you feeling?"

Rubbing my forehead to push back a headache, I say, "Like I got hit by a truck."

Charlie turns slightly to says, "So, pretty normal, then?"

I wince as I try not to laugh. "Very funny." Otus grabs my head to stare into my eyes, inspecting me. "What are you doing?"

"We can't ever do that again. It might kill you next time."

A flash of hope sears through me at the idea, but I try to joke to distract the others. "Don't tempt me with a good time."

Charlie slaps Otus to back off. "Give him a moment to breathe, man."

Leaning back into my seat, I say, "But it didn't, Otus. It wasn't even as bad as last time."

"Well, we're still not doing it again."

"It may be our best chance of standing up against the Titans."

"Doesn't matter. It's not worth the risk, especially with you being out of action for the next 40 hours."

Shock floods through me. "I've been asleep for 40 hours?"

"Yeah."

"Whoa."

Charlie shakes her head, lost in thought. "The thing I don't understand is, people pray to Athena all the time and it's never made you go nuclear besides the twice. I've prayed to her before, I'm sure Otus has too, and even Arien did before it happened."

After a moment of thought, I laugh slightly, understanding. "I'd never prayed after a suicide attempt."

"What?"

Otus nods in agreement. "He's right. He had the divinity down so deep that it couldn't hear the prayers. His body knew the best way to protect itself from all that energy would be burying it so deep he had no idea it was there. But the suicide attempt brought his walls down enough for it to hear his prayer. Can you imagine the amount of endorphins and adrenaline going through his body at that time? His body was a mess and the walls cracked. Now that they're cracked, anyone can give it psychic energy if they're close enough, like us."

I turn to stare out the window, horrified by the thought of what damage my depression had caused. "So, none of this would ever have happened if I didn't want to die? Medea, Rachel, and everyone the ghost killed would still be alive."

Otus purses his lips before saying, "And we'd never have any hope of stopping the Titans from killing any more people."

"That's little comfort to the dead."

Charlie sighs, her body tensing at the mention of Medea. "What happened, it's not your fault. If not them, then someone else would have died." Otus and I share a meaningful look, me asking for permission to tell her. Charlie notices the look and says, "What is it?"

I take a deep breath, preparing for the pain to come. "One death is unquestionably my fault."

Otus interrupts to stop me. "Don't do it, Arien. It's just gonna make things worse for both of you."

Charlie glances back at me from the road. "What are you talking about?"

"It's about Medea."

Otus sighs as he gives up.

"What about her?"

"Her death's my fault."

"No, it's not. I mean, no more than the rest of us. Apollo told Rachel where we were going, so our being there is what put her in danger. But we couldn't have known what would happen."

"Rachel would never have been there if I hadn't made a mistake."

"What do you mean?"

"When we were in Amber with Molly, we captured Rachel."

"What?"

"I let her go. I couldn't bring myself to kill her. I thought there might have still been a way to save Rachel herself. I was wrong."

Otus tries to take the blame by saying, "It's not all his fault. Molly and I helped him."

Charlie clenches her jaw as she stares out the window before she suddenly relaxes. "What about Atlas?"

I raise an eyebrow, confused. "What?"

"I'm not going to say that you didn't fuck up, because you did. But Atlas would still have been there and Medea would still be dead. You can't stop fate."

Otus and I stare at Charlie, in awe of her maturity and self-control. "Thank you."

"I haven't forgiven you, but I will."

A smile cracks my lips a little. Turning, I stare out the window at the approaching city.

CHAPTER 27: GOD OF TRAVELERS

<u>**Arien**</u>

Carlie pulls Becki's car up in front of Hermes's modest house. We all get out and stare at it for a moment. Otus says, "Is this it?"

I nod slowly, saying, "According to his file." We all feel the anticipation of meeting another god, all grounded to the spot, none wanting to be the first to open the can of worms that inevitably accompanies a god. After a long pause, I finally sigh and take the first steps toward the door.

Raising my hand, I knock firmly. We wait until a small, squirrely man I assume is Hermes's, answers the door. He lets out a big sigh as he looks up-and-down his visitors.

I smile and say, "Hi, my name's Arien. And this . . ."

Hermes interrupts, saying, "Yes, I know who you are."

"How?"

"It's my job. Come in." Hermes steps aside to allow us to enter. As we come in, he motions for us to sit down. "Please, have a seat." We all awkwardly sit down and stare at each other. "Would you guys like anything. Coffee? Tea? Beer? I am the god of travelers."

Charlie shakes her head and says, "No, thank you. We'd just like to talk."

Hermes's face constricts a little as he attempts to hide his emotions. "I know why you're here. You want me to become a god again to help in your struggle against Timorian. Tell me, what's your plan?"

My mind stumbles, stopped in its tracks by a question I'd never considered, preoccupied with my own death. "What do you mean?"

"How do you intend to defeat Timorian? What secret weapon, what master plan, or giant army do you have up your sleeve that you believe will tip the balance that hasn't been in our favor for 2 thousand years? What hope is there?"

Sweat beads down my temple; I look away, embarrassed. "None."

"None?" Hermes lets out an exasperated laugh.

"Aren't you tired of hiding? Tired of living a life that wasn't yours. We may not have much hope of winning, but we have hope for the pain to end. The endless methodical centuries coming to their inevitable close. This is the final chapter in the tragedy of Greek faith. Help end the story on our feet. One last chance to stick it to Timorian and give him a run for his money."

Hermes sighs in resignation. "The centuries have become tedious."

"So, you'll help?"

He pauses for a second before nodding. "You can only lose so much." I notice Charlie giving Hermes a curious look as he stands. "I'll grab my divinity and we can get started." He walks into the kitchen as we stare at each other, dumbfounded.

"That was easy."

"Too easy."

I shake my head, not believing our luck. "Yeah, we should be pulling teeth at this point."

Charlie smiles slightly. "Maybe it was your rousing speech."

Otus sighs more resigned than confused. "He's gone."

"What?"

"No god has their divinity with them, that defeats the whole purpose. Plus, he took my wallet."

"He what?" Charlie and I check our pockets, confirming our wallets and other valuables are gone. "He stole our stuff."

"God of thieves."

"That bastard."

We all stand and rush into the kitchen, but Hermes is gone. My eyes flash black as I scream. "Dammit. God, dammit. Fuckin' shit."

Charlie grabs my shoulder, trying to calm me. "Whoa, calm down. We'll find him."

"Whatever. Let's just go." Angry seems to come off me in waves, controlling my actions.

Otus says, "Go where? He took our money. We can't afford a hotel."

Charlie cautiously watches me, appalled by my overzealous outburst. "We'll just stay here. That'll give me enough time to figure out how to find him. Or he may come back."

I tersely say, "Fine," before storming into the next room, feeling Otus and Charlie's concerned looks on my back. Sitting on the couch, I stare at the wall.

Charlie tentatively smiles and approaches me, sitting beside me and stroking my shoulder. "Hey, I'm gonna go get my stuff from the car. You gonna be OK?"

I sigh, releasing some of my pent-up anger. "Yeah, no. I'll be fine. Thanks."

"OK." She nods, stands, and leaves. I smile after her as Otus takes his turn, sitting across from me.

Otus smiles sadly, saying, "Careful, it looks like you care."

"What do you mean?"

"You play the tough guy and act like you have nothing to live for, but I think you do. You'll need to be careful, or you'll find a reason to not let yourself die."

I give Otus a look that dispels all his hopes that I don't want to die. "I'm from a past too dark to be changed this easily. I want to die so much. To have it all end. I want all the voices to stop and all the responsibilities to end."

"Voices?"

I ignore Otus's question, saying, "I just want . . . I just want to sleep. Just that. Nothing else. An endless dreamless sleep where nothing matters and nothing is. I'm just unworthy of the gift of life." I turn, a single tear leaking out of the corner of my eye. "I still expect you to keep your promise and kill me if we survive all this."

"How?"

"Find a way."

The pain I pour into my gaze makes Otus's eyes fill with pity. "Why?"

"Why? I've told you why. I'm a monster."

"No, you've told me conclusions. Tell me why you believe you're not worthy to live."

I let out a quiet sigh. "I don't know, at least not entirely. There's the people I've let die, my depression, and a belief that there's something wrong with me. . . I have no memories before the age of 7 except for blood, death, and chaos. I did something. Something horrible and that's why my parents did what they did to me. I was so evil the devil wouldn't take me. Am so evil. Death follows me like a cloud. I have no reason to live. The world will be better off without me. People will be safer."

Otus goes to speak but is interrupted by Charlie walking in from the car, carrying our gear. She smiles and says, "Hey."

Standing, Otus says, "What took you so long?"

"Well, the neighbor girl's got a nice ass. Had to talk to her."

"Nice."

Charlie pauses, noticing my tears. "Are you guys OK?"

"Yeah, we're fine," I say, wiping my eyes.

CHAPTER 28: FOR THOSE WE'VE LOVED

<u>Arien</u>

Tears fill my eyes, responding to the impossible memory before me. I'm back to the day I got my heart broken, sitting upon a fence overlooking the Marks farm. Anna smiles at me, turning to gaze up at the twinkling stars far above. Her smile widens as she says, "They're beautiful."

My body is longer my own, acting out the memory as it had played out. I stare at Anna, lost in her beautiful, supple cheek. "They aren't the only things tonight."

Anna looks at me, blushing before glancing down. "Aw, thanks." She reaches out and gingerly touches my hand. I smile down at our hands, grabbing hers with mine. She smiles again, returning her gaze to the stars, our hands still clasped tighter.

"Anna?"

"Yes?" Anna looks back at me, curious.

"Can I kiss you?"

Her smile broadens as her eyes flutter. "Do you have to ask?"

I smile again, leaning in for a kiss.

When I pull back, Anna's eyes go distant and she stares past him. "I've . . . ah . . . I've got to go, Sam." She jumps off the fence and runs away, leaving me alone and broken-hearted.

***

With a start, I wake on the couch of Hermes's house. Sighing to compose myself, I get up and head to the kitchen for a beer. After taking a sip, I lean against the counter, breathing slowly to reign in the anger coursing through me, anger not my own.

An old black-and-white photo on the wall catches my attention. Stepping closer to inspect it, I see that it's a photo of Hermes with a woman in a white dress. A wedding photo. "You can only lose so much."

My angry builds as realization that Hermes's motive for denial is the love of a woman long dead. "You selfish cunt."

Screaming in rage, my eyes go black, and I punch the photo.

I stumble, suddenly lost in the endless darkness, Hermes's house nowhere to be seen. "Not again."

Turning, I see the Empty-Man huddled upon the ground, rocking himself. My anger rising again, I approach the Empty-Man. "What do you want from me? Huh? What the fuck do you want? Tell me something. Anything. Who are you?" I scream again, throwing a firebolt at the Empty-Man.

The Empty-Man screams back and blasts out a dark shockwave that sends me flying.

I fall to the ground, suddenly in a hotel room.

Slowly sitting up and rubbing my head, I freeze as I see Hermes lying in bed watching TV. He doesn't seem surprised or upset; he just switches off the TV and looks at me. His voice dripping with sarcasm, he says, "Oh, no. You found me."

Shock is replaced with my familiar anger. "What the fuck's wrong with you? Why'd you leave us hanging like that?"

"Like you said so poetically, there's no hope. I like my new life and I don't want anything to change. Anyway, Timorian may not be that bad. He made a great religion that's done a lot of good in the world. Humanities atrocities have been kept to a minimal for the last 2 thousand years."

His words fill me with utter confusion at their idiotic stupidity. "Where have you been? No, they haven't. Look no farther than the world wars."

"Ah, yes. Those were awful, but Timorian needed to clean house after Judaism abandoned him."

"And you don't think he should be stopped for that, if nothing else?"

"It's not my place anymore."

"I think you're just a coward."

Hermes smiles, un-offended. "The god of liars cannot be offended or baited by such childish and simple insults."

"What about the picture of the woman in your kitchen?" He immediately clams up, turning away. "You should be fighting for her, if for no other reason. You owe that to her."

Anger laces Hermes's words as he responds. "You don't know what you're talking about. I'm *not* fighting because of her and our child." I look down in embarrassment at the mention of a child. "Nancy. Her name was Nancy, and she was my wife. She knew who I was, and she didn't want me to ever get dragged back in. I don't really like the man I become around my family." His eyes get a little distant. "It was cancer. A brain tumor. I will honor her memory by never becoming a god again. I just want to die and see her again."

My anger ebbs, finding comradery in his death wish. How can I ask him to go against a desire I so dearly share? A desire that I'm moving mountains to achieve. "God's don't go to the Underworld when they die."

"Who told you that?"

"Charlie."

"Your witch friend? She's very talented, but she's wrong. When we ripped out our divinities, we torn our souls apart and literally became different people. I have a human soul and a godly one. If I take my godly one back, it will destroy my human one. Effectively killing me with nothing remaining to send to the Underworld. I don't know if I'll care about Nancy anymore as the god I'd become."

I shake my head in confusion, remembering Apollo's death. "But Apollo was killed and when we put his divinity back into his body, he came back to life with all his memories."

"Memories are in the mind and the soul. There's a version of Apollo banging on the gates of hell as we speak. Our human selves can still find peace or torment in death, just like any mortal."

"Then we'll find a way. Helping us will be the best way to ensure your death and see her again. And there's honor in death. You'll die a hero. I think she'll appreciate that man."

"What honor? There's no honor. We honor the dead by living as best we can." Hermes sighs as his emotions start to overwhelm him. "People always pity the dead, but they shouldn't. The greater trial is living as a good person. That's the best way to remember them. By being kind. Just kind. I can't do that dead. Even if we're together, we'll never be happy knowing I gave up. That I didn't try to be a good man. She would want me to stay alive. That's the only reason I haven't killed myself. Because I'm afraid of losing her."

"I don't understand. It's not giving up, it's fighting back."

"As soon as I take back my divinity I can't die, so I'd never see her again. And if I let myself die as a mortal, I'll never be able to look her in the eye knowing I could have done more."

I finally nod in understanding. "I get it."

"Good. Now leave me alone." Hermes turns the TV back on and starts ignoring me. I stare at him with pity for a moment before walking into the corner and taking out my phone to call Charlie.

She answers, saying, "Arien, what is it?"

"I found Hermes."

"What? He came back?"

I notice a hotel pamphlet on the dresser and pick it up. "No, I'm at a hotel. The Legacy Inn, apparently. Should be nearby."

"What are you doing there?"

"I just had a hunch, I guess. It's a long story. It doesn't matter. Can you summon the dead?"

Her voice becomes strained as she says, "What? Ah, I guess, with a nekyia, yeah. Why?"

"Do you have everything you'd need?"

"Yeah, I think so. Except a photo or item that belonged to the deceased. Arien, what's going on?"

"Get what you need and meet me in room 444. I have an idea. Hurry. Oh, and bring the broken photo from the kitchen." I hang up, turning to stare at Hermes.

CHAPTER 29: TORTURE FOR THE GOOD

<u>Arien</u>

Answering a knock, I open the door, letting Charlie and Otus into Hermes's hotel room. Hey, thanks for coming. You have everything you need?"

Charlie nods in confusion. "Yes, but what are we doing?"

"You'll see."

Hermes stands and glares at us as we approach. "What the hell is this? I told you to leave me alone, not bring all your friends over."

"They're not here for you."

"What?"

I turn to Charlie. "You have the picture?"

"Yeah."

Charlie pulls the photo of Hermes and Nancy from her bag. Hermes's eyes widen as he realizes what I'm planning. "No!" He tries to grab the photo, but Outs and I hold him down on the bed. "You can't do this."

Charlie stares at me in shock, comprehending my plan. "Arien, this is wrong."

"Just do it."

She shakes her head in resignation, tears streaming down Hermes's face.

Charlie grabs a wooden bowl from her bag and sits on the ground, placing it on the floor in front of her. She takes out a candle and puts it behind the bowl before lighting it. "To all the souls of those who've gone before, I humbly give this offering." She takes 5 urns from her bag, slowly pouring a libation from each into the bowl. Libations of milk, honey, mellow wine, water, and then of barley.

Charlie raises her arms and closes her eyes, beginning a prayer to Thanatos:

"Hear me, O Thanatos, whose empire unconfined, extends to mortal tribes of ev'ry kind. On
thee, the portion of our time depends, whose absence lengthens life, whose presence ends.
Thy sleep perpetual bursts the vivid folds, by which the soul, attracting body holds:
common to all of ev'ry sex and age, for nought escapes thy all-destructive rage; Not
youth itself thy clemency can gain, vig'rous and strong, by thee untimely slain. In
thee, the end of nature's works is known, in thee, all judgment is absolv'd alone: No

suppliant arts thy dreadful rage control, no vows revoke the purpose of thy soul; O

blessed power regard my ardent prayer, and human life to age abundant spare."

Charlie places the wedding photo in the bowl before reaching into her bag and pulling out a squirming bird.

Hermes whimpers softly. "Please, don't."

Charlie glances up at him, grimacing before proceeding. "Aa emptokom basym, protect me." She takes out a knife and slashes open the bird, letting its blood pour into the bowl to mix with the other ingredients. Putting aside the bird and knife, she raises her hands and closes her eyes. "Eláte, psychí aftoú pou agapísame kai échasa."

Charlie's eyes glaze over as she starts to seize.

I scream, "Charlie" with worry.

Hermes turns away, hoping Charlie fails. "Oh, god."

Charlie stops shaking long enough to say, "It's all right. I'm just having trouble calling the spirit here. She's farther away then she should be."

In confusion, I say, "What does that mean?"

Before Charlie can respond, a ghostly aura wafts through the window into the room. Hermes pulls away from the spirit, crying, "No, please, no." He curls up to hide as the spirit forms into a faceless, transparent body to lean down and drink the blood from the bowl.

The spirit solidifies into Nancy before standing and turning to Hermes. "Hello, Herman."

Hermes looks up at Nancy with anguish. "Nancy."

"I missed you."

"I've missed you too."

"Why am I here? Have you not moved on?"

"How could I?"

"Oh." Nancy looks away in embarrassment.

More tears leak out of Hermes's eye as he looks up at her in pain. "Have you?"

"I was assigned a beautiful man who takes care of all my needs."

"Assigned?"

Nancy nods slowly, her expression blank, emotionless. "Things are different there then you'd think."

I step forward to say, "Ma'am?"

Nancy turns to look at me. "Yes?"

"My name's Arien, and this is Otus, and Charlie. We need your husband's help."

"With what?"

"We're gathering all the gods together for one last struggle against Timorian. This may be our best chance to fix everything that's gone wrong. To be free again."

"And Herman doesn't want to help?"

"He says it would disgrace your memory."

Nancy looks back to Hermes with sadness. "For the person I was, it would. But I've seen so much, and learned more, since I died. The world isn't as black-and-white as I had always believed. It's a rainbow. There are so many possibilities and so many ways to do right. In my afterlife, we forgive everyone because no one makes mistakes. I hope by your efforts that you can make this place a little like that. Herman, my dear, sweet husband. I give you my blessing and let you go. You should do the same."

Tears stream freely down Hermes's cheeks as he stands up and reaches out to stroke his wife's face one last time. "I'm not strong enough, Nance."

"No, but you can be."

"I'll never see you again."

"But you'll have done the right thing. You'll have been kind. I'm going to be alright without you. And so are you."

"Don't leave."

"I can't stay. Be strong, for me."

"I will."

"I love you, Herman."

"I love you, Nance."

"Goodbye." Nancy fades away.

We stare after her, tears threatening all of us after what we've done. Turning to Hermes, we wait for him to speak. He finally says, "You are all horrible people for making me go through that." We all avert our eyes in shame. "I'll help, but not out of duty or loyalty. Or to help you get that death you crave." He glances at me, seeing through me. "But because my wife told me to, and I do what I'm told."

"Thank you," I say solemnly.

"Don't thank me. Don't ever thank me. I'll never forgive you for this. Any of you." Hermes glares at each of us in turn. "My divinity is in a Galápagos tortoise on Isla Isabela."

I turn to the others, diverting us away from our shame. "Of course, it is."

Otus shakes his head to clear it, saying, "How are we supposed to get there?"

Charlie accepts our silent agreement to ignore our actions by saying, "We'll have to fly, I guess."

Thinking it over, I shake my head. "I can't show my face in an airport. I'm a dead man, remember."

Hermes sighs, drawing all our attention. He says, "You won't need to fly." We all stare at him in confusion. "Arien can just teleport there."

Charlie and Otus turn to me in shock. "He can what?"

"How do you think he found me?"

"What's he talking about, Arien?"

I bite my lip, still in denial. "I'm not sure. I mean, I don't understand what or how. . ."

"Luckily, I'm the god of travelers. I know how." Hermes pauses, deciding every moment whether or not to help us. "You're somehow connected to Erebus."

Otus gasps in horror. "No."

Charlie cocks her head, trying to comprehend. "*Erebus*, Erebus?"

I glance between all of them. They all seem to know who this Erebus is. "Who's Erebus?"

Otus turns to me, concern written all over his face. "He's the primordial deity of darkness."

"Is that bad? That sounds bad."

Charlie says, "Darkness and night have always been associated with evil. He might be the reason for that."

Hermes shakes his head before saying, "Erebus rules, or *is*, a, sort of, half-dimension. A fundamental part of our own dimension, but just a little off. All shadows and darkness are Erebus bleeding throw cracks in the dimensions. Cracks appear and close based on if there's light. The light keeps the dimensional barriers closed. He covers all the earth. He's everywhere. He's the space between atoms that build our world. He is neither good nor bad. He just is. Arien seems to have the ability of stepping into Erebus and his dimension fully. My divinity will be like a dark beacon in there. The dimensional barriers there will be stronger than anywhere else. Arien can go into Erebus, appear in the Galápagos, find my divinity, and bring it back here."

I glance at Charlie for strength, afraid of going back into the darkness. "I'm afraid. You don't know what being in there does to me. I see things. Horrible things. It's turning me into something dark and evil."

"What do you see?"

"Everyone I've let die standing in judgment. A man getting tortured for years. A church bathed in blood. And a woman."

"What woman?"

"I don't know, but I feel like I've done something to her. Something unspeakable. Something so bad my visions won't even show me."

Hermes says, "You can navigate it if you just try."

My face constricts, the decision to try made. "Alright."

"When you get there, find a cliff where a caduceus is carved. Say a prayer and give an offering of blood to me. A cave mouth will open. My divinity is in there, guarded by some unorthodox creatures, but nothing you can't handle. Bring the tortoise here and I'll take the divinity out of her."

I nod, turning to accept the Aegis and the spear from Otus. Closing my eyes, I imagine all the horrible things I've seen in the darkness, letting them play before my eyes, darkening me. Flashes of Brittnie, the Temple of God's Time suicide, Erebus getting tortured, and me killing Molly all appear before my gaze.

The shadows darken and grow; a scream is torn from my throat by the psychological torture that I'm putting myself through. A light bulb explodes above us, plunging the room into darkness.

Charlie rushes to the light switch, turning on a hallway light. They all stare down at me, curled up on the floor, crying against the bed. She hurries to me, cradles me, and whispers soothingly, "It's alright."

Turning, I sob violently into her shoulder. "It didn't work. It's too horrible to be controlled."

Standing, Hermes stares down at me with contempt. "Why are you trying to control it?"

"What?"

"Are you trying to control your memories and emotions?"

"Yes."

"Why?"

"It's my only connection to the darkness. I can't feel it unless I'm afraid, angry, or in pain."

"That's not true. Like I said, Erebus is not evil but necessary. He's A-moral. You need to think of nothing. Become a-moral. Not happy or sad. Become one with the emptiness. Otherwise, it'll just happen randomly. It's the only way. Don't control it, become it. Emotions control your encounters with Erebus if you let them. But if you have no emotions, you can navigate Erebus on your own and can avoid the apparently insane piece of him that your emotions are drawn to."

"I can try."

Charlie shakes her head, forcing me to look into her eyes. "No, not now. You need to rest, recuperate."

I reach out to grab her hand. "It's OK. I need to figure this out, or I don't know what I'll become."

Pushing Charlie away, I cross my legs and close my eyes. The lights start to flicker as the shadows grow. I breathe in-and-out slowly, starting to meditate. The darkness thickens, ignoring the bounds the lights have defined. I open my eyes, dark as night. A bright flash of black light illuminates the room, blinding us all. I vanish within the light.

CHAPTER 30: BLURRED HISTORY

Arien

The flash of darkness clears, leaving me on the shores of a sea. I stare around in awe at the beauty of the Galápagos Islands. "Oh, my god. I did it." Turning, my gaze traces up the curves of a cliff to the edge high above. A caduceus carved into the cliff at eye-level catches my attention. My fingers run along the caduceus before I say, "A caduceus."

Setting aside the Aegis and the spear, I pull out my bear-bone-knife and cut my hand, smearing the blood over the caduceus. I kneel down and start chanting a prayer to Hermes:

"Hermes, draw near, and to my pray'r incline, angel of Zeus, and Maia's son divine; Studious of contests, ruler of mankind, with heart almighty, and a prudent mind. Celestial messenger, of various skill, whose pow'rful arts could watchful Argus kill: With winged feet, 'tis thine thro' air to course, O friend of man, and prophet of discourse: Great life-supporter, to rejoice is thine, in arts gymnastic, and in fraud divine: With pow'r endu'd all language to explain, of care the loos'ner, and the source of gain. Whose hand contains of blameless peace the rod, Corucian, blessed, profitable God; Of various speech, whose aid in works we find, and in necessities to mortals kind: Dire weapon of the tongue, which men revere, be present, Hermes, and thy suppliant hear; Assist my works, conclude my life with peace, give graceful speech, and me memory's increase."

The caduceus shimmers and glows before fading to reveal a cave mouth. Picking up the Aegis and the spear, I descend into the dark, weapons raised.

The tunnel mouth opens up into a massive cavern lit by numerous holes to the outside world through the ceiling. I stare down at a small habitat at the center of the cave where a tortoise lounges amidst grass, trees, and a pool of water. Cautiously, I approach, expecting danger.

A deep animalistic voice echoes from the darkness at the edges of the cave. "Who goes there?"

Crouching behind the Aegis, I prepare to fight, looking around for the source of the voice. "I am here at the command of Hermes to collect his divinity."

A second, higher voice responds. "Hermes? That monster locked us up here for thousands of years with nothing to eat. We're hungry."

The first voice says, "So hungry."

"Has Hermes at last sent us a meal?"

I try not to show fear as I say, "No, I'm here in peace."

"Hermes said this day would come. He'd send a hero to kill us and rid the world of our filth."

"I'm sure he didn't mean it." I whirl as I see movement in the shadows.

"Then why are you here and armed?"

"For my own protection."

"Hermes has taken everything from us. Our Mother, our freedom, our form, and the love of my life."

The higher voice says, "Calliope was the love of my life, not yours."

"She loved me."

"She despised you."

I interrupt their argument, saying, "I'm sure she loved you both."

"Silence."

I stare around frantically, looking for the monsters.

"Even after Hermes defeated us, he could not give us the honor of death. He had to take away our form, our strength. Then he took our Mother and Calliope and transformed them too and we become omens to humanity to not become beasts. But we didn't ask to be born. We didn't ask to be monsters. We were just kids."

The deeper voice responds. "After all that, Hermes had the gall to ask us for our help."

"And when we said no, he transformed us into greater monsters and locked us in here alone with that horrible tortoise."

An idea for escape comes to me, so I say, "I can set you free. Just let me take the tortoise."

"Once you see us, you'll never let us live."

"We're going to kill you and get out of here. Then we're going to find that monster and kill him. Without his divinity, he's just a man."

"And we're quite good at killing men."

"Oh, yes. But our hungry hasn't been satiated for millennia. We'll need to eat a little before we find Hermes. How do you care to be cooked?"

I quip to offset the horror overwhelming me. "I've always been partial to being grilled."

"You're a funny one. We'll see who's laughing once you see us."

Two monstrous forms step out of the shadows in front of me. I gasp and stare in horror at their hideous bodies. They're twenty-foot-tall bear-men with contorted bird parts sticking out of them, each a grim distortion of all things natural, instinctively feeling wrong and vile.

The monster with the higher voice smiles and says, "Look what Hermes has made us. Neither man, nor bird, nor beast. We were proud of our heritage of man and bear, but he had to corrupt us with these broken and useless things." The monsters unfurl their wings. "We are Agrius and Oreius, the sons of Polyphonte, and the mighty grizzly, Deimosi."

Oreius says, "What type of monster do you serve?"

My voice quivering, I say, "I don't serve Hermes or any other god. I just do what I think is right. And right now, that means ridding the world of you."

"So be it."

Agrius and Oreius roar as they charge.

I heft the spear and scream, rushing at the monsters. As Agrius swings for my head, I baseball slide under the blow and stab the spear into his ankle. Agrius whirls to face me, but I'm already out of reach.

Blood drips from the spear's tip as I climb a small pile of boulders to get the high ground, the monsters close behind. I turn and swing several deterrent blows as I climb. My foot catches and slips, nearly causing a rock slide. I quickly catch my balance and continue up.

Oreius side steps a jab and grabs the shaft of the spear, pulling it free. Oreius tosses the spear off the boulder pile to my horror. Drawing the bear-bone-knife, I continue upward. When I reach the top, I turn to face the monsters.

"There's nowhere else to run."

"I'm not running. Just getting to eye level."

"What?"

Leaping forward, I slam the Aegis into Agrius's face before letting it go and vaulting over his shoulder. As we fall, I plunge the bear-bone-knife deep into his eye, pushing off to land on my feet on the ground. Agrius smashes against several boulders as he hits the ground.

Agrius stumbles to his feet, slashing about wildly with his claws. I rush to the discarded spear as Agrius cleans the blood off his working eye. "I can see you."

Charging with the spear, I falter when Agrius picks up the Aegis and points it at me. He swings the shield as a weapon, striking me full in the chest. I go flying back as Oreius climbs down off the boulder pile.

Rolling over, I moan and spit up blood.

"You're just a boy. You cannot stand against us."

"No, but I can outsmart you."

Standing, I throw the spear like a javelin at the precarious boulders I'd nearly slipped on, now positioned just above Oreius's head.

Oreius looks up in horror as the spear bounces off a boulder above, starting a rockslide that rolls down, crushing him.

Agrius screams, "Oreius?" He frantically digs to free Oreius. Agrius turns just as I charge and jump at him, plunging my dagger deep in his throat.

Agrius roars and throws me off, stumbling.

I struggle to my feet and watch Agrius starting to bleed out. He falls to his knees, the blood loss becoming too much. Picking up the spear, I walk back to Agrius, who says, "Please."

I drive the spear into Agrius's heart.

I pull both my weapons out of Agrius's corpse, stumbling back and staring at the blood all over me clothes.

The rocks above Oreius shift violently.

"Ah, fuck."

Oreius bursts out of the rumble, roaring.

I sigh, hefting the spear and charging at Oreius.

Oreius lowers himself onto all fours as he charges to meet me.

At the last second, instead of diving to the side, I plant the spear in the ground and raise the point like a boar hunter.

Terror fills Oreius's as he runs onto my spear and is skewered. His forward momentum sends me flying.

I again struggle to my feet and dust myself off. To my shock, Oreius is still alive and dangerous. He pulls himself up and starts dragging himself toward me. "Oh, come on."

Walking forward, I easily dodge a swipe from Oreius before vaulting onto his back. I reach back and snap a broken wing, making Oreius scream and buck.

Wrapping my arms around Oreius's neck, I hold on as Oreius bucks harder. My grip tightens, choking the raging monster. When Oreius realizes what I'm doing, he rolls over and tries to crush me beneath his weight.

I grunt, the gigantic monster crushing me, but I hold on.

Oreius continues to struggle, but his strength starts to fade under my immense pressure. His struggles slow as his life leaves him. I hold on for another second before letting go and pushing Oreius's corpse off me.

Quickly gathering and cleaning my weapons, I walk to the tortoise, untouched by the raging fight. Crouching in front of the tortoise, I slowly stroke its shell. "I don't know if you like that, but it feels right." I glance over my shoulder at the mess behind me. "Sorry about the mess. Those guys were awful, weren't they?" The tortoise ignores me. "Right. Well, let's get going."

I stand, preparing to leave.

***

In another dark flash, I appear back on the floor of Hermes's hotel room, riding the tortoise. I gasp and slide off the tortoise, my body spent. Warm hands cradle me, lifting me up. I stare up into Charlie's eyes, happy to see her.

Behind Charlie, I see Hermes kneeling to stroke the tortoise. "I missed you, old friend."

I catch my breath, anger flooding through me. "A little warning next time would be great before sending me in like Goldilocks."

Charlie looks between me and Hermes in confusion. "What are you talking about?"

"Trickster here sent me into a trap. There were these giant winged bear-men guarding his divinity. And they were not too fond of me because I had anything to do with their arch enemy."

Hermes smiles with something akin to pride. "But you took care of them?"

"Yeah, I took care of them. Still have no idea how, but I did. You've got some friends there, pal."

"As you said, they aren't my friends. Keep your friends close, your enemies closer. Ever hear that? Who better to guard me divinity than people who won't even let me near it."

"That's a terrible plan."

"Worked for 2 thousand years."

Charlie glares at Hermes. "You could have gotten him killed."

"No, I couldn't have. He can't die, remember? But he may have been tortured repeatedly until the end of time."

I slowly stand, horrified realization flooding me. "You wanted that to happen."

"Either way would have been fine with me."

"What kind of god are you?"

"One that just had his dead wife paraded before him to manipulate him. Got a right to be pissed." I look down in shame. "Now, if you can all step back." We move back as Hermes starts stroking the tortoise again. "It's time, my friend. We're going home."

The tortoise glows bright white, forcing us to avert our eyes. Hermes and the tortoise are engulfed in a pillar of white fire. Hermes is lifted off the ground and spread-eagled in the center of the burning pillar.

The fire and light fades leaving Hermes standing on the ground, unharmed. He snaps his fingers and the tortoise is returned home. He whispers under his breath, "I'm sorry, Nancy."

I slowly stand before saying, "How's it feel?"

"Wrong, but I'll get used to it."

"If it means anything, I am sorry about Nancy."

"It doesn't. I'll never forgive you, but I will help. Dionysus is in London. Last I heard, he's somewhat of a gentleman. A man named Benjamin Yard. Apparently, quite friendly with Prince Charles. It shouldn't be too hard to find him. Good luck."

"Thank you."

Hermes nods in acknowledgement. "I'm going to gather my forces and meet up with Apollo. I hope to never see you again, but I'm never that lucky."

The glass of the window explodes as Hermes disappears.

Otus smiles, shaking his head. "He knows how to make an exit, if nothing else."

"What now?" Charlie says, lost.

"We go to London, I guess."

"How?"

"I take us."

Charlie looks at Otus, nervously, before saying, "Are you sure that's a good idea?"

"No, but what choice do we have?"

"I just don't trust these visions you're having. I don't trust Erebus. I don't think he can be trusted."

"I didn't see any visions this time and I think Erebus is too far gone to be a threat."

"Gone?"

"He's insane, at least, as far as I can tell. I think a lot of what I see are his nightmares. When I see him, he's a huddled mess. I don't think we need to worry about him."

"Why are you even connected to him?"

"I don't know."

Otus sighs, a look of understanding as he says, "It's because of Athena."

"What?"

"Before Kronos revealed himself, Erebus got a little out of control."

"How?"

"This was about 50 years before Timorian was born. Erebus came to Olympus, for the first time ever, screaming about a coming darkness. He said, 'Utopia is coming to destroy us.' He wanted the gods to allow him to show them a vision of the coming calamity. Only Athena agreed and Erebus brought her into himself to see what he saw. She refused to speak to anyone about what she saw except to say, 'everything will happen the way it should.' I always assumed the calamity Erebus spoke of was Kronos, but Athena would never confirm it. She said that she had to leave a piece of herself, her blood, inside of Erebus to guide a hero to him when the time came. That must be you. Her blood in Erebus must be connecting to her divinity inside of you and connecting you with Erebus."

I rub my temples to push back a headache; Charlie shakes her head in confusion, saying, "That doesn't make any sense. I know magic and there's no blood magic that could connect them like that."

"With all due respect, you're only a first-life witch. There's a lot you don't know."

Charlie nods a little in agreement before I say, "She's right, that doesn't feel right."

"It's what happened. Athena wouldn't lie to me."

A loud pounding on the door interrupts our conversation, a woman's voice echoing through, "Excuse me, is everything OK? We heard glass breaking."

"Shit. We've got to get out of here."

"Mr. Schou, are you in there?"

I reach out for Charlie and Otus's hands; they hesitantly stare at me. "Come on. We need to leave. The Titans will be here soon tracking the power surge. We're putting these people in danger."

"I'm opening the door, sir."

Charlie nods, trusting me. "OK. I trust you."

Charlie and Otus grab my hands. The lights flicker as we disappear in a dark flash.

Part 4:

DIONYSUS

CHAPTER 31: ANCIENT NEEDS

<u>Otus</u>

Soaring high above a beauteous English countryside, I let the breeze roll over my wings, ruffling my feathers. Gliding down toward a medieval castle tower, I gently land on a window ledge, transforming back into a man.

Posing sexily, I stare across the room at a scantily clad princess waiting for me with her leg up on a stool. I smile at Princess Isabella, winking as sexily as I can. "Hey, baby. I'm here to rescue you."

"My hero. Thou hast thwarted the diabolical scheming of my fiendish fiancé, the ogre prince."

Sliding of the window ledge, I strut to Isabella. "It's nothing."

"Oh, but it is. A feat worthy of the noblest of knights."

I puff out my chest, staring off into the distance. "You're right. I am quite magnificent."

"You are indeed. I must find some way to repay your heroics."

Looking up and down Isabella's body, I reach up to stroke her cheek. "The gift to look upon your beauty is reward enough."

"You are far too kind, dear knight. But I cannot allow it to be so. My conscience demands it."

"What do you have in mind?"

She smiles and says, "The best gift a maiden can bestow."

"Groovy."

"Indeed."

"Very well, then. Proceed."

Isabella steps back, slipping the straps of her dress over her shoulders, letting it fall to the ground, leaving her naked. She smiles before standing on tiptoe to kiss me. I wrap my arms around her and pull her tight. Our passion rivaling that of the fiercest of lovers.

Isabella pulls back and kneels down to pleasure mw. My jaw drops as I scream.

A loud knocking echoes through the tower door.

***

My passion has built too far to stop. The knocking continues as someone bangs on the hotel room door. I try to ignore it, my eyes closed, lost in my fantasy.

Arien's voice echoes through the door, laced with concern. "Otus, we heard a scream. Let us in. The door's locked."

My passion climaxes, spraying my ready tissue. I scramble to pull up my pants and clean up. I smile at Isabella across the Skype call, pausing to appreciate her; she's dressed as a princess and sucking on a dildo.

She looks up at me and says, "Otus, what is it?"

"Nothing. Just give me a second."

The door unlocks as Charlie finishes her spell. Arien and Charlie hurry in and freeze when they see what I've been doing.

Arien turns away, horrified. "Oh, come on, man. Seriously?"

Charlie lips curls, trying to maintain her decorum. "Were you jerking off on my bed?"

"What? No, of course not."

Isabella's voice echoes from my laptop, surprising Arien and Charlie. "Who are you guys? It'll cost more for extra people."

Arien raises an eyebrow before saying, "She's live. What're you thinking, Otus?"

"Give me a break. I'm 2 thousand years old, but I still have needs."

Charlie gives me a disappointed look before picking up the laptop and carrying it away so Arien can start lecturing me. "You know live streams like that can easily be traced. What if the Titans find us because of your porn addiction?"

"It's not an addiction."

"Yes, it is. A little porn is healthy, but you take to a level that I didn't know was possible."

"Well, you know why."

Arien looks down and sighs. "Yes, and I am sorry about your family. I am. But you need to switch to magazines from now on. OK?"

I can no longer meet Arien's gaze, my heart filling with shame. "OK."

"And stop screaming too. That's weird." I nod slightly. "Good. Now, wash your hands. I've got pizza." Arien goes into the hallway to grab the pizza from where he'd left it while I wash my hands.

Charlie sits down at the table and continues talking to Isabella.

"That's a pretty good deal. Do you do women too?"

"Of course, they're a huge part of my audience."

"Well, then maybe we can work something out."

"There's still some time left on Otus's clock."

"Really? Then let's . . ." Arien shuts the laptop and puts the pizza on top of it. "Hey!"

"The Titans can track that."

"Wouldn't they already have? What's five more minutes?"

"We have work to do."

"Fine."

I sit down next to the others, reaching out to get a slice of pizza.

Arien nods and moves on. "Good. Now, while Otus was in fairyland, I found Dionysus. Benjamin Yard is going to be at the Queen's Edinburgh estate, Holyrood palace, for an event in two days. It's a week-long event that happens every June where the Queen meets with all the Scottish lords, and Benjamin Yard happens to be a minor one."

I smile, remembering my days in 16th century England. "I was somewhat of a British gentleman back in the day. I can help us blend in, but those parties are extremely exclusive. How do we get in?"

"I can get into the RPG's system and add your names to the guest list and forge invitations. I'll stay back as tech support to monitor on the security system and make sure you both get in to find Benjamin."

Charlie tenses, nervously. "You really think I should go in?"

"Yeah. Why not?"

"It's just, I don't really know how to be a proper lady."

I smiles, saying, "I can teach you. You'll be fine."

Arien nods and turns to Charlie. "You OK with that."

"Yeah, I guess. It'll be fine."

"You sure?"

"Definitely. Always wanted to meet royalty." Charlie smiles unconvincingly before shaking her head and changing the subject. "Anyway, am I gonna be the one to mention the elephant in the room?"

Smiling at the compliment, I say, "Oh, why thank you." I adjust my seat, nodding at my pants.

Charlie grimaces, "Oh, no. Gross. No, can Arien actually teleport us all to Scotland?" She turns to Arien. "I'm sorry, but we barely made it to the Nevada border last time."

"It's not about distance. It's about focus and serenity. Last time I didn't have enough time to focus, but I can do it now."

"If this works, it'll give us an edge in staying ahead of the Titans."

CHAPTER 32: DAYDREAMS

Atlas

The grey dust of asteroids long since destroyed gently depresses into footprints beneath my feet, never to change again. I trek across the rim of a lunar crater, the earth framed above my shoulders, reminding me of my age-old punishment.

I freeze, the sound of ocean waves crashing against a shoreline filling my head. Looking into the crater, I see wispy waves flowing across its surface. A dolphin crests above the intangible waves and chirps before diving back into the water.

Reaching down, I grasp the dolphin pendant hanging from my neck. I turn away from the ghostly lake to see Calypso standing before me. A tear slips out of the corner of my eye.

"Calypso?"

"Dad."

"I'm sorry."

Calypso smiles softly, fading away. I am again alone in the barren expanse of the moon.

Arien

In a dark flash, we appear atop a grassy hillside. "Welcome to Scotland."

Charlie shivers violently, saying. "Where are we?"

"Pentland Hills Park outside Edinburgh. I wanted to stay away from populated areas so we wouldn't be seen."

"Well, its fucking cold. Which way do we go?"

"The town of Roslin is about a mile east of here."

"Alright. Let's go."

After a long, arduous hike, we reach the Original Rosslyn Hotel. We enter and approach the front desk, where the concierge smiles and says, "Good evening. Welcome to the Original Rosslyn Hotel. How may I help you?"

Otus, with an impeccable English accent, says, "Forsooth, fair maiden. We have journeyed here from London town in search of lodging 'twere for the Queens visitare."

The concierge smiles, utterly confused before saying, "Pardon?"

Charlie shakes her head, stepping forward. "We'd like a room."

"Of course, ma'am."

The concierge types on her computer as I lean over to whisper in Otus's ear. "Been a while since you were in England?"

"Oh, shut up."

The concierge glances between us, focusing on Charlie and me. "Any couples in need of shared beds?"

Charlie blushes, saying. "What? No. No couples. All single here." I give her a curious look, confused by her reaction. Once Charlie has finished checking in, we take our keys, thank the concierge, and head up to the rooms.

I unpack my gear, saying, "Alright. I'm gonna try and find a place to print out the invitations before people start closing for the night. Otus, you still on recon?"

"Yeah, if there's a Titan around, I'll know."

"Good. And Charlie, you good with watching those videos Otus recommended?"

Charlie smiles, unconvincingly. "Oh, yeah. I'll be a proper lady in no time."

"OK. I'll see you guys later." Otus goes to the window, transforming into an owl and flying off. Nodding to reassure her, I walk out, leaving Charlie alone.

Charlie

My hand twitches, only refraining from reaching down my pants by sheer willpower. Whenever I'm this nervous, some alone time with a vibrator is the only thing that can calm me. The memory of Isabella's nude form, not helping my self-control.

Sighing, I give in, grabbing Otus's laptop and signing in. To get Arien off my back, I log into a VPN before opening the video call.

After a minute, Isabella answers, saying, "Oh, hello again. I expected Otus."

"Yeah, well, he's busy now. It's just me."

"Can't say I'm disappointed."

"Really?"

"Of course."

"Thanks. Well, I bought an hour with Otus's money, so let's not let it go to waste."

Isabella giggles a little. "Alright. Do you want me to follow the same script Otus typically has me do?"

"Sure, we can try it."

I reach down the front of my pants, but Isabella interrupts, saying, "Hold on. This is still two-way. I'll need to see something too."

"Alright." Smiling, I take off my shirt and bra.

I close my eyes, entering into the fantasy.

***

In a puff of green smoke, I appear on the ledge of a medieval tower, Isabella waiting for me, her legs spread.

"Hey, baby. I'm here to rescue you."

"My hero. You have thwarted the diabolical scheming of my fiendish fiancé, the ogre prince."

I slide off the ledge, strutting to Isabella. "It's nothing."

"Oh, but it is. A feat worthy of the noblest of knights."

Puffing out my bare chest and staring off into the distance, I say, "You're right. I'm awesome."

"You are indeed. I must find some way to repay your heroics."

"Anything in mind?"

Isabella smiles up at me. "The best gift a maiden can bestow."

I reach out to stroke her cheek, pulling her in for a kiss. "I accept."

Isabella steps back and slips the straps of her dress over her shoulders, letting it fall to the ground, leaving her naked. She smiles before kissing me again.

Pulling back, she kneels in front of me, her hands lifting my dress.

I moan softly, Isabella's tongue sliding in.

CHAPTER 33: MY FAIR LADY

<u>Atlas</u>

Limping to a rocky ledge, I wince, sitting down, the fresh scars and bruises covering my body aching. I spit out blood and watch it float out in a long arch to the ground.

The dust on the surface of the moon shakes, swirling up and forming into Selene. I sigh, looking up at her. "Hey."

"Hey." She sits down next to me, mopping up the ichor running down my cheek. "He's really upset with you this time?"

"For good reason too. I've been subpar recently."

"Even so, he shouldn't treat you like this. You're his most loyal follower."

"He's on edge. She's been telling him that this boy can stop Utopia, and that has him scared."

"What makes this boy so special?"

"I don't know. I like him, though. He's got heart."

"He reminds you of her, doesn't he?" Stiffening, I recoil from her touch. "I'm sorry. I know you don't like talking about her."

"It's alright. It's hard fighting for someone without an end in sight. Let alone a happy one."

"You'll see her again when Utopia descends."

"Will I? All we get are empty promises that haven't been fulfilled in 2 thousand years."

Selene reaches up and places a finger over my mouth. "Shush. You mustn't speak of such things. Not where she can hear. You never know when she's listening."

I pull back and bow my head. "It's just hard having faith after all this time."

She smiles a little, wrapping her arms around me and pressing our heads together. "Do you remember when you found me?"

"Of course."

"Did I ever tell you why I was in Idaho?"

"No."

"It was the only place that reminded me of home. Craters of the Moon, they call it now. When the gods took my home and cast me to Earth, I tried to act grateful and fit into their story with the humans, but that wasn't meant to be my life. I was meant to rule and roam these endless craters. With this beautiful view before me every day." We both look up to see the Earth suspended on the edge of the horizon. "I never thought I'd have it back. Not with Artemis as its new queen. I even asked to just live here since Artemis was always in the woods with all her lady friends anyway. But they refused. They were afraid that I'd plot against them. No Titans could really be trusted in their eyes. I went to a very dark place after that. I lost all hope and will to just live. And do you know what got me out of that mindset?"

"No."

"It was you, you idiot." Selene playfully nudges my shoulder. "Something you said really hit me."

"What did I say?"

"You said, 'Be who you were meant to be.' It was pretty corny, but it meant something to me. I'm a fucking Titan. I shouldn't bow down and grovel before anyone. I'm strong and powerful and the moon is my domain. You gave me hope and the strength to leave that cave and be myself again. So, when you say, 'it's hard having faith after all this time,' remember you gave me my faith back. Not faith in a cause, or Kronos, but faith in myself. I think that's all you need. What do you believe? What do you want? Because, someday, this war will be over, and you'll only have yourself to guide you. Where does your heart lie?"

I turn to stare into Selene's eyes. "Right here." Leaning in, I kiss her.

"What I say? Corny."

We both smile before kissing again.

Arien

The waiter approaches our table, menus in hand. He passes them out to the three of us before saying, "Good afternoon, everybody. What are we starting with to drink?"

I turn to the others, "A round of Guinness?"

Otus and Charlie nod as the waiter writes it down. "That'll be right out."

"Thanks."

Otus arranges some silverware around Charlie's plate before saying, "Alright, there'll be dinner at the event and you're going to have to learn how to eat properly. Did you watch those videos I gave you?"

Charlie smiles and nods, unconvincingly. "Oh, yeah. Definitely watched them."

I smile and lean back, watching.

"Alright, then which dish will come first?"

"Salad."

"Very good. And which utensil will you use first?"

"The salad fork."

"OK. Point to it."

Charlie looks at the silverware in front of her. "That one."

"No, it's the other one."

"Why? Salad is so much easier to eat with a big fork."

"But it's not proper."

"Who decided what's proper? Some self-centered douche bag was like, 'let's fuck with everyone and make their lives miserable.' I feel like that's how half of all etiquette came about."

"Despite that, it's what needs adhered to."

"Why?"

"Because customs and manners dictate it."

"Who dictates them?"

"It doesn't matter."

I laugh, saying, "She's trolling you, man. Calm down." Otus stares between us, confused as we start laughing softly. "She'll be fine."

"I don't know."

"She's got the dress, she watched your videos, and you'll be there all night to coach her."

Charlie tries to give Otus a reassuring smile. "I won't be a proper lady and I'll probably make a fool of myself in front of the Queen, but that'll happen either way. Besides, none of this matters if Arien can't get us in."

I open my bag and pull out two invites. "I got into their system and added your names. Amy Gillan and Arthur Williams, the newly elected officials to the Aberdeen city council, guests of the honorable Lord Provost." I hand Charlie and Otus their invites.

"This is really good. Will it fool the guards?"

"There's a barcode on the back that connects them to your name on the guest list. Their guest list wasn't on the intranet server so multiple agencies could add to it, making it easy for me to slip in a few extra names. This event is so massive that it'll be impossible for security to be perfect. You'll get in, then it'll be up to you to find Benjamin."

The waiter brings over our drinks; Charlie takes hers and raises it for a toast. "I'll drink to that. God save the Queen."

"God save the Queen."

We clink our glasses together before drinking.

CHAPTER 34: BEING POSH

Arien

Gentle rain patters against the hotel window, foretelling a greater storm coming. I stare out the window at the rain, embracing its calming nature, forgetting all my problems for a moment. Sighing, I put in my Bluetooth earpiece before saying, "Charlie, you there?"

Charlie's voice echoes through the earpiece, saying, "Yeah, I'm here. We're just pulling up to the gate."

Turning, I sit in front of my open laptop. "Alright, I see you on the security camera."

Charlie

Taking a deep breath, I brush the dust off my beautiful blue dress.

Otus swats at my hand, saying, "Stop fussing. A lady is confident and still."

"You try wearing all this shit. These pantyhose itch."

Otus adjusts slightly in his seat, entirely at home in his elegant tuxedo. "I have, and I quite enjoyed it."

I smile broadly at Otus. "Otus, you?"

"Shakespeare had strange tastes and those corsets were far worse than anything you're wearing."

Laughing softly, I'm put at ease. "Point taken."

Our limo driver pulls up to the gate and rolls down his window to talk to a guard, who says, "Invitations, please." The driver hands the guard our invites, who quickly scans them and looks into the back of the limo at us.

Another guard checks under the limo for explosives with a wheeled mirror and a sniffer dog. Once the second guard finishes his round, he waves at the first guard. We hold our breath as the guard hands back the invites. "You're clear. There's no public parking in front of the palace, so you'll need to pull around back to the servants' entrance."

"Thank you."

"Have a pleasant evening." The guard tips his hat as the driver pulls forward. Otus and I let out our pent-up breath.

Otus reaches up to press his Bluetooth earpiece. "We're in."

I shake my head, saying, "You don't need to touch it, it's always on."

"Oh, right." He drops his hand, embarrassed.

Arien's voice comes over the earpieces, saying, "Good. Keep me posted."

"Will do."

The limo pulls up to the entrance before we get out. I feel Otus's eyes drilling into my back, judging my unladylike walk toward the door. Ignoring him, I walk into the palace.

Otus and I stand amidst the bustling crowd of Scottish nobles as we collect ourselves. Otus says, "We're in."

Arien replies, "OK, I'm checking through the security footage for Benjamin. Looks like everyone is congregating in the throne room and the gardens while the staff prepares the gallery for dinner. You two split up and look too."

"OK. I'll take the garden. Charlie, you got the throne room?"

I nod, saying, "Sure. Is the Queen there?"

After a moment, Arien says, "No, looks like Her Majesty is entertaining a more exclusive party in the privy room."

"Oh, good."

"Good luck." Otus squeezes my elbow, heading toward the garden, leaving me to find my way to the throne room.

With a little help from Arien, I find the throne room and start flitting from group to group, looking for Benjamin and occasionally engaging in conversation.

A group of women is gathered around a beautiful lady, hanging on her every word. She says, "That's when Johnny proceeded to try and kiss me." The group of women around her gasps. "I know. The impropriety. Of course, I denied his advances. Americans are so incorrigible."

Joining in with my terrible accent, I say, "I find their prevalence for vulgarity and sexuality most despicable."

The group of women turn to look me up and down with mild disgust. The lady says, "And who might you be, miss?"

"My apologies. I am Miss Amy Gillan of the Aberdeen City Council."

Another woman replies, saying, "An elected official? I was unaware any got invitations, especially those as low as the city council."

"You'll find that we are as essential to the governance of Scotland as any other."

"But you are not Scottish."

"Pardon?"

"Your accent is not Scottish. It's unfamiliar to me but is definitely English."

"My parents are from Croydon, but moved to Aberdeen when I was an infant. I assure you, I am as Scottish at heart as any other."

"Perhaps, but that remains to be seen. I'm sure you deeply care for all the sheep and goats within your care."

A woman with kind eyes interrupts, coming to my defense. "Ladies, I implore you to remain dignified and not resort to the baseless superiority of our ancestors that divided this country, common from noble. We are all the same, as we must all remember."

The other women look down in mild shame at these words. "Of course, my lady."

"Good. Now, Amy. Are you enjoying yourself?"

I smile in thanks, saying, "In truth, this lifestyle is unfamiliar to me and I find myself disheartened."

"We cannot have that. We must find a way to put you at ease. What is something that you care deeply about?"

"My work."

"Indeed? Well, how may we help you with your work?"

"My lady, there is but one thing that I stand in need of. I have been tasked to acquaint myself with a Benjamin Yard and I am unable to find him."

One of the snobby women says, "His lordship is far too busy to meet with one such as you."

The kind woman gives the other women a reproachful look before turning back to me. "Though her manners are somewhat lacking, Ann is right. Lord Yard will be entertaining the Queen for most of the night. I'm afraid we cannot help you with this."

"My thanks for your kind words and your time, but I must contact my leadership and inform them of this."

"Very well. It was a pleasure to meet you, Amy."

"The pleasure was mine, my lady." I curtsy slightly, retiring to the drawing-room for privacy. Taking a glass of champagne from a passing waiter, I drink it greedily, saying, "Did you get that, Arien?"

"Yeah, I got it. I'll let Otus know."

Sighing, I continue drinking.

A beautiful lady looks up at me from her seat on the settee before saying, "It's exhausting, isn't it?"

I turn to the lady, confused. "Pardon?"

"Hanging out with these people. They mean well, but they'll never understand what it's like to be ordinary."

"And I suppose you do?"

"More than some, less than others."

"That's a very diplomatic answer."

"This is a very diplomatic party."

Smiling, I sit next to the lady, shaking her hand. "Hi, I'm Charlie."

"Deni. Pleasure to meet you."

Arien's voice buzzes over my earpiece, worried. "Charlie, what are you doing? You can't use your real name."

I take out my earpiece, putting it in my purse as Deni waves down a waiter. "We'd like a bottle of the Australian Pentfolds Grange. Any year pre-1980 will do."

"I'm sorry, ma'am. That vintage is reserved for the privy room."

"Of course. Then we'll have the finest Pinot Noir you have."

"Very good, ma'am."

As the waiter leaves, I give Deni an impressed look. "You know a lot about wine."

"It's somewhat of a passion of mine."

We gaze into each other's eyes a moment longer than necessary before I blush and turn away.

Otus

Walking around a hedge, I pause, seeing Benjamin Yard talking with a group of people. I whisper through my earpiece, saying, "Arien, I found Benjamin."

"Good job. I'm having issues with Charlie, but try to get him alone to talk. I'll send her to help as soon as I can."

"Copy that."

I start walking toward Benjamin but am accosted by a guard, preventing me from entering the inner garden. "Can I help you, sir?"

In my English accent, I say, "No, I'm just here to see Lord Yard."

"This part of the garden is reserved for royalty and friends only."

"I'm sure he would make an exception for me."

"I'm afraid I cannot let you pass."

"Very well. Thank you for your time." Retreating behind a bush, I transform into an owl and fly into the restricted part of the garden. I quickly return to my human form before adjusting my bow tie and approaching Benjamin. "Excuse me, your lordship."

Benjamin turns to me. "Yes?"

"My name is Otus Sowa. I'm here in regard to the Greek restoration."

Benjamin's expression darkens slightly. "I'm afraid I don't have time to speak with the press."

"Oh, I'm not with the press. I'm with the ambassador for the pantheon."

"You'll have to make an appointment with my people. I'm due in the privy room." Benjamin and the rest of his group head to the palace while the guard escorts me back to the public gardens.

Waiting till I'm alone, I say to Arien, "That didn't go well."

"Hermes wasn't easy to get to either. You'll just have to try again."

I shake my head, heading back toward the palace.

Charlie

Our infectious laughter echoes through the drawing-room, the wine starting to affect us. I struggle to speak through my laughter, saying, "In front of everyone?"

Deni smiles and says, "Yeah, that was the best thing to ever happen in parliament."

Our laughter slowly subsides as we stare longingly at each other. I look away and rub my head, swirling my wine glass. "This wine's really done a number on me."

"The ultimate party starter."

"I never would have called wine that before, but maybe you're right."

We sit in awkward silence for a moment, only sipping our drinks before she says, "So, any husband or boyfriend in your life?"

I chuckle to myself. "Nah, not really my thing."

"Girlfriend then?"

I look at Deni in surprise, hearing the hope in the question. Smiling, I start to understand. "Not currently, but you never know when that can change."

"Fate is a fickle master. Makes anything possible." We lean into each other, our voices growing softer.

"Like meeting a beautiful woman at an awful party."

"For example."

"It'd be a shame to pass up such an opportunity."

"Such a shame."

We give in, kissing fiercely.

Otus

Peering around a corner, I see a guard posted outside the door to the privy room. Sighing, I retreat behind the wall. "Arien, do you copy?"

"Yeah, what's up?"

"Benjamin just went into the privy room. I could really use Charlie's help with that love bracelet thing she has."

"I still can't get a hold of her."

"Well, where is she?"

Charlie

Deni pushes me firmly against the back wall of the closet, leaning in to kiss me. We kiss passionately for several seconds before she pulls back and takes a strap-on from her purse. My eyes widen slightly. "Should I be worried that you just carry one of those around?"

"Let's just say I had a premonition that I needed to buy one for tonight."

"It's like fate."

"Exactly."

Smiling, I hike up my dress. She lifts me up and drives forward, thrusting into me, her head planted between my breasts. I bounce up and down, my moans increasing. Deni's thrusts grow faster as she lifts her head to kiss me.

We both moan loudly into each other's open mouths.

CHAPTER 35: CHANGING PARTS

Charlie

Deni and I step out of the closet once the coast is clear, kissing once more. I smile and say, "It was great to meet you, Deni."

"And you, mystery girl."

"Mystery?"

"You dropped your accent."

I awkwardly run my fingers through my hair. "Yeah, well . . ."

"Shush. I like a mystery."

Smiling nervously, I stammer, utterly infatuated. "OK, yeah. Well, you got my number?"

"I do. I'll call."

"OK, do that."

"Denise, there you are." I turn to see Benjamin walking down the hallway toward us. "I've been looking everywhere for you."

Deni winks at me and says, "I've been busy."

Benjamin curls his lip at me before turning back to Deni. "Yes, I can see. Sleeping around again?"

Deni straightens in defiance. "Charlie, this rude man is my brother Benjamin."

Smiling, I extend my hand. "Benjamin? Lord Benjamin Yard?"

Deni smiles, saying, "Oh, don't call him that. His head's big enough as it is."

Benjamin ignores my outstretched hand and says, "Perhaps, but we are expected elsewhere, so we must bid adieu, Miss Charlie." Benjamin herds Deni away before I can say anything else.

I frown, taking out my earpiece and putting it back in my ear. "Hello, Arien?"

"Charlie, where are you? Otus needs your help."

"Calm down. I'm in the hallway outside the drawing-room."

"Otus'll be right there."

After a moment, Otus walks up to me and pushes me back into the closet. "Ow." He rips out both of our earpieces, glaring at me. I say, "What's your problem?"

"My problem, what the fuck? You could have jeopardized the mission. What the hell is wrong with you?"

"Nothing."

"Don't lie to me. You're a witch. In 2 thousand years, I've never met a good witch. I was opposed to letting you come along from the beginning, but we needed you, so I bit the bullet. Turns out I was right all along. Turns out you're more interested in fucking any pretty ass you see than saving the goddamn world."

"That's not true."

"Then what is the truth?"

"Susan broke up with me. OK?" Otus immediately clams up in embarrassment. "That's why I wanted to come with you guys. That's why I'm sleeping around." Tears start to well in my eyes. "I caught her cheating. It wasn't bad enough that I thought my best friend was dead, but then the woman I loved betrayed me. Then I have some rebound sex and that woman gets murdered because of my not dead best friend. I'm not in a good place right now. I just needed . . . need to feel something. Anything. I can't keep living like this."

"I'm sorry."

Sniffling, I wipe the tears from my eyes. "Anyway, while you were messing around, I found a way to get close to Benjamin. That woman, Deni, is Benjamin's sister and I've got her phone number."

"Really?"

"Yeah. Let Arien know while I text her."

I step away to text Deni as Otus puts his earpiece back in. "Arien, we have a way in."

***

Otus and I wait outside the privy room as Deni walks out to talk to the guard. "It's alright. They're with me."

"Yes, Lady Yard."

Deni motions for us to follow her. I say, "Thank you, Lady Yard."

"Oh, shut up."

Inside the privy room, we follow Deni through the bustling crowd toward Benjamin. "Is Her Majesty here?"

"No, she just went to the garden. The Lord Provost brought his hawk to try and impress her."

"His hawk?"

"I know, but some of these lords do whatever they can to stand out." We reach Benjamin, so Deni says, "Benjamin, you remember Charlie?"

"Ah, yes."

I curtsey, saying, "A pleasure again, my lord."

Deni motions to Otus and says, "And this is her friend Otus. He'd like to talk to you."

Benjamin looks Otus up and down, mild contempt barely hidden in his gaze. "We've met, and I'll tell him what I did before. I have no wish to talk business now, so if you'd like to talk, please make an appointment."

Otus says, "But, sir, this is about restoring the Greek gods."

Benjamin raises an eyebrow, utterly confused. "What?"

"We need your help to restore all the gods for one last conflict with Timorian."

"I haven't the faintest idea what you are talking about. If this is a joke, it must desist. If you'll excuse me."

Benjamin tries to walk away, but Otus follows. "But you're Dionysus."

I move to follow, but Deni grabs my arm. Turning, I give her a curious look. She smiles and says, "Round 2." She nods to the door; I look back-and-forth between Otus and Deni, conflicted.

Deciding, I let Deni lead me back to the closet, where I take out my earpiece again and say, "A little early for round 2, but I think I can manage."

Moving to kiss Deni, I pause, her finger raised to stop me. "We need to talk." I raise an eyebrow as Deni walks around me, stroking her chin nervously. "You're looking for Dionysus?"

I stare at Deni, dumbfounded. "Ah, yeah. Do you know him?"

"Better than anyone and it's not Benjamin."

"Then who is he?"

Deni smiles nervously. "She."

Taking a moment, my eyes widen in understanding. "What? No, Dionysus is a dude."

"Was. I switched before tearing out my divinity to throw them off my scent."

I start to pace back-and-forth as the questions swim through my head. "But how?"

"I was the god of all gays and transgenders. I had to pretend to be a girl for the first 15 years of my life. You kinda get flexible after that."

"But Hermes said Dionysus was Benjamin."

"Ah, yes. I told the other gods I was a man because not all of them are as open to the idea as others. Plus, that way they can't give the Titans anything if they're captured."

"What about Benjamin? How are you his sister?"

"I'm not. I'm his great grandmother, but I pretended to be his long-lost half-sister to explain the not aging." I make confused noises, starting to come to terms with this. "What about you?"

I look up in surprise. "What?"

"Who are you?"

"I'm a first-life witch. My group and I are goding up all the gods and stuff." I return to my contemplation.

"I see. But why?"

"Arien can tell you."

"Arien?"

Looking up, anger floods through me at the realization of what I've done, my Father's face flashing before my eyes. "You'll meet him soon, but first. Why didn't you tell me you were a man? I'm a lesbian. I don't like men and you let me go along with it anyway. Some might call that rape."

Deni steps back nervously. "I'm transgender, literally. I am physically a woman. I didn't lie or mislead you."

"Well, what if I get pregnant?"

"Again, I'm physically a woman. Don't have the parts."

My anger and confusion subsides, but not my annoyance. "Whatever, but it's still not cool."

"What was I gonna say? Oh, by the way, I'm an inter-dimensional ancient god that can change my gender whenever I want, but I was born a man. I didn't know you knew stuff like that was possible."

"I don't know, but you could have said something."

Deni sighs, saying, "You're right, I'm sorry." She looks down in shame; we stand in awkward silence for a moment before she says, trying to joke, "I do miss my cock sometimes, though."

I shake my head with little humor before looking up as I remember something. "Earlier, you said you had a premonition that you'd need that strap-on. So, did you know we were coming using your god powers?"

"No, I just always carry one around, hoping I'll get laid."

"That's gross."

"I clean it."

"Fine. . . I don't know how I feel about all this, but we have work to do."

"I don't know if I want to help."

Laughing sinisterly, I say, "Oh, buddy. You're helping after the shit you pulled on me. Let's go."

I lead the way out and to the privy room door where Otus is being escorted out by a guard. I rush to him and say, "Otus, what happened?"

"I don't think Benjamin is Dionysus."

"He's not."

"How do you know?"

Deni steps forward, a thin smile on her face. "Because I'm Dionysus."

Otus stares at Deni, perplexed. "Excuse me."

"I'll help you with Timorian. No parties last forever and I have a debt to repay." Deni gives me a sad, guilty look.

I look down, shaking my head before glancing at Otus. "Anyway, we should go."

As we leave, I can hear Otus whispering under his breath. "Oh, he's a girl. Yeah, let me explain. No one tells me shit. Wouldn't that be something worth knowing, but no. Let's go. Fuck explaining. It's not like its earth-shatteringly confusing, but what do I know. I'm just the 2 thousand-year-old Gandalf of this group. Not like I'm important at all."

"Shut up, Otus."

CHAPTER 36: MODERN DYSPHORIA

<u>**Arien**</u>

The door opens; I leap to my feet, confused and worried as Charlie, Otus, and a strange woman walk in. "What, the hell's, going on, guys? What was too weird to tell me while you were driving? And who's this?"

The strange woman smiles awkwardly and waves. "Hi, I'm Deni, or Dionysus."

I take a moment to process, floored by this revelation. "Of course, you are. My life used to be so normal. Now you can't even depend on genders."

Charlie's dark gaze lifts from the floor for a moment to say, "Hey!"

"Sorry, I didn't mean it like that."

Deni steps forward, almost protective of Charlie. "I get that it's weird."

"No, it's fine. I'm just surprised. So, did they tell you what's going on?"

Deni looks to Charlie for confirmation, but she refuses to look up, her gaze returned to drilling holes in the floor. "Yeah, Otus gave me the low-down in the limo."

"And you're willing to help?"

Deni again glances at Charlie. "Seems I must."

"Good. OK. Well, where's your divinity?"

"Mount Nysa in Ethiopia."

I nod, thinking of the logistics. "OK. I can swing it."

"It's where I was raised as a mortal. I can show you where."

Charlie finally re-engages, her anger cowing all of us. "She's not coming with us."

Turning to her in surprise, I wonder what could have caused this rage. "Charlie, we may need her help. I'm sure there's something guarding it."

Deni nods, her eyes hopeful, in search of redemption. "There is."

Charlie dismisses our pleading, saying, "I don't care. She's not coming. End of story."

Cautiously, I say, "Why?" She glares at the wall past me, ignoring my question. "I'm sorry, Charlie. But if you can't tell me why, I'll have to bring her. She knows what's there."

Her jaw clenching, Charlie walks to her bag and pulls out a red curse tablet with glowing letters. Deni and Otus scream, diving for cover, leaving me just standing in confusion. Charlie's eyes flash as she menacingly says, "This is not a debate. She's not coming."

Without knowing my reason for fear, I step forward and say, "What is that? A curse tablet?"

Deni's voice quivers in a most ungodly way as she says, "Not just a curse tablet. It's the katares tablet that Hecate herself used to transform the witch Gale into a polecat."

"That doesn't sound so bad."

"A polecat eternally raped by every beast it comes across with no chance to die."

Dread freezes the blood in my veins at the thought, the horror. Slowly stepping back, I say, "OK, that's bad. Charlie, put that away."

Tears start to fill Charlie's eyes. "She's not coming with us. Not after what she did."

"OK, we'll manage without her. We always do. You, me, and Otus. Always us against the world."

Charlie shakes her head in confusion, dropping the tablet. "I don't know what's wrong with me."

Otus gingerly grabs the tablet with a pillowcase. "Where did you find this, anyway?"

Sitting with a sigh, Charlie says, "It was my mentor's."

Deni looks down at Charlie with perplexed shame before turning to me. "I should go. Charlie's got my number, so call me when you have it."

Nodding in thanks, I respond, "OK. Thank you."

Deni nods, leaving. Kneeling, I try to comfort Charlie.

After a moment's hesitation, Otus turns to follow Deni.

Otus

Hurrying out of the hotel room, I chase down Deni. "Hey, wait up." She turns back, slowly, broken inside. I say, "What's she going on about? What happened?"

Her eyes downturned in shame, she says, "She's upset that I didn't tell her that I was born a man before having sex with her."

"Oh, OK." Scratching my neck uncomfortably, I continue, "I get why she's upset, but isn't she taking it too far? Being a little irrational?"

"Our reaction and interpretation of trauma is rarely rational. And maybe it shouldn't be. It's an emotional response. I think she's a lesbian, not because she felt it her entire life, but because of a traumatic experience. I think I may have opened up some old wounds, making her reevaluate her life and sexuality. She's going to need some time and I only remind her of her problems and make her cycle through them."

"What makes you think she's had trauma?"

Deni looks up at the door as if she can see Charlie. "You can see it in the eyes. And I understand homosexuality. It's not all black and white." Nodding my understanding; Deni shakes her head to clear it. "Good luck, Otus."

We shake hands. "Thanks. You too." I stare after her as she turns and walks away.

CHAPTER 37: HIDDEN SON

In a long-dead language, a woman not whom she seemed, said, "No, Dye. You must keep your stitches closer together." Blood dripped from Princess Dye's young fingers, splashing to the hard stone ground. "Ow." Without looking up, Dye's nanny, Zoe, wiped up the blood and returned to her tutelage of sewing for the young princess.

The ornate ancient palace glistened with silver and gold in the sun's twilight rays. The princess pouted, throwing away her needle and thread to nurse her still bleeding finger. "This is too hard."

Sighing, Zoe set aside her own work to respond, "I understand, but you must be persistent if you ever want to make a good wife someday."

"But you're not a wife. Why can't I be like you and never marry and never learn this stuff?"

Sighing once more, Zoe said, "You don't want to end up like me, your ladyship. I was deemed too ugly to win a husband, so I was sold as a slave to ensure my parents didn't lose the profit owed to them by my marriage."

Dye looked down, chastened, and ashamed of the horrors her Father's kingdom allowed. "I'm sorry."

"Don't be. When your parents freed me, they gave me a good life and a reason to keep living."

Looking up hopefully, Dye said, "They did?"

"Why, of course. Nurturing you has been the greatest joy of my life."

Smiling uncomfortably, Dye looked away. "I can be rather horrible sometimes, though."

"True, but the moments you aren't would be worth nothing if you were never bad. You need true sadness in this life to experience true joy. Or else your joy will be empty and meaningless. Remember that. No matter how dark your life can get, it only means the sun will shine even brighter when you get out of the dark."

Before Dye could respond, Queen Ino paraded into their chambers, flanked by her personal guard. Dye and Zoe stood and curtsied to the Queen, Dye saying, "Mother, we did not expect you home until tomorrow."

Ino's dead eyes tightened, maliciously, "No?" She started laughing hysterically as insanity has overwhelmed her.

"Mother?"

King Athamas entered behind Ino, covered in blood. Zoe and Dye gasped at the King's gruesome visage.

"Father!"

"I am no Father now." Athamas cackled, wiping the blood from his shirt and smearing it over his lips. "My seed bore wholesome fruit."

Ino laughed at Athamas's joke, leaning in to kiss him. "Indeed, our son is so sweet."

Dye looked on in horror, gagging at the sight of her parents. Ino and Athamas both turned to Dye, lust in their eyes. Ino said, "Should we taste the girl as well?"

"Aye, I think we should. But first."

Athamas drew his sword, cutting down both of Ino's guards. Ino laughed uncontrollably as Zoe dragged the horrified Dye toward the door.

Once safely in the hall, Zoe waved her arms over the door; it glowed with a godly light as it turned to solid stone. Dye looked on, dumbfounded, at Zoe's sudden power. "Who are you, Zoe?"

Zoe grabbed Dye's hand, leading her away from the door. "My name's not Zoe, it's Pandia. Our Father asked me to protect you."

"Our Father?"

"Yes, our Father, Zeus. He asked me to protect you."

"My Father is King Athamas. The man trying to eat me."

"No, Zeus asked Athamas and Ino to raise you because his wife, Hera, would love to kill you. She doesn't really like his bastards, and there's a lot. She's cursed the king and queen to try and kill you, so she's not directly responsible. Olympian laws allow you to get away with arranging someone's death, but if you do it yourself, there will be consequences. Not a great system, if you ask me. The only reason she hasn't tried to kill me is because I'm a god and you're just a demi-god."

Dye faltered, awed. "You're a god?"

Zoe slowed enough to grab Dye again and continue dragging her to safety. "Yes, minor goddess of the moon. Keep up."

"Where are we going?"

"Father told me to send you to the nymphs of Nysa if you were ever in danger. They can protect you."

"Why didn't he send me there in the first place?"

"They don't allow men there."

"I'm a girl, though."

"Sorry, you're a boy. Zeus thought it would fool Hera if you were raised as a girl. Didn't really work."

Dye stopped again to Zoe's annoyance. "Hold on, I'm a boy? But I look like a girl . . . down there."

"Oh, that's an illusion I made." Zoe waved her hand over Dye. "There, you have your cock back." Dye started walking strangely as he had to adjust to the new limb. Zoe sighed, tugging on Dye's arm. "Keep up."

Taking all this information in very well, Dye said, "If they don't like men, why will the nymphs take me now?"

"They won't, but they're vegetarians, so we have a plan."

"What?"

"As soon as we get outside, I can make a portal to take you to Nysa."

They reached the palace doors, going through them. In the courtyard, Zoe and Dye raced out but stop as soldiers poured out of a garrison, surrounding them. Zoe turned to Dye and hands him a potion. "Drink this."

"What is it?"

"Just do it!"

Ino and Athamas exited the palace, standing atop a flight of stairs, looking down at Zoe and Dye, their clothes soaked in blood. Athamas cackled, saying, "You cannot flee from this place. There's no escape."

Zoe smiled as she saw that the moon has risen in the evening sky. "Not for me, but for the son of Zeus, maybe."

Dye collapsed, seizing as the potion took hold, transforming him into a ram. Ino and Athamas screamed; the ram struggled to its feet and bleated in confusion.

Ino, horrified, said, "What have you done to our daughter?"

"Saved him."

"Kill her!"

The soldiers rushed forward as Zoe raised her hand in the air. A pillar of light shot down from the moon and engulfed the ram. The light disappeared, leaving Zoe unconscious on the ground, surrounded by the confused soldiers.

CHAPTER 38: VEILED CONFUSION

<u>**Arien**</u>

My body tenses, waiting for Deni to finish her horrifying story. She says, "I get so confused when it comes to matters of gender and their apparent differences. That's why I didn't think about the consequences of my actions with Charlie. We were just two people having sex, but these days nothing is ever that simple." She turns away, her face constricting with the guilt she feels. "How is she doing, anyway?"

Smiling in pity, I sigh and say, "I don't know. I always know what Charlie's thinking, but this is something different that I don't understand. I don't think it has anything to do with you. It's a lot deeper than that. I caught her alone in the room staring at her reflection and repeating, 'never helpless again.' Over and over. You should have seen her eyes. We all have our demons, and it seems that Charlie's just woke up. I just don't know how to help her."

Deni reaches across the table to squeeze my hand, comforting me. "We'll figure it out together."

Staring down at our hands in surprise, I smile. "We can touch?"

"What?"

My thoughts clearing, moving past the shock of feeling a woman's touch, I say, "Ah, nothing. So, tell me about Nysa."

Deni shakes her head in confusion before focusing. "There's a village at the foot of the mountain. The way up can be very dangerous, so you'll need to find a guide from the village. There's a vineyard at the top, where the nymphs lived, with an oak pedestal in the center. My divinity is in a box on the pedestal."

I say, "And?" expecting a twist or challenge.

"And there's a dragon guarding the gate to the vineyard."

I sigh. "Of course, there is. How are we expected to fight a giant, flying, fire-breathing lizard? We have nothing to defend against that."

"It can't fly. Greek dragons are just giant snakes. This one's about 180 feet long."

"Not much better."

"Perhaps Charlie can make the same sleeping potion that Medea used on the dragon guarding the Golden Fleece."

"I can ask her, thanks."

I stand to leave, but Deni reaches out to stop me. "If I may ask, how are you planning on getting there? Can't imagine you guys flying commercial with all that gear."

"I can teleport us there."

Deni's eyes widen in shock. "You can what?"

"Teleport. I'm somehow connected to Erebus and can travel through his dimension to anywhere on Earth."

"That's not possible."

"That's how we got here from Vegas."

"How do you navigate it?"

"I can't really explain it, but I can sense things like magic and people in there when I let my emotions go. I got here because I could feel that people were thinking about Edinburgh. I found Hermes's divinity by sensing it when I got close. I'll just try to sense any locals thinking about Nysa to find yours."

After taking a moment to process, Deni says, "You said you can sense magic?"

"Strong magic. It creates an almost impenetrable barrier in there. I get as close as I can, then look around on this side."

"The village Elders have a stuffed magic bull. The last, I believe. It may be enough for you to latch onto."

"That might work. Thank you."

"Before you go, I should tell you, the locals aren't what you'd expect."

"How do you mean?"

Deni hesitates, ashamed. "I froze them. I prevented them from ever evolving. Generations later, their culture is still identical to what it was when I left. It ensured that they'd never decide to leave and stop protecting my divinity."

"That's horrible."

"I felt it was necessary, and I was a different person back then. We all were. People believed that the gods could ask anything of them, so we believed it too. We're slaves to humanity and their moral evolution, which can be fickle at best."

I crack a thin smile, my eyes daggers as I say, "Sounds like an excuse."

"It's what helps me sleep at night after remembering all the terrible things we did in the name of divine retribution."

Sighing, I let go of my resentment, remembering all the times the idea alone of the gods had saved me. "You guys weren't all bad. There's a reason I wanted you to be real when I had no hope. You gave me hope and something to live up to. That can't be a bad thing."

Deni smiles at me in thanks before I turn, leaving her alone.

***

Walking into the hotel room, I stop, feeling the tension in the air. Charlie and Otus are sitting in silence, uncomfortable in their seats. Otus leaps up when he sees me, latching onto a distraction. "You get what we need from . . . *you know who?*"

Charlie scoffs, her veiled annoyance clear to see. "Brilliant code there, Otus. I'm never going to break it. Just say her name. It won't make a difference."

Grimacing, I say, "Yeah, I've got what we need. There's a dragon. Deni thought you could make the same potion Medea used to get the Golden Fleece."

Nodding, Charlie says, "I can make it."

"There's a village at the foot of the mountain. We'll need to go there and find a guide to get up to the vineyard at the peak."

"No time to waste."

We pack only what we need for the journey, leaving the rest of our gear. Once ready, we reach out to hold hands.

The lights flicker as we disappear in a dark flash.

CHAPTER 39: RUNNING OF THE BULLS

<u>Arien</u>

We appear in the endless darkness, stumbling apart. Struggling to our feet, Otus says, "Arien, what's happening?"

Charlie turns to me, overcome with fear. "I thought you had this under control."

Thinking for a moment, I force past my emotions to find the cause of this. Suddenly, I realize it's the emotions themselves that are the cause. I turn back to Charlie, saying, "It's you."

"What."

"I'm sorry, but I'm worried about you."

"You're worried about me? Well, don't be. I'm fine."

"No, you're not."

"You want to do this now?"

Otus steps between us, trying to be the voice of reason. "I'm with Charlie. We need to get out of here."

"Alright, come here." I reach for the others' hands but stop as a loud ringing echoes through my head, shattering my focus. Covering my ears, I fall to my knees. Through the tears of pain streaming down my face, I say, "No, not now." Leaning over, I sprawl on the cold obsidian ground, convulsing violently.

Iapetus's voice screams out of the darkness, saying, "Seed planted in the dark."

The fog billows up and forms into the Temple of God's Time.

Struggling against the noise in my head, I get to my feet and stumble to the others, who are staring around at the ghostly church around them, petrified. I force myself to say, "We have to get out of here."

Suddenly, the pews are full of hooded figures, all chanting and staring at the altar at the front of the room. A small boy is tied spread-eagle on the top of the altar with several hooded figures standing around him. I turn to stare at the boy, lost in a trance. "Don't hurt the boy."

A hooded figure by the altar mumbles something before lifting a knife above his head. A wild, feral feeling encompasses me as I stare at the boy. "No, I must protect the boy. Orphans don't have parents."

Rushing to the altar, I shove the figure with the knife. As he stumbles back, his hood comes down to reveal his face. He's me.

I stare at my doppelganger in horror. The Evil-Me smiles, looking past me at the boy. He says, "The boy must die. His soul has been corrupted."

"I won't let you touch him."

Evil-Me gaze returns to me. "I will kill the boy." He lifts his knife and stabs himself in the heart. I scream, collapse, and clutch at my chest. Charlie and Otus rush to my side as blood starts to pool in my shirt.

Evil-Me stares down at me, unaffected by the knife still lodged in his heart. "Not made for bliss." Evil-Me turns to his hooded followers and smiles. All the hooded figures slide off their hoods to reveal dozens of men with my face. "As God sent forth the angel Samael to kill every firstborn of Egypt, I prepared a new angel of death and darkness to serve our Lord in these harrowing times. But our angel has shunned the power of the divine and must henceforth be destroyed, for the darkness within overcame the pure soul God gifted him."

Evil-Me turns back to me, pulling a gun from his robes and placing it against his own temple. "As the coward tried to take his own life, I take his." He fires the gun, blowing his own brains out.

My body shudders, a blinding pain radiating through my head before all becomes nothing.

Charlie

A bullet hole appears in Arien's head, leaving him limp. Tears run down my face falling onto Arien's breathless chest. I hold him tight, unwilling to let him go.

I hear Arien's killer turn to his faceless followers and say, "Samael no more."

Looking up, I see the killer stab the boy on the altar. Arien's corpse flinches slightly, filling me with a moment's hope before remaining still.

I lift my head to whisper in Arien's ear, confessing something I've kept secret from even myself.

Arien gasps as he wakes up.

I smile and laugh through my tears, relieved.

Before the killer can turn, Arien has grabbed our hands. We all disappear in a dark flash.

***

We appear at the foot of Mount Nysa. Otus turns to Arien with shock and fear written all over his face. "What the hell was that?"

Arien lowers his eyes in shame. "I . . ."

Looking past Arien, my heart falls to my stomach, fear gripping me. "Shut up." I swat at Arien to quiet him.

"What?" He follows my gaze, his jaw dropping. We're standing in the middle of a herd of giant red bulls. A nearby bull looks up from his meal of lion at us. In an unmanly, high-pitched voice, Arien says, "Fuck."

The bull gets to its feet and roars. The other bulls all turn, surrounding us. Arien hefts his spear and the Aegis. "Deni said the last bull was dead."

"Apparently not."

A few bulls start pawing the ground as if preparing to charge; our bodies tense, preparing for a fight.

Arien breathes out slowly, relaxing his shoulders. "Alright, I'll distract them, you guys make a run for it."

I shake my head, saying, "No, I'm not going to leave you."

"I'm the only one who can teleport."

"You can't go back in there."

"It'll be alright. We'll survive." Arien gives me a reassuring look.

Nodding, I accept the plan. "Do it."

Arien nods, turning to the bulls and banging his spear against the Aegis, yelling, "Come on, then."

The bulls shift around to get closer to Arien, opening an escape path for Otus and I. Arien lunges forward to stab a bull with his spear, but it just bounces off the bull's hide. "Shit." The bull roars and charges Arien. He sidesteps at the last second before starting to scream and run around randomly, striking at the bulls to distract them.

Taking our chance, Otus and I run down the hill away from the bulls. Glancing back, I see Arien struck by the side of a horn and flung out of the circle of bulls. He rolls to his feet and stares at a bull charging him.

With no time to think, he plants the shaft of his spear in the ground by his foot with the tip pointed at the charging bull in the classic boar hunter's stance.

The bull rams the spear.

The spear shatters and blasts out a shockwave that flings Arien to safety as the bull continues, unfazed.

Arien struggles to his knees and stares down at the pieces of the spear still in his hands. Hoping he can handle himself, I turn back and continue running. A moment later, Arien appears in a dark flash beside me, his bear-bone-knife in hand.

The sound of the stampeding herd echoes from behind us as we see a village at the foot of the hill come into view. A local warrior waves at us to come toward him.

"This way." Otus turns and leads us toward the waving warrior. As we near him, the warrior points down at massive trenches in the ground in front of him. "Jump."

We all jump over the trench with the bulls just behind us.

The bulls, unable to stop or change course, fall into the trenches, but a single large bull jumps and makes it across. Otus changes into an owl and flits around the bull's eyes, trying to distract it as the rest of us surround it. The bull spins, deciding who to kill first. It chooses the warrior, ramming him and sending him flying.

"Hey, you. Look at me." The bull turns to stare at Arien. "Shit."

An idea springs to me, so I yell, "Arien, the Nemean Lion." I can just make out the grimace on his face as he remembers the story.

The bull charges.

Arien sidesteps at the last second, reaching out to wrap his arms around the bull's neck. He's dragged along for a while, but as soon as the bull stops, Arien pulls it to the ground. He squeezes, the bull struggling violently. After a long battle of strength, the bull falls still as it suffocates.

Arien slowly gets to his feet, staring down at the bull before looking at the bulls in the trenches. I look down as well, surprised to see them seemingly choking to death on their rage.

The warrior approaches Arien, saying, "Impressive."

"I guess."

"My name is Hakeem."

"I'm Arien, and this is Otus and Charlie."

Hakeem nods at each of us in turn. "I don't mean to be rude, but why are you here?"

"Dionysus sent us."

Hakeem tenses as he hears the name. "What does she want?"

"She said we need a guide to get to the vineyard at the peak where the nymphs used to live."

"No one goes into the vineyard. Her orders, actually."

"When we're done, there will be no reason not to."

"You intend to take the divinity." We all glance at each other, surprised and confused by Hakeem's knowledge. "She's known here. She's told us many things about the war and her enemies."

Otus steps in, misreading the situation; he says, "Timorian is the enemy to all of us."

"Is he? I've never seen him do harm." Otus looks down uncomfortably before Hakeem continues, "I digress, this is no place to speak of such things. I will take you to see the Salgan ya'ii Borana, or chiefs as you would know them. They will decide if we can help you."

"Thank you."

"Follow me." Hakeem turns, leading us toward the village.

CHAPTER 40: TRIBAL SCHOLAR

<u>**Arien**</u>

A sense of foreboding pervades through the chambers of the Abbaa Gadaa of the village; the nine Salgan ya'ii Borana file in and sit at the head table. The chief among them leans to speak in their tongue to Hakeem, who turns to us, translating, "He says to tell him your story."

Turning to Otus, our best storyteller, I nod at him. He steps forward and says, "We humbly come before the Salgan ya'ii Borana to ask for aid on our quest." Hakeem translates to the chiefs while Otus continues talking. "We've been sent by the Hellenic gods to find their divinities and restore them in hopes of finding a way to defeat Timorian and bring peace to all the lands. We ask for a guide to take us to the peak of Mount Nysa, where Dionysus's divinity resides. By doing so, the curse that has afflicted your tribe will be lifted."

Hakeem finishes translating and listens as the Chief of Abbaa Gadaa replies. "He wishes to know what curse you speak of."

Otus looks around awkwardly, turning to Charlie and me for help. Charlie's eyes are dead and haunted, so he focuses on me. "They don't know about the curse."

I say, "How do you know about it? I didn't tell you."

"I've lived long enough to know when people aren't progressing. Has to be magical because of how far behind they are."

"It was Deni. She wanted to make sure they'd never decide to leave and stop guarding her divinity."

"That's horrible."

Hakeem steps away from the chiefs, saying, "You know of our curse?" Otus glances up at the chiefs, silently asking if the question comes from them. Hakeem shakes his head and says, "No, this is from me. I thought you were going to say the bulls, but listening, you know of the evolutionary lock."

"How do you know? The others don't seem to notice."

"I'm just observant."

We don't believe him, but we move on anyway. I say, "Will we be able to convince them, or should we say the bulls are their curse?"

"They'd believe the bulls."

"Where'd they come from? Deni said that this stuffed one was the last magic bull." I motion at the giant stuffed magic bull mounted behind the chiefs' judgment table.

"They appeared when Aura did."

"Who's Aura?"

Charlie perks up, finally paying attention. "She's another victim of Dionysus." With pity, I struggle for what to say, tears welling in her eyes, stumping me. She stands, saying, "I'm sorry." She flees out of the chamber.

Waiting a moment, I stand to follow, but Otus grabs me and says, "She still needs time."

"No, she was there for me. Now, I need to be there for her." Ignoring his advice, I follow Charlie.

After searching for a while, I find her crying in the shadow of a barn. "Charlie?" She turns to me; I say, "Come here."

She runs to me, hugging me tight, tears flowing freely down her cheeks. "I'm not the first."

Giving her a second to breathe, I respond, "What do you mean?"

"Dionysus raped Aura. She had sworn off men and he hated that. He drugged her and raped her." My face constricts in barely contained anger. She continues, "Why do we help people like them? Why are they better than the Titans? They're monsters too, not gods."

I'm lost for words because I've often asked myself the same question. In the end, I tell Charlie the same excuse I tell myself when I question. "They're human."

She pulls back and stares up at me. "What?"

"They're human. That's why I fell in love with them before all of this. They make mistakes and do terrible things, but they also do wonderful, beautiful things. Just like any person. They're a reflection of us. They understand what it means to struggle. They understand what it's like to always try to be better and that makes them far more worthy of praise than any perfect god. Titans don't understand, can't understand what it means to be human. Which is why they are unfit to rule. The gods aren't perfect. They can be monsters, but they learn from people like you. People with pure hearts. That's why you'll survive this."

She hugs me again, a stillness overwhelming her. "Arien, this isn't the first time I've been . . . Or thought I'd been . . ."

Otus rushes over to us, interrupting Charlie. "We've got a problem."

Charlie and I awkwardly pull apart before I say, "What is it?"

"Aura. We're going to have to get past her to get to the vineyard."

"Who is she? What can she do?"

"She was a goddess of the breeze, but after trying to kill herself, Zeus transformed her into a spring."

Utterly lost, I respond, "How is she here then?"

"My guess, the Titans let her loose to hunt Dionysus for them."

"Where is she?"

"She's gone to the vineyard itself."

"We'll deal with her after the dragon. Did they decide to help us?"

"They want your oath that you'll rid them of Aura and the bulls."

"Let's go."

I start back toward the town hall, but Charlie's hand pulls me back. "I'm going to start working on the potion for the dragon."

Giving her a concerned look, I say, "Are you gonna be OK?"

"Yeah, I'll be fine now."

"OK. I'll be right here if you need me."

"Thanks." Charlie turns away as Otus and I return to the town hall.

Once inside, Hakeem approaches us to say, "Can you really do all of this? Rid us of the bulls, Aura, and the evolution lock?"

Nodding as convincingly as I can, I say, "I can try."

Hakeem turns and talks to the chiefs in their native tongue while we watch. Hakeem turns back to us, saying, "They will deliberate on this and return shortly with a verdict. I don't see this taking very long, so you should stay here." The nine chiefs stand and file out with Hakeem close behind.

I sigh, sitting down to wait. Otus stares down at me for a moment before sitting next to me. "We need to talk."

"Not now, Otus."

"This might be our only chance."

Sighing again in resignation, I say, "What do you want to know?"

"What did we see in Erebus?"

"I don't know. . . It feels like a memory, but I don't remember it."

"That's not an answer."

"I feel like I'm always on the verge of insanity. A dark well of horror that feels foreign to me, as if it's not my own. A depression that I don't remember not having. Being in Erebus just makes it all worse. Whenever I go in there unprepared, I see things. I just want it to end. That's why I want to die. To get rid of the darkness."

"What did Charlie say that pulled you back in there?"

Biting my lip, I hesitate, her words so powerful to me. "That she loved me. That she needed me. That she'd never survive without me. I don't think she was talking about the vision."

Otus stares off while he thinks before turning back. "I want to limit your exposure to Erebus. We can't teleport everywhere anymore."

"No. We can't afford to risk the mission for my sanity. I . . ." I stop talking as Hakeem walks in. "Any news?"

"They're still discussing. They just asked me to leave. . . They don't really trust me." Hakeem sits down next to the fireplace, stirring the coals.

"If I may ask, how do you speak English so well? It looks like you're the only one in town who does."

Hakeem sighs, saying, "I'm not like the others. That's why they don't trust me. I'm immune to the evolution lock, so I'm always pushing against tradition and trying to get them out into the world. As a young man, I couldn't take it anymore, so I left to look for my Mother in England."

Otus says, "Dionysus is your Mother?"

Nodding, lost in his thoughts, Hakeem says, "Yes. She comes to the village every few years to check her divinity. I think she really comes because she feels guilty about what she did to my people. When I went looking for her, I didn't understand what she was or why she did what she did. I just wanted to leave, and she was the only person I knew. I stayed with her for a few years. I went to med school and that's why my English is so good. Eventually, I started to understand what she had robbed my people of. When I confronted her, she refused to try and find a way to fix it. I left and came back to fix it myself, but they won't listen to me. I just can't leave them like this."

Hakeem stands, the chiefs filing back into the room. The Chief Abbaa Gadaa speaks to Hakeem before waiting for him to translate. He turns to us, saying, "They are sending me as your guide, but we must leave soon. Night is the only time safe from the bulls."

"Alright, let's grab Charlie and we can go."

Otus, Hakeem, and I head for the door.

CHAPTER 41: MOUNT NYSA

Arien

Once night has closed in, we sneak past the sleeping bulls up the mountain. As we round a boulder, we stop in surprise, seeing an entrance to a giant maze that weaves up the mountainside toward the peak. I whisper, "Holy, fuck."

"I see why we needed a guide."

"Who built this?"

Hakeem stares at the maze, his eyes swimming with haunting memories. He sighs and says, "Dionysus before she tore out her divinity. He always loved to drive people mad and a maze is a quick way of doing that."

"And you know the way through?"

"It's our test of manhood to find our way through the maze and return with a dragon scale. As boys, we dared each other to try. I got lost in there for 3 days. You can't imagine how mad you become after wandering through a maze for that long."

"That sounds terrible."

"But I couldn't leave it alone. I had to come back again and again. It called me. I supposed that's because of Mother. I eventually learned its secrets." Hakeem sighs again, shaking his head before lighting a torch and heading into the maze. "Come on."

We follow him into the maze.

Hakeem leads us through the twisting passages. Whispering coming from behind the vines on the walls makes us all uncomfortable and skittish.

"What are those voices?"

"The vines. They're alive. Hera had her revenge on the nymphs who protected Dionysus as a child. She changed them into these vines to mock Dionysus with his own symbol. If you get too close, they'll grab you."

Otus takes a step further away from the vines. I smile slightly before saying, "What else is in here?"

"With Aura here bringing monsters back to life, anything." We all hold our weapons tighter, our eyes darting about, looking for danger.

The maze walls open up before us into a strange clearing. Hakeem stops at the entrance, confused. I lean to him and say, "What is it?"

"This shouldn't be here. Someone's managed to tear down the maze walls to make this clearing."

"I have a bad feeling about this."

"It'll be fine. I can see the right passage on the other side. Let's go." Hakeem leads us across the clearing; Charlie reaches into her bag and pulls out a roman short-sword and a bundle of alchemy grenades, I draw my bear-bone-knife, Otus a small dagger, and Hakeem hefts his spear.

We freeze, a cracking noise echoing from beneath Charlie's foot. Looking down, we see the skeletons of dozens of Greek warriors half-buried in the ground. Charlie carefully lifts her foot off the bone before looking up.

"What happened here?"

Hakeem stares down, just as lost as us. "I don't know."

A rustling from the passage mouth ahead makes everyone back up in fear. Charlie's eyes widen as she realizes what the skeletons are. "Stay away from the bones!" She herds us as far away from the bones as she can before forcing us to circle up.

"What is it?"

"They're not dead."

Otus's eyes widen in fear and understanding; Hakeem throws his torch away to grab his spear with both hands. "Fuck."

I'm still lost, so I say, "What do you mean, they're not dead?"

"Well, they were never really alive."

"Spit it out, Charlie."

"You said there's a dragon up ahead."

"Yeah, why?"

"Dragon teeth, when buried, grow into Spartoi. Skeleton warriors."

"Fuck." We look on in horror at the bones starting to move, standing into the Spartoi. An unearthly howl echoes through the maze as a horde of Spartoi rush from the passage mouth ahead to join their brothers in a charge toward us.

"Stand back!" Charlie screams, throwing a lit alchemy grenade into the Spartoi horde.

BANG!

Several Spartoi blast apart in the explosion, but the surviving pieces merge together to make new Spartoi. Charlie throws her remaining grenades, only damaging the horde slightly. She steps back, hefting her sword as the Spartoi reach us.

We heave and slash as best we can against the horde, but any bone we break is replaced by another. I drop the bear-bone-knife, beginning to use the Aegis as a weapon, smashing skeletons apart. The broken bones pile up around us, hindering our movement. Several of their attacks slip through our defenses, striking us. More and more Spartoi pour from the passageways and from holes in the ground.

Charlie screams as her ankle is smashed by a Spartoi mace. She falls to her knees before springing up and slicing her attacker in half.

I scream over the cacophony of battle, "This isn't working." Stealing an ax from a Spartoi, I swing it with more success, but there are just too many Spartoi.

Charlie limps back, the Spartoi horde pushing us toward the wall. "Does anyone have any jewelry?"

"What?"

"They like shiny things. They'll turn on each other if we throw something at them."

"I've got nothing."

Hakeem slices through an enemy before answering, "Nor me."

I sense the sudden pang of sadness coming from Otus; he says, "There must be another way."

"There isn't."

I realize what Otus is thinking, saying, "Otus, your owl." Heaving back the enemy, I glance at Otus, continuing, "I'm sorry, Otus. It's the only way."

Otus stabs a Spartoi in the head before stepping behind us. I hear him whisper, "I'm sorry, Eve." He pulls out his silver owl figurine from inside his shirt, dropping it to the ground and transforming into an owl.

A Spartoi breaks through the line, rushing Otus.

"Otus, watch out."

Otus picks up the figurine and tries to fly off, but the Spartoi grabs his wing and yanks him back to the ground. Otus screeches as his wing is nearly torn off.

I turn to help, but my distraction allows a Spartoi to impale me through the stomach with a sword.

Time seems to freeze, my gaze focusing in on the sword sticking out of me. Blood gurgles through my lips; I fall, collapsing to my knees.

A glint of silver rolling past me catches my lethargic gaze.

The Spartoi standing above turns away, leaving me alive, rushing toward the silver. Bones fly past me, exploding from the Spartoi tearing each other apart to get to the silver. A faint smile creases my lips before my vision goes black, and I fall back.

***

I was only out for a moment, but it felt like an eternity. When I awake, Charlie is putting the final touches on my bandage, tightening it. I look past her at Otus nursing a dislocated shoulder, and at the last Spartoi standing over the shattered remains of his brothers with the silver figurine held high in his hand. Several Spartoi limbs still thrash, but none have enough support to stand.

The Spartoi smiles before eating the silver for safekeeping and reaching out to his brethren. Any remaining limbs of the fallen Spartoi roll across the ground and connect to the last Spartoi, making him larger and stronger than ever.

I struggle to moan and motion at the growing giant Spartoi, its body bulbous and misshapen, random arms and legs sticking out at odd angles, more mountain of bone than a giant skeleton. Charlie and the others turn to look at the giant in horror. I try to stand, but Charlie pushes me back and says, "Stay down."

Hakeem, the limping Charlie, and the injured Otus advance to meet the charging Spartoi Giant.

They circle it, swinging at any bone they can reach, breaking many, but not enough. Hakeem is struck and thrown but quickly gets back up and charges.

Her ankle slowing her, Charlie is hit and flatten beneath one of the giant's massive feet. She screams under the immense weight but manages to pull a potion out of her pocket, smashing it against the giant's leg. The acid in the bottle burns away the bone and forces the giant to retreat in pain. Charlie screams, the acid burning her skin as well.

Otus rushes to her side, but the giant swings an arm and sends him crashing into the maze wall. He sits up, shaking his head to clear it, and yelling as the wall vines reach out, grabbing him. He's silenced, the vines shutting his mouth, dragging him behind them.

With all my strength, I struggle to my feet, limping to Otus's aid. I reach out, grabbing hold of Otus's hand and trying to pull him free. His eyes bug out, the vines strangling him. They reach out for me, dragging me in too. I struggle to free myself to no avail.

Otus closes his eyes as he passes out.

Turning, I to try to call for help, but the vines close around my jaw, silencing me.

The flames of Hakeem's discarded torch catches my eye. The firelight dances in my eyes, encompassing all my gaze, soon burning from within as well.

My hands steam with a newfound heat.

Screaming, a shockwave of fire bursts out from me. The vines screech and retreat from the flames, letting us go.

The fire dies down enough for me to see Otus's limp body. I rush to him, patting his clothes to put out a few small fires. I tap his face to try and wake him. "Come on, buddy. Wake up." He gasps as he awakes. "Oh, god. You good?" He stares around for a moment before nodding. "Good."

Standing and turning from Otus to the giant, I sigh in ecstasy, my wounds healed by fire. Lifting the Aegis, I shout at the giant, "Hey, over here."

The giant turns to face me just as I charge, the Aegis lifted in front of my face. I slam the Aegis into the giant's gut, pushing it forward toward the wall. Arms attached to the giant's legs claw at my face, leaving me bloody. I continue on until the giant crashes into the maze wall. The vines shoot out and wrap around it, constricting it down.

Bones crack as the giant is compacted into dust, leaving nothing to reform.

Turning, I see the stunned faces of my companions.

Charlie smiles, wincing as she lowers herself to the ground. Everyone rushes to her side to help. She tries to wave us off, saying, "I'm alright. It's probably just a sprain."

Hakeem says, "Let me see," before carefully taking off Charlie's shoe to check the injury.

Charlie looks up at Otus and I in confusion. "What happened to you? You were injured."

I shake my head, equally bewildered. "I don't know, but it's gone." I lift my shirt to prove it.

Nodding, Charlie turns to Otus. "Otus, you alright?"

"My shoulder was just dislocated. I'll be fine once Hakeem can set it."

"Hakeem, take care of him first."

Otus steps back, not having it. "No, you're more important."

Charlie smiles slightly for the first time since Deni. "Thank you."

Hakeem leans back and says, "Your ankle's broken."

"Fuck."

"Walking around on it for as long as you didn't help, but I think it'll still heal. I'll need to set it and splint it."

Otus grabs a few broken bones, saying, "Will these do?"

Hakeem takes the bones and places them beside Charlie's foot. "They're great." He turns to Charlie. "This is going to hurt. Don't bite your tongue."

"You counting from . . ." Charlie screams as Hakeem sets her ankle. "Fuck!"

Hakeem makes a splint while Otus walks over to the torch and takes it to where the giant had been destroyed. He blows into it to brighten the flames before waving it by the vines to make them retreat. Among the giant's remains, he finds the broken pieces of his silver owl figurine. He picks them up and stares down at them, a single tear leaking out of his eye as I walk up to comfort him.

"I'm sorry, Otus."

"It was the only way."

"I know, but it's alright to be sad."

Otus sniffs and puts the remains in his pocket before turning. "It's time I moved on, anyway. 2 thousand years is enough."

"It's never enough. She was your daughter. You never fully get over that."

Anger flashes in Otus's eyes as he says, "Don't you think I know that? You act like you've had it so bad that you have to die, but you forget the rest of us have gone through some shit too and we haven't given up."

"I haven't . . ."

He interrupts me, saying, "Just leave me alone."

Otus walks back to Charlie as Hakeem finishes her splint. "That feel good?"

"Yeah."

"We'll make you a crutch. You'll need to stay off of it for a few weeks. Go to the hospital if you can." Hakeem stands and turns to Otus. "Ready."

"Just get it over with." Otus doesn't even scream as Hakeem sets his shoulder.

"You good?"

Otus rolls his shoulder to test it. "Yeah, I'm good."

"Alright. You wanna help me make a crutch for Charlie."

Otus nods, helping Hakeem fashion a crutch before giving it to Charlie. They help her stand and let her test the crutch. Otus says, "How's that feel?"

"It's good."

I approach, pushing past Otus's words still swimming in my head to say, "Hakeem, why don't you take Charlie back to the village? Otus and I can deal with the dragon."

Charlie protests, saying, "Don't I get a say?"

"He's your doctor and knows best." Charlie goes silent, taking my logic.

Hakeem shakes his head and says, "You'll need all the help you can get with the dragon. Besides, I don't want her walking that far yet."

"OK. Let's go."

Hakeem leads the way back into the maze.

CHAPTER 42: DRAGONSLAYER

Charlie

We trek through the maze until we hear the loud breathing of the dragon coming from up ahead. Hakeem whispers, "That's her."

Arien turns to me and says, "You have the potion?"

"Yeah." I hand them all a vial. "Get the dragon to smell it and it'll knock him out. You have to get close, though."

"Do we need to worry about smelling it ourselves?"

"It doesn't affect humans."

"Thank you. You should stay here. You're no good to us out there."

Nodding, I sink to the ground, taking the weight off my ankle. "Yell if you need me."

Arien smiles down at me before turning to the others. "Ready?"

Otus's face sets in slight anger, surprising me. "Come on, already." He leads the way around the corner, stopping suddenly. I glance round the corner to see the enormous 180-foot-long dragon coiled over the walls of the maze. "Fuck."

The dragon's burning eyes turn on Otus and the rest of us; lifting its massive head, it roars.

Arien shouts, "Hakeem, can you distract it?"

Hakeem nods, screaming and running out to the side. The dragon turns to pursue the screaming Hakeem as Arien rushes in. Arien tries to throw his potion at the dragon, but he misses, and his potion smashes to the ground.

The dragon whirls, sending Arien flying with a blow from its massive head.

Otus turns into an owl and dive-bombs the dragon to distract it from Arien. The dragon ignores him as it slides toward Arien. Arien moans and rolls to his feet, the Aegis in hand. The face of the Aegis makes the dragon hesitate just long enough for Hakeem to charge in from the side, grabbing its neck.

The dragon thrashes and bucks to lose Hakeem, clearly struggling with his weight. Otus is struck by the dragon's flailing head and sent flying over the edge of a nearby cliff.

Arien sees the dragon's struggle, so he drops his weapons and jumps onto the dragon's neck, helping to weigh it down. "Hakeem, your potion."

"It's broken."

"Otus, can you hear me? We need you!"

When Otus doesn't respond, I know what I have to do. I struggle to my feet, an extra potion in hand. Limping around the corner, I approach the dragon's thrashing body.

"Charlie, no. It's too dangerous."

Ignoring Arien, I continue on. When I near the dragon, I throw my potion into its mouth. The dragon screeches and bucks hard enough to send Arien and Hakeem flying. Hakeem is thrown into the ground; his head hit hard, leaving him unconscious.

The dragon rolls over as it falls asleep, crushing Hakeem beneath its enormous body.

"Hakeem!" Arien rushes to Hakeem's side, attempting to push the dragon off him, but to no avail.

Hakeem gasps as he comes to. "Fuck." He takes a moment to assess his situation. "This is bad, isn't it?"

Smiling, I kneel and say, "No, you're going to be fine."

Hakeem coughs up some blood. "I think I have a punctured lung and a concussion, but I can't be sure."

"We just need to find a way to get it off of you."

"How?"

"Maybe pry it up with our weapons."

"They'll break before you can."

"Our weight was enough to slow it, so it can't be that heavy."

Otus flies up and transforms into his human form, crouching next to us. "What happened?"

"Hakeem, he's . . ." I sigh instead of finishing.

Arien turns to Otus with hope. "Can you carry him back to the village?"

Otus stares at Arien in confusion. "I'm just an owl, and we have to get him out from under it first."

Hakeem wheezes, saying, "Just go on, guys. I promise not to die until you come back."

Anger fills me, strengthening my resolve, and giving me an idea. "No. Not going to happen." Standing, I limp to the dragon's mouth while pulling out a curse tablet and a saw from my bag. I cut a tooth out of the dragon's mouth with the saw before using it and the subsequent blood to write on the fresh curse tablet. "Ópos écho grápsei, as eínai étsi." I stab the tooth into the bottom of the tablet. The dragon's skin starts to smoke and burn away until nothing but ash remains.

Everyone stares at me in awe as I return my gear to my bag. "Arien, take Hakeem back to the village. With Otus and I here, you should be able to return without appearing in the maze."

Arien nods, disappearing in a dark flash with Hakeem. Otus stares at me with curiosity, saying, "What's wrong?"

Not meeting his gaze, I say, "You have to ask?"

"It's just, you're not acting like yourself."

"I'm just done losing."

Arien appears in a dark flash. "He's going to be OK."

"Good. Let's go."

Arien picks up his weapons, following me through the vineyard gates.

I lead the others down the center path through the vineyard. The grapevines whisper at us as we pass before becoming voices from our pasts. I hear a little girl scream, "Daddy, Daddy, help me."

Otus shudders at a voice, covering his ears.

Arien cowers at the multitude of voices attacking him, driving him mad.

Out of the cacophony, I hear one voice, a voice that chills me to the bone and brings tears to my eyes at the mere sound. I hear the memory of my father saying, "Lie still, girl," as he rapes me.

We all try our best to ignore the hauntings of our pasts as we continue on. Arien snaps, stopping to lean against a grapevine, laughing hysterically. Otus and I turn to him, but freeze as the grapevines grow and reach out for us. We all struggle against the vines and slash at them with our weapons, to no avail.

Otus transforms into an owl and flies toward an oak pedestal at the top of a flight of stairs with a small box on top. The box is open and emanating a godly light. My view of him is obscured as we're buried by the vines, constricting our throats, choking us.

All the vines vanish, and the voices stop. Arien and I clutch our throats, our breath coming back. I glance up at Otus, who has closed the box, closing in the godly light.

Arien coughs and says, "What was that?

Otus sighs, overcoming his memories to say, "None of it was real. It was his divinity. The madness he loves to cause."

A hauntingly beautiful voice echoes from the shadows behind the pedestal. "Very good." The ghostly figure of Aura glides toward us, her body neither water nor air, but continually shifting between the two. She casually takes the box from Otus and flings him down the stairs.

After checking on Otus, I look up and say, "Aura?"

"Yes. . . Have you come to kill me?"

"No."

"Then, why didn't he come to get his own divinity?"

"I wouldn't let him."

"You? How did you command a god?"

"He's not a god now. He's human. I think that's why you're here. Why you're bringing back these monsters. You hope to kill him while he's a mere man."

Aura hesitates for a moment, her water gaining a reddish, angry hue. "After what he did, he deserves it."

"Yes, he does." I turn to glance at Arien before looking back at Aura. "But he learns and deserves a chance like any mortal."

"You would forgive my rape?"

"No, nor would I forgive my own." Aura looks down for a moment in recognition. "Despite how we feel, we both know it wasn't his fault either time."

"How do you mean?"

"You heard how he was cursed by the hands of Eros to rape you at the request of Nemesis because of what you said to Artemis?"

"So, it's my fault?" Aura's water turns fiery blood red as she takes a menacing step forward.

Ignoring her threat, I start walking up the stairs toward her. "Not in any way. But maybe it's not his either. When I was raped, it was by a man I trusted and believed in. I've never trusted a man again until Arien. Because of him, I've begun to hope again. To trust again. To see past my own pain and see the truth. Maybe Dionysus raped me too, or maybe he didn't. I don't know. But what I do know is, he deserves to prove if he hurt you of his own choice."

The fire in Aura fades, turning sky blue. "What would that change?"

"Whether or not I stand with you as you try to kill him." I reach Aura and grab her hand to comfort her.

"I can't forgive him."

"Nor should you, but maybe you can let him go. I know there's things you've done that you believe you need punished for. Do you think these thousands of years have changed you?" I slowly open the box in Aura's grip, letting the light of divinity wash over her, the full force of Dionysus's defensive madness washing over her.

I hear a baby's cry echoing from the light before seeing an image appear.

Aura, as a young woman and a solid being, cackles in the vision as she bashes her baby's brains in. She crouches down with the baby's corpse, eating it while the baby's twin brother cries from his crib.

Once she finishes her meal, Aura turns to her other child. She screeches; the baby has vanished. She howls, searching for the child. "Artemis, bring him back."

Aura wanders to the riverbank and freezes, seeing her own reflection. She reaches up to wipe the blood from her mouth in shame, wailing in realization of what she's done.

Her wailing suddenly stops as a fish swims past in the water. Smiling slightly, Aura stands and strips naked.

Wading out into the river, she lets herself sink to the bottom.

Aura stares up at the surface of the river, her air running out. A single bubble escapes her lips and floats to the surface.

Thunder shakes the sky far above before a bolt of lightning crashes down into the water and through Aura's heart. She gasps, letting the water rush into her lungs.

Her eyes glaze over as her life leaves her.

A single bubble pops out of her exposed nipple, floating to the surface. Another bubble follows until water is pouring from both of Aura's breasts as she is transformed into a spring of water.

Aura's body settles into the riverbed, staring up at the sky, completely at peace.

I stumble back from the divinity, escaping from the vision, back in the vineyard.

Aura looks down in shame and says, "You're right. I believe that he should die for what he did to me, but then I should die for what I've done. I was at peace when I was gone."

My gut sinks, realizing what Aura plans to do and the hand I played in her choice. "Don't do it."

"Thank you, strange girl."

Aura thrusts her hand into Dionysus's divinity. She screams, a white light creeping up her arm and through her whole body. She holds on far longer than I had with Apollo's divinity. She becomes solid for a single moment before flaking and turning to dust.

The box falls to the ground by a solitary pile of ash.

Arien rushes to the box, closing it while I kneel in solidarity. "I used her trauma against her. What kind of person does that? I didn't want it to go this far." Turning, I sob into Arien's comforting shoulder.

***

We appear in a dark flash, back in our Scottish hotel room. I ignore Deni sitting on the bed, turning to putter with my things, unwilling to talk. Deni stands and says, "Did you get it?"

"We got it." Otus steps forward, handing Deni the box with her divinity in it. She smiles in thanks, opening it.

We're forced to avert our eyes as a bright light begins emanating from the box. Deni is engulfed in a pillar of white fire. She's lifted off the ground and spread-eagled in the center of the burning pillar.

A sharp pain pierces through me, emanating from my gut, the divine radiation washing over me.

The fire and light fades, leaving Deni standing on the ground, unharmed.

We all stare around the room awkwardly, not knowing what to say. Eventually, Arien says, "What now?"

Deni sighs, saying, "Well, I could join you."

Finally acknowledging her, I say, "No."

Deni nods and takes a pendant out of her bag, giving it to Arien. "This should help you find Hephaestus. He gave it to me and said if I was ever in danger, he'd know. He mixes magic with technology, so between you and Charlie, you should be able to back-trace it. He's stubborn, so it'll take a lot of convincing to get him to help. He never really believed in the gods and our right to power. No one really respected him. He won't want to bring that back. You'll need an olive branch if you want him to help."

"Thank you. What will you do?"

"Find the others, I guess. Help where I can."

I turn and approach Deni with fire in my eyes. "I'll tell you what you're going to do. You're going back to that village and fixing everything. The evolution lock, the bulls, and you're going to heal your son."

"The bulls?" Deni looks at me in confusion.

"Aura came back." Deni's eyes fill with pain and fear. "Don't worry. We took care of her, but she brought back some nasty shit to try and kill you. You're going to do right by those people. You owe them that much."

Deni nods as she accepts my orders. "OK."

"Good." I return to puttering with my gear and ignoring her. I hear Deni open the door before pausing to say, "I'm sorry, Charlie."

When I don't respond, she quietly leaves.

***

"I'm gonna go get some food from the vending machine. It looks like you guys need to talk." Otus leaves, giving Arien and me some privacy.

Arien sits across from me and says, "How are you feeling?"

I take a moment to respond before saying, "I can't keep doing this, Arien?"

"What do you mean?"

My mind made up, I continue, "I have to leave, at least for a little while. I have some things to work out on my own. If Aura couldn't move past her trauma after thousands of years, how can I hope to? I need time to find a way."

Arien nods in understanding. "OK."

I pick up a notebook, giving it to Arien. "I already finished decoding the magical runes on Hephaestus's pendant. Everything you need is in there."

"Thank you." We stand and hug in farewell. "I'm going to miss you, Charlie."

"It won't be for forever."

"I hope you find what you're looking for."

"Thank you."

"Do you want me to take you?"

"No, I need the time on the plane to think. Thank you, though."

Arien nods at me as Otus walks in. "What's going on?"

I walk to Otus and say, "I'll be leaving for a little while."

"Oh, I'm sorry to see you go."

"I know we've had our weird moments, Otus, but I'm going to miss you."

We hug briefly in farewell. A single tear leaks out of my eye as I grab my bag and walk out, leaving Arien and Otus alone.

.

Part 5:

HEPHAESTUS

CHAPTER 43: LIQUID COURAGE

Charlie

Limping past security on new crutches with my hand bandaged up, I stop, a bar catching my eye. Sighing and shaking my head, I go in, sit at the bar, and lean my crutches against a stool before waving down the bartender. "Whiskey on the rocks and make it a double." The bartender nods, making my drink.

I nurse it sullenly, lost in my own mind. Soon, I finish it and order another. The bartender refills my drink before saying, "Rough day?"

Snorting in exacerbation, I respond, "Life, actually."

"Sorry to hear that. Boyfriend trouble?"

"Girlfriend, among other things."

"Wanna talk about it?"

"I'm sure you don't want to hear about my problems."

"I'm a bartender. It's kinda my job, and I come way cheaper than a shrink, with booze included. Tell me about it."

Taking a moment to decide and take another sip, I say, "My girlfriend cheated on me."

"Shit."

"Afterwards, I took my first chance to run away. I thought I was helping people and figuring out my shit, but it's never that easy or simple. I just started sleeping around and hurting more people. I've realized that I need to go home and come to terms with it before I can move on, in any way."

"That why you're here?"

Putting on a brave smile, I toast my drink and say, "A little liquid courage before I go see her, yeah."

"This may be detrimental for me to say, but I've never seen liquid courage help anyone."

I stare down into my glass, swirling it around. "You're probably right." Pushing my drink away, I pull out my wallet.

"It's on the house."

Giving the bartender an appreciative smile, I say, "Thank you." Standing to leave, I continue, "Wish me luck."

"Good luck."

After calling an Uber, I wait on the curb for a minute. When I turn back to the bar, I'm surprised to see the windows boarded up and a sign saying 'Coming soon' on the door. Before I can give this oddity another thought, my Uber arrives.

***

A strange new feeling has me rooted to the spot as if my legs were stone and jelly simultaneously. Just one more step forward and a knock and the door will open, opening upon pain I've ran round the world to flee.

Before I muster the courage to knock, a strappingly shirtless young man opens the door, faltering when he nearly runs into me. He apologizes then freezes as he seems to recognize me. "Charlie, right? What are you doing here?"

"I . . ." trying to speak, I can't manage a single word; his form matches that of the man that had driven Susan and me apart, making me falter.

Susan's voice echoes from inside, piercing my heart with ice. "Chad, who is it?" Susan steps into the doorway, her eyes widening as she sees me. "Charlie?"

Sniffing back my tears, I turn and flee, limping away.

Susan cries after me, "Charlie, come back."

I don't stop until I'm blocks away, hidden under the shadows of an alley. Leaning against a wall, I let the sobs overwhelm me. I frantically dig through my pockets until I find and pop a couple painkillers.

A scuffle at the other end of the alley begs for my attention, but I ignore it. It's just some middle-schoolers bullying a kid. One of the bullies presses a scrawny redhead kid against the wall, saying, "Fucking ginger doesn't know his place."

The redhead sobs out, "Stop." His tears amuse the bullies; they slow their torture to enjoy his pain.

The bully turns to his friends and says, "His mom probably fucked a trucker while she was on her period." I finally look up, realizing they're bullying him because of his hair. Shrugging anyway, I turn to leave,

I hear the redhead kid say, "Please, leave me alone."

"People say gingers ain't got souls. Maybe we should test that. If we kill the little cocksucker, maybe he'll go to hell, or maybe he'll just disappear. Should we try it?

Mumbling under my breath, I say, "Hmm, fuck." I sigh and turn to help the kid. "Hey!"

"Fuck." The bullies scramble away as I approach.

The redhead kid wipes his eyes, staring up at me, his supposed savior. "Thank you." Turning without saying a word, I walk away, the kid close behind. "I'm in your debt."

"Fuck off, kid."

"I can't do that."

"Why not?"

"Have you seen the Kevin Costner Robin Hood? According to it, I have to serve you until I save your life."

"I can see why those kids were bullying you."

The clearly asthmatic kid struggles to keep pace with me, breathing hard as he says, "I know I'm a nerd, but there's nothing wrong with that anymore."

"But if you're an annoying prick, there's something wrong with that."

He stops and stares after me. "Please, I don't have anyone else."

I sigh, stopping, but refusing to turn. "I'm gonna need another drink before I can deal with this shit."

"There's a diner round the corner that serves alcohol."

I finally turn to look at the kid, sighing again.

CHAPTER 44: PHANTOM OF THE WICKED

Charlie

The strange kid leads me into a stereotypical 60's diner and to a booth where I prop my crutches, sit, and pop a few more pills, leaving the bottle on the table. The waitress, Ava, walks over to us, her notepad ready. "Hi, welcome to the Raven Diner. I'm Ava, and I'll be your server. What can I get started for you guys?"

"I'll have a beer."

"OK, can I see your ID?" I show Ava my ID. "Thank you." She turns to the kid. "And the regular for you, Ty?"

Ty nods, saying, "Yeah, thanks, Ava."

"Yeah, no problem." Ava smiles, walking away.

Once she's gone, I turn to Ty. "You come here a lot, *Ty?*

"More than most."

"Your parents bring you?"

Ty shakes his head and averts his eyes, embarrassed. "No, I'm an orphan. Those boys and I live at an orphanage together."

I glance away, uncomfortable. "Sorry."

"You get used to it. It's not so bad."

"I guess." Ava brings over our drinks, breaking up the tension. I take my beer, drinking greedily. Ty smiles before glancing at my bandaged ankle sticking out into the aisle. "What happened to your leg?"

Taking a moment, I decide not to elaborate more than saying, "Long story, and it's too bat-shit crazy to believe, anyway."

Ty stares knowingly at me, his gaze filled with knowledge well beyond his years. "You know, I'm a smart kid."

Raising an eyebrow, I say, "Yeah?"

"I can tell when people are hiding from something."

Looking away in shame, I snarkily say, "Got ourselves a fucking Einstein here."

"What are you hiding from?"

"I'm not gonna talk to a fucking shrink about all my shit. So, I'm sure as fuck not going to spill my guts to a snot-nosed kid who thinks he's Dr. Phil."

"Do you normally talk to people this way?"

I sigh, shaking my head and releasing some of my anger. "No. If you'd met me a few months back, I'd have been the classic shallow 20-year-old girl pretending not to be freaked out for being responsible for a kid your age. I'd never have sworn, never have yelled, and never have hesitated to help you with those kids earlier. I'd have taken you straight back to the orphanage because it's the *right* thing to do. But people change after getting cheated on and raped. So, forgive me if I'm a little coarse."

"You were raped?"

Realizing what I said, I quickly cover, not fully believing what happened had been raped. "Yes, well, I don't know. It's complicated. The first time, I definitely was."

"First time?"

My jaw clenches; I turn to stare out the window, a tear leaking out of the corner of my eye.

Once Ty realizes that I'm not going to answer, he smiles and slaps the table. "Well, looks like you need a good time to cheer you up."

Glancing back, I say, "Huh?"

Ava puts a quarter in a jukebox, selecting a song. The music echoes through the whole diner as Ty starts to hum along. Turning in surprise, I see that all the customers at the bar have started tapping their feet in sync with the music. The clinking of silverware on plates from the other customers chimes in to the beat. Ava takes off her apron, throwing it on a hook before running down the aisle and doing a back handspring.

Ty stands, singing, "There's ice cold steel . . ."

My jaw drops, and my eyes widen as Ty steps back, the booth seats behind him pulling away into the wall.

Ava joins in the song, singing, ". . . in my heart."

The center of the diner is suddenly a well-lit dance floor with an audience straight out of a 60s blues club. Ty and Ava start dancing across the floor and singing to a happy tune of a depressed soul.

My chair folds out from underneath me, forcing me to stand and step forward, my crutches unneeded, as all the customers join Ty and Ava on the dance floor for a choreographed dance. I stare, dumbfounded, at the joyous laughing and dancing of everyone to lyrics of suicide and pain.

The crowd sweeps me away, the music encompassing me. I strangely know the dance and join in as we all frolic around the diner. I smile ever so slightly before everyone stops, a spotlight leaving Ty alone on the dance floor. He says, "The brightest smiles hide the darkest pain."

Realizing the comment is for me, I turn away, embarrassed.

Ty starts to sing a sober solo about a friend he lost taking his own life. He stops singing, but his disembodied voice continues as Ava steps out to join him for a waltz. The sober music and the beautiful dancing has the audience members reaching for tissues, tears overwhelming them.

Ty spins Ava out, kneeling and staring at the floor. "I just can't go on."

Ava runs at Ty; he stands as she reaches him, lifting her up to soar high above the crowd. The lighting morphs into that of a happy sunset party.

The lyrics change to sing of hope, the crowd starting to synchronize dance again. I join in, smiling through my tears.

The diner suddenly reappears, and everyone starts to dance on their own. Ava and I end up sitting next to each other with Ty across from us, back in our booth.

Ty and Ava hold hands across the table as Ty sings to her, asking for her to give him another chance after all his issues hurt them too many times. The light lowers until Ty turns to me, asking me to forgive him one more time.

He stops singing, and the music winds down; Ava stands, walking away, holding onto Ty's hand for as long as possible.

The lights return to normal as the music ends.

I stare around at the customers, utterly confused. They're all again ignoring us and eating their food. Ava puts on her apron, returning to work.

My eyes darting about in shock, I say, "What was that?"

Turning back to Ty, I see him take a sip of his drink before cocking his head at me. "What?"

Staring down at my pill bottle and beer, I shake my head, comprehending why alcohol and pills should never mixed. "I got to get out of here." I gag, rushing out of the diner, limping without my crutches.

Rounding the corner of the diner, I vomit into the bushes. Ty walks up behind me and holds back my hair, patting my back as I continue throwing up. "Everything ends, even the bad. Especially the bad."

I finish, turning to stare up at Ty in horror. "Who are you?"

"Ty."

I stumble away from him. "Leave me alone. You need to stay away from me. I'm not safe to be around. I'm seeing things, and I could hurt you. I'm not going to be your new fucking Mother."

"I know, I just want to help."

"You can't help. You're just a kid. Sorry, but you don't know shit about what it's like being cheated on and raped."

"I've been raped too."

I freeze, staring at Ty. "What?"

"I was raped too."

I look down in shame. "Sorry."

"Yeah, the headmistress of my last orphanage had me dress up like a girl all the time, then she'd do things to me. Things I didn't want to like. I knew I shouldn't. I didn't, but there were things I couldn't help."

"That's horrible."

"I may be a kid, but I get it, and it sucks. We just have to take it day-by-day." I stare off, embarrassed, and lost in my memories. Ty smiles and says, "Why don't you start by coming inside?"

"OK."

"Come on." Ty takes my hand and leads me back inside and to our booth.

Ava walks over, smiles, and says, "You're back. Is everything OK?"

"Yeah, we're fine, thanks." Ty gently slides me into my seat.

"Is there anything I can get you guys?"

I sigh, leaning back in my seat. "Could I get a burger and some water?"

"Course, I'll bring it right out." Ava leaves as I turn to stare out the window.

CHAPTER 45: LITTLE ORPHAN TY

<u>Charlie</u>

Finishing my food, I push my empty plate away, saying, "Ah, that was good."

"Yeah, it was."

Looking up at the clock on the wall, I sigh. "It's way too late for a kid your age to be out. Your orphanage must be freaking out."

Biting his lip, Ty shrugs and says, "I doubt they've even noticed."

"Come on, they can't be that bad."

"I've told you how bad they are."

I look away, embarrassed, remembering what he had told me about his headmistress. "Right. So, what do you want to talk about?"

"If you don't mind, I'd like to talk about what happened to you." Squirming in my seat, I snort uncomfortably. Ty adds, "It helped me a lot when I just had someone to talk to about it." He reaches across the table to squeeze my hand.

I look down at Ty's hand before looking up into his eyes, smiling. "There was this woman. Well, sort of woman. We, ah, had sex. But there were some things that she didn't tell me beforehand. Do you know what a transgender person is?"

"Yeah."

"Well, she was one, sort of. I felt lied to afterward and violated because she was really a man."

"I don't understand. How was that rape?"

"It's not, not really. I don't know." I decide to trust Ty, expounding, "I had a horrible experience with a man when I was young. I swore off men after that. She made me break that promise without even giving me the chance to choose. . . That's rape, sort of. Right? The lie brought down my very carefully built walls that kept me safe from everything that happened to me."

"I don't think she meant to hurt you. She couldn't have known."

Sniffing, I force back my tears before they can overwhelm me. "I know. But every time I saw her after that, all I could think of was the man who ruined me. Made me what I am. It took me so long to trust another man again after him. Now, that's all gone. I know it's not any of their faults, and most of them aren't bad. I just see the one man who was a monster, and I forget that they can all be special and pure too. They're all monsters again to me because I can't see them without seeing him. It's wrong, but I can't help it. A man did this to me, now all men must pay his debt."

"But she isn't a man."

"I know. I'm just so confused and angry I can't separate reason from fantasy. There's too much going on inside me to be rational."

Ty leans back, thinking for a moment, calculating his response before saying, "You just have far too much baggage. You need to shave it down a little, so you can think clearly and heal. You said your girlfriend cheated on you? Have you talked to her?"

I wipe a few tears from my eyes that had slipped through my walls. "No. I just ran. This all happened because I ran. Because I couldn't face my problems like an adult."

"I don't think you can decide how you feel about whether or not this was a rape or get past your childhood trauma until you face your ex and try to heal, just a little. It doesn't mean forgiving or forgetting. Just not re-living it anymore."

My walls crumble, the sobs racking me. "I know you're right, but I don't know if I can." Ty moves around the table to hug me; I turn and sob into his shoulder.

My tears slowly subside until I can lean back and wipe my eyes. "I'm going to get you home, then I'm going to go see Susan."

"I think that's best."

I wave down Ava. "Check, please."

Ava smiles and says, "It's on the house. Any friend of Ty's is a friend of ours."

"Oh. . . thank you."

I raise an eyebrow as Ava walks away, Ty watching me curiously. "What is it?"

"I've never had my check covered before and now it's happened twice in one day."

Dismissingly, Ty says, "Weird. Should we go?"

"Yeah, let's go."

We get up and leave, ambling along in silence, Ty leading me back to his orphanage, the sun's morning rays just peeking over the buildings.

Reaching the orphanage, Ty stops on the steps and turns to say goodbye. "Well, this is it?"

"This place, really?" I look up at the dilapidated building, looking like something out of a horror movie, a seething menace under the surface.

"I know, it's not very nice."

"It's a shit-hole." Ty giggles in agreement. My phone buzzes violently, interrupting us and making me rush our goodbye. "Oh, yeah. Well, it was great to meet you, Ty."

"I'll see you around." We both nod in farewell, Ty walking inside as I answer my phone.

CHAPTER 46: FACING THE SHADOW

<u>Arien</u>

Otus and I sit in silence, brooding over Charlie's loss, and working on locating Hephaestus. Otus sighs, leaning back from reading Charlie's notebook. "You find anything?"

Looking up from my laptop, where I've been trying to hack into Hephaestus's pendant, I say, "It's brilliant tech, but it's got a USB output. That's how I got into it. From what I can tell, the magical runes act like a perfect WI-FI equivalent, so the device never loses signal back to Hephaestus. The device monitors the wearer's medical vitals like a Fitbit and sends the data over the runic WI-FI. If I can break the internal algorithm that's translating the data from binary to a signal the magic can understand, I can send a ping request back to the source."

"That's where Charlie's translations come in?"

"Right. They should help me understand the algorithm."

"How long's it gonna take?"

"Not sure. Depends on the complexity of the algor . . ." I pause when my computer dings. "I got it."

"What?"

"I broke the algorithm. I just need to ping for Hephaestus, which shouldn't take long." Typing for a second, my computer dings again. "I found him."

"Where is he?"

"Turkey."

"Turkey?"

"Yeah, Istanbul. It looks like he's in a steel mill. And he's . . . fuck."

"What?"

Sighing, I push the computer away. "I was worried about this. Hephaestus got notified that I pinged him. He shut down his system, so I can't track him anymore."

"But we know where he's at?"

"Sure, but will he stay there. He might be driving down the street past the mill for all we know."

"It's a lead, we'll have to start there."

"Yeah, you're right. Let's go." We quickly grab our stuff before holding hands and disappearing in a dark flash.

***

I'm suddenly floating alone in the endless darkness, my eyes closed. A soft voice echoes through the nothingness; the voice opening my eyes. "*. . . the poor in spirit: for theirs is the kingdom of heaven. Blessed are they that mourn: for they shall be comforted. Blessed are the meek: for they shall inherit the earth. Blessed are they which do hunger and thirst after righteousness: for they shall be filled. Blessed are the merciful: for they shall obtain mercy. Blessed are the pure in heart: for they shall see God. Blessed are the peacemakers: for they shall be called the children of God.*"

My feet gently touch the ground, the fog forming into an Israeli hill in 30 AD. A figure who can be none other than Timorian is sitting at the top of the hill teaching his disciples. "*Blessed are they which are persecuted for righteousness' sake: for theirs is the kingdom of heaven. Blessed are ye, when men shall revile you, and persecute you, and shall say all manner of evil against you falsely, for my sake.*"

I tentatively walk toward Timorian and the gathered crowd. Timorian continues his sermon, saying, "*Rejoice, and be exceeding glad: for great is your reward in heaven: for so persecuted they the prophets which were before you. Ye are the salt of the earth: but if the salt have lost his savour, wherewith shall it be salted? It is thenceforth good for nothing, but to be cast out, and to be trodden under foot of men. Ye are the light of the world. A city that is set on an hill cannot be hid. Neither do men light a candle, and put it under a bushel, but on a candlestick; and it giveth light unto all that are in the house. Let your light so shine before men, that they may see your good works, and glorify your Father which is in heaven.*"

Timorian turns to stare directly at me. "Arien."

I stumble back in surprise.

***

Otus and I appear in a dark flash, hidden in a Turkish alley. Stumbling to the ground, I stare around in shock, Otus turning to raise an eyebrow at me. "You good?"

Gulping, I calm myself. "Yeah, yeah, I'm good."

"Alright," Otus says before reaching out to help me up.

We wander about for an hour until we find the steel mill I traced Hephaestus to. We watch the mill workers file out at the end of their shifts from the safety on a bus stop across the street. I say, "Can you see him?"

"I don't know what he looks like."

"We got to find a way to recognize him."

"Got any other ideas?"

"Fraid not." I stare to the side as I think. "Unless . . ." Turning back to Otus, I smile, a glint in my eye. "What if we get a job in the factory and put ourselves in a very dangerous situation which will force out the only fireproof guy in there to save us?"

"You forgot that we're not fireproof."

"We can have Charlie make us a fireproof potion or something," I say, shrugging.

"This is asinine. You got this from a movie, didn't you?"

"It's from a bad X-men movie. Sorta."

Rolling his eyes, Otus responds, "Course."

"You got anything better?"

"Just because I don't have any ideas, doesn't make this a good plan. Yelling his name from the rooftops would have a better chance of success. But Hephaestus may not even be in there."

"That's a chance we'll have to take."

Sighing, Otus runs his fingers through his hair. "Fine. Call her."

I smile before looking at my watch. "Well, it's 1 here, so it's 3am back home. We'll wait till she wakes up to call her."

"Alright. Now what?"

"We'll need to find some uniforms to wear, so we can sneak in."

"I think I can help with that."

I give Otus a curious look.

***

I knock on our hotel door, waiting for Otus to let me in. He answers it and stares at the bag of money under my arm. "Where'd you get all of that?

"I don't want to talk about it." Shame fills me, tensing my muscles and restricting my breathing. I throw the money on the bed, going to the bathroom to wash my hands vigorously.

"What's wrong?"

"I feel sick, OK. I hate using my skills to rob people. I know I have no other choice, but it feels awful and wrong."

"I get it."

"Just give me a minute." Otus lets me have some privacy as I finish washing my hands. Once done, I dry off and walk to Otus. "So, did you find anything?" He smiles, showing me 2 sets of uniforms from the mill. Smiling to repress the shame still flooding me, I say, "How'd you get these?"

"Gave a few workers bird flu and stole their gear."

"Great. Now, all we need is a potion from Charlie." I take out my phone and dial.

Charlie answers, saying, "Hello?"

"Charlie, it's Arien. How's it going?"

"Fine."

"Have you seen Susan?"

Charlie takes a minute to respond, breathing hard. "Not yet. Not really."

"That's too bad. Is there anything I can help with?"

"No, thank you, though. I'm fine."

"Good. I'm sorry to bother you, but this wasn't simply a social call."

"What do ya need?"

"We were wondering if you knew of any fireproof potions or ointments."

She sighs, and I can hear her rubbing her face. "You never have any easy requests." I wait to respond, my contrition clear in the silence. She continues, "I can give you the ointment that Jason used to plow a field with fire-breathing bulls."

"That's perfect."

"You're going to make a sacrifice to a god at a crossroads to get their blessing, use one we've already restored just to be safe." Charlie lists the steps of the potion while I frantically write them down. "Before you craft the ointment, you'll need to cleanse yourselves in the waters of a spring and invoke Hecate with an offering of incense and mead. Then, you'll create an altar that you purify with candles. This will be your workspace. You'll craft the salve in honor of the god you made the sacrifice to. The ingredients are mandragora root, virgin olive oil, and beeswax. Finally, you'll bathe naked in the ointment then wash your clothes in it. I'll text you the full spell to make sure you got all of that."

Nodding as I think, I say, "Where do we get mandragora root?"

"My storage locker in Phoenix. I'll text you the address and the codes. Otus should know what it looks like."

"That all sounds doable. Thank you, Charlie. You're a life-saver."

"I do what I can."

"Let me know if you need anything. A character reference to Susan or just someone to listen to you. Just let me know."

"I appreciate it."

"Take care, Charlie. Bye."

"Bye."

I hang up the phone, turning to Otus. "You get all that?"

"Yeah, and I know what mandragora root looks like."

"OK. Which god do you think we should make the sacrifice to?"

Thinking, he says, "Well, Apollo hates witches and magic, Hermes hates you, and Deni is off-limits. So . . .?"

"I think we'll have to use Deni. We just can't tell Charlie."

"On your head be it."

My phone buzzes, receiving a text from Charlie. "It's the storage locker codes."

We hold hands before vanishing in a dark flash.

***

Appearing in a dark flash, I stumble again slightly, shaking my head before walking to Charlie's locker. I mumble the code to myself as I unlock the door. "69, 80, 0, 8." Smiling, I stop and shake my head.

"What?" Otus says, confused.

"Charlie, she's such a child inside."

"What do you mean?"

"The numbers. It's 69 and boob."

"Really? Sounds about right."

I yank on the padlock to unlock it, sliding the door open to reveal an empty locker.

"This the wrong one?" Otus goes to walk forward, but I stop him. "What?"

"Charlie said there's a magical defense system." Walking to the door frame, I stroke a series of carvings engraved around the door's edge. "Min eíste mónoi." The air in the locker shimmers, revealing the secrets held within.

We survey the many items in the locker; items from potion ingredients to weapons, curse tablets, and books. In the air in the center of the room is a shimmering portal into Charlie's bag. "Impressive," Otus says, turning to me for verification.

"It's safe."

He nods, walking to get the potion ingredients as I wander, looking through random items. A book on a shelf catches my eye; I pull it down and leaf through it, soon realizing it's Charlie's diary. With great effort, I put it back on the shelf.

"I got everything." Turning, I walk to Otus, who continues, "Wine for the sacrifice, candles, a portable altar, mixing bowls and tools, incense, mead, mandragora root, virgin olive oil, beeswax, and a couple vials. Anything else?"

"No, that's all."

We load up the items into a bag, preparing to leave.

***

Kneeling at the center of a crossroads, a vial of wine in hand, I raise my voice in prayer to Dionysus:

"Dionysus I call, loud-sounding and divine, fanatic God, a two-fold shape is thine: thy various
names and attributes I sing, O, first-born, thrice begotten, Bacchic king: rural, ineffable, two-
form'd, obscure, two-horn'd, with ivy crown'd, euion, pure. Bull-fac'd, and martial, bearer of the
vine, endu'd with counsel prudent and divine: Triennial, whom the leaves of vines adorn, of Zeus
and Semele, occultly born. Immortal dæmon, hear my suppliant voice, give me in blameless plenty
to rejoice; and listen gracious to my mystic pray'r, surrounded with thy choir of nurses fair."

I pour the wine into the dirt in front of me. "Arien?" Standing at the voice, I turn to see Deni in the shadows behind me.

"Hey, Deni."

"What are you doing?"

"We're making a fireproof potion to help us find Hephaestus. The recipe included making a sacrifice to a god to start it and get their blessing. You were the best option."

"Does Charlie know you chose me?"

"No. I don't think she'd approve."

Deni's eyes fall from my gaze, filled with shame. "I don't imagine so."

"So, do we have your blessing?"

"You do. Add a bit of that winery dirt to the recipe, and it'll work."

"Thank you."

She nods and vanishes. I scoop a bit of dirt back into the vial before standing and walking to Otus. "Here." Handing the vial to Otus, I strip to my underwear and walk to the spring of water. Kneeling on the bank, I light the top of a sprig of incense that's resting in a goblet of mead. *"I call*

Einodian Hecate, lovely dame, of earthly, wat'ry, and celestial frame, sepulchral, in a saffron veil array'd, leas'd with dark ghosts that wander thro' the shade."

I blow on the incense, sending a cluster of sparks out across the spring's still surface.

Wading into the water, I spend some time washing myself before walking out of the pool and going to our portable altar.

I light a series of candles around the edge of the altar before beginning to mix all the ingredients and mash them together with a set of mixing tools.

Once finished, I lean back and stare into the night sky. "In the name of Dionysus, god of wine, I invoke the power of Mother Gaia for the means of saving a man's life from the flame." The mashed ingredients pop and sing, melting into boiling liquid. The boiling continues as I stand and get dressed.

Staring curiously, Otus says, "How long did she say to wait?"

"3 to 5 minutes."

"Great."

Finished dressing, I sit on a log beside Otus, staring off, lost in thought. "What's Athena like?"

"What?" says Otus, turning to me in surprise.

"All this time, I've had her divinity inside me, but I never asked you what she's like. Some of the gods seem good, some bad, confused, or broken. What is she?"

Sighing, he runs his fingers through his hair. "Honestly, she's a lot like you."

"Really?" I respond with raised brow.

"Yeah. I don't know if that's just you, or her divinity rubbing off on you, but yeah. She went through a phase where she gave up. Where she just wanted it all to end."

"How'd she get out of that?"

"I don't think it's true, but she said I got her out of it. She said that her part in ending the calamity had almost ended, then she'd have no more reason to go on. I just reminded her of all the good she'd ever done and all the good she could do again once this was all over. She'd smile at me and say my part in salvation would make all the difference. If I still had hope, then maybe she could have some too. I think she just said that for my sake, to keep me going, but I think something else saved her. When she thought I couldn't hear, she spoke about her son. I think he's what made her go on. I think her son is the one destined to stop the calamity she saw in Erebus."

"I thought Athena is sworn to her virginity."

"She is. I always assumed it was more like an adopted son, but maybe now that she's not divine, the rules are different."

Turning, I stare off as I think. "Did she have black hair?"

"Yeah. Why?"

"It's just, there's this woman I keep seeing in my visions that I don't know. She's always talking about her son."

"You think it's Athena?"

"I don't know. I saw part of her life. She had a family. So, I don't think so. But, maybe it's connected, somehow."

"What's this woman say?"

My body tenses, remembering the feeling of her anguish and pain. "That I destroyed her son. Corrupted him. She's always in pain. Always burning."

"Burning?"

"I don't know. It just feels like the right word." I pause for a moment, the strength of her feelings flooding through me again. "Could I be Athena's son and these visions are trying to tell me that?"

"Well, it does seem like you're gonna be the one to stop all of this. And it would explain why her divinity was drawn to you. But I don't know. Maybe."

Snorting to myself, I say, "Does seem very cliché. Demigod out to save the world. I always hoped my story would be something special."

"It is. You're a hero like no one's ever seen before. You're out to do more than any hero before you. There's no future without you."

My very body rejects the idea of a compliment, so I deflect. "I'm not a hero. I'm just a coward who can't manage to die." Otus stares sadly at me, but I stand and walk to the altar before he can speak. "It's done."

I feel his eyes on my back as I pour the ointment into a vial.

CHAPTER 47: ANGEL ON OUR SHOULDER

Charlie

The now-familiar feeling of stone and jelly in my legs once again has me rooted to the spot outside Susan's door. A door opening to my old life, the life I've fled from, but must face to clear the way forward to confront my age-old trauma.

Sudden confidence pushes me to knock soundly. After a moment, Susan answers, wiping the tears from her eyes. She gasps, saying, "Oh, hi, Charlie."

"Hi." We stand in awkward silence for a moment before I say, "Is he here?"

"Chad? No, I asked him to leave."

Averting my gaze, I say, "Oh."

"You could, ah, come in."

"OK." Susan steps back to let me in, awkwardly trying to hug me as I enter, but I pull back and shake my head. "Not yet."

She nods, looking away in disappointment before motioning for me to sit down. "I'll get us some drinks. You still like cosmos?"

"More of a whiskey on the rocks girl these days."

"Oh, OK." Susan makes drinks for both of us; returning, she hands me a whiskey and sits down across from me.

I take a sip and say, "So, who's Chad?

"My cousin."

Gargantuan embarrassment floods through me, forcing my eyes to avert in shame. "Oh, I thought he was your boyfriend."

"No, he's in the marines and just got back from a deployment. He needed a place to stay. He's out with his marine buddies for the night, so you don't need to worry about him walking in on us."

"I'm sorry, for how I acted earlier."

"You're fine. It looked bad. Chad's blonde just like . . ." Susan stops, looking away in shame.

Continuing for her, I say, "The guy? You're right, I never saw his face in the dark. It could have been Chad for all I saw."

"I'm so sorry. You didn't deserve that."

"No one does. Especially not on their anniversary."

"I know, I did something terrible."

Tears well in Susan's eyes, threatening pity from me, but I force the feeling down; instead, I continue my judgment and condemnation. "I wanted to be spontaneous and romantic and surprise you after canceling our date because of Arien. But what I saw . . ." Tears well up in my own eyes. "You cheated on me with a man. Was I so bad I turned you straight?"

"No, of course not. You just miss what you don't have. The grass is always greener. I forgot what men were like, and I couldn't help myself. It's no excuse, but I was weak."

"I've been through so much recently. Losing my best friend on the same night I catch my girlfriend cheating, having one lover murdered, one turning out to be a man, and all this reminds me of my Father and what he took from me."

Full sobs rack Susan as she says, "I know, and I'm sorry. I always admired how strong you are after surviving what you did. I feel awful for bringing that all back up for you."

Finally giving in to my pity, I say, "It's not all your fault." I laugh slightly, wiping my eyes. "We were good together, though. Before all this. We made a good couple."

Susan smiles softly too. "Yeah, we did."

My gaze goes distant, remembering what Ty had said to me. *Everything ends.*

Nodding in contemplation, Susan says, "Yeah, it does."

Thinking for a moment, I reach out to squeeze Susan's knee. She looks up in surprise as I say, "I'm willing to give you another chance, I care too much for you not to."

"Thank you," she says, smiling in relief.

Smiling awkwardly, I finish my drink for a distraction. Once I do, Susan reaches for the glass. "Here, I'll take that for you." She carries it to the kitchen, returning a minute later, completely nude.

I scramble to cover my eyes, saying, "Whoa, whoa. What the fuck are you doing?"

"Oh, sorry. I thought we were getting back together."

"No, no. I'm just ready to be friends again." Susan grabs a blanket to cover herself before I lower my hands and continue, "I can't be with you in that way yet. Not for a while, if ever. I don't know if I can trust you yet. I've forgiven you, I haven't forgotten."

"I understand. I'll just, ah, get dressed, I guess." She says, leaving me to get dressed, her eyes averted in shame.

***

Susan walks me out and stands on the doorstep as I walk away. Stopping, I turn to look back at her and say, "Thank you. This was good for me."

Biting her lip to contain her emotions, she says, "Me too."

We smile softly at each other, both saying, "Goodbye." I turn and walk away, Susan going back inside.

Before I can reach the end of the block, Ty jumps out from behind a bush. "Hey."

I stumble back in surprise, nearly falling off my crutches. "Jesus, Ty. Don't do that. How'd you find me?"

"I followed you."

"That's kinda weird."

Ty shrugs, dismissing the idea. "Sorry."

"Why didn't you go home?"

"I was worried about you."

Sighing, I shake my head. "I'm gonna have to take you back again. And make sure you stay this time."

I start walking, but Ty steps out in front of me. "Wait. I, ah, lied before."

Tensing in repressed anger, I say, "About what?"

"I ran away from the orphanage weeks ago because of the headmistress. I'm homeless."

Looking away, embarrassed, I check my watch. "Well, I don't see why we can't have an early lunch."

Ty looks up and smiles at me. "Really?"

"Yeah, why not?"

"Cool." He leads the way back to the diner.

When we get to the diner, I look around curiously as Ty and I sit in our booth. Little details seem out of place, nothing I can really put my finger on, more a feeling that it's changed. Ty notices my behavior and raises an eyebrow, saying, "What is it?"

"Oh, nothing. It's just . . . this place seems different somehow."

"What do you mean?"

"I can't really put my finger on it."

"OK. Anyway, how'd it go with Susan?"

This pulls my attention back to Ty and away from the diner. "It went well." Smiling a little, I continue, "It really, really, did. And you were right?"

"About what?"

"Certain things are a little easier to address now. Maybe I was too hard on Deni. Maybe it wasn't her fault."

"I've been waiting for you to say that."

Breaking from my happy trance, I say, "What?"

Ava walks up and smiles, interrupting us. "Hey, you guys are back. What can I get you?"

"Same as before, but hold the beer."

Ava nods, turning to Ty. "Alright, and for you, ma'am?"

"Ma'am?" My brow furrowed, I turn back toward Ty and jump in my seat when I see Deni sitting where Ty had been. "Jesus fucking Christ."

Her eyes sad, Deni glances up at Ava. "I think we're gonna need a minute, Ava."

Ava nods, saying, "That's fine, just let me know when you're ready."

Ava walks away as I come to terms with Ty's change into Deni. "I should have fucking known."

Deni can't meet my gaze, her eyes glued to the table. "I'm sorry. I didn't want to do that."

My body shakes, my rage fighting to burst forth. "Do what? Manipulate me into forgiving you? But you did it anyway." Turning, I shake my head, pushing down the anger. "Costner should have tipped me off."

"Costner?" Deni says, raising an eyebrow.

"Ty was too young to quote Costner's Robin Hood."

Nodding, she says, "I decided to risk it."

An idea comes to me, so I say, "You were the bartender too, right?"

She takes a moment to respond, but Deni eventually replies, "Yeah."

"Why? Why'd you do it?"

"I couldn't bear . . ."

I raise my hand, interrupting her. "You know what? I don't care. Just stay away from me." Standing, I rush outside, Deni following.

Stumbling away from the diner as best I can, I try not to scream. Deni cries out behind me, "Please, stop. We can talk about this." I ignore her, so she continues, "At least let me fix your leg so you can run away properly."

Horrified, I stop and turn, yelling, "No!"

It's too late; Deni has already waved her hand, my hand and leg popping loudly back into place, forcing me to grunt harshly. I glare at Deni as I tear off my braces, throwing my crutches away and screaming, "Jesus, I don't need your charity. I'm a fucking witch. You don't think I could have healed myself? I wanted the pain to remind me how fucked up I am inside. Now you've stolen that from me too."

Deni looks away in shame. "I'm sorry."

Getting in her face, I continue, "No, you don't get it. You don't get to be sorry. I was prepared to forgive you for the sex cause that wasn't your fault. But this, this is fucked up." I wave my hand at the diner. "Even by a god's standard."

"I thought it was the only way."

With a short bark of laughter, I say, "The only way to what? Get me to forgive you? There's a hundred better ways you could've used that humans have to use every day. But you chose to do it like this. By tricking me and taking advantage of me. That's not what a god should do. Gods are supposed to be better than us to give us something to strive to be, but you're no better than the rest of us. Worse even. Stay away from me."

I turn to leave, but Deni calls after me, "I thought you'd forgiven me."

Turning back, I respond, "I forgave you for the old, now there's a whole lot of new to hate you for." Her look of shame forces me to sigh and shake my head. "Look. I was wrong to call it rape. That was harsh. But I do feel violated. I don't understand what I'm thinking or feeling right now. And this little stunt has only made things worse. You made up a fucking child to trick me. To manipulate me and pull at my heartstrings with your made-up stories about being a sexually abused orphan."

"I didn't make up Ty, or create him, or lie, or anything like that." Deni whispers softly.

Lost, I say, "What are you talking about?"

"Ty was me as a little boy."

Horror and embarrassment blot out my anger. "What?"

"Everything I said happened to him, happened to me."

"All of it?"

"I was dressed as a girl and raped by my adopted Mother. I was raised as an orphan. I was bullied for being different. Ty is me."

It's my turn to avert my eyes and say, "I'm sorry."

"Don't be. We all have our past, and yours was worse than most. I can't imagine going through everything you did."

My rage dissipated; I give her a little ground but don't let her off the hook. "I feel bad for you too. That sounds awful, but that's still not an excuse."

"I know what I did was wrong."

"I just need time. I'm sorry." Deni looks down sadly as I turn and walk away.

CHAPTER 48: STRIKING STEEL

<u>Arien</u>

Trepidation fueling me, I pour the fireproof ointment into the bathtub. Staring at the unchanged water for a moment, I say, "That's it, I think."

"I'm surprised it was this easy," says Otus.

A single bubble rises and pops on the liquid's still surface. Bubbles explode in the water as the ointment boils; Otus and I jump back in surprise. "Holy shit." I tentatively reach out to touch the water's tumultuous surface, surprised by its coolness. "It's fine." Turning to Otus and undressing, I say, "Can you give me a minute?"

"Sure."

Otus leaves me alone to strip and get in the tub.

***

Otus and I slip into the crowd of people heading toward the mill gates, dressed in matching uniforms, now immune to fire. At the entrance, the workers start scanning their IDs, unlocking a turnstile. As we approach, we pull out our stolen ID cards and scan them to get into the mil.

For the first hour, we try and blend in, working and helping where we can while we take the lay of the land. Soon, our ineptitude draws the attention of the floor manager, who approaches us. He says something in Turkish, but all I can do is stutter out, "We . . . ah."

Otus steps in front of me to speak to the manager in another language. They talk for several minutes until the manager nods and leaves. Once he's out of earshot, I turn to Otus and say, "I didn't know you spoke Turkish."

"Arabic, actually. Most of these guys speak Arabic as well as Turkish. They're all Bi-lingual, so I took a risk. I spent a few years in the Middle East back during the crusades. I try to keep up to date on it still."

"Full of surprises, you are. What did he say?"

Smiling in self-pity, he says, "We're going to mop the floors."

"What?" I stare down at the disgusting concrete floor. "He knows that we'll never be able to get this clean?"

Otus shrugs slightly, saying, "He's doing us a favor. Or the workers we got these uniforms from, rather."

"How's that?"

"Places like this, you work, or you get fired. Taking sick days is unacceptable. So, people send in their family members when they have to. If the manager reports that it's not the workers hired, people get fired. He gave us busy work, so the guys we stole the uniforms from don't lose their job. He's a good boss. Cares about his people."

"That's crazy. Feels like a different world here."

"I've seen many countries around the world across thousands of years, and I've never seen anything that compares to the US. Don't forget how lucky you are, and fight to keep it from people who want it to become like the rest of the world. That didn't work so well for countries like this."

I nod, slightly embarrassed by Otus's extreme sounding beliefs. He leads the way to the broom closet before we start cleaning. The furnaces reach heat, so workers add in metal for melting; Otus stares up at the liquid steel, fear in his eyes. "What's the plan?"

The molten steel striking fear in me too, my voice trembles as I say, "I read up on the controls online. I'm going to realign the internal axis, so it starts to pour in the walkway rather than in the smelting pot."

"I got that, but how are you going to get near the controls?"

"Working on it."

"Great," says Otus, his eyes rolling.

Staring around for a bit, an idea strikes me, remembering the bad X-men movie. "We're in a steel mill with molten metal."

"Right."

"And we've got a bucket of water." I grin, drawing Otus's gaze down to our mop bucket."

His eyes widening in shock, Otus says, "No, no. Our guys will lose their jobs."

"How will they know who we're replacing unless they see the IDs?"

"That's pretty thin." His face constricts in torment before he sighs and shakes his head. "Oh, alright. What're you thinking?"

"You start mopping the upstairs walkway, then accidentally tip the water into the far melting pot. That'll distract everyone while I mess with this first one."

"Fine." Otus puts his mop back into the bucket, wheeling it toward the stairs while I hurry over to the first melting pot, waiting for Otus. After pretending to mop for a minute, Otus pours his bucket's content into a melting pot. The water boils and steams, drawing everyone's gaze.

The workers all scream and run toward Otus to check if the metal is contaminated, distracting them long enough for me to climb up to the controls of another melting pot. Starting the function, I jump down into the walkway as the melting pot moves to be taken to its next stop.

I scream, real fear racking me as the pot pours, molten steel cascading down directly toward me. "Help!"

A lone worker sprints toward me, ramming me; the worker sends me flying just as the molten steel pours out. He's knocked over by the force of the metal, but he doesn't scream or cry out.

The worker crawls out from under the metal, standing and wiping himself off. Everyone stares open-mouthed that he's still alive. I smile up at Hephaestus, saying, "I can't believe that worked. That should not have worked." Looking down, I notice the leg braces revealed by Hephaestus's now burning pants. "It is you."

Hephaestus turns without a word, limping out of the mill, Otus and I close behind.

When we get out to the parking lot, we hurry to Hephaestus, who's at his truck changing out of his burning clothes. "Hephaestus!" He freezes, slowly turning to me as I approach and say, "Hi, sir. My name's Arien. You're Hephaestus, right?"

Hephaestus smiles coldly, grabbing me by the throat and shoving me up against his truck. "So, you ruined my life on purpose. Huh? Well, no good deed goes unpunished." My fingers pry and clasps at the hand round my throat, straggled breaths breaking through his grip.

Otus runs up to stop Hephaestus, saying, "Let him go."

"Why?" Hephaestus says, his burning eyes never leaving me.

"Because we need your help stopping Timorian."

Hephaestus suddenly lets me drop to the ground, where I gasp, clutching my throat. He says, "Not interested," before turning to get in his truck.

"But you have a responsibility to Olympus to try. It's your destiny. It's all of our destinies to try and undo all of this."

Hephaestus slams his door shut, turning to Otus. "I have no responsibility to anyone, let alone Olympus. I have no love for them. Not after how they treated me for thousands of years. I'm good with how things are. Kronos hasn't done too badly by humanity. Better than the gods ever did. I don't care if he stays in power, as long as he leaves me alone. As long as everyone leaves me alone."

He turns to leave again, but I struggle to my feet and manage to say, "Maybe you're right." Hephaestus turns back, giving me time to rub my throat and clear my voice. "Maybe Kronos isn't that bad. But that's never what you cared about. You always cared about the craft. The art. The ability to take something insignificant and make it magnificent. That's what you care about. Not the war or the politics. The beauty of working with your hands to make something amazing."

"I still have that."

"What? Making bolts and beams for other men to build with. Where's the beauty in rebar. No, I'm talking about crafting you could only ever do as a god in the heart of a volcano with your Cyclopes and hundred-handed-ones. That's what you can have again if you help us. The power of pure creation again within your grasp."

Hephaestus sighs, looking down. "You make a good speech, kid. But, no. Those days are long since gone."

For a third time, he turns to leave, but I say, "Wait." Disappearing in a dark flash, I leave him confused, soon reappearing with the Aegis in hand. "Remember this." I hand the Aegis to Hephaestus, continuing, "You made this, right?"

Smiling slightly, Hephaestus takes the shield. "Yes, I did. A long time ago."

"It's a beautiful piece of craftsmanship. Saved my life a number of times." He strokes the cravings around the edge of the Aegis, reminding me that I never knew their meaning, so I say, "What do those say?"

"It's ancient Algarren. Means: *for my love, Aphrodite*."

"You dedicated it to your wife," I say, brow raised.

"I dedicated everything I made to her."

Otus and I smile slightly in pity. "Would you like to see her again?"

A distant look in his eyes, Hephaestus says, "No. She divorced me before we became mortal. She's not even my wife anymore."

Otus clenches his jaw in worry, but I press on. "Maybe, with a truly beautiful piece, you could win her back."

A single tear slips out of the corner of Hephaestus's eye. "A rose."

My rhythm lost, I say, "What?" in confusion.

"*A rose by any other name*." He raises his eyes to meet my gaze, saying, "She always hated that I could never make anything grow. Only life was beautiful to her. I was working on building a garden for her. No powers or magic. Just my hands. I built the architecture, but I never got to plant the roses. I think I'll start that again." Otus and I glance at each other, hopeful as Hephaestus continues, "Maybe life will lead to love."

Smiling, I say, "Where was this garden?"

"Off the coast of a great lake in America. I believe it's Detroit now."

Trying not to laugh, amused the shit-hole Detroit was a godly garden, I say, "Detroit?"

233

"She always loved it there. She never wanted anyone to know that, but I knew. The snow made her sad, and that made her happy. Goddess of love should never be sad, or so people thought. But there's a certain lovely beauty in being sad, and I think she knew that. She'd have seen me bring life to the flowers, then watch them wilt in winter's melancholy. Joy and sadness hand in hand. Something she didn't think I was capable of, but I'd have given it to her. Anything to make her feel loved." Shaking his head, Hephaestus snaps out of his melancholy. "And if I'm to be with her, I must be a god."

The bait hooked and taken, I bring him in, saying, "So, you'll help."

"If it gives me another chance with her, yeah. My divinity is in a pocket-watch at NORAD's new Top Secret base in Texas."

My gut sinking and my head dizzy, I say, "What?"

All business now, Hephaestus says, "It's been passed down from brilliant inventor to brilliant inventor. Christiaan Huygens found it and used it to make the first human clock. Some of my genius bleeds through to the owner. From him, it passed down through the years until Einstein had it. Through him, it got into project Manhattan, then to America's nuclear program. Where it ended up in NORAD. I believe NORAD's head scientist has it now."

I lean against Hephaestus's truck, dropping my head into my hands. "It's hopeless. There's no way to get into NORAD; let alone for me, I'm dead."

"That's your problem, I'm afraid. Now, please get off my truck."

Stepping forward, I take back the Aegis while secretly slipping a tracking device into Hephaestus's pocket, unnoticed. He gets in his truck and drives away, leaving us alone.

Otus says, "Did you put the tracker on him?"

"Yeah." Sighing, I look after Hephaestus. "We need a miracle."

"Good thing we've got a witch on our side." I turn to Otus, surprised at his trust in Charlie.

CHAPTER 49: ANOTHER ROUND

Charlie

Sitting at the bar, I take a deep breath, trying not to cry. The bartender walks over, saying, "What can I get you?"

"Whisk. . ." Stopping, I look aside, laughing softly. "A Cosmos, please."

"Coming right up." The bartender starts making my drink. "Rough day?"

I look up, suddenly concerned, remembering Deni's bartender trick. "What makes you say that?"

The bartender sighs, shrugging. "Dunno. Start to just tell in this job. Wanna talk about it?"

Turning away, I shake my head. "No, not really."

"Alright." He hands me my drink, continuing, "Let me know if there's anything else I can do for you."

"Thank you."

The bartender nods, walking away as I stare into my drink, swirling it around. A drunk walks up behind me and touches my shoulder. "Charlie right?"

I turn to look up at Chad. "Yeah. You're Chad, right? Susan's cousin."

"That's me. Do you mind if I . . .?" He motions to the seat next to me.

"Oh, please."

Chad sits down, waving down the bartender. "A refill, please. Thank you."

Listening to his slurred speech and looking up and down his swaying body, I say, "You don't think you've had enough?"

"Me? Never." He gets his refill before continuing, "If you don't mind me asking, how'd things go with Susan?"

"Why don't you ask her?"

"I did. She's being very tight-lipped about it. Can't tell if it was good or bad."

Embarrassed, I look away, changing the subject. "You're here with your marine buddies, yeah?"

"Ah, yeah."

"Didn't you go drinking with them last night too?"

"Don't judge. We're marines. It's our therapy." Chad takes a big drink, my eyes following the glass up, pity filling them.

"And it works for you?"

"Not remotely, but the pain in my head drowns out everything else in the morning. So, maybe it does, a little."

"You've seen a lot of bad shit over there, huh?"

Chad gives into melancholy for a moment. "Well, sure. But I can handle all that. It's the stuff here that makes me do this."

"What do you mean?"

"Just this morning, I was jogging in a shirt with a marines logo, and someone threw a bottle at me as they drove by. They yelled, 'why don't you go back there and murder some more kids.' I can't deal with that."

I gasp horrified. "That's awful."

"You get used to it. It happens a lot, especially when I was stationed in California." He shrugs slightly, his eyes distant. "What I saw over there was tough, but I always thought I could get through it if I knew I was doing something good. But I come back here, and people make me feel like a monster. The shit I saw suddenly loses that filter of hopeful morality when people say stuff like that. If they don't want me to fight for them, then what's the point? It's just blood, and death, and mangled friends." He looks away as his emotions overwhelm him.

"Maybe that's why you need to keep going."

"Whaddya mean?" Chad says, his eyebrows raised.

"I think you fought so pieces of shit like them have the freedom to talk shit. Without people like you, maybe more 911s happened and maybe those losers would have died. Just smile when the shit rolls and know they don't roll without you."

Chad smiles a little, saying, "That's not a bad way of looking at it. Is it what you do?"

I tense, worried of his meaning; my tone biting, I say, "What makes you say that?"

He leans back from the tone and explains, "Whoa. What's the matter? I just . . ."

Turning, I shake my head, realizing he must be Deni again. "How could I have been this stupid?"

"Huh?"

"I suspected the bartender, but you're not dumb enough to play the same trick twice. Are you, Deni?"

Chad reels, backtracking, "Deni? Who the fuck is Deni?"

"Oh, stop pretending. I caught you."

"I just meant letting the shit roll off of you, but clearly, you marinate in that shit. Cause you crazy." Chad stands, continuing, "See ya, Charlie. Maybe Susan was right about you."

Realizing my mistake, I reach for his arm, a pained expression on. "Wait, Chad. I'm sorry." He hesitates, so I press on, "I'm just really strung out right now, and I'm having issues trusting anyone. Please, sit back down."

Chad nods, sitting back down. "OK. Who's Deni?"

"Oh, it's a long story. Most of it, I don't even believe. But yes. I used to try and let the shit roll off me, but I don't anymore."

After a long pause, Chad says, "Then maybe you need to remember what you're really fighting for." I raise an eyebrow at him as he explains, "About *who* you're fighting for."

Understanding strikes me, "I don't know if Susan and I can ever be together again, but maybe you're right."

"Well, I'm not good at letting the shit roll either. But, two things seem to help, at least trick me that they're helping."

"What are they?"

"Drinking and working. I drink like a sailor, then I work like a marine. Keeps me sane. So, why don't we get you something stronger and ensure you'll be in pain at work tomorrow."

I smile at the thought, saying, "I like that idea."

"Great." Chad waves down the bartender, "We'd like a hell of a lot of tequila shots down here, please."

My purpose finally clear to myself, I whisper quietly, "Tonight we drink, then it's time to get back to work."

"What'd you say?"

I look up, snapping out of my trance. "Oh, nothing. Let's drink."

We both lift our shots high, Chad saying, "I'm not a religious man, but there's one scripture I love to misinterpret as a toast. *'Let us eat, drink, and be merry, for tomorrow we die.'* Cheers."

"Cheers."

We down our shots, Chad's face constricting as he finishes. "Wow! God, I forgot how much I hate tequila."

I whoop loudly, grinning widely. "I fucking love tequila."

"Want another one?"

"Fuck, yeah." We do a couple more shots before I drag Chad to the dance floor, where we both thrash and scream, the alcohol taking over, my vision blurring.

After a while, I stumble and nearly fall, but Chad catches me and screams to be heard over the music. "You good?"

"Hell, yeah. Whoo whoo."

Laughing to himself, Chad says, "I think that's enough dancing."

I pout, "No!" but my knees give out, and I nearly fall again. Once stable, I nod, saying, "You right." Giggling, I let Chad help me off the dance floor. I wrap my arms around his body, feeling the muscles bulging through his shirt. Sudden desire fills me, so I lean in for a kiss.

"What, the fuck? What are you doing?" Chad pulls back, blushing and confused.

"I haven't been with a man since I was a kid. Or last week. Depends how you look at it. But I want to feel a big strong man inside me again."

He pushes me away gently, saying, "Alright, time to get you home and to bed."

"That's what I've been saying."

"No, I mean, go to sleep."

"Booo! But I don't want to."

"Come on." Chad herds me toward the door, saying, "Do you remember where you live?"

"No, I don't. I haven't slept since I got back in town. Maybe I should get a hotel."

"I'll take you back to Susan's, then."

My speech slurred and drool running down my face, I say, "Oh, for a threesome? I'm down."

Chad grimaces in disgust. "What? No, that's gross. She's my cousin."

"You guys are Alabaman, though?"

"No, we're not."

"Then we'll just pretend to be in Alabama."

"No, I don't think so." Chad stumbles violently; I look up at him, finally noticing his slurred speech. He's just as wasted as I am. We both start laughing hysterically.

"You can't stand up either."

"I told you. I've been seeing three of you since we got on the dance floor. I still have no idea how I caught you when you fell." We continue to giggle as we stagger outside.

My memory and vision blur; nothing but flashing lights and guttural noises remaining. Next thing I know, we're trying to quietly sneak into Susan's house, but to no avail. We wake her; Susan storms out of her room, wrapping herself in a robe. "What's going on?"

Chad leans to me to whisper, "Ooh, fuck. I think she heard us."

"I think she did," I say, giggling.

Turning on the lights, Susan walks to us, saying, "Are you guys drunk?"

I straighten, offended. "Absolutely not."

Chad and I burst out laughing as Susan rolls her eyes. "I'll make up the couch." She grabs a blanket and a pillow, making a bed for me. "Come here." Hoping she'll feel me up, I let her tuck me in and say, "You good?"

"Yeah. Thanks, babe."

I feel Susan hesitate for a moment as I call her 'babe.' She shakes her head, leaning down to kiss my forehead. "Good night."

"Nighty night." I roll over, closing my eyes and letting myself drift off into the buzzed haze clawing for my embrace.

CHAPTER 50: REPRESSED LOVE

Charlie

The light streaming through the window and the sound of cooking makes me slowly open my eyes. I sit up, rubbing away the sleepiness still clinging to claim me.

"Oh, you're awake." I look up to see Susan bringing me a plate of food.

"Oh, thanks." I can sense Susan's eyes on me, but I'm too tired to care, digging into my food.

"How'd you feel?" Susan says, concern emanating from her.

"Like shit." We both laugh softly at my pain.

"Thought so. You were pretty drunk last night. Chad doesn't even remember most of it."

I grimace, remembering some of the night's adventures with Chad. "Oh, Chad. Is he here?"

"No, he had to do some paperwork on base. Why?" Susan's face constricts as a dark thought comes to her. "Did he take advantage of you?"

I lean back, shocked. "What? No. Why would you go there?"

Susan turns away, suddenly very uncomfortable. "Well, we're both thinking it?"

"What?"

"Well, he's a man. It happens."

Rage foreign to me floods through my veins; rage I'd never have felt before more than happy to blame and hate men for all hardship. "No, he was a perfect gentleman. If anything had happened, it would have been just as much my fault. He was wasted too. Like you said, he barely remembers last night."

"It wouldn't have been your fault. He's bigger than you."

"But he couldn't stand. I could have just as easily taken advantage of him."

"Yeah, but that would have been different."

The double-standard drawing bitterness to my tone, I say, "Why?"

"Well, cause he's a man."

To work off the anger, I stand and pace. "I don't wanna have this conversation with you right now."

Susan's eyes are filled with confusion and worry as she says, "What did I do?"

"I've always had my issues with men because of what happened to me, but they never deserved my wrath. And you only helped me treat them like shit. You made me a worse person. This is why it's better that we broke up."

Susan stands, her eyes matching my rage now. "Wow. Great thanks I get for taking you in last night and feeding you."

I pause, repentant, letting the anger go. "You're right. I'm being a bitch. I'm sorry. Can we just not talk about this anymore?"

"Whatever." We both sit back down, awkwardly avoiding each other's gaze for several minutes. Eventually, Susan says, "Then what do you want to talk about?"

"I, ah. I don't know."

"That's great."

We sit in another prolonged silence, only broken when my phone rings, the tension dissipating. Before answering the phone, I turn to Susan and say, "Sorry, I got to take it."

"Fine."

I answer my phone. "Hello."

Arien's voice comes through the phone, saying, "Hey, Charlie. It's Arien."

"Hey, Kevin. What's up?"

Picking up my meaning, Arien says, "Have you heard if the current situation is one-sided or two?"

I take a moment to understand Arien's code before responding, "One-sided. Yup. All good."

"OK, so no one can hear me, but someone can hear you."

"Gotcha."

"Right. It's probably better this way, so you can't freak out too much."

A knot forms in my stomach, preparing for the news. "What do you mean?"

"We found Hephaestus's divinity, but it's in NORAD."

My face constricts; all my willpower put into not losing my shit. I manage to calmly gulp and say, "You sure?"

"That's what he said. We'll need your help getting in."

"Fine. Great. Coolio." I notice Susan raise an eyebrow at my use of 'coolio.' Smiling and shrugging, I turn away from Susan to say, "I have an idea, but I'll need to call someone else."

"OK, we'll be in Phoenix later today. Do you think we can meet for lunch and talk it over?"

"Yeah, just let me know."

"OK. Thanks, Charlie. See you then. Bye."

"Bye." I hang up, turning back to Susan. "Sorry, I've got to go. It's work."

"You got a job?"

"Ah, yeah. Just your run-of-the-mill job. Boring. Very boring. But thank you so much for everything. I owe you one."

A ghost of a smile traces Susan's face. "Anytime." We stand, hugging before I gather my stuff and walk to the door. "Wait." I turn back to Susan, watching her run into her bedroom, soon returning with the Power Ranger toy from her headboard. "I want you to have this."

Taking the Power Ranger, I stare at it in shock. "I can't take this."

"It's something to remember me by."

"You really love this guy."

"Then you'll have to bring him back to me sometime."

I smile a little, understanding Susan's desire. "I'm sorry. I can't."

Susan looks down in disappointment, taking the toy back. "No, I get it. You're not there yet."

Reaching out, I squeeze her arm. "Sorry. . . Goodbye."

"Bye."

I leave Susan alone; my need for closure fulfilled, no thought or desire to ever return, but hopeful that she'll find happiness again with another.

Another need for closure drives me into the nearest alley, where I look up to the sky and pray to Dionysus:

"Dionysus Perikionios, hear my pray'r, who mad'st the house of Cadmus once thy care, with matchless force, his pillars twining round, when burning thunders shook the solid ground, in flaming, founding torrents borne along, propt by thy grasp indissolubly strong. Come mighty Dionysus to these rites inclin'd, and bless thy suppliants with rejoicing mind."

"Charlie?" I turn to see Deni standing behind me. "What's going on?"

"We need to talk."

"OK." Deni shifts on her feet, worried.

Taking a deep breath, I press on, "I don't know if I can ever forgive you, or ever forget. But I think I can work with you."

Nodding in thanks and acceptance, Deni says, "OK."

"We need to get into NORAD, and I think you can help with that."

***

Arien waves me over to his table with Otus. I sit next to them; my eyes averted, I say, "Hey, guys."

There's genuine concern in Arien's voice when he says, "Hi. How'd it go?"

Not wanting to expound on the last few days, I cagily say, "Different than I expected."

"Really? How?"

"I'm not ready to, ah . . ."

Understanding dawning, Arien changes the subject. "It's fine. We already ordered, but do you want anything?"

"I'm good, thanks."

"Alright. To it then. You said you had an idea to get in?"

"Yes." Reaching into my purse, I pull out a bundle of stuff. "I've got military IDs for everyone." I pass those out, continuing to list my gear, "An introduction letter from General Goldmier saying we're doing an unscheduled COMSEC inspection, which should get us to the heart of NORAD. And finally, this."

I hand Arien a mirror. He stares at it, utterly confused by it. "What's this?"

"If you stare into it long enough, it'll create an illusion that you're the mirror's owner. You're dead to the government, so we can't afford to show your real face. I'm sorry, Arien, but the mirror's owner is a woman. So, you'll need to wear a female uniform."

Otus giggles, so Arien turns to smack him. "Oi, shut up." Turning back to me, he says, "Fine."

"The problem is, they'll call General Goldmier's office to verify our visit. He's in a Top Secret teleconference every day at 10, so that's when we should go. But, as soon as they get through to him, we'll be caught. We'll have to be fast."

Nodding, his mind running through the plan, Arien says, "We can do that. Only thing, we'll need a government car to get in."

"Right." I pull a set of keys from my bag. "There's a car hidden a couple miles outside NORAD's gate waiting for us with all of our uniforms."

Arien shakes his head, awed at the detail of my plan. "This is amazing. How'd you pull this all off?"

Deflecting, I say, "Doesn't matter. So, we doing this tomorrow."

Arien and Otus give each other concerned looks before nodding. Otus says, "We'll need to go over the details a little more before then, but I think it might work."

"Yeah, I'm in." Arien says, smiling.

Glad they're not pressing me for details, I say, "Cool. So, what are we looking for?"

"The head scientist has a pocket watch. The divinity's inside it."

"Doesn't sound too bad." I smile slightly at the absurdity that stealing a pocket watch from NORAD doesn't seem too bad.

***

I straighten my tie in the reflection of the car window before tightening my bun, the brisk Texan breeze constantly blowing it into disarray. Giving up, I turn to Otus, who is trying on his OCP cap, saying, "I really miss the BDUs."

"You were in the Air Force?" I say in surprise.

"No, I just had a really close friend who was."

Posing, I wait for Otus to inspect my Air Force blues uniform. "How do I look?"

"Really good, except . . ." Otus reaches out to rotate my occupational badge. "There. All good now."

"Thanks. I'm just going to recheck the dress code." Turning back to the car, I yell for Arien to hear, "What'd you call it, Arien? An AFI?"

Arien, with Deni's face and voice, steps out from behind the car in full dress blues. "I don't think this mirror thing works. Cause I've been staring into it for a few minutes and nothing's happened."

Otus's face constricts in laughter as he sees Arien. "Oh, it worked"

"Really?" He turns to look at his reflection in the car window. "Wait. But I'm Deni." He turns to me, confused. "You got this all from Deni?"

Looking down in shame, I say, "Yeah."

"Why didn't you tell us?"

"I was ashamed. After all the railings I'd done against her, it felt like a sign of weakness to accept her help."

"Oh, Charlie." Arien grabs my shoulders and says, "It's a sign of strength. I'm proud of you."

Otus steps forward, saying, "You must've known we'd find out when he changed, or we looked at the CAC cards."

Sighing and shaking my head, I concede, "I know. I just wanted to push it off for as long as possible."

Smiling, Arien stares into my eyes and says, "It's fine."

I shake my head to clear it, stepping back. "So, which of us will be the Major and which the Lieutenant?"

"Well, it should be on our CACs." Arien pulls out his ID and pauses. "Hold on. The ranks are blank."

"I had her leave it blank so we could decide. I was hoping since it was my plan, that I could be the Major."

"Fine."

Otus disagrees, "I don't think that's a good idea."

"Why not?"

"It may be Charlie's plan and her gear, but Arien's the only one with military experience. So, if anyone questions him, he'll know the lingo. Plus, Deni looks older. Sorry, Charlie, but you don't look old enough to be a Major."

I nod, accepting his logic. "You're right."

"You sure?" Arien says.

"Yeah." I hand Arien 3 gold oak leaf pins.

"Alright, then. We ready?"

"I just need to finish the CACs."

"And I need to make a call." We ignore Otus, too wrapped up in finishing the CACs and pinning on our ranks as he steps away to make his call.

CHAPTER 51: MUTUALLY ASSURED ENDS

<u>Arien</u>

We stare up in awe at the new Top Secret NORAD base as Otus drives toward it. The front gate is tucked away at the bottom of a massive hidden dam that's powering the base buried in the mountainside beside it.

Otus approaches the gate, rolling down his window to hand the guard our CACs. The guard says, "Morning."

"Morning."

"Please roll down the back windows." Otus does this so the guard can see Charlie and me as other guards check around the vehicle with mirrors and dogs. "What's your business?"

"An unscheduled COMSEC inspection from General Goldmier."

"Your orders, please." Otus hands the guard the introduction letter. "Why wasn't this digitally signed?"

"Huh?"

"We usually require digital signatures to verify the DODID number."

Scrambling, Otus says, "The General must not have had access to his computer."

"Then how'd he type it up?"

"Well . . ."

"I'm going to have to call this in."

I lean out the window, hoping to convince the guard of our authenticity. "Is there a problem, Airman?"

"No, ma'am. I'll just need to get the General on the phone to verify this."

"Is that necessary? The General's in a secure VTC every day at this time."

"Then we'll have to ask you to wait here until he gets out, ma'am."

"This is ridiculous. The point of an unscheduled inspection is to catch everyone off guard. They'll be able to cover up god knows what before we get in."

"I'm sorry, ma'am. But that's the policy."

A staff sergeant Engler approaches the guard, saying, "What's the problem, Airman?"

"Their orders are wet signed."

Engler takes the orders, looking over them. "I'll take it from here. Go on to the next car."

"Yes, sir." The guard walks away as Engler hands Otus back the orders. "Colonel Noble sends her regards." He turns to the guard manning the gates. "They're good. Let them through."

Otus drives forward as Charlie and I share surprised looks.

We soon park in the garage; getting out, Charlie says, "What was that? Who's Colonel Noble?"

I shrug, just as confused. "I don't know."

We both turn to Otus, who says, "She's that friend I have in the Air Force."

"And you told her about us?"

"It worked out, didn't it? We'd never have gotten in if I hadn't."

"Whatever, just let us know next time."

His eyes averted, Otus says, "OK."

"Good. Now, can we keep going?"

"Yeah. Let's go."

I lead the way toward the door. Outside the garage, a golf cart pulls up to drive us up the hill to the massive vault entrance. When the cart stops, we get off and are greeted by the base commander. We all salute each other before the General says, "Ma'am, I'm Brigadier General Alistair Steward, the installation commander. It's a pleasure to meet you." Steward reaches out to shake my hand.

"Major Samantha Winchester, the pleasure's mine."

"I must admit, we were not expecting an inspection."

"With the recent uptick in North Korean activity, General Goldmier felt it best to keep you all on your toes."

"Of course. If you'll follow me, we can begin immediately. Unless you'd like to rest and begin tomorrow?"

Smiling poignantly, saying, "And lose the spontaneousness? No, thank you, sir. We can begin now."

"As you wish. Please," Steward motions for me to walk beside him as we head into the vault.

We pass through many winding corridors, like something out of a Star Trek film, until we reach the control room. Steward says, "This is the command center, but we've come to call it the NEXUS. Everything comes through here. It's usually the first stop for inspections."

Despite my strong desire to explore this mind-boggling awe-inspiring room, I say, "We actually want to take this in another direction. We'd like to interview your people first."

Steward raises an eyebrow before responding, "Of course. Is there anyone you'd like to start with?"

"How about your head scientist?"

"Of course. You can use my office."

"We'd actually prefer to use his."

"Very well. Right this way." Steward leads the group through more passageways into an office to meet the head scientist. "Dr. Falken, this is Major Winchester. She's here for an unscheduled inspection and would like to interview you."

Falken looks up from his workbench, his eyes crazed with a mad scientist look. "What? No, no. Far too busy. Please come back later."

I step forward, saying, "Afraid we're not asking, doctor."

Sighing, he says, "Very well." He looks around his cluttered office for suitable seats. "Have a . . . ah, well. I'm afraid I don't have anywhere for you to sit."

"Not a problem." I turn to Steward, saying, "Could you give us a minute, sir?"

Hesitating for a moment, Steward concedes, "I'll be across the hall if you need me."

"Thank you." Steward walks out as I turn back to Falken. "Doctor, it's a pleasure to meet you."

A computerized voice suddenly echoes over the intercom throughout the vault. "Vault door closing."

I look to the others, wondering if we should be concerned. Deciding to dismiss it, I continue, distracting Falken so Otus and Charlie can casually search the room. "How long have you worked here?"

"Oh, near 10 years now."

"That's incredible. And you intend to stay."

"For as long as I can."

"But aren't you a pacifist?"

"How do you . . .?"

I motion to the necklace around his neck. "The eight-spoked dharmachakra around your neck. A Buddhist symbol, yes?"

Falken reaches up to clutch his necklace. "Indeed. Most people don't recognize it."

"I'm very familiar with Buddhism."

"It's true that Buddhists are inherently peaceful, but that doesn't mean pacifist."

"Of course, to fight in defense of a just cause. And what cause is that for you?"

Sighing, a faint smile tracing his lips, Falken says, "My grandkids. People find it strange that I build and support the worst weapons in history to defend them, but I don't see it that way."

"You make sure that we never need them by making them the best."

"Mutually assured destruction, yes. I maintain the peace by making war an impossible option. I'm also the man who can turn them off if the impossible option is chosen."

"Isn't that treason?"

"Not to my grandkids."

I smile at Falken as Charlie finds the watch in a glass case under the workbench. I press on, saying, "If only we all were a little more like you, doctor."

Sirens blare loudly throughout the vault. "What is that?"

Falken has gone deathly pale, worry crippling him. "The alarm. Someone's launched a warhead at us."

Charlie grabs the watch before rushing out with the rest of us.

CHAPTER 52: WAR GAMES

<u>**Arien**</u>

We rush into the NEXUS amidst a horde of scrambling technicians and blaring sirens. Steward shouts from his command pedestal, "Get those sirens off." After a moment, the sirens go silent. "Good. Now, Captain Rogers report."

Rogers turns from his station at the front of the room. "North Korea has fired 12 warheads from various locations at our western seaboard, one on course for us."

"Engage ground-to-air defense, and get me the White House."

"External communication has been cut off."

"How is that possible?"

"We don't know. It shouldn't be."

Steward paces for a moment before saying, "Well, what *is* working?"

"Our lines to the nuclear silos seem clear."

"Dammit. It falls to us, then. Take us to DEFCON 2."

"Yes, sir."

Otus leans toward me and whispers in my ear, "What do we do?"

My gut is wound tighter than the Gordian knot, but I manage to say, "We have to help."

"How?"

"I don't know, but I have a feeling this has something to do with us." I look around the room, searching for anything or anyone out of place. An Airman by the door catches my attention; he's grinning, overseeing the catastrophe with unrestrained glee. "Gotcha." I rush over to the Airman, pinning him against the wall. "Who are you?"

The Airman laughs and spits in my face. "It's too late."

"Too late for what?"

"The War Games Protocol can't be stopped."

Hope loosens the knot in my stomach, possible freedom within reach. "Hold on. War Games? This isn't real, is it?"

Cackling maniacally, the Airman says, "I'll never tell."

"Who are you?"

Before he can respond, Charlie walks up and slips a mini curse tablet into his pocket, chanting, *"Aletheia, who art the beginning of great virtue, keep my good-faith from stumbling against rough falsehood."* A light burns inside the Airman's pocket as he grimaces from the pain.

"Thanks, Charlie." I say before turning back to the Airman. "Once more, who are you?"

A distant, dead look in his eyes, he says, "I am Gegar, a Gargarean."

I turn to Otus, who expounds, "The Gargarean's were all wiped out in the war."

Gegar's unsettlingly haunting voice echoes out despite his lips barely moving. "Not all of us. The ones who sided with Kronos were given eternal life. I serve at the will of Hyperion."

"What's the mission? What is War Games protocol?"

"To start a war and make many souls to feed our Mother."

"Mother? What Mother?"

"Our Mother. In all and through me and you always."

"Why now? Why'd you do this now?"

"As a distraction, while I destroy the base to kill you."

Horror re-tightens the knot in my stomach; the missiles may be fake, but our deaths are nigh none the less. "This is for us?"

"You have no idea how much Hyperion wants you dead." Gegar laughs hysterically, his eyes rolling back into his head as he collapses.

I look at Charlie, concerned. "That you?"

"Yeah, it's a nasty spell. He's alive, though." Charlie says, her jaw tight with self-disgust.

I let go of Gegar, rushing back toward Steward, but Roger's voice interrupts us, saying, "Countermeasures have been deployed." Everyone watches the screens as radar tracks the countermeasure missiles, our more impending doom forgotten for a moment. We sigh in disappointment, the missiles missing the incoming warheads completely. "Countermeasures ineffective. Firing secondary countermeasures." Rogers initiates the countermeasures, rotating in his chair to look up at Steward. "Sir, the procedure is to go nuclear."

His face set in stone, Steward says, "We can't do that, not without POTUS's approval."

"Command falls to you in case of a communication malfunction."

Steward looks down for a second before nodding. "Prime the warheads."

I approach Steward, my hands raised, pleading, "General, you don't want to do that."

"This is no longer an inspection. This is real-world, so you must stand down."

"I . . ." I groan and collapse, a blinding pain searing my face. Once the pain subsides, I look up; gathering from the looks of shock, my face is my own again.

Steward goldfishes, near lost for words. "What devilry is this?"

"Dammit." I slowly stand, straightening my dress. "General, I have reason to believe that the incoming missiles are fake."

"That's impossible. Guards, restrain him." Guards grab and cuff me as Steward steps in close. "Now, I don't know what trickery this is, but I'll have to sort you out later. Take him away."

"General, stop." We all turn to see Falken standing behind Steward.

"Stay out of this, doctor. This is a military matter."

"Sir, he, or she, or whatever, is a good person. I can feel it." Falken reaches up and clutches his necklace, making me raise an eyebrow. "Give him five minutes."

Steward hesitates for a moment, staring into my eyes. Sighing, he says, "Release him. You've got five minutes to prove those missiles aren't real. Rogers will continue the countdown procedure while you work, in case you're wrong."

The guards uncuff me, letting me stand and rub my wrists. "Thank you. Which desk is sergeant Gegar's?"

"That one. Why?" Steward says, pointing at a desk at the end of a row.

"He initiated this." I sit at Gegar's desk, typing furiously, searching for the War Games protocol. "Doctor, I need you." Falken hurries over before I continue, "You said you control the final option. A backdoor, I presume. What's the account?"

Glancing between Steward and me, Falken says, "But the General said . . ."

"I know what he said, just give it to me."

Steward steps forward, ready to intervene. "Are you counteracting my instructions?"

"I've got to get into the system, is all."

Steward nods at Falken, who says, ".\westernworld. Password, \benedictarnold1."

I pause, looking up at Falken. "Benedict Arnold?"

"That's who'd I'd be if I ever used it."

Nodding, I sign into the system. *"Shall we play a game?"*

I type mindlessly for a minute, every second pounding out like a beat in my head.

Rogers suddenly stands, confused. "Sir, the countdown procedure has stopped."

Steward turns around my chair, his eyes boring down into mine. "What is this? Is that you?"

"I can't have the Korean's actually firing because of you scrambling our missiles."

"It's too late for that. They'll have already seen our countermeasures fire. Guards, take him away."

Charlie and Otus both step between the guards and me as I stand, gently pushing Steward back. "Sir, you've got to trust me because I'm the only person who can stop World War 3."

"That's not within the procedure."

It's my turn to bore into his eyes; trusting my gut and intuition, I say, "No, but you've been a soldier a long time. You know that procedures and policy don't matter when life and death are in the balance. Only your gut and your will to survive matter. What does your gut say about me?"

Steward's face constricts as he thinks for a moment. "You've got three minutes left of your five. Don't dawdle."

"Thank you, sir." I sit back down and continue typing. Suddenly, I find what I'm looking for, and hope once again prevails. "Gotcha. I found the virus that's making our systems see the missiles."

"Can you shut it down?"

I check the virus code, hope receding at the pure magnitude and brilliance of the code. I grunt, giving up. "No, it's as part of the system as your code, doctor. It's almost alive, constantly updating all sections of the system. There's nothing I can do." I feel the blood drain from my face, turning me pale, a revelation in the code striking fear into my very soul.

Charlie notices my body language, saying, "Arien, what is it?"

"Remember when Gegar said he was going to destroy the base?"

"Yeah."

"There are explosives linked to this code. When the warhead is set to impact here, is when they'll go off. Appearing to the rest of the world like an attack and justifying our last act of firing our nukes, sparking a war. By the time they figure out what really happened, it'll be too late."

Falken and the others go pale before I hear someone whisper, "Oh, my god."

"Can't you reboot the system or something?"

I shake my head, totally lost on what to do. "There's a series of redundancies. The system is continually signaling our nukes and the explosives down here. If either loses the signal, they'll both be set off. We'll die, and World War 3 will start either way."

"What do we do?"

An idea coming to me, I turn to the side, saying, "Rogers?"

"Yeah?"

"Can you bring up the estimated time of impact of the main screen?"

Rogers looks to Steward for permission, who says, "Do it." Rogers turns to his computer, a countdown clock soon appearing on the main screen with 10 minutes remaining.

"Alright, that's the time to beat. We need to find the explosives and disable them, while connecting the nuke signal to a server separate from the rest of the system without interrupting the signal. Giving us time to free the main system of Gegar's code and contact the outside to shut everything down. All before the time runs out. Dr. Falken, the NIPR servers are in a separate vault from the SIPR, yes?"

"That's correct."

"Can you replicate the signal uninterrupted through a NIPR server, which should be free of Gegar's code?"

"With a little help, yes."

With thought of others forgotten by me, Otus says, "Can we evacuate non-essential personnel in case things go wrong?"

Steward looks down in embarrassment, confessing, "The vault door malfunctioned. We're sealed in."

I nod, saying, "That's probably part of Gegar's plan."

"How do we find the bomb?" Falken says, his voice trembling.

"Is there somewhere here where one explosion could blow the entire base?

Steward shakes his head, saying, "No, we're built to withstand heavy damage. Unless . . . fuck."

"What is it?"

"If you blow the dam at the right place and set the system to open all blast doors, you could flood the base."

Otus says, "How does that help justify us starting a nuclear war to the outside world?"

I shrug, thinking aloud, "We just need to be dead. By the time the world knows we drowned, it won't matter. The war will have started." Turning to the computer, I type through the code, checking for blast door controls. "There's a command to open all blast doors."

In military, problem-solving mode, Steward says, "The bomb will be in the turbine room."

"Can you show me?"

"Yes."

I stand, saying, "Dr. Falken, Charlie and Otus will go with you to the server room to assist you. Once the bombs are deactivated, try rebooting the servers. Hopefully, that'll be enough to get the vault door open and comms back online."

Falken nods, trying not to hyperventilate. "Very well. I can also power on the emergency generator for the servers in case we lose the turbines."

"Good idea." I turn to Rogers, continuing, "Rogers, keep working on getting communications back online. Tensions will be tight out there with the countermeasures having been fired. We need to let them know what's going on."

Charlie raises a concern, "With comms down, how will you let us know when the bomb is deactivated?"

"Do you guys have radios?"

Rogers wheels to a wall cabinet, grabbing radios for everyone. "For emergencies, but with all the stone, their range is limited. You'll never get a signal from the turbine room to the server room."

"Could you get a signal from here to both places?"

"Maybe."

"Then you'll be our middleman as well. Transfer all info between us." Turning to the others, I say, "Everyone know what they need to do?" Waiting until everyone has nodded, I continue, "OK. Good luck."

We split up, heading to our separate destinations.

CHAPTER 53: WORLD WAR III

Otus

Charlie and I follow Falken through the base's winding passageways until we reach the server room. Falken hesitates in the doorway for a moment, deciding how to proceed. Eventually, he sighs and says, "You two, in that closet, is a generator. Can you get it started?" Charlie and I nod, following his finger to the closet.

Falken turns to the server farm, starting his search for the signal's origin.

Rogers

I type frantically, muscle memory and training overwhelming the fear that would paralyze me given the chance. Until I re-establish our communications, there's no sure chance of success or survival. They're relying on me.

My radio crackles, Falken's voice echoing through, saying, "Rogers, you there? Over."

I lift the radio, pressing the button to respond, "I read you. Over."

"Let Steward and Arien know, I found where the signal's coming from, and I'm starting to replicate it on the NIPR now. I just need to reconfigure the gateway first. Over."

"Roger that. Over and out." I glance up at the main screen, pausing when I see the countdown is down to only 6 minutes. Snapping out of my fearful trance, I get back to work.

Arien

Steward and I step into a massive room at the heart of the dam; giant turbines turn around us, powered by the water flowing through. I quickly oversee the room; if the reservoir side wall was blown, water would rush in, stopped by the reinforced far side. With the blast doors open, the water would funnel down into the tunnel, flooding the base.

Rogers's voice buzzes over the radio. "General Steward, do you read me? Over."

Steward lifts his radio to reply. "I read you. Over."

"Dr. Falken has found the signal and he's working to replicate it. How are things at your end? Over."

"We just reached the turbine room. We'll keep you posted. Over and out." We hurry to the reservoir side of the room, searching for explosives. It's not long before we find several bombs beneath the floor grating. "How many are there?"

Quickly counting, I say, "I see six. We'll have to be fast." One-by-one we gingerly take the explosives from the flooring, deactivating them.

Stopping, Steward glances up at the nearby dam wall, saying, "Can't we just move them away from this wall? They're not large enough to bring it down from the other side."

Doing quick calculations in my head, I respond, "We risk blowing the turbines before Falken can get the generator on and the missiles will fire."

Steward nods, returning to disarming a bomb. "We'd better hurry then."

Otus

Charlie and I are working on getting the generator started with little success; it clearly hasn't been used or inspected in a while. Falken yells from the other room, saying, "Can one of you come out here and help me." Getting a nod from Charlie, I go out to the main server room.

Falken motions for me to stand in front of a computer terminal, adding, "I'm going to the NIPR server room to duplicate the signal over there. When I call over the radio, read me the info off this screen. OK?

"Got it."

Falken nods in thanks, hurrying through a security door to the NIPR room. As he walks away, I hear him whisper, "I'm gonna hate my next Tempest inspection."

"What's that?"

"Never mind." A minute later, his voice comes over the radio, saying, "Alright. I've pinged the SIPR gateway. I'm connected. Otus, read me those IP addresses from the top down, starting with the subnet mask."

Taking a moment to understand what I'm looking at, I say, "193.49.3.45, then 193.49.397.8, that's the last one."

"Alright." I can hear him typing furiously before laughing and saying, "I'm connected to the nuclear net. Sending duplicate packages to all stations." He presses one more key. "Otus, disconnect power from that entire server tower." I crouch, unplugging the server. A moment later, he adds, "It's working. The signal's disconnected from the timer so the nukes won't go off as long as this station's not destroyed or loses power."

The sound of the generator winding up echoes through the server room. Charlie whoops and yells, "I got it."

Hopeful melancholy in his voice, Falken says, "Now we just need to make sure we all come out of this alive."

Arien

I stop, staring down at the bomb I'm diffusing, suddenly realizing we won't make it. "We're not going to have enough time."

Over the radio, Rogers says, "Falken got the signal replicated and the generator on. Over."

I click my radio, replying, "That's great. How much time is left? Over."

"Just over 3 minutes. Over."

"We have a problem. I don't think we'll have enough time to disarm all the bombs. If we do, it'll be close. We need a backup option. Can you get the blast doors closed? Over."

I wait for a response while Rogers thinks. "Maybe. If Falken could disconnect the security system from the rest of the network, so the virus won't keep updating it. But, I'll have to go through line-by-line to delete the code that's already there. Over."

"Alright. Get Falken on that. Over and out." Returning to disarming the bomb, I freeze; a loud beeping fills the room, partially coming from the active bombs in front of me. Horror fills me and the scale of the noise. "That's way too loud for just six bombs." The muffled beeping is coming from everywhere. I stand, stroking the dam's concrete wall; there's a small flashing light embedded in the concrete. "Turn off the lights."

"What?"

"Do it!"

Steward runs to a massive power switch, turning the lights off. The reservoir wall of the dam lights up with a hundred little lights embedded in the concrete. "Shit."

Steward turns the lights back on, saying, "We'll never disable all of those. We can't stop it."

Lifting my radio, I call Rogers, "How's it coming along? Over."

"Falken just disconnected the security system, but there's too much code for me to go through alone. Over."

"There's nothing more we can do here. Falken and I will come help you. Otus and Charlie can reboot the servers alone. Let them know. Over."

"Roger that. Over and out."

I hurry to Steward and out of the room.

Charlie

Falken wipes the sweat from his forehead as he talks to Rogers over the radio, "Roger that. I'm on my way. Over and out." He turns to the admin terminal and types a few commands before turning to Otus and I. "When the bombs go off, just press enter. I've already loaded the script."

"Got it."

Falken nods, heading for the door.

Arien

Steward and I rush into the NEXUS to see only 2 minutes left on the clock. I turn to him and say, "There's nothing more you can do here. Get everyone down behind the second blast door in case things go wrong. And take Gegar with you."

Steward nods, turning to his staff. "Alright. Everyone except Rogers, follow me." He leads everyone away as I sit down at Gegar's computer, starting to sift through the security systems code, deleting Gegar's commands.

After a moment, Falken rushes in and joins us in the hunt. Rogers continues typing while turning to give me a concerned look, "You know we only have time for one door, right?" I nod slightly, not responding, so he adds, "And that it'll have to be the one after ours because ours will only seal us in."

"I know."

"We're going to die."

Falken pauses for a second, looking up at us in solidarity. I quickly shake my head, an idea coming to me. "No. When we reach 30 seconds, you both will go down to the others. I can't die, so I'll finish this."

They both give me a confused look before Rogers says, "Putting aside not dying, you'll never finish the code in time. We're staying."

Falken nods, adding, "That's right."

I shake my head, determined not to let anyone else die. "I can't let you do that."

"Arguing is just wasting time."

Giving in, I nod in thanks, turning back to the code. We work for the next minute and a half as time runs out.

BEEP!

The timer reaches zero.

BOOM!

All the bombs explode, the sound of rushing water following soon after, funneling into the base.

Charlie

Steward, Otus, the rest of the NORAD staff, and I all flinch at the sound of the bombs going off.

Otus screams, "Now, Charlie!"

I press enter to run the reboot script. The servers shut down before powering back on, hopefully clearing the virus, opening the vault entrance, and bringing comms back up. But none of that will matter if Arien didn't get the blast doors closed.

Otus runs to the hall and peers out at the blast door. "It's still open!"

Arien

"Almost got it." I remove the last of the code. Screaming and jumping to my feet, I shout, "Got it."

Falken presses enter to start closing the blast door.

I leap to grab the other men just as the water rushes into the NEXUS. Water slams into Rogers, killing him instantly before hitting Falken as I grab him.

We both disappear in a dark flash.

CHAPTER 54: AMONG US

<u>Arien</u>

Falken and I appear in a dark flash atop the NORAD mountain. Falken collapses to the ground, spitting up blood. Realizing his condition, I kneel, cradling the dying man and checking his injuries to find that his ribs were crushed by the water. Tears filling my eyes, I say, "I can heal you."

To my surprise, he says, "No," coughing up more blood.

"Why not?"

"I don't know what you are or what you have the power to do. But death is a natural part of living. Preventing it at a moment like this is an affront to nature."

"What about your kids, your grandkids?"

Falken smiles slightly. "They'll know I died well and am going to a better life."

"Please don't make me let you die. I couldn't save Rogers, but I can save you."

"It's alright. It's my choice." Falken's gaze turns to look at the sun as his expression glazes over. "It's so beautiful." He lets out his final breath.

I slowly lay the corpse to the ground before standing and disappearing in a dark flash.

After many trips, I appear in a dark flash for the last time, with all of the survivors safely on the mountain overlooking the reservoir far below. At the mountain's base, the vault door slowly opens, and water spews out, draining the base.

I walk to my friends while I feel Steward's eyes boring into my back. Charlie hugs me, saying, "Are you OK?"

"I couldn't save Rogers or Falken."

"I'm sorry."

"Did you get it?" Charlie lifts the pocket watch to show me. "Good. We should get out of here."

"Can we pay our respects first?"

Nodding, I lead them over to Rogers and Falken's bodies. We stand in a moment of silence.

"Arien!" I freeze, hearing Steward yelling my real name. We turn to him; he motions for his guards to stay back a little, saying, "Stay here, but keep them covered."

"Yes, sir," the guards say, hefting their weapons.

Steward walks across the intervening distance to me. "Not too many Arien's in the military, and you are clearly a military man."

"You know who I am?"

"Heard your friend say your name, looked you up, but I haven't the slightest idea who you really are. A dead man wearing another's face, stopping World War 3, and saving everyone's lives in there."

I look down, shame filling me. "Not everyone's."

"I have no idea who or *what* you are."

"I'm nobody, other than what you said. That'll have to be enough. If I were a terrorist or dangerous, why would I have done what I did?"

Nodding, Steward says, "You were right earlier. I can't stand the pomp and circumstance, or the bureaucracy. When it comes down to it, I trust my gut, and it's never led me wrong. You have my thanks." Smiling, Steward puts as foot forward as if preparing to fight. "For appearance's sake, I have to pretend to follow procedure and try and capture you. I can't stop people knowing you're alive, and I can't stop them from chasing you."

"I know."

"But I can give you a head start."

I raise an eyebrow. "What?"

"Hit me."

Smiling in thanks, I say, "Thank you. You're a good man."

"I try to be, but it looks like you're the good man here."

My face constricts, revolting at the idea that I am good. . . That I'm clean. "I try to be."

I punch Steward in the face, knocking him to the ground. The guards raise their weapons and shout as Charlie, Otus, and I disappear in a dark flash.

***

Floating empty in the endless darkness, I hear Timorian's voice in the dark, saying, "*Let not your heart be troubled. Trust in God; trust also in me.*" He pauses before adding, "Trust me."

***

I go through the next hour in a veil, my mind barely present. I'm ripped out of my reverie by the blinding light of Hephaestus goding out in the center of the room. Once the light fades,

Hephaestus turns to me, saying, "I'll go talk to my Mother, see if she's willing to help. Until then, good luck." He disappears in a flash of light.

I stare off into space after Hephaestus leaves, Timorian's voice echoing in my head, "Trust me."

I stand suddenly, saying, "I'm going to get food." I walk out, leaving Otus and Charlie alone in Hephaestus's apartment.

Otus

Charlie and I look at each other, worried about Arien's strange behavior after Falken's death. Charlie sighs, dismissing Arien for the moment, and saying, "I've got to go call Susan. Do you mind if I . . .?" She motions toward the door.

"That's fine. I'm just going to crash here." I sit on the couch as Charlie leaves. Once she's gone, I get up and go to the window, transforming into an owl and flying off.

I circle the house high above, following Charlie as she walks to the back for privacy. When she stops, I land nearby, transform into a man, and take out my phone to record. Charlie kneels and calls out in prayer:

"Come mighty Dionysus to these rites inclin'd, and bless thy suppliants with rejoicing mind."

Deni appears behind Charlie and says, "How'd it go?"

Charlie stands, turning to Deni, and saying, "Not bad. Thank you. We couldn't have done it without you."

"I had a debt to pay."

"And you've paid it. I'm not angry anymore, and we're even. I'm not fully over it yet, but I will be. It really meant something that you helped us. But I do want you to be a man around us from now on."

Deni looks down, uncomfortable. "Really?"

"I'm sorry, but seeing you like this is too painful."

Deni nods, "OK." Her skin glows softly, transforming her into her male form, Dionysus.

"Thank you."

They hug briefly, Dionysus saying, "Goodbye."

"Bye."

Dionysus disappears, Leaving Charlie to sigh and head back into the house. From the shadows, I finish recording Charlie, uploading the video, and texting it to my boss.

<u>**Arien**</u>

I stumble down the streets of Istanbul, fighting back the insanity. I freeze as I see Timorian standing underneath a streetlamp. He says, "Trust me."

My vision warps and blurs, the lights of the street flickering violently, making me lean against a streetlamp for balance. Looking up, I see that Timorian is gone. Everything slowly settles, my balance and sight returning.

I stare out into the night, my soul lost in the darkness.

Part 6:

HERA

CHAPTER 55: THE WAY, TRUTH, AND LIFE

Arien

After a week without incident, I find myself back in the endless darkness, lost in the horrors of Erebus. Timorian's voice echoes out of the black, saying, "*I am the Way, the Truth, and the Life.*"

I scream out in utter frustration, "What do you want from me?!"

The fog rushes in and forms into a hill outside of ancient Jerusalem. "Arien." I turn to see Timorian standing behind me.

"You? How are you doing this? Why?" I say, not sure if this is dream or vision.

"It matters not. You must watch for my coming, for it shall not be as you foresee. The Earth is not all that we may lose in the coming war, nor humanity only. But all our souls we shall lose on the last day if the final judgment is bestowed on us from above."

"Why are you telling me this? I'm gonna try and stop you."

"Oh, my son. You shall do far more than that once the day is done. Thy trust must needs be with me. Trust that I know best."

"I can't."

"Then you shall surely die."

The fog floods in, consuming us both. It pulls back, forming into my childhood home, my nightmare life back in tangible horror. I stare around; each toy, carpet hair, and stretch of wall, even the very flecks of dust floating in the air reflecting in the light, hold memories I long since wished to forget. I reach out to stroke a door frame, the sound of screaming and laughter echoing through my head.

"Arien." I turn to see my Mom standing behind me.

"Mom? . . . You called me Arien."

"It's what you want to be called, right?"

"Yes."

"Why have you shirked your name?"

Tears start to overwhelm me as I struggle to say, "Because of what you did to me. What you made me do."

"Everything I did, I did because I love you. I'm your Mother. That's never going to change."

"I can't forgive you."

"But we're family."

Unable to look her in the eye, I turn away, guilt and confusion flooding me. "You made me into a monster. That's not what family does to each other."

"You're not a monster."

"That's not what you said."

"I was afraid."

"Of what?"

"Your Father. He made me, but I loved you so much that it destroyed me inside."

"Oh, mom." I let her pull me into a hug, sobbing into her shoulder.

"I'm your Mother. I'm always going to be here for you."

My tears slowly subside, allowing me to say, "Would either of you have done what you did if the Temple didn't tell you to?"

She pauses for a second before responding, hate dripping from every word. "Yes, because you're a sickness. A disease that needed to be purged at birth." I pull back from the hug in shock to see Mom's face has turned into one of rage and hate. "How could we ever love a disgusting monster like you? You don't deserve the breath we gave." I stumble back, Mom slowly following, each step precise and intentional. "You destroyed our lives and our reputations with your filth. We should have smothered you as a baby. Any good Mother would have. But we thought we could change your nature. No good deed goes unpunished. Your Mother will forever be cursed because of you."

Huddling down into a corner, I cover my ears to block her out. "Stop."

"I wish I'd have died in childbirth like Brittnie, so I'd never have had to see your revolting face."

I lunge out, screaming, "Stop!"

The fog explodes and disappears, leaving me alone in the darkness.

My heavy breathing and tears slow as Brittnie's voice echoes out of the darkness, calming me. "My son should not feel pain. What have you done to my beautiful baby boy?"

"I haven't done anything to him."

Her voice fading, Brittnie says, "Yet."

***

Stumbling, I appear in a dark flash in a Baltimore hotel hallway. Leaning against a wall, I try to catch my breath and act normal as a maid steps out of a room, saying, "Are you alright, sir? Too much to drink?"

"I'm fine. Thank you."

The maid nods, continuing her rounds. Once my body settles, I enter our hotel room. Inside the room, Charlie is trying her best to work out in the small space. She stops, walking toward me when she sees the expression on my face. "What's up?"

"Oh, nothing. Just saw something weird outside. Where's Otus?"

"He's still at the library doing god knows what."

I smile, holding up a brown paper bag. "Well, I've got food."

"Nice." She takes the bag, grimacing when she sees what's inside. "It's Chinese."

"Yeah, so? I thought you loved Chinese."

"I did . . . Do. I'm just not feeling it now." Charlie smiles, shaking it off. "Probably nothing."

"I can go get something else if you need me to."

"No, it's fine. I'll manage."

Nodding, I take off my coat, freezing as I see the bloody figure of a Temple of God's Time victim staring at me out of the mirror. My body seizes, the very breath in my lungs revolting. I flinch violently, drawing Charlie's gaze, but she says nothing.

Otus flies in through the window and transforms into a man, distracting Charlie and I. Stepping forward, I say, "Hey, you find anything?"

"No gods anywhere."

"No surprise. I've got food."

"Oh, good. I'm starving. It's really hard to catch mice in the daytime."

We all sit to eat, Charlie watching us with a slight look of disgust. "So, what's our plan moving forward?" she says.

"Keep doing what we're doing and hope we find something. Unless you guys have any new ideas?"

"I've been reading some old spellbooks and have a few spells I'd like to try."

"Anything we can help you with?"

"No, it's complicated stuff." Otus raises an eyebrow at Charlie, so she says, "What?"

He shrugs, saying, "Oh, nothing. I was gonna say, I've got a few contacts I can reach out to as well."

Charlie and I look curiously at Otus, Charlie saying, "That's great."

We finish eating in silence before standing to clean up. I awkwardly say, "I'm gonna head to the library. You guys need anything?"

"No, we're good."

"Alright. See ya."

As I prepare to leave, Charlie grabs her books, sitting down to research, but Otus reaches out and touches her shoulder, saying, "Are you alright?"

"Yeah, fine. Why?"

"Nothing, it's just . . . I can sense something different about you. I'm worried, is all."

I sense the anger coming off Charlie as she says, "Well, I'm fine. Totally fine. Don't you have work to do?"

Otus nods, backing off and transforming, flying off. I watch Charlie work for a minute, worried about her. Eventually, I sigh and head to the library.

Outside, I walk down the street toward the library, just breathing in the air and enjoying the walk. I halt; clouds of darkness roll in, darkening the street to twilight. The streetlamps respond to the darkness, turning on. I wander around through the dark, looking for a cause before stopping, my reflection in a Christian bookstore window catching my attention; it's laughing hysterically, independent of me.

Focusing past the reflection, my blood runs cold. In the window is a small statue of Jesus, one that I've seen before.

My reflection changes, becoming the Temple of God's Time mass suicide with that same statue resting behind the altar, covered in blood. The screams of the suicide victims start to echo through my head.

I cover my ears to try and block out the noise, to no avail. Screaming, my eyes turn black as night, darkening my gaze.

The streetlamps start to flicker violently as the darkness thickens.

A priest steps out of the bookstore, staring at me and screaming hysterically. "Demon! Demon!" He pulls out holy water, dowsing me.

My body not my own; it falls still, slowly raising my gaze to stare deep into the priest's soul with the eyes of a monster; no emotion in my face and nothing but black in my eyes. I spit out a little holy water back at the priest.

The priest moans, pissing himself.

Stepping forward, I press a single finger into the center of his forehead, a dark wave traveling down my arm and into his head.

The priest steps back, giggling and raving like a madman. He turns, running out into the street in front of an oncoming car. The already confused driver swerves to avoid the priest, crashing into a power pole. Smoke billows out of the car as the driver scrambles out and opens the backdoor to pull out a baby. She steps clear just as the car explodes.

The fire reflects eerily in my blackened eyes, drowning out everything in my sight. Soon, the fire feels like it's burning my very soul; I look down at my hands to see that they're on fire.

Staring around, I finally realize the fear and chaos I've caused, the horror crippling me. All sound around fades away as I stare deeper into the flames.

Molly's voice echoes in my head, saying, "You're a good man . . . Arien."

A single tear leaks out of the corner of my eye, the fire and darkness leaving me. The darkness in the street recedes until it's full day again.

The priest stops laughing and stares around in shock before rushing to comfort the crying baby and its Mother. He looks up at me, pointing an accusing finger. The crowd of people gathered by the freak events all turn to look at me as the priest shouts, "It was him. Devil! Demon! Be gone!"

Turning away, the tears overwhelm me. I whisper, "I'm sorry," as I flee into an alley. Once safe, I lean against a wall, letting my sobs rack me with full force. Suddenly I remember the only thing had that pulled me out of my trance and saved those people. "Molly."

I disappear in a dark flash, returning to the only family I have.

CHAPTER 56: SKELETONS OF BELIEF

Arien

Appearing in a dark flash, I stumble into Molly's diner, searching for her. Tiffany, a waitress and old friend of Molly's, smiles at me, saying, "Hi, handsome. Would you be needing a table, or would you like a seat at the bar where you can see all the goods?" She leans forward, propping her plump breasts against the counter, her top buttons undone, leaving little to the imagination.

Surprised she doesn't recognize me with my beard, but going along with it, I say, "No . . . thanks. I'm actually here to see Molly."

Licking her lips and leaning closer, she responds, "Oh? There's nothing Molly has that I don't have better."

Molly walks out of the kitchen, freezing when she sees me. She rushes over, grabbing Tiffany's shoulders and hissing, "Tiff, stop bothering him and button-up your shirt."

Tiffany lets Molly button up her shirt, shivering as her hand brushes her boobs. "Oh, Molly. Buy me dinner first."

"Shut up, Tiff."

"You're no fun." Tiffany glances back at me, saying, "How come you bagged such a hottie?"

"It's not like that."

"Oh? Well, I've told you before, if you ever get tired of being a virgin, let me know. I can show you a few things."

"Really, shut up, Tiff." Tiffany traces a finger along Molly's cheek, walking away. Molly turns to me, grabs my hand, and says, "Come on." She drags me into the backroom before continuing, "You can't let people see you. You know that. That beard's probably the only thing saving you right now." Once we're alone, she turns back to me, gasping slightly at the sight of the tears filling my eyes. "Oh, Arien." She pulls me into a hug, saying, "What's wrong?"

I just sob into Molly's shoulder for a moment, letting it all go. Eventually, my tears subside, so I can say, "I've been seeing things." I have to pause for a second, the emotions threatening to overwhelm me again, but I proceed anyway, "I've been seeing Him. Jesus."

Molly pulls back to stare into my eyes. "What?"

Looking away in shame, I say, "I've seeing visions of Jesus. He just keeps telling me to trust him."

Molly smiles slightly; the skeletons of her belief that have been clawing to regain dominance have finally been confirmed, reasserting meaning for her life and her past devotion. She pulls me back into a hug, saying, "Maybe God's reaching out to you. Telling you to believe. I've been forced to believe the Greek gods are real because of what I've seen, but I've read the Bible too many times to believe that Jesus is evil. Maybe he wants to help you. Whether or not Christianity is true, Jesus was a good man. He did too many good deeds for him not to be. I have to believe that, so my life doesn't become a waste. From what you said, Kronos is possessing him, right? I think He's reaching out to help from underneath Kronos's control."

Rejecting this idea, my belief threatening to become skeletons if she's right, I respond, "I can't accept that."

"Why not?" She says, pulling back, confused.

"Christianity has condoned so many evil things for thousands of years. There's monsters in the Bible that we put up as heroes. No good man could start all that."

"I believe that every religion has skeletons in its closet. Things that they'd rather forget. But that doesn't make the good things they've done unimportant or irrelevant. It doesn't make any religion false. Humanity is flawed. Belief isn't. You can't tell me Zeus has always done right. Even the Temple of God's Time has done some good. And that's the point. We all try to be the best we can be, and if religion helps that, it's not a false religion."

I tense at the mention of the Temple of God's Time, memories of horror flooding me. Finally admitting my past, I ask, "Do you remember the Temple's suicide?"

Molly shivers, pulling back as she thinks about it. "That was the worst thing to ever happen here. Everybody lost somebody. We still haven't recovered."

"Do you know if I was there? I don't remember it. Just what people have told me."

"I don't think so. Why?"

"I see it in my visions too. It feels like it was somehow my fault. If my visions are from Jesus, why would a good man make me see that?" She turns away, embarrassed, so I continue, "And now the visions aren't enough. It doesn't end there. The last vision of him I had led to something horrible. I drove a priest mad, nearly killed a baby, and brought darkness to a whole street." Molly gasps in horror, pulling my tears out again. She bites her lip, pity overwhelming her fear; she pulls me into a hug again, letting me sob into her shoulder. I mumble, "I'm a monster. I'm too dangerous to be around."

"It's not your fault."

"Then who's is it?" Molly remains silent; she doesn't have an answer. I wait for a second, my tears subsiding enough for me to say, "How can I fight this?"

"I'll be here for you, always." Molly thinks for a moment before pulling back as an idea comes to her. "Do you know the scripture, '*Through the valley of death*' from Psalms?"

I raise an eyebrow, confused. "Yeah."

"Anytime you feel another fit coming on, I want you to quote it over and over until you regain control. I think it'll help."

I turn away to think, interrupted before I can respond by the door chime ringing. Tiffany calls from the front, "Molly, I need you."

"Be right out." Molly looks back at me, saying, "I've got to go. You gonna be alright for a minute?"

"I'm actually gonna head out."

"You sure?"

"Yeah. You've helped a lot."

Molly nods slowly, deciding to let me go. "Homeless Harry is out back today, and he'll definitely recognize you, so you should hurry through the front without anyone seeing you."

"Oh, I miss Harry. How is he?"

"Depressed since you left. You were his only friend." She smiles slightly before leading me back to the main diner, where she hugs me one last time, saying, "Goodbye."

"Bye."

Molly goes to help a customer as Tiffany walks up to me, smiling and saying, "You leaving so soon, hot stuff?"

"Fraid so."

"Why don't you stay? I can take you to the back too, if you like."

I look down, embarrassed. "I'm fine, thanks."

"You sure?" She reaches out, grabbing my arm before her eyes go distant. Turning, she walks away without seeing me anymore. I sigh, running my fingers through my hair, heading for the door.

I stop, rooted to the spot in horror; the woman who got away, Anna just walked into the diner, froze, and stared open-mouthed at me. "Sam?" I gently grab her arm, dragging her outside and around the corner where no one can see us. She pulls against me, screaming, "Ow, you're hurting me."

Letting her go, I turn to stare at Anna; struggling to keep my emotions in check, I manage to say, "I'm sorry. I'm not gonna hurt you. We just couldn't talk where anyone could hear."

"What are you talking about? How are you here? How are you alive? I mean, I went to your funeral."

I start pacing, lost in thought. "I knew coming back here was a bad idea."

"It was you that I saw a few weeks ago. Wasn't it?"

Stopping, I turn back to Anna, shocked. "What? You saw me?"

"Yeah, you were riding a motorcycle through town."

"I thought my beard and hat would throw people off."

She averts her eyes, saying, "Not me. Not after what we . . . Ah."

"How am I supposed to fix this? Huh? Now that you've seen me."

"How are you here?"

I hesitate for a moment, deciding to trust. "We should go somewhere quieter."

There's only one place that makes sense for us to go, back to where it had all ended the day she forgot me. We walk in silence through town, avoiding people, until we reach Molly's family farm, where we climb a fence and turn to watch a pair of horses prancing in a field.

Without turning to me, Anna says, "Now, we're alone. What the hell is going on?"

Sighing, I run my fingers through my hair. "There are things about me that are completely mad, and I don't fully believe them. Some things, you saw in me before I even did."

"How do you mean?" She says, her brow furrowed.

I sigh again, bracing myself to say, "Did you ever love me?"

Her body tenses, confused, and embarrassed. "I don't know. Maybe. But one day it felt like you'd disappeared to me. From me. It's almost like I saw right through you. I can't really explain it. And I think I treated you horribly because of it. I'm sorry for that." She finally looks at me, worried. "Is that what this is about? Is that why you tried to . . .?"

"No, not at all. It's not your fault. Not what happened or how you treated me. There was more going on that you didn't even realize. There's something inside of me that drives people away."

"No, don't think like that. That's not true. Your perfect woman is out there."

"No, no, hold on. That something makes me dangerous. I get people close to me hurt, so it's better this way. People are better off without me."

Anna suddenly realizes something, wrapping her arm around me in comfort. "Is this about suicide? Because that's never an option. Too many people love you."

Surprised that she can still see me, I stare down at her arm, tears threatening at the corner of my eyes. "It is, to a certain extent, about that, but I'll never be brave enough to do it myself. I want to, but I can't."

"Is it my fault?"

"No, it's so much more than that. I have a destiny to do something great, but my inner darkness and madness are too strong to be let to continue."

"What do you mean?"

My fist tightens, and my breath thins, admitting my pain is causing me agony. "I faked my death and ran to leave it all behind. To find a life worth living . . . and a death worth dying."

Anna snuggles up next to me, whispering, "You've always had a life worth living. I'll always be your friend, no matter how bad the darkness gets."

I sigh, accepting my path. "I know what I have to do."

Anna turns her deep brown eyes to stare up at me; I nearly lose myself and my will into their swirling, stark beauty. She says, "What do you have to do?"

Lifting her chin, I gently kiss her.

Anna's eyes go distant as if she can't see me anymore. She mumbles something, getting off the fence and walking away.

I jump off the fence to watch her go. "Goodbye. You'll forget for now, but you'll always have a place in my heart."

I disappear in a dark flash.

CHAPTER 57: MOTHERHOOD

Charlie

Flecks of discolored vomit splash out of the toilet; my stomach revolts at the sight, making me throw up again. I hear the hotel door open but am too weak to stand and shut the bathroom door. Arien walks into the bathroom and stops, looking down at me in surprise. "Charlie?" He rushes forward, pulling my hair back from my face and saying, "Are you OK?"

Trying to laugh, I say, "I think it was that damned Chinese food."

"I thought you weren't going to eat it."

"I was lazy and hungry so . . ." I'm interrupted by another spout of vomiting. When it subsides, I turn slightly to look at Arien. "Where were you all night?"

His eyes refusing to meet mine, he says, "I was at the library."

"It closed at 9 so you could have only been there for a few hours before you had to . . ." Vomiting interrupts me again.

Stroking my back, he clarifies, "I broke back in to keep working."

"You find anything?"

"No. You?"

"Just the inside of my stomach."

"Right. Sorry." The vomiting stops, I wait for the next bout, but it doesn't come. Checking me, Arien asks, "You good?"

"I think so." I lean back against the wall, finally relaxing after a night of pain.

Once I'm settled, Arien looks around, saying, "Where's Otus?"

"Don't know. He left when you did and hasn't been back."

Arien takes out his phone to text Otus. "I'll text him. We need a new plan." I struggle to my feet with his help. I stand steady for a moment, making sure I'm good before taking another step. He asks again, "You good?"

"Yeah, I just need to lay down."

Helping me to one of the beds, Arien tucks me in before sitting in a chair to start polishing the Aegis.

I try not to look, but the face of the Aegis unsettles me, reminding me of my Father, curdling my stomach, and threatening another wave of nausea. "Can you not do that? Sorry, it just freaks me out."

Arien glances down at the Aegis, nods, and puts it down. "Sorry. It just calms me."

Otus crashes through the open window as an owl, transforming into a man. Arien and I both stand, worried. "Otus, what's wrong?"

"I'm being followed."

Drawing his bear-bone-knife and picking up the Aegis, Arien turns to the window as I draw a roman short sword from my purse. A large golden bird flies up and lands on the window sill. We stare at it, realizing it's made of metal. "What, the hell?"

The bird goes rigid, its jaw dropping, revealing a speaker; Hephaestus's voice echoes out, "I have found Hera. She is a Lamaze instructor in Tokyo. Details are carried within." A flash drive pops out of the bird's stomach, dropping to the floor. "I have already spoken to her, and she has agreed to help. This message will self-destruct in 10 seconds."

We stare at each other, confused. Suddenly, Otus dives at the bird, transforming into an owl and flying it high into the sky, dropping it.

The bird explodes harmlessly in the air.

Otus flies back in, transforming and sitting on the bed. Arien shakes his head and says, "He must' be a Tom Cruise fan."

Shrugging, Otus responds, "Or he really doesn't like us. He probably hoped it would hurt us."

"That too." Leaning down, Arien picks up the flash drive and plugs it into his computer. A moment later, he reports his findings, "Everything's here. Hera's even put out some magic to guide us in."

"Aright. You guys ready?"

Arien looks up at me, a question in his eyes. "You don't need to come if you don't feel up to it."

"No, I feel fine now."

I feel Otus giving me a curious look as Arien nods, saying, "OK. Let's go."

We grab our stuff before holding hands and disappearing in a dark flash.

***

Arien, Otus, and I flash into a dark Tokyo alley. A homeless man stares at us in shock; ignoring his palpable fear, Arien turns to him, saying, "Oh, sorry. Do you speak English? Do you know where the Lamaze studio is?"

The homeless man backs away, shaking his head, and screaming in Japanese.

Otus steps forward and smiles at the man, speaking to him in perfect Japanese. The man slowly calms down, talking to Otus for a minute. When they finish talking, Otus takes off his jacket, handing it to the man. The homeless man nods in thanks, walking away.

Otus turns to meet our shocked stares. "What? It was a long 2 thousand years."

Arien shakes his head, saying, "Glad you're on the team. What'd you say to him?"

Smiling, Otus says, "That we're filming a movie and what he saw was a visual effect. The studio is just up the road a little."

He leads the way out of the alley to the studio where Hera is teaching a Lamaze class as we walk in. "You're just in time, we're about to start."

Hera walks over to us as Arien quickly shoves the Aegis into a corner behind our bags, saying, "Oh, we're not here for class."

"Don't be silly, of course, you are. You're a pregnant couple here for my American military class, right?" Before we can answer, Hera grabs Arien and me, dragging us into the class. "Now, if all the men will sit cross-legged and all the women lay with their heads in their partner's laps." Arien and I look at each other, eventually shaking our heads and complying with Hera's instructions. "Good. Now, ladies bring your heels up to your bottoms and spread your knees. Letting your vaginas blossom like flowers." I hear Otus smirking from the doorway as Hera continues, "Now, men, please massage your partner's shoulders. Ladies, we're going to start with some breathing exercises. Take a deep breath in. Hold it. And out."

Arien massages my shoulders, helping me relax and breathe along with the others.

Otus

My enjoyment of watching Charlie and Arien's torment is broken by my ringing phone. I discreetly step out of the studio to answer it. "We found Hera. We're told she's willing enough, but we'll still need Intel to find the others."

I wait for a response before saying, "That's great. Can you send Hermes to deliver the news after this is cleared up? The others may start to get suspicious. And Arien's still not ready to trust you, or any gods yet."

Charlie

Hera cleans up the studio as her students leave. Once we're alone, Arien walks to her and says, "Hello."

"Hi, did you enjoy the class?"

"We didn't actually come for the class."

"I know why you're here, but you needed the class, even still." Arien raises an eyebrow at Hera, so she continues, "Hephaestus sent you, yes? He told me to expect you. My divinity is with a cow herder in Denmark. A few miles south of the town of Vojens."

"Why are you so eager to help us? And why didn't you just send us straight there first?"

"I agreed to help because of all the crying children in the world. I hope, as a god, I can do more to soften their tears then I can as a mere mortal. I wasn't that great as a god before, but this mortal coil has given me perspective." Hera turns to look at me, seemingly staring into my very soul. "And I had you come here because of you." She reaches out to stroke my cheek.

Lost in her soothing gaze, I say, "Me?"

"Maybe I can stop men and women from getting taken advantage of when I'm a god again."

I look down in shame, unable to take the pity in her eyes. "How did you . . .?"

"I can see the pain of a child. I'm the goddess of Motherhood. I can also tell that you needed this class today."

My head snaps back up, horrified of her meaning. "What?"

"You bare Dionysus's child."

I gasp as Arien and Otus stare, dumbfounded. Trying to stop my head from connecting the dots, I say, "No, no. That's not possible. It's too soon to know, and we were both women."

"It's a demigod turned god, irradiated by Dionysus's divine light when he ascended in front of you, so you'll have an accelerated pregnancy. As for the women aspect, magic is sometimes unnatural."

Tears threaten at the corner of my eyes; remembering my morning sickness and my skipped period, I'm forced to flee from the studio, running from what I know to be the truth.

Arien

I go to follow Charlie, but Hera reaches out to grab my arm, saying, "Let her go. She needs time. Then, she'll need you more than ever. You're not the Father, but you shall be as the Father to this child. And the destiny of the child shall surpass the Father's." I stare at her in complete confusion, so she continues, "You should go get my divinity and leave her be. You won't need her. There's no monsters or anything." Hera goes to her desk, pulling out a cow pin and a parchment; handing them to me, she says, "I hear you can sense divinities within Erebus? Just get to Vojens, and you should be able to sense it. Find the cow herder and tell him, '*all love begins and ends there. With Mothers.*' He'll take you to my divinity. You'll need to sing from this parchment to release it into the pin.

I nod before glancing outside, hoping to see Charlie.

Hera reaches out to squeeze my hand in comfort. "She'll be alright. I'll look after her. Go."

Nodding again, I grab Otus's hand and disappear in a dark flash.

Charlie

Storming into an alley, I scream into the sky, "Dionysus, get your ass down here." After nothing happens, I take a deep breath to calm myself, praying:

"Dionysus Perikionios, hear my pray'r, who mad'st the house of Cadmus once thy care, with matchless force, his pillars twining round, when burning thunders shook the solid ground, in flaming, founding torrents borne along, propt by thy grasp indissolubly strong. Come mighty Dionysus to these rites inclin'd, and bless thy suppliants with rejoicing mind."

CHAPTER 58: THE IMPOSSIBLE CHILD

The Litai dangle from the ceiling, Charlie's prayer echoing through their heads. They scream and thrash, lights blazing round them. Koios rushes in, staring up at them in awe. He reaches out to rest his hand on one's head, Charlie's prayer echoing through his arm to his head. Listening to it, he smiles and says, "Oh, the pain and fear here. Hmm. Delicious." Tracing the prayer back to its source, he continues, "Where are you?"

Darkness fills the room as Koios projects his thoughts into a physical image that he alone can see. Out of the darkness, a ghostly version of the Tokyo alley can be seen with Charlie praying in a loop. *"Come mighty Dionysus to these rites inclin'd, and bless thy suppliants with rejoicing mind."*

Koios's smile widens, letting the image fade. "Thanks for the tip."

In the neighboring asylum cell, Iapetus puts on a medical mask; turning to his bound and gagged patient, he says, "You know, I miss the days when lobotomies were legal. I invented them, you know. Well, a few of them. It's become more of an umbrella term now. Lucky for us, I continued my experiments to perfect them, so when humanity eventually comes back to the practice, it will be perfect. But, until then, I must hide away and do my research with the likes of you." A gruesome smell wrinkles his nose. "I really should have had you bathed first, but no matter."

Iapetus picks up his drill and approaches the thrashing man, continuing, "This is an old one, but a classic. I drill into your skull and pour ethanol in. It'll destroy the fibers connecting your frontal lobe from the rest of your brain, thereby curing you of all ailments." Turning on the drill, he pauses to stare into his patient's eyes. "You think that's a bit basic, huh? Well, you may be right. I have a new method that's not quite ready yet. Do you think it's time to test it?"

Nodding as if he got a response, Iapetus picks up a shock therapy device. "I know this looks like an ordinary shocker, but it's not. I'm trying to perfect the voltage to do something amazing." He takes off his mask to sit next to his patient and parade his invention. "I've come to learn that human emotions are the root of all your ills. We could make a truly perfect world if emotions could be eradicated, and that's what I'm trying to do here. With the right chemicals and voltage, I can permanently kill all emotions in a human mind, while also disabling nerve endings, so pain is a thing of the past. Unfortunately, my other test subjects had severe scarring, so if you survive, you may need to wear a helmet for the rest of your life. I'm also working on a helmet that will be able to maintain the emotional dampening in case of a malfunction. What do you think? You want to try it? Maybe you'll survive."

Iapetus goes to put on his mask but stops as Koios walks in and says, "Sorry, sir. I've got something."

Glancing between Koios and his patient, Iapetus whines, "Can't you see I'm busy?"

"It'll only take a moment."

Sighing and putting down his tools, he leans in to whisper to the patient. "I'll be back." He playfully bites the patient's ear before walking to Koios. "What is it?"

"A prayer from the girl just came in. I know where they are."

"Are you sure this time? You've led us round the bend a few times. That incident in Turkey wasn't pretty."

"They were there, but they can teleport. I think they'll stay in the same place this time. The girl's crying in an alley alone. They're not leaving anytime soon."

"Very well. Hyperion is still injured, so you'll need to go." Koios nods, turning to go but stopping when Iapetus grabs his arm to say, "If you fail to capture them again, I'll send you lunar-side, but not before I get a taste first."

Koios shivers as Iapetus licks his lips. "I understand."

"Good." Iapetus lets Koios leave, turning back to his patient, and saying, "Where were we, sexy?"

Charlie

Rocking myself back-and-forth, I sob into my arms. From above me, Dionysus says, "Hey, Charlie." I look up, wiping the tears from my eyes to clearly see Dionysus.

I leap to my feet, screaming, "You bastard." I start punching him repeatedly; he just stands and takes it, unhurt. "Why did you have to do that to me?" Leaning forward, I sob into his chest.

"What's going on?"

"I could get over and bare that we had sex because you were a woman, but that's not true so. . ."

"What are you talking about?"

"I'm pregnant."

Dionysus stumbles back in shock. "What? No, that's not possible. Have you slept with anyone else?"

"You know you're the only man I've been with. Willingly, at least."

Pacing, he says, "No, no. This can't be happening."

"You think it's bad for you. I swore to never sleep with a man, then that choice was taken from me, and I got pregnant. This ruins my whole life."

Dionysus stops pacing, turns to me, and says, "I know, and I am so sorry. It shouldn't have been possible. But I am a god. I may have accidentally imbued the toy with some of . . . Well, my essence."

My tears turn to rage, putting fire in my voice, "Your essence?" Drawing my knife, I repeatedly stab Dionysus in the gut. This hurts him no more than my fists had, but he lets me get it all out.

My thrusts slow as my tears well again.

"I am so sorry."

I lean in and sob into his chest again.

CHAPTER 59: INTO THAT GOOD NIGHT

Arien

Otus and I wander through the field until we find a cow herder just sitting and watching his herd. I awkwardly wave and say, "Hello." The cow herder ignores us, so I lean in to whisper into his ear. *"All love begins and ends there. With Mothers."* He finally acknowledges me, standing and leading us to his nearby barn.

Inside the barn, we find a mother cow nursing her young calf. I look to the cow herder, who nods, giving us confirmation and consent. Handing Otus the parchment and pin, he kneels in front of the cow and places the pin in the hay, starting to sing off the parchment in ancient Greek.

The melody echoes through the barn with magical sincerity, unknown instruments joining Otus in the song. I smile, breathing in the serenity.

Otus leans forward, pressing his forehead against the cow's head as the song ends.

The cow moans, a bright light passing from her into the pin. The cow seems to age instantly, losing her color, fading away until all life has left her. The calf rises to its feet and wobbles over to its Mother as the cow herder kneels to hug the cow's body.

Tears in his eyes, Otus says, "We need to bury her."

"OK." I roll up my sleeves to help the cow herder, grabbing a shovel.

Charlie

I'm once again alone in the alley, clutching my stomach, when the pendant around my neck starts to hum. Reaching up to grab it, I turn to see a Titan standing behind me, a giant sword strapped to his back. I gasp, recognizing him. "Koios."

"Pleasure to meet you. I do so love your prayers. The ones about your Father are particularly entertaining."

Reaching into my bag and pulling out an alchemy bomb, I throw it, a plume of gas enveloping us both. I roll behind Koios, slashing at the back of his knee with my short sword.

He grunts, falling to his knees, the poison on my blade infecting him. He says, "What is that?"

"The blood of Tartarus. Stings, doesn't it?"

"How did you . . .?" He moans softly, preventing him from speaking.

"I know a guy." I go for another blow, but Koios rolls clear. He grows to the towering height of a giant before kicking me in the chest, sending me flying.

Koios waves his massive hand to clear the fog from my bomb, shrinking back to his human form. "Your cheap tricks and poisons are no match for a Titan." He kneels next to me, holding me down. "Stay still. This will hurt more if you struggle." He presses a finger into the center of my forehead; both our eyes roll up into our heads.

***

There's nothing but blackness; all I feel are my thoughts and emotions; until, now connected to him, I can sense Koios smile, flashes of my past amusing him. These memories strengthen, engulf my view, and swirl past, all tangible and deadly, and all phantoms, unable to be changed.

The first memory blows past like breath on a mirror; I try to touch, to feel my last moment of happiness, but the past is gone and cold. Deni pushed me firmly against the back wall of the closet, thrusting into me; driving deep for the beast residing in my screams.

A new memory takes hold, a memory of when I thought my world had ended. Recently returned from Arien's home, I heard moaning echoing from the bedroom. I walked slowly toward the door; opening it, the light from the hall spilled over Susan, naked, and getting pounded from behind by a man hidden in shadow.

Susan gasped when she saw me. "Charlie!"

I turned, unable to see the betrayal, running away as fast as I could.

This memory of betrayal evaporates, leaving behind flashes of my time of wonder held within Medea's arms. The flashes end, and I see her death. A scream was torn from my throat as Medea was impaled through the chest from behind. She spit up blood before collapsing, Rachel standing behind her.

I'm suddenly returned to the Tokyo alley, but it's also a memory. Drawing my knife, I repeatedly stabbed Dionysus in the gut. This hurt him no more than my fists had, but he let me get it all out.

My thrusts slowed as my tears welled again.

"I am so sorry," he said, his soul as bared and broken as mine.

I leaned in and sobbed into his chest again.

My tears continued, but the memory becomes distant, disconnected, as Koios's laughter echoes through my head. He says, "Ooh, this one looks really fun."

We're sucked into another memory, this one of 15 years ago, the day I died.

I'm once again a child, no older than seven, cowering from my Father, who's beating my Mother with his belt. He sent her to the ground with a punch to the gut; Mom gasped and huddled up as he approached to continue the beating, yelling, "You'll never forget the beer again, will you?"

Sobbing, Mom struggles to say, "No, Mason. I'm sorry. Never again."

"Good. But I need you to remember this, so a little longer, I think."

He raised his belt to strike again, but I leapt between my parents, screaming, "Please, daddy. Stop. You're hurting her."

The belt came crashing down, sending me flying. He roared in rage, barely managing to say, "Don't interrupt me when I'm disciplining! Understand, girl?"

I sobbed, cradling my throbbing head. He walked over and picked me up by the front of my shirt, lifting me to stare directly into his eyes, his beer-ridden breath stinging my cheek. He whispers, "I said, do you understand?"

I nodded vigorously through my tears, but he cuffed my ear, saying, "I can't hear you."

"Yes, daddy. I understand."

"I don't think you do. I think you require a further lesson."

Turning to leer momentarily at Mother, he waited for her to stop him, but she only cowered away, silent. Accepting her obedience, he dragged me into the bedroom, slamming the door. The memory goes black, but the sound of my childlike screams still echoed through the darkness.

My mind crippled by the memory, I barely notice another forming around my sight. My teenage-self sat across from the witch, Morgan le Fay, telling her the story of my rape. "I want to be like you, so that never happens to me again. Never helpless again."

Morgan spoke with a voice akin to an old oak that long since should have rotted away, yet clinging to existence, "And you've sworn off men because of this?"

I looked down in shame, saying, "Yes."

"I will help you so no man or woman can ever treat you like that again."

Koios's voice again interrupts the memory, saying, "Enough. Where is Arien?"

The final memory is of meeting Hera in the Lamaze studio; Arien raised an eyebrow at Hera, so she continued, "Hephaestus sent you, yes? He told me to expect you. My divinity is with a cow herder in Denmark. A few miles south of the town of Vojens."

***

We return to the alley in the present, the echoes of my memories still bouncing around in my head but no longer drowning out the now. Koios pulls back, releasing me from my past; my eyes return to normal as I roll over to vomit into the street.

His eyes distant, almost dreamy, Koios says, "A god, here? This is far better than I could have dreamed. Two birds with one stone."

He presses his finger against my head again, everything goes black; I fall over, losing consciousness.

CHAPTER 60: DARK DISEASE

Arien

Resting against my shovel for a moment, I wipe the sweat from my brow, basking in the sun's warmth, reminding me of home. Drawn from my reverie, I glance down at the nearly finished grave for the mother cow who had given her life for the future we hope to build. Leaning into the work, we soon complete covering the grave. Turning to Otus, I say, "Is that good?"

"Yeah, we can go."

As we prepare to leave, the cow herder approaches me, staring into my eyes. "Do not forget your Mother. She gave all for you, and you shall need her again before the day is done. You will never be truly alive or fit for life so long as you shun your Mother's love."

My face constricts in pain, rejecting everything he's saying. I'm incapable of loving the monster that bore me. I struggle to say, "My Mother never gave a damn about me."

Grabbing Otus's hand, we disappear in a dark flash.

***

We appear in a dark flash; I glance around to see Charlie and Hera standing behind the front counter. Approaching them, I say, "Hey, guys. We got it." I freeze, noticing their stiff bodies and blank expressions. "What, the hell?" I hurry over to see if they're OK while Otus looks around for a threat. Tapping Charlie's face, I try to wake her, saying, "Charlie? What's going on? Wake up."

A deep voice behind me fills my heart with ice, burning my soul, and filling me with fear. "I'm afraid that won't wake them."

I turn to see a Titan walking in through the back door. Trying not to show my fear, I say, "Who are you? What have you done to them?"

"I've taken them from you. Completely." The Titan walks to Charlie and runs his fingers through her hair. "She's so pretty. I know you've thought so. I hear all of your prayers. And you know what, she fancies you too. Just a little."

Anger replacing fear, I growl, "Don't you touch her."

Grinning, the Titan responds, "Why don't you stop me?" He strokes Charlie's hair for a moment longer before stopping. "Because you know you can't. You don't know what I've done to them and if it can be undone. Until then, you're in my power."

"You have no power over me."

"Don't I?" He turns to Hera and Charlie, saying, "Raise your right arm." Charlie and Hera follow all instructions given them. "Now, your left. Now both. Do a jumping jack. Spin around. *'Ayy, Macarena.'* Ha." Charlie and Hera start dancing the Macarena while the Titan claps, giggling with childlike glee.

"Just stop!"

He raises his hand, and the women stop dancing. Leaning in close, he stares into my eyes, whispering, "I have complete power over you because you care about them. Bad move to care. You never can win when you care."

"Please."

The Titan cocks his head as if seeing something in my eye. "Fascinating. There's a strength or power inside of you that your prayers don't convey." I stare back in confusion as he continues, "You know, I've been a step behind you for so long. I always get just within reach, then you're on the other side of the world. But that's done because I finally have you. Your friend prayed to Dionysus, and oh the pain and hatred in that prayer. So delicious." He moans, licking his lips, and letting his eyes roll back in pleasure. "I knew this was my chance because she wasn't going anywhere till she got an answer."

Suddenly, I recognize the Titan. "You're Koios."

Smiling broadly, Koios says, "I'm impressed. No one ever recognizes me over my more famous brothers. I'm flattered."

"But you're the Titan of the mind. How do you read prayers?"

"The Litai spirits are quite useful. They get the prayers and I read them. Quite ingenious of me, if I do say so myself. But Iapetus stole the credit for that as well." He shakes his head, walking over to Otus to distract himself. "Anyway. What should I do with this friend?"

"Don't touch him."

"What? Like this?' Koios taps Otus's forehead, making him go stiff and blank like the others.

Lost and without hope, I say, "Let them go." Grabbing the Aegis, I tilt the face to show Koios; he just laughs loudly when he sees it.

"I'm the Titan of the mind, and fear is only in the mind. Your trinket won't affect me."

"No, but maybe this will."

Picking up Charlie's discarded sword, I charge.

Koios smiles, stepping back to avoid my first swing. Screaming, I swing again and again to no avail.

Switching from the sword, I use the Aegis like a battering ram, slamming it into Koios, sending him off balance while I slice the Titan's ankle with the sword.

Koios stumbles back, growling through the pain. "Enough!"

Growing to a height of 25 feet, he kicks me, sending me flying into the wall. Following, he yells, "You're no match for a Titan, even with all your power." I moan, trying to get up. Fed up with my entertainment value, Koios says, "Stay down, or they die."

Charlie and Otus draw knives, pressing them against their throats, while Hera breaks a bottle and prepares to slit her wrists with the shards.

"They will die unless you yield."

I hesitate for a moment, so Koios waves his hand at Hera. She slits her wrists, starting to bleed out, her expression still blank.

Screaming, I say, "Alright, I yield."

Smiling down at me, Koios coos, "Very good."

Hera continues to bleed out, but my friends all drop their weapons. I stand, unarmed, and hands raised. "I surrender."

Koios walks up to me and grabs me by the throat, pressing me against the wall. "You know who I am, what I am. I was always going to kill your friends, and you knew that. But you gave yourself up anyway. Like I was saying, caring leads to burying." He taps my forehead to take control; both our eyes roll up into our heads, my vision darkening, and Koios's body tensing suddenly.

***

Koios and I are standing alone in the endless darkness; he stumbles back in fear, saying, "No, not him, not here."

I smile down at Koios, lost in the madness of Erebus, my eyes black as sin. "Caring doesn't mean burying when you have the strength to change it. I have the strength, the power to make a difference."

"This is impossible. He's supposed to be crippled and useless." Tortured screaming echoes through the endless darkness.

"I think he remembers you."

Iapetus's voice claws through the cacophony of screaming to say, "Seed planted in the dark."

"No, please stop," Koios screams, curling up in fear as the fog forms into hands, grasping for him and tearing at his flesh.

I crouch down in front of Koios, lending no aid, just smiling at him. "Not made for bliss, or Utopia as I've heard."

He whimpers in pain and fear, blood starting to pour out of his eyes and ears. "Please, make it stop."

I reach out and touch Koios's forehead with a single finger; his eyes turn black as mine.

***

We're back in the studio, both touching each other's heads, our eyes black as night.

The lights flicker violently as the shadows deepen. Koios screams, his eyes melting before he collapses, laughing hysterically in complete insanity.

Charlie, Otus, and Hera collapse, released from Koios's control.

I pull the mighty sword off Koios's back, swinging it to take the Titan's head off with one clean stroke. The others stare at me in shock as I pick up the still laughing head.

Turning my blackened gaze over to my friends, I disappear in a dark flash with the head.

***

Appearing in the darkness, I drop the head and fall to my knees, reaching up to clutch my head as manic screaming echoes through it.

I vomit blood, curling up, a seizure taking me.

All sound fades, leaving only Molly's voice ringing through the pain, saying, *"Yea, though I walk through the valley of the shadow of death, I will fear no evil: for thou art with me; thy rod and thy staff they comfort me."*

Fighting through my clenched jaw, I say, *"Yea, though I walk . . ."* I spit out blood from biting my tongue before forcing myself to continue, *". . . through the valley of the shadow of death, I will fear no evil: for thou art with me; thy rod and thy staff they comfort me."*

The blackness in my eyes slowly fades.

Part 7:

ARES

CHAPTER 61: STRANDED

Arien

A car whizzes by, breaking through the shrouds of consciousness, awakening me. I open my eyes, sit up, and stare around, surveying my surroundings; corn and brush are all that can to be seen. Crawling out of the bush I find myself in, I get a better look at the fields of endless corn surrounding me.

I'm alone in the middle of nowhere, with nothing but corn and a solitary road in sight. Shaking my head, I close my eyes, trying to teleport away.

When nothing happens, I open my eyes and stare about, confused. "What, the . . ."

Searching my pockets for my phone and coming up empty, I sigh and turn to stare at the road itself. Pausing for a moment, I decide a direction and start to walk out through the plains.

Another car zips by, ignoring my raised thumb.

After many hours of walking, a town pokes above the horizon, giving me hope.

Charlie

Hera and I work tirelessly to clean the remains of her studio post Koios's attack. Taking a break, I pause, staring down at the bloodstained carpet. Hera walks up behind me, hugs me, and says, "He'll be alright. We'll find him."

Guilt and tears threatening, I respond, "We wouldn't need to if I hadn't led Koios here."

"You couldn't have known they can track prayers. This isn't your fault."

Closing my eyes, I take a deep breath, forcing myself to say, "Then whose is it?" Our conversation is interrupted as Otus walks in through the backdoor.

Hera turns to him and asks, "How'd it go?"

His eyes rolling, full of sarcasm, Otus grunts, "Have you ever tried to fit a 25-foot-tall Titan into a human sized incinerator, especially with it still thrashing? Not easy, but it's done."

"Mrs. Sakurai will be very confused about the mountain of ash left behind, but she shouldn't ask questions. You'd be surprised how many strange things happen at a morticians."

Going to the front counter, Otus takes a health food drink to re-hydrate. He gags and grimaces when he tastes it. "What is this stuff?"

"Pureed Caesar salad with hummus."

"That is disgusting."

"My clients requested it. I don't really understand it either. There's PowerAde in the cabinet below."

"Thanks." Otus pulls out the other drink, swallowing it greedily. I sense them both pausing when they notice that I'm still staring at the bloodstain. Otus walks up beside me, saying, "We're going to find him. No matter what. It's what we're good at. Tracking people down."

No hope left, I say, "What if he doesn't want to be found?"

"Why wouldn't he want to be?"

"Because he's angry at me."

Otus grabs my shoulders, forcing me to look at him. "He has no reason to be angry. You did nothing wrong."

"I nearly got everyone killed, just because I couldn't deal with this as an adult." I cradle my stomach, revolted by it and what it's wrought.

Otus glances down at my stomach before staring up into my eyes. "It's going to be alright. We're all here for you."

The sobs take me; Otus pulls me in for a hug, holding me tight until my tears subside. I manage to sniffle out, "How are we gonna find him, Otus?"

I feel him staring off, just as lost as me. "I don't know."

Hera steps forward, saying, "If I may, if I had my powers, I could help look for him."

Otus and I pull back from each other to look at Hera, Otus responding, "Of course." He pulls out the cow pin and hands it to Hera.

We are forced to avert our eyes as Hera is engulfed in a pillar of white fire. She's lifted off the ground, spread-eagled in the center of the burning pillar.

The fire and light fades, leaving Hera standing on the ground, unharmed. "I'll start looking for him. You have my word, I will do everything within my power to bring him back to you."

I nod in thanks as she disappears.

Sighing, I walk over to the Aegis and Arien's bear-bone-knife, kneeling down to hold them. Crouching next to me, Otus tentatively says, "Charlie, how much do you remember while Koios had control over us?"

"Most of it. But it felt like a dream. Like I knew what was happening, but couldn't do anything about it."

"There's something that Koios said that confused me. He said that you have feelings for Arien. Is that true?"

Letting myself be vulnerable, I sigh and say, "I don't know. It doesn't feel like I have a choice; that someone else made my decision of love for me. Sometimes I think maybe. But I can't. Not after everything that's happened." Shaking my head, I stand. "So, what's our plan? What're we gonna do?"

Otus purses his lips, standing as well. "If he's not still in Erebus, he'll go somewhere familiar. Somewhere in the U.S. for sure. Probably Amber to see Molly."

"Great! Let's go." I start packing our stuff before lifting the Aegis. "How are we gonna get this on a plane?"

"Big suitcase, I guess," he says, shrugging.

"Yeah, good idea." I continue packing and talking to distract myself, "Glad you had us start carrying our passports when we travel. We'd be stranded otherwise."

"Yeah."

I feel Otus's sad eyes following me, but I can't acknowledge them now, not yet.

CHAPTER 62: INNER NELLY

<u>**Arien**</u>

Passing a sign designating the town as Lawrence, Kansas, I walk down the near-deserted main street, staring at the buildings around me. The town looks like it's straight out of the 1950s; old cars, old buildings, old diners, and the few residents I see, dressed in 50's apparel.

Everyone in town suddenly steps outside to stare at me as I pass, with looks from passing curiosity, to outright hatred. I try waving, but they all continue to just stare.

At the end of the road is an old phone booth that I climb into. I dig through my pockets for change but stop when I remember they're empty. Staring at the phone, I scream, hitting the glass.

A tapping of glass comes from behind me. Turning, I see a beautiful young woman standing outside the phone booth. She says, "Yo, idiot. Whatcha doing?"

Stepping out of the booth, I say, "Nothing, I guess."

She raises an eyebrow, appraising my disheveled clothing and messy hair. "Damn. You look like shit."

Glancing down at myself, I laugh, responding, "Well, thanks for noticing."

"Why are you using a phone booth? No one even knows how they work anymore."

"I, ah . . . lost my phone," I say, awkwardly.

"That's rough. Can't imagine losing my phone. I'm Cornelia, but everyone calls me Nelly." Nelly reaches out to shake my hand.

"Arien."

"Arien? That's a funny name."

"So is Nelly."

She laughs loudly, saying, "You right. Here, you can borrow my phone."

Accepting her phone, I try to make a call but stop when I realize there's no signal. "There's no signal."

"What?" Nelly takes the phone back to check, staring at it in confusion. "That's weird. That's never happened before."

"Thanks anyway. It was a pleasure to meet you, Nelly, but I'm gonna go find some food now."

"There's a diner nearby. My treat."

Pausing to think, I again remember I have no money. Nodding, I accept her offer. "I appreciate it. Thank you."

"Of course. Come on."

Nelly leads me around the corner and into the diner where a waitress curls her lip at me, saying, "Sorry, we don't serve your kind here."

Near at a loss for words, I manage to say, "What kind?"

"Homeless."

Nelly steps forward, sticking her finger into the waitress's face, and whispering menacingly, "Back off, Darth Barbie. We're paying customers, so give us a table."

Rolling her eyes, the waitress says, "Whatever. Follow me." She leads us to a table before leaving us alone.

Daggers in her eyes, Nelly watches the waitress walk away, saying, "What a bitch."

Embarrassed and thankful, I say, "I'm not, you know, homeless."

Shrugging and turning to her menu, Nelly responds, "I wouldn't care if you were."

"I just got kinda mugged, basically, and left in the middle of nowhere."

"That's horrible."

"It's not so bad. Gives me an excuse to escape all my problems."

"I get that. So, where do you live? Topeka, I'm guessing."

"Well, nowhere, I guess. I'm not homeless. I just travel a lot for, ah, work. There's no point to getting tied down with how much I travel."

"So, you're rich, then?" Nelly says, brow raised.

Laughing lightly, I say, "No, far from it. I just like what I do, so I put up with it."

"What is it you do?"

"Ah, private investigator, basically. I find missing people."

Nelly tenses suddenly. "Were you working when you got mugged?"

"Yeah. I had just found the woman I was looking for when it happened. Didn't get a chance to finish the job, though."

Relaxing a little, she says, "For a moment, I thought you were looking for me."

My turn to raise my brow, I say, "Why?"

"I'm taking a year off school to travel the country. I didn't tell anyone I was leaving. I just up and left. Trying to see the sights, you know. Breathe in the culture. Trying to meet as many interesting people as I can. Of whom, you are by far the most interesting."

Laughing and taking it as a compliment, I say, "I have my moments. Why'd you decide to leave, if you don't mind? Most people don't up and leave their lives without a reason."

Her gaze wandering sadly, Nelly responds, "Someone very close to me died recently. If I'd have stayed where I was, where everyone pitied me so much, I don't know what I'd have done to myself." Rubbing her wrists, I notice several jagged scars tracing the veins of her arms, matching my own. Suddenly realizing I have a sister in suicide, I listen closely as she continues, "Living on the road is better for me than that."

"I get it. I wish I could do the same."

"Aren't you kinda doing it already?"

"I still need to go back, for my friends. They need me. But I'm afraid of everything that comes with going back."

"Maybe you should let them live their lives. Maybe the world is better off without people like us."

"That's why I keep going. To end it."

Nelly looks at me, confused. "How do you mean?"

"My job, it's going to kill me someday. That's why I do it."

She nods, getting it. "I wish I had a way out like that. A way out while trying to help other people. I can't bring myself to do it myself, so I wander. But I can't keep it up forever." We both stare off in thought for a moment before she whispers, "Do you believe in the afterlife?"

Sighing softly, I say, "I don't know, but I've seen things to lead me to believe there is one."

"That's one reason I haven't done it. Fear of the unknown. Fear keeps me alive. If I were certain it was good, I don't know if I'd be here."

"Maybe that's why we can't know for sure."

"Maybe," she says, tears glistening in her eyes.

"I'm hoping that if there is an afterlife, I get a few points for what I'm trying to do."

"If life means anything, I think it will."

"Let's hope it does.

The waitress returns with food, interrupting our train of conversation. Nelly stares at her burger in confusion, saying, "Oh, we didn't order yet."

Smirking, the waitress says, "We're a burger joint. It's kinda obvious." She walks off before we can respond.

"Well, doesn't look too bad."

"No, it doesn't."

Inspecting her burger, Nelly says, "Let's just hope she didn't spit in it, or anything."

"Oh, why did you have to say that? I don't know if I can eat it now."

Nelly laughs at my discomfort, saying, "I'm sorry. I'm sure it's fine."

Shaking my head with a smile, I take a bite; my mouth full, I struggle to say, "Does this town seem weird to you?"

"What?"

Swallowing to clear my voice, I repeat, "Does this town seem weird to you?"

Smiling broadly, Nelly snarks, "The whole 1950s anti-outsider deal? Yeah. I'm glad I'm not the only one who noticed it."

Finding validation, I quietly exclaim, "It's so weird."

"At my hotel, they didn't even take card. Everything here's cash only. I'm gonna run out before I can leave and find an ATM."

"Maybe they're Amish."

"Or Mormon." We both laugh together before Nelly changes the subject, "Speaking of my hotel, do you think you'd wanna come up and see it when we're done?"

I smile sadly but nod anyway, deciding to take a risk. "Yeah, I'd like that."

Smiling timidly, she mutters, "Great."

We continue eating, the tension strong, both anticipating the end of the meal.

With few more words, we finish, pay, and head up to Nelly's hotel room, where she gently presses me against the door and slowly leans in to softly kiss me. The kiss doesn't end, surprising me; Nelly hasn't lost focus or walked away.

Noticing my tension, she pulls back, asking, "What's wrong?"

Finally accepting this gift, I decide to take advantage of my first chance at physical intimacy. I proudly state, "Nothing's wrong," before pressing in to passionately kiss her. A heat foreign to me builds as we tear off each other's clothes.

I have trouble with Nelly's bra, but she just smiles, whispering, "It's alright. Let me." She removes it to reveal her perfect breasts and hard nipples.

I stare down at them for a moment before tracing my eyes up her supple skin to look deep into her eyes and express, "You're so beautiful."

Nelly smiles, looking away, embarrassed. "Thank you."

Leaning in to kiss her again, I move my lips along her skin to her jaw and up to her ear, gently biting before continuing down her neck to one of her breasts. Nelly moans softly as I take a firm nipple in my mouth, my tongue swirling over the toned ridged.

Picking her up, I carry Nelly to the bed and gently lay her down. I unbutton her jeans, gingerly sliding them off, her slightly moan driving me to go further. She giggles softly as I pull her panties off too.

I'm forced to pause, basking in the almost tangible light of my first pussy; it's ruddy flesh beckoning the primordial nature in me, driving me to enter and bathe in its flowing love.

Smiling, Nelly asks, "You like?"

The beast in me utters, "I like," before kissing her inner thin just above the knee.

Sitting up, Nelly crawls forward to unbutton my jeans, pulling them off, revealing my manhood. She stares at my cock in unabashed wonder. Forcing her gaze to look up into my eyes, she ejaculates, "Wow! Thank you."

Leaning in, I enter her mouth, her head starting to bob against me. I reach down to run my fingers through her hair, moaning softly, fire flowing through my veins.

I shudder suddenly, horror filling me as my spent load leaves me, emptying my will and passion.

Nelly pauses in surprise, swallowing, pulling back, and wiping my seed from her mouth. "Is that it?"

Looking down, ashamed, I confess, "Sorry. I've never done this before."

"Never?"

"No."

Smiling slightly, she pulls me down on top of her. "In that case, I'll give you a minute." She goes to kiss me, but I stop her. Raising an eyebrow, she asks, "What is it?

"I don't really feel comfortable . . . Well, ah, kissing after oral."

Nelly laughs softly, saying, "Seriously? You really are a virgin."

Turning away, I nod slightly. "Sorry. I just don't want to taste myself."

She nods in acceptance, conceding, "Whatever. Then you're gonna warm me up with your fingers."

"OK." Rolling off Nelly, I kiss her breast, reaching down to caress her inviting pussy. Nelly moans softly, her pleasure building.

CHAPTER 63: SEEN HORNS

<u>Charlie</u>

Traffic clears enough for me to cross the road into the airport parking lot where Otus is calling Arien. "Any luck?" I ask, worried.

"No, he still hasn't answered. And I can't get Molly either. What about you?"

"I got a rental car."

"Alright, let's hope he's there."

"Come on." I lead the way back toward the car rental.

<u>Arien</u>

Nelly and I are snuggled up against each other, only partially covered by the sheets. My eyes closed, I feel Nelly move, lifting the sheets to look down at my body. Noticing my erection, she asserts, "You're awake, I see."

Giggling softly, I open my eyes, confirming, "I don't need to be awake to be turned on by you."

She purses her lips, trying not to laugh. "That was pretty bad."

"I know. Not my best line."

We laugh together, snuggling closer. Nelly starts twisting her finger through my chest hair as she thinks. Eventually, she asks, "Arien?"

"Yeah."

"Do you want to come with me?"

Sitting up a little, I stare down at Nelly. "What?"

"I know we haven't known each other long, but I trust you. I told you more about myself last night than I tell anyone. Maybe you can leave your job and we can work through our issues and find a reason to live, together."

It only takes me a moment to think before I agree, "OK."

Nelly sits up to look in my eyes, affirming, "Really?"

Smiling broadly, I say, "Yeah, let's do it."

"Oh, big boy deserves another blowjob for that."

"Big boy, huh?"

"What else do you call the beast that had me screaming all night?" She bites her lip, glancing back down at my crotch.

"Not this time."

Nelly looks away, disappointed. "No?"

"It's your turn."

Turning back, surprised, she gushes, "Really?"

"Yeah."

"OK."

Nelly giggles, laying back to let me crawl under the covers on top of her. She moans and tenses up as I start.

***

We're still buttoning up all our clothes when we walk down the stairs to the lobby. I turn to Nelly, asking, "So, you got a car?"

"Of course, I have a car. What, you think a pretty lady like me feels safe hitchhiking?"

"True."

As we head for the door, I accidentally bump into the mailman. He turns to me, growling, "Hey, watch yourself."

"Sorry, that was my bad."

"Of course, it was your bad. I didn't slam into you. What kinda person does that?"

"Sorry, it really was an accident."

Reacting to the kerfuffle, the hotel manager walks over and intercedes, "Excuse me. Is there a problem here?"

Grabbing me, Nelly says, "No problem, we were just leaving."

The mailman contends, "Yeah, we have a problem. This cunt hit me."

Utterly confused, I retort, "Whoa, whoa. I bumped into you on accident. I didn't hit you."

"Well, the cops will have to determine that, won't they?"

"The cops?"

The manager interrupts, reasoning with the mailman, "Now, hold on. There's no need for that. I can take care of this."

"But . . ."

"It's OK. Go."

Nodding, the mailman leans toward me for the last word, "This isn't over." He turns, leaving as the manager takes a deep breath to compose himself.

Thankful, I turn to the manager, saying, "Thank you for that, sir. It was just a big misunderstanding."

"While I don't agree with his methods, I do agree with him that we have a problem."

Again confused, I reply, "What?"

"I can't believe the cops let someone like you in town, let alone let you wander. I am equally as disgusted that you spent a night beneath my roof. I want you to leave and not come back."

"Are you serious?"

"Deadly. Or I will call the cops."

"Why? This is insane."

"You're rude, impertinent, and foul to look upon. Our town maintains the highest standards, and a homeless bum like you is not welcome.

Lost, I exclaim, "Why does everyone think I'm homeless?"

Nelly steps closer to the manager, declaring, "I don't agree with how you're treating him. I can vouch for him. He's not homeless."

"Even still, his appearance is too awful to be allowed to remain. If you associate yourself with him, I must ask you to leave as well."

"This is rich. What is this? The 1950's where you could just walk all over black people?"

"I don't have a problem with you, ma'am. But I cannot have the likes of him around. It hurts business."

"Whatever. We were leaving anyway. Come on, Arien." Nelly grabs my hand, dragging me out.

Stumbling behind her, I follow Nelly toward the diner, mumbling, "What the hell, was that?"

"People don't like what's different. You're as different as people get."

Laughing softly, I say, "Thanks for that."

"No, I mean it in a good way. Your magnum dong makes you different enough for me." She slaps my ass, laughing.

We reach the diner, walking in to be greeted by the same waitress from last night. She sneers, "Ah, great. You guys are back. You going to waste more food today?"

Shaking my head, I respond, "We didn't . . . Whatever. We'd like a table."

"Oh, so you do have the balls to talk for yourself? I thought you were her little sex slave she found on the street."

"I'm not homeless. Do I look that bad?" I say, turning to Nelly.

"Well . . ." Nelly is clearly trying not to be rude, so she won't answer me.

"Great. Well, I'm burning these clothes when I get the chance."

"You're better off without them."

Nelly smiles up at me, making the waitress gag. "I'm gonna be sick. Table's over here." She leads us to a table and waits for us to order this time. "We got a few more options for breakfast. What do you want?"

"Biscuits and gravy for me."

"Ooh, nice. The same for me. Oh, and coffee. Lots of coffee."

"Fuck you. I'll be back." The waitress walks away as we stare after her in shock.

I mutter, "What is this fucking town?"

"Maybe it's hell and we've both actually died."

I laugh for a moment before pausing, realizing that might actually be true. "No service, no powers, and the way I left my friends. Maybe you're right."

"What do you mean, powers?" Nelly asks, brow raised.

"Oh, nothing. Never mind."

CHAPTER 64: VOID WITHIN

Charlie

Otus and I pull up to Molly's house in our rental car; Molly rushes out, waving for us to hurry, yelling, "I'm so glad you guys are here."

Getting out, I ask, "What's going on, Molly? We've been trying to call."

"Sorry. It looks like he's absorbing any type of signals."

"What? He? Is he here?"

"You should come see." Molly leads us into the house and to her bedroom, where Arien is passed out on the bed. Molly explains, "He just appeared in my living room like that and hasn't moved since. It's been awful keeping him hidden from my parents. He moans occasionally, so I know he's alive, but he won't wake up. And all the signals in the house won't connect. Radio waves, cell signal, even our TV doesn't work. How is he doing that?"

Sitting next to Arien, I place a hand on his head, immediately pulling it back, singed. "He's burning up."

"I try to keep him cool, but it won't go down."

"This isn't an ordinary fever. Have you measured how hot it is?"

"200 degrees."

Otus exclaims, "Holy shit. How is he not dead?"

I speculate, "Probably the Phoenix inside of him." Taking saliva from my mouth, I rub it onto Arien's forehead before doing the same with his saliva on mine.

Molly grimaces, "Gross."

"Shh." I place my hand back on his forehead, ignoring the searing heat. Closing my eyes, I chant:

"Make me know in advance the things in this one's mind, today, for I am of Hecate.

IAO SABAOTH IAO THEASETH . . . M ADOUNAI BATHIAO . . . EATHOE IABRABA

ARBATHRAS IAO BATHIAOOIA ZAGOURE BARBATHLAO AEI AAAAAAA

EEEEEEE . . . OE . . . SOESGSISIETH . . . SABAOTH IAEO."

Losing myself in Arien's mind, I search for his consciousness. Pain stabs through me, I scream, tears streaming down my face.

Otus shouts, "Charlie!" rushing forward to drag me back, breaking my connection to Arien.

Moaning, I rub my head, pushing back a migraine. I feel the others staring at me, but all I can manage to say is, "Thank you."

"What happened?" Molly asks.

"He's not here. Well, his body's in a coma, but his mind is somewhere else. I nearly found it, but the walls between his mind and body were destroying me. Walls of pain, grief, and anger. That's what is happening to your signals. They're being drawn through the well of his body to where ever he is."

"Is there any way to reach him?"

Sighing softly, I confess, "Yes, maybe. Now that I know what to look for, I should be able to get through."

Otus contends, "You sure? You didn't look pretty before."

Deflecting with a joke, I reply, "Thanks."

"You know what I mean. It looked dangerous."

Accepting his concern, I affirm, "Thank you, but I can handle it."

"OK." He helps me up and back to the bed. I reconnect the spell, mumbling the verse over and over again to maintain the connection.

Arien

The waitress mutters, "Fucking pagans," dropping our food on the table and walking away.

I watch her go, my hand clutching the owl pendant around my neck, comforting me.

Nelly consoles, "Don't listen to her. It's fine believing whatever you want." She stiffens suddenly, her jaw dropping and her eyes blanking. Charlie's voice echoes out of Nelly's mouth, full of apprehension. She calls, "Arien!"

I stare at Nelly in shock, replying, "Charlie?"

"You have to wake up. Wake up, Arien." The connection is lost; Nelly shivers to clear her thoughts, starting to eat as if nothing had happened. She pauses when she notices me staring at her. "What?"

Shaking my head, utterly confused, I rationalize, "I don't know. Nothing, I guess."

Charlie

"Dammit!" I expound, leaning back from Arien, the connection lost, and my hand seared.

Cradling me, Otus asks, "You OK?"

"Fine, but this isn't going to work." Looking up at Molly, I continue, "Molly, I need your help making a potion."

Her Christian prejudice flashes across her face, adverse to doing magic, but Molly shakes her head to banish it, accepting her task, saying, "Sure, anything. But I had an idea."

Otus and I look at her, surprised. I affirm, "OK, go ahead."

"If signals are getting sucked into him, can't we use a device to send a signal to him?"

My utter stupidity crashes against me, validating Molly's genius; sometimes science trumps magic. I nod, controlling my excitement, articulating the plan, "You know, I think we can. That's brilliant. The hardest part would be choosing something that would drown out the noise of all the other signals. Something a lot less one-sided, simple, and personal."

"What about my voice on a walkie talkie? That might work."

"I think so. Do you have one?"

"Yeah, we use them to herd cows. I can grab one."

"Great, do that." She turns to leave, but I call her back, "And Molly, good job."

Molly smiles in thanks, "Come on, we can use the kitchen for your potion." She leads the way, leaving Otus to stare down at Arien, worried.

Arien

Gingerly taking a bite of my food, I stop eating when across the diner, a customer stands, storming over. He looms over me, staring down, eyes full of malice. I tentatively mumble, "Can I help you?"

He growls, "Do you mind keeping it down? You're chewing like a fucking horse. It's disgusting."

Staring up at the customer in shock, I concede, "I'm sorry, I'll try and keep it down."

"You so fucking important that you don't need to follow proper etiquette, huh? You think you own this fucking place. You should just go and leave us all the fuck alone. Go die in an alley with the other trash."

The waitress storms over, joining in the tirade, "That's it. That's the last fucking straw. I want you both out of here. I never want to see either of you in here again. Disturbing our regulars. It's bad for business to keep a couple of cunts like you around."

I carefully try to stand without bumping into anyone, rejoining, "This is crazy, but we'll leave."

Nelly contends, "We don't need to. They're being the cunts."

"We should really get out of here. Things are getting out of hand."

Giving in, Nelly says, "OK," getting up and following me outside.

CHAPTER 65: SELF ODYSSEY

Arien

Nelly and I walk out into the street, leaving the diner. I turn to her, pleading for answers, "What the fuck is going on in this town? Everyone just hates me for some reason."

"No, they don't. You're being crazy."

"I guess."

BOOM!

The ground shakes and trembles, booming footsteps echoing through the town. I whisper, "What the fuck is that?

Tears threaten to overwhelm Nelly, fear gripping her. "Arien! What's going on?"

Out from behind a building, a mighty beast steps. I stare up at it in horror; it's a dark, almost gaseous, bear-like creature with spiked tentacles flailing out from all over its body, standing over 20-feet-tall.

Saliva drips from its fangs as it turns its solitary glowing red eye on me.

I exclaim, "Holy shit. What is that?"

The hotel manager steps onto the street, screaming at me, "This is your fault. You brought this upon us. You've killed us all because of your filthy soul."

Turning my guilt-ridden gaze from the manager, I stare up at the monster. I say, "Any ideas?" When I get no response, I turn to see Nelly frozen by fear. "Didn't think so. Well, me either. I really wish the others were here."

Nelly stammers, "How . . . how . . . Ah."

"If I had my powers, I could send it somewhere, or if I had my weapons, I could fight it. But I have nothing." Looking about for help, I notice a lumberjack truck parked in front of the diner, a dent in its side. Recognizing it from the Arimaspi bar, I utter, "What?"

Hurrying over to it, I find a chainsaw covered in griffin blood in the truck-bed. Shaking my head, I pick it up, powering it up. "Here goes nothing."

Chainsaw raised, I charge the beast.

I duck the first swinging tentacle before blocking the next with the chainsaw. A third one swipes at me, sending me flying back into the side of the pickup where the dent already was.

Moaning, I struggle to my feet, shaking it off and charging again. Bobbing, weaving, and blocking through the tentacles, I finally get close to the body to jab at it but am again sent flying by an unseen tentacle.

Through my blurred vision, I glimpse Nelly standing behind the beast, waving at me. Blinking to clear my sight, I shout, "What?"

"It's got fur."

"Yeah."

"Fur plus gas plus spark equals . . .?"

Grinning, realization setting in, I whisper, "Fire."

Nelly points at the town gas station not far from the beast. "Draw it in, I'll douse and light it."

"OK." Pulling myself back to my feet, I charge the beast again, this time staying back and trying to draw it toward the gas station.

Nelly takes a while to figure out the 1950's pump, but once she does, she waves at me. With a final lunge, I force the beast to take a final step back. I shout, "Now!"

I dive to the side as Nelly engages the pump, dousing the beast in gasoline. The beast roars and stumbles forward.

Nelly jumps back, the beast taking a swing for her. Missing, it tears open the gas pump, sending gas high into the air, dousing itself even more. It roars, scrambling back, but Nelly ignites her lighter, throwing it at the beast.

The beast howls in rage and pain, engulfed by a pillar of fire.

I run around the burning beast to Nelly, asking, "You alright."

"Yeah."

"Good job."

The beast stops screeching, turning to look at us, now ignoring the flames enveloping it. "Shit." It roars and charges.

Pushing Nelly to safety, I run and draw the beast away. It ignores me, focusing its wrath on the source of its agony, Nelly.

She's cornered against a wall, sobbing as the beast's fiery breath brushes her face.

"No!" I shout, my face setting in rage, eyes turning black.

Screaming, I charge for a final time.

I grab hold of the beast and pull its fiery form away from Nelly; clutching its head and pressing our foreheads together, I merge my thoughts into its mind.

***

I'm standing alone among the bodies of the Temple's suicide. I mutter, "No, this isn't my mind. My insanity."

My evil doppelganger is standing at his place behind the altar, laughing. He exclaims, "There's nothing else here but your own madness."

Tears threaten to overwhelm me. "No." Huddling up, I cover my ears to block out the pain as Evil-Me laughs manically.

***

I stumble back, released from the beast's mind, alone and defeat, my darkness gone. Kneeling, I accept my fate, waiting in despair for the final blow to be cast. The beast's maw opens wide, ready to swallow me whole. I plead, "I give in. I'm done fighting."

The beast screams, its body disintegrating.

I stare in shock; the beast turns into a whirlwind of dust, driving down my throat. I'm thrown back by the whirlwind's force, all the dust coursing into my veins.

A shockwave blasts out of me, the beast finally vanquished.

Nelly hurries to my side, helping me sit up. "You alright?"

Coughing violently, I smile up at her, replying, "Yeah, I think so."

She smiles in relief. "Oh, thank god. I thought I'd lost you."

"That's not going to happen." I lean in for a kiss, but she pulls back right away. Hurt and confused, I ask, "What?"

Giggling, she whispers, "You've got monster dust in your mouth."

"Oh, right."

"But I'm happy to do other things with you as soon as we get some privacy."

"Oh, yeah?" I say with a sexy brow raised.

"Oh, yeah."

My smile widens, motivating me to stand. "Then I'd better get up." Nelly helps me to my feet as the entire town pours out of every building, rushing toward us. They're all screaming hate at me.

"Everyone around you ends up dead."

"Why should your parents ever love trash like you."

"You killed all those people. They had families and you fucking killed them."

"You should just fucking kill yourself and rid this world of you. It'll be a far better place."

"Your Mother is rolling over . . ."

Every self-conscious and suicidal thought I've ever had is thrown back at me. I reach for Nelly's hand, but she's nowhere to be seen.

I bend down, covering my ears as the hate continues to pour out. A person at the back of the mob picks up a rock and throws it at me.

Soon the whole town has joined in, stoning me.

Charlie

Arien starts seizing violently in the bed. Otus jumps on him to hold him down as Molly and I rush in to help. I shout, "Molly, the walkie talkie."

"Right." She grabs the walkie talkie, speaking into it, "Arien, it's Molly."

Arien

I'm huddled, battered, and broken on the ground, the town screaming and throwing rocks at me. Molly's voice starts to echo through the streets, whispering, "Arien, it's Molly."

I open my eyes when I hear the voice.

She continues, "I need you to calm down. Take a deep breath." People start disappearing one by one around me as I slow my heartbeat. "We're trying our best to help you on this end, but you need to stay calm."

The crowd dissipates completely.

Slowly raising my head, I check if it's safe before stumbling to my feet.

Molly's soothing voice consoles me, "Thank you, Arien. We're going to save you."

Turning, I see Nelly alone in the street with me. "Nelly?" I hobble over to her, staring down at her. "What's going on, Nelly? Who are you?"

She smiles up at me, whispering, "I'd have thought you'd have figured it out by now." Nelly reaches up to stroke my face; suddenly, all of my wounds are healed. I gasp, staring down at my body. She answers, "I'm you?" I smile softly, understanding. She continues, "I'm your subconscious. Your voice of reason. This town is your mind, and these people are the voices in your head that you've had to deal with your whole life, telling you that you aren't good enough."

Snickering softly, I jokingly ask, "Why is my mind a 1950s town from hell?"

"That's a question you'll have to answer yourself."

The beast reforms in the street behind me, towering over us. I tense for another fight, but it just stares down at me. Turning to Nelly, I ask, "And what is this thing supposed to be?"

"Your depression. You've pushed it back again and again, but you've never been able to defeat it. It's always right there ready to destroy you." Nelly waves her hand, and the beast backs off, lying down behind a building. "Your voice of reason can only help so much against that."

Nodding, I look away, tears threatening to overwhelm me. "Why?"

"Why?"

"Why is this happening? Why am I doing this to myself?"

"This is your subtle way of telling yourself to give up. To stop fighting."

Laughing softly, I say, "I've been telling myself that for years."

"No. To stop fighting in another's war and find a simple life with someone like Nelly. You shouldn't let the voices in your head drive you to suicide by heroism."

I understand but reject it, contending, "You know I can't do that."

"I know. I'm you, remember." Nelly and the entire town start melting away.

"Wait. If you're me, or part of me, then we didn't . . . I'm still . . ."

"A virgin? Yes."

Nelly and the town fade away completely.

***

Sitting erect, I violently spit out the potion that Charlie's force-feeding me. Everyone around sighs in relief as I start to breathe normally. Otus gushes, "You can't believe how happy we are to see you, mate."

Molly weeps, "We've been so worried."

"Thank you. All of you." They all pull me in for a hug; I breathe in their scent, basking in reality restored.

Charlie asks, "What happened to you?"

"I'll tell you guys later." All I want to do now is hold them and enjoy our closeness for a minute.

CHAPTER 66: TEMPTED NORMAL

Arien

We quietly wait in Molly's room for the all-clear. Eventually, Molly calls from the living room, "They're gone. You guys can come out." Otus, Charlie, and I walk out of the bedroom to join Molly in the parent-free house. Molly says, "It's date night, so they'll be gone for a while."

Hugging Molly, I say, "Thank you, for everything, but we should go. It's not safe for us to be here."

"Please, stay for dinner. You all need a good home-cooked meal."

I pause for a second, so Charlie cuts in, "We'd love to."

"Great. I'm making pizza. Charlie, you wanna help?"

"I'm not that great of a cook."

"Nonsense. You brew all those potions, and they take precision, and pizza's nothing special."

"I guess." Shrugging, Charlie follows Molly into the kitchen, Otus and I following.

Molly grabs everyone a beer, exclaiming, "Nothing better than a beer while cooking."

"I thought you don't drink?" I ask, concerned.

"I don't usually. But you gotta live a little."

"You're parents let it in the house?"

"What they don't know . . ."

I smile broadly, glad Molly is finally loosening up. "Good for you."

"Can you check if there's any eggs in the coup?"

"I gotcha." Taking my beer, I head outside.

Enjoying my alone time after such a crazy day, I take my time gathering the eggs, searching in every nook and crevasse of the coup.

Once my basket has a few eggs in it, I head back toward the house, pausing when I see the stretch of fence I often go to with people to talk. Putting down the basket, I climb up to drink my beer and look up at the moon.

"It's beautiful, isn't it?" I don't even flinch as Hermes climbs up to sit next to me.

I say, "Sorry, I don't have a beer for you."

"I don't really need to eat or drink anymore and I'd rather not, anyway. Reminds me of being mortal and everything I lost."

We sit in silence for a moment, my guilt threatening to flood through me. Eventually, I confess, "I'm sorry about what I did."

"I know, but that doesn't change how I feel. How I'm always going to feel. It was a pretty awful thing to do."

"I'd offer you revenge, but apparently, people need me, or whatever. So, I'm fine, thanks."

"I already took my revenge."

I turn to Hermes in surprise, asking, "What?"

"I knew what condition Erebus was in from the beginning. I knew the things his madness would drive you to do. To become. I taught you how to navigate him to destroy you."

Smirking, I turn back to the moon. "I'm impressed."

"Thank you."

"I still have to keep using it. I don't have a choice. I need those abilities if we're ever going to finish all this."

"I know and it will be your end."

"More power to you, man."

We again sit in silence, staring at the moon, until Hermes asks, "I heard that you were able to defeat a Titan, thanks to Erebus's insanity. That true?"

"Yes. Koios isn't dead, but he's as close as a Titan can get."

"Well, maybe you owe me thanks for being able to do that. My revenge led to your victory."

"Maybe, but I would have discovered how to use the ability on my own."

Smiling slightly, Hermes agrees, "You're probably right." He slides off the fence and stares up at me. "Best be careful, or your desire to die will get other people hurt."

He turns to leave, but I call after him, "You just come to gloat?"

Hermes sighs but doesn't turn back. "I also came to . . ." He swallows violently, trying not to gag. "I came to help."

I laugh softly, saying, "What? You?"

"Ares is a marine fighting in Syria. Gunnery Sergeant Hannibal Sparta."

"Well, if that's not on the nose . . ."

Hermes turns, giving me a parchment. "I was told to deliver this to you. It has all the specifics."

"Who sent it?"

"Who do you think?"

"Right. Tell them thanks for me."

Hermes nods and vanishes. I wait for a while longer, basking in the moonlight. Eventually, I sigh and head back inside.

Everyone pauses when I walk in. I ask, "What?"

Molly asks, "Are you alright?"

"Yeah. Why?"

"You were just gone for a while."

Holding up the parchment for them to see, I explain, "Hermes came. We know where Ares is now." Handing the basket of eggs to Molly, I continue, "Sorry, I know you can't get far without these."

"Thanks, but I found some eggs, so the foods almost ready. Sorry." She takes the eggs, finishing the cooking while Otus and Charlie step closer to talk to me.

Otus asks, "Where is he?"

"Syria."

Charlie closes her eyes in exacerbation, exclaiming, "Of course, he is. He a marine, navy seal, or what?"

"A marine."

She shakes her head. "I never liked Ares, and now he's perpetuating a godless war."

Not wanting to awaken mine and Charlie's subject of most contention, I plead, "Let's not talk about this now. Let's just have a nice dinner."

"OK. You're right. Sorry."

Molly calls, "Food's ready." We all help set the table before sitting down to eat. Otus reaches out to start digging in, but Molly slaps his hand, scolding, "We're going to say grace first."

"But . . ."

"No buts. I'll say it because I know how you all feel about it."

I shuffle awkwardly, contending, "It's not how we feel about it. The Titans can read prayers. If you pray, they may find us."

Life-crumbling horror crosses Molly's face. "Really?"

"Yeah, sorry."

Recovering, she suggests, "Oh, well, perhaps a moment of silence then?"

"That be great."

Bowing our heads in reverence for a moment, Molly says, "Amen," giving us permission to eat.

We all dig in, laughing together. I smile, overlooking my new family.

CHAPTER 67: CRUSADE

Arien

Holding Molly tight, I say farewell. She squeezes me, asking, "You going to be alright?" Times like these, no one tells the truth. I can't leave her knowing how broken I am, how without hope.

To put her mind at ease, I affirm, "Yeah, I'll be fine. Thank you for everything you've done for us."

"You'd have done the same for me." Giving her a solemn nod, I step back, allowing the others to say their farewells.

Otus pines, "Until the next time, Molly."

Raising an uncomfortable eyebrow, Molly responds, "See ya, Otus."

They hug briefly until Charlie steps in to kiss Molly's cheek and embrace her, saying, "If you ever want to experiment a little, let me know."

Molly smiles broadly, taking the joke. "I'm flattered. I'll keep that in mind."

"Good. You got all the information you need for the car?"

"I got it." Molly insists, her eyes fluttering strangely.

"Thanks for doing that for us."

"Of course. I needed an excuse to go into the city anyway."

Molly and Charlie continue talking softly as Otus turns to me, asking, "Are you sure you won't reconsider? It's not safe for any of us to be traveling with you in there."

Accepting the risk, I state, "We can't afford not to. It's the only edge we have. How else are we going to get on base in Syria? Besides, the darkness itself isn't what caused my coma. If I minimize contact with it, I can manage it. It's worth the risk."

"I feel like this is going to come back to bite us in the ass later."

"You may be right." Charlie rejoins us, interrupting our conversation. I smile, asking, "Ready?"

"Yeah."

Turning to Molly for a final goodbye, I say, "I'll see you around, Molly."

"You'd better."

Otus, Charlie, and I all hold hands, disappearing in a dark flash.

***

We appear in a dark flash in the middle of the Syrian Desert. Staring about in confusion, Charlie asks, "Is this the right place?"

Trying not to show the large, ragged breaths I'm taking, pushing back the insanity threatening, I manage to say, "We must be close. I didn't have any magic to lock on, so I had to guess, but we shouldn't be too far off."

His eyes closed, and his breaths deep, Otus whispers, "We're close."

"How do you know?"

"I remember coming through this desert during the 2nd Crusade."

"Can you get some altitude and check if you can see the base?" Otus nods, transforming into an owl and flying off, soon returning to the ground in human form. I ask, "Did you see it?"

"It's over the hill. We're really close. Come on." He leads the way through the desert toward the nearby military base.

When we reach it, a voice over a megaphone screams at us, "Halt. Raise your hands, or you will be shot."

We comply; I shout back, "It's OK, we're Americans."

"What are you doing here?"

An idea coming to me, I let my voice crack and my eyes well with tears, answering, "We were prisoners and we just escaped. We've been wandering out here for days. Please, help us."

"Do you have any ID?"

"No, they took anything we had. Please, we just want to go home."

"Hold on. I need to call this in." I give the others worried glances as we wait. Soon, the voice returns, "You're clear. Proceed to the gate, hands still raised. Before you enter, you will be searched."

"Thank you. Thank you very much."

I lead to the gate where a band of marines come out, guns raised, and shouting, "Bags on the ground." They quickly search us and our bags, finding our weapons and the Aegis. The marine who uncovers the Aegis from its suitcase shutters as a memory overwhelms him. He mutters, "What is this stuff?"

Thinking quickly, I reply, "They were holding us in a museum, so we took any weapons we could when we escaped."

"We'll hold onto your gear for now." The marine nods, turning toward the compound, shouting, "They're clear."

DOWN IN FLAMES

He leads us through the base and to the commander's tent, where Colonel Jessup and Sergeant Sparta are waiting for us. If Hermes was right, Sparta is Ares. His demeanor is not what I'd expected from the god of war; he couldn't be more than 6'1", clearly strong but not a muscle-bound hulk. He's very unassuming; the only sign of the extraordinary is in his eyes. There's a bottomless intensity and knowledge in his gaze, power within them, far beyond what his appearance would suggest.

Jessup introduces himself and invites us to take a seat before continuing, "Now, would you care to explain who you are and what's going on?"

Still floundering for answers, I respond, "Well, sir, I'm Nathan Drake, this is my wife, Lara, and this is our friend, Jones. We were archaeologists working in Jerusalem when we were captured and taken to Syria. We've been prisoners for months. We only just escaped."

"What did they want you for? I never heard of any ransom notices for you three."

"They had us excavating a religious site. Apparently, they believed there is a lost book of the Quran, which would, without doubt, support their war upon the western world. They believed that it could be used as a rallying cry for the millions of Muslims who would not follow them."

"How'd you escape?"

"We found underground ruins beneath the Palmyra Museum, where the lost book was reported to reside. We got away from our guards and managed to find a secret exit that came out in the desert, where we wandered for days until we found you."

"You're lucky that you didn't go through the minefield on your way in."

Going a little pale, I whisper, "Minefield?"

"Yes, you must have past right next to it on your way in."

"Huh, lucky."

Jessup glances up at Ares to speculate, "These are very concerning reports. If they can rally more radicals to their cause, we may not be able to hold out." Turning back to me, he continues, "Did they find the book?"

"No, but if it's in the caves, they'll find it."

"Very well. You all did good. We have a helo departing first thing in the morning. It'll take you to the forward operating base where you will debrief the general before getting sent home. Until then, you must be tired. Sergeant Sparta will show you to the barracks where you will sleep." Jessup stands, shakes all of our hands. "Thank you for bringing this to my attention."

"Thank you, sir. For helping us."

Jessup nods as Ares leads us out of the tent.

321

CHAPTER 68: RAINING MORTARS

Once we're alone and walking through the compound to the barracks, I turn to Ares, saying, "Sparta is a pretty on the nose name for you, Ares."

He stops, slowly turning to me. "What?"

"We know who you are. We're here for you. To get your power restored."

"That whole spiel back there was a lie?"

"I didn't want to get arrested."

Ares smirks, muttering, "I knew there was something different about you. An air of fire and night."

Ignoring his insight, I press, "We need your help."

His eyes prepping to disappoint, Ares says, "I don't really . . ."

BOOM!

A mortar explodes against the side of a tent nearby as gunshots ring through the air. Ares shouts, "We're under attack!" He points to the hardened shelter, screaming over the noise, "Take cover in there. I need to defend the base." A crazed look in his eye, bloodlust swelling within him, Ares shouts again, "Go!" He runs to defend the walls while we stare at each other.

Charlie frantically asks, "What do we do?"

"We have to help them."

"How?"

I glance around until I see our gear, discarded in the center of the yard. "There. We need to get our stuff." I lead the charge to our bags, arming up.

Charlie grabs me, pointing, and screaming, "Look!" I turn to see insurgents climbing the back wall.

Otus ask, "Why is no one over there?"

"Doesn't matter. That's where we're going." I race to the wall, quickly climbing up to the catwalk. Roaring, I barrel into a man with the Aegis, sending him flying back over the wall. Another insurgent opens fire on me, but I block the bullets with the Aegis.

Charlie stabs the insurgent in the leg, making him fall to his knees before she slits his throat. Nodding at her in thanks, I knock aside an insurgent's gun, stabbing him with my bear-bone-knife.

As a bird, Otus dives the insurgents' faces, pecking at their eyes to distract them while Charlie and I cut them down.

I soon sheath my knife, picking up a fallen insurgent's gun and starting to fire at attackers below trying to climb up the wall.

A group of insurgents approach with a slab of metal on their backs, protecting them from my hailstorm of bullets. I look up as Otus hoots and drops a grenade into my hand. Smiling, I pull the pin and throw it down below the metal slab.

BOOM!

The grenade explodes, sending chunks of insurgents everywhere. The survivors of the grenade are crushed by the metal slab dropping onto them.

The remaining insurgents pause as I show them the face of the Aegis. Fear overwhelms them; they all turn tail and flee from the sight of the shield.

"Ha!" I turn to smile at Charlie, who finishes off the last insurgent on the wall as a motor shell crashes into the catwalk at my feet.

I don't hear the explosion; my vision blackens, the concussive blast knocking me off the wall. I hit the ground hard, rolling for several yards. When I stop, I'm only a shattered heap in the dirt.

I moan, my death coming.

My shallow breaths echo through my head like the pounding of a mighty drum set to my fading heartbeat. The smell of my burning flesh hurts more than the burns themselves, leaving my nostrils screaming. My vision is only flashing light and warped clouds. A single image burns through the fog enough for me to make it out; the tent next to me is alight with flames bright and yellow. I reach my mangled fingers for the fire, the only chance for my survival.

The flames ignite something inside of me, burning my very soul, burning my eyes.

The pain and stench leave me, only a feeling of serenity left in their place.

My hand catches fire, burning bright as I'm lifted into the air. The flames spread, engulfing me high above the base.

My burning gaze is drawn to the insurgents reengaging their assault of the back wall. I raise my hand, a blast of fire and night shooting out at the insurgents, the fire around me spreading like phoenix wings.

The insurgents scream as they're vaporized.

Once all threats are eliminated, the fire in me fades, dropping me back to the ground.

Charlie rushes over to check if I'm alright. I moan as she props me up, my chest riddled with shrapnel wounds. I manage to whisper, "Is it over?"

Tears falling from her eyes, Charlie replies, "Yeah, it's over. We won."

"Good. I think I need a medic."

She smiles slightly, turning to shout at the nearby marines, "Medic! I need a medic!"

Several marines hurry over to help me into the medics tent. I'm lifted up onto a table where a medic takes a look at my wounds, saying, "Damn."

"What?"

"How are you still conscious or not screaming your head off right now with wounds like these?"

In a drug-like fog, I say, "I don't know. It doesn't hurt too bad."

He gives me an anesthetic before starting to dig around in the wound for shrapnel. "I don't believe it."

"What is it?" Charlie asks.

"There's no shrapnel. It looks like it all melted away. He'll need an x-ray to be sure, but I'm going to have to sew up these wounds first to stop the bleeding. There's a helo in the morning that can take him to a hospital to get the x-ray, but for now, he should be fine." The medic starts to sew up the wounds. Once he's done, Ares walks in and waves for him to leave.

Ares shouts, "What were you thinking?"

My mind barely present, I mumble, "Did they see me?"

"A few of them. I convinced them it was just an explosion. Why didn't you tell me you were a phoenix?"

"We didn't exactly get a lot of time."

"That's what you start with. *Hi, I'm Nathan, and I'm a phoenix.*"

"Oh, my name's Arien. This is Charlie and Otus."

"Whatever."

Still searching for answers on my immortal condition, I ask, "So, what is a phoenix, anyway? Otus sensed it in me when we met, but he said that it was impossible."

"You didn't even know?"

"Not really. I mean, I've sparked in a weird way every now and then, but nothing like what just happened. How am I an ancient firebird?"

Signing, Ares explains, "When Timorian first came to power, he started hunting down all magic to keep his control of the hearts of his followers. Most creatures went extinct, or nearly so. But phoenixes decided to evolve instead. The next time a phoenix died, it chose not to regenerate. It chose to meld its soul with the nearest worthy mortal. Thereby hiding itself and giving the mortal a means to defend itself if the need ever arose. Eventually, the consciousness of the phoenix faded, but its power remained, passed down Mother to child down the generations. Your Mother must be a phoenix. Another reason they're so rare is if a Mother's first child was a male, the bloodline would end there. For you to be a phoenix is 2 thousand years of coincidence."

"That's impossible. My Mother would kill herself if she had any pagan abilities."

"It can lie dormant as you've seen. She may not have even realized it."

I tense up, glancing away to process this.

Ares asks, "Athena is inside of you as well, yes?" I purse my lips in acknowledgment, so he continues, "And a darkness not of this world. What is that?"

Otus steps in, answering, "Erebus. He's connected to Erebus, somehow."

I give Otus a dirty look for speaking on my behalf before turning to Ares and confirming, "Yes, I don't know why, but I can travel through Erebus and call upon his abilities at times. It's dangerous, though. He's gone insane, and sometimes, if I let my emotions get away from me, his insanity rubs off on me."

Ares turns away, exclaiming, "God, you're a cocktail of chemicals waiting to explode. How have you stayed sane?"

"I haven't. Not really."

"I see. Well, I can help a little. At least with the physical ailments. If I had my divinity, I could heal you."

Charlie gives Ares a curious look, asking, "But you're the god of war?"

"And wars need medics. Our powers are not all mutually exclusive one god to another."

She nods in understanding as I try to sit up, saying, "Alright, then. Let's go." I fall back to the cot, unable to stand.

"Whoa. You're not going anywhere. Otus and I will get it." Turning to Ares, Charlie continues, "Where is it?"

"In the sword of Mars in the tomb of Attila the Hun."

Stepping forward, Otus notes, "But no one knows where the tomb is."

"I fought with him, and I buried him in Budapest. After I tore out my divinity, I couldn't sit idly by and watch Timorian win, so I helped Attila attack Rome to try and defeat his human forces and free as many people as I could. It worked, for a while, at least." Sighing, Ares shakes his head and states, "No one can win a war forever. I know that better than anyone." We all remain silent for a moment, letting Ares reflect on his past.

Eventually, Otus says, "Well, we don't have time to fly to Budapest, and Arien can't take us. How are we going to get there in time?"

Snapping out of his reverie, Ares asks, "Can't one of the other gods you've restored help you?"

"No. The Titans have found a way to eavesdrop on prayers."

"Shit."

Charlie looks up, eyes wide, an idea coming to her. "Wait. There's a talisman that I can make that will bypass prayer completely to communicate with Hermes. It was a way for mortals to request that he deliver messages directly to Olympus. I need a few ingredients, but I can do it."

"Great. If they're nearby, I can help you look for them." Charlie and Otus leave to make the talisman, Ares and I now alone.

"Do you know how you used your phoenix abilities back there?" Ares asks, almost like an aside.

Shaking my head, I reply, "I don't know. It just, sorta, happened."

"I can help teach you, if you want."

"How?"

Ares smiles, turning to rummage through the tent until he finds a spoon. *"Do not try and bend the spoon. That's impossible. Instead, only try to realize the truth. There is no spoon."* I take the spoon, my brow raised in question, so he expounds, "Sorry. Keanu's the man."

I smile and shake my head, staring at the spoon. "What am I supposed to do with this?"

"You're a phoenix, yes. But you also have Athena's wisdom and craftsman's talent. You should be able to melt the spoon and reforge it into something else."

"OK. I can try." Shrugging, I shake my head again to focus on the spoon. A ringing starts to fill my ears as my focus hardens.

Giving up, I grunt and lean back, nothing having happened.

"That's alright." Ares furrows his brow, thinking. "What was going through your head when you phoenixed out?"

I sigh, trying to remember. "Just rage and the desire to survive."

"But you've had all that before and nothing's happened. Besides, we can't afford to let you get angry because of Erebus, like you said. What was different?"

My gaze goes distant, remembering. "I lost control a few days back and the only thing that stopped me killing a lot of people was the phoenix. There was a car accident and a fire." I look back to Ares, realizing the spark of my fire. "Every time I've used the phoenix, there was fire and the flames seemed to light something behind my eyes."

"Really?" Ares fishes around in his pockets until he pulls out a lighter. "Maybe this will work." I take the lighter and prepare to ignite it, but Ares interrupts me, saying, "Remember, fire is not evil or destructive. It burns away the old to create something new. It's pure magic. Focus on the flame and the feeling of creation."

Nodding, I ignite the lighter and stare into the flames. Everything but the flame seems to fade away. Soon, I feel it burning from behind my eyes. I turn from the lighter to the spoon, focusing my fiery gaze upon it.

The spoon glows, starting to melt before reforming into a fork.

I allow the flame behind my eyes to fade, glancing up at Ares. "I did it."

Sarcasm dripping from every syllable, he mumbles, "Astounding creativity you've got there."

CHAPTER 69: SELF OR FUTURE

<u>Charlie</u>

Hiding in an empty tent, I prepare the potion and spell to create the talisman. I stand to grab an ingredient, gasping, and clutching my stomach. A heavy wave of nausea crashes into me, forcing me to lean against the tent-pole for support. Tears well in my eyes, glazing them over and opening my mind.

***

I'm suddenly alone in the white expanse of my own mind; mist swirls around me, forming into visions of the future, of a life to be had.

The mist forms into a hospital, where a ghostly version of me is giving birth. I'm sucked into my doppelganger, becoming her.

I'll scream, the final contractions racking my body. A nurse'll smile, pulling out my newborn baby, saying, "He's beautiful." She'll clean up the infant, leaving me to pant heavily, recovering from the agony of birth. Once clean, the baby will be handed to me with a question, "Congratulations. What's his name?"

I'll smile, staring down into those deep ocean blue eyes, and say, "Adonis. His name's Adonis."

The mist reforms the vision into a quaint country home, where I'll be happy raising Adonis with a woman named Emma, gruesome scars cut deep into her face.

I'll rock baby Adonis to sleep on the couch.

Emma will walk in from the kitchen and sit down next to me, saying, "Hi, honey."

She'll kiss me gently, her lips tasting of rose petals, and I'll whisper, "Hey, Emma. Got the popcorn."

"Of course." She'll say, lifting the popcorn bowl.

"Great. Just let me go put him down real fast."

"Aww. He's so cute when he's sleeping. Here let me. I'll put him down."

"Thanks, babe." I'll hand her my baby, trusting her implicitly with everything I am.

The mist transforms everything to a grassy hilltop, where Emma and I will watch Adonis, as a young boy, running around trying to get a kite into the air.

We hold on this future for but a moment before it's Adonis's first day of school.

I'll kiss his head, letting him run off to join the other kids running into the school. The feeling of letting go will be too much for me to bear, so I'll cling to Emma's loving embrace to quench the burning guilt and pain of seeing my angel grow up.

With a flash of mist, I'll sit with middle-school-aged Adonis at the kitchen table, working on his homework together. "So, X=25."

"Yeah, you got it."

This last happy vision is interrupted by another bittersweet one.

I'll adjust high-school-aged Adonis's bowtie before looking up and down his suit. "You look so handsome."

"Thanks, Mom."

"Abigail's a nice girl. I'm happy for you."

"We're just friends, Mom."

"Sure." Tears'll start to swell in my eyes as I pat Adonis's chest. "Alright. Off you go then. Be back by 2 and no fooling around. I don't want to be a grandma yet."

He'll smile broadly and say, "No promises," before kissing my forehead and grabbing his corsage, heading out, leaving me to smile after him.

My last glimpse of the future is the final goodbye, the final letting go.

I'll sob into my handkerchief and grasp Emma's wrinkled hand harder as I watch Adonis get married.

The priest'll say, "Do you take Abigail to be your lawfully wedded wife?"

Adonis will say, "I do."

***

I collapse as the vision ends, returning me to the empty tent. Tears streaming down my face, I try to get my bearings, freezing when I see Apollo standing in front of me. He says, "Hey, Charlie."

Pulling myself up onto a cot, I stare up at Apollo, asking, "What was that?"

"The moment your child was conceived, I had a Delphic vision. My first since regaining godhood."

"A vision of what?"

"Your child will be very important. Essential even to the survival of all of us. Way beyond this Titan war. I needed you to know that, and see all that because there's a possible future where you decide not to keep him."

I gasp in shock, horrified that he knows the desire of my heart. "What are you saying?"

"I need to ensure that doesn't happen, so anyone can have a chance for a future. And I'm sorry; he will be the death of you, whatever you choose."

Otus walks in, and Apollo disappears. I cry out, "Wait, we need your help."

"What?" Otus asks, utterly confused.

Turning away and wiping the tears from my eyes, I mumble, "Nothing. You get what we need?"

"Yeah, I got it." He holds up a bag as proof.

"Good. Let's get started."

Arien

I smile, holding up a newly forged silver bullet to show Ares. He says, "Very good. A little more creativity there."

Putting aside the bullet, I ask, "Why are you so willing to help us?"

He shrugs unconvincingly, answering, "I miss fighting like a god and the power I could wield."

I stare into his eyes for a moment, shaking my head. "No, that's not it."

Sighing, Ares gives in. "At the battle of Pompeii, I was a coward, and I ran away. I'm ashamed of myself. But these marines, they inspired me. No powers or protection and they are constantly willing to run headfirst into danger in the defense of others. They're the modern-day 300. I want to be more like them. I want a chance to prove I'm not a coward and takedown Timorian once and for all, or die trying. All these brave men will be able to go home to see their families, to be able to tell them, 'I proved myself.' I just want a chance to do the same."

I smile, accepting his reasoning. "I think you'll get your chance."

We're interrupted by Charlie and Otus rushing in. "We finished it."

"Great."

Otus asks, "Who's going to use it?"

Thinking for a moment, I say, "I think Ares should."

"What?"

"Hermes has a bit of a problem with us. It'll sound better coming from you."

Ares accepts the talisman and says, "I'll tell him where it is and have him watching nearby when you're ready to leave. OK?"

Charlie and Otus nod, clutching their weapons tighter. "What can we expect?"

"There's a dragon, but it should be long dead by now."

"Should?"

"That's the best I can do."

"Whatever. We're ready."

"OK." Ares closes his eyes, calling out to Hermes with his mind. After a moment, Otus and Charlie disappear.

CHAPTER 70: SWORD OF A HUN

<u>Otus</u>

Charlie and I appear in a pitch-black cave, stumbling to get our bearings. I whisper, "Shit. Do you have a light?"

"Yeah. Hold on." She rummages through her bag and pulls out a flashlight. When she turns it on, a series of torches ignite around the edge of the cave, bathing us in light. "OK. Won't be needing this." Returning the flashlight to her bag, she stares around at the massive cavern around us. "What is this place?"

"It looks like it's a natural cave. They probably found it then caved in the entrance to keep it hidden."

"So, there's no exit?"

"Not without Hermes."

"Great."

I point across the cavern to a pedestal where a skeleton is lying, clutching a massive red sword; a giant dragon's skeleton wraps around the pedestal and around the edge of the cave. "That must be it."

"Let's go." Charlie leads the way down a pile of rubble and toward the pedestal. I go a bit slower, preoccupied with staring at the dragon's skeleton.

My eyes widen, realizing it's missing all its teeth. I shout, "Charlie, wait."

She turns just as a skeleton hand bursts from the ground and latches onto her foot. "The fuck?"

"They're Spartoi."

She swings down and cuts the hand off the arm before scrambling back. Dozens of Spartoi start crawling from the dirt as Charlie and I look on in horror. "I really wish Arien was here."

Lightening the mood, I say, "I wish I'd taken Fiore dei Liberi up on his offer of fencing lessons."

"Now's not the time."

"Right. What are we going to do?"

"Try, I guess."

"Brilliant."

We both scream and charge the Spartoi.

Charlie throws an alchemy bomb, taking out several Spartoi before lifting her sword and slashing through another. I transform between man and bird, flitting around the Spartoi, killing where I can.

Soon, all the Spartoi are dead.

Relieved, I gloat, "Is that it?"

"Oh, Otus. You did not just jinx us?"

The sound of creaking makes us both turn. Attila the Hun's corpse is sitting up and staring at us.

"Shit."

He pulls himself off the pedestal and reaches back to heft the sword of Mars. An unearthly howl echoes from his gaping maw before he charges us.

I meet Attila head-on and barely manage to keep off his swinging blade. Weaving between man and bird, I jab and peck wherever I find an opening.

Attila whirls and spins violently, hitting me with the flat of his blade and sending me flying.

Charlie throws a bomb at Attila's feet, blasting him apart.

Moaning, I struggle to my feet, hobble over to Charlie, and say, "Good job."

"Thanks." Attila's bones creak, rolling across the cave floor toward each other. "Oh, hell no." He reforms, standing tall above us.

"Keep him occupied."

"What?"

I turn into an owl, flying off behind Attila. He circles to confront me, but Charlie picks up a rock and throws it at his head. "Hey." His attention latched, he turns back to Charlie. "It's probably been a long time since you had a woman. Why don't I bend over right here, and you stick your bone in me?" Attila cocks his skull at Charlie, processing the joke. "That's right. Some nice warm pussy for ya. Come and get it." He starts walking toward her, but she holds her ground, her voice cracking. "Premium cut pussy here." Charlie starts dancing sexily. "Oh, you like that." She turns, grinding on Attila's boney leg, and singing, "*I'm all about that bass, 'bout that bass. No treble.*"

Attila slams a fist into Charlie's back and sends her sprawling. She rolls over, staring up at Attila, who's raised his fists for the killing blow.

I swing the discarded sword of Mars and slice Attila in half.

He roars and explodes into dust.

Charlie sputters and spits out a mouthful of his dust, saying, "Oh, gross. . . You took your time."

Reaching out, I help Charlie to her feet. "I was stunned by your performance. What the hell was that?"

She shrugs, replying, "It was the first thing that came to me."

I smile and shake my head. "Whatever. We've got the divinity, let's go."

Charlie pulls out the prayer talisman, closing her eyes to mumble a prayer to Hermes. After a moment, she opens them. Nothing happens.

"What's wrong?"

"I don't know."

I reach out and take the talisman. "Here, let me try." I pray too, but to no avail.

"This is bad. What's going on?"

"Hermes's revenge, maybe."

"Whatever it is, we need to find a way out." A single torch on the wall flickers out. Charlie and I stare at it, worried before she adds, "And fast."

We search the cave, soon coming across the cavern entrance, buried under mounds of rubble. We just stand and stare at the mound for a moment. Eventually, I say, "That's probably our only way out."

"I know."

"We're going to have to dig."

"Yup."

"We only have so much time before the air runs out, and the torches go out."

Charlie sighs loudly, whispering, "Then let's get started." We shake off our worries and start moving boulders from the top of the pile.

CHAPTER 71: MASTER SMITH

Arien

$\mathbf{A}$res stands near as I hobble out into the yard on crutches. We stop in a clearing, glancing round to ensure our seclusion. I ask, "You sure no one will see us."

"I have them all doing an exercise on the other side of base. We'll be fine."

Ares hands me the metal tent pole he's been carrying. I take it, trading it for my crutches before igniting my lighter. I stare into the flames until the fire lights behind my eyes. Turning to the pole, I concentrate my fiery gaze on it. It glows, melting down and reforming into a short sword.

Ares smiles broadly, affirming, "Good job. Test it out. See if the balance is good."

I take a few practice swings, measuring its weight and balance. I stop, reaching out to run my fingers along the blade. "It's sharp."

Ares points at a target set up a few dozen yards away, saying, "Make something that can hit that."

I morph the sword into a spear, throwing it at the target. I miss entirely, but we both smile none the less.

His eyes pondering, Ares suggests, "It's possible if you memorize the internal workings of a firearm, you could make a gun."

"What about the gunpowder in the bullets?"

"I think, in theory, you can someday reforge the atomic structure of particles themselves to create new compounds. Making dirt into gunpowder. Wood into bread."

Rejecting the idea of possession of such an awe-inspiring power, I contend, "I don't know. That seems too crazy, even for us."

"Perhaps, but the possibilities are endless."

I stare at Ares curiously; my mental picture not remotely met. "You know, you're a lot different than depicted."

"How's that?"

"You're nerdier."

Fake outrage flashes in his eyes as he pleads, "No. Don't say that. I'll rip your arms off."

I laugh softly, taking the joke. "Hey, there's nothing wrong with that. I'm a huge nerd, and proud of it."

He shakes his head, smiling. "I am not a nerd. Marines pull code reds on nerds."

I raise an eyebrow, asking, "Code reds? Like from *A Few Good Men*?"

"Yeah. They're rare and far between. We stop them when possible, but we use the threat of them to keep certain people in line."

"Wow. Glad I joined the Air Force."

"You're in the Air Force?"

"Was. They think I'm dead so . . ."

"I thought I detected the air of a warrior about you. I assumed it was from your quest, but maybe not."

A massive siren blares throughout the base.

I shout over the noise, "What's that? Are we under attack?"

Ares smiles and laughs at me, answering, "No. That siren is much louder. That's the half an hour warning till lights out."

"That apply to us?" I ask, surprised that it's already so late.

"I'm afraid so."

Worry for Charlie and Otus floods me; they shouldn't have been gone for so long. "What about the others? I didn't think it would take this long."

"They're probably just searching the caves. It's a bit of a labyrinth down there. But Hermes is watching them. They'll be fine."

"What about the dragon?"

"Like I said, I'm sure it's dead. They'll be fine."

"If you say so."

"Come on. I'll help you back to the med tent." Ares hands me back my crutches and helps me hobble back toward the med tent.

***

Dreamless sleep pervades until strong hands grasp me, yanking me from my cot, binding and gagging me. I'm held down, a sharp thumb pressed into my wounds. Pain paralyzes me, preventing me from struggling. A harsh voice whispers into my ear, "Quiet. We wanna talk." The thumb pulls back, the pain subsides, and I lie still, so the voice continues, "Good. We're going to beat you senseless if you lie, or we don't like your answers, or if you scream. Agreed?"

I nod slightly.

"Good." My gag's taken out, and my eyes adjust enough to make out the faces of my attackers, a group of marines. The apparent leader continues his interrogation, saying, "Now, we saw your little fireworks show during the attack and your weird session with Sergeant Sparta. Who and what are you?"

Knowing they can't harm me, I bid my time, replying, "My name's Arien Vlahos. I'm an Airman in the Air Force."

The marines laugh and snicker to themselves. "Chair force, huh?"

"Yep. Brain over brawn."

"Why you little cunt." The marine digs his thumb into my wound again to my great discomfort.

"OK, OK. Sorry."

He lets up, asking, "What are you?"

The truth too strange to be believed, I decide to go with a believable lie. "I'm a test subject."

"What?"

"A test subject for a secret government super-soldier project. You know, Captain America, Spider-man, Batman, and the like. Sergeant Sparta is my handler. This is the first field test of the experiments."

The marines glance around at each other to see if they all believe me. "What abilities do you have?"

"Fire. That's it. Just fire stuff. Like the Human Torch."

"So, you could burn us all and get away if you wanted to?"

Ice in my tone, I affirm, "Yes."

"Why haven't you?"

"Cause we're all on the same team here. We're all here to protect our loved ones at home. We are the 300 standing on the walls fighting chaos itself."

The marines again look at each other for agreement. "I don't see why they chose some Air Force brat over an American-blooded marine, but you're alright."

The marines let me go; I sit up, moaning, and cradling my side. "We cool?"

"We cool. Sorry, we had to be sure."

"I get it. I might have done the same thing in your shoes. Now, does anyone have any whiskey?"

The marines look at each other before bursting out laughing and patting me on the back. "You're alright, man. You're alright."

<u>Charlie</u>

Otus and I sit alone in the near darkness, huddled together against the cold. Only a few torches are still lit, and they continue to go out one by one. I timidly ask, "Otus?"

"Yeah?"

"I'm terrified."

"Me too."

Baring my soul in confession, I continue, "No, I'm afraid of having this kid. Of the type of mother I'm gonna be and just everything that comes along with it. What it means for my life. But I guess I may not need to worry about that anymore."

Otus sighs softly, saying, "I am so old and so tired. I act all weird and innocent on purpose. It helps mask all my issues and regrets. My biggest regret is losing my family. They were my everything. Sure, my life changed when they came into it, but that's not a bad thing. The fact that I had someone that loved me unconditionally made all the difference. Made it all worth it. I don't know what the future holds for you, but I promise it will be so much better, and so much worse than you can possibly imagine. Mostly better because you choose if it's better, and I know you'll make the right choices."

I smile slightly, snuggling closer to him. "Thank you, Otus. You're a good man."

He kisses me on the head, holding me tighter.

The torches slowly start to relight and get brighter; Otus nudges me, saying, "Charlie, the lights." We stare around at them in confusion.

We freeze and turn slowly as the giant dragon skeleton creaks loudly.

CHAPTER 72: TO BE 300

Arien

I hobble across the yard toward Ares, who finishes talking to a marine, sending him away as I reach them. I ask, "What's going on?"

"Helo's been delayed. There's a sandstorm coming. Look." He points out into the desert where massive sand clouds are billowing toward us.

"Shit."

"Yeah. Can't get you to the hospital, so we'll keep training. I assume you practiced last night."

"Kinda hard not to." I say, shrugging.

"I can imagine. Reforming objects is just one small aspect of being a phoenix, and you'll have the rest of your life to discover them all. Take it slow."

"I get it. It just feels so familiar. So much like that's who I am. I feel alive for the first time in a long time. I don't know how to explain it."

"It's your heritage. Are you going to talk to your Mother about it?"

I look down, uncomfortable, unable to meet his gaze. "We don't actually talk, especially since she thinks I'm dead.

"I get it. I don't usually get along with my parents." We smile at each other in shared pain.

CRASH!

We turn to see Charlie and Otus collapsed on the ground. I hurry over to them and help them up. "You guys OK? What's going on?"

"It's right behind us!"

"What is?"

"The dragon!"

Through a fissure in the air above us, a dragon skeleton begins to materialize.

Charlie screams, "Get back," and helps everyone run as the dragon continues to come through the gap.

Tears in his eyes, Otus pleads, "I'm sorry, Arien. We didn't know it could follow us."

Ignoring his guilt, I focus on the sword in his hand. "Is that it?"

Otus hefts the sword of Mars. "Yes."

"Give it here." Ares says, taking it from Otus.

We're all forced to avert our eyes as Ares is engulfed in a pillar of white fire. He's lifted off the ground and spread-eagled in the center of the burning pillar.

The fire and light fades, leaving Ares standing on the ground, unharmed. He grimaces, moans, and stumbles, whispering, "I missed this more than I should have." He turns to me and places a finger against my forehead. I'm immediately healed with no more need for crutches. Ares explains, "I really wish I could help more, but fundamental laws of the god's state, we cannot destroy symbols of our divinity. It destroys people's faith in us and diminishes our power. I've done all I can to help. I'm sorry." Ares glances up to see the dragon's skin and venom glands regrowing rapidly. "There's one more thing I can do." He snaps his fingers, and my weapons appear in my hands. "Good luck."

Ares disappears as I heft the Aegis and draw my bear-bone-knife, turning toward the dragon. I close my eyes and sigh to myself. "Fuck."

Otus and Charlie draw their weapons, standing beside me. Charlie asks, "Got a plan?"

"I've got a few new tricks, but considering how much bigger this one is compared to the last dragon, I doubt it'll be enough."

Otus mutters, "Way to instill confidence."

"Sorry. You guys have anything?"

Charlie says, "Nothing new. You do all the work while Otus and I do our best to distract it."

"Worked before."

"But not on this scale," Otus contends.

"Nothing else we can do."

"You're right."

I step toward the dragon, flashing the face of the Aegis at it. The dragon ignores Medusa's face, spewing a stream of venom at me. I only just get the Aegis up in time to block the stream of venom.

I maintain my distance as I circle round the dragon, occasionally fainting an attack, but none of my weapons have enough reach. "Ready?"

"Ready," Charlie shouts.

"Now."

Charlie throws a smoke bomb at the dragon's head as owl Otus swoops in at its eyes. While the dragon is distracted, I charge in, shield raised.

I stab at the dragon's hide, but my knife just bounces off. It whirls and sends me flying with a flick of its head.

Crashing into a tent, I knock it down. Moaning and struggling to crawl out of the collapsed tent, I quickly block a stream of acid with the Aegis as I fight onward.

I drop the bear-bone-knife, pulling out the lighter, and igniting the phoenix within me. My eyes burning, I stand straight among the steaming ruins of the tent.

Charlie and Otus stare in awe as I step out of the tent and toward the dragon.

I spread my shield arm wide, leaving myself open for an attack. The Aegis starts to glow brightly before it melts, reforming into a massive broadsword with the face of Medusa carved into its hilt.

The blade drips molten drops of steel as I continue to advance, ignoring my burning hands, the flesh melting.

Spinning to avoid a stream of venom, I scream and charge, dodging several venom sprays. I duck a swipe of the dragon's paw and slash upward with my molten blade.

The dragon screams and retreats, spraying an endless stream of venom at me. I morph the Aegis back into a shield to block the massive stream, nearly knocked off my feet by the force.

Crouching down to protect my legs, I dig in against the onslaught.

BOOM!

The dragon stumbles back, an RPG rocket exploding into it. I turn to see the marine from my code red, lowering the RPG, smiling. He nods at me, turning to a group of his friends, and shouting, "Open fire!"

The group of marines fire their weapons at the dragon. It roars, stumbles, and struggles against the onslaught, allowing me to continue my charge.

The Aegis a sword again, I swing it through the air, sending several molten darts hurtling toward the dragon's eyes. It dodges and sends a bolt of venom in return, making me reforge the Aegis into a shield to block. I roll from in front of the blast of venom and continue my charge.

A fresh onslaught of marine gunfire draws the dragon's attention away from me. It sends a stream of venom hurtling toward the defenseless marines as I stare in terror.

The marine grunts and collapses as he takes the venom in the chest.

"No!"

I grab a horn of the dragon's head to hold it down as I repeatedly chop at its throat. The dragon screams as I finish chopping its head off.

Now covered in dragon blood, I defuse the phoenix, rushing to the fallen marine and clutching his hand as he dies.

The medic does what he can while I try to keep him awake. "Hey, hey. You're OK. You're good. Come on, look at me. Stay awake."

"Did I do good?"

I smile and laugh softly. "Yes, yes, you did good. You're a hero. You saved everyone on this base."

His eyes, distant and unseeing, fill with tears of joy. "Really?"

"Yes, you did. You've got a Medal of Honor or a Purple Heart coming your way for sure."

The marine smiles, spitting up blood. "That'll be nice. Spruce up my uniform a bit. I don't have many ribbons yet."

"Yeah, it'll look really good on you."

"Am I dying?"

"No, you're going to be alright."

"To be 300."

"What?"

Interrupted by a fit of coughing, he struggles to continue, "You said we're the 300 standing on the walls against chaos. To be 300 is to die for others. I'm glad it went this way. Fighting a motherfucking dragon. How many guys can say they went out like this?"

"No one. That's your honor."

"To be 300."

"To be 300."

The marine smiles again, his eyes emptying, the life leaving him. I smile a little and kiss his hand, reaching up to close his eyes.

The medic tentatively says, "I'm sorry. There's nothing that could have been done."

I stare down at my burnt and blood-covered hands in horror; reaching out, I take the marine's gloves, putting them on to remember him. "What was his name?"

"What?"

"His name, what was it?"

The medic looks for the marine's nametape, but it's melted off. "I don't know."

Another marine steps forward, saying, "He was *The Marine*. That's all anyone need know."

I glance up and nod, affirming, "The marine."

Standing, I step back toward my friends.

The other marine utters, "To be 300."

"To be 300."

The entire base is standing there, staring at me and the dragon. The howling of the sandstorm is near upon us when I raise my hand to salute all the marines.

They all salute in return.

I reach out to grab Otus and Charlie's hands, preparing to leave, but the medic stops us, "Wait. Who are you?"

I smile as the sandstorm envelopes us, and we disappear in a dark flash.

***

I'm walking alone down a Kentucky sidewalk with takeout when Ares appears behind me, saying, "Arien."

I pause, turning to look at him. "Ares."

"I'm sorry for what happened. He was a good friend of mine." I look down in regret, the memory of the marine still haunting me. When I don't answer, he continues, "I didn't think Hermes would bring back the dragon."

Looking up suddenly, I ask, "Did he do it on purpose?"

Ares pauses for a moment but affirms, "Yes."

My face constricts as I try to hold in my rage. "Jesus! And the little bit about leaving them in that cave overnight. Was that on purpose too?"

"Apparently, he thought that was funny."

"Funny? He got the marine killed."

"I think he regrets that, but I've never seen him hate anyone as much as he hates you."

"His reasons don't excuse this." I struggle to control my emotions with little success.

"You know, I was impressed with what you did with the Aegis. How did you know it self-replenishes its metal?"

The change in subject helps me calm down a little. "A guess. With how you guys can change your size and all. Figured there had to be a way that it grew with you."

"Ah."

I take off my gloves to show Ares my burnt hands. "Did you know this would happen?"

Ares reaches out and examines my hands. "It shouldn't have. You should be immune to fire. Something's holding you back somehow."

"What does that even mean?"

"I don't think these burns were an accident. I think you're trying to tell yourself something."

"What could I possibly be trying to tell myself?"

"That's a question that you'll have to ask yourself."

We're silent for a moment, thinking. Eventually, I ask, "Have you seen the news?"

"No. Why?"

"The dragon's all over it. Apparently, someone recorded the whole thing. Luckily, no one saw my face. . . No one understands what it is or what happened, but the death of a marine pisses some people off. They're going to start asking questions. Questioning everything they know about the world."

"That's a good thing."

"How?"

"If people start to believe in magic, we take just a little belief away from Timorian. We take a bit of his power. There's a shot of winning if we can get people to believe in the impossible. To believe in you."

I snicker softly, saying, "Why would anyone believe in me?"

Ares looks at me curiously, asserting, "You know, I sensed your lust for your own blood the moment we met. It pulsates from you like a crimson fog. You're so close to the end of your journey, and there's always the possibility that you'll survive." I don't respond, just turn away in shame. Ares shakes his head, realizing he won't be able to get through to me. "Aphrodite is in Mexico. She has a cottage on the slope of Cerro de la Viga. She's changed a lot since the old days. She's not what you'd expect."

I nod in thanks at Ares. "Thank you."

He nods in return, vanishing, leaving me to just stand in the street, thinking.

Charlie

I'm vomiting profusely into the toilet again. Once finished, I flush and stand to stare at myself in the mirror. I fight to keep my gaze on my guilt-filled eyes, but I'm inevitably drawn to the bottle of abortion pills on the counter.

Tears overwhelm me as I take a pill out of the bottle and place it against my lips. I pause, my gaze again latched to my guilt-ridden eyes, Apollo's words of prophecy echoing through my head.

Sobs rack my body; I throw the pill away and collapse to the floor. I huddle against my knees, sobbing violently.

Part 8:

APHRODITE

CHAPTER 73: ANCESTRY

The fog thickened darkly on old London-town, obscuring the bright moon, leaving the alleys in shadow, letting all manner of monsters roam unseen. The Greek goddess Aphrodite, hidden as Emma in traditional 18th-century woman's garb, walked alone down one such alley after a night of theatre.

The ancient serial killer Procrustes, then in the body of Jack the Ripper, peered round a corner to stare at Emma. He licked his lips, stepping out into the alley behind her, whispering menacingly, "What's a pretty lady like you doing in a place like this?"

Emma didn't stop or turn; she just lifted her skirts and walked faster.

"Now, is that how you treat a gentleman courtier?"

Jack burst into a run and tackled Emma. She screamed and thrashed as Jack flipped her over and drew a knife. He went to slit her throat, but her thrashing made the knife slip, carving up her face.

Emma screamed louder as blood covered her face.

Jack smiled, an idea coming to him. He continued cutting her face, making patterns in her flesh. Emma brought a knee up and slammed it into Jack's groin. He didn't even flinch; he just smiled, revealing a mouth empty of teeth.

Jack raised his knife for the killing blow. Emma covered her mutilated face in a vain attempt to block the blow.

SMACK!

A club swung out of nowhere, slamming into Jack's head, sending him sprawling. A prostitute rushed forward to help Emma up, shouting, "Come on!" and pushing Emma to run in front of her.

Jack stumbled to his knees, grabbing hold of the prostitute's legs. She fell, and Jack climbed on top, raising his knife.

Emma turned back to look just as the prostitute's throat was slit. Emma fled as Jack enjoyed his kill. He got to his feet to follow Emma but stopped when he saw that she was already gone. Turning back to the prostitute's corpse, he disemboweled her.

Emma made it to the mouth of the alley where the bustle of people concealed her. She leaned against a wall and sobbed.

<u>Atlas</u>

Appearing on the asylum steps, I stumble, clutching my injured side; my body is covered in a multitude of fresh wounds and scars. Grimacing, I shove down the pain, standing straight and walking into the asylum. I find Iapetus in his room, sitting cross-legged in the center of the cold ground. He smiles without opening his eyes, asking, "Where have you been?"

"Where do you think?"

"I don't appreciate your tone."

Fiery anger coursing through my veins, only just restrained, I whisper, "What?

"I'm still your Father, and I deserve your respect."

I smile slightly, my rage spurning control; I kick him in the face, sending him crashing back. Rushing in to clutch his throat, I lift him up against the wall, whispering menacingly, "You lost the right to parent me a long time ago. We only work together because He demands it. . . And that may not be for much longer. First, you lose Erebus. Now, you've lost the boy twice. I leave for a month, and everything goes to hell."

Coughing violently past my grasp, Iapetus manages to say, "Losing the boy was Hyperion and Koios's fault, not mine."

My grip only tightens, my words lethal, "I don't have time for your shit. Where are they?"

I loosen enough for him to speak. "Hyperion has returned to D.C., and Koios is missing."

"Missing how?"

"Scattered."

Dropping Iapetus, I stumble back in horror. "How?"

"His head is trapped, and his body incinerated. The worst fate for a Titan."

"Did Arien do this?"

"Yes." He struggles to his feet, continuing, "He's far more powerful than we imagined. And there are reports of a darkness following him."

I go pale, considering the implications. "That's impossible."

"The timeline matches. The child was born before we captured him."

"But he's insane. He can't have done all this."

"He wasn't back then." Iapetus says, an almost playful smile creasing his face. He's enjoying this; the chase, the hunt for Him.

"We need to track their prayers. Now!"

"We can't. Not with Koios gone."

"Kronos is on the verge of coming down himself to deal with this."

Iapetus stiffens in fear, saying, "Then we'll have to catch the boy before that happens. We both know how little he likes distractions from Utopia."

Reaching into my pocket, I pull out a small vile, explaining, "This wasn't my first stop. I visited Hecate and got her to cook this up for our guest." Iapetus nods in understanding, following me to Medea's cell.

I stop in the doorway, staring down at the feral, animal-like Medea, struggling against her chains and growling at me. I step forward, and she cowers against the back wall away from me, whimpering. Crouching down next to her, I stroke her hair like a dog, whispering soothingly, "Does this still hurt?" I poke the gaping hole through Medea's chest, making her hiss. "I guess so. Well, I have something that can help with that."

Grabbing her jaw, I force her to drink the potion from Hecate's vial. She struggles and thrashes, to no avail.

The wounds covering Medea's body start to heal, revealing her beautiful nude form.

A green light flashes in her eyes, and her body stiffens, falling still. "I am ready to serve, master."

"I need you to find Arien."

"I shall need ingredients."

"I'm sure we have everything you'll need."

CHAPTER 74: BE NOT BLIND

<u>**Arien**</u>

I'm alone in the endless darkness. Suddenly, the fog rushes in to form the streets of Jerusalem where Timorian is walking down the street, surrounded by his followers. A disciple comes to him with a blind man, asking, *"Master, who did sin, this man, or his parents, that he was born blind?"*

Turning to address the gathered crowd, Timorian expounds, *"Neither has this man sinned, nor his parents: but that the works of God should be made manifest in him. I must work the works of him that sent me, while it is day: the night cometh, when no man can work. As long as I am in the world, I am the light of the world."* He crouches down and spits into the dirt, making the ground wet enough to make clay. Taking the clay, he rubs it upon the eyes of the blind man, whispering, *"Go, wash in the pool of Siloam."*

"Thank you, master. Thank you." The blind man kisses Timorian's hands before being led away by the crowd of disciples.

Once we're alone, Timorian stands and turns to look at me, saying, "It warms my heart to see thine-self before me."

Keeping calm, my heartbeat steady, I ask, "Why are you showing this to me?"

"To remind you, punishment is not bestowed on a child due to a parent's sin and that all wounds may be washed clean."

"What do you want?"

"I desire to change the world. But I require thine assistance. When the time of reckoning comes, we shall stand together."

***

Otus gently shakes me awake, whispering, "It's time to go." I nod, scratch my hands beneath my gloves, and roll off the couch to start packing. He watches me for a moment with concern, asking, "What's with the gloves?"

"Oh, it's just to help me remember."

"Remember?"

"Ah, yeah. The marine."

Knowing he'll get nothing more from me, he nods and turns away.

Charlie

Pounding knocking echoes through my dreams, shaking me awake. I'm sprawled on the bathroom floor, lying in a puddle of my own sick. I had fallen asleep last night, too tired to drag myself back to bed after a wave of nausea.

Another knock pounds against the door; I go to answer but freeze; baby Adonis is asleep on the ground in front of me. I scream, "No!" shoving the baby away.

It disappears as Otus's voice echoes through the door, asking, "Charlie, are you OK?"

Shaking my head to clear it, I stand, responding, "Yeah, sorry. Just got dizzy when I stood up." I flush the toilet, quickly clean the floor, and wash my hands before opening the door.

Otus looks me up and down, saying, "You were in there a while. Are you alright?"

I shrug, shouldering past him. "Fine."

We all pack in sullen silence, Arien and I moving slower than usual. Otus watches us closely; eventually, groaning and saying, "I'm worried about you guys. We've been through a lot recently."

"We're fine."

"Go downstairs and get breakfast. I'll finish packing."

Arien and I glance at each other before nodding. "Fine."

As we leave, I look over my shoulder to say, "Just don't go poking through my underwear."

"I won't. Go."

Otus

I stare after the others as they leave. As soon as I'm alone, I start going through their stuff, trying to understand what's wrong. All Arien has are weapons, clothes, and porn. Suddenly, I find a Sermon on the Mount doodle among Arien's stuff. I stare at it for a moment, trying to comprehend the implications of drawing the enemy.

I take a picture of it, abandoning the rest of Arien's stuff to start digging through Charlie's. I carefully pick up a pair of her panties, enjoying the view for a second before throwing them aside.

In Charlie's purse, I find a set of abortion pills. Horrified at my actions, knowing this is none of my business, I return the pills, take a few more pictures, and send them to *her*, deleting the messages after.

Arien's porn catches my eye again, my hand twitches, craving action. Giving in, I go to my laptop, open it, and connect with Isabella. She smiles and waves, "Otus, long time no see."

"Yeah, it's been awhile. How you been?"

"Good. Pretty busy."

"Ah. . . Well, can we start?"

"Of course."

We both start getting undressed.

<u>Charlie</u>

Arien and I have gotten our food and are sitting together, eating in silence. Arien carefully tries to eat through the clumsiness of his gloves, wincing occasionally as if in pain. I nod at the gloves, asking, "Why are you wearing those?"

"No reason."

"Really?"

"I just don't want to forget the marine."

Raising an eyebrow in disbelief but not wanting to press the issue, I return to my food in silence.

CHAPTER 75: WEBS OF REGRET

Arien

We return to the hotel room after breakfast, finding the window broken and Otus missing. "Otus!" I rush to the window, trying to see Otus, but he's gone. Several large spiderwebs and rotting egg-sacks are scattered through the room, blowing in the breeze. "We've got to find him."

"I made you all eat small tracking amulets that latch to your stomachs. We should be able to find him."

"You did what?" I ask, annoyed.

"Well, we lose you so much, we needed an easier way to find you. Just give me a minute to activate his tracker."

Deciding to be patient and not explode in anger, I wait as Charlie starts digging through her stuff.

Otus

The aching in my skull slowly pounds loud enough to wake me. Upon seeing my surroundings, my breath catches, and my body thrashes in fear. I'm suspended from a cave ceiling, wrapped in spider webs, unable to move.

Below, a gargantuan spider hisses up at me, paralyzing my body with terror.

I watch in horror as the monster's body convulses and gives birth to an egg-sack. She roars in agony, her body shuddering. Once the egg-sack is fully out, it rolls away and cracks open to reveal all the eggs are rotted through. A ghostly male spider appears and uses its palps to shove its sperm up into the female's abdomen. She screams in pain before the ghostly male spider vanishes.

I look on in sadness, almost sorry for her.

Arien

Charlie is holding a string attached to a glowing and floating amulet, leading her to Otus. I follow her through the hotel and out to the street. The amulet stops, pulling Charlie toward a sewer manhole. I stare at the manhole; worried, I ask, "Down there?"

"Looks like it."

"Dammit." I check the manhole, surprised to find that it isn't bolted down. "Are we expected?"

"We'll find out."

Pulling the manhole cover off, I glance down into the sewer. The tunnel walls come to life in the light, crawling with spiders. I stumble back in fear, exclaiming, "Jesus!"

Charlie looks down and gasps when she sees all the spiders.

"I am not going down there," I add, terrified.

Charlie checks the amulet to make sure it's pulling us down there. "I don't think we have a choice."

Shivering in fear, I mutter, "I hate spiders."

"They don't seem to like the light, so hopefully, our flashlights will be enough to hold them at bay."

My face constricts as I psych myself up to go. "Fine." Accepting a flashlight, I jump down the manhole, followed by Charlie.

The spiders flee before us as if guiding us on. "This isn't creepy at all," I note, all my willpower poured into every step forward. A single spider descends from the ceiling, landing on my neck. I jump and scream, frantically trying to flick it off.

Once free of its hairy grasp, I smash it underfoot repeatedly, well beyond the point of death. My heavy breathing slows as I look up at Charlie, who's laughing profusely. "What?"

"I think it's dead."

"Shut up."

Charlie continues laughing as we start walking again.

Atlas

Medea is sitting cross-legged on the floor, staring into a blue fire, when her head snaps back, and her eyes glaze over, a deep-pitched voice echoing from her open mouth, "The one you seek meets an old enemy in the bowels of the earth. An enemy with the power of 8 and the soul of a victim. They meet beneath the halls of Lexington, of Kentucky."

Her skin melts as she screams.

I turn away from the horrific sight of Medea reduced to ash. Iapetus stares with sick satisfaction at Medea's remains. Crouching down, he runs a finger through the ash, licking it, and whispering, "There's a new taste here that she didn't have before. Lilac and gooseberries, yes?"

"Stop. We have work to do."

Iapetus stands, brushes the ash from his knees, and follows me out.

<u>Otus</u>

I watch the spider give birth to another rotten egg-sack, only to be rapped again. A few of her eggs survived this time and hatch, revealing healthy spiderlings. She glances up and meets my gaze. I smile slightly, seeing the sadness in those many eyes. A single tear leaks out of the corner of my eye.

Arien and Charlie step through the cave entrance, staring in awe up at the mighty spider towering over him. Arien whispers, "Shit," wholly intimidated. He lights the phoenix and hefts the Aegis, ready to fight. The female hisses, and hordes of spiders prepare to attack.

"Wait!" I shout, getting everyone's attention.

Charlie yells back, "Otus! Are you OK?"

"Yes. Don't hurt her. She needs our help."

"Our help?"

"Cut me down."

Arien walks to me, using his bear-bone-knife to free me. I rub my wrists to restore their circulation before walking toward the majestic beast I now know is Arachne. I point at the mounds of rotting egg-sack piled up behind her, saying, "Look. She gave birth twice since I got here and nearly all her eggs died. Every time she gives birth, she's raped by a phantom. Over and over again. Only of few of her eggs survive. Can you imagine?"

Arachne roars as she gives birth again, then is raped by the ghostly spider again. No eggs survive this time.

I walk to Arachne's face, reaching out to stroke her hairy cheek. "I think she just wants her suffering to end. I think you can both understand." Arien and Charlie look down in shame, both remembering the trauma they have in common with Arachne. I continue, "I think this is Arachne, the weaver cursed by Athena."

Arien's face constricts in anger upon hearing this. "Athena did this to a woman?"

"Yes."

Charlie steps closer to Arachne, asking, "May I?" Arachne nods slightly, so Charlie reaches out to stroke her face as well.

"She's in pain all the time."

Arien steps forward with an upraised hand, but Arachne retreats from him.

I explain, "She's afraid of you. You've got Athena inside of you. The god that did this to her. You have the power to make her eternal misery worse, or end it."

Tears welling in his eyes, Arien asks, "End it? How?"

"I think she kidnapped me to force you to kill her. Only Athena can kill her, and you are Athena."

Arien nods, taking off a glove, trying to hide the many burns crisscrossing its flesh. He lights the phoenix, quickly transforms the Aegis into a sword, and steps closer to Arachne. She nods in thanks, leaning her head back and roaring.

The walls come to life with spiders coming to say farewell to their queen and mother.

Arien thrusts the Aegis deep into Arachne's brain, making her go limp.

Thousands of spiders swarm forward and cover Arachne's corpse. Arien steps back to watch as all the spiders flee, leaving the cavern forever.

Arachne is gone, eaten by her children.

Charlie turns and sobs into my shoulder; Arien puts back on his glove, looking on in sadness, and whispering, "We should go. I can't be in this town a moment longer."

I nod, holding hands with Arien and Charlie. We disappear in a dark flash.

Atlas

I gently push the slightly ajar door open, glancing into the hotel room. Quickly searching it, I find no one. My expression tightens as I attempt to hold in my rage.

"Atlas!" I fall to my knees, Kronos's voice echoing through my head.

"My lord, Kronos."

"You must not fail me again, or your daughter shall not achieve Utopia beside you."

"Yes, my lord."

Kronos's voice fades; struggling to breathe normally, I pause, seeing an overturned laptop on the floor. Standing and picking it up, I see it's still connected to a personalized pornographic website.

I smile, hope restored.

CHAPTER 76: SCARRED BEAUTY

Charlie

We appear on a hill overlooking a small cottage with smoke billowing from the chimney, a garden of lettuce and roses growing beside it, and a small lake glistening beyond it, several swans gliding across its surface.

A woman is bent over, pruning her roses in the garden, ignoring our appearance. We approach her; she stands to stare at her visitors. Her beautiful, scarred face strikes something inside of me, reminding me of someone I once knew or will know; all these feelings cause the strongest sensation of Deja Vu I've ever experienced.

Arien steps forward, asking, "Hello. Are you Aphrodite?"

"Yes, but you can call me Emma."

"Well, ah. It's nice to meet you, Emma. I'm Arien, this is Charlie, and Otus. We're here to . . ."

"I know why you're here. There're rumors circulating of a boy with Athena's soul trying to restart the Titan War."

"Well, yeah . . ." Arien looks down, nodding.

Otus is staring at the massive scars covering Emma's face, so she turns to meet his gaze. He adverts his eyes, embarrassed, whispering, "Sorry."

"Don't be. I've become a different person since I lost my beauty. I don't mind so much anymore."

Under my breath, too timid to speak up, I mumble, "You're still beautiful."

Emma looks at me in surprise, gratitude in her gaze.

"We need your help," Arien says.

"Would you like tea? I've got a pot on inside."

"OK. We'd love some."

Emma leads us into her cottage and pours tea for everyone, our eyes staring into her back whenever it's turned; all our expectations of her shattered, leaving us empty of momentum.

"Cream or sugar?" she asks me.

Still without out the nerve for volume, her radiate beauty and air of Déjà Vu crippling my charm, I whisper. "Cream for me."

Emma nods, adding cream to my tea.

Persistent as ever, Arien presses, "We need to know your answer. Will you help us?"

Emma sighs, her back turned to us. "No."

"No?"

"I just want to be left in peace."

"If you do this, it may kill you and give you eternal peace."

Emma smirks slightly, turning to Arien and contending, "Does that really work on anyone? I'd never die as a god and who said there's peace in death. I want to have peace here. Just me and my garden with no one to judge my scars."

I stare up at Emma in confusion, asking, "Wouldn't your divinity heal your scars?"

"Yes, but not the damage they've done. When your ugly, you see what people love you for who you are. Everyone only ever loved my beauty. I'm not the same person anymore. No one will ever love me again. I'll never be the charismatic free-spirited slut I used to be. No one will accept the new me."

Arien looks at her scars intently, asking, "How'd you get the scars, if you don't mind me asking?"

". . . The Titans got a tip that I was in London in the 1880s. They sent Procrustes to hunt down the most beautiful women in town to try and find me. He became Jack the Ripper. . . So many women paid the price for my safety. He did eventually find me and gave me these before a woman saved me. And he ate her." Emma clenches her fists, trying to hold in her emotions. "I still see those women every day, reminding me that beauty is a curse that got them killed."

"All those women will have died for nothing if you don't fight."

I glare at Arien as Emma tries to hold in her tears, saying, "You're welcome to stay for lunch, then you'll need to be on your way." She walks to the kitchen to start preparing the food.

I smack Arien upside the head, pissed at his insensitive and cavalier approach. He rubs his head, saying, "Ow. What was that for?"

"You're not helping. Stay here and drink your tea." I stand, going to help Emma, who's sheering corn. "Hey, Emma. About Arien, he means well."

"It's fine."

I stare at her for a moment, trying to remember where I've seen her before. Giving up, I say, "You know, you're nothing like your myths."

Without turning from her corn, Emma responds, "Yeah. How's that?"

"You're not bitchy and self-absorbed, and they definitely didn't do justice to your beauty." Emma pauses but still doesn't look up, her cheeks blushing profusely. I continue, "You should never let anyone try and convince you that you're not beautiful."

Emma slowly glances up into my eyes.

A strong primordial force is drawing us together, something beyond space and time; it just feels so right, like destiny, yet so much more. Her eyes tell me she feels it too. The call of ages. The lust of eternal passion. I slowly lean in and kiss her gently.

Emma smiles and looks away. I ask, "What is it?"

"That's my first kiss in 150 years."

We both laugh softly together before I get sober suddenly, saying, "You know, you don't need to help us. You can stay here forever with your swans and roses, telling yourself you're hideous. Or you can show the world just how beautiful you are. Where it counts."

A few tears leak out of the corner of Emma's eyes. I pull her into a hug, sobs overwhelming her.

Arien

Otus and I wait for Charlie and Emma, just sitting and drinking tea. I lift my tea for a sip but stop when I see my hands shaking violently. Putting the tea down, I clench my fist, trying to hide it from Otus. Shadows deepen slightly as my knuckles turn white, and I whisper, *"Yea, though I walk through the valley of the shadow of death, I will fear no evil: for thou art with me; thy rod and thy staff they comfort me."*

The shadows return to normal; Otus turns to look at me, but before he can say anything, Charlie and Emma walk back in, hand in hand. Emma says, "My divinity's in Paris, in the Eiffel Tower spotlight."

"Makes sense."

Emma hands me a small vial, adding, "You can store it in there."

I stand, preparing to leave, and asking, "Alright. You guys ready?"

Unable to meet my gaze, Charlie mumbles, "I'm staying."

"What?"

"I'm going to stay with Emma."

Hesitating for a second, I shrug, saying, "OK. We'll be back." Otus and I hold hands, disappearing in a dark flash.

***

With a dark flash, we appear in an alley of Paris, framed in evening light. Otus smiles, stepping to the mouth of the alley to stare at the city, breathing it in, and whispering, "Oh, I love Paris."

While he's distracted, I turn and vomit up blood, quickly finishing and walking to stand beside him. I confirm, "It is beautiful."

"We'll need money to get up the Eiffel Tower. 30 or so euros should do it."

I smile, brilliance with a dash of madness and flare striking me, "I have an idea."

I put my plan in motion. Soon, I'm dressed as a street performer with a mask, and Otus is in owl form beside me. I close my eyes, drawing on Erebus to darken all the streetlights except the one above me, which I brighten. In broken French, learned from a crabby aunt in middle-school, I shout to passersby, "Ladies and gentlemen. Come one, come all and see the phoenix."

A crowd gathers around me and Otus, so I continue in English, "Good evening everyone. Tonight, we have a very special performance planned for you. The phoenix and the owl." Taking out my lighter and igniting the phoenix, I breathe fire into the air. "For one night only, you shall see the power of a mythical bird meet the mundane skills of modern avifauna."

In a screeching bird-like voice, owl Otus cries, "Whooo dares challenge me?"

"Oh, I do, fair avian."

I create a ball of fire that I fling at Otus. He leaps into the air, flying over the crowd in circles, the fire close behind. The crowd oohs and ahhs as Otus dances in the sky, the fire tracing the pattern of giant wings in the air. He dives to the ground, turning at the last second, avoiding a wall; the ball of fire continues on, missing the turn and exploding against the wall in a dazzling display of colors.

The darkness thickens until I am spotlighted by our lamppost. I shout, "Die, foul bird." I lift off the ground, fiery wings expanding behind me, blazing with light.

Otus dives toward the cobblestone beneath me; I throw another fireball that envelopes his landing. Hidden within the explosion, he transforms into a man again. Feigned shock in my voice, I cry, "Ha. The beast reveals his true face." Letting the fire and darkness fade, I glance at our collection can, filling quickly with euros.

Addressing the crowd, I render, "The prologue of this mighty avian battle is done. But fear not, for act 1 begins with mighty kings and queens returning from the dead to choose sides in the battle betwixt mythic and mundane. And for the royal pleasure, act 1 of 'The Shifter's Salvation' will commence on the steps of the Louvre itself. Come one, come all, and behold, 'The Shifter's Salvation.' Coming at midnight."

I throw down a fireball at my feet; when the smoke clears, Otus and I are gone. The crowd continues clapping profusely as they pour more money into the collection can.

Back in the alley, I stumble against a wall, vomiting more blood before taking off my gloves to see the massive burns covering my hands and arms have grown. I shake my head to try and clear it, but my eyes start to glaze black. Fighting the insanity, I whisper intently, *"Yea, though I walk through the valley of the shadow of death, I will fear no evil: for thou art with me; thy rod and thy staff they comfort me."*

I stabilize just as Otus walks around the corner with our collection can. He pauses when he sees me, asking, "Are you alright?"

Quickly pulling my gloves back on, I turn and say, "Yeah, fine. How much did we get?"

"I'll need to count it, but it's a lot. Maybe we missed our calling. Street magicians may have served us better."

"Maybe," I say, smiling slightly.

Otus quickly counts the money, pausing when he finishes. "300 euros."

"Really? Holy shit. Is that enough?"

"10 times as much as we need."

"Maybe we really did miss our calling. We should go to the Louvre and finish the show. We'd make a killing there."

"Yeah, if we had any idea where the story was going."

"True. . ." With a sharp inhale, I have to pause for a moment, pain coursing through my body. Otus looks curiously at me, so I quickly change the subject, "We'd better get going. We have no idea if that performance will attract the Titans."

Otus pockets the money as I change out of my magician outfit.

CHAPTER 77: LOVE AND HATE

<u>Charlie</u>

Emma and I are bent over in the garden, pulling weeds, occasionally glancing up to smile at each other. Continuing my intense line of questioning, I ask, "Alright, so your favorite food is quesadillas?"

"Right. Why do you think I live in Mexico?"

I laugh softly, continuing, "And your favorite city is Barcelona?"

"So much to do there."

"Let's see. How many more basic bitch questions can I ask you before you get bored?"

"As many as you like."

We smile at each other again, lost in each other's eyes. Eventually, I say, "OK. Here's a goodie. What's your favorite book?"

"Pride and Prejudice, obviously."

"Really?"

"Oh, hell yeah. Mr. Darcy gets me all tingly. I may have even helped Jane Austen write it."

"Shit."

"What?" Emma asks, curious concern in her gaze.

"That's my favorite book too."

"No way?"

"Yes way." We both burst out laughing before I ask, "You helped her write it?"

"Parts. Lydia's story-line was my idea."

"Oh, I hated that part, but in a good way. Like, it's one of those parts that pisses you off, but you enjoy the way you're pissed off. You know what I mean?"

Emma smiles broadly, saying, "That's what I was going for. Jane threw out most of my ideas cause they were rubbish, but just sitting and listening to her talk about her writing was magical."

"I can't imagine."

We work in silence for a minute as we think, until Emma looks up, uncomfortably. "Charlie?"

"Yeah?"

"Is there something between us?"

I sigh softly, appreciating her candid approach but not trusting the raging fire of lust burning in my gut. Overall, I'm just lost and unsure. I mumble, "I don't know. Maybe. I'm happy to see if there will be."

"Then, I have to ask, and please forgive me."

"What?"

"You're pregnant, yes?"

I turn away, embarrassed. "You sensed it?" She simply nods, so I continue, "It's complicated."

"I'm a good listener."

"It's Dionysus's baby. . . When we meet him, he was a woman and I slept with her. But something happened and he impregnated me somehow. I don't really understand it."

Her jaw tense and unyielding, Emma mutters, "I never liked him."

"He didn't do it on purpose. The big thing is . . ." I sigh, deciding to trust Emma. "I was raped by my Father growing up."

"Oh, my god."

"And ever since, I swore never to be with a man again, and I swore never to have kids. Because I never knew if I would turn out to be a monster in my own way like him." Emma's eyes drop down in pity, but she remains silent, so I continue, "With this child, I don't want to have it. I'm afraid of what it will mean for me, and for him."

"I can relate to not wanting to have a child. I've had my fair share, many were forced upon me, but I believe every child deserves a chance, health withstanding."

"I've always been a feminist and pro-choice and all that, but when the moment came for myself, I didn't know if I could do it. I think I'm starting to agree with you."

"I believe pro-choice is important when the health or welfare of the parties involved is at stake, but when it isn't . . ."

"Every day I wake up and decide what I'm going to do. Give into my fear, or hope that I can be better than my Father." I turn to stare out over the hilltops, smiling when I see child Adonis running with a kite along a hill. Suddenly, I remember where I'd seen Emma before. She'd been in my visions of Adonis, living happily-ever-after by my side. Perhaps it is destiny drawing my heart to her.

Otus

The elevator slowly rises, lifting Arien and I to the top of the tower, a group of girls with us. The girls glance at us, giggling to each other. I smile at Arien for permission to approach them, but he shakes his head, leaving me to stand in disappointed silence for the rest of the ride.

When we reach the top, we get off, heading up all the sub-levels to the highest of the visitor platforms. Waiting till no one is watching, I transform into a bird and fly through an open window into the employee only section. After a moment, as a man, I open a restricted access door to let Arien in.

Grabbing a toolbox, we climb a few service ladders until we reach the very tip of the tower where the spotlight is. Arien turns to stare out across the beautiful night lights of Paris. He starts laughing profusely, bracing his legs against the railing and spreading his arms wide, screaming, *"I'm the king of the world!"*

Smiling, I let Arien enjoy the view, turning to the spotlight and unscrewing the cover, taking out the lightbulb. I stare down at the still glowing bulb in my hand, whispering, "I wonder why no one noticed that they never needed to change this."

"Because I never told them that I wasn't changing it." Arien and I turn to see a tower mechanic standing by the ladder mouth.

Arien asks, "And who are you?"

"Himeros, god of sexual passion."

"Don't you appear as a winged child?" I ask, stepping forward.

"Times have changed. Now, you should put that back."

"We can't do that."

His fist clenched menacingly, Himeros calmly says, "I was tasked by Aphrodite herself to protect it. I will not allow you to take it."

"Aphrodite sent us. There's a war coming, and she needs to be prepared."

"How can I believe you?"

Arien states, "Because, you know as much as I, that she needs to feel beautiful again. She can't live any longer as she is now before she does something drastic. She believes her scars have doomed her, and healing them is the only way to be loved again."

Himeros sighs, accepting Arien's statement. "I believe you, despite myself." He looks up at the lightbulb, continuing, "Do you know why it's called the city of love?"

"No."

"Because her divinity comes with a curse to all that bear it. Only my presence and a whole city to disperse the curse has saved you from its power. If I let you take it, that protection with evaporate. You will be hit with the full power of the curse, and Paris will no longer be the city of love. Are you prepared for that?"

Arien hesitates for a moment before nodding. "Yes."

"Very well. Be warned, if you feel any un-reciprocated love, there will be consequences."
Himeros spreads his hidden wings for the first time in centuries, diving off the side of the tower.
We watch him fly away, waiting for something bad to happen. Nothing does.

I tentatively ask, "Do you feel any different?"

"No. You?"

"No."

Arien suggests, "Maybe we're immune. With your age and Athena's virginity, we may be fine.
Here, let me hold it."

I hand Arien the bulb; we both gasp as we touch it together. The light within the bulb splits
and flows up our arms into each of us. We stumble back, dropping the now empty bulb to shatter
against the ground.

We grab our heads, voices shouting in our ears.

Arien whispers, "Anna," and vanishes in a dark flash.

I muddle down the ladder back to the tourist observation deck, searching until I find one of
the hot girls from the elevator. She smiles; her melodious French accent lilting through my head
like a song never to be forgotten, she asks. "Oh, hello, handsome fella."

All tact lost, I drool, gushing, "Wanna fuck?"

"Pardon?" she says, her eyes wide in surprise.

"Can I bend you over this railing and fuck your brains out?"

"Oh, monsieur." She slaps my face, walking off with her friends. I continue wandering
around, asking men and women for sex. The fringes of my consciousness still fighting through
the rosy hue of lust permeating my mind, I notice that several couples are now arguing with each
other. The magic of Paris is gone, and love has left it. Only hate remains.

I approach a husband and wife arguing; grabbing the wife's arm, I ask, "Can I stick my
magnum dick in your mouth?"

"What?" She replies, her eyes bulging, flitting from anger at her husband to revulsion
from me.

The husband pulls her away from me, shouting, "Oh, so you're fucking him too. My brother
wasn't enough, now random trash in Paris."

"I never fucked this guy. I don't even know who he is."

"Liar!" He grabs me, shoving me against the railing. "Did you fuck my wife?"

No fear present through my lust, I say, "No, but I was about to, unless you'd rather."

The wife yells as the husband shoves me off the Eiffel tower. I scream, falling, fear finally
breaking through my fog.

Remembering my powers later than I'm proud of, I transform into an owl and fly off before hitting the ground.

I soar above Paris, tonight not as an owl but as a hawk, hunting for prey. A group of lovers catch my piercing gaze; I glide down to land as a man on the Pont des Arts Bridge, its many padlocks glistening in the moonlight.

To my surprise, the many couples I'd spied from above are all engrossed in lovers' quarrels, blind to the better prospects begging for their attention. I ask all I come across to release the burning passion engorging my loins, but none have the desire to bite.

I really think I am the last person in Paris interested in sex.

All hope of peace slipping away, I'm rescued by a neon sign cutting through the encircling darkness. It's an open internet café, odd as it seems, but a starving man does not question the hand that gives him bread.

Hurrying inside, I steal the first computer I see; my theft unnoticed because its owner's whole world is the phone from which a screaming sexual partner raves hate. In mere moments, I'm signed into my pornographic site and connecting to Isabelle. She flashes onto my screen, asking, "Oh, Otus. What the hell happened earlier?"

"Shut up and get naked." I start masturbating, ignoring the gasps of horror echoing through the café, my sexual desire breaking them all out of their hateful trances. Several take out their phones, but I cannot worry about that for now; I must finish or burst.

I close his eyes, thinking the moment is close, but to no avail. Shouting, I beg Isabelle, "Get another girl."

"What?"

"I'll pay double, just start fucking someone."

Isabella calls another porn star into the room to fuck her. I tug on myself violently as the passion builds.

I'm grabbed from behind and pulled away from my source of salvation, a cop's voice in my ear, hissing, "Sir, you need to stop this."

Screaming and thrashing violently, I cry, "No, I'm almost there. I'm not done yet."

"The city is falling apart. I don't have time for this." The cop tases me; my whole world goes dark in a blinding shock.

Arien

My mind's not my own, my whole person stripped down to a singular desire to fuck. But not only to fuck, but to fuck the one I love above all else. I'm wandering through the streets of Amber, looking for Anna, and shouting her name.

Stumbling across her house, I bound up the stairs, banging firmly on the door. After a moment, Anna opens it and stares at me, tears welling in her eyes as she says, "Sam, you're alive. . ." She shakes her head, struggling to remember me. "What are you doing here?"

My last modicum of decorum fighting through the urge to take her here and now, I ask, "Are your parents home?"

"No. What's going on?"

"Fuck me."

Of all the words to come from my mouth, I think those two had not been guessed because her whole body shudders, rejecting me with her every cell. "What?"

Feeling my chance of release slipping away, I beg, "Fuck me. Please. I've wanted to fuck you for 10 years. Please fuck me." I lean in and kiss her, but she pushes me back. She stares at me in shock as I kneel down in front of her, grab her knees, and beseech her, "Please. I need you to fuck me. Oh, I need it so bad."

"Let go of me!" She struggles out of my embrace, slamming the door shut in my face.

I sob against the door, still imploring, "Please. I might die if you don't." When Anna doesn't respond, I scream, running away.

Through the town I run, the friction of the race temporarily satiating my desire.

I end up behind Molly's diner to be greeted by Tiffany, Molly's coworker, smoking on her break. "Oh, hey, hot stuff. What are you doing back here?" Remembering her proffered sexuality, I rush in and kiss her. She hesitates for but a second before kissing back, grabbing me and shoving me against the wall to kiss harder.

Tiffany lowers to her knees and quickly unbuttons my pants, leaning in to take my erect cock in deep. I moan, my passion building on my first real blowjob.

When I climax, I throw my head back, my eyes clearing of all lust.

I wince, something burning in my pocket. Taking it out, I find the vial that Emma had given me, now glowing with a godly light.

Realizing what I must do, I disappear in a dark flash, leaving Tiffany staring at where I'd been.

***

Appearing in a dark flash back on the steeple of the Eiffel tower, I stare around at the empty visitor balcony. I call and search for Otus to no avail. He's gone. Going to the railing, I oversee this once mighty city of love, now debased to hate; the only flame left are the flames of many raging fires engulfing the city; the once many whispers of love replaced by the screaming of looters guided only by greed. Horrified at the destruction I've wrought, I whisper, "What the hell is happening?"

"Love and hate." I don't turn, waiting for Himeros to walk up beside me and stare out across the city.

I finally speak, replying, "You warned us, but I had no idea it was going to look like this."

"It's chaos down there. Lover against lover, friend against brother, Mother against son. No one's died yet, which is a miracle, but things are escalating."

"Why is it happening? These people loved each other before they were close to Aphrodite's divinity. Shouldn't it just become like any other city?"

"Emotions are like pendulums. Love and hate are so alike yet opposites." He explains with the voice of a teacher educating a childhood too young to grasp the complexities of life. "When you take someone off of a high of one, they spiral into a high of the other, leaving them vulnerable to the divinity's magic. Which has also pendulumed to hate. When you took away the divinity, you took the rose-tinted filters off peoples' eyes, and now people can't make the distinction between love and hate.

"They can't tell the difference anymore. Aphrodite is the goddess of love, hate, and jealousy. Right now, people think they're all 3 the same thing. As long as Otus is out there with the divinity, it will continue to confuse them. Once the full divinity is contained, people's natural distinction will return. Otherwise, its raw power will destroy that distinction in this city forever. It will leave Paris a ruin, an emotional wasteland to dwarf Chernobyl."

"Do you know any way to find him?" I ask, defeated.

"No, I don't. But the one you're attracted to may?"

"Anna?"

"No, there is another. One that you can never have."

My eyes widen in understanding and horror at my deepest secret laid bare. Pushing my emotion down deep, I say, "The amulet! I gotta go. Thank you."

"Good luck."

I disappear in a dark flash.

CHAPTER 78: DENIED CRAVING

Charlie

Emma stands, wiping her brow and staring at the setting sun; it's rosy light softening her scars, making them nigh invisible. She bathes in the warmth for a moment before whispering, "I think that's enough for the day."

I throw a few final weeds into my bucket; standing, I ask, "You think so?"

"Yeah. Wanna settle in by the fire with a bottle of wine?"

"Oh, hell yes. And maybe a back rub too."

"Don't push your luck." We both laugh together, heading back to the house.

Arien appears in a dark flash in front of us, stumbling. I rush forward as he wipes blood from his mouth, trying to conceal it from me. I frantically ask, "Arien, are you OK?" helping him to stand straight.

He mumbles, "Yeah, I'm fine. We have a problem."

"What is it?"

"When we took the divinity, it caused chaos in Paris. People have gone crazy. They're going to start murdering each other if we don't contain it. Otus has half the divinity, and I've lost him. I need the amulet to track him."

"Of course. Here." I dig out the tracking amulet, hand it to Arien, and turn to Emma, asking, "Did you know this would happen?"

"Himeros should have been there to help you put the divinity directly into the vial."

We look to Arien, who nods, adding, "He was, but he just said some vague warning and left."

"I wonder what he was thinking. Himeros was always radical, but I can't believe he did anything on purpose to hinder you."

"Why don't you come with me and ask him? Help us fix the city while you're at it."

"I can't. If I go anywhere near my divinity right now, it'll only make it more powerful."

"On my own, then. I'll be back." He disappears in a dark flash.

Transfixed with worry, I ask, "There's nothing we can do to help?"

"I'm afraid not."

"Still offering wine? I need it for another reason now." Emma nods, leading me back toward the house.

Otus

My hand itches, and my leg bounces, my raging erection unsatisfied. The gathered assortment of depraved miscreants in my holding cell become more and more attractive by the moment despite my higher taste in sexual flesh. The only thing preventing me from leaping atop the bull of a man beside me is the small fear that has managed to burrow through my lust, terrified at his hulking form, unsure of the damage he could cause if provoked.

Before a victim can be chosen, Arien is escorted into the cell by a police officer. He rushes to me, helping me up, and asking, "Hey, man. Are you good?"

My lust now like a drug or alcohol, slurring my words and clouding my judgment, I grin, grab Arien's crotch, and whisper, "I'm good, big boy. Are you?"

He carefully pries away my hand and leads me out of the cell. As we pass my arresting officer, I mumble, "That guy tased me."

Sighing, Arien says, "I'm sure he had reason. Come on."

"But I didn't like it."

Arien turns to the police officer, his brow raised. "Did you guys drug him, or something?"

"No, he's been acting super weird, though. There's something glowing in his chest. That may be causing it."

"What?"

Arien turns, opening my shirt to reveal a pulsating white light emanating from my chest. I stare down and the light and coo, "Ooh, pretty."

"Fuck. His body can't handle the divinity."

It's the cop's turn to raise his brow and ask, "The what?"

"Nothing. I've got to get him out of here." The police officer helps carry me out of the cell, locking the door behind us.

Arien

With the police officer's help, I manage to carry Otus to the street curb. The cop turns to me and says, "Thanks for taking him off of our hands. We're way too overwhelmed with violent offenders here to worry about public nudity."

"I'm sure things will calm down soon."

"I hope so." A voice comes over the officer's radio, calling him inside. After responding, he turns back to me. "I've got to go. Will you be OK?"

"Yeah, go. Thank you." The officer runs off as I try to find a quiet place to teleport away, an alley catching my eye. "Come on, Otus. Just walk until we get to the alley."

"You're so pretty. Kiss me." He tries to kiss me, but I fend him off until his strength leaves him.

"Maybe when you're sober, man." I help him walk across the street until Himeros appears in front of us. Happy for the help, I say, "Himeros, great. Help me get Otus to the alley so we can get out of here without anyone seeing."

"I'm afraid I can't do that."

"What?"

"Otus, come." Himeros waves his hand, and Otus goes stiff before running to Himeros's side. Otus goes to all fours, pawing up at Himeros's crotch.

"What the hell?"

"Down boy." Otus leans back, staring up at Himeros.

"What have you done to him?"

"Oh, I've made him my sex slave. It's crazy the type of fetishes that I can inflict people with. Except for you. For some reason, I can't affect you."

"I have a virgin goddess inside of me."

"Really? I see now," he says with intense fascination.

"Give me back Otus so we can restore Aphrodite before anyone dies here."

Anger constricts his face, overwhelming him. "Aphrodite? Now, why would I help her?"

"Because she's the goddess of love."

"Goddess of love. You know, I used to think that meant something, a couple thousand years ago." Rage shakes Himeros's body violently, tensing his every muscle as he continues, "But now, I've spent too much time watching these mortals with their meaningless life flit past me, dreaming of a better tomorrow. A tomorrow full of love and hope. . . There's no tomorrow. Not for them. Their lives are so short and empty. It's enough to drive you mad just watching the cycle over and over again.

"I want Aphrodite to suffer like she cursed me to suffer. Eternal, monotonous boredom. And I want the humans in this city to burn. Better now than suffering through their lives, devoid of true passion. Humans used to be so magnificent. Sexually free. Sexually beautiful. But now it's all so . . . vanilla. Times have changed slightly, but it's too little, too slow. There are just so many rules. Rules like consent. In ancient days, marriage and sexuality meant nothing. Just endless pure, passionate, and beautiful fucking. You saw what you wanted, and you took it, and everyone else did the same. It was infinite ecstasy.

"Aphrodite disproved of my more radical sexual beliefs. As such, she never really trusted me. But when the war came, she didn't have a choice. I was the only one left beside her to entrust her divinity to. To ensure I never used her divinity to create a world free of sexual laws, she placed a shield around it. I couldn't touch it. Until you came and broke the shield and unleashed love and hate onto this city. . . I'm going to make this city fuck itself until there's nothing left but ash and blood. And I shall be the sole god of love, burdened with freeing the world of all its laws of love."

Horrified at the prospect, I contend, "We need those laws. It's what it means to be human. It's why we're not still apes."

Himeros gives me a curious look, saying, "No, there's a law that's defining you. Making you different than all the rest of them. I can remove your sexual barrier. Aphrodite's raw, unchecked power broke it down, just a little. It must have, or you wouldn't have been able to free yourself from it. But with me to control it, I can remove the barrier permanently. You can be normal. You can fall in love. Have a family. Fuck a godless amount of whores. That all could be yours." I hesitate, struggling with the choice, tempted by the prospect of love. Himeros adds, "Let me show you."

He waves his hand, and a crowd of naked women materialize around me; among them are Anna, Charlie, and Nelly.

The crowd dances seductively for me, the 3 I know surrounding me and stroking my thighs, breaking down my resistance. Giving in, I let each of them lean in one-by-one and kiss me. I turn to stare into Charlie's eyes, whispering, "No," the sight of her breaking through my reverie.

"No?"

"Not Charlie." I shake all the women off me. The vision fades, leaving me alone. Turning to Himeros with newfound confidence, ash from a burning building falling down on me like snow, I proudly say, "I've been a virgin so long, I don't know any other way." I take off my gloves, revealing my burnt hands. "A friend said, these burns were me trying to tell myself something. I've finally realized what I was trying to say. . . I've been fighting who I am for so long. I'm a fighter. I'm a phoenix. I'm a martyr. I'm a killer. And I'm a virgin."

The light of a burning building ignites the phoenix within me. My hands blaze white-hot as they're healed. "I'm not afraid anymore. Afraid to admit that I'm a monster. But I'm the monster that monsters fear."

His voice trembling, Himeros tries to bravely say, "I don't want to fight."

"Neither of us gets to choose now." I take a step forward, stopping as Himeros presses a knife against Otus's throat.

"I'll kill him. I will."

Smiling, I raise my hand. Otus disappears in a dark flash, leaving Himeros without protection. Before he can react, I rush in, pick him up by the throat, and lift him high into the air.

Himeros claws at his throat, my hands burning his neck. I whisper, "Tremble before the beast."

I reach up and place a single finger against Himeros's forehead. He screams, bursting into flames and turning to ash.

"As you prophesied, there is nothing left but ash and blood."

With Otus gone and Himeros dead, people stop fighting and stare around in shock. I let the phoenix fade and turn to smile at the city, now safe from love and hate.

I disappear in a dark flash.

***

Charlie and Emma are drinking on the couch when Otus and I appear in a dark flash. Charlie rushes forward to catch the collapsing Otus, crying, "Otus!"

He stares up at her and smiles, whispering, "Oh, hey baby. Wanna bagpipe me?"

"What?" Charlie turns to stare at me, asking, "What's wrong with him?"

"The divinities eating him up. We need to get him to ejaculate to release it."

Her jaw drops in disgust, again saying, "What?"

"Do you have any adrenaline, or something? To get him enough energy to masturbate."

"Ah, sure."

Charlie digs through her bag, pulling out a potion, and making Otus drink it. His eyes come into focus as he stares up at us. "Hey, guys. What's going on?"

"Otus, look at me. We need you to go into the bathroom with this vial and masturbate." I say, handing him the vial.

"What?"

"I know it's weird, but it'll save your life."

"Ah, OK." I help him stand, leading him to the bathroom.

When I return, Charlie grabs me and makes me look at her, asking, "What happened?"

"Himeros. He's dead."

Emma turns from watching the bathroom to stare at me, grief filling her eyes. "What? Are you sure?"

"He made us release the divinity on purpose. He wanted to be the only god of love and bring humanity back to our carnal roots. So, I killed him"

"I knew he was extreme, but I never thought he'd go so far."

"I think he was amplifying the divinity, as well. Because as soon as he was dead, things went back to normal."

"It's possible." Pushing past her grief, concern for Paris replacing it, she asks, "Is everyone alright?"

"No one died, as far as I know."

"That's something, at least."

"Yeah, something." Otus returns from the bathroom holding the glowing vial. I ask, "Did you . . .?"

"Get to cockroaches? Yeah." Everyone raises an eyebrow at him, confused by his terminology. He clarifies, "I jerked off."

Charlie curls her lip, staring at the vial. "Is that your. . .?"

"No, I didn't do it into here. It just sorta happened."

I interject, assuaging Charlie's concern, "Same thing happened to me."

We turn to Emma, who explains, "The orgasm released the energy, and the vial drew it in." She takes the vial from Otus, opening it.

We're all forced to avert our eyes as Emma is engulfed in a pillar of white fire. She's lifted off the ground and spread-eagled in the center of the burning pillar.

The fire and light fades, leaving Emma standing on the ground, unharmed.

Charlie steps forward, reaching out to stroke the scars still on Emma's face. "You kept them?"

"As a reminder. . . I need to make things right with that woman who saved me. I don't even know her name."

Charlie nods in understanding, validating, "Do what you need to do." They kiss in farewell.

Emma disappears, leaving Charlie alone, a tear escaping the corner of her eye.

Part 9:

HESTIA

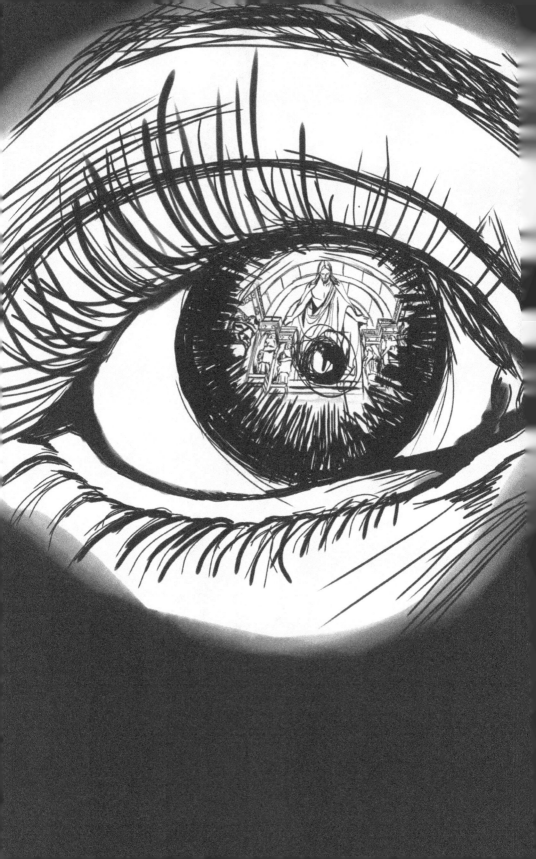

CHAPTER 79: CLARA

Clara

I shed my morning tear, the ringing of my alarm clock blasting through my dreams of Henry Cavill breaking me in half. Sighing, I roll over and stare at my clock; it's 5am. Why the fuck do I undergo such self-flagellation?

I smile and remember the answer. I'm still alive!

Jumping out of bed, I begin my day happy and right. I'm soon naked, turning my shower to full heat, and jumping in. I smile, enjoying the heat cascading down my shoulders. Pouring out my shampoo and massaging my hair, I start to sing:

"Busy days and later nights

Check the time

Watch the clock

Cross my fingers so my heart won't stop

Thinking of knives and rope

Remind myself don't lose hope"

Once my hair is clean, I turn to my newly installed water-proof TV, turning it on. This TV has but one purpose; its presence plus the boiling water against my shoulders creates the most sensual scene. I press play, gently rubbing my clit to warm up, soon driving several fingers deep into my pussy, a Dick Van Hugo gay porno exciting me.

Faster than imaginable, I moan my last, finishing. With a minute longer to complete a deep scrub, I climb out of the shower, dress in semi-formal business attire, and do up my hair.

I stop for a moment, smiling at myself in the mirror. "Hey, sexy." With a set of finger-guns and a click of my mouth, I add, "Who's getting laid tonight? Ah, you." I smile a final time before checking that the dog's food and water bowls are full. "See ya, Hodor."

Hodor doesn't even open his eyes to say goodbye. Smiling at him, I grab my stuff and walk out.

After an uneventful car ride, Adam Levine the only entertainment, I reach my favorite coffee shop. The bell above the door announcing my arrival, I'm greeted with waves from the baristas, one among them saying, "Morning, Clara. Your usual?"

"You know me so well."

"Then why don't you go out with me?"

Smiling and taking the joke, I reply, "As I constantly remind you, you're married, dingus."

"What can I say? You're a heartbreaker."

"I'll be sure to tell your husband that. Maybe I can win both rings from you guys."

Everyone in the shop laughs at this as the barista says, "No complaints here. We can be a thruple, or something."

"But I'm a top. Hard to be a top for 2 people."

"I'm sure you'd find a way." The barista finishes my drink, handing it to me, and continuing, "Think about it. I need a woman to rock my world."

"Well, I've got a date tonight. If it goes badly, I'll give you a call."

"Score. Who's the lucky fella?"

"A handsome guy I met down at the station."

The humor gone, disdain dripping from her every word, she asks, "Another cop?"

"What? I guess I have a type."

"You never used to."

Trying not to remember the night my whole life changed, not remember the girl with no face, I whisper, "Things change."

"What're you guys going to do?" she asks, accepting my deflection.

"Shooting range."

"Again? Is that cops' go-to date spot."

"I guess." I say, looking away, uncomfortable at the anti-cop atmosphere.

"The cops aren't suspicious yet at why you're hanging out at the station so much?"

"I volunteer with family advocacy at the station. A great cover. No one knows I'm there for prey."

"I'm going to get a uniform for my husband and I. That'll get you into bed with us."

Laughing, the light-hearted atmosphere restored, I say, "It just might. You guys have a good day." I wave at the other baristas as I walk out.

Another boring drive follows until I reach Tennant tower, glistening high above the rest of the city. I wave at the security guard as I approach the turnstile, saying, "Morning, Henry."

"Morning, Clara."

"How was your weekend?"

"My arthritis is killing me."

"Sorry to hear that." Running my ID through the scanner, I walk through a turnstile, adding, "You should try Icy-Hot patches. Those helped my Mom a lot."

"I'll have to try it."

"You coming up for lunch?"

"I'll try, but the new guy is late all the time. I might need to cover down here."

"Alright, let me know. Good luck."

"See ya, Clara."

Getting in the elevator, I wave goodbye to Henry as the doors close. With a ding, I reach the IT floor. I step off and am immediately bombarded by Phyllis rushing at me, asking, "Morning, Clara. Want a donut?" She holds up a box of donuts for me to choose from.

"Ooh, yeah. Thank you." I take a donut, and Phyllis flies off to pass out the rest. Shouldering my way through the bustling room, following in Phyliss's wake, I reach my desk, sit down, and situate myself, pausing when I see my photo of Mark Gibbs on the desk.

I sigh, letting myself have my daily moment of silence and melancholy in his honor. My reflection in the photo's glass is broken by my boss Jerry standing behind me.

I turn, and he asks, "Clara, did you get those reports finished?"

"Yeah, I got 'em." Picking up a binder from my desk, I hand it to Jerry.

He opens it and quickly flips through, saying, "I thought we said we were going to use Python on the Smith server?"

"We did, and I included the framework to do so in there, but I feel like Ruby would be a better option. So, I made a mock-up for that as well. The senior team members can choose, and we can go from there."

"Sounds good. I'll let them know. Good work."

I smile after him as he walks away. "Thanks." Drinking my coffee and eating my donut in my first peaceful moment, I sign into my computer.

Jesse pokes her head over her cubicle wall, looking down at me and asking, "So, you excited?"

I smile without looking up from my screen. "It's just a first date, nothing to get too excited over."

"I don't know, you seemed to glow when you told me."

Finally looking up, I let my eyes get dreamy. "He is pretty great. You know, he saved someone's life once."

"Really?"

"Rushed into a car about to explode and pulled a woman from it before it blew."

"Real hero that man."

"Yeah. Yeah, he is."

Phyllis waves at everyone, turning up the TV in the corner and saying, "Everyone be quiet. Listen to this."

Jesse and I nod in promise to continue our conversation before turning to watch the news.

The customary unemotional voice dominating, the reporter says, "We're just getting the report in now. There's been an explosion in Hong Kong, in the heart of the technology manufacturing district. No news yet on which factories were destroyed or who is behind this. The prevailing theory among locals is, it's the Chinese government attempting to cripple Hong Kong's economy after the series of riots beginning back in 2019."

Everyone in the office looks at each other, worried; Jesse voices our concerns, saying, "Isn't our factory in that part of town?"

"Yeah, it is," I say, turning to my computer.

"What are you doing?"

"Afraid I can't tell you that."

"Is it illegal?" I glance up, giving Jesse a look to shut up. She adds, "I'm cool with it if it is. I just didn't see you being OK with it."

"You should just shut up now." I disconnect my monitor cables and plug them into a second computer hidden in my drawer. The monitor brings up an interface for a dark web node.

Quickly navigating through the dark web, I locate the Asian servers. Once there, I pull up a connection to the Hong Kong police database. Exiting the dark web through the Asian gateway and sifting through the police files, I find the reports on the explosion.

After reading the report and smiling, I stand, rushing to Jerry's office, leaving Jesse to stare after me.

I knock on the open door, stepping in, pausing when I see Todd sitting and talking to Jerry. I fluster, saying, "Oh, I didn't realize you had company."

Waving me in, Jerry responds, "It's fine, Clara. What's up?"

"I need to tell you something in private."

Jerry raises an eyebrow, turning to Todd. "Was that everything you found?"

"Yes," Todd replies.

"Good work." They stand and shake hands before Todd leaves, giving Jerry and I some privacy. He asks, "What's up?"

"That explosion, that wasn't our factory."

"How do you know that? The news doesn't even know that yet."

I just purse my lips, giving him a knowing look. He nods, implying his understanding. "Anything else?"

"It was a gas explosion. Looks like an accident."

He nods again, saying, "I'm afraid Todd beat you to the punch. He brought this to me already."

"Really?" I ask, my eyes falling in defeat.

"Yes. We'll have a lot of work to do. Even though it's not out factory, our stock will go down a little, and we need to be prepared for that."

"I understand. I'll get the team to start making market projections."

I turn to go, but Jerry stands to stop me. "Wait. I've been meaning to talk to you, and now's as good a time as any. Please, shut the door and sit."

I comply, giving him a curious look, and asking, "What's this about?"

"Well, I got a new job."

"Really? That's awesome. Congratulations. Where?"

"Director of transportation at Downey Industries."

"That sounds . . . fun," I barely muster up an encouraging smile, the mere thought of that job boring me.

"It's boring, I know. But with the baby coming, I need the bigger paycheck."

"I'm happy for you."

"I was given one last assignment before I leave. To choose my own successor, and I couldn't think of anyone better than you."

My eyes wide in shock, I stammer, "Me? Why?"

"You're good at what you do, and you're good with people."

"Thank you, sir. I won't let you down."

"I know you won't."

It's our turn to stand and shake hands before I go to leave. Hesitating at the door, I turn back. "Sir, does this have anything to do with the new Diversity and Inclusion policy cooperate just pushed down?"

His eyes wide and darting uncomfortably, Jerry says, "What? No."

"Because if it is, I can't take the job. I worked hard for where I am and don't want anything handed to me on a silver platter."

"Why would you say that? You're more than qualified."

"But I'm not the most qualified. Todd's been here 3 years longer than me, and he got the Hong Kong info before I did. And Blaine has 5 years more. And Phyllis has 10. Why me? Is it because I'm the only African American candidate? Cause they'll think that, if I get the job and resent me forever. I want to win the job fair and square."

Jerry sighs, sitting back down and taking out a cloth to clean his glasses. "Honestly, it's not because of that policy, though corporate will give me brownie points for it anyway. No, it's because you're willing to say things like what you just did. That was one of the most selfless, compassionate, and prideful things I've ever heard. You found a way to care about your co-workers while simultaneously saying that you worked hard to get the job. Sure, they have more experience, but you have more talent and more heart. And that's what this place needs. That's what I never had.

"I believe you can direct this office in a better direction than any of the rest of us. Todd only beat you to the punch cause his husband is rich enough to buy him the best computer on the market. Tools not skill won. So, don't ever accuse me of being so shallow as to pander to my superiors' politics at the expense of this office. I always choose who's best for the job. I don't give a flying fuck what color your skin is, what you have between your legs, or who you sleep with. I care about what type of work you do. So, never insult me like that again. You've earned this job."

"I'm sorry," I whisper, my eyes downcast in shame.

"I get why you said it. There would be reasonable doubt. Now, go direct your team. Get to work."

I smile at Jerry, walking out, going to direct my new team.

***

I open my door, smiling as Hodor rushes me, licking violently. Crouching down to pet him, I say, "Who's a good boy? Huh? Who's a good boy? Ooh, enough kisses." I laugh, standing, freezing when I see the shadow of a man sitting on my couch.

I quickly turn on the lights and stare in confusion at the empty seat. "That's weird, huh, Hodor?" Shaking off my delirium, I go to refill Hodor's food and water bowls, adding, "I'm sorry I'm home so late tonight, buddy. I had a crappy date, then I went out celebrating. I got a big promotion at work." Changing into some comfy clothes, I go to my gaming computer setup, put on my headsets, and listen to my mates all say hello.

"Hey, Clara. Where've you been?"

"Partying. I got a promotion at work."

The sound of all my friends cheering drowns out the speakers before William can continue, "That's awesome. . . So, I assume the mod isn't done yet. It's fine, if not."

"What mod?" I grin, enjoying William's flustered moans.

"You know which mod. For 'The Lost World' multiplayer level."

"You know it's super racist, right?"

"No, more nationist."

Fred chimes in, asking, "What does that even mean? Nationist?"

"You know what I mean."

I start typing in a coding panel, saying, "It's done except for one final touch."

"Awesome. Finish it and upload it."

Finishing the code, I export the file and upload it to the server. "Ready."

A round of 'The Lost World' starts; my team spawns in a cavern in Atlantis. We rush around a corner and are attacked by a horde of Russian bears with William's face on them.

All my teammates burst out laughing, while Williams cries, "Hey, that's not funny. That wasn't the plan."

"It gets better."

The bears heft balalaika musical instruments and fire colorful musical notes at us. The laughing becomes deafening as the team fights back.

WHOOSH!

The power in my house shuts down, disconnecting me from the game and my friends. "What, the fuck?" I get up and head for the door to check the breakers. Opening the box and using my phone's flashlight, I search for the problem.

With a faint rustle of a bush, heavy breathing brushes my ear, tickling my neck. I freeze, paralyzed with fear, breathing softly. My survival instinct takes over, pushing my hand down into my pocket, grasping for the taser on my keychain.

I scream, whirling to zap the shadow behind me in the chest with the taser. It has no effect. The shadow reaches past me, ignoring my quivering form to switch the breaker back on.

The lights flicker on, revealing my assailant. Fear clouds my eyes; I can't make him out clearly; the only thing I see is the dolphin pendant dangling from his neck.

I quietly stammer, "What do you want?"

"A hacker," he hisses, striking lightning fast at my head.

Everything goes black.

CHAPTER 80: ROBBED HELL

Charlie

Arien, Otus, and I are gathered around our hotel table, researching gods' locations, having no luck. Arien slams his new laptop shut with a growl, bemoaning, "I can't work on this fucking thing anymore. It's got Windows 8 on it. I can't use Windows 8."

"Sorry, it's all we could afford," Otus defends.

"Maybe we can break into the police station and steal all our old gear."

I contend, "We drew enough attention to ourselves in Lexington with the whole Arachne situation. Military police will be there soon after a sighting of you. We can't afford to give them anything more."

Arien sighs, re-opening his laptop. "Fine." His eyes seem to go out of focus, shadows in them darkening. He shakes his head as if he can no longer read his screen, clenching his fists to regain control.

Otus glances up at Arien with concern, asking, "Are you alright?"

Arien looks up, squinting like he can barely see us. "Fine. I just need some fresh air." He stumbles to his feet and grabs his coat, going outside.

Before I can go after him, my stomach growls violently, nausea washing over me. Otus turns in concern as I rush for the toilet, just in time to catch the stream of vomit that explodes out. Soft hands stroke my neck, pulling back my hair. Emma runs her fingers through my hair like a massage, calming me and settling my stomach.

Many excruciating minutes later, I finish, leaning against the bowl to regain control. Smiling up at Emma, I whisper, "Hey." Without a word, she places a glowing hand against my stomach, ending the morning sickness. I pause for a moment to ensure I'm better before leaning back against the wall and saying, "Thank you. I'm so sick of throwing up."

"I'm glad you're feeling better."

She leans against the wall beside me; we each lay a hand against the other's knee and squeeze it in comfort. After enjoying our silent intimacy for a moment, I ask, "You find that woman?"

Emma sighs and shakes her head. "The gates of the Underworld are sealed, but the caves before them are more dangerous than I've ever seen them. Timorian's forces are everywhere. It's where he's been keeping the monsters he sparred so they wouldn't affect humanity's belief." Tears threaten at the corners of her eyes as she struggles to continue, "Things are wrong down there. There are no new souls. No souls have gone to the Underworld since Timorian took power.

"With the gates sealed there should be billions of souls waiting there to get in, but they're nowhere to be found. Souls aren't making it to the Underworld because no one cares. No one's managing hell." She smiles slightly, moving past her grief. "I found Hecate down there, and she helped me summon the woman's soul. I tried to talk to her, thank her, but she just kept rambling about Utopia. I suppose anyone would go mad after wandering for as long as she has. With Hecate's help, I got her into Elysium. I think my debt is paid, as best as it can be."

I smile at Emma, snuggling up into her shoulder, and confirming, "You did a good thing."

She wraps her arm around me and rests her head against mine. "Thank you."

Breathing in her rosy scent, I whisper, "You know, I'm ready for all of this to be over. This quest. The war. Even the pregnancy and everything else. I just want to retire somewhere with the woman of my dreams."

"Who's this woman?"

I look up to stare into Emma's eyes, gushing, "I don't know, but I have an idea."

She smiles and kisses my forehead, turning to rest her head back down. We hold each other close, both dreaming of our futures, and fighting to ignore the darkness of our pasts.

Otus

With time alone, I send several update texts to my unsaved number, deleting them as Charlie and Aphrodite step out of the bathroom. I stand, staring at them in surprise, asking, "Aphrodite?"

"It's Emma, please."

"Emma, what are you doing here?"

Charlie interjects, saying, "Emma's going to be traveling with us for a while. If that's alright?"

"Yeah, that shouldn't be a problem."

Emma smiles, nodding in thanks, and adding, "Great. And I can help too. I know where Hestia is."

"I'll let Arien know. He'll be excited to get back to work." I get out my phone to call Arien.

Atlas

I drag the girl into an empty cell, throwing her against a wall. She moans and pulls herself upright as I drop a laptop beside her. Tears filling her eyes, staring up at me, she pleads, "Please, let me go."

"I can't do that. I have work for you to do. Magical tracking has failed me, so I need to try more human methods to track down my fugitives."

"Why me?"

"My family and I control the government . . . well everything. And we've had our eye on you for some time. You're a very promising hacker, one of the best we've seen. We need the very best, or our master with end us all."

"How can I find these people?"

"One of them frequents a certain pornographic site." I motion to the laptop beside her, continuing, "We have his laptop. He'll use the site again. We want you to find him when he does, unless you can find them another way sooner. And don't try and call for help. Like I said, we control everything. You'd only make things worse for yourself, and your little dog."

Her eyes widen at the threat. "Hodor?"

"Better get to work."

She gulps, opening the laptop.

CHAPTER 81: FAMILY TIES

<u>Arien</u>

Stumbling from our hotel, I barely make it into an alley and safely out of sight before collapsing against a wall. All the shadows around me darken, my eyes going black. I manage to whisper, *"Yea, though I walk through the valley of the shadow of death. . ."* A racking seizure interrupts my scripture, thrashing me to the cold ground.

I spit out blood, painting the snow before me, marking my fading breath. Gently snowflakes fall down around me, adding chills to the seizure writhing me.

I'm violently grabbed and flipped onto my back, strong hands grasping for my throat. Through my bulging eyes and halted breath, I stare up into my Father's face, contorted in murderous rage. He hisses, "Why won't you just die?"

Ephraim vanishes suddenly, allowing me to roll onto my side and gasp. In the whirling snow, I have other visions of horrors seen before. Like Iapetus torturing Erebus, and Brittnie chained down screaming as a fireball surrounds her.

A single tear leaks out of the corner of my eye.

My frost frozen fingers clambering, I manage to slip out my lighter. Once free of my many layers, I try to ignite it, but my hands are shaking too much from the seizure's remnants.

A set of ancient sandals appear in the snow before me, the pair of feet in them unaffected by the biting cold permeating. The figure kneels in the snow, lowering his face to my view. Hermes leans closer to gloat, asking, "How's it feel, Arien? To have a fate worse than death coming for you. Insanity." He vanishes just as Emma rounds the corner behind him, gasping at the sight of my prone form in the snow.

She rushes forward, cradling my head in her lap, whispering, "Come on, Arien. Stick with me." Her warm embrace seems to stave off the darkness, letting my eyes return to normal. Noticing my recovery, Emma coaxes, "There you go." I sit up and shake my head to clear it as she asks, "Are you alright?"

Pressing the palm of my hand against my head to push back a headache, I affirm, "Yeah, I'm OK."

"What the hell was that?"

"It's nothing."

"Arien?!"

I glance up into her firm, loving eyes, giving in. "I get seizures sometimes because of my connection to Erebus. It's fine."

"Do the others know?"

"Not really."

"Jesus. You realize this could put them in danger?"

Worried that she'll divulge my secret, I attempt to convince her, "I know, but I have it mostly under control. Please don't tell them. I don't want to worry them."

She stares into my eyes for a moment, nodding. "OK. I'll keep your secret, but I don't like keeping anything from Charlie."

"Thank you."

She helps me stand before getting out her phone and texting Charlie. After a moment, Charlie and Otus walk into the alley. Charlie cries, "There you are? Where have you been? Why aren't you answering your phone?"

"Sorry, the battery died. I just needed some air."

Otus jumps in, distracting Charlie, almost like he knows he needs to cover for me. "Well, Emma has a lead on Hestia in Frankfort, Germany, so we brought your gear." He hands me my bags, asking, "We ready?"

"Yeah."

We all hold hands, Charlie and Otus closing their eyes, ready to teleport. Emma gives me a knowing look, so I nod in acceptance.

She teleports us away without the others realizing the difference.

***

We appear behind a bush in a beautiful park; dozens of children run wild, playing as parents and nannies watch. Emma explains, "Hestia's a nanny here. We just need to find out which one."

I take charge, saying, "Let's split up and ask around. Just make sure to stay in sight."

"OK."

We split up to look for Hestia.

Atlas

Few geniuses are born each generation, but this Clara is one, no doubt. I watch over her shoulder as she works, typing furiously at her keyboard, making me afeared the keys will alight in revolution.

Before that eventuality, she stops and exclaims, "I found something." Briefly forgetting our captive captee relationship, she turns to me to explain her triumph, bathing in the success of such an accomplishment. "I got this Otus guy's username and password from his laptop. Then, I created a program that will notify us when and where it's used again."

Slightly underwhelmed by her revelation, I reply, "Very good. Is there no way to find them faster?"

"Not with the information you gave me."

Ice in my tone, reinforcing our dynamic, I whisper, "Are you saying it's my fault?"

She cowers in horror, pleading, "No, of course not. But if I had pictures, names, known aliases, I could use facial recognition, track credit cards, and tag passports."

I nod, setting aside my brief enjoyment at making her squirm. "I'll get you what you need."

<h3 style="text-align:center;"><u>Otus</u></h3>

I watch Charlie and Emma walking around together hand-in-hand, worried about the implications of their relationship. Setting aside my concern for a moment, I sit down on a bench beside a beautiful young nanny, asking, "They're beautiful, aren't they?"

"Pardon?" she replies, her accent heavy and difficult to make out.

"The kids. I love kids; they're great."

"Yes. . . You are American?"

"I'm Greek, actually. But I've lived in America for the last few decades."

She nods, accepting my presence and turning back to watch her charges. "Ah. Which one is yours?"

"Which what?"

"Child. Which child is yours?"

"Oh, none of them."

The nanny raises an eyebrow, concern written in every crease. "You just come to watch children play?"

Realizing my mistake, I ramble, "No, no. Of course, not. That'd be weird. No, what I meant was, they aren't mine, but I nanny a few of them."

"You are a nanny?" she asks, disbelief replacing concern.

"Yes. Why? Can't a man be a nanny?"

"Of course, but most people don't trust men with their children."

"That's very sexist . . . and you'll find I'm very trustworthy." I say, leaning in and smiling.

Now distracted from my blunder, she smiles and tucks her hair behind her ear, reveling in my advances. "Indeed?"

Arien

Turning away from Otus's ill-timed romance, I cross the park to search the far end. When I reach the other side, a square woman, built like Mrs. Doubtfire with silver-grey hair, waves me over to her bench. I approach, and she says, "Hello, Arien."

I pause before sitting down next to her. "You must be Hestia."

"Indeed."

"How'd you know it was me?"

"I can see the darkness hanging round you. I've heard rumors about a boy bathed in fire and night who wants to lead the gods into suicide. But no one seems to know where you came from, who, or what you are. Some believe you are the son of Kronos, risen to destroy him."

A short bark of laughter is torn from me. "No, my parents are ordinary. Evil pricks, but ordinary."

"Perhaps. . . Your darkness is powerful. You need to be far more careful with it, or it may consume you. I can see how much you've embraced it."

"I don't have a choice."

"I never believe that's true. There's always another way. Sometimes infinitely more difficult or beyond imagining. But there's always another choice."

Uncomfortable with her motherly advice, I change the subject, pleading, "Help us, then. Help us end this."

"I know what you want from me, and all I want is my family to be together again, even if it's only in death. Never let Molly go, or your new family that you've found with these people." She briefly motions to Charlie and Otus across the park, continuing, "You'll need them if you hope to have a chance of holding back the darkness and defeating Kronos."

"I'm worried about them. I'm dangerous to be around. I might get them killed. And there's only one end to the path I'm going down."

"I don't believe that. There's always another way," she says, leaning in to emphasize her point again.

"I don't want another way. I want it to just be me in the end, alone. So, I get my wish, and no one else gets hurt."

"That's some pretty flawed logic. You're embracing the darkness and its insanity in order to be free of it, free of yourself. It doesn't make sense."

"The insanity isn't all the darkness's. It's mine too. I tried to kill myself once before, after a rough fight with my parents, I slit my wrists." I lift my sleeves to show Hestia the scars. "But I got scared and showed my parents. They patched me up, but wouldn't take me to the hospital. That's when I knew I'd never be able to take my own life. That's why I joined the military. That's why I joined this quest. A life worth living and a death worth dying. Death by heroism." A few tears leak out of the corner of my eyes while Hestia stares at me with a somber gaze. Wiping the tears, I confess, "I've never told anyone that before."

"What about your family?"

"What about them? They never cared."

"Your new family."

"I'm a danger to them. They're better off without me." Before Hestia can respond, Charlie and Emma walk up to us.

Emma asks, "Hestia?"

"Aphrodite."

They nod to each other in greeting. "It's been a few hundred years."

"Thousand, actually." Hestia smiles, standing to hug Emma. "It's good to see you, auntie A."

"Please, we're more like sisters."

While they catch up, I go and drag Otus away from his nanny friend back to the others. Once rejoined with the others, he asks, "Is this her?"

"Yes."

Otus bows slightly to Hestia, declaring, "My lady."

Hestia nods at Otus before turning back to me and saying, "My divinity is in a home hidden in the Gobi Desert. Only people sharing familial love may enter the house. And, as far as I can tell, only Emma and Charlie may enter from this group. The rest of you aren't there yet."

Charlie turns to stare at Emma in amazement, asking, "You love me?"

Her eyes downcast and her cheeks flushed, Emma affirms, "Well, yeah. Do you?"

"Of course, but I didn't think you would, since we just met."

"I don't understand it either, but it just feels right."

Hestia interjects, explaining, "You've met before." We all wait for Hestia to elaborate, but she refuses, sitting silently.

Eventually, I move on, leaning forward to ask, "Could I enter with Molly?"

"Yes," she says, nodding. She glances up at Otus and says, "But he cannot enter with anyone."

Otus's eyes lower in shame as he whispers, "I understand."

Her eyes full of guilt, Charlie consoles, "Oh, Otus. We . . ."

"No, it's OK. It's not you. I haven't been able to really love anyone since my family. . . I've still got some euros left over from Paris. I saw a hotel over there on the corner. I'll get a room and wait for you guys."

"Otus, you don't have to . . ."

"There's not really a better option."

To distract us from our guilt, Hestia pulls 4 torches from thin air, handing them to me, explaining, "You'll need these. The house is in the exact center of the desert. You should be able to sense it when you get close."

I nod, but not accepting her distraction from Otus, I stand to hug him. "We love you, man."

"Yeah, we do," Charlie adds, hugging him too.

After our goodbyes, Charlie, Emma, and I hold hands, teleporting away, leaving Otus and Hestia alone.

CHAPTER 82: CONSEQUENCES OF LUST

Arien

Molly is alone, unlocking the diner's back door when, Charlie, Emma, and I appear behind her. She flinches violently, whirling, pepper-spraying Emma in the face. I cry, "Whoa, whoa! Jesus, Molly. It's us."

"Oh, my gosh. I'm so sorry. Are you OK?"

Emma wipes the pepper spray out of her eyes, affirming, "I'm fine. No harm done."

"Sorry. I've been really on edge lately with everything that's happened. With Rachel and finding out monsters are real." Molly leans back, taking a better look at Emma, still unaffected by the pepper-spray. "Are you . . .?"

"A monster? No, a god actually. Aphrodite," Emma explains.

"I was going to say magical, but holy cow. A god?"

I interject, "Focus, Molly. We don't have time for this. We need your help."

"With what?"

"There's this place in China that we need to get into that can only be entered by those sharing familial love. And since you and I . . . you know."

"Love each other?" Molly asks, her brow raised.

"Yeah. It's not dangerous or anything."

"I'd love to help, but I can't just abandon all my responsibilities here."

My temper on a much shorter fuse of late, I struggle to calmly say, "We understand, but this is about saving the world."

"Can it wait till I get off at 2?"

"I suppose so."

"Great. Until then, come inside and get some breakfast." Giving in, I sigh and allow Molly to lead us inside and set us up in a booth for breakfast and coffee. Charlie and Emma sit together, fawning over each other, whispering and giggling like honeymooners lost in love, completely ignoring me.

Boredom soon sets in; the only noise, the obnoxious lovers' whispers. Their infatuation boils my blood, every second reminding me how alone I really am.

The monotony is shattered when Tiffany strolls in, waving at Molly and freezing when she sees me. "You?"

All I can give her is a stupid grin and an awkward, "Hey."

"Hey, yourself, you little shit."

"Tiff!" Molly roars from the back.

"No, this little butt-bloat lets me blow him and up and vanishes like a ghost before I get anything in return. I had to masturbate alone for an hour because of you."

I can sense Charlie and Emma struggling not to laugh as Molly looks on in horror, exclaiming, "That's enough, Tiffany. Go to the back and get changed. I'll talk to you about this later." Tiffany sticks her tongue out, obeying. Once she's gone, Molly turns to me and asks, "The heck was that?"

My eyes downcast, I whisper, "Well, when we restored Aphrodite's divinity, some of her sexual energy rubbed off on me. Tiffany was just the first person willing to satisfy it."

"I thought you couldn't have sex because of your whole maiden goddess thing?"

"Seemed to be OK with a blowjob."

The scale of gods and magic overcoming comprehension, Molly sighs, shaking her head. "Whatever. It'd probably be better if you leave. I'll grab some boxes for your food and coffee-to-go cups."

"I'm sorry."

"It's not your fault."

Once she's gone to gather our food, Charlie and Emma burst out laughing. I turn a look of disdain on them, snarking, "Go on. Laugh it up."

Falsely assuming this would be the low point of my day, I'm soon corrected by Anna driving by and slamming on her brakes when she sees me leaving the diner. She bursts out of her car, exclaiming, "Sam!"

"Shit."

She slaps me in the face, screaming, "You wanna explain the other night, huh? Why'd you come to my house all hot and bothered?"

"I'm sorry. I can explain."

"You'd better, or I'm going to call the cops on you. An AWOL Airman rapist won't look good for you."

Horrified by her accusation, I stammer, "I never tried to rape you."

She relents only slightly, still shouting, "Alright. Just a pervert, then."

Charlie and Emma's looks are now of pity, not humor, as I whisper, "You're right."

My confession stumping her, Anna's voice softens slightly, saying, "I just want to know what you were thinking."

"I don't really have a good answer."

To my surprise, Anna breaks out into tears, barely managing to sniffle out, "I'm disappointed that you have nothing to say."

"You'd only forget it again," I admit, my heart tight with the prospect, unable to act.

"What?"

Emma takes control, touching Anna's arm with a glowing hand, sparing me the guilt of hurting her again.

Anna's eyes go distant, all memory of me slipping away like footprints washed away by the ocean's ebbing tide. She looks at me, all recognition and identity blank. She mumbles an apology, climbing into her car and driving away, not even a backward glance to mark the loss.

Emma turns to me, whispering, "I'm so sorry I put you through that, Arien."

"It's not your fault." I stare after Anna, becoming regret itself, void of personality, or other emotion.

CHAPTER 83: HEARTH FIRE

Otus

My master remains silent, the only sign of her presence muffled breathing over my phone. Taking her silence and permission, I report, "We found Hestia. The others are on their way to retrieve her divinity because they share familial connection. I'm worried that they won't all be able to finish the mission. Some of them are too wrapped up in their own issues."

A text buzzes my phone, her only response. It reads, '*Trust and be patient.*'

"I'll try."

When no further reply comes, I hang up, staring at my hotel wall. My eyes trace over the engraved wooden wall panels, letting the patterns and symmetry calm my rattled nerves. The final days of our quest are approaching; only five gods remain, each one drawing Arien closer to my betrayal, closer to the truth.

My nerves no longer quelled by the wall's splendor, I turn to the only respite from my loneliness, Isabella.

Atlas

"Yahtzee!" With this exclamation, Clara declares, "I found him. He signed into the porn site."

My blood pounding, the noise beating a drum in my ears, ready for a fight, I calmly ask, "Where is he?"

"Frankfurt, Germany."

Without another word, I grab Clara, dragging her to a neighboring cell where dozens of starving sirens are stacked in cages, screaming and wailing at the scent of fresh human blood. "Arien's power has surpassed the level at which I'd wish to face him alone. I shall lead the sirens into battle with you at my side. If they move, I want you to track them."

Clara stares at the sirens in horror, their sight opening her life into the world of magic and monsters, not yet knowing of the game of gods, Titans, and primordial deities that she is now a player in.

<u>Arien</u>

The whole day is passed in strained silence, none of us willing to brooch the subject of Anna, choosing to stare at the ground instead. 2 o'clock finally arrives to our visible relief. Molly steps out of the diner, asking, "So, do I need to bring anything?"

"No, you're fine as you are."

"OK. Ready to go?"

We hold hands, disappearing in a flash from Emma.

***

The sparkling waves of the Gobi's sands cascade down to meet red rock valleys, colliding in rustic beauty. Across the rocky expanse, a lone home resides, defiant against the harsh, empty desert. We appear, our dark flash stark against the landscape. Molly turns, vomiting into the sands, her body rejecting the darkness. I cry, "Molly!" rushing to her side. "Are you alright?"

Her body calming, Moly stands straight, whispering, "Yeah, I'm fine. Is it always like that?"

"You get used to it." Once I'm sure she's alright, I turn slowly, walk up to the screen door, and knock. It gently opens to reveal a small patio where several lone chairs sit. Lost by the sight, I ask, "What are we supposed to do?"

Emma steps forward, a solemn smile cracking her still depressed demeanor. She says, "Sit and talk as family groups. Prove to the house that we love each other despite any quarrel."

Grasping the idea, I nod, saying, "OK. Do you mind if we go first?"

"Not at all." Charlie and Emma step back, giving Molly and I privacy to sit and talk.

Molly glances around, the warm aura of the house flushing her cheeks and pulling out a smile. She finally asks, "So, what, ah, do we talk about?"

"I'm not sure. Just talk about what we're feeling, about our problems."

"Well, right now, I'm a little upset about the whole situation with Tiffany. I know you explained it, but it's going to make things difficult for me with her."

I nod, conceding my guilt. "I get that, and I'm sorry. My line of work gets . . . complicated for the people around me. I hate to see what it does to all of you. I'm afraid of what I'm becoming. What my actions will mean for you. If they will make any worse problems for you than a coworker dispute."

Her eyes swell with pity, her anger ebbing, my fear scaring her. "Oh, Arien. Don't be worried about hurting me. I'm always going to be there for you while you're out saving the world. That can never change."

Simply smiling at each other, tears welling in our eyes, I mumble, "Thank you." We pull each other in for a hug, holding tight for a moment until the front door of the house opens. I stare at it, standing and leading Molly inside. There's a small flash of white as we each cross the threshold, final proof of our love.

Clara

With a jolt, we travel around the world in a blink of an eye, instantaneously going across an ocean to appear in Germany. I stumble, terrified and shocked by the move; trying not to fall on a siren cage near their thrashing claws, I back toward Atlas, who whispers, "He's here?"

My eyes darting, I frantically search the deserted park for help, but there's no one. Resigning to my fate, I sit, opening my laptop to ping Otus's IP, confirming, "Yes, the hotel on the corner."

"He's alone?"

I turn on Otus's webcam with a few quick commands, curling my lip at his exposed cock, his hand rubbing it gently. "He's alone, just masturbating."

"Very well. We'll wait here until Arien and the others return."

The sirens start to sing a sad song, their soprano voices stirring something primordial inside me, calling the animal within. Warmth fills me, numbing my skin, and blurring my gaze. When my sight clears, the sirens are gone, replaced by a crowd of lounging, beautiful, nude women. I stare transfixed by their beauty, an unbeknownst wetness tingling my pussy. Reaching out, I try to grasp one of their perfect, supple breasts.

Atlas's hand darts forward lightning-fast, catching my hand and hissing, "That's not a good idea."

I shake my head to clear it; the sirens return to their bulbous, translucently scaled, sea-monster forms. Fighting their still wafting tune, I mumble, "I know. I couldn't help myself. I'm not gay, but there's something about them . . ."

Atlas smiles in the slightest amusement, explaining, "Their song can turn the straightest women and the most homosexual men to attraction. I've even been tempted, but this protects me." Reaching up, he points to a dolphin pendant hung round his neck, a small scroll dangling from it. He adds, "The pendant protects me from most magical interferences, and the scroll allows me to control them. As you can see, they all have similar scrolls."

He motions to the sirens' to confirm his words. I stare at them, an idea for salvation coming to me.

Arien

After Charlie and Emma join us inside the house, we walk down the house's long, dark corridors, all holding hands for comfort. A lone hearth fire claws out of the dark, beckoning us onward. We stop before the hearth and its lone rocking chair. Emma kneels before the fire, whispering, "It's the hearth of Olympus, the fire of the gods. How is it here?"

Hefting a torch from Hestia, I bend to light it. The fire blazes blue, forming small figures acting out a vision of Brittnie and Erebus walking hand-in-hand down the beach, a baby in her arms. They're both laughing and smiling together.

With a kiss goodbye, Erebus goes to buy ice cream, leaving Brittnie to lean down and whisper in the baby's ear, "Hey, Jules. Your mommy and daddy love you so much. We'll never let anyone hurt you, no matter what."

My evil doppelganger flashes out of nowhere, brandishing a sinister smile. He hisses, "I need the boy."

"You can't have him," Brittnie cries, cradling down to protect Jules.

Evil-Me smiles wider, relishing in the hard way. He lashes out, blasting Brittnie with a shockwave of fire and night. She's thrown back, screaming as she disintegrates. Sauntering maliciously, Evil-Me bends over, picking up the motionless and alone baby Jules. Smiling, Evil-Me puts his hand over the baby's face.

Jules kicks and struggles, soon falling still and lifeless.

Discarding the baby's corpse into the hungry surf, Evil-Me turns to enjoy the sight of Iapetus and other Titans dragging Erebus away. He smiles again, the flames of the vision fading.

Molly

Arien stumbles back from the hearth, tears in his eyes. I grab him, asking, "Hey, are you OK?"

Struggling to control his ragged breath, he mumbles, "Yeah, I'm fine."

"What did you see?"

"I don't know. Some family on a beach. The worst thing I'll ever do." He backs away without another word, Hestia's lit torch in hand, allowing Charlie to take her turn.

The fire blazes blue again, the flames forming visions seen only by her. Charlie steps back, turning to smile at Emma, who asks, "What did you see?"

"Memories. All my happy memories with you guys."

Charlie goes to hug Emma, leaving the way clear for me to approach the pagan fire and light my torch touched by the hand of a god.

In the flames, I see my worst day, the day I embraced the lie that would destroy Arien.

I was a little girl, not more than seven, roaming through a blank landscape, the true scene too horrible to even show. Out of the dark, Arien appeared, again as the boy Sam that I think of him as. He knelt in a massive pool of blood, sobs racking him as I rushed forward to hug him. He cried, "It was me. I did this."

My younger self recoiled from Sam, horrified by the sight of him, now covered head-to-toe in blood. I looked down, shocked to see the same blood running down my body, soaking me. I screamed in anguish.

Ripped from the vision, the blue fire fading, I stumble back, my lit torch still in hand, the lingering shivers washing away.

Unable to meet the others' gazes, I look down, stepping back to give Emma her turn.

CHAPTER 84: RABID TITAN

Emma

We appear in Otus's hotel room, guided by magic left for us. Otus slips, falling off the bed, his fingers scrambling to pull up his pants, cum stains all around. His pungent aroma tingles the lust within me, watering my pussy. We all turn away, Charlie exclaiming, "Jesus, Otus. Again?"

Trying to remain calm, Arien says, "We talked about this, man."

Once decent, Otus stands, mumbling, "I know, I'm sorry, but I can't help it."

As Arien reiterates the risks of being tracked through a porn site to Otus, I pull Charlie to the side, my lust needing satisfaction. With raised brow, she asks, "What's up?"

"I was thinking, since we know how we feel about each other, we could get our own room and . . . you know." I wink slyly, selling my point, but Charlie turns away in embarrassment.

"I'm sorry, Emma. I'm not ready. After Susan, Deni, Medea, and the pregnancy I . . . I just can't. I'm sorry."

I avert my gaze, disappointed and embarrassed by my lust. "No, I get it. I shouldn't have asked. Being taken advantage of like you have leaves scars. I should know. I'm sorry."

"Don't be. I want to. I really do, but I'm not there yet. Soon, though."

"OK."

Arien grunts, throwing his hands in the air, drawing us back to him. He cries, "Whatever. We need to find Hestia. Did she tell you anything about how to find her?"

"Just that she goes to the park at the same time every day," Otus replies.

"Well, then we'll just need to . . ." Arien stops; the most melodious and smoothing song in creation wafts through the open window from the park below. The notes numb my senses drawing me forward. We gather round the window, staring down at dozens of nude women basking and singing in the sunlight.

There's something familiar about them that I can't quite place, my unsatisfied lust clouding my reason and driving me forward. Arien climbs out onto the windowsill, prepared to jump down to the women.

His imminent danger snapping me out of my trance, I see the sirens for what they truly are. "Arien, wait!" I cry, reaching out to grab him.

My cry seems to momentarily break the siren's hold over Arien. "What?"

BOOM!

Atlas crashes through the hotel door, charging us, a shield raised to ram us. Arien grabs Molly, teleporting away just as Atlas slams the rest of us through the wall and down to the street below.

Arien

Molly and I appear in the park, just in time to see Otus transform into a bird and fly to safety. Emma and Charlie are not so lucky. Emma grabs Charlie in the air, twisting, so she lands first, breaking Charlie's fall. They slam into the hood of a moving car on the semi-busy street.

Emma rolls off the vehicle, turning to the oncoming traffic, yelling, "Arien!" She grabs Charlie, throwing her to me.

I gently catch her as Emma braces herself, another car slamming into her. She's sent flying by the force of the blow.

Before I can run to her aid, Atlas leaps from the gaping hole in the hotel wall, sirens grabbing and restraining us all save Emma.

Emma struggles to her feet, meeting the gaze of horror that Atlas lays upon her. He whispers, "You? Why are you here? The only god I actually hate." He grabs the dazed Emma, laying in, beating her face in with his fists, then lifting his shield to bash down with it.

Emma goes limp, and Atlas slowly stands, hands covered in her ichor. He lifts her body, throwing it to the sirens. "The time of my revenge has not yet come. One final task must I complete before I revel in your blood." I struggle and thrash, Atlas's piercing gaze turned upon me. He continues, "Because if I lose Arien again, Kronos will continue to be distracted from Utopia, and that would spell doom for all of us."

Letting my fear go, I focus on Emma's limp form, anger surging through me, calling upon the darkness. My eyes go black, and I scream, the sirens grasping me vaporize into clouds of night. I stand, slowly walking toward Atlas, whispering, "Doom is already here."

Atlas smiles softly, drawing a massive Scythe from off his back.

The darkness within me retreats, fleeing until I am left without its power. Collapsing, I vomit violently, unable to stand or fight.

Atlas strokes the blade of the Scythe, explaining, "Iapetus and I used this to torture Erebus for 20 years, and it's from him you derive your dark power, though I still don't know why. Erebus's insanity cannot overwhelm his fear of this." I stumble to my feet, fighting for every inch against the pure terror coursing through me.

Pulling out my lighter, I attempt to ignite the phoenix, but Atlas smirks and smacks the lighter out of my hand, saying, "And with no fire, no phoenix. And your weapons are up there in the hotel room." I reach behind my back and draw my bear-bone-knife to Atlas's amusement. "You're persistent, aren't you? What is that, a bear's jawbone?" Determined no matter what, I spit out some blood and struggle to take another step toward him.

A slightly impressed look replaces Atlas's amusement as he asks, "Why do you fight so hard for the gods? After they've committed more atrocities than the Titans ever could." He walks to Emma, dragging her and throwing her down at my feet. "What about her? Why do you ally yourself with child murders like this one?" My resolve stalls, the accusation halting me. With brow raised, Atlas continues, "You didn't know? She killed my daughter Calypso out of jealousy."

A sob and a cry are torn from Charlie, her tear-filled eyes fixed upon Emma. She utters, "No, that's not true. She couldn't. . . Otus! The power of prayer."

Charlie and Otus start mumbling a prayer to Athena, to Atlas's annoyance. He commands, "Be silent!" With a wave of his hand, the sirens holding Charlie and Otus slit their throats.

A rage-filled scream is torn from deep within my soul; Molly sobs the only sound I can hear, everything else fades away. Charlie and Otus struggle, but they're slowly bleeding out.

A bright flash rips me from my trance; we all turn to stare at the crowd gathered around, recording everything. Atlas falters, muttering, "Sometimes I hate our rules regarding mortals. Luckily, nothing's happened here that their simple minds won't explain away. Some nude cult killing people, but nothing magical. . . And a man beating a boy to death." He grabs the front of my shirt, striking me repeatedly in the face.

I go limp, all will gone. He drops me to the ground, where my vacant gaze turns to stare at the crowd.

Kneeling, Atlas whispers in my ear, "Why would you want to save them when they're so useless. So immaterial." My gaze drifts from the crowd to Charlie's fading eyes. Her hands clutch her throat, but she's fallen still, save for the occasional blink to stave off death. With a moan, my will returning, I roll over, spitting up more blood and standing. "Again?" Atlas cries in amazement.

I turn to face Atlas; tears streaming down my face, I manage to say, "We're all damned the day we're born. But if any of them accept that, just for a moment, they end up like me. A useless, decrepit, suicidal bitch with nothing to live for. They all decide every day that they're going to try and be happy, denying their inevitable doom. That's why I fight for them. To protect the lie. To let them live in their own deception. There's beauty in their fight. They're so beautiful, and that's why I fight. That's something I think you understand more than you realize."

Atlas grimaces, replying, "Now, who's lying to themselves?"

BOOM!

A single gunshot rings through the park.

I turn to see a strange girl standing in tattered rags, her heel pinning down a tased police officer, the officer's still smoking gun pointed at Atlas.

Without pain, Atlas snaps, "Damn you, girl. You realize what you've done? Now, these people have seen something impossible. You must have known bullets wouldn't hurt me. But, I admit, I'm impressed with your zeal."

The girl smiles broadly, explaining, "I wasn't trying to hurt you."

Atlas stares down at his shattered dolphin pendant, the attached scroll completely destroyed. "No, no, no!" He kneels down to pick up the pendant's scattered pieces but stops as the siren's full song hits him. Covering his ears, he attempts to block out the song, but to no avail.

The sirens scream and charge their abusive master. Atlas is overwhelmed by the rabid sirens clawing at him.

While he's distracted, I hobble to my friends. The girl rushes over to help, asking, "What do we do?"

"Get everyone to hold hands."

"What?"

"Just do it." Molly, the girl, and I grab the unconscious Charlie, Otus, and Emma. I cry, "Ready?"

"For what?"

Atlas finishes dispatching all the sirens, roaring and charging his lost prey. We all disappear in a dark flash

***

We're hit by a wave of ice-cold water, slamming us down. Struggling against the riptide, we drag our unconscious companions out of the surf and onto the welcoming sands of a beach. Seagulls caw and swoop low, seeing us as a source of food. Ignoring them, I fumble, trying to see through my swollen eyes, finally managing to heal my friends with my tears. They all gasp in turn, the life restored to them.

I collapse to the sand, unaffected by the icy water washing over me, clawing for me to rejoin it.

"Charlie!" Emma crawls to Charlie, kissing her and holding her tight, tears streaming down both their cheeks. Once their relief is spent, Emma heals the bruises on my face, helping me to stand.

Hestia appears next to us, standing as if nothing had happened. Anger bubbling from the darkness now reunited with me, I ask, "You? How'd you find us?"

"I planted the idea to come here while you were fighting Atlas. I saw the whole thing. I used your distraction to get into your hotel room, where I found my torches still lit."

"Why didn't you help us?"

"I'm not a fighter, I never have been. I would have only hindered you."

Shaking my head, I turn away to help the rest of my friends up. "Fuck off."

"I brought your gear with me, at least. I figured you didn't want to lose it." Our bags materialize in the sand behind her. When no one speaks to her again, Hestia sighs and disappears.

The strange girl stares around, disbelief still shaking her to the core. "Is this normal for you guys?"

Molly stands beside the girl, shivering, her disbelief matching her's. "This was my first time too. It's a bit much."

Helping Otus up, I respond, "It's never been that bad before."

Emma leans closer to Charlie, but she won't even look at her. "What's wrong, honey?"

"Is it true?" Charlie asks, still not meeting Emma's gaze.

"Is what true?"

Charlie lifts her eyes to glare at Emma, exclaiming, "Don't bullshit me. Did you kill Calypso out of jealousy?"

All eyes now on her, Emma looks down in shame, affirming, "Yes."

For a moment, Charlie's eyes are locked on Emma's, as if confirming her words, before she turns and walks away. Chasing her, Emma cries, "Wait, Charlie."

I reach out and grab Emma, stopping her and saying, "Best let her go. She'll need some time."

"But she knew I was a god. She knows all the other bad things I've ever done."

"She didn't want to believe they were true. She was living in denial about your sins. She had to. Everyone she's ever trusted has betrayed and hurt her. She hoped you'd be different. Now, she can't deny what you are. She'll have a hard time trusting you, knowing you killed a child."

"She wasn't a child," Emma whispers, trying to defend herself.

"It was a jealousy kill either way. If you're capable of killing out of jealousy, what else are you capable of? She'll come around. She's not a saint either. She just needs to reinvent her image of you."

Emma nods slightly, conceding, "OK."

"Help me get our gear away from the water."

Once our gear is safely out of the surf's reach, I sit beside Molly, who's on a brick wall, staring out into the ocean with a blank expression. I quietly ask, "Are you OK?"

"Take me home, Arien, and never ask me for help again."

I nod sadly, saying, "I think it's better if Emma took you home. I don't want to risk taking you into the darkness right now."

"Whatever." I stand, trying to hug Molly, but she walks past me, disappearing with Emma.

Staring after Charlie for a moment, I turn to Otus, asking, "How are you?"

"I'll be alright. I just need to be alone." I nod as Otus transforms into an owl, flying off.

Now alone with the strange girl, I walk to her, sitting in the sand beside her. "It's just us now."

"I guess so."

"Who are you? Did you know Atlas?"

"He kidnapped me. Forced me to track you guys down using some porn site."

I roll my eyes in annoyance, whispering, "Damn you, Otus."

"I would have found you anyway, eventually. I'm too good of a hacker."

"Hacker, huh?"

"One of the best, according to Atlas."

"I did some hacking for the military a while back. Maybe we could compare notes sometime."

She turns, smiling at me. "I'd like that."

I smile back, sighing, and standing. "So, where's home for you?"

"Miami."

"Really? I was in Miami recently. I hated it."

"Why?" she stands, asking.

"I pretended to be a gay porn star to get close to a god, but this crazy serial killer bitch hunting me killed a lot of people."

"That's horrible."

"Yeah, lots of bad memories." Pushing down the memories, I change the subject, "Anyway, you ready to go?"

"You going to zap me there like you did here?"

Her discomfort showing, I attempt to console her. "Zap? Basically. It's kinda complicated how I do it, but yeah."

"OK, go ahead."

I reach out, taking her hand; we disappear in a dark flash.

***

We appear in her living room as a storm rocks Miami. She stumbles slightly but soon regains her grounding, saying, "Wow. That was disconcerting." With a loud bark, a Pitbull rushes into the room. "Hodor!" she cries, crouching to hug the dog, who repeatedly licks her face. "Good boy."

"Cute dog."

"Yeah, he's the best."

"Well, I should get going."

"Wait." She stands, rushing to her desk, where she grabs a piece of paper and writes something down, handing it to me.

"What's this?" I ask.

"My phone number. If you need anything, let me know."

I smile, nodding, and tucking the number into my pocket. We hug in farewell, somehow a familiar connection already between us. "Wait, I don't even know your name."

"Nor I yours."

"I'm Arien."

She reaches out to shake my hand, saying, "Hi, Arien. I'm Clara."

I raise an eyebrow at her name, remembering Apollo's prophecy. "Clara?"

"Yeah. Why?"

"A friend of mine recently told me that I'd soon meet a Clara and that she'd change my life."

Clara smiles, slightly uncomfortable, asking, "Is that some sort of pickup line?"

"No, it's just . . . Whatever. A pleasure to meet you, Clara. I'll see you around." Unable to understand the repercussions of her name, I step back and disappear.

Part 10:

DEMETER

CHAPTER 85: LOVE BETRAYS

Long ago, Odysseus of Ithaca stared out upon the blue expanse of the Aegean Sea, a look of longing for home wrinkling his chiseled face. Calypso walked up behind him, wrapping her arms round his waist, a dolphin pendant dangling from her neck. She breathed in deeply the scent of Odysseus's long flowing hair, whispering, "Hmm. Thy scent is most refreshing." Odysseus continued to stare out across the sea, barely hearing her. "My love, what troubles thee?"

She walked around to stare up into Odysseus's eyes, forcing him to acknowledge her, though his eyes remained fixed upon the sea. He finally relented, answering, "My time to journey home is upon us. I must go."

"Nay. Thou must needs stay here with thine true love. You shan't leave."

"Verily, my son requires a Father," he expounded, a father's love twinkling his eyes.

"Thy son tis a man grown. He hast no time to learn the dawdled lessons of a Father. The lessons others bestowed upon him while his Mother still suckled him."

Tears welled up in Calypso's eyes as Odysseus finally turned his gaze from the sea to stare down at her. "I fear that I must hasten away despite thine true words. I must needs do this."

Calypso paused before sprinting away, sobs overwhelming her. Once she's gone, Odysseus fell to the sand, burying his head in his hands.

In the nearby cave, Calypso screamed violently, tearing out her hair, collapsing in tears. Calming, she went to her loom, weaving to calm herself. As her breathing slowed and her tears subsided, Calypso began to sing a melodious song in a language unknown to mortal men.

Hermes flew through the cave mouth, borne on his winged sandals, landing next to the blazing hearth.

Calypso turned and smiled up at Hermes, saying, "God of golden wand, why have you come? A beloved, honored friend, but it's been so long, your visits much too rare. Tell me what's on your mind, I'm eager to do it, whatever I can do, whatever can be done."

As Calypso talked, she had Hermes sit at her table, heaping endless food before him. He ate briefly but stopped when he saw her expecting gaze. "As one god to another, you ask me why I've come. I'll tell you the whole story, mince no words, your wish is my command. It was Zeus who bade me come hither against my will. Who of his own will would speed over so great space of salt seawater, great past telling? Nor is there at hand any city of mortals who offer to the gods sacrifice and choice hecatombs.

"But it is in no wise possible for any other god to evade or make void the will of storming Zeus. He says that there is here with thee a man most wretched above all those warriors who around the city of Priam fought for nine years, and in the tenth year sacked the city and departed homeward. But on the way they sinned against Athena, and she sent upon them an evil wind and long waves. There all the rest of his goodly comrades perished, but as for him, the wind and the wave, as they bore him, brought him hither. Him now Zeus bids thee to send on his way with all speed, for it is not his fate to perish here far from his friends, but it is still his lot to see his friends and reach his high-roofed house and his native land."

Calypso shuddered in despair at Hermes's words. "Cruel are ye, O ye gods, and quick to envy above all others, seeing that ye begrudge goddesses that they should mate with men openly, if any takes a mortal as her dear bed-fellow. Thus, when rosy-fingered Dawn took to herself Orion, ye gods that live at ease begrudged her, till in Ortygia chaste Artemis of the golden throne assailed him with her gentle shafts and slew him. Thus too, when fair-tressed Demeter, yielding to her passion, lay in love with Iasion in the thrice-ploughed fallow land, Zeus was not long without knowledge thereof, but smote him with his bright thunder-bolt and slew him. And even so again do ye now begrudge me, O ye gods, that a mortal man should abide with me.

"Him I saved when he was bestriding the keel and all alone, for Zeus had smitten his swift ship with his bright thunder-bolt, and had shattered it in the midst of the wine-dark sea. There all the rest of his goodly comrades perished, but as for him, the wind and the wave, as they bore him, brought him hither. Him I welcomed kindly and gave him food, and said that I would make him immortal and ageless all his days. But since it is in no wise possible for any other god to evade or make void the will of thundering Zeus, let him go his way, if Zeus thus orders and commands, over the unresting sea. But it is not I that shall give him convoy, for I have at hand no ships with oars and no men to send him on his way over the broad back of the sea. But with a ready heart will I give him counsel, and will hide naught, that all unscathed he may return to his native land."

Hermes was taken back by Calypso's fury but soon recovered, nodding. "Even so, send him forth now, and beware of the wrath of Zeus, lest haply he wax wroth and visit his anger upon thee hereafter." He stood, bid farewell, and flew off, leaving Calypso to deliver Odysseus the news of his salvation, her tears only just held at bay.

Calypso walked across the gleaming sands to where Odysseus was still huddled and sobbing. She sighed, resigned to her grief, kneeling to stroke his back, whispering, "Unhappy man, sorrow no longer here, I pray thee, nor let thy life pine away; for even now with a ready heart will I send thee on thy way. Nay, come, hew with the ax long beams, and make a broad raft, and fasten upon it cross-planks for a deck well above it, that it may bear thee over the misty deep. And I will place therein bread and water and red wine to satisfy thy heart, to keep hunger from thee. And I will clothe thee with raiment, and will send a fair wind behind thee, that all unscathed thou mayest return to thy native land, if it be the will of the gods who hold broad heaven; for they are mightier than I both to purpose and to fulfill."

Finally raising his teared-filled eyes, Odysseus stared up at Calypso in amazement, his way home clear.

In the far distance, Emma watched the couple say goodbye, anger overwhelming her.

***

Once the way to Calypso's heart was free of competitors, Emma approached the cave, Calypso's grief palpable in the air. Calypso weaved alone to calm her shaking hands, oblivious to Emma standing behind her, just enjoying the sight of her lover freed.

Her desire fulfilled, Emma reached out to brush Calypso's pearly-white shoulder. She turned, smiling up with love, her grief forgotten. "My love. Tis been an age since thine last visit."

A strained smile concealing her anger, Emma replied, "Tis because mine heart grew cold when word reached on high of thy human bedfellow."

Calypso's expression was replaced with one of worry, her hands shaking again. "Twas not Lord Zeus nor Lady Athena that brought about the departure of Odysseus?"

"Nay, but mine steady hand upon Lord Zeus's staple of manhood," Emma said, her fist raised tight, the skin turning pale.

"My heart never desired to deceive nor betray thee, but the heart leads us down uncertain paths that none can know nor escape from."

Releasing her fist, Emma's face softened, the anger ebbing. "My rage has lessened since beholding you and your beloved together."

"Thou wast upon mine island in days past?"

"Yea, for my heart burned to know if thine happiness was with another. To mine sight, it doth. Verily, I called upon my uncle for aid in finding a path toward thine happiness."

"Forsooth, thou hast?"

Emma slowly took Hades's Helm of Darkness from within her robes, holding it out to Calypso. "Odysseus fled not for lack of love, but for fear of losing you whilst he grew old. With this, thou mayest become mortal and join thy beloved in Ithaca for a mortal life lived in happiness. If your desire is thus, thous mayest end thy isolation and live as a mortal."

Her eyes fixed upon the Helm for a moment, Calypso made her decision, her gaze lifting to meet Emma's eyes. "Thy wouldst do this for me, despite mine betrayal of thee."

"My love for thee doth burn too bright. I must see thee happy, at any cost," Emma replied, tears of love in her eyes.

Calypso smiled in thanks, taking the Helm and putting it on. She closed her eyes as she focused, beginning to glow with a godly light as her divinity left her. With raised hands, Emma washed the divinity down toward her Cestus, the girdle round her own waist, to hold it close.

Calypso sighed, collapsing into Emma's arms. Her eyes slowly fluttered open, staring up at Emma, whispering, "Aphrodite?"

"Yes?"

"My love for thee still burns. It shall burn through the ages despite my now feeble form and my mortal husband to be."

Emma smiled down at her love, grief in her eyes. "I know." Her eyes inverted, the pupils turning white, Emma stabbed Calypso in the heart.

Gasping softly, barely noticeable, Calypso stared up at her once and always love, releasing her final breath.

Her grief and guilt awoken by the warm blood flowing down her hand toward her lap, Emma released a howl of anguish, holding tight the corpse of her lover.

CHAPTER 86: DENIED FORGIVENESS

Charlie

My soul feels dead and empty, devoid of life, my emotions too strong to comprehend or grasp. I sit with my friends, hearing Emma tell the story of her murder of one she called love. How sure am I that I would not end likewise?

"Calypso had sided with the Titans during the first Titan war," Emma continues, "She was exiled for it and needed a prison. I made a curse surrounding Ogygia that made mortal men come and fall in love with her to torture her. But I don't know if my curse worked too well because I fell in love with her too. We had a secret affair for thousands of years. Calypso never fell for any of the men stranded on her island. Until Odysseus, that is. It broke me. I was a very different person back then. So, I killed her out of rage and jealousy. The gods helped keep that story secret from the mortals; even they would have a hard time worshiping after a lesbian love affair turned murderous. But Atlas found out somehow." Grief and fear twinges at the edges of my empty soul, releasing a single tear down my cheek.

Noticing the tear, Emma pauses, unable to continue for a moment, genuine regret in her eyes. Eventually, she explains, "We were all different back then. We evolve with humanity. At the time, any mortal would have done the same. I did it because my morality was humanity's. I've tortured myself for millennia because of it, none the less. I'm sorry you found out this way. My biggest regret and my biggest secret. Can you find it in your heart to forgive me, Charlie?"

I just turn away, afraid to meet Emma's gaze. Arien stands, pacing, rage in his eyes. He asks, "Why should we help the gods if they act like you? Like Hermes or Dionysus? How are any of you better than the Titans? The Titans haven't done such a bad job the last 2 thousand years, at least compared to you. Christianity has done endless good because of them. It's made the world a better place."

"Christianity got away from them after the Reformation, they can't be credited for the good it's done since."

Her excuses irritating Arien, he cries, "Now's not the time. No time for excuses. Regardless, why should we serve and worship you over them, or ourselves?" She looks down, her shame preventing her from meeting his gaze. When no answer comes, Arien sighs in exacerbation, continuing, "It's up to Charlie what happens with you, if you get to stay with us."

Both Emma and I look up, meeting each other's gazes. Emma asks, "Charlie?"

"I think you should leave, for a while at least."

"Not you too," she whispers, hope gone.

My eyes lower again, no longer able to look at her. "You hurt me. I believed you were a good person, but I'm dating a murderer. I almost wish you'd cheated on me like Susan."

"I'm a god. We all murder. We have to sometimes."

"It's no excuse. You have to be better. There can't be a statute of limitations on murder. Please, just go."

Emma sighs, vanishing without another word.

Wallowing in his anger, Arien turns and leans against the windowsill, his eyes flashing black for a moment until he regains control.

Otus tentatively asks, "What's our plan? Are we moving forward?"

With a nod, Arien affirms, "Nothing's changed. It's too late to stop. We need to find the rest of the divinities."

"Alright. I'm going to reach out to my contacts again. Maybe they've found something."

Arien lets Otus leave before he sits beside me, putting an arm around me and whispering, "It's going to be alright."

"I know. I'm just going to need some time."

He smiles, standing and saying, "I'll go and get some food for you then." Squeezing my shoulder, he heads for the door.

Arien

Fighting my mounting anger with every step, I walk to a vending machine, getting some food. I pause when I hear Otus's voice coming from around the corner.

Stepping closer, I hear him say, "No, Charlie didn't take it very well, and Arien started yelling at Aphrodite. I don't really understand it. They know the myths. They know the types of things that were done. But they're still determined to finish the quest. Any more distractions, though, and they'll lose faith. They've been through so much already." His phone buzzes as if in response. Otus checks it before continuing, "We're at some motel outside Boston. Blue Hills off I-93." With another text, he says, "Excellent. I'll be ready, but Arien won't understand." One finally text comes; Otus replies, "I understand. It's the best thing. I'll wait a while, then tell them."

I hide as Otus hangs up the phone and walks back toward the hotel. Once he's gone, I stare after him, contemplating the ramifications of his conversation, his betrayal.

Charlie

I hold the pills tight, unable to let go, nor to take them. My stomach tightens, revolting against me and bringing sobs to my eyes. Through my watery gaze, I stare at the selfie Emma and I took in the Gobi, back when we were on top of the world.

Arien rushes in; I quickly hide the pills and wipe my eyes, but he ignores me, going to his laptop. Trying to act casual, I ask, "I thought you were getting food?"

"I was, but something came up. We may have a problem."

"What?"

"I think Otus may be spying on us for the Titans."

Balking at the idea, I contend, "That's ridiculous."

"Is it? Remember how many times we've been found because of Otus. Just yesterday, he led Atlas to us."

"But neither of us would be on this quest without him."

"Kronos could be using us to draw the gods out of hiding to defeat them once and for all. He's decimated them once and nothing's changed."

"Yes, it has."

He finally pauses his furious typing to turn and stare at me, asking, "What?"

"Emma said the Titan's lost Christianity after the Reformation. They've lost the power of belief that sustained them in the last war. That's why he's having our culture destroy Christianity. Using the only thing he has. It's dangerous out there outside of his control."

Comprehension dawning, he tentatively deduces, "Does this mean we have hope?"

"Maybe. . . I think the gods knew there was hope this whole time, but lied to us because of you. Your death wish. Only a hopeless cause would have convinced you."

Arien bites his lip, anger surging through him. "Fuck them." He turns back to the computer, signing into Otus's phone carrier account, and bringing up today's call history. A number with a Colorado area code catches his eye. He mumbles, "Colorado?" Cross-referencing the number with the calls Otus made in Germany, Arien exclaims, "See. He called this same number just before Atlas showed up. Clara said they found us from his porn site, but maybe he did that on purpose as an alibi."

"But Atlas had his throat slit too."

"It's good tactics to kill an informant that knows your secrets when their usefulness expires."

"If you're right and they want us to drive the gods out, why would he kill Otus and stop us before we finished?"

Arien doesn't answer; he just stares at the ground, fighting his instincts to distrust Otus.

CHAPTER 87: RAT IN THE HOUSE

Arien

Prepared for Otus's return, I stand waiting to accuse him. He enters, stopping; sensing the tension in the air, he asks, "Is everything alright?"

Without a word, I turn the open the laptop to show him, saying, "You want to explain why you called this number before Atlas show up in Germany?"

Not missing a beat, he explains, "That's my therapist."

"Therapist?" I whisper, my now close compatriot rage bubbling up. Giving in, I leap across the room, grasping Otus and pinning him against the wall, my bear-bone-knife pressed into his jugular.

"Arien!" Charlie cries, unheeded.

Focusing on Otus, I whisper, "Don't bullshit me, Otus. You're spying for the Titans, aren't you?"

His eyes go wide in shock as he stammers, "What? No. How could you think that after everything we've been through?"

My vision focuses on the throbbing vein in his throat, my eyes turning black, and my mouthwatering. I lick my lips, my hand itching to cut it, my lips throbbing to taste it.

Wrestling back control, I shake my head, clearing my eyes. "I'm not in the mood for having my emotions played on. I overheard you telling someone where we are. Who was it?"

Sighing, Otus gives up, confessing, "Athena."

I drop Otus, surprise overtaking my other emotions, my anger and darkness gone. He crumbles to the ground, rubbing his throat as I stumble back, and whisper, "Athena? I thought she was missing like the other gods."

"I've never lost contact with her since Pompeii. I was the guardian of her divinity when the tornado came. She had to know where I was to ensure her divinity's safety. And she's how I found you when this all started. She sensed you use her power."

"If that's true, why wasn't she our first stop? Why didn't we already restore her?"

His eyes lower, the confession too far to stop but sticking in his mouth none the less. "Athena didn't want to take your powers and cripple your ability to restore the other gods. . . And it might have killed you."

"What?" I stammer, tears of anger and hope welling.

"We wanted to hold it off for as long as possible. Make her the last god to restore."

No longer able to stand, I slowly lower to the bed, staring blankly at a wall for a moment. "You should have told me."

"We weren't sure you'd go on. Not sure if your death wish was only surface level. An undefined possible future death is a lot less frightening than a sure thing at a specific time."

"Did you tell her everything?"

"Everything?" He asks, confused by my change of direction.

"About my darkness, about what Deni did, what Emma did, and all the rest?"

His eyes downcast again, he mumbles, "Yes. All of that, the pills, and more."

Charlie's rapid jolt catches my attention, so I ask, "Pills?"

"Nothing."

"We trusted you with our secrets, and you betrayed us. That's what hurts." Resigned to our new dynamic, I continue, "Who is she?"

"Colonel Iliana Noble." Otus answers, saying, "She's an instructor at the Air Force Academy. You can check her out. That number's listed as hers on the AF Global directory."

Without another word, I get out my laptop to research her. Charlie tentatively asks, "That's the woman who got us into NORAD?"

"Yes."

"I found her," I exclaim, turning the laptop to show Charlie.

"She even looks like the statues," Charlie notes, the ghost of a smile on her lips.

Thinking our anger's passed, Otus says, "I was on the phone with her earlier because Demeter reached out to Athena. She's a potato farmer in Idaho, and her divinity's on a mountain in Peru."

Forgoing politeness, I accept, "OK. We'll go . . . but you'll stop telling her our secrets. It's none of her business."

"I get it. I betrayed your trust. Can you forgive me?"

I stare at Otus for a moment before standing and saying, "We should get going. Checkout's soon. Don't want to pay for another day."

"I checked out before I came back." Otus mutters, hurt by my deflection.

"Then grab your stuff. Let's go."

We all grab our gear, holding hands, and vanishing in a dark flash.

CHAPTER 88: PRECIOUS DOVE

<u>Arien</u>

An icy grip rips us from our path, pulling us deep into the darkness. We all stumble, horrified by our arrival. Erebus appears, grasping Otus's wrist, who cries, "Let me go." The rest of our hands still conjoined, I kick Erebus, freeing Otus.

"Get us out of here," Charlie screams.

I close my eyes, attempting to free us, but to no avail. "I can't."

Erebus starts walking toward us; Otus whimpers, "Run!" We all turn and flee into the endless darkness.

The asinine nature of our plan strikes Charlie as she asks, "How do we run from him, when we're literally inside of him?" Everywhere we go, Erebus appears before us. We change directions, and there he'd be, forever our fate. With inhume speed, Erebus slides across the obsidian ground, reaching out for Charlie. "Do something," she begs.

I'm rooted to the spot in fear, unable to stop the claws nearing my friend's vulnerable flesh.

A sudden scream rings through the empty, shaking Erebus to his core. He roars and collapses to the ground, muttering, "Never, never, never. She's coming. Take the boy, her boy. Blood, blood, so much blood. My blood, her blood, his blood, our blood. Blood burns, blood black. Forever is ahead. Utopia burning, killing, feeding, being. Fight the light. Be the empty. Don't blink. Blink and you're dead. Baby in womb, fed by fire and night. Baby makes no Utopia, dystopia. Protect the boy. Don't let the boy burn."

My body freed by Erebus's distraction, I disappear, the others in hand.

***

Appearing on a majestic Peruvian peak, we stumble apart, blind to the beauty all around. Charlie staggers away from me, desperate for distance; she screams, "What the hell was that?"

"I don't know."

"I thought you had this under control."

Sick of defending myself, I contend, "Well, you try controlling an insane primordial deity inside your head. It's not easy."

Staring at our surroundings, Otus whispers, "Guys."

"We can't keep going in there if we nearly die every time," Charlie continues, ignoring Otus.

"What choice do we have?" I rebuff, "We don't have time or the capability to fly commercial to Peru. We're wanted for what happened in NORAD, remember?"

"We'll think of something. I can find a spell."

"Guys!" We finally turn to Otus, freezing as we see a massive wheat field, impossible in every way, foreign to the snowy mounds all around.

"Holy shit," I whisper in awe. "Why aren't we freezing? How's wheat growing up here?"

"Demeter," Otus whispers with a smile.

Charlie notices several basins surrounding the wheat field, walking to inspect them. Following, I ask, "What is it?"

"These carvings, they're magical in nature." She dips a finger into the potion filling the basin, licking her finger. Gagging profusely, she spits it out, trying to vomit.

"What is it?"

"This spell, it's disgusting. Salt, snake's tongue, animal blood, and literal human shit."

Otus and I grimace. "Fuck. You ate that?"

"It's why we were fighting with each other. It's a spell to cause hate. It's meant to keep people away from this place."

"Why wasn't I affected?" Otus asks.

"Because you're partially a bird, and this ecosystem needs animals to feel welcomed." Taking out her dagger, Charlie scrapes at the runes on the basin before standing. "There. With one basin down, the whole spell is lifted."

I nod, feeling the difference.

A wave of power washes over me; I tense, my eyes drawn skyward to a turtle dove soaring above. Swooping down, it lands on a large oak tree in the center of the wheat field. "Look," I whisper.

With his brow raised, Otus asks, "Is that a turtle dove? They shouldn't be on this continent."

"Check it out."

He nods, transforming into an owl and flying toward the dove. The moment Otus touches it, he's blasted backward and thrown to the ground. Limping back as a man, he sits beside us, defeated.

"Are you OK?"

"I'll be fine. That was godly power. Only someone who can withstand divinity can touch it."

Both their eyes are drawn to me. "I got it."

"Here." Charlie digs through her bag, pulling out a mint seed and handing it to me. "Take this as an offering, but be quick. The Titans can still track prayers. We'll want to get out of here fast."

I nod, taking the seed and walking through the wheat field, stopping at the base of the magnificent oak. Kneeling, I plant the mint seed, praying:

"Oh, universal Mother, I give thee praise and offer up this gift of
mint seeds that I may be graced by thy presence."

The seeds sprout and spread until the base of the oak is surrounded by mint plants, a warm bush to the oak's sturdy base. The dove perches on a branch above my head, cocking its beak. I raise my arm in invitation. It swoops down, landing on me, and glowing as it transforms into a small statue.

I stand, carrying the statue back through the field to my friends. Charlie asks, "Got it?"

"Yeah."

"Let's go before the Titans get here." With a dark flash, we abandon the already wilting wheat field.

CHAPTER 89: TRUTH WILL OUT

<u>**Arien**</u>

Pain! Pure, unadulterated pain racks my body. I scream, collapsing in the empty, stranding my friends in my landscape of insanity. They watch on in horror as I curl up, convulsing violently. Echoing through the rising fog unseen, Erebus whispers, "No more. No more. A son must know his Mother. Brittnie die, Brittnie live. Him born of fire and night needs loved." Blood pours from my every orifice, my thrashes slicing my virgin skin upon the cold obsidian.

Charlie clutches me, trying to hold me tight, to protect me. "Come on, Arien. Focus." She cries, slapping me in the face. When my seizure only grows in intensity, she turns to Otus, asking, "Any ideas?"

"The shadow of death," he replies.

"What?"

He crouches beside us, explain, "Whenever he's losing it, he quotes the shadow of death scripture. I think Molly told him to. It reminds him of her."

"Do you know it?"

"I helped Shakespeare write it."

"What?"

"Nothing. *Yea, though I walk through the valley of the shadow of death, I will fear no evil: for thou art with me; thy rod and thy staff they comfort me.*" Slowly, my trembling subsides, the image of Molly pulling me through.

"Are you alright?" Charlie asks, barely daring to hope.

"I think so." They help me to stand and find my balance. "We should get out of here." We hold hands and attempt to leave, to no avail, we are once again trapped.

"Arien, what's happening?"

"I don't know."

"Are we trapped again?" My eyes answer her question. She mutters, "Fuck," lost for other words. Gentle voices start to echo through the darkness, all too low to make out. "What is that?"

Before I can answer, the fog rushes in, surrounding us all, forming the alley across from Molly's diner, its paint still new in burgeoning youth. Oblivious to our presence, Erebus, as a handsome young man, and a woman shrouded in darkness, stare across the way at the diner. The woman I feel is Nyx, the goddess of night, asks, "Are you sure it's her?"

"It's her. The phoenix is inside," Erebus replies, his voice un-muddled by insanity for the first time.

"Why is she so important?"

"Because Chaos is coming, and we need someone to stop it."

"How can she stop it?"

"By making the future happen in the only way that anyone survives."

"Do as you wish." Nyx shrugs, disappearing, leaving Erebus to step out of the alley and walk toward the diner. With silent agreement, my friends and I follow him into the diner.

Inside, Brittnie is working as a waitress; dropping off food for a customer, she approaches Erebus, saying, "Good evening. How can I help you?"

"Table for one."

"Very well. Please follow me." She leads Erebus to a table in the corner and seats him.

I stare at Brittnie, confused by her presence in Amber. Noticing my perplexion, Charlie asks, "What is it, Arien? Who is she?"

"I don't know, but I've been seeing visions of her ever since Canada. . . How can she be here in Amber?"

The fog shifts slightly, and Erebus is suddenly done eating, and Brittnie is giving him his check, asking, "Is there anything else I can help you with?"

"How about your phone number?"

Brittnie grins and blushes. "What?"

He stands, stepping just a little closer to say, "I'd love to see you again and get to know you. Would that be alright?"

Brittnie's lower, her cheeks blushing brighter. "Yeah, yeah, I'd like that."

"Great. So, how about the number?"

"Check your receipt." He checks to confirm that she had already written her number on the receipt. "Don't call too late. My parents don't like me talking to boys . . . Well, men."

"You still live with your parents?"

"It's alright. I'm 19."

"Great. I'll call you."

"You'd better."

Erebus smiles, walking past Brittnie to pay at the front counter. She stares after him, giggling to herself.

Suddenly, there are dozens of versions of Brittnie and Erebus throughout the diner having several dates. Some are making out at closing, some are just talking, some are cleaning together, and some are just smiling at each other from across the room.

All but one couple fades as the fog morphs into Brittnie's bedroom at night.

A rock taps the window, waking the sleeping Brittnie. She gets up and opens it to see Erebus in the yard below. "What are you doing here?"

"I wanted to see you."

"My parents will kill us."

"I'll be quiet."

Taking only a moment, she nods, waving him up. "Alright. Climb up, but be quiet."

"I brought a ladder."

"What?" Brittnie tries not to laugh too loudly as Erebus sets up his ladder and climbs up. He slips through the window, and they kiss fiercely.

"I brought this." Erebus holds up a condom, awkwardly stating his intentions.

"Oh," Brittnie mumbles, her eyes lowering.

"It's fine if you're not ready, totally fine."

"No, it's not that. I've just never done it before."

"What?"

Looking back into his eyes, proud and ashamed, she affirms, "I'm a virgin."

"That's OK. We don't need to do it. It was a stupid idea."

Erebus goes to put the condom away, but Brittnie reaches out and grabs his hand. "No, I want to . . . with you."

He smiles, leaning in to kiss her. "I love you." Their kissing becomes more passionate, Brittnie pushing Erebus toward the bed.

I usher my friends back through a doorway concealing our view. Otus objects, "Hold on, we were just getting to the good part."

"It feels wrong, somehow. Watching them."

Sunlight streams through the windows, the night changing to day. I reopen the door back to the bedroom; Brittnie and Erebus are sitting in bed together in their underwear. Brittnie awkwardly says, "You should go. My dad wakes up at 7 and comes to check on me."

"It's only 5. We've got time."

She smiles slightly, enjoying being rebellious. "OK." Thinking for a moment, she looks up into Erebus's eyes, asking, "Did you mean what you said last night? Do you love me?"

He smiles, looking down a little. "I do. I really do. I didn't think I would because I never have before, but I really do love you."

Brittnie smiles broadly. "I love you too." They kiss briefly. "I've never said that to anyone before."

"Neither have I."

Eyes lowering, abashed, she tucks her hair behind her ear. "There's something I want to show you."

"What?"

Grabbing a lighter from her nightstand, she ignites it, fire lighting within her eyes. She creates a fireball in the palm of her hand, swaying it back and forth.

With feigned surprise, Erebus says, "That's incredible."

Closing her fist, Brittnie puts out the phoenix. "I've never shown anyone that before. You're not afraid of me."

"No."

"Why not?"

"Cause I'm like you." The shadows in the room lengthen and deepen, the lights flicker, and the sun itself appears to recede.

"Whoa. How are you doing that?" Brittnie whispers, an awe-filled smile tracing her face.

"I was born like this."

My grandma and my teenage Mother burst through the door, deadly rage in their eyes. I start and stumble more than the lovers at the sight of them. Horrified, I mumble, "Mom?"

Grandma Ada cries, "Demon!" She rushes forward, a knife raised to stab Erebus.

"Mom, no!" Brittnie screams just as Erebus dodges the attack, backing away with his hands up.

He reasons, "Hold on. Let's be civil."

"You're trying to corrupt my daughter and steal her away." The word daughter shatters me, every vision falling into place. Brittnie is my long-lost aunt my Mother never dared mention.

"No, I'm not," he defends.

Brittnie jumps between her Mother and Erebus, yelling, "Get out of here, Jason. I'll be fine." He hesitates before jumping to the window and escaping. Once he's gone, Ada turns to Brittnie, slapping her and sending her to the ground.

Charlie and Otus only just manage to hold me back from leaping at Ada and tearing out her throat. Charlie tries to calm me, saying, "It's just a memory. You can't do anything."

Cooling off, I watch Ada circle Brittnie and command, "You will never see that monster again. Understood." Brittnie mumbles something, so Ada grabs her by the hair and stares into her eyes. "You will live in this house until your marriage, at which time you shall obey your husband, but until then, you obey me. . . So, do you understand?"

"Yes, mamma."

"Good." She drops Brittnie, walking to an altar in the corner, kneeling to pray. "We shall now pray for your forgiveness." My Mother and aunt Brittnie kneel beside grandma, joining hands in prayer. "Oh, Lord, who art in heaven. We ask that you heal my daughter's corrupt and base soul and cleanse her of all rottenness. We ask that you send swift judgment on her and the foul creature that has the power to bathe our house in darkness. We ask that you destroy the monster and rid the world of his filth that he may no longer tempt young girls into sin. This we pray, in Jesus's name, amen."

"Amen."

Ada stands, gliding to the door with Dinah in toe. "Your Father will be by to put bars on your window. After that, you will see no one for a month. Understood?"

"Yes, mamma," Brittnie mumbles.

Accepting her submission, Ada nods and walks out with Dinah, locking the door behind them.

The fog shifts the room; bars appear on the window, and night closes in again. Brittnie is once again asleep in bed when the shadows meld together to create Erebus. He leans down and places his hand over her mouth. She thrashes violently but stops when she sees him. When her silence is assured, he releases her. Collecting herself and taking a breath, she says, "Jason? What are you doing here? How did you get here?"

"I'm making the future happen. And I'm sorry, it won't be pretty for either of us."

"What do you mean?"

"People are coming, monsters really. They want me, and they're coming here because of your Mother's prayer."

"My Mother's prayer?" Brittnie asks, lost by his words.

"I can't explain, I just want you to know that I love you. I really do. I didn't intend to fall in love, but I did. I won't be myself anymore soon, maybe for forever, so I wanted you to know that before I lose myself."

"What are you talking about?"

"They're here."

The window explodes inward, glass showering the floor. Koios and Iapetus leap through the gaping hole, wrapping Erebus in golden ropes and pressing the blade of the Scythe against his throat. Iapetus hisses, "Erebus. Good to see you. . . Why are you causing so much noise? You could have lived your life in peace. But Lord Kronos believes you are a threat to Utopia. Why is that?"

"You'll have to ask him."

"Our Lord does not take kindly to questions, but as that we cannot risk killing a primordial deity, I will have eternity to cut it out of you with this." Iapetus tilts the Scythe, its blade reflecting in the moonlight. "Do you recognize it? What's on it?"

He presses the blade closer to Erebus's throat, barely letting him reply, "The blood of eternity, of Chaos."

"That's right. Which means I can return you to that same blood from which you formed at the beginning of time, or at least parts of you." Brittnie screams as Iapetus slashes Erebus's ear off. "Silence!"

"No!"

Iapetus swings the Scythe, stabbing Brittnie in the heart. She gasps, slowly sinking to the floor. Iapetus laughs evilly over Erebus's violent sobs. "Forever is ahead, Erebus."

The Titans and Erebus vanish as Ada and my Mother rush in to stare down at Brittnie's corpse. Mother stammers, "What happened?"

"Our Lord has spoken, and she has paid for her sins. Do you understand?"

"Yes, mamma."

Brittnie gasps and screams in torment.

She convulses violently, her eyes beginning to glow with a fiery light, the carpet around her bursting into flames. The air shimmers, lifting her to float up off the ground and stretching her spread-eagle. Her skin catches fire, and she lets out a silent scream.

Ada grabs Mother, pushing her out of the room to avoid the flames.

All the light is sucked towards Brittnie before blasting outward in a massive explosion. When the light dissipates, she collapses in the burning room, unconscious.

I try to call out, to help, but the past is dead and cold, only breath on a mirror.

The fog transforms the room into the basement of the house, where Brittnie slowly opens her eyes, sluggishly pulling on the chains around her wrists and ankles. "What's going on?"

"Repentance." Brittnie looks up, her eyes struggling to focus on Grandpa Nephi standing in front of her, his Bible in hand.

"What?"

"The only cure for your sin is deep meditation and self-flagellation."

"No, dad, please," Brittnie begs, her will nearly spent.

"Look above you." Glancing up, she sees dozens of sprinklers set on the ceiling, pointing down at her. "Those will pour gallons of holy water upon you if you attempt to escape or use the hellfire that Satan has gifted you. You lay with a demon, and this is your punishment." Nephi turns to Ada, who places a robe around his neck, handing him a scepter and a vial of holy water. He returns to Brittnie, circling her, spraying her with holy water, and chanting:

> *"Exorcizamus te, omnis immunde spiritus, omni satanica potestas, omnis incursio*
>
> *infernalis adversarii, omnis legio, omnis congregatio et secta diabolica, in nomini*
>
> *etvirtute Domini nostri Jesu Christi, eradicare et effugare a Dei Ecclesia, ab*
>
> *animabusad imaginem Dei conditis ac pretioso divini Agni sanguini redemptis."*

Nephi backs off, continuing to chant under his breath, his hands repeatedly making the sign of the cross. Ada crouches and hands Brittnie a whip, which is refused. "Take it. You will not be feed unless you do this." Begrudgingly accepting her fate, Brittnie accepts the whip, lashing herself to the mantra her parents chant. With each lash comes a muffled scream, but Brittnie uses all her will to not show the pain; pain reaps only pain in this house, misery your only companion.

My Mother stands in the corner, chanting with her parents, a sick grin transfixing her alabaster cheeks, the sight of her sister's torture, arousing a primordial lust for suffering she'd carry into my youth.

The fog shifts as time passes. Weeks of torture, starvation, and rituals unfold before us. I force myself to watch every moment of the horrors, a throbbing need to know the end of this tale driving back my nausea.

The vision suddenly slows until it's only Brittnie alone in the basement, trying to sleep. When the vision doesn't progress, I approach her, kneeling to look into her face, not at peace even at rest. Feeling somehow responsible for her suffering, I whisper, too low for the others to hear, "I'm sorry they're doing this to you. Tell me how I can help. Please."

With a jolt, Brittnie's eyes open and stare into mine.

Once I recover from the shock, I ask, "You can hear me?"

"Hey, Brittnie." I turn and follow Brittnie's eyeline to my young Mother standing atop the stairs, gloating.

I step aside as Mother approaches, and Brittnie mutters, "Sister, please, help me."

Apparent pity in her eyes, Mother kneels to spoon-feed soup to Brittnie, saying, "Why? You sinned against God and our parents. We were taught how to treat such sinners."

"But you know it's wrong. That they're wrong."

"I don't know that. I do the Lord's will, and the will of my new master."

Brittnie's eyes raise from the soup, her turn to show pity. "You got married?"

"Yesterday. Papa arranged it. He's one of the 12's great-grandsons. His name's Ephraim."

"Are you happy?"

"I am happy serving the Lord's will."

"Then I'm happy for you."

Dinah pauses the feeding, her expression slowly darkening. "You aren't, not truly. I serve a Lord you despise."

"I do care about you. I'm happy for you if you're happy. Can I meet the lucky fellow?"

"Papa has forbidden it. We must hide the dark stain upon our honor, even from Ephraim. For now, at least." Resuming the feeding, Dinah waits in silence until the bowl is empty before standing to leave.

"Wait, Dinah." Brittnie cries after her sister. "Please help me. Not for my sake, but for my child's." I stare at Brittnie, realization slowly dawning, hope blooming, but muted by the impossibility of it.

Dinah pauses, slowly turning to look back, an expression I know well gracing her face; she's found her enemy's weakness. "You're pregnant?" Brittnie's silence speaks louder than words ever could. "The demon is the Father?"

"He's not a demon, but yes."

"I saw the contraceptive that night."

"It was broken."

"Mother must know of this."

"No, please!"

With a vengeful flourish, Dinah glides up the stairs to report her good news. A moment later, Ada storms down the stairs, screaming, "Is it true? Are you bearing the child of the demon clouded in shadow?" Brittnie's sobs escalate beyond the capability of speech, so Ada bends to yank her daughter's hair, forcing her to meet her icy gaze. "Is it true?"

"Yes, mamma."

Ada throws Brittnie down in disgust, disparaging, "Another stain upon our family." She paces, her mind racing for a route forward containing honor for her public façade. Eventually, she declares, "Your penance has not yet been met, but we do not wish to harm the child, even if it comes from corrupt stock. You shall flagellate yourself 5 times a day now in exchange for more food. We shall be back in an hour to start the next session."

Ada and Dinah leave Brittnie alone with her tears, each one burning the concrete as it splashes down, a dark tribute to the torture inflicted.

I stand, dumbfounded, rooted to the spot, only broken from my trance by Charlie's soft touch and quiet words, "You realize what this means?"

"She's my Mother," I whisper, not daring to believe. Throwing aside my doubts, I let the happiness and grief consume me, my knees buckling, crashing me down before my true Mom. "That's why Erebus has been showing me her all this time. He was trying to tell me, in his own insane rattled way, that he's my Father and she's my Mother.

"That's why I have a connection with the darkness, why I have a phoenix, why the monsters who raised me hated me despite everything I did to win their favor. I was cursed from the beginning in their eyes." I reach out to cup Mom's cheek, her tears gliding through my translucent fingers to drop upon the cold ground. "It's alright . . . Mom. I turned out alright."

Tears to match her's run down my cheeks, Mother and Son re-united. I press our foreheads together, confessing, "I miss you." I stand and step back, hurrying away before I lose all will to move again. "We don't need to see how this story ends."

Despite my wish, the fog rushes in and transforms the basement into an olive grove. I stare around at the un-familiar scene, shouting to be heard over the howling wind shaking the grove, "What is this place?"

"This is where I kept the divinity." Otus replies. "This is the night I lost it."

In the distance, an F-5 tornado begins to form. I glance up at the statue of Athena in the center of the park, a small owl statue perched upon her shoulder. "Is that it?"

"It's in the owl."

The tornado hits the grove, tearing up everything in its path. The past version of Otus rushes from a shed and stares in horror at the tornado. He transforms into an owl and flies toward the statue to retrieve the divinity, but the winds picks him and the owl statue up and fling them apart.

The rest of us cover our eyes as the tornado swirls around us, tearing away our surroundings and dropping us back into the basement, where Ada and her family are cowering from the coming tornado, with the very pregnant Brittnie still chained in the corner. The sound of stone cracking echoes from the window. We all look to see the shattered owl statue outside on the lawn, a glowing light floating above it.

The light passes into the basement, drawn to Brittnie. The family stares in horror as Athena's divinity is sucked into Brittnie. She screams, her water breaking.

The screams continue, contractions racking her body. Fire burns in Brittnie's eye, a whirlwind of flames swirling around her. Her body convulses and heaves, her very life force getting sucked into her child.

The sprinklers spray down, dousing Brittnie, but to no avail.

"Not again," Ada whispers, barely heard.

The shadows in the basement deepen and grow, darkness swirling with the flames around Brittnie.

With no one to come to her aid, Brittnie attempts to catch the baby that is now crowning. The whirlwind of fire and night condenses down and funnels into the baby, along with the glow of Athena's light.

With a final scream, the baby slides out completely, the tornado and other sounds fading, leaving just the infant's cries.

Knowing her time with her child is short, Brittnie pulls the baby to her soaking chest to whisper in his ear. Realizing these last words of my Mom are meant for me, I struggle against my grief to approach, tears streaming down my face, listening, "Hey, hey, it's OK. Mommy's here. I'm going to have to leave you now, but you're going to be alright. You have an impossibly hard life ahead of you, but I have faith that you'll be fine. No matter what happens, know that your life is the most precious thing to me, and I am happy to give mine to bring you into the world. Someday, your Father will find you and make this all right. Until then, you're going to live a life of torment, but you'll live, and that's what matters for now. Do your best to be kind, but never fail to hold your ground. Fight for those who can't, and show mercy when you can. Never be cruel or cowardly, or you'll become the monster that you'll be raised to be. Love hard, live well, and above all, be happy, my little Julian." She continues to rock her son slowly, the life fading from her. Eventually, she falls still, giving her life for her son.

Baby Julian sobs profusely, sensing his Mother's death.

My sobs match his, the sorrow of meeting my Mom and losing her in a single day too much for me to bear. I collapse into Charlie's warm embrace.

Ada slowly stands and approaches her daughter's corpse, reaching out to take Julian. She turns to Dinah and hands the baby to her, commanding, "You will take the child and raise him as your own. He still has our righteous blood and therefore has a chance to choose right. We still have a chance to root out his Mother's evil."

Dinah shushes Julian, swaying slightly. "Hey, Julian. I'm your new mommy."

"No, we shall not call him by the pagan name chosen by the whore."

"Then what shall I call him?"

Ada thinks for a moment, contemplating the choice. "Samael, after our Lord's dark angel that took the firstborns of Egypt. He shall be our angel of darkness that serves the light."

Dinah nods, turning back to Julian. "Samael, I'm your new mommy."

I fall to my knees and vomit, my history complete, the fog receding completely, leaving us in the endless darkness. Charlie strokes my shoulders, whispering, "It's alright. I'm here."

"Everything makes sense now. My whole life finally means something."

"She really loved you."

"Yeah, she did."

Ephraim's voice echoes through the empty, shaking me from my grief, "There's only one way to move forward." His voice marks the change from Erebus's memories to mine.

"What is that? Is there more?" Charlie asks.

"This is my memory, not Erebus's."

The fog solidifies into my childhood home. Adult Dinah and Ephraim are in the kitchen talking while they watch me, a boy of no more than seven, reading scriptures on the living room couch. Ephraim states, "We took him out of that school and brought him home to get away from those heathens, yet he still yearns for their friendship and their sin."

"It's because he doesn't believe in our Lord. His Father's darkness may be taking over. If he continues to reject our teachings, he may be beyond saving. I don't know if we can risk leaving him alive."

"There's only one way to move forward."

Without regret, Dinah affirms, "I agree, there's no saving him. He must be sacrificed to purge the bloodline."

"I'll call the Brothers."

The scene shifts into the chapel of the Temple of God's Time, where Ephraim guides boy Sam down the center aisle toward an altar with a familiar statue of Christ behind it, passing dozens of hooded figures in the pews. I stare in horror, realizing, "This is it. This is what really happened."

The crowd starts chanting in Latin, and Sam goes pale as he sees a row of knives beside the altar, realizing what's about to happen. He struggles to free himself from Ephraim's grip, but to no avail. "No, Dad. Please, stop." Ephraim lifts Sam onto the altar while several priests tie him down. The crowds chanting gets louder and faster.

Ephraim slips into a robe and lifts the hood over his head, grabbing a knife and stepping to the altar. "As God sent forth the angel Samael to kill every firstborn of Egypt, I prepared a new angel of death and darkness to serve our Lord in these harrowing times. But our angel has shunned the power of the divine and must henceforth be destroyed for the darkness within that overcame the pure soul God gifted him." He raises the knife and hovers it above Sam's chest. "As Abraham was commanded to kill his own son, so am I, for the good of the community, and the good of the Temple of God's Time."

Ephraim brings the knife down and stabs Sam in the heart; I shudder as if the knife had stabbed me as well.

Leaving the knife in the corpse, Ephraim steps around the altar to address the now cheering crowd. "We shall now feast in celebration of a bloodline cleansed."

Sam's finger twitches almost imperceptibly, a priest notices and steps forward to investigate.

With a scream, Sam convulses, a black shockwave blasting outward from him and enveloping the collected disciples. The darkness is sucked into the disciples' eyes, turning them black.

Roars of rage and bloodlust echo throughout the room, violence culling their newfound appetite. The disciples tear each other apart; friend turning upon neighbor, son on father, and secret lovers upon each other. The bodies begin to pile up; blood starts to fill the room, spraying onto every surface.

Otus screams and turns to vomit into a corner. Charlie's eyes go distant as she sits in a pew, blood splashing all over her.

All sound seems to fade away from me, though, the carnage I'd caused as a child falling upon dead eyes. Someone is decapitated in front of me, coating my face in the grey matter of a monster undeserving of death.

Sam is still seizing on the table, his restraints the only thing stopping him from hurting himself. I walk forward through the carnage toward Sam.

When I reach the altar, I am barely recognizable from all the blood soaking me. Looking down at Sam, I see the pain in those blackened eyes, pain reflected in my own eyes, Erebus's insanity racking us. I turn my empty gaze onto Ephraim, who's cowering in a corner, unaffected by the insanity. He stares in horror at the carnage around him before focusing on Sam's thrashing body. Getting up, he rushes forward to push a lantern stand down onto Sam.

Sam screams even louder with a primordial roar as he's enveloped in flames.

His restraints and the knife in his heart burn away, and he's lifted into the air. I stumble back to avoid the flames, looking up into Sam's eyes, now glowing with a godly light. The drapes of the altar burst into flame, spreading across the room.

Sam rises up and is stretched spread-eagle, his skin catches fire, and he lets out a silent scream.

The people left alive continue to kill each other despite some catching fire and melting.

Ephraim manages to hide in the corner away from the flames, any other survivors burning away.

Sam slowly lowers down to stand on the steps beneath the altar, raising his hand to extinguish all the flames. His eyes clearing, he collapses into a pool of blood. Molly, as the child I remember, walks in and screams.

Sam's sobs draw out Molly's maternal instinct; fighting past the terror of the blood, she rushes forward to hug her cousin. "It was me. I did this." Sam stammers.

Molly pulls back in fear, only to be distracted by an insane laugh starting to echo through the chapel, seemingly without source.

Sam's eyes turn black again. He stands, walking to Ephraim's cowering form and crouching down in front of him; his voice warped with that of Erebus, Sam says, "Do you realize how hard it was for me to reach out from my cage to save my son? No?" Sam bares his teeth, reaching out as if he wants to rip Ephraim's throat out. "I already feel myself slipping into insanity. I may not have the faculties to be as forgiving next time you try to kill my son. Do we understand each other?" Ephraim nods vigorously. "Good. I'm not asking you to love him, but just raise him, as normally as you're capable of, or my wrath will make this day pale in comparison to the horrors I will inflict. Julian will not remember this, and you won't ever tell him. Understood?" Ephraim nods again. Accepting his submission, Sam stands and turns to Molly, his expression softening. "And you, please don't tell him either. It'll destroy him."

With understanding far beyond her years, Molly nods, affirming, "I won't."

"Thank you." Sam's eyes clear, and his body goes limp.

I turn my gaze onto my friends as the chapel dissipates into fog, returning us to the empty. I let a single tear leak out of the corner of my eye. "I don't remember anything before I was 7. Now I know why."

"Oh, Arien." Charlie steps forward, hugging me tightly, I finally let the flood gates open, and the sobs pour out.

"Hey Arien." My emotional breakthrough cut short, I turn to Otus, who's pointing across the darkness to Erebus's huddled form.

Wiping my eyes, I approach and collapse in front of my Father. "Hey, Dad."

Erebus only mumbles, "Must protect the boy. Boy must know. Boy makes the future. Boy needs help. My help. Protect the boy. Save the boy."

I reach out and clasp Erebus's hands tightly. "You did protect the boy. He's safe."

Erebus looks up into my eyes, asking, "The boy?"

"The boy is safe."

Erebus smiles, slowly fading away into darkness. I turn slightly to my friends, saying, "I don't think we'll have to worry about traveling through here anymore. My visions . . . my insanity, was just my Dad trying to talk to me. He finally mustered up the focus to show me what I needed to see. It's safe now."

When no response comes, I stand and turn to see that my friends are gone.

I suddenly appear on the moon's craggy surface, the Earth framed before me in unmatched glory. Unable to comprehend the sight, I turn away, my hands clutching my throat, surprised that air is passing normally through my lips.

"It's beautiful, isn't it?" Timorian is standing a few yards away, smiling at me.

"Jesus?"

He laughs softly to himself, and I realize this is Kronos himself. He chuckles, "No, I'm afraid not. I am Kronos, Lord of . . . well, everything." His gaze shifts to the Earth, now setting in the distance. "So, isn't it beautiful?"

I turn back to the Earth, forcing myself to take it in without the urge to vomit. "Yes, it is."

"It's part of the reason I've stayed up here for so many years. All of its problems and faults seem so small from up here. Almost toy-like. Like I could just reach out and rebuild it in any way I see fit."

"How am I breathing?"

Kronos chuckles again, "No imagination with you, huh? No desire to just soak it all in and enjoy the impossibility of it? I created an air bubble for you. But that means you don't have much time here with me before the air runs out. So best breathe shallow."

"So, I'm really here? This isn't a vision, or anything?"

"It is, and it isn't. You are, and you aren't. I doubt you'd understand. All you need know is, neither of us are capable of hurting each other. It's like a parley spell, let's say."

"I didn't agree to this."

"No, but the one who shares her soul with you did." I look down at my chest, not believing Athena would do this. He continues, "It was her idea, really. She left me a message in the form of a tortured and mutilated Gargarean. I believe you met him in NORAD. I think she suspected that your commitment was failing, so she wanted me to prove to you that the Titans are worse than the gods and deserve destruction, or some such idea."

"Really wasn't necessary. Not after what you did to my parents."

"You've found out, have you? I only just discovered your lineage myself. Most unfortunate what happened to them. I apologize. Iapetus is very unstable, but useful in certain situations. . . My intention is not to do as Athena desires. I wish to explain why I've done what I've done. While I was in Tartarus, I learned that Chaos herself had turned her gaze to Earth for the first time since creation, and that she intended to destroy it. The gods wouldn't listen, so I had to take matters into my own hands. I started the war so that we could prepare for when she came. I let the gods live and helped humanity. Have you heard of the 5-thousand-year leap? That was me helping and guiding humanity. The gods didn't do that. They did more horrendous things than we Titans ever could."

"Like killing Calypso?" I ask, my resolve waning a little.

"Like killing Calypso," he affirms.

"But you ate your children."

"So did Zeus. I'm not proud of what I did, but I was young. You do terrible things when you're young. It only matters that you learn from them. Immortals mature at a similar rate to humanity itself. Humanity wasn't even created yet to forge our morality when I did that, so we had none. We learned morality from humanity."

"Atlas has done some horrific things to us under your instructions. Immoral things."

"And for that, I apologize. Atlas is a double-edged sword. Please forgive me and help me protect the world from the coming Chaos."

He extends his hand to me; I look at it with temptation twinging at my belief, but I stand firm. "I know you aren't pure evil, and the gods aren't pure good, but after seeing everything I have today, I can't. My Mother wouldn't want me to."

Kronos's face darkens slightly, but he manages to smile through it. "I expected nothing else. Our time is up, but I am glad to have met you, Arien. A worthy foe you will make. We shall meet again soon."

I begin to fade away as Kronos turns and walks away.

CHAPTER 90: MATRICIDE

<u>Arien</u>

My friends and I appear together in the rolling green of an Idahoan farm. Charlie turns to me, smiling and asking, "How are you?"

Unable to respond, I'm relieved to see a tractor pull up beside us, a woman jumping out. She says, "Hello, I'm happy to see you guys. I've been expecting you." Demeter raises an eyebrow upon seeing how emotionally drained we are. "Are you guys alright?"

"Fine. Here," I reply, handing her the turtle dove statue.

We're all forced to avert our eyes as Demeter is engulfed in a pillar of white fire. She's lifted off the ground and spread-eagled in the center of the burning pillar.

The fire and light fades, leaving Demeter standing on the ground, unharmed. "Ah. It'll feel so good to put some things right. This world needs a god to support her again. Keep her from dying. I must leave at once and heal this sick planet." She disappears without another word, leaving us alone.

"What now?" Otus asks.

"There's something I need to do." I say, a dark intention in my heart.

***

With a dark flash, we appear in front of my childhood home. Charlie turns to me in surprise, exclaiming, "I don't think this is a good idea."

"I need to do this. Please, wait here." I squeeze her hand, walking away to confront my demons, their claws too long in my flesh. Opening the unlocked door, I step into the home of my many nightmares; the air itself desperate for my blood, racking down my throat as I approach my once parents. They're standing, oblivious to me, in the kitchen, cleaning up from dinner. My breath becomes ragged, and my muscles tense at their very sight. I force myself not to lash out, the Valley of the Shadow of Death echoing through my head.

Eventually, Ephraim turns to me and gasps, drawing Dinah's attention. She cries, "You're alive. How?"

"Does it matter?"

The shock wearing off, their faces set in a familiar hatred and rage. "Why are you here?" Ephraim hisses. "It's not enough for you to shirk your destiny and commit mortal sin, now you've come back to what, taunt us?"

My jaw clenches, my nearly spent will containing my wrath. "I needed to look you in the eyes when I asked you why you did it. Why you tortured my Mother? Why you let my Father get taken?"

Without missing a beat, he says, "What are you talking about? We're your parents."

"I remember what you did. I remember how you tried to kill me when I was only 7. No parents would have done that."

Ephraim pales, a gun from nowhere appearing in his hand, pointing at me. Bleeding impudence, I grab the gun, melting it, using the phoenix for the first time without a spark.

Dinah watches, no fear nor worry in her eyes as Ephraim cowers. She confesses, "We did what we did because you're a monster. No more seen than now."

With a primeval roar, my hands ignite into flames, burning testaments to my rage and hatred.

"Arien, no!" My fire dissipates, the rage replaced by confusion at Molly's cry. I turn to see her in the doorway with Charlie and Otus.

Tears welling, I ask her, "Why didn't you tell me what you saw? What I am?"

Her eyes filling with companion tears, Molly renders, "I thought it was for the best, and I didn't really know what you were until Rachel. I was afraid that you were possessed. I'm sorry, I should never have thought that. I should have trusted you and been there for you, but I'm here now. You should leave them alone. They don't deserve your time."

I stumble into her warm embrace, the torment of ages flooding down my cheeks, moistening her pure skin. "I wouldn't. I couldn't. I'm not a monster."

"But you are. A monster cursed by God." I fight the anger Dinah's declaration recalls.

"Dinah, don't," Molly begs.

"It was a mistake to let you live. Your destiny is to be slain by a righteous follower of God. That might be me, it might not. But the end is the same. You in hell forever."

Molly grabs my head, forcing me to stare into her eyes. "Arien, look at me. It's not true."

"How soon before you get your due? We should have let you die with that cow of a Mother of yours."

An animal shriek is torn from me; I whirl, sending a dark shockwave out toward Dinah and Ephraim. They're thrown back, and Dinah's head crashes into the counter, her eyes emptying.

I breathe heavily, feeling everyone's stares of horror.

Ephraim crawls to check his wife's pulse, whispering, "Dinah, my love. Speak to me."
Her eyes just stare blankly as if gazing through the roof to the stars above, her view beyond
imagination. Once her death is assured, Ephraim's maleficent leer fixes upon me. "Get out of
here."

"Is she . . ."

"Get out!" he screams. "Get out and never come back!"

Charlie grabs our hands, dragging us out of the house of horror.

Outside, Molly slumps against the railing, her blank eyes transfixed to the ground in shock.
The barbarity of my actions finally setting in, I collapse before Molly, stammering, "Molly, I . . ."

"I never want to see you again."

"Molly?"

She doesn't look up or move; my existence gone from her. Police sirens ring out in the
distance, marking our departure.

"Arien, we have to get out of here," Charlie says, dragging me away.

"No! Not without Molly."

"There's nothing we can do. Come on."

She manages to drag me away while Otus stays with Molly to plead, "You should really leave
too. You don't want to be here when the cops show up and have to lie to them."

"Why would I lie?" She asks, utter confusion in her eyes.

"The cops will never understand."

She nods, conceding, "I'll leave as soon as he's gone."

Otus returns to us, grasping our hands. I cry, "I'm sorry, Molly." We disappear in a dark flash,
leaving Molly alone to flee before the police arrive.

Part 11:

ARTEMIS

CHAPTER 91: IGNORANCE WAS BLISS

Atlas

Family has never been my crutch nor firm ally through the ages, but a plague to be reviled. Sympathy of blood does not supersede rage at betrayal. Thus, the sight of my starving and beaten Aunt Mnemosyne draws no pity from my cold heart. She's dragged motionless by Iapetus into the Litai's cell and thrown down beneath them.

I crouch to whisper in her ear, "Dear aunt, it's time for you to redeem yourself. Your decisions to side with the gods can be forgiven now. We need you to read these prayer spirits' thoughts and learn where Arien is. . . Or Iapetus can spend some alone time with you before you're thrown back into your Tartarus cell." Iapetus hefts the Scythe menacingly, smiling as he runs his finger across the blade. "So, what shall it be? Will you help us and redeem yourself?" Mnemosyne nods sullenly in submission. "Good."

Charlie

The week's events have left us all cold, empty, and distant, none knowing if we can trust one another. Otus and I sit alone in awkward silence, perusing ancient texts for the whereabouts of gods; the silence of our hotel deafening, almost echoing in the air, demanding reconciliation.

Otus sighs softly, putting his book aside to look at me and break the silence, "We can't keep doing this. We're not going to find anything in these books. We need to move on before the government or the Titans catch up to us."

"Tell that to him."

"I would, but he hasn't come down from the roof or spoken in days. I can't get through to him. I think he's still upset with me for the Athena situation."

"He's afraid if he tells you how he feels, you'll just tell her, breaking his trust."

His eyes lower in shame, conceding, "I know."

"I'll go talk to him," I say, standing.

Contemplating a path toward resolution, I walk noiselessly to the hotel service ladder, climbing to the roof and walking to Arien, who's sitting with his feet dangling off the edge. Sitting beside him, I sigh, staring out at the beautiful view of a sagebrush desert. "It's beautiful." When he doesn't respond or acknowledge my presence, I peer down over the edge at the ground below, noting, "Pretty far down. Are you thinking about seeing if your phoenix lets you fly too?" Again, he ignores me. Giving in, I stare out into the desert, breathing it all in while I wait for him to speak.

Nigh an hour later, he mutters, "I've been thinking about jumping." I turn in surprise, listening intently. "But I don't because I know it won't kill me. I'd just regenerate. . . For so long, I thought I didn't kill myself because I was too afraid, but I must have known deep down that it would take a lot to do it."

Wrapping my arms around him, I let him lean his head against my shoulder. "I'm glad it would take a lot; that way, you're here with me."

His eyes still lost in the desert, he whispers, "I don't know what to believe in anymore. Or do. . . I'm glad I'm adopted, but I managed to lose the only family I had left because of how I handled the knowledge. Molly will never speak to me again. Now even the gods have betrayed and lied to me. They have hope of winning this war, and they thought I couldn't handle . . . hope. Even though the Titans tortured and killed my parents several times, they may be better than the gods. . . I'm just so lost and confused." A tear leaks out of the corner of Arien's eye, sliding down to splash upon my coat.

"You know, I've been thinking about killing myself too."

Arien smirks slightly, disbelieving. "Why? You have everything."

"It's complicated, with everything that's happened with Emma, Susan, and Deni. But more than just killing myself." Deciding confession breeds trust, I say, "I've been thinking about having an abortion." I reach into my pocket and pull out my abortion pills. "Every day, I take these out and decide whether or not to take them. I've always chosen not to, but I can never escape the want.

"It's destroying me. I think the only thing that's stopping me are the visions of my son that I'm having. Of everything he'll become. Of how happy of a family we can be. I'm still tempted, though." Tears well in my eyes, a horse laugh torn from me. "I don't even know if these will work. Hera said I'd have an accelerated pregnancy, so I may be beyond the point that these'll do anything. But, despite that, I can't bring myself to get rid of them. They're the choice. Whether to keep the baby or go in and get an abortion. As long as I have them, the choice hasn't been made." Giving in, I hand the pills to Arien, continuing, "I'll promise not to choose if you promise to keep fighting . . . for yourself. Not for gods or man. But for you. To be happy."

He stares down at the pills before looking up into my eyes and nodding. "OK. But you'll need to call Emma too. Her mistakes are millennia old, and you need her."

I turn away, saying, "I don't know if I can forgive her."

"I've realized that it's too hard to be apart from the ones you love. There's no reason to fight without them. You're just living a death wish without hope if you don't have someone to live for, or die for."

Tears stream down both our faces as we start to heal, just a little. "I'll call if you call. You need Molly."

He smiles, nodding. "OK." We hug to seal the deal. Arien's phone rings, interrupting our cathartic moment. He takes it out, explaining, "It's Clara."

I wipe my eyes, laughing softly. "Now, you'd better tap that, or I will."

Laughing for the first time in a while, he affirms, "I'll see what I can do."

"I'll give you some privacy," I say, standing to leave.

He stops me, asking, "Will you stay?" Nodding, I sit as he answers, "Hey, Clara. How's it going?"

Her voice faint, I hear Clara reply, "Good. What about you?"

"Good. How'd your first day as the new boss go?"

"It sucks. No one likes me anymore. I told you about Jesse, right? We used to eat lunch together every day, now she won't have anything to do with me."

"The price of leadership."

"I just didn't expect it to be this bad. But that's not why I called. I think I found a god for you. You think you can come to my house now?"

Arien checks his watch, calculating. "Yeah, I can be right there."

"Great. I'll see you in a sec." He hangs up, turning to ask me, "Did you hear?"

"Yeah, go."

He smiles, disappearing in a dark flash.

CHAPTER 92: FALLING FOR HER

Arien

Startled by my apparition, Clara jumps. When she's recovered, she notes, "I'm never going to get used to that."

"Sorry." We hug briefly before I add, "Good to see you."

She looks away, blushing. "It's good to see you too."

We stand in awkward silence for a moment until I cough and rub my chin, stammering, "So, ah, you said you had something for me?"

"Yeah." Walking to her computer, she starts typing, continuing, "So, I, ah, hacked into the FBI and stole their facial recognition software."

"You did what?" I exclaim awed.

"What? Saving the world from ancient Titans comes first."

I grin broadly down at Clara, gushing, "You're awesome. Now you'll be a wanted criminal like the rest of us."

She smiles in appreciation for a second before moving on, "I managed to get a few rough matches off an ancient statue of Artemis. Only one matches the M.O. and style of Artemis." A list of five names with pictures and personal details appears on her screen.

"I'm impressed."

"I'll give her to you only if I can come along. Already got a dog sitter and everything."

Surprised, I ask, "What? Why would anyone ever want to get involved in all of this?"

She stares at me, genuinely confused by my statement. "Why? It's the coolest thing to ever happen to me. I have a chance to do something incredible and be a part of something amazing. It's the dream of every 21st century nerd." My look unconvinced, she gives in, confessing, "I had an encounter with a couple cops a few weeks ago. One of them died to save my life. After that, I knew it was time I tried to do the right thing and help other people. I couldn't keep living just for myself, or his sacrifice might be in vain."

Understanding and accepting her answer, I nod, conceding, "Alright. You can come."

"Really?" She cries, leaping to her feet with an infectious grin.

"Really. You'll need to pack a bag. We never know how long these things last."

She pulls a packed bag from under her desk, declaring, "All ready."

"You have Artemis's details?"

"In the bag."

"OK. Let's go." I grab her hand, and we disappear in a dark flash.

***

My friends and I appear in the forests of Yellowstone, the sulfur in the air twinging our noses and drawing several gags. I take out a map and compare it to the surrounding terrain. "All right, looks like Artemis's rangers station is a mile or so that way." I say, pointing down a nearby trail.

"Couldn't get us any closer," Clara teases.

I smile at the grinning Clara, explaining, "What I do isn't all that precise."

"I don't know. You always seem to find what you looking for round my parts."

Charlie's head snaps around, obviously thinking the reference was sexual in nature. Ignoring her, I say, "Well, I was trying to impress you."

Clara giggles, punching my arm before grabbing it. "Oh, stop it."

"Come on. We should get going," Charlie states, dissolving our moment.

I shake my head to clear it. "Right. Let's go." Clara releases my arm, letting me step forward to lead the group deeper into the woods. Charlie and Otus fall back a little to give Clara and I some privacy. A single dark question sticks in my mind, and I force myself to ask it, "You really think you could risk your life for strangers?"

Taking a while to respond, she eventually says, "No, not really. I don't know. I just want to feel like I did something worth doing with my life. Life's too short, and I don't want to waste it." To diffuse the solemnity of the moment, she adds, "Plus, I really enjoy the company." She reaches out and grabs my hand.

I stare at our conjoined hands, fearful of my divinity's intervention. When our contact persists, I decide to confess my worries, none the less. "Clara, I, ah, need to tell you something."

"What?"

"Any girl I've ever tried to be with, it's ended badly. I'm just worried about being with you because of that."

Anger flashes in her eyes; she yanks her hand back, offended. "What are you trying to say? Are you talking about sex? Are you calling me a whore for holding your hand?"

"What? No."

"You know, I don't sleep with guys on the first date. I have standards." She picks up the pace, hurrying down the path ahead of me.

449

"Clara, wait!" I cry, running after her. Catching up, I gently make her stop and look at me. "That's not what I'm trying to say at all. I told you Athena's divinity's inside of me, right?"

"Yeah," she replies, her eyes avoiding mine.

"Well, what I didn't tell you is, she's a maiden goddess. Which means, so am I. Whenever I get close to a girl, even kissing her, or holding hands sometimes, it intervenes to preserve its purity. It makes the girl forget about me in that moment. Then it muddles all her past memories of us. I just don't want to see that happen to you. You're too special to lose. If we say we're dating, or kiss, or anything like that, you'll lose all your emotional connection to me. Good or bad. I just wanted you to know what you're getting yourself into. I like you. I like you a lot, but I don't see how we can possibly move forward."

Understanding dawning, her embarrassment grows. "Sorry. I overreacted. I've been called a whore a lot, even by my Mother, so I'm really sensitive about stuff like that."

"That's alright."

"Maybe because now that I know, the divinity won't affect me."

"I don't think so."

"It's my decision, and I choose you because you're worth the risk." She reaches out and retakes my hand. "We'll take it slow and see what happens."

I smile, staring down at her. "Thank you."

Charlie runs up, interrupting, "Sorry, guys, but we should keep moving. It's getting dark."

I shake my head to clear it again. "Right. Let's go."

After a largely uneventful hike, we reach the ranger's station. With a knock, a ranger answers, "Can I help you?"

"Yeah, we're looking for Phoebe," I explain.

"She's not here right now. How do you know Phoebe?"

"I'm her cousin. We just need to get a hold of her cause her grandfather's having problems again."

"Oh, my god. Is he OK?" He asks, genuine concern on his face.

"For now, but we're not sure what the future holds."

"Of course. Well, she's been up at our mountain cabin doing a survey for the last few days. The radio's down, so I was thinking about going to check on her in the morning. I can take y'all with me, if you like."

"That'd be great."

"I have some tents I can let you borrow and set up in the back."

"Thank you. We'd appreciate it." Our path clear, we settle down for the night.

CHAPTER 93: SECOND START

<u>**Arien**</u>

The flames of our campfire dance and sing, each spark holding the power to unlock my soul. I bore into them, determined to not miss a single wisp, the flames warming more than just my body. My reverie is interrupted by Clara sitting beside me and snuggling with me under her blanket. "Hey."

"Hey."

I continue to stare into the fire as Clara closes her eyes and whispers, "Are you OK? I'm getting a little worried."

Carefully constructing my answer, I eventually reply, "I fought my whole life for meaning and purpose to explain the horrors of my childhood. When I finally do, it seems so empty."

"What do you mean?" She asks, her eyes opening to meet mine.

"I believed the gods were real for so long, but when I finally met them, they don't seem to be much better than the Titans."

Closing her eyes again, she starts rubbing my chest softly, saying, "Maybe that's why they're better. Maybe they're beautiful and worthy of praise because they fail. If even gods make mistakes, it might not be so bad that we sometimes do too. As long as we keep trying to be better, just like they do. Their flaws make them magnificent. Like you said, gods mature with humanity. There's beauty in that. It shows that we actually mean something in the grander scheme of things. There's beauty in their failings."

I tear my eyes from the flames for the first time, impressed by her wisdom. Despite agreeing with her, I ask, "What about the Titans?"

"There's a reason part of the last 2 thousand years was called the dark ages. So much death, famine, disease, and insanity. Recent humanity has become apathetic, resigned to their lot. That's why they need you. To fight for them when they can't fight for themselves."

"But I'm not doing it for them."

"Then why are you doing this?"

"To die."

My confession makes her stiffen; her eyes lift to stare into mine, filled with pain. "What?"

"I'm not a hero. I'm not a good man. I'm just a coward who's doing this as a way to commit suicide. There's just so much pain that I have to leave behind." She sighs, snuggling back up to me, surprising me. "You're not going to try and convince me that I have something to live for? That it's wrong to kill myself?"

"Why? Do you want me to?"

"No."

"Then there's no way for me to convince you. From what I know of your childhood, you have more of an excuse to do it than anyone. Do I want you to? No, of course not. But I'm with you, through all of it, any of it."

I smile, snuggling up to her as well.

Charlie

Sneaking out of my tent, past Clara and Arien, I slip into the woods. Once alone, I pull out the prayer talisman, closing my eyes to pray:

> *"Heavenly, illustrious, laughter-loving queen, sea-born, night-loving*
> *Aphrodite. Come and attend thy humble servant, I pray."*

"Humble servant, huh?"

I turn to Emma standing behind me and explain, "It's how the prayer goes."

She smiles slightly, a touch of worry wrinkling her eyes. "I'm so happy to see you. Does this mean we're good?"

"I'm not ready for things to go back to the way they were, but I've forgiven you. I realize it was unrealistic of me to judge you for such an old crime. It was a different time, and right and wrong were different. I can't expect an immortal goddess to share all her dark secrets with me."

"That's good to hear. Thank you."

"I can't just go back to where we left off, but I can start anew. Rebuild."

"I can work with that."

Atlas

With a great bellow of pain, Mnemosyne groans, her voice cracking as she mumbles, "Heavenly, illustrious, laughter-loving queen, sea-born, night-loving Aphrodite. Come and attend thy humble servant, I pray."

A strange presence fills the air, something so familiar but lost to the ages of my memory. I ask, "What is that?"

"The girl has prayed. But you shall lose yourself in the mighty forest, in which they reside, and you will not reach them in time before the might of 3 gods joins them in defense. You must not go, or failure will be all you find."

Hesitating, I decide to take her at her word, moving on to contemplate a plan forward. "Where are they?"

"Yellowstone."

I nod, walking to the privacy of the alley behind the asylum to pray. Kneeling, I extend my arms and stare up at the bright moon, willing my words to reach my uncle far above:

"Etherial Father, mighty Titan, hear, great fire of Gods and men, whom all revere:
Endu'd with various council, pure and strong, to whom perfection and decrease belong.
Consum'd by thee all forms that hourly die, by thee restor'd, their former place supply;
The world immense in everlasting chains, strong and ineffable thy pow'r contains
Father of vast eternity, divine, O mighty Kronos, various speech is thine: Blossom
of earth and of the starry skies, husband of Rhea, and Prometheus wife.
Obstetric Nature, venerable root, from which the various forms of being shoot; No
parts peculiar can thy pow'r enclose, diffus'd thro' all, from which the world arose,
O, best of beings, of a subtle mind, propitious hear to holy pray'rs inclin'd; The
sacred rites benevolent attend, and grant a blameless life, a blessed end."

Ending my prelude, I ask, "Oh, mighty Kronos, I ask that you send me aid to track and defeat the phoenix and his companions in the mighty forest of Yellowstone. I ask for the hunter."

My gaze shifts slightly from the moon's splendor to its sister's, the stars. Suddenly, the constellation of Orion warps and shifts, the lights appearing to coalesce and cascade down toward the Earth. The stars themselves remain in the sky, but their inherent shape can no longer be sensed.

The light crashes to the ground before me, its brilliance fading until it becomes a giant, seemingly made of black glass, lights glowing inside his chest, marking the points of the constellation. The spirit of Orion himself stands before me.

I smile, preparing to send the greatest tracker in history after the boy.

CHAPTER 94: MARIAS RIVER

<u>**Arien**</u>

The sun's morning rays are barely cresting over the peaks of the mountains when we start our long hike to the ranger's cabin. Along the way, Clara and I walk hand-in-hand in silence, just enjoying our closeness.

When we finally reach the cabin, Artemis is waiting for us, her eyes filled with curiosity. "Justin? Is everything OK?"

The rangers hug briefly before Justin explains, "Hey, Phoebe. No, we're good. With the radio down, I wanted to make sure everything was OK, and these people say they're your relatives. They have some news about your grandfather."

"My grandfather?"

"I'll let you guys have some privacy. I brought some parts for the radio, so I'll take a look."

Artemis nods as Justin goes into the cabin. Once he's gone, she turns back to us, asking, "What's this about? I don't have grandparents."

Stepping forward, I explain, "Isn't Kronos your grandfather?"

She stiffens slightly, turning to yell into the cabin, "Justin, I'm going to take these guys to the geyser. You good?"

"Yeah, go for it."

Without another word, Artemis grabs her pack and guides us through the woods to a secluded geyser, its warmth emanating through the clearing and its bubbling making a calming steady echo.

Our enjoyment of the scene is cut short when we notice a mighty grizzly lounging on the geyser's bank, sunning itself.

I draw my bear-bone-knife, ready to fight, but Artemis reaches out and places a hand over mine, whispering, "Don't you dare. She's a descendant of Callisto, and she's been my only friend for many years."

Before I can respond, Apollo appears next to me, smirking to himself. "Nice bear, sis."

My face darkens, every ounce of my self-control taxed to restrain my anger. "Apollo?"

"Long time no see, my friend. How've you been?"

Letting the anger flood free, I roar, pinning Apollo against a tree, my knife pressed into his jugular. He cries, "Whoa, hold up, buddy. What's wrong?"

"You knew there was hope this whole time." I hiss, rationale fleeing me. "You knew that Kronos had lost the belief of humanity. That we had a shot. But you and the other gods failed to mention that, for what? To test me?"

Not even trying to deny it, he sighs and confesses, "You're right. Most every god you've come across has tested you in their own way to decide whether or not they trust you. We all saw your potential, and we needed to know if you could do it."

"Do what?"

"Kill Kronos."

Stumbling back, my shock releases my grip, letting Apollo slump down. I stammer, "What? He's a Titan. Even all the gods couldn't kill him."

"No, we couldn't," he explains. "We can't, but maybe you can. We all saw that potential and needed to be sure you were ready. If you still continued on without hope, your resolve would be strong enough to do whatever was needed to kill him."

"How?"

"Your connection to Erebus. That gave us far more hope than the loss of Christianity ever could. You can atomize Kronos and scatter him inside of Erebus. A chance of resurrection always exists, but his essence will be far more secure than in Tartarus. He'd stay dead forever this time."

"But I've been fighting this whole time because there wasn't hope, so I'd end up dead. Now, what motivation do I have to go on?" Glancing at my friends, I see Clara's disheartened gaze and Otus's downcast eyes. Noticing his shame, I ask, "You knew too, didn't you?"

Otus concedes, "It's the only motivation that would have worked on you."

"What about the whole extracting Athena will kill me thing?"

"Part of the same lie. You'd just regenerate. But I will still keep that promise I made you. That wasn't a lie. I'll find a way."

"How can I trust that, or trust you anymore? None of you are any better than the Titans. You're all just manipulating me for your own ends."

"Well, boohoo," Artemis cries, drawing all our attention. "God, no one told me you'd be this whiny. It's been a while since anyone stood up to your tantrums, hasn't it? We gods aren't perfect. I'll be the first to proudly admit that. But we try and improve. We've accidentally and purposely killed so many people over the years, yes. But we ensure the worthy have an afterlife worth living in exchange. That's something the Titans don't provide. That alone should be enough."

"What are you talking about?" I ask.

Artemis turns to Apollo, commanding, "Show them what you came for." He nods, waving his hand, making us all disappear.

***

In a split moment, we appear on the banks of a river far from Yellowstone. Charlie asks, "Where are we?"

"This is the Marias River in Montana," Artemis answers. "The site of the Marias Massacre. Over 200 Native American women and children killed by an Army detachment led by Koios." Apollo again waves his arm; a ghostly image of the past massacre overlays itself over our surroundings.

A group of Titans watch from a hilltop, overseeing the Army company opening fire on the sleeping Blackfeet. Dozens of women and children try to escape but are shot down.

Koios stops the firing to issue the command to charge.

The Army mounts their horses and rides into camp, slaughtering the fleeing Blackfeet.

Tears fill Clara's eyes as she watches the murdering of so many innocents.

Artemis explains, "The Titans did this for sport. And they didn't even allow the souls to go to the Underworld to find peace." Apollo waves his hand a third time, revealing the ghosts of the dead over the scene. More and more ghosts appear as the massacre continues.

On the hilltop, Iapetus raises his hand; the ghosts scream, catching fire and burning away. Artemis continues, "The gates of the Underworld are closed. The Titans steal the souls of the dead and torture them for their own amusement. No one is finding peace in death." The vision fades, leaving only the modern-day Marias River. "There have been battlefields like this all over the world for the last 2 thousand years. This was small-time compared to some of the horrors the Titans have caused. Senseless murder so the Titans could be amused by the dead. We gods have had our issues, but we were never this evil. The Titans deserve to be destroyed." Tears stream down my face, the horrors I'd just witnessed haunting me.

Turning to boor her gaze into my soul, Artemis solidifies her point, "Even in death, you'd be miserable. You have to defeat the Titans so that when you do kill yourself, it won't be for an even worse existence."

With a sniff, I suck in a trail of snot threatening freedom. Realizing my errors, I turn to Otus to make amends. "You lied to me, but you always did what you thought was right to help stop more battlefields like this one. You did what you had to to make me into the man I needed to be. . . I think you did a good job. I'm sorry I ever questioned you or your loyalty." He nods in thanks.

Thinking she's unnoticed, Charlie takes out the prayer talisman and whispers, "Emma." Emma appears beside her, holding her hand. I smile and nod at them, happy that our many bridges are being mended.

***

All back from the Marias River with newfound looks of resolve and determination, we stand united again. I walk to Emma and extend my hand in reconciliation, saying, "I'm sorry for what happened. I was wrong."

"No need."

Nodding in thanks, I turn to Artemis with a questioning look. Superiority dripping from her attitude, as if a favor, she declares, "My divinity is in the Indian jungle outside of Kolkata. Only a maiden may retrieve it."

Charlie steps forward, volunteering, "I'll go."

"No witch will touch my divinity," Artemis replies with a sneer.

"I'll go," Clara offers.

Artemis sneers even more at Clara, hissing, "You are far from a maiden. Far from it."

Not taking any shit, Clara leans closer to Artemis, hissing back, "Are you slut-shaming me?"

"Your words, not mine."

Fighting to maintain the hard-won peace, Emma intercedes, "Then who can go, Artemis?"

"What about Molly?" Otus suggests.

Unable to meet their questioning gazes, I mumble, "She won't help us. Not after . . ." When the words catch in my throat, Clara reaches out to comfort me.

"There's always Arien." Everyone stares at Apollo in confusion, so he explains, "He's a virgin, and if we kill him, he can regenerate into a woman."

I stumble back in shock, horrified by the prospect. "That's the fucking stupidest thing I've ever heard. I mean, who would even like watching that."

To my surprise, Clara spanks my butt and whispers seductively, "Well, I would, a little." I stare down at her, turned on my how she's biting her lip.

"Really?" I ask in a moment of weakness before turning back to Apollo to say, "No. Not going to happen."

Throwing his hands in defeat, Apollo concedes, "Whatever. It's quite enjoyable to switch things up."

"You're a virgin?" Artemis finally asks, somehow floored by the revelation.

My eyes downcast in shame, I affirm, "Yes."

"I'm surprised."

"Why?"

"You don't seem like the type to have that much self-control."

Not sure if her words are compliments or not, I explain, "I don't. I have Athena's divinity inside of me, and she's a maiden goddess, so . . ."

"A maiden goddess?" she interrupts, excited.

"Yeah."

My eyes widen, realizing what Artemis is getting at. She confirms my suspicions by saying, "It might be enough to retrieve my divinity. Here." With a flourish, she unstrings her bow and hands it to me. "This may tip the scales in your favor to the judges."

"Judges?" Understanding my task, I nod, preparing to depart, but Artemis cries after me, "Wait. You'll need to leave everything behind. Even your clothes."

"What?" I ask, mortified.

"The judges need you to bear yourself before them. No secrets. No disguises. No sin."

"I'll strip when I get there."

"Don't be ridiculous. Do you really want to carry your clothes through a jungle where you need both hands for defense in case something attacks?"

Unwilling to bare myself before the others, I contend, "I'd rather not be naked if something attacks."

"Greek warriors went into battle in the nude all the time. Are you less than them?"

"Yes. Those guys were beasts."

"Whatever. Take them off. We've all seen penises before. Nothing to be ashamed of."

Finally giving in, I mutter, "Fuck it," and begin stripping, handing my discarded clothes to Clara. "Happy now?" I ask.

Feeling everyone's eyes on my cock, I attempt to cover him with my hands. Apollo commends, "Good on you, mate," and Charlie remarks, "I may not be gay anymore," her eyes filled with fake admiration.

"Shut up, Charlie."

Charlie laughs and turns away. "Sorry. Couldn't help it."

"Mary, Mother of god. Whoa." I turn, surprised by Clara's response.

"Really?" I ask.

She gulps and nods slowly. Wanting to satisfy her, I remove my hands, letting her get a full view, the attention making him grow to full salute.

Her eyes fixed, she steps closer, but I retreat, muttering, "No touching. I told you what would happen."

"I'm not going to touch it." She leans in and kisses me on the cheek. "Go be a virgin."

"Thanks," I whisper before vanishing in a dark flash.

CHAPTER 95: STARLIGHT

Arien

I appear in a dark Indian jungle in the dead of night. Standing still, I wait for my eyes to adjust to the darkness, the sound of my breath and heartbeat echoing loudly, magnified by fear of attack while blind. Ahead, three giant statues of fair maidens guarding the entrance to a forest garden are revealed by moonlight.

I take a single step forward but freeze when a loud CREAK echoes through the jungle. The statues moan and sway slightly, seemingly taking their first breaths in 2 millennia.

"Who dares enter the garden of our fair lady?" the first one asks.

My voice quivering slightly, I reply, "I am Arien, fair maiden of the phoenix. I come at the behest of Lady Artemis herself. I humbly beg you leave to retrieve our lady's divinity and return it to her."

The third cries in defiance, "But you are a man. A man cannot be a maiden, so cannot enter here."

"Lady Artemis said you could sense maidenhood. Sense it in me." I extend my arms in invitation, waiting as the statues fall silent to scan.

"You are what you say," the second one reluctantly affirms.

"How is that possible?" the third asks.

I explain, "Lady Artemis is not the only goddess I serve. I bear the divinity of another, destined to remain pure."

Apparently the level-headed one of the bunch, the second one declares, "He speaks the truth. I can sense our lady Athena inside of him."

"He's still a man. We can't let a man in."

Lifting Artemis's silver bow, I extend it to the statues. "I was told to show this to you, and it would tip your judgment in my favor."

"That's not possible. Our lady would never part her bow to a base male. We should kill him. He probably killed her and took it from her corpse."

"No human has skill enough to kill our lady. I believe him."

"As do I."

"We should kill him for merely being a man. They're all monsters."

The first must be the leader, for she raises a hand to silence the bloodthirsty third. When silence is assured, the first scolds, "That's exceedingly narrow-minded of you, Hecaerge. We know not what today's society looks like. There are no absolutes in either gender, good or bad. There are good people and bad people. Gender doesn't come into it. Just because you were spurned by one man, does not make all him. We cannot kill him merely for what his Mother gave him betwixt his legs. I say we let him pass."

"I say aye," the second agrees.

Hecaerge sighs softly but concedes, "Very well. I say aye."

Bowing in thanks, I proffer, "I thank thee, honorable maidens." The statues return to stone, allowing me to enter the garden.

The scenery changes as if I'd been transported across the world to the Rocky Mountains of Colorado. None of the beautiful streams, trees, nor hills belong in the jungles of India. I stare around, awed by the magic at play to protect this small sliver of paradise safe from the outside world. My reverie breaks at the sight of a glowing silver doe grazing in the distance.

Crouching down, I sneak closer to the doe, bow raised. The moment a kill shot is possible, I suddenly realize I am without arrows. "Fuck." After I moment of thought, I decide a peaceful approach is necessary.

I stand and simply walk to the doe, bow held out. It raises its head to stare at me, its eyes piercing my soul, somehow understanding me better than I do myself.

The doe begins to crystallize into shards of pure light, shattering and funneling into the bow.

Once the doe is gone and the bow glows brightly, I sling it over my shoulder and disappear in a dark flash.

***

I materialize onto a scene of chaos and horror. Otus and Charlie have both been shot with arrows; Emma's tries to stop the bleeding, but to no avail. Artemis and Apollo have disappeared, and Clara is limping alone toward the trail.

Running to Clara, I let her lean against me before asking, "Clara! Are you alright? What's going on?"

"It's Artemis. She's been taken," she mutters in a delirium.

"By what?"

"I don't know. It was like it was made of starlight."

Not understanding her meaning but not wanting to press, I help her to sit down. "Where's Apollo?"

"Left after you did. Done what he came for."

"Alright, stay here. I'm going after Artemis."

"But you don't have any real weapons. You left the Aegis behind."

"Did I?" In answer, I extend my arm and the Aegis appears on it in a dark flash.

Clara smirks slightly. "Show off."

After making sure she's comfortable, I hurry over to Emma and ask, "How are they doing?"

"He had some kind of poison on his weapons that prevent me from healing them, but they'll be fine."

"Yup, totally fine here," Charlie groans.

"He?"

"It's Orion," Emma explains. "Pulled down from his place among the stars. That shouldn't be possible. No god or Titan has that power."

"We'll worry about that later. You think they're going to the rangers station?"

"That be my guess. He'd have just teleported away if he could, so he probably has a car."

"How far ahead do you think they are?"

"5, 10 minutes. No more than that, but he's fast. Impossibly fast."

"So, I have time to put some pants on?" Emma returns to her patients, and I quickly get dressed. I pause, meeting Clara's gaze. "I'll be back."

"I know," she whispers as I disappear in a dark flash.

***

Appearing at the station, I'm just in time to see Orion shove the bound and gagged Artemis into the back of his SUV. I race after him, but the SUV pulls out of reach, leaving me in the dust.

I stare after them, losing hope until I see Justin's motorcycle.

Moments later, I'm speeding down the road on the motorcycle, the Aegis propped up on the handlebars. With one hand, I reach into my pocket and pull out my lighter, igniting the phoenix. Now aflame, I grab the Aegis, melting it into a sword and holding it out beside me, molten droplets trailing behind me.

Catching up to Orion, I pull up behind him. He shudders, his form blurring. Orion splits into two smaller versions of himself; one keeps driving while the other stands in the sunroof to siege me with a hailstorm of arrows. I weave back-and-forth to dodge the arrows, returning the Aegis to shield form and jamming it back into the handlebars in defense.

Pressing forward, I draw up alongside, ready to attack, but the driver's door opens, and he slams on the breaks. I crash into the door, tearing it off; the bike tips, sending me flying.

The Orions merge as they drive away.

I stumble to my feet, moaning. An idea striking me, I pull Artemis's bow off my back, forming arrows from the Aegis. I pull back the drawstring and breathe out slowly, taking aim. The glowing light of Artemis's divinity moves from the bow, melting into the arrow.

I fire.

The arrow releases, flying through the air and crashing through the SUV's back window. Smiling, I wait.

The SUV explodes in a pillar of white fire as Artemis gods out. Orion swerves and crashes into a ditch, the SUV burning around him.

Rushing forward to the wreck, I find Artemis dragging Orion out of the flames. Horrified, I shout, "Why are you helping him?"

"He was my friend once and it's my fault that he's like this."

Orion's eyes open and he kicks Artemis, sending her flying. I help her up, turning to stare at the 3 small versions of Orion approaching us. "Oh, you've got to be shitting me."

I side-step the first attack, driving the Aegis forward. That Orion dodges as another slashes at my leg with an arrowhead. Falling to one knee, I roll back out of range.

Artemis is having no more luck in her defense. Whenever she or I nearly land a blow, the third Orion slashes at us. We're pressed back toward the road, the Orions taking their advantage. I land a blow, but the Orion turns gaseous, unharmed by the strike. Artemis growls, anger welling in her.

Without hope, I remember Artemis's past, so I cry, "Aren't you a space goddess? Can't you do anything?"

"My things the moon, not stars."

I'm pressed back further, my injuries from the crash slowing me. "Would sending them to space help?"

"It'll slow them down, at least."

"I'll try, but I can't leave Earth's atmosphere. Erebus doesn't reach that far."

"Shut up and do it."

Changing the Aegis into a shield, I ram it into an Orion, sending us both to the ground. I pin the Orion under the Aegis using my weight, freeing my hands.

I scream as I'm impaled from behind, but I continue on, reaching up to place my hands on the head of the trapped Orion, making both of our eyes turn black.

The Orions all scream, Erebus's insanity overwhelming them. The two free ones fall to the ground, convulsing violently, turning gaseous, and getting sucked back together beneath me, reforming back into the single giant Orion.

He screams and disappears in a dark flash.

I sigh and lean back, nursing all my injuries. "He's back in space."

For the first time, Artemis seems impressed. "Maybe we gods weren't wrong to place our faith in you. You're not so whiny when it comes down to it." I laugh, moaning when the laughter strains my cracked ribs. Artemis kneels to inspect my wounds.

Remembering what Emma had said, I say, "There's some sort of poison on his weapons that prevent magical healing."

She laughs softly to herself, explaining, "It's Norse eitr. I taught him that. There must be some of the old Orion left in there."

"Is there an antidote?" I ask, almost not wanting the answer.

Broken from her reverie of the past, she affirms, "Theriac should do it, but it's near impossible to make."

"Do you know the recipe?"

"Sure, but no one's seen the herb of Moria in ages."

"Charlie will know. Help me get back to her."

Artemis grabs me, and we vanish.

CHAPTER 96: EITR

Arien

Everyone is resting comfortably when Artemis and I appear next to the geyser. The grizzly bear rushes to Artemis, snuggling up to her, clearly glad to see she's alive. Artemis purrs, "Hey, hey. Good to see you too, girl."

Moaning, I hobble to Charlie, who's propped up on a rock beside Otus and Emma. When I reach them, I ask, "How you guys doing?"

"Better than you, it looks like," Charlie replies.

"Funny. Artemis said the antidote for this poison is theriac. Do you know it?"

"Theriac?" Charlie asks, confused. "No one knows the full recipe anymore. The one widely known is missing the magical ingredient that does the true healing."

"It's the herb of Moria." Artemis says, walking over. "That's the missing ingredient. You also need a sample of the poison to make the antidote." She holds up one of Orion's arrows.

"The herb of Moria?"

"Do you know it?"

"Yeah, but I've only ever found dried out seeds. No blossoms. Any idea where we could find blossoms?"

Sighing, Artemis shakes her head. "I don't know. I haven't seen it in a thousand years. That's why I stopped using eitr as a poison."

"Eitr's the poison?" Charlie asks, an idea brightening her gaze.

"Yeah. Why?"

"It brings life, as well. It's pure creation. That's why it's used as a poison. It freezes the body's functions, waiting for the instruction to create."

"So?"

"Only a primordial deity can instruct such creative power. It's how they were created and how they created everything."

Everyone turns to stare at me; realizing the power I hold, I ask, "Erebus is a primordial deity. Could I do it?"

"Not fully." Charlie says. "Not on something as complicated as a human. Erebus himself would have to do that and we know he's in no condition to help. What you can do is make the herb of Moria."

"How?"

"With eitr and you, we could revive the dried out seeds I've found."

"Where are they?"

"In my storage locker." Charlie opens her satchel and pulls out a handful of dried out seeds. She places them on a rock, takes Orion's arrow from Artemis, and pours a few drops of poison onto the seeds. "Now, Arien. Surround the seeds in Erebus and will them to grow. It may take a while, so Artemis and I will work on getting the other ingredients ready."

I'm left alone to create life. Picking up the rock, I stare at the seeds and whisper, "Grow." When nothing happens, I sigh. My eyes turn black, and a cloud of darkness swirls around my fingers. All sound around fades as I close my eyes to concentrate. "Erebus, come to me."

I open my eyes to see nothing has happened.

I sigh again, thinking.

My eyes narrow, an idea striking me. Again closing off the outside world, I let darkness swirl around my fingers. "Mom?"

I open my eyes to see a vision of my Mom sitting in front of me. She smiles lovingly and whispers, "You're a smart guy. The act of birth is the most important creation there is, and I created you. With your memory of me, your Father's power, and the eitr, you can do anything. You'd be a god. More than a god. Gods would fear you. You could do or become anything you wanted." I raise an eyebrow at Brittnie's now venomous tone. The shadows in her face deepen as she becomes a great temptation. My hands tingle from the Eitr crawling up them toward my chest.

Fighting my new desire for power, I mutter, "You'd never say that."

"Why not? I made you, the most important and powerful man to ever live. You're potential is limitless. You can remake the world in any way you see fit. You only need to find more eitr. You must find more."

I start to twitch, the eitr crawling up my arms, acting like a drug in my system. "I can't. That'd be wrong."

She laughs loudly, declaring, "Right and wrong mean nothing. They can become whatever you want them to. You just need more eitr. Get eitr. I need eitr."

"No!" I scream.

Brittnie lashes out, making me recoil in horror. Suddenly, she's gone, and the eitr has returned to the rock where the seeds have bloomed into the herb of Moria.

I shout for Charlie, and she hurries over with a mixing bowl full of ingredients. She bemoans, "I forgot how many ingredients there was in this shit. Did you get it?"

"Here," I respond, handing her the herb.

"Great job."

Nodding in thanks, I turn away, still haunted by my drug-induced vision. Noticing my state, she asks, "What's wrong?"

"Nothing. Just that stuff made me see something that I didn't want to."

Overhearing me, Artemis comments, "Eitr is poison to mortals, but it's a drug to the gods. I guess you're enough of both that you get both symptoms."

"Will you be alright?" Charlie asks, concerned.

"Yeah, I'm fine. Just . . . making me, ah, sluggish, I think. Go ahead." The drug's effects slow me, but I attempt to focus, watching Charlie mix a few of the herbs into her bowl, grinding it together into a salve.

"It's ready." She moans, rubbing the salve on her own wound before doing the same for the rest of us.

Artemis follows behind her, healing once we're free of poison. When her work is done, she turns her gaze to me, no longer the look of a superior but of a peer. "Thank you, for everything you've done."

"Of course."

"I need to go see Apollo now. We have some catching up to do. Farewell."

I nod, and she vanishes.

Otus grumbles, "Why do all the gods just up and vanish after we restore them?"

I laugh in response, but Emma contends, "Hey, we have important stuff to do too."

Atlas

With a roar, I slam my fist through the asylum wall, breathing hard. Wrestling back control from my darker impulses, I manage to hiss, "Why the fuck did that star-studded freak go after Artemis instead of Arien, like he was supposed to?"

Reveling in my base rage, and relishing in his deduction, my Father gloats, "It was personal to him. She got him killed after all. You should never have let him go alone."

"Mnemosyne said I'd fail if I went with him."

"And you believed her?"

Understanding my mistake, my jaw clenches. "An err I don't intend to repeat. No matter what, I must be the one to defeat Arien. I cannot trust any other. I'm going to tear him and that monster he travels with a part as soon as I find them."

"4th time's the charm."

I growl, "Make sure Mnemosyne knows not to lie again."

Iapetus bows, backing out of the room, sarcastically proffering, "Yes, my lord."

He leaves me to stew in my anger. The rage seethes and froths, every second a darker memory of these so-called heroes driving me further into madness.

Arien

Clara and I appear in her house. She stumbles less than before, saying, "That was . . . eventful."

"Yeah, not what I had in mind." I smile down at her, asking, "Are you sure you don't want to join full-time?"

With a sigh, she affirms, "I love it, but I still have a life here. I still have bills to pay. I can't. Sorry."

"I get it," I reply with a nod.

We stand in awkward silence for a while before Clara throws her hands in defeat, muttering, "Aw, to hell with it."

"What?"

Expertly stripping off her clothes, she explains, "I saw you naked. Only fair to even the score. We might not be able to touch, but we can do other things." She poses nude for me, declaring, "There."

My eyes are transfixed on her supple, perfect mounds of erotic flesh, their sight watering my mouth and engorging my pants. I whisper, "They're my first."

"What do you think?"

"You're beautiful."

An unconscious hand reaches out to hold, to grasp, to be one with, but she recoils, saying, "No touching, remember."

With a shake of my head, I regain control. "Right."

"This is the most we get to do for now." Flowing in slow, deliberate motions, she re-dresses and leans in to kiss my cheek. "Now, go save the world. I'll be here."

I smile and disappear.

Part 12:

POSEIDON

CHAPTER 97: A FATHER'S LOVE

Atlas

Child's laughter brightens all dark days, and its absence disheartens the blackest of nights. I did not comprehend the importance of this day, this last day I'd hear my daughter laugh. "8, 9, 10. Ready or not, here I come," I shouted, beginning my search for my young daughter Calypso in the gardens. "I'm coming for you." I searched high and low, under palm and fen, standing straight to nod profoundly at passing nymphs and satyrs.

To my surprise, a lone bush giggled softly, giving away its occupant. Noticing my approach, Calypso bolted from her hiding spot, racing deeper into the garden.

CRACK!

She screamed, the ground beneath her giving way and devouring her. "Calypso!" Whirling at her cry, I leapt into the expansive sinkhole to cradle her sobbing form. "Are you alright?"

"My ankle hurts."

Gently lifting her, careful of her injury, I carried her to the clearing at the garden's center, putting her down on the edge of a fountain to appraise her ankle.

Kronos and my Father were waiting for me beside the fountain, but I ignored them, first tending to my daughter.

"Atlas, we must talk," Iapetus growled, angered by my dismissal.

Continuing to ignore him, I gently rolled Calypso's ankle, asking, "Does that hurt?" She only yelped in response. "It must be sprained." I waved at a passing nymph, pleading, "Lady of the Anigrides, please heal my daughter."

With a smile, the nymph nodded and knelt beside Calypso, humming as she worked.

Iapetus's face darkened even more, displeased with my disrespect of choosing daughter over Father. He stepped forward to reprimand me, but Kronos merely raised a hand to stop him.

Once Calypso is settled, I finally stood and ushered the other Titans away from her. To Kronos, I proffer, "My lord, Kronos. Mine apologies for keeping you waiting."

Stepping close, Iapetus hissed, "How doth not shame riddle thee for requiring your masters to stand by while thou dost tend to a mewling child?"

Before my own rage got the better of me, Kronos again raised his hand and said, "No apology necessary. I honor thy choice of choosing your young over thy duty. If I had only been a Father like unto thee, this war may have been averted."

Suitably chastened, Iapetus slinked back, his eyes downcast. Allowing myself to gloat for but a moment, I turned to Kronos with raised brow, asking, "What war is it that you speak of?"

"Thou has not heard? Mine children are waring to overthrow me."

"Did my lord not devour them as thou had supposed?"

A flash of annoyance and embarrassment crossed Kronos's face, but he quickly regained his composure, explaining, "Forsooth, my bride did deceive and betray. From her scheming, a son survived and rescued his siblings from mine bowels. The how holds no sway over these events. This war is waged for control of this world. All its elements and dominions are at stake. The hole that swallowed thine daughter is but one of many as this war racks the land itself. I desire a general to lead the forces of the Titans against our foe. I can think of none better than thee."

Before I had time to make the choice, Iapetus hawed, "My lord, thy hast said unto me in all the days gone by that I shall lead thy forces. A son cannot command his Father. Especially as skilled a Father as I."

Kronos's venomous gaze turned upon Iapetus, cowing him. "Doth thou question mine authority? Mine choice?"

"Nay, my lord."

"Atlas bears more skill of command than an army of thee. He is the only one I can trust."

Bowing in similitude, I say, "I humbly accept my lord's call. I shall depart at dawn."

"I fear time is not on our side. My children have begun an assault of the forges of Tartarus. We must depart immediately."

Turning to stare at my daughter, smiling at the sound of her laughter, I whispered, "My lord, grant me time to bid my daughter farewell, at least, I beg." He nodded slightly, allowing me to bow and return to Calypso.

As I approached, the nymph stood and declared, "Thy daughter is whole."

"My thanks." Once the nymph had taken her leave, I sat beside my daughter, smiling as I asked, "Are you feeling better?"

"I'm fine." She turned her gaze across the garden to where the other Titans waited for me. "Who are they, papa?"

"They're your grandpa and great-uncle."

"Can I meet them?"

"I don't think that's wise." I sighed softly, continuing, "Calypso, some bad people are doing some bad things and those guys need my help to stop them."

"Does that mean you're leaving?"

"I'm afraid so."

She grabbed me and hugged me tight, whispering in my ear, "I love you, papa. You're my hero, but it'd be selfish of me to keep you. Go be someone else's hero for a while, as long as you always come home." Tears welled in my eyes as Calypso pulled back to gaze into my face with profound wisdom. "I will be scared for you, though."

I smiled, deciding a premature birthday gift was in order. Pulling a dolphin pendant from my tunic, I fastened it around her neck, consoling, "There. As long as you're wearing that, nothing can hurt you, and I'll always come back to you."

Her eyes transfixed upon the sapphire dolphin, Calypso cooed, "I love it."

We hugged again.

Unable to prolong my departure any longer, I stood and walked away to stand beside my kin. With a solemn wave goodbye, I vanished.

***

I'm sitting alone, crying in the dark, cradling the shattered remains of Calypso's dolphin pendant, reliving the sound of her simple laughter.

CHAPTER 98: EMBRACED PASSION

Charlie

The warm embrace of our souls uniting draws goosebumps to my flesh, Emma's soft touch tracing my rocky surface. Her moist tongue glides deep within my throat, playing my pleasure like an instrument. She presses me against the now-closed door, greedily trying to devour me. We barely breathe, neither wanting to interrupt our soft touch.

With a few deft motions, Emma undoes my pants and is slow tracing her fingers down my naval to my moist and welcoming pussy. She twirls the neat curls of my landing strip but pulls back before journey's end.

Finally breaking our kiss, Emma starts to kiss me in a line from my chin to my ear, which gently bites, continuing down to my collarbone. There she stops to free a breast from the insulting confines of my bra. Unable to restrain her lust any longer, she devours my boob, taking it whole in her mouth. I moan sharply, surprised by her gusto. Her expert stirring ignites the fire within me, inciting my nipple to grow in thanks.

Drawing back, Emma smiles up at me, kneeling to finish removing my encumbering pants. Once I'm bared before her, she stares in awe-filled wonderment, licking her lips to stave off her desire. She glances up into my eyes to ask, "Is this OK? Are you ready?"

I bite my lip, only managing to mumble, "Yeah."

"Alright. Here I go," she exclaims with a smile.

With a solitary lick, she traverses my entire length, familiarizing herself with my terrain. She follows up with several small kisses around my exterior, slowly exciting my flesh and heating my desire.

Many minutes and screaming moans later, I pull Emma to her feet, not wanting to finish yet. With a gentle shove, I push her down onto the bed, where she grins up at me, excitedly awaiting my approach.

An idea comes to her, so she reaches into her bag, pulling out a strap-on. "You want this?"

I'm suddenly yanked my sensual trance, remembering the last time I answered yes to that question. "No, nothing like that."

Emma frowns but nods and throws it aside.

Trying to regain the magic, I finish stripping before crawling atop Emma. I rotate atop her, bringing my near throbbing pussy to her lips as I start to work on hers.

Arien

Otus and I sit alone in awkward silence. He taps a finger on the table to stave off the boredom, but my sharp gaze stops him. He sighs, shaking his head, and asking, "Where's Charlie?"

"Her and Emma got their own room," I reply. "Looks like that'll be the new normal."

"Ah." He nods, and the awkward silence continues.

Fed up, I growl and slam my fist down into the table, exclaiming, "What the hell is going on? Why are you being so awkward?"

"Well, I, ah, wasn't sure if we were friends again or not. I know we shared a moment with Artemis, but I'm not sure that it stuck."

"First of all, super weird you're calling that a moment. Secondly, of course we're friends again. I want everything to go back to the way it was."

"Does that apply to everyone?"

My face darkens, realizing who Otus is referring to. "Some things can't be fixed. But you and I are good as long as you stop being weird about it."

"Great." Otus pauses for a second as if psyching himself up. Eventually, he asks. "Have you called her?"

"I don't want to talk about her."

"OK, sorry I asked." Before another word can be said, Otus's phone buzzes violently. He looks up to meet my gaze, asking for permission, expecting that I know who it is.

I nod, saying, "Remember our deal. Nothing personal."

He answers the call, "Hello." Otus listens patiently as I look on. "Very good, my lady. I'll let them know. Goodbye." He hangs up.

"What she have to say?"

"She found Poseidon. He's a surfing instructor in Sydney that got killed by a shark. She recognized his picture on the news."

"That complicates things."

"Poseidon was always tricky. He may have faked his death."

"Either way, he can wait. We haven't had a good night's sleep in a while and Charlie needs some personal time. We'll leave in the morning."

Otus nods in understanding.

Atlas

Despite the battle raging at its gates, Mount Othrys stood unaffected by the slaughter.

My daughter, now too grown to hide but still young to me, stood defiantly in full battle armor before me, her military commander. I shouted over the noise of war, "Calypso? What are you doing here? You were assigned to Lord Kronos's personal guard."

"He sent me into the fight. I bring word from the gate. A captured satyr says this attack is merely a diversion while the hundred-handed-ones climb Mount Olympus."

"Olympus?" I asked, confused. "What can they do from down there?"

"The gods think the hundred-handed-ones can launch boulders at the city, weakening our defenses."

"Oh, great Mother Chaos," I cursed. A horn from the gates drew my gaze down the battlements toward it.

Calypso asked, "What is it?"

"The gods' forces are retreating."

"But that means . . ."

I lift my gaze across the valley at Mount Olympus. "Look to the sky." Out of the smoke of battle, giant boulders soared, flying toward us. "Get down!" I cried, covering Calypso with my body.

BOOM!

When the dust settled, I pushed Calypso back toward the keep, shouting, "It's not safe here. You have to get out of here."

"I'm not leaving you."

I smiled, ignoring the boulders still raining from the sky. "Please. I can't help anyone here if I know you're in danger. The best way for you to save lives is to save your own. Please."

Before she could respond, a boulder crashed directly into us, sending us both flying.

Calypso was thrown down to the street below and through a wall. The wall crumbled, bringing the building down on top of her. I roared and leapt from the battlements to the street below, quickly digging through the rubble until I freed her.

Her injuries were severe, her mind barely conscious. I turned and shouted to the empty air, "Medic! I need a medic!" My cry was heard, and a daemon of healing rushed to our side, crouching to inspect Calypso. "Can you help her?" I asked frantically.

"I can ease the pain, but the wounds are too severe for me to heal."

"Is there anyone who can?"

"Not that we can get to."

I grasped the front of the daemon's tunic, growling, "If you let her die, I will tear you limb from limb."

Fear shrouded his eyes as he stammered, "If we can get her out of the city, there's a grove full of Anigrides nearby, but all the exits are blocked."

"There's a secret tunnel under the walls leading into the woods. I can show you the entrance." Lifting my daughter, I led the daemon away from the assault.

Charlie

Emma and I lie naked, intertwined, sleeping peacefully until I am roused by gentle kissing on my exposed nipple. With a giggle, I open my eyes and whisper, "Morning." Emma doesn't respond, only sucks harder, taking in the entire breast, making me gasp slightly. "Oh. . . This is definitely the best way to be woken up."

Finally releasing her grip, Emma crawls up to kiss me, saying, "I love you."

I grin broadly, teasing, "Oh, yeah?"

"Yeah."

"What do you love about me?"

We both giggle softly before Emma replies, "Well, I love your passion and your heart." We kiss again. "And these lips." She continues kissing body parts as she lists them. "These little ears. This neck, and this shoulder. I really love these girls." She briefly sucks on each breast, making me giggle again. "This itty-bitty bellybutton. And most of all . . ." With unrestrained eagerness, she kisses my clit, making me moan violently. I arch my back and sigh while running my fingers through her hair.

A knock comes from the door, followed by Otus barreling in. "Hey, Charlie?"

"Otus!" I shout, scrambling to cover our nakedness.

He turns away crying, "Fuck! Sorry."

"Wait till we answer next time."

"I will definitely do that."

Emma grins, mocking my anger with laughter. "It's not funny, babe," I contend.

She replies, "It's a little funny."

I scowl at her before looking back at Otus. "What do you need, anyway?"

"We need to get going soon. We know where Poseidon is."

"We'll be out in a minute."

"Alright. I'll be in the other room."

He scampers off as fast as he can while I turn back to Emma. "I guess we'll have to cut this short."

"I'm a goddess. I can make it short." She pulls the covers up over her head, going back down on me. I gasp, the passion building.

CHAPTER 99: PLAYING DETECTIVE

<u>Arien</u>

Molly, the only family I had left, now gone from me too. I stare at her number on my phone, fighting for the will to simply press call and salvage what I can. My decision made, I take the leap and call. Before she can pick up, Otus rushes in, and I hang up.

His terrified gaze gives me pause and distracts me from my pain. I ask, "Otus, what's going on?"

"I think Charlie is going to kill me."

Deducing the problem, I smile and prompt, "You walked in on them having sex, didn't you?"

"Yes," he replies, his eyes downcast in shame.

"Why didn't you knock?"

"I did. I just didn't wait for an answer." My grin widens, followed by ruckus laughter, making Otus turn bright red and say, "It's not funny. I think she might really kill me. And not in a pleasant way. She'll use some, like, witch's spell to turn me into a mouse, or something. Then let an actual owl eat me."

His prediction only heightens my laughter. "If you're lucky."

"What am I going to do?"

"Lick her boots for as long as she wants."

"Or maybe I can move back to England. I loved it there. I could hide away there. She'd never find me."

"She's got a tracking amulet in your stomach, remember."

"Then I'll find another witch to dig it out. Or . . ." He freezes as Charlie and Emma walk in. Charlie has a dazed look in her eyes that's not allowing her to focus on anything. Otus stammers, "Charlie! Hey!"

"Huh?"

"Are you OK?"

"Fine," she mumbles.

"Are you still mad at me?"

"What? Oh, whatever."

I turn to stare at Emma in pure wonder, guessing the cause of Charlie's trance. "What?" Emma asks coyly.

"What did you do?"

"I'm the goddess of love." She smiles and shrugs it off.

Moving on, I address everyone, "Right. So, we found Poseidon. He's in Sydney. The problem is, he's dead. The coverage of his death is how we found him."

"Why not just do that thing we did with, ah . . . What's his name?" Charlie slowly articulates.

"Apollo?"

"That's the one."

"Poseidon's not a god of healing, so his divinity won't heal something that complicated. Neither can Emma. Though, Otus thinks he may be faking his death. We'll need to go to Sydney and figure it out from there, either way. If he is dead, we'll find some other way to resurrect him, then."

Charlie snorts and caws, "So, the normal impossible bullshit?"

"Looks like it."

"No time to, ah, waste, I guess."

Emma

We appear in my nephew's Sydney apartment; Charlie stumbles violently, only kept upright by my quick reflexes. "I'm fine," she insists.

Arien ignores Charlie, going to inspect the police tape on the door and the forensic equipment scattered throughout the room. "Wow. What is all this about? I thought you said he was killed by a shark?"

"He was," Otus replies.

"Then what happened here?"

"I don't know."

"Alright. Spread out. See if we can find anything." We all nod and start our search.

The men step into other rooms before Charlie grabs me and whispers seductively, "How about a quicky in the closet?"

I glance down at her with worry, regretting my previous gusto. "I may have taken it too far with you."

"What? Pssh, naw. I'm good." Raising a single finger, I tap her forehead, clearing the lust from it. Charlie gasps and steps back, exclaiming, "Wow. That was weird."

"Sorry."

"No, you're fine. I trust you."

"Guys! I found something," Arien shouts from the other room.

We follow his voice into the bedroom, where we're greeted by the sight of a massive bloodstain in the center of the floor. "Oh, my god," Charlie cries.

"This explains the forensic equipment."

Still not comprehending, Otus contends, "The news said a shark killed him. I don't understand."

"I don't think a shark did this. Charlie, can you do your thing?"

Charlie nods, reaching into her bag, she pulls out a prayer mat and a series of incense candles. Kneeling on the mat, she lights the incense and starts chanting a prayer under her breath. The rest of us quietly search the room while she works.

Otus pulls back the bedcovers, gagging at the smell and the bloodstain hidden within. Inspecting the sheets, I whisper, "That smell. Whatever wound Poseidon had got infected and that's what likely killed him."

Charlie stops chanting, her voice trailing into confusion. We turn to her, freezing at the sight of a forensic tech pointing a gun at us from the doorway.

"Whoa, take it easy," Arien says.

"No one's supposed to be up here." The tech shouts, her hands quivering. "What are you doing here?"

Taking control, I declare, "I'm with ASIO. I'm going to slowly reach into my pocket and pull out my badge, OK?"

The tech nods, allowing me to reach into my pocket and pull out an ID badge. "Toss it here." I comply, and she catches it. With several glances between me and the badge, she confirms my identity and lowers her gun. "Sorry, Agent Rossum. Can't be too careful."

"No, you can't."

"I'm Mia Hemsworth. I'm a forensic tech working on this case. I just came here to collect more evidence before the cleaners came. I am confused why ASIO is involved in a shark attack."

"We don't believe it was a shark attack."

Mia gives me a curious look, saying, "That's not possible."

"We're still going to need to see the body."

CHAPTER 100: LAND SHARK

Atlas

Waves of light descended from the sky, coalescing into a transparent avatar for me to possess. I stood still for a moment, taking in my surroundings and acclimating myself to my new form. A scream tore me from my preparation; I ran forward, barreling into my daughter's cave. Inside, I found not blood nor pain, but passion and love. My daughter was entwined with the body of a god, embraced in making love. Horror and disgust riveted me to the spot, ashamed that my daughter would fall for a god after all they'd done.

Turning, I fled the cave, retreating to the welcoming surf to calm my aching nerves. I took a moment to stare across this strange little island, neither part of the world nor separate from it; a place beyond time. As prisons go, I was glad Calypso got one so bright and lovely. Despite the gods' kindness to her, she still should not have forgiven them and lain with one.

Deciding to confront my daughter, I waited until the god, Aphrodite, said her goodbyes with a kiss and vanished.

"Calypso!" I cried, revealing my presence.

"Father?" Calypso ran to me and tried to embrace me, but my starry form was immaterial. "What's wrong with you? How are you here?"

"I'm a star projection. Something I picked up while holding up the sky."

"So, you're still . . .?"

"Imprisoned," I finished for her. "Yes. But more importantly, what on Earth are you doing with a god?"

"Have you been spying on me?"

"Not intentionally."

"I love Aphrodite, and that's my business. Mine alone."

"I'm just worried about your safety. Gods can't be trusted."

She smiled, her sudden anger dissipating, replaced with affection. "Don't worry about me. I can take care of myself."

I stared down into her eyes, reluctantly nodding and conceding.

<u>Arien</u>

Mia pulls back the sheet covering Poseidon's corpse, revealing its mutilated and gruesome visage to us, the massive bite mark in his side of particular interest. "Jesus!" I mutter.

"No, that's definitely a shark," Emma affirms.

Mia shakes her head, confused by our reaction. "That's what the autopsy said."

"Then why is there all that blood at the apartment?"

"He was found there. He was bit then went home without telling anyone. It appears that he went to bed and rolled out in the middle of the night, dying on the floor."

Still confused and grieving for her kin's death, Emma stammers, "Why . . . How would he do that?"

"You guys should know all this from the report. Didn't you read it?"

"Oh, ah, we only got the initial police alert. The finished conclusion never made it to us. Would you mind taking me to your lab so I can review the forensic data?"

"I don't think I should leave anyone alone with the body."

"Don't worry about it. They're professionals." Emma guides Mia to the door. Once they're gone, Charlie gets out her prayer mat and incense, starting to check for magical interference of the body.

Otus and I wait patiently until she stands and says, "There's nothing here. Looks like he was really killed by a shark."

"Then what do we do?" Otus asks.

I suggest, "We'll have to try a nekyia," and Charlie agrees.

"What about praying?"

Thinking for a moment, Charlie explains, "The only prayer the spell requires is to Thanatos to grant the spirit's safe passage from the Underworld. With the gates of the Underworld closed, we can skip that part." Without another word, Charlie pulls a few of Poseidon's hairs before grabbing a wooden bowl from her bag. She sits on the ground, placing it on the floor in front of her, and lighting a candle behind it. "To all the souls of those who've gone, I humbly give this offering." Taking 5 urns from her bag, she slowly pours a libation out from each into the bowl; libations of milk, honey, mellow wine, water, and then of barley.

Finally, she places Poseidon's hairs in the bowl and reaches into her bag to retrieve a squirming bird. "Aa emptokom basym, protect me."

Hefting a knife, Charlie slashes open the bird, letting its blood pour into the bowl to mix with the other ingredients. Setting aside the corpse and her tools, she extends her arms and closes her eyes, whispering, "Eláte, psychí aftoú pou agapísame kai échasa." Her eyes glaze over as she starts to seize a little.

A ghost passes through the wall into the room and leans down to drink from Charlie's bowl. The ghost of Poseidon materializes in front of us, exclaiming, "Oh, wow. . . Took you guys long enough."

Charlie stares at Poseidon in confusion, muttering, "What?"

"I've been following you since my apartment. I've been waiting for you to do this ever since. And, may I say, I am not impressed with the performance that I've seen so far."

"How could you be following us? Your soul should at least have been drawn to the gates of the Underworld."

Poseidon's swaggery demeanor falters for a moment; his eyes lower, and he mumbles, "Someone's kidnapping spirits and taking them somewhere. I only escaped because I knew what to look for in death. No one else that I saw was that lucky."

"It's the Titans taking the spirits."

"I figured as much."

"How did you die?"

Happy for the change in conversation, Poseidon's confidence returns. "Acheilus, a shark-daemon son of Zeus. I was teaching some beginners how to surf when he knocked me off my board. Before I could react, he got me. I knew if Acheilus had attacked me, then Oceanus had finally chosen a side in this war. Kronos must have offered him something he couldn't refuse. I think Kronos isn't leaving anything to chance with you all running around restoring gods. He needs all the help he can get. Everything got a little hazy after that. I went home because I needed to contact my divinity's guardian to have her move it. With Oceanus on the Titan's side, the ocean isn't safe for it. I must have passed out after that because the next thing I remember is being dead. Now, we just need to find a way to bring me back."

"I know a spell." Charlie declares. "After Apollo's death, I made sure I had all the ingredients. The blood from the right side of a Gorgon was the hardest thing to get, but I found it."

"How the hell do you have Gorgon's blood?" Otus asks, awed.

She shrugs mysteriously, deflecting, "I get around."

Poseidon interrupts, "Great. Let's do it."

"The problem is, the spell requires a prayer to Hecate."

"Dammit," I mutter.

"No, no dammit. Why dammit? Why can't you pray to Hecate?" Poseidon asks.

"The Titans can track prayers."

Poseidon's jaw drops in horror. "What? That's horrific. Even the gods could only do that if prayers were directed at us."

"We can try to use the talisman, but Orion still found us the last time I used it." Charlie suggests.

"Talisman?" Charlie takes out the prayer talisman and shows it to Poseidon. He glances at it before asking, "Ah. Who'd you pray to the last time with this?"

"Aphrodite."

"That's your problem. It's specifically for praying to Hermes. It won't work otherwise."

"Fuck."

Otus's eyes widen, an idea coming to him. "I have a plan. You're not going to like it. Emma goes after the divinity while Charlie brings him back. You and I will buy everyone enough time from the Titans until he's restored, and we can all teleport out of here. We don't really have any other options."

"That's your big plan?" I rejoin. "Hope Atlas doesn't destroy us like he has every other time we've met?"

"With one major difference. We'll be waiting for him this time."

My brow raises at the thought.

Emma

With trained skill, Mia brings up more crime scene photos on her computer for me to review. Watching me closely, she explains, "According to the M.E., the bite is approximately 1.5 meters wide. Rather large for a Great White, but nothing unheard of."

"How on earth did he get home with a hole that large in him?"

"Adrenaline, I guess. We've seen people do some pretty insane things on adrenaline."

"I suppose." Charlie, Otus, and Arien walk in, interrupting my review.

Mia asks, "Did you guys find what you were looking for?"

"Yes, I believe we have everything we need," Arien affirms.

"Honey, could you?" Charlie asks with a nod to me.

"Course," I reply, tapping Mia's forehead, wiping her memory. Her eyes roll back, and she collapses to the floor. Turning back to Charlie, I ask, "Did you find him?"

As if in answer, the ghost of Poseidon floats into the room, much to my surprise. He stops and nods in deference to me, rendering, "Aphrodite."

"Poseidon. Been a while."

"Indeed."

"I missed you."

"So did I."

I can sense Charlie's uncomfortable gaze flitting between to two of us, so I cough slightly and say, "Anyway, what's going on? How are we going to fix your, ah, body?"

Jumping in, Charlie explains, "I know a spell, but it'll take a while and involve praying."

"OK. Any ideas?"

It's Arien's turn to jump in, saying, "Charlie resurrects Poseidon, while you get the divinity, and Otus and I distract the Titans."

I hesitate for a moment, not sure how to respond to such a simple and doomed plan. "It doesn't sound easy."

"It's the best we have."

"OK. Where's the divinity?"

"Challenger Deep, the bottom of the deepest trench on Earth," Poseidon mumbles, with an awkward grin.

"Fuck." Taking a moment for my task ahead to sink in, I concede, "Fine. I might as well leave now. It'll take me a while to find it." I turn to say goodbye to Charlie, whispering, "I love you."

"I love you too." We kiss briefly before I step back and vanish.

Charlie

With a kiss, the woman I love abandons me to dangers unknown, not that her path is any more secure. Brushing off my dread with a sigh, I say, "I'll go down to the morgue and start the spell."

"Alright." Arien replies, turning to Otus. "Otus, go with her. You're going to be the last line of defense."

"That wasn't the plan," Otus contends.

"I know, but Atlas will follow me. Anyone with him will come for her. We can't leave Charlie alone while she works."

Otus nods without another word. Arien goes to defend the front door, but I stop him. "Wait." I hand him a packet of alchemy bombs, explaining, "These'll put the locals to sleep. Let you do what you need to."

"Thank you." He heads out while the rest of us retreat back into the morgue.

***

After what felt like days, I've finished mixing the concoction and have started drawing with it on Poseidon's corpse. I draw a trident on his head, a butterfly with crossed torches behind it on his chest, and an array of gorgon snakes crawling up from his groin. "Are you sure this is going to work?" he asks.

"Shh."

"Sorry."

Finishing the drawings, I rub the excess potion into my hands and arms, asking, "Otus, will you help me?" Otus helps me drag Poseidon's body onto the ground, where I sit cross-legged with Poseidon's head in my lap and my hands covering his ears. Closing my eyes, I begin my prayer to Hecate:

> *"I call Einodian Hecate, lovely dame, of earthly, wat'ry, and celestial frame, sepulchral,*
>
> *in a saffron veil array'd, leas'd with dark ghosts that wander thro' the shade."*

The concoction drawn on Poseidon and covering my arms glows with a godly light. I open my eyes, and they blaze with a bright fire.

The shark bite in Poseidon's side begins to stitch itself back up slowly.

CHAPTER 101: BLOOD OF A DOLPHIN

Atlas

I again descended from the sky, occupying my starry avatar. I gasped, seeing the sight of my blood-soaked daughter lying motionless upon her cave floor. Rushing forward, I tried to cradle her head in my lap, but my hands passed right through, never able to touch again. Tears streaming down my cheeks, I cried, "No, no, Calypso. Come on, honey. Please." I was lost for what to do.

She coughed and spat up a mouthful of her sparkling blood, human blood and not ichor as she had before. "Father?" she whispered, staring blankly up at me.

"Yeah, baby. It's me. I'm here."

She smiled slowly through the pain, her mind fading. "Father."

"Yes, it's me. Who did this to you?"

"Aphro . . . Aphrodite." She coughed more violently, barely keeping it together.

"Come on, stay awake."

"I love you."

Recognizing her words as farewell, I demand, "Don't say that. You'll be fine."

"No, please say it back. Just this once."

Tears streaming down my cheeks, I accepted that I was watching my daughter die. "I love you."

Calypso smiled again. "Thank you." She sighed, releasing out her last breath.

"Calypso. No, no, no." I struggled to touch my daughter one last time, to no avail. "No!" I howled, collapsing in upon myself.

***

Still alone in the dark, I'm staring blankly at the wall when Iapetus rushes in, exclaiming, "Mnemosyne has found them. They're in Sydney."

Simply nodding, I stand slowly. "I want the harpies ready to depart immediately and standing by if I cannot handle them alone. With them being in a large city, the harpies must be the absolute last resort. We can't have anyone seeing anything too impossible."

"I could still go with you."

"I will never fight beside you. I've told you that for eons. I cannot trust you."

"Take someone else then. We've seen how this plays out before."

"Koios is gone and Hyperion is injured. Who else is ready and trustworthy?"

Iapetus nods in acceptance, conceding, "Fine. Good luck."

Arien

I hold my breath, not out of need; fear has nigh crippled me, the anticipation of Atlas's attack making my hands tremble and my nerves heighten. I'm standing alone in the police lobby, shotgun in hand, the stations' inhabitants all unconscious and tucked away in closets out of danger.

Suddenly, Atlas appears outside on the street; I stiffen, my adrenaline kicking in and drowning my fearful nerves. From outside, he shouts, "Arien, come out. I don't want to hurt any of you. You don't know any better. The gods have brainwashed you. Please, let me help you." With a sigh, I comply, exiting the station. He smiles and says, "It's good to see you." I don't speak in reply; my reply is unloading a round of buckshot into his gut. He stumbles back and grunts as I empty all my rounds into him. "You done? You know those can't hurt me."

"No, but it's a start," I respond, pointing up at the station's security cameras focused in on Atlas. "Reporters are on their way and they'll have a video to baffle the world."

"That doesn't prove anything. I could be wearing a vest."

"Like I said, a start. They're about to know that magic is real, and Kronos will hate that, won't he?" I take out my lighter and ignite the phoenix.

Atlas snarls and charges.

The Aegis appears on my arm just in time to block Atlas's vicious downswing with the Scythe. He kicks at me from beneath the Aegis, sending me flying. I roll to a stop and vomit, drawing a smile from Atlas. He gloats, "Erebus still won't help you, huh? And you're body doesn't know how to operate without him inside of you."

I struggle to my feet, declaring, "True, but I still have the phoenix."

"Will it be enough?"

I charge this time, morphing the Aegis into a sword. He blocks my first attack, but stumbles, realizing my skill has grown, and we may have a fair fight.

News reporters pull up all round us, getting out their cameras to record the fight. Atlas stares at them in horror before his face sets in determination. "Fuck this." He slams into me, pushing me back and gaining a brief reprieve in which he turns and raises a fist to signal someone. Atlas turns back to me and grunts as our blades clash again.

Otus

I turn on a TV to monitor the fight, flipping through until I find the battle on the news. A reporter narrates, "We still of no word yet on who these two incredible beings are, or the cause of their conflict. The most we can say at this moment is, the world is so much stranger than we could have known."

My guilt and fear prevail; I stand suddenly, turning to the door. "I have to help him."

"Whoa, you need to stay here." Poseidon exclaims. "Remember what Arien said? You're the last line of defense."

I hesitate for a moment.

BOOM!

The back door explodes off its hinges and dozens of harpies pour in. I draw my knife and charge, seamlessly weaving between bird and man as I fight, but the harpies soon overwhelm me; their claws tear at my flesh, making me scream.

Arien

Atlas towers over me, raising the Scythe for the killing blow. "Don't worry. You'll only be dead long enough to get you to Lord Kronos."

The flash of the reporters' cameras distracts him long enough for me to reach into my pocket and press the remote turn-on.

Dozens of floodlights in the station windows blaze to light, blinding him. I manage to land a blow with the Aegis as a mace, which sends him to the ground. Before he can react, I've stabbed him through the chest with the Aegis.

I pull out the sword and press it against Atlas's throat, making him look at the cameras as I whisper, "The whole world has seen me beat you. Can you actually feel it? The strength of belief that Kronos gives you dwindling away. Making you weak enough that an untrained boy like me could defeat you."

Shame fills his eyes.

The lights from the station suddenly go out as a power surge knocks out the building. "What, the fuck?" I mutter.

SCREECH!

Dozens and dozens of harpies swarm forward, surrounding us. I grunt, their claws slashing at me and driving me back from Atlas. Covering my eyes, I attempt to swing at the harpies, but there are too many of them. I'm being torn to shreds.

A light brighter than the floodlights pours from the station, bathing me in light. The harpies screech, the light burning their skin. They all flee or evaporate before the fully powered and alive godly Poseidon steps out of the station.

Once the storm of harpies disappears, I turn to look for Atlas, but he's gone.

The reporters turn the cameras onto Poseidon as he approaches me. I stumble to greet him, fighting past my numerous injuries. Offering my hand, I proffer, "My lord, Poseidon. It's a pleasure to finally meet you, for real this time."

He smiles and shakes my hand. "The pleasure's all mine." Turning the reporters, he ponders, "I don't know what I should do. Should I talk to them?"

"I think you should."

"But what could I say that they'd understand?"

"Just tell the truth. Give people a little credit. It may take them a little while, but they'll figure it out."

"I don't know if I can do that. I've been living in the shadows for so long."

"The only way we can win this war is if humanity is on our side."

He nods, transforming his swimsuit into something more appropriate. "Thank you." Poseidon heads off to talk to the reporters as Otus, Emma, and Charlie walk up to me.

Emma asks, "Where's Atlas?"

"He's gone, but he'll be nursing his wounds for a little while."

"I'm impressed."

"Don't be. I can't even stand anymore." Charlie grabs me before I collapse. I gratefully accept her help, hobbling to a bench. When I sit, my phone rings. Checking it, I freeze, seeing the caller ID. "It's Molly."

"We'll give you a little space," Charlie whispers, herding the others away.

CHAPTER 102: STRENGTH OF BELIEF

Charlie

While leading the others away from Arien, Poseidon runs over to ask Otus, "Hey, why don't you join me?" Otus smiles and limps back to the reporters with him. I smile at Emma and lead her to a bench, muttering, "It's been a long day."

"It really has."

We sit in silence for a moment until my need for confession overrides my better judgment. "Emma, there's something I need to tell you."

She glances at me in surprise, asking, "What is it?"

"When we were in Poseidon's apartment and I did the detection spell, I didn't tell you, but I found something." Emma just sits and waits expectantly, so I continue, "While I was scanning, I sensed a lot of magic coming off of you, which isn't uncommon for a god."

"But?"

"There's a blood-lust curse on you."

"A what?"

"A curse that makes you kill a specific person."

Emma's eyes widen in shock. "Who?"

"From what I sensed of the spell, I think Ares cursed you to kill Calypso, and its effects still remain.

Tears threaten at the corners of Emma's eyes as she stammers, "No, he wouldn't do that. He loved me."

"Love makes people do awful things. Especially when jealousy gets involved. I don't think he wanted to share you with Calypso."

"Ares isn't like that. I had tons of boyfriends and girlfriends back then."

"I can't be sure it's him, but either way, you're not a murderer."

She turns to stare into the rising sun, her face flushing with anger; the shadows darken strangely on her face, but I dismiss it as a play of the light. Her voice as cold as steel, she whispers, "I need to talk to Ares."

"Of course."

With a smile and a kiss, she says, "Thank you," and vanishes.

<u>Arien</u>

Fighting back my tears of joy, I listen to Molly ask, "Is that really you on TV?"

"Yeah, I'm still in Sydney at the scene."

"You saved a lot of people?"

"In a way. Atlas would have killed everyone inside the police station if I hadn't stopped him."

She pauses, obviously struggling to continue, "You always try so hard to be a good man. I'm . . . I'm sorry for what I said. I know it was an accident."

"It was. I never wanted to hurt anyone."

"Did you hear what the police are saying here?"

"No," I whisper, not wanting to hear the answer.

"When your dad said you, ah, did it, they didn't believe him. He's been arrested for her murder." I don't answer because the words I want to say would enrage her and undo today's progress. Eventually, she demands, "I want you to confess to get him released."

"What?" I exclaim, not believing she would ask something so terrible of me.

"Not turn yourself in, or anything. Just give them enough proof to release him."

Sighing, I try to articulate my feelings, "I don't know if I can do that. They probably haven't released him yet because they think I'll let my guard down to get him out. I can't risk getting anywhere near this."

Her tone biting, she hisses, "So, you're willing to let your own Father go to prison for a crime he didn't commit?"

"He's not my Father," I whisper.

"An innocent man, then."

"They know I'm alive and dangerous. They won't keep him any longer than they think he's useful as bait."

"That's awful." She sighs, calming herself before adding, "I'm sorry. I guess you're right. I know it's dangerous for you to come to town, but is there any way for me to see you."

"I'll come as soon as I can."

"OK. I'll see you then. Love you."

"I love you too. Bye." I hang up, staring into the rising sun to process my emotions.

Mia and the other police officers slowly walk from the station, dazed expressions on their faces. Mia notices me sitting alone and approaches to ask, "What happened? What I miss?"

"Turns out, your victim was the god Poseidon. He's come back to life and just battled the Titan Atlas for the hearts of humanity."

She snorts derisively, jeering, "Come on. What really happened?" When I don't answer, she looks down at my injuries, exclaiming, "Fuck, you mean it."

"Afraid so."

The information overwhelming her, she leans against a wall, baffled. "Shit. This is . . . a lot."

"Tell me about it."

"And you guys knew who he was?"

"It's kinda our job to find all the gods and reunite them with their godly spirits."

"Wow. . . And you like doing this?"

I glance down, lost in thought. "As much as the next guy likes his job. I like what I get out of it."

"You're paid?"

"No, I get something a little more personal out of it."

"Ah." She stands in silence for a moment before asking, "What's this going to mean for everyone?"

"I'm not sure yet. Everyone will have the chance to make their own decisions. Some will deny, some will fight, and some will just choose to believe and hope. Which group wins that fight will determine who wins the bigger war. The war that could destroy us all."

"Who with?"

"The Titans, and, believe it or not, Jesus Christ."

"Really?" she utters in shock.

I giggle softly, realizing the insanity of my statement. "Yeah. You'd be surprised the role he's had in humanity."

"Do you think we'll be OK?"

I stare up at Poseidon talking to the reporters. "Yeah, I do. Some of us, at least."

Mia sighs again and shakes her head. "This is too much for me to handle. I think I'm going to call all the guys I know and get them to gang-bang me. I need to lose myself a little."

"Have fun with that."

She goes to walk away but stops and turns back. "You could always join us."

I smile sadly, again reminded that I will never feel a woman's touch. "I'd love to, but I need to heal up a bit before I try anything that intensive."

"Maybe just a blowjob, then? You look like you need it. I need a distraction and I've always wanted to do a famous person."

"It's OK. Thank you, though."

"You sure I can't change your mind?"

"Yeah."

"Alright. Good luck with all of this, then."

"Thanks."

She walks away, leaving me alone as I always shall be.

Part 13:

ZEUS

CHAPTER 103: FOREIGN DELIGHTS

Arien

How can air itself feel so different when separated by space alone; its weight, touch, and taste? I breathe deeply of this Brazilian air, enjoying the difference of it, the romance of it. To enhance the feeling it gives, I take a swig of beer, enjoying the cold trickle down my throat. "You look like you're about to orgasm," Clara says with a giggle.

"Can you blame me?" I ask with a happy sigh.

She appraises our view and affirms, "It's beautiful, isn't it?"

Turning from our mountain view of Rio, I stare deep into Clara's eyes, whispering, "Yeah, very beautiful."

She blushes, realizing my words are of her, not the view. "Stop."

I smile slightly and take another sip of my drink. We stare from her car hood down the mountain to the bright flashes of the city far below. Enjoying our shared silence for a minute, I eventually ask, "Clara?"

"Yeah?"

"I was wondering something. I'm not trying to be offensive, just curious. Clara isn't really an African American name."

She sighs, seemingly remembering a profound and personal memory. "You're right. I'm actually named after my great-great-grandmother, Clara Belle Williams. The first black woman to graduate from New Mexico State University."

"Oh, wow."

"I know it doesn't sound that cool or important, but my family is really proud of it."

"No, it's pretty cool. Did you ever meet her?"

"No, she died before I was born, but she's my hero." Clara's eyes go distant, reliving her heritage. "She defied all expectations and did something extraordinary. I want to be like that, more than anything. To have made a difference and be remembered after I'm gone. Things may have changed since her time, at least a little. It's not as bad anymore, not in the same way, so I'll have to be remembered for something else. That's why I jumped at the chance to help you. A life worth living."

We sit in silence for a moment, both staring off in thought. ". . . And a death worth dying," I eventually add.

She nods slowly. "Sometimes that's what I want. I was suicidal once too." With a smile, she laughs softly, heartlessly. "Why are we so messed up? We're terrible for each other, but perfect at the same time."

"Yeah, I guess we are."

Clara stops smiling to turn and look at me. "I don't want you to die. Neither does Charlie, Molly, or Otus."

It's my turn to sigh softly and say, "I admit my will to . . . die has faltered a little. You're a big part of that."

"I'm glad to hear that," she whispers with a broad smile.

"With Erebus's insanity gone, all that's left is my own pain. And I might be able to handle that."

"I think you can too." We sit in another prolonged silence, neither wanting to ruin the closeness of the moment. Once the moment begins to fade naturally, Clara says, "Charlie told me about Dinah. I'm sorry."

I stiffen suddenly, the moment dead. "I'm surprised you're not angry with me, for doing it and not telling you."

"I'm sad, not angry. I know that it was an accident and that she kinda deserved it. I'm sad that you have to live through it. Through killing your Mother."

"She was never my Mother."

She concedes with a nod, affirming, "I still feel bad for you." She waits a second for my strained breathing to slow before asking, "Has Molly forgiven you yet?"

"No, but she's speaking to me again. She's the only family I ever had. I can't lose her."

She reaches out and grasps my hand in comfort. I glance at our hands, concerned of my divinity's intervention, but Clara consoles, "It's alright." She snuggles up to me and smiles, staring out at the beautiful city again.

Our moment is again interrupted, this time by my buzzing phone. I sigh and answer, "Hello."

"Hey, Arien," Charlie replies. "There's something on the news. You should come take a look at this."

"Ding."

"What?"

"Sorry, YouTube joke. I'll be right there." I hang up, turning to Clara. "Sorry, looks like I'll have to cut this short."

"It's alright. Can we drop off my car before we join the others?"

"Sure."

We disappear in a dark flash, the car with us.

***

Clara and I appear in our Texan hotel room. Emma and Charlie don't even react as they continue watching the news; I briefly notice how much Charlie's pregnant belly has grown, now starting to push out her shirt. "What's going on?" I ask.

Without looking up, Charlie replies, "It's about what happened in Sydney. Watch."

Turning to the TV, I see it cut to Robin in the studio, explaining, "What we're seeing around the world right now is unprecedented. People are flocking to their local demos just trying to learn more about the supposed gods and how to survive the coming war that the man claiming to be Poseidon predicted. Many remain skeptical, but millions of people are being converted. Countless reports of sightings of magical creatures and of gods are flooding social media. It appears that gods are among us.

"Many established religious groups are having difficulties with this new wave of Hellenism, though. The Temple of God's Time is calling for a purge. A violent and decisive eradication of anyone preaching in support of what they deem to be pagan heresy. Other church leaders in America are united in a less violent abolishment of these pagan beliefs. Calling it; 'the work of the devil.' Only the Catholic Church has not spoken out against this reformation. The contrary, in fact. The pope himself has claimed to have been visited by the god Apollo, and is currently converting to Hellenism. No matter your opinion on this reformation, we must all agree that these events will leave the world changed forever. Nothing like this has ever been seen before."

"This is amazing," I mutter.

Emma nods, saying, "I haven't seen anything like this since ancient Greece. I can feel their belief strengthening me." I look to her in time to see her eyes briefly invert into blackness with a milky white pupil before she blinks, and they return to normal. I assume the change is caused by the influx of belief flooding her and ignore it, returning to stare at the news.

"Where's Otus?" Clara asks. "He should see this."

"He hasn't answered his phone," Charlie responds.

"You should track him. This is important."

Charlie sighs and stands, moaning, "Fine." She digs out her tracking amulet to find Otus.

After a quick search, we discover Otus in an empty room. I push open the slightly ajar door and freeze upon seeing him jerking off to his laptop. "Jesus Christ, Otus," I exclaim, rushing forward to take the laptop. "We talked about this. Your porn addiction keeps putting us in danger."

"Remember how I tracked you through that website before?" Clara affirms. "Who knows if the Titans can do it again."

His eyes downcast in shame, Otus mutters, "It's not porn, per se."

"What?" I lift the laptop to get a look at the screen; on it is a photo of Molly naked. "Oh, fuck," I cry, throwing it away in disgust and gagging a little.

"What is it?" Clara asks, picking up the laptop. "Is this . . .?"

"Molly? Yeah." I glare down at Otus, continuing, "Molly wouldn't take these kinds of photos for anyone. She's too much of a good girl. How'd you get them?"

Still unable to meet my gaze, Otus mumbles, "I photoshopped them."

"You fucking what? That's disgusting."

We all cringe slightly, so Otus attempts to defend himself, "Oh, come on. You guys can't tell me you've never tried something like this before."

"Well, not with my cousin," I rejoin.

Clara whirls to face me, a strange look in her eyes. "Wait, what? You've made photos like this of women before?"

Shocked how it's about me now, it's my turn to defend myself, "What? I was young. And it was mostly celebrities who were already naked. I just added myself."

"That's weird."

"I'm being forced to be a virgin, remember? I have a good excuse. But we're talking about Otus here, and he doesn't have one."

"I'm sorry, but I really like Molly," Otus says.

"Then you ask her out," Charlie contends. "You don't make a porno with her as the unknowing star."

Otus again looks down in embarrassment. "I didn't want to ask her out without Arien's permission, and with everything going on between you two, I didn't think it was the right time."

I sigh, restraining my anger. "You have issues, man."

"Yeah, I do. A few millennia of only whorehouses can lead to a lot of problems."

We all recoil in disgust and Charlie pleads, "Ah, fuck, man. We did not need to know that."

Ignoring the STD comment, Clara sits beside Otus and says, "I'm going to help you ask her out. OK?"

Glancing up, Otus smiles and nods in thanks. "OK."

Clara smiles before turning to look at me and ask, "You're going to take us, right?"

I sigh softly, giving in. "Fine, but we need to be careful. The FBI might be there waiting for us."

"OK. We'll need to go shopping first, though."

Otus gives Clara a curious look as I say, "Come on."

We three hold hands, preparing to leave, but first, Clara asks the others, "You guys want to come?"

Charlie and Emma turn to each other, shaking their heads. "No, we're good, thanks." They try to act coy, but we all know they'll be taking advantage of the empty room as soon as we're gone.

"OK. See you guys later." We disappear in a dark flash.

CHAPTER 104: TWILIGHT CHOICE

<u>**Arien**</u>

We appear in a dark flash behind Molly's diner. Clara turns to inspect Otus's new clothes, saying, "OK. Looking good. You remember what I said?"

"Confidence, confidence, confidence," Otus replies. "And women these days like a little aloofness."

I step round the corner of the diner, checking for cops while Otus keeps talking. An FBI squad car goes by but doesn't notice us. I groan, noticing Anna stepping out of the post office on her lunch break. "Jesus. My fucking luck."

Clara's hand on my back makes me jump; I turn as she asks, "Honey?"

"Yeah?"

"Is there anything you want to say to Otus?"

"Right." I glance past her to Otus. "You'll do good. She'll say yes."

"Thank you." Clara smiles and briefly hugs me. "I'll go in with him and watch. You OK staying here?"

"I'll be fine."

"OK." Clara and Otus head into the diner as I look back at the post office. Anna's gone. "Thank god."

I jump again; Anna steps round the corner directly in front of me, exclaiming, "Sam."

"Jesus!"

"Sorry. I didn't mean to startle you."

I shake my head to clear it. "You're fine."

"I can't believe that you're here. . . I didn't believe it when they said you were still alive."

"It's complicated."

"I can only imagine. Did you come back for the funeral?"

"No, I missed it. I only just got here."

Anna reaches out to grab my hand, much to my surprise. "Losing a parent can be hard. I don't know how you're alive or why you're hiding from the FBI, but I know it's what you need to do. I can't imagine what you're going through."

"It's, ah, difficult, but I just found out I was adopted. It's just making all my feelings way more complicated."

"That's crazy," she says, staring in confusion.

"Yeah, I guess it is. I just don't know how I should feel right now."

She pulls me in for a hug, consoling, "I'm here for you if you need me."

"Otus is going for it," Clara shouts from behind me. I turn to see her standing by the back door, her gaze dark. "Oh."

I quickly pull back from Anna, stammering, "Hey, Clara."

"What's going on here?" she asks.

"This is Anna. She's an old friend."

"Girlfriend?" My worry deepens, uncomfortable with the things about to come to light.

Otus

My nerves tremble more than they ever did going into battle, for winning a woman's heart is the fiercest of battles. I take a deep breath and approach Molly, who's cleaning an empty table. She turns to me in surprise and asks, "Otus, is that you? Is Arien here?"

I feel the sweat running down my face and the breath catching in my throat. I fight to reply, "He's nearby, but it's actually me who's here to see you."

"You? Why?"

"I wanted to, ah, well . . ." I pause, trying to build confidence.

"Are you alright?"

"Yeah, I'm fine. I'm here to ask you out."

Her eyes widen slightly.

Arien

Clara has her arms crossed, and she's glaring at Anna and me. "Fucking hell, Arien."

"It's not his fault," Anna intercedes. "I hugged him, but nothing else happened or will happen. I was just trying to comfort him."

"Comfort him?"

"He just lost his Mother."

Clara falters a little but still steps forward to get in Anna's face. "Just so long as you know who he belongs with."

"It's completely clear."

Clara opens her mouth to reply but stops when Otus walks out of the diner, his head bowed. She rushes to him, leaving Anna to finally take a breath. "Otus, are you alright?"

"She said she's not interested," he mutters.

Clara's face darkens, and she cries, "That bitch."

"I just want to leave."

"Alright. We should get back to the others."

"You're leaving already?" Anna asks. "Shouldn't you go see your Father?"

I shake my head and say, "No, that wouldn't be a good idea. We're going to leave town before things get messy. It was good to see you again. I'll see you later."

"OK. I'll see ya." Anna and awkwardly shake hands under Clara's watchful gaze. My friends and I head down an alley to get some privacy as Anna turns to go. Once we're alone, we grab hands and disappear. As we do, I briefly catch a flash of movement from where we'd come.

***

Charlie and Emma are waiting for us when we appear in a dark flash. I pause and raise an eyebrow, noticing the strained look on their faces. "What's going on?"

"Zeus called," Emma answers. "He's waiting for us in New York."

CHAPTER 105: THE KING OF WALL STREET

Arien

Staring up at the towering facades and achievements of Wall Street, I remember the words of a mad man, poignant to all life, "There's no nobility in poverty. I've been a rich man and I've been a poor man. And I choose rich every fucking time." In my life before my first death, I was like Jordan Belfort, a man who'd crawled from nothing into comfort. I always thought I make the same choice as him, rich over poor, but I'd thrown away all I'd worked for and achieved for a simple death, valued above all the riches in the world.

Equally entranced by the street of wealth, Clara whispers, "Wow. Is this Wall Street?"

"Yeah. Impressive, isn't it?"

"I'll say."

"Figures that he came here," Emma mutters. "It's right up his alley."

"You guys have a rough relationship?"

"Not back then. We were pretty similar. Had sex with anyone we wanted to. I only hope he's changed as much as I've tried to in recent centuries."

Charlie reaches out to take Emma's hand, consoling, "You're perfect now."

To distract the others from Emma and Charlie's moment, I point to a nearby building, explaining, "He's on the top floor using the name Leo Fitzsimmons."

They all nod, following me inside and up to Zeus's office, where a secretary greets us, "Good afternoon. How may I help you?"

"We're here to see Mr. Fitzsimmons."

The secretary looks up and down our rag-tag group, disdain curling her upper lip. "I'm sorry, but Mr. Fitzsimmons is very busy. Do you have an appointment?"

"He called us and asked us to come."

The secretary now raises an eyebrow in disbelief. "That's odd because I call clients and associates to schedule appointments."

"We're something special."

"I highly doubt that. How did you get past the front desk and to the private elevator? They usually call me if someone with an appointment arrives."

"Our name was left with the front desk to hurry us up with all haste. Perhaps you should look us up."

Conceding, the secretary sighs and asks, "Very well, and the name is?"

"Phoenix."

Searching her computer for the name, she freezes when she sees it, stammering, "My apologies. The name is indeed in our database, granting you immediate access to Mr. Fitzsimmons. I'll buzz him immediately." She picks up her phone, rotating her seat to speak to Mr. Fitzsimmons in private. When she turns back, she has a forced smile on her face. "Mr. Fitzsimmons is on his way presently."

The inner office door opens and Zeus, limping heavily on a cane, steps out, saying, "A pleasure to meet all of you. Please come in." Expecting us to follow, he turns and walks back into his office. We follow, all awed at the massive and decorative office, filled with bookcases, antiques, and fine alcohol. He motions to a large sitting area, offering, "Please, have a seat." Otus jitters as he sits, drawing Zeus's attention, "Are you alright, child?"

"I just can't believe you're Zeus, the king of gods."

With a boisterous laugh, Zeus lowers himself into a chair, explaining, "The stories about me are a little blown out of proportion. Good and bad. Anyway, I am happy to meet all of you. I've followed your work as best as I can with great respect. Some of which, I've been able to watch on the news itself. I'm very impressed." Emma sighs softly, sarcastically. Zeus notices and rejoins, "My dear aunt, Aphrodite. I'm so happy to see you again."

"Are you?"

"Of course. Why wouldn't I be?"

"A lots changed in the last few millennia."

"Indeed."

"Including a limp. What happened to your leg?"

"Oh, this thing?" Zeus whacks his leg gently with his cane. "It was nothing. Just a little workplace accident 20 or so years ago."

"You're not immortal anymore, but it still takes a lot to maim you."

Zeus shrugs, conceding, "I used to work in the Twin Towers before they fell."

"You were in a tower on 911?" I ask, surprised.

"No, but I came to help dig people out. I was a volunteer firefighter. Apollo called me that day, the first time in a millennium, and told me to call in sick. He saved my life. A chunk of debris fell on my leg during the digging, though. Didn't get a chance to really help get anyone out before it happened, kind of embarrassing actually. Now I'm permanently stuck with this limp." We're all moved and surprised by this story, making Zeus uncomfortable, so he shakes his head to clear the melancholy, continuing, "Anyway. That's not why you're here. You're here to do something important. You're here to defeat Timorian."

Emma's eyes invert black and white again. I seem to be the only one who notices, though I dismiss it again as she cries, "You're a fucking drama queen. Where's your divinity?"

"Very well. It's in Crete guarded by Talos."

Everyone besides Clara and I turn pale. Otus whispers, "Talos?" Zeus nods slightly to their collected horror.

"Who's Talos?" Clara asks.

"He's basically a giant ancient murder bot from Asimov's nightmares."

"But the Argonauts destroyed him," Emma contends.

His eyes downcast, Zeus says, "I had Hephaestus repair him."

"Well, we're screwed," Otus mumbles, throwing his hands in defeat. "Even an army of demigods barely took him down. How are we supposed to?"

"Talos is in a cavern beneath the island that can only be accessed during a lightning storm. If you get past Talos, you'll have to lift my Lightning Bolt, which will kill any mortals and most non-mortals."

"Why did you make it so hard?" Emma hisses.

"Why else? So, no one could steal it. I thought I'd be the one to go and get it, but with my leg, I'd never get past Talos."

Clara checks Crete's weather, exclaiming, "There's a 70% chance of a thunderstorm next week."

"What are we supposed to do till then?" I ask.

Before any of our party has a chance to voice options, Zeus offers, "Well, I have a house upstate where I summer. You're all welcome to stay there for as long as you need to."

"Thank you, it be great to stay somewhere besides sleazy motels."

"What's mine is yours. Let me just write down the address and the security codes." He stands and hobbles to his desk, starting to write. When he finishes, he hands the paper to me and shakes my hand. "If you guys ever need anything, let me know."

"We appreciate this, sir."

The group stands and walks out, leaving Zeus to stare after us.

CHAPTER 106: LIVING

<u>**Arien**</u>

Delirious and sleep-deprived, my eyes bleary, I stumble into the manor kitchen, stopping when I see Otus and Clara sitting together at the table watching a video. I hear a voice say, "Seduce the desk and fuck its brain's out."

Raising an eyebrow at the voice, I ask, "What is that? Porn?"

Clara and Otus laugh to themselves as they continue watching. "Basically."

I hear my voice from the phone say, "There's no hole." My eyes widen, recognizing the sound of the video. "No, turn it off." I rush forward to grab the phone, but Otus pulls back out of reach.

Courtney said, "Just hump under the countertop, or something. You're not doing anything for real, it's just for appearance's sake. Figure something out. Make it a distinctly you performance."

Barely able to speak through her laughter, Clara gushes, "Hold on, babe. This is great."

I sigh and shake my head. "Whatever. Just know, that was the only way to get close to Apollo."

"Doesn't mean you didn't enjoy it."

"Hey, baby. Have you been wicked?" My past words break Clara, drawing an outburst of raucous laughter. She watches me sexily stroke my fingers along the edge and moan softly. "You're so soft." Sliding the very tips of my fingers under the edge of the countertop, I said, "So wet." I took off my shirt before sliding down to my knees. "You're so goddamn beautiful." With a tentative kiss on the lip of the desk, I reached up and traced a single finger over the curves of the edge. I stuck out my tongue and licked the desk's soft lips. "Ah, yeah. You like that, baby. You dirty slut. Take it."

Unable to watch anymore, I walk to pour myself some cereal, mumbling, "You try fucking a desk."

Clara cheers, "Oh, yeah. Take it, baby." Seconds later, she moans, "Oooh, mama." Looking up, I recognize the moment I took off my pants; Clara's ogling my cock.

Finally, the video ends, and they look up at me. "What?" I ask.

They burst out laughing again. Clara caws, "Take that big cock."

"How long it take you to get the splinters out?" Otus asks, drawing a haw from Clara.

"There weren't any splinters," I replied.

"Cause she was sooooo wet," Clara rejoins. They continue laughing uncontrollably.

"Very funny."

Charlie

My large pregnant belly encroaching my movements, I gingerly crouch to weed the flower beds beneath the windows. Laughter echoes through an open window, making me smile, glad despite our hardship, we can still laugh.

Feeling Emma's eyes upon me, I turn to see her grinning at me. I smile back and ask, "What?"

"Nothing. You're just so beautiful."

Blushing, I push a loose lock of hair behind my ear. "Really? Maybe dating the goddess of love and beauty has its perks."

"It does, but only for the goddess of love." She leans in and kisses me.

I smile again but sense something is bothering Emma, so I demand, "Stop."

"What?"

"Is everything alright with you?"

Raising an eyebrow in confusion, she affirms, "Yeah. Why wouldn't it be?"

"It's just, you've been acting strange recently."

With a sigh, she looks away, admitting, "It's just everything with Ares and Calypso. I'm getting too much in my head. I can't think straight, and I don't know what I feel yet."

"You're sure that's everything?"

"Yeah. I'll always tell you if anything's bothering me." She kisses me again, adding, "Now, back to work." Despite her words, she starts softly nibbling my ear.

My cheeks flush, filling with lust. "We'll never get any work done at this rate."

"Who cares, this is the work I love." She kisses me yet again. I sit with my back to the wall, letting Emma mount me to continue the kiss.

I embrace it until I hear a soft meow. "Whoa, whoa, stop. What was that?"

"What?"

"Listen." We both listen intently until we hear the meow again. "There it is again. Help me up." Assisting me up, Emma helps me search for the cat. "Here, kitty, kitty, kitty." Following the meows, we eventually find a black cat caught in a square of a wire fence. "Aw, poor thing." Crouching, I pet its soft fur and am met with a quiet purr.

"Here," Emma says, handing me a set of wire cutters.

"There you go," I mutter, freeing the cat. Once free, I hold him tight, letting his warmth fill me. "Aren't you a handsome boy."

"He have a collar?"

Checking, I reply, "No."

"Then what are you going to name him?"

"We can't keep him."

"Why not?"

"He must have a home," I rejoin, my will not in the words, though.

"If he does, how are you going to find it?"

"I don't know. Besides, our lives are too hectic to worry about a cat."

"With your pregnancy so far along, you won't be able to go on any more missions. You'll need some company while the others are gone."

Realizing she's right, I nod sadly, thinking for a second as I stroke the cat. "What about Pluto?"

Emma raises an eyebrow in surprise, asking, "Won't that get confusing? With Hades and all."

"No, I don't think so. I'm naming him after the planet, so we're good."

She shakes her head in confusion. "OK, if you say so."

"Let's introduce him to the others." With a hand up, I carefully carry Pluto inside.

Arien

I eat in sullen silence, still listening to Otus decry my most embarrassing moments. "He's literally standing in the middle of an orgy, and no one wants to have sex with him."

Clara's smile fades as she looks sadly at me. "Really?"

"Yeah. Most guys there had 2 or 3 girls while he couldn't even get 1."

I clench my jaw, embarrassment overwhelming me. Trying to assuage my pain, Clara consoles, "That's awful."

"It was hilarious." Clara nudges Otus's leg, confusing him. "What?"

She motions at me, saying, "That's enough."

"Oh, right. Sorry."

Charlie and Emma walk in, pausing as they feel the tension. Emma asks, "Is everything alright?"

"Yeah, we're fine."

"Look what I found," Charlie exclaims, hefting a jet-black cat with murder in his eyes. Clara squeals and rushes to pet him, gushing, "Aw, he's so cute."

Otus cowers away from the cat, annoying Charlie. She asks, "What's wrong, Otus?"

"Cats and birds aren't known for being friendly," he replies.

Charlie laughs softly, to everyone's surprise, she hasn't been this happy in a long while. Embracing my dislike of cats for Charlie's sake, I stand to pet him. "Is it a familiar?"

"A what?" Clara asks.

"A witch's animal companion. Said to have magical abilities that help the witch."

Charlie shakes her head, explaining, "No, those aren't really a thing, so far as I know."

"Oh? Huh."

Otus quietly slips out of the room. Clara notices his departure and says her goodbyes before following him.

Clara

Racing after Otus, I find him by a window, leaning against the frame. "Hey, Otus. What's the matter?"

"There's something wrong with me."

"No, there isn't. Why would you say that?"

"There is. I'm social cancer. I tell myself that I'm from another millennium, so it's OK, but so are the gods, and they're doing fine. I just never say the right thing at the right time. I was hurting Arien, and I didn't even notice till you pointed it out. It should have been obvious. Now I get why Molly couldn't stand the sight of me."

Pained by his hurt, I ask, "Is that what this is about? Molly?"

A single tear escapes out of the corner of Otus's eye as he shakes his head. "No, not completely. She's just the drop that made the cup run over."

Raising an eyebrow in confusion, I say, "OK."

"There I go again. Using idioms your grandparents were too young for."

"No, it made sense."

He shakes his head again. "You're too kind to me."

Lost for how to help, I think for a moment, suddenly finding enlightenment. "You know what I think we all need?"

"What?"

"Titties."

He turns to me in surprise. "What?"

"Titties in our faces. We're going to Vegas."

His eyes light up a little as he gushes, "Really?"

"Yeah. It'll be fun. We all need a vacation." Grabbing his hand, I drag him back into the kitchen, where I declare, "I have an announcement. We've been cooped up here for too long. We need to go out and have some fun. We're going to Vegas to see some titties."

Arien grins and stands. "Really?"

"Yezzir."

"You're the best girlfriend ever." He leans in and kisses my forehead, making me go stiff with worry.

"Whoa, careful."

"Right," he mutters, his face constricting slightly.

Breaking the tension, Charlie says, "That sounds like so much fun, but I'll have to stay here." She motions down at her pregnant belly in explanation.

"Oh, right. Sorry," I stammer. "As soon as the baby's born, we'll go again. Celebrate."

"That'd be fun."

Emma wraps her arms around Charlie, squeezing softly. "I'll stay with you, honey."

"No, you should go have fun."

"Vegas pales in comparison to the parties that I used to go to. I'll have more fun here with you."

Charlie smiles, leaning in to kiss Emma. "Alright."

Pluto jumps up on the counter next to Otus, making him scream and stumble back. We all burst out laughing as Otus struggles to recover from his fright.

CHAPTER 107: EAT, DRINK, AND BE MERRY

Arien

From the dark recesses of a coat closet, Clara, Otus, and I file out, having discreetly teleported into a bustling Vegas strip club. Clara grins broadly at the strippers dancing on stage, exclaiming, "Oh, I love strip clubs. . . Ooh, there's a table." She grabs my hand and drags me to the table, Otus close behind. As soon as she sits, she starts dancing with her hips to the rapid beat of the music. I smile at her, a little embarrassed to be enjoying this as much as I am.

A waiter approaches, and Clara orders, "Oh, we'll all have a tequila shot platter, thank you." The waiter nods and leaves just as a stripper struts to our table, stroking Clara before dancing just out of reach. "Oh, yeah." Clara slips some ones into the stripper's panties, buying a single lick of a nipple. The stripper continues around the table, giving Otus the same treatment.

When it's my turn, the stripper dances for a second, stroking my arm. Her eyes go distant as she forgets about me and walks away.

I can feel Clara's stare of pity but refuse to meet her gaze. She mumbles, "Oh, I'm so sorry, babe. Maybe this wasn't such a good idea."

"No, I'm having fun. You get used to it."

The waiter brings over our tequila platter, interrupting our melancholy. Clara shouts, "Ah, ah, shots." We all down multiple shots.

A new stripper saunters to Clara, rubbing her shoulder. Clara coos, "Well, hello, beautiful."

"I've been asked to show you a good time," the stripper replies, provocatively climbing into Clara's lap.

"Oh, really?"

"The woman at table 3 told me to give you whatever you want."

We glance over to see a smiling woman watching us from table 3. Clara nods in thanks before turning back to the stripper. "What's your name?"

"Jade."

"Well, Jade, show me what you got."

Jade smiles, starting to grind into Clara's lap. She leans forward and gently bites Clara's ear, making her eyes flutter. With a flourish, Jade spins, twerking into Clara's face. Whooping, Clara's slaps the perfect ass.

"No touching."

"Sorry."

The dance soon ends with Jade letting Clara motorboat her and suck on a nipple. "I had fun. Thank you."

"Thank you." Clara smiles, watching Jade's ass walk away. She turns back to my grinning face, asking, "What?"

"Are you BI?"

"No, I just like to have fun."

"Noice."

She laughs at me, saying, "Shut up and take a shot."

"As you wish." I comply, joining the others in another shot.

"OK. We're here for you, Otus. So, I'm going to buy you a private show in one of the back rooms."

"You don't have to do that," Otus balks, his eyes flitting.

"No, I want to." She grabs a passing waiter and asks, "How much for a VIP room for 1?"

"15 minutes, $125. 30 minutes, $250," he replies.

"My friend here will have 30 minutes." Clara pays, and Otus is taken away for his dance. "Another shot," she turns and asks.

"Maybe we should slow down."

"No way." She takes another shot, explaining, "I can hold my liquor like no one else."

Not ten minutes later, she's bent over a toilet, vomiting profusely. I hold back her hair, whispering, "There you go. Get it all out."

Lost in a pain-filled, drunken delirium, she mutters, "You're a really great guy, you know."

I look away, not believing but yearning to hear it again. "I don't know about that."

"You're here, aren't you?" Before I can respond, she vomits again. Eventually, it stops; she sighs and leans back against me, trying to fall asleep. I think I may even be falling in love with you."

I raise an eyebrow in surprise but don't say anything. Smiling down at her, I start stroking her hair. When I'm sure she's done throwing up, I stop and sigh, saying, "Come on." I gently pick her up, disappearing in a dark flash, taking her back to the mansion.

***

We appear in her room, and I help her change into her pajamas. While she's undressed, Clara sways and smiles at me, cooing, "You can look if you want."

My eyes lifted above her head, I reply, "That's alright. Thank you, though." I finish getting her changed before tucking her into bed. She snuggles up to her pillow and smiles. Looking around the room, I find a garbage can and place it beside the bed in case she vomits again.

"Goodnight," she mutters as I walk out.

I smile softly. "Goodnight." Shutting off the lights, I leave her.

***

Back in the club, I search for Otus. When I can't find him, I ask a passing waiter, "Hey, have you seen my friend? The short birdy guy with me."

"Yeah, he got tossed out for being too handsy."

I roll my eyes, saying, "Of course, he was. Thanks."

The sun is just peeking over the horizon when I find Otus passed out on the side of the road. "Oh, great." I help him up, leading him to an alley where we disappear in a dark flash.

***

"You smug, son of a bitch. Motherfucking whore." My head throbs, aching from the hangover, the shouts from downstairs not helping my stability. The sound of glass breaking echoes through the house; I struggle to my feet, hurrying downstairs to investigate, Charlie close behind. I find Ares, his arms covering his face to protect against the projectiles Emma's hurling at him while shouting, "How could you think that just cause we're gods again that we'll be together, especially after everything you've done? I've been looking for you for weeks and you just show up wanting to fuck."

Shouting over her, I ask, "Whoa, whoa. OK. What's going on here?"

"I've been looking for this cunt for weeks and he just shows up wanting to fuck."

Charlie walks to Emma, trying to calm her. "OK, let's go upstairs and talk. Arien will take care of him."

"OK," Emma mutters, her eyes lowering. She allows herself to be led away as I turn to Ares.

"Ha, women, huh?" Ares quips.

"What are you doing here?" I ask.

"I just wanted to see Aphrodite. What did she mean, she's been looking for me?"

"She heard some pretty terrible things about you and wanted to know if they were true."

"What she hear?"

"It's better if it came from her, but it's pretty bad."

"Fuck." He turns away, lost in thought. "You know, I wasn't just here to fuck her. I really did just want to see her."

"I know." Sighing, I shake my head and add, "You better wait till she cools down. Don't want her to try and kill you."

"What am I going to do while I wait?"

"I've been watching Friends in my spare time."

We consider Friends for a moment, but both realize how awkward that would be. "We could spar," he suggests.

"Good call."

We're soon in the gym, dressed in workout gear, and set up on a sparring mat. Ares says, "No powers, just wrestling. Do you know how?"

"No, not really."

"That's fine. We won't worry about the rules too much, considering we're both immortal. Just pin me or incapacitate me and you win the round."

"OK." Worry fills me; I've never fought without my powers before, relying heavily on them and brute strength to see me through any fight. Because of my lack of finesse, Ares has me pinned to the floor within a couple of seconds. I tap out and roll free.

"That's OK," he supports. "We're just warming up."

"This is starting to sound more like a training session than sparring."

"Necessity demands it." He pins me again.

I'm pinned over and over again, barely putting up a defense. But once, I manage to sidestep a blow and get a lucky shot in on him. He reacts with anger and kicks me in the chest, sending me flying into a padded pillar.

Darkness overwhelms me, the world lost to my sight.

***

I slowly come to, my eyes blinking hard against the bright sunlight streaming down onto my face. When my sight clears, I roll to my feet, shocked to see the rolling hills of Calvary in Israel. Suddenly realizing the culprit, I turn to the man standing behind me. "Kronos?"

"Nay, it is I, Timorian," he replies. "I'm afraid our previous chats were but shallow reflections of what I desired to communicate with you. It hath taken many a month, but I have finally siphoned enough strength from Kronos to fully communicate with thee. I'm glad to truly meet thee."

"So, you and Kronos are separate, and you're trying to help us?"

"Indeed."

I look away, thinking for a second. "Despite that, I can't trust you. I can never be sure you're not Kronos, and you alone have caused endless suffering and heartache. So much death. You're evil too, just like Kronos."

Timorian looks down in sadness, whispering, "I only asked men to love one another."

"Why? What's the point of a message like that in a world like this? Especially if it's twisted into an ugly shape. How could Kronos think a message like that could defeat the gods?"

"Kronos inspired good people to commit horrific acts throughout the ages. Never the less, it took his shattered body millennia to create me, his masterpiece. It took all his strength to pull the seed of Hades, Tartarus, Typhon, and himself mixed with the waters of Lethe to corrupt the child's mind, my mind, and fertilize Gaia's egg before impregnating the Virgin Mary. From thence came my birth, under the celebrating star of the Titan Astraios. With all that effort put in, Kronos cared little for the goodness of my message as long as it called to men's souls. My mind was mine own for many years thereafter.

"I beheld visions of a God promising greatness of me. Weaving tales of my role as the Son of God. Mine belief was strong there onward. I fulfilled the Messiah prophecies that Kronos had created. Even unto mine death. It was only then that the gods knew of the plot. Zeus sent a mighty storm to stop my death, to no avail. When I rose on the 3rd day, I went to my Father and said, 'thy work is done.' It was only then that his role became manifest unto me. He wast God and the devil playing man's souls like unto a fiddle. To my horror, I realized all the good I had tried to do was for naught. I attempted to stop him, but to no avail. My Father took over my mind to create the most powerful being who had ever lived. I was merely a passenger as I watched mine body do such heinous things that would chill thy soul. It takes all I am to merely speak with thee like this."

My face is full of anger, I shake my head, rejoining, "I don't pity you. The religion you created still did some terrible things. It's killed so many people."

"Christianity and Judaism are good and true at heart, but as a wise friend once said, 'the church is true and good, but the people aren't always.' Once Kronos no longer had a hand in them, they shined out to the world and made it a better place."

I look down in sullen agreement, muttering, "What do you want?"

"I want to lend my hand in aid."

"How?"

"I have found a way to fight Kronos for control of my body and I finally have hope to be free, but I need thine help to do it."

"What do you need from me?"

Timorian's eyes go wide as a loud ringing fills the hilltop.

***

I slowly open my eyes again, this time onto reality. Shaking my head to clear it, I glance up at Ares towering over me, smirking down at me, "Not much without your powers, are you?"

Struggling to my feet, I'm interrupted by Emma and Charlie walking in. Ares slowly approaches Emma, waiting for her to speak. Charlie cautiously strokes Pluto as Emma takes a deep breath, asking, "Did you make me kill Calypso?"

Ares's eyes go wide in shock before settling into defeat. He slowly turns to look at Charlie, noting, "You're a good witch. You found the inactive blood curse, didn't you?"

"Yes," Charlie affirms.

"You, in particular, should be thankful it's inactive."

Charlie raises an eyebrow in confusion, not comprehending the cause for her supposed gratitude. Before she can ask, Emma interrupts, "So, it's true?"

Turning back to Emma, Ares answers, "Yes."

Emma gasps and stumbles back, tears welling in her eyes. Her face sets in anger, and her eyes briefly invert again as she steps forward into Ares's face, screaming, "How the fuck could you do that to me?!"

Unable to meet her gaze, Ares mumbles, "I don't have a good answer."

Emma breathes heavily, attempting to contain her emotions. "You're a monster."

Charlie checks her buzzing phone, explaining, "It's raining in Crete."

Emma nods at Charlie and turns back to Ares. "We have work to do. I want you to leave and never show your miserable face here again."

He nods sadly in acceptance, stammering, "OK. . . I'm sorry." He vanishes.

Trying to shake off her pain, Emma turns to me, asking, "You ready, Arien?"

"Sure, but don't you want some time?"

"No, you need me since Otus is down and who knows how long the storm will keep up." She turns to hug and kiss Charlie, saying, "Goodbye."

Emma grabs my hand, and we disappear in a dark flash.

CHAPTER 108: THE BOLT

Arien

We appear on the island of Crete in the midst of a raging thunderstorm. Emma points up at a large cliff with a giant lightning bolt carved into the side, shouting, "That must be it." She leads the way to the cliff, reaching up to touch the base of the bolt.

"What now?" I ask.

A flash of lightning explodes to life in the sky, the cliff face briefly disappears in the light of the bolt, revealing a cave mouth. "We gotta be fast," she replies.

I roll my shoulders, preparing to jump.

A series of lightning bolts ignite, giving us enough time to jump through into the cave. We stand near the entrance to the cave, waiting for our eyes to adjust. Suddenly, several magical torches ignite, lighting the cavern. There's something unsettling about the lights, like an itch in the back of my mind I just know it's wrong. "What's wrong with the lights?"

"Nothing. It's the shadows, they aren't cast. There's no darkness in here, no Erebus." She runs her fingers over a series of runes carved around the cave mouth, explaining, "These keep everything out when the cave's sealed, including your Father."

"So, if I go in there, I won't have access to my Erebus abilities."

"I'm afraid not."

I shake my head in acceptance. "Let's get this over with then."

We look deeper into the cave until we see Talos. I stop and cock my head in surprise at the mere 8-foot-tall bronze automaton. "I thought he'd be taller."

"People always exaggerate these types of things. Makes for better stories."

I light the phoenix and reach my arm out of the cave in a flash of lightning, connecting to Erebus to conjure the Aegis. I nod at Emma once I'm ready. We tip-toe our way down a ramp from the cave entrance toward Talos. To my surprise, he doesn't move at all as we approach. We stop in front of him, waiting for something to happen. "Maybe he's broken." I take a few tentative steps forward to get around Talos.

Fast as lightning, he lashes out and sends me flying with a kick to the chest. I crash into the cave wall, moaning and struggling to sit up. My voice high-pitched, I observe, "Nope. Not broken."

"Are you alright?" Emma asks.

"Yeah, fine." I pull myself to my feet, hefting the Aegis. Taking a deep breath, I charge at Talos.

I transform the Aegis into a sledgehammer and bash it against him, but it barely fazes him. I drive forward again and again before being beaten back repeatedly. Emma helps where she can, but it's clear that she's not a fighter. Falling to my knees from a gut punch, I'm kicked again.

I roll back to my knees, spitting up blood and saying, "This isn't working. We need a plan."

"Any ideas?"

"One. Just before he hits me, try and distract him." I get to my feet and morph the Aegis back into a shield, whispering, "Ah, fuck." Ducking behind the Aegis, I scream and charge.

Talos turns and prepares to push me back.

At the moment before I crash into him, Emma slashes at Talos's arm with her sword. He turns slightly, distracted as I slam into him. The force of the blow doesn't even rock him, but I drop the Aegis and roll around to stand behind him. Jumping up on him piggy-back style, I grab his head for dear life as he starts bucking violently. I concentrate, my hands burning with phoenix fire, melting his head.

Talos falls to his knees, his head melting away completely.

Once he's still, I step back, smiling in victory.

Emma cries, "Good job."

My leg explodes in pain, the bone shattered. I crumple, smashing my head against a rock. Fighting a concussion, I stare up at the headless Talos towering over me. I blink violently to clear my vision as he hefts a boulder to crush me with. Unable to defend or escape, I raise my arms in pointless instinct.

The boulder crashes down, shattering my body; I can't even cry out I'm so broken. I'm struck again and again, my nerves dead, the only thing saving my consciousness.

Talos stops his assault; my eyes flutter just enough to see something gleaming protruding from his chest. Talos turns to face the now unarmed Emma behind him, her sword trapped in Talos's bowels.

A voice not my own echoes in my head, reminding me of the myth of Talos and of Achilles. With my final bit of strength, I lunge forward, grabbing hold of Talos's ankle, my bright burning hands melting the foot.

Talos screeches with an inhuman scream, slowly sinking to the ground and melting completely until there is nothing left.

I stumble to my feet and stare down at the pool of liquid metal before me. Emma's eyes flit between me and the pool in slight amazement. Smirking through my deformed face, I ask, "What? I remembered that's where his weak spot was, the heel. Pays to read sometimes."

She shakes her head, hurrying to support me as I stumble. "You alright?"

"I'll be fine. He was a tough bastard."

We both freeze, the sound of grinding stone echoing through the cavern. Turning, we see a massive door opening at the back of the chamber, revealing Zeus's crackling Lightning Bolt on a pedestal. "There it is," she whispers.

Hobbling with me to the pedestal, she turns to me expectantly. Realizing her intent, I contend, "I'm in no condition to lift it. You do the honors."

She nods, helping me prop myself against a wall. She turns back to the Bolt and takes a deep breath as she reaches out to grab it.

BOOM!

An explosion of light fills the cavern, nearly blinding me. When the light fades, I stare in awe at Emma, lightning flowing through her veins. Tentatively, I ask, "Are you alright?" She turns a power-hungry gaze on me, her eyes inverted black-and-white, but she doesn't respond. "Emma?"

"I never knew Zeus had this much power at his fingertips. I could do so much with this power. I could defeat Timorian myself and bring peace to this world."

"It's not for you."

Her face fills with anger as flakes of burning skin float off her body. "Why not? Cause I'm a woman?"

"No. Because it's changing you."

Emma smiles with an evil light. "What's life without a little risk for what you desire?"

"What about Charlie? She needs you."

This makes her falter for a moment. "Charlie?"

"Yes, think about Charlie."

Her face sets in determination. "I'm going to bring an end to this war for her."

"No!"

Emma explodes in a blast of lightning, sending me flying yet again. When the light fades, I struggle to sit up, stopping when I see that Emma is gone.

CHAPTER 109: FIRST TO LOVE THE SAME

Ruins of a bygone age quiver against the torrent of heavenly wrath, windswept rain and thundering lightning tearing at its core, demanding satisfaction. This heap of rubble is all that remains of the once-great Titan capital Mt Othrys, lost in eons past. Eris, goddess of strife, stands atop the ruins, staring across the plains of Greece far below.

She smiles softly as a hooded figure appears behind her. "Do you ever miss when this ruin was the jewel of Earth? A shining city on a hill. When blood ran freely over these battlements. When gods and Titans clashed in a bitter struggle for dominion of Earth. I do, and I think you do too. Because love and hate are so deeply intertwined." When the figure doesn't respond, Eris continues, "Well, mourn not, for that time has come again. All the Earth will burn before the day is done, and there will be no peace no matter who rises from the ashes. And the pain--oh, the pain. . . I get off on it, you know. Listening to the screams of the innocent makes me burn with passion. But my supply of pain has become stagnant in recent millennia. My steady stream of agony since humanity could comprehend its own existence has gotten stale. I need more."

Eris finally turns to look at the figure, explaining, "Which is why I'm glad you're here, and with all your power back--Ooh, maybe a little more." The figure looks up to reveal her face from within the shadows of her hood. It's Emma.

Eris walks to Emma, circling her and stroking her shoulder, saying, "I see you're back in your goth phase. Not what the kids call goth these days, but true demonic darkness. The last time you were like this was when we first met, yes? After you lost your lady love. Calypso, wasn't it?"

Emma uses all her will to not speak or react to Eris's words. Eris stops circling Emma to stand in front of her. "You come to me in your darkest hour. You really know how to pull on my heartstrings."

With a grimace, Emma pushes down on Eris's head, forcing her to kneel. Smiling, Eris ducks beneath Emma's cloak, greedily satisfying her sexual desire.

Emma grunts, staring out into the distance. The sound of waves crashing on a beach echoes through her head, building louder and louder.

**

The waves become real, framing a memory of death. Emma stood on the beach next to Hermes and the bound Calypso. She waved at Hermes to untie Calypso, saying, "Those are no longer needed." He nodded and untied the golden ropes binding Calypso's arms. "My thanks, Hermes. Thine help is no longer necessary." Hermes nodded again and vanished.

Calypso rubbed her sore wrists, starring around at her new home with an empty expression. Emma smiled awkwardly before looking around the island too, consoling, "Tis but a humble abode. None the less, I attempted to make it as congenial as possible." Calypso continued to stare without any emotions. So, Emma grunted and sighed, embarrassed, adding, "This land twas the abode of Ananke, where she came to rest. Therefore, she engendered it separate from the rest of creation to ensure repose from time itself. As such, none can find this place save for those chosen by mine curse. A lone derelict man that thou must restore shall wash ashore once a millennium to fall madly in love with thee. The Olympians believe this will torture thee, but I hast made a change. Thou whilst not be cursed to fall for them and suffer when they depart from thee." Calypso finally turned to look at Emma in surprise. Emma continued, "I wish not to be cruel." Calypso still didn't say anything. Clearly uncomfortable, Emma motioned at a cave mouth, saying, "Perhaps thou desirest to inspect thy new home."

With only the slightest of nods, Calypso responded. Taking it as progress, Emma smiled and led her into the cave. Calypso stared around at her abode, finally breaking down and crying violently. Emma rushed forward to hug Calypso tightly. "Tis alright. It will not be unbearable here."

Through her tears, Calypso muttered, "But it will not have mine Father."

Emma looked down, ashamed. "Even so, thou mayest find happiness."

Calypso sniffed and wiped her eyes before looking up into Emma's. "Why doth thou care for one such as I?"

Emma's eyes fluttered softly, unsettled by her own feelings. "When I came to thee in prison for thy essence, I felt a strange stirring in mine heart. I came back to thee again and again for no purpose other than to understand mine stirring. Therefore, I feel I knoweth thee well, which only heightened mine confusion. I understandeth not what mine feelings mean; I just knoweth I relish mine time with thee."

"What art thou saying?"

In a moment of passion, Emma leaned in and kissed Calypso. Calypso pulled back in shock and stared up at Emma in confusion. Emma grimaced and turned away in shame, saying, "Mine apologies. Tis improper of me."

With a slight smile, Calypso understood. She slowly leaned in to kiss Emma back. Tears flowed freely from both as they kissed again and again, the passion building. Slowly and cautiously, they started undressing each other until they're naked. Emma pulled back to look up and down Calypso's nude form, whispering, "Thou art beautiful."

Calypso blushed in thanks. "How canst we do this?"

Her brow furrowed in thought, Emma said, "Perhaps we approach this as if twere an intimate moment with a man."

Calypso tensed slightly in embarrassment, confessing, "I haveth no more experience with a man than I do with one such as thee."

"Lie thy head upon thy pillow," Emma said with a nod. "I shall showeth thee how."

Lying down, Calypso allowed Emma's nude form to crawl on top of her and gently thrust their hips together. They both moaned in anticipation, but it was soon clear neither were enjoying this. Emma sat up and rotated Calypso so they could try pressing their moist pussies together, again to limited success. "I imagined not the difficulty of this," Emma said with an awkward giggle. Calypso's face constricted in shame before rolling away to cry into the pillow. Emma tried to comfort her by stroking her back and whispering, "Mine apologies. I knoweth how hard twere for thee to try this."

Calypso rolled back to look up at Emma. "I feel great love for thee as well. I wanteth this to be."

Emma started to gently knead one of Calypso's breasts, asking, "May I try but one thing more?" After a nod of permission, Emma smiled and crawled down Calypso's body, gently biting her thigh before kissing her groin.

Calypso suddenly moaned and arched her back, grabbing Emma's hair. Her passion built until she screamed.

***

Emma screams, a blast of light exploding from her groin, sending Eris flying. Eris rolls to a stop and sits, wiping blood from her mouth. "Neat trick. Getting kinky, are we? I'm down." Rushing forward, Emma grabbed Eris by the throat, lifting her into the air. Choking, Eris manages to mutter, "This is pretty sexy."

"Where's Atlas?" Emma asks.

"Why would I know?"

"Anywhere there's pain, you'll be there, and Atlas has caused his fair share recently." Emma tightens her grip around Eris's throat, electricity surging through her body, violently shocking Eris.

"Alright, enough." Emma drops Eris to the ground, where she rubs her bruised throat.

Emma crouches in front of Eris, smiling as she raises an electrified finger up to her face, hissing, "Where is he?"

"His headquarters is a mental hospital in Charlotte, North Carolina. More of an insane asylum, really. He tortures so many people there. The pain is always . . . exquisite." Without another word, Emma stands and turns to walk away. Eris coughs violently, struggling to her feet and shouting, "Do you know why you came to me?"

Emma stops but doesn't turn back. "Why?"

"It wasn't to find Atlas. If fact, you didn't come here. I've been inside of you since the moment you found out what Ares had done to you." Emma turns to stare at Eris in shock. Eris continues, "What most people fail to understand is, I don't cause pain. I've always only fed off of what is already there. More like a parasite than anything. I latched onto you and fed off your desire for revenge. But when you touched the Bolt, I changed just like you did. I fed off its power. I can now cause pain through you. I created this vision just to tell you where Atlas is. You want revenge on him. I deliver."

***

Emma opens her now permanently inverted eyes while standing in the middle of a lightning storm. She stares up into the rain for a moment before vanishing.

CHAPTER 110: GUILTLESS MURDER

Arien

Fighting for every inch, for every moment of consciousness, I crawl toward the cave mouth. When lightning flashes, it opens the cave, and the light dances around the shadowless room. Suddenly, the lightning stops; I look up at the sealed cave mouth in horror, comprehending my doom. The storm is over, trapping me. I close my eyes and try to teleport, but there's no connection to Erebus in the cave.

There is no way out.

Clara

Walking into the kitchen, I run my fingers through my disheveled hair, muttering, "Arien?"

Charlie looks up from the table where she's petting Pluto. She says, "He's gone. Him and Emma went to get Zeus's divinity."

"Oh, OK." I pour myself a cup of coffee, moaning as I sip it.

"I'm starting to get worried. They've been gone too long."

"You try tracking them with your amulet things?"

"I tried that, but I can't get a signal. He must be shielded by something."

Otus stumbles into the room, clearly hungover, crying, "Hmm, coffee."

Charlie and I watch Otus greedily down a cup. I shake my head, turning back to Charlie to ask, "What can we do?"

"Well, we can't teleport ourselves, and we can't pray to a god who can."

"Maybe we should give it a few more hours before we start worrying too much." Charlie hesitates for a moment before nodding.

"Sounds good," Otus affirms. "I'm going to be waiting in the hot tub if you need me." He stumbles to the back door while Charlie and I trade worried glances.

Atlas

Pain shoots through me, emanating from the sword wound in my chest. I grunt quietly, reacting to Iapetus putting the finishing touches on my bandages. He smiles at my discomfort, gloating, "Painful, is it?"

I growl, "I hope I get to be the one to kill you someday."

"And sin against your Father? I don't think so."

"Shut the fuck up."

The power in the building shuts off, plunging us into darkness. We sit still, waiting for a change.

SCREECH!

The sound of distant inhuman screams echo through the asylum. We leap to our feet and rush into the hallway, where we stop, listening to the screaming fade. At the end of the hall, crackling blue light flashes from within the Latai's cell.

The screaming fades completely.

The light gets brighter as Aphrodite steps out of the Latai's cell, covered in blood, with Mnemosyne's severed head in hand. Iapetus conjures a spear, steps forward, and commands, "I'll hold her off. Get the Scythe."

For once obeying, I flee as Iapetus continues to approach Aphrodite. She drops Mnemosyne's head, conjuring the Bolt of Zeus from within her body.

The sound of combat follows me while I search frantically for the Scythe. When I find it, I return to the battle just in time to see Aphrodite impale my Father through the heart. Stopping in my tracks, I watch on with a feeling akin to happiness.

Iapetus gasps, collapsing to the ground.

Smiling, I say to Aphrodite, "Despite all that you've taken from me, you may have just given me something special."

She pulls the Bolt from Iapetus's chest, letting the lightning fade into her. She hisses, "He was but an obstacle to get to you."

"None the less, before we fight, I thank you."

Aphrodite looks down at Iapetus's body, seeing his chest rising and falling. "He's not dead yet."

"Give it time."

"I'm here for you."

"Then do what you came for."

With a deep breath, the electricity surges through her again. She screams, sending a bolt flying down the hall at me. I raise the Scythe to absorb the bolt, swinging to send the bolt back at Aphrodite. She's briefly pushed back by the returning bolt, drawing only a snarl from her.

We both charge, weapons raised with bloodlust in our eyes.

The Scythe and I hold our own against Aphrodite and the Bolt as we destroy the asylum around us. We both manage to land several small blows on each other, but neither can get the upper hand until I hook the Scythe behind her ankle and yank her feet out from under her.

She slams into the ground while I raise the Scythe for a killing blow. Roaring, she sends a bolt up through her arm into my chest, sending me up through the ceiling onto the roof.

Smoke billows off me in waves, the smell of burnt hair filling my nostrils. I roll over just in time to see Aphrodite jump through the hole, electricity burning through her.

I shake my head and pull myself to my feet.

Aphrodite smiles, raising her arms to the heavens. Storm clouds gather, bringing lightning, thunder, and rain.

I look up into the rain, letting it run over my burns, soothing them. She screams, sending a massive lightning bolt down on me. I raise the Scythe high above my head in futile defense.

CRACK!

A blinding explosion engulfs the roof.

When the light fades, I fall to the ground, covered with burns. The Scythe falls away, discarded and crackling with lightning. I moan, starting to drag myself across the roof toward the Scythe. Aphrodite steps on the Scythe, staring down at my beaten form.

Looking up into her eyes, I freeze, recognizing their inverted look. "Eris?" Aphrodite's face darkens before she kicks me, sending me flying. She picks up the Scythe and raises it for the killing blow. "Stop," I cry. "I know what happened to Nyx." She falters in shock, so I continue, "She's your Mother, right?"

Aphrodite kneels on my injured chest, placing the blade of the Scythe against my throat, asking, "Where is she?"

"Before the last war started, Ares was ordered to imprison her."

"You're lying. How could you know that?"

"When we killed the Fates, they told me."

"How'd you kill the Fates?" She asks, her eyes wide in shock, momentarily forgetting her Mother.

"Chaos is beyond the Fates' control, and that Scythe is filled with her blood. It shields the bearer from their power."

Aphrodite leans back, staring at the Scythe. "Why would the gods imprison her?"

"That's a question for a god."

Taking advantage of her distraction, I stab her in the ankle with a hidden dagger. She screams and falls back, dropping the Scythe before I push her. She rolls back, tumbling off the edge of the roof.

I struggle to my feet and rush to the edge to look after her, but she's gone, teleported away. Breathing heavily in recovery, I turn and stare down at the Scythe, discarded on the ground. An idea comes to me; an idea not fit to think, to base and low for any monster, but sweet-sounding to my soul.

I jump back down through the hole in the ceiling, Scythe in hand. Walking to my Father, I kneel next to him, listening to his strained breath. He moans, "My son, help me."

"Why? What have you ever done for me?"

"I gave you life. Now's the time to give me back mine."

Clenching my fist, I turn to stare at the wall, whispering, "That's not a debt a child owes their Father. It's a gift. That's what made me at least a little of a better Father than you."

He coughs up ichor as he laughs at me. "Is this still about Calypso? When will you get over that little whelp?"

I tense even more, turning back to look my Father in the eyes. "I've struggled with being a good person like she would have wanted, while still getting my revenge. But what's the point? She's gone, and even if I get her back when Utopia rises, she'll never be alright with how I made it possible. So why should I care? I'm just going to take what little happiness there is in revenge and leave it at that." I swiftly raise the Scythe and stab my Dad in the chest.

He grunts, fading into death.

His body turns black as night, stars twinkling deep within. The blackness shatters, transforming into star-filled smoke, drifting up through the hole in the ceiling into the sky, returning to Chaos, the first Titan to ever be killed.

I smile, relishing in patricide.

CHAPTER 111: MISCONSTRUED

Emma raced through the forest of Ogygia, running from the things she'd done. She collapsed on the bank of a stream, sobbing violently. Lifting her hands, she stared at the blood of Calypso coating them. Her sobs increased as she struggled to wash them clean in the stream. Her tears overwhelmed her, racking her too much to focus on being clean. When her eyes finally opened through the tears, she flinched when she saw Eris's face reflected back to her from the water.

***

In the present, Emma stares down at a puddle into Eris's reflection, her injured ankle bleeding unnoticed. Emma's eyes are no longer inverted, but they're filled with madness. Eris cries, "We must have our revenge."

The lines between the two blur, their vengeance and anger merging, focusing on the smell and taste of blood, fueling every hateful desire. The rapid pumping of the bloodlust in her veins excites Emma; she reaches down her pants and deep into her folds, relishing in lust and hate. She shouts, "Ares will pay for what he's done to us."

"Then, we will finish what we started with Atlas."

"He will pay for his deceit."

"My Mother shall be freed, that is what I ask for my help."

"All but Nyx shall burn in our wake. None shall escape. Our revenge will sweep the Earth and purge it of all who have done us wrong."

Arien

Every breath I take feels heavy and empty, the oxygen thinning. I'm lying on the ground, struggling to breathe and trying to conserve the little air left.

A child's sobs clear my fading consciousness, pulling my focus from the sweet embrace of nothingness. I force myself to stand and stumble toward the sound, finding a little boy sitting in the cave corner, sobbing into his arms. "Hey, hey, it's OK." Sitting beside the boy, I extend a comforting hand. He looks up, making me gasp. The boy is me; my child face stares up at me, his eyes imploring for help, his lip quivering in fear.

He whispers, "I'm scared."

Regaining control, I ask, "Of what?"

"Of dying."

I turn to lean against the wall next to my younger self. "Me too."

"Really? You?"

"Yeah, me to," I answer with a slight smile.

"Can't we just regenerate?"

"Maybe once or twice, but then the air will run out. Without air, there's no fire for regeneration."

"Why did this happen to us?"

Sighing, I answer with the grim truth that he has ahead of him. "It's what we wanted."

"I never wanted this."

"No? Well, the days are coming that you will. When the blood flows and the pain becomes immeasurable, you'll pray for death, despite yourself. That's your future." My own nihilism deepens the depression already chilling my heart. A single tear runs down my cheek.

"I'm scared of my future."

"Don't be. There are good days too. The days you'll share with Molly, Charlie, Clara, and even Otus. They'll make your life a little more livable."

"I'll have friends?"

"More than that. . . You'll have the family you never had." My face constricts, struggling with my emotions. "And I don't want to leave them. Not like this." My eyes widen, an idea coming to me. Standing, I hobble to the golden puddle that had once been Talos.

I take a deep breath and hold it to limit my air intake as I ignite the phoenix with the feeble flame of my lighter. Reaching down to the pool of molten life, I dip in my hand, setting it alight with a new type of burning life, phoenix fire. The beautiful work of Talos's craftsmanship will not be in vain; he's given his life that I may live.

Like the Nile of ancient days, I trace the gold into a molten river of life, each drop baring my future, flowing it toward the cave mouth. Still holding my breath, the phoenix giving me strength, I run the liquid gold up around the mouth, filling in the runes that surround it. The letters blaze to life from the flaming gold that fills them.

Unable to hold my breath any longer, I breathe deep but hardly get any air. My vision hazes; I collapse against the cave wall.

My last vestige of consciousness, of life, fights to remain, each second of warfare a contradiction of my life's goal.

My boy-self kneels in front of me and smiles, saying, "I'll help you." He lifts my limp hand to touch the glowing runes one last time. The runes start to melt as the temperature rises.

The molten gold sloughs off the stone, wiping it bare of runes.

The cave mouth doesn't open, but shadows fill the room, and darkness returns. With a smile, I disappear in a dark flash.

***

Breathing deep, I let the soft touch of fresh air fill me, rejuvenating my mind and flesh. As my mind clears, the cold touch of familiar concrete drowns out my other senses. Realizing where I am, I scream, opening my eyes and huddling against a wall. The cold ground, the piles of musty boxes, and the rock-hard cot; this was my childhood room.

Soon recovering from the shock, I stand, a pained smile crackling my shaking demeanor at the sight of my Bible still tucked away beneath my cot. There's no anger at the sight; nostalgia can warp even the darkest of memories.

Turning away, I go to the water heater in the corner, pulling off the front plate to check if my secret stash was still there. To my surprise, my searching fingers touch the hot steel of the box containing all my secret memories and wants. Gingerly pulling it out, I open it, smiling at the photograph of me and Molly as children resting on the top. Tears bittersweet well, fighting to break loose and moisten the damning evidence that I ever felt love.

Moving farther down into my subconscious made tangible, I find a child's drawing of Brittnie, the beautiful woman that haunted my dreams since birth, the Mother I never had a chance to love.

Beneath the drawing is an owl feather and a dilapidated army man. I smile slightly at each item before a noise in the hall makes me stand.

Ephraim opens the closet door and stares at me, stammering, "You? . . . You shouldn't have come back here." He smiles, stepping aside for several FBI agents to rush into the room and tackle me. I'm unable to struggle or fight back, my injuries too severe. Within a moment, they have me pinned to the ground.

The agent in charge struts into the room, a look of joyous success plays in his eyes as he says, "I can't believe you came back here. The Nuclear Spectre made a mistake. Thanks for the promotion."

"Don't call him that," Ephraim whispers. "He's nothing but a devil's mistake."

The agent glares at Ephraim, hate already burning in the look. He turns back to me, kneeling to add, "Arien Vlahos, you're under arrest for trespassing on government property, tampering with government property, desertion, and the murder of Dinah Mathus." Ephraim gloats down at me as I'm cuffed. The agent continues, "OSI will try and take this from me, but the Bureau will take good care of you."

Seeing the unadulterated glee in Ephraim's eyes, I give up on my walk down memory lane. In a dark flash, I vanish, leaving the agents behind in confusion.

***

Appearing on a Kansas hilltop, I light the phoenix to melt the handcuffs, rubbing my wrist to restore circulation.

"Arien."

I whirl to stare at Apollo standing behind me. "Apollo, what are you doing here?"

"I saw what happened in a vision. We have to stop Emma. She's putting the future at risk. There's a bigger war coming that can only be won by delicate manipulation of the future."

"Do you know where she is?"

"My last glimpse of her was at an asylum in North Carolina."

I clench my jaw, preparing for the fight ahead.

Charlie

I yelp, scaring Clara from her worried stupor. "I've got a signal," I explain, motioning to the glowing amulet in my hand.

"Really?" she asks. "Where is he?"

Holding the amulet tight in my hand, I mumble the spell under my breath. I drop it down on a map spread across the table and watch as it slides around looking for Arien. "There's a slight delay on the tracking. With his teleportation, we've got to be fast to make sure he hasn't left before we get there." The amulet stops. "He's in Kansas."

"Kansas? What's in Kansas?"

"I don't know." Thinking for a moment, I remember something. "When he was in his coma, he said he had of vision of a Kansas town. Maybe his subconscious associates it with safety."

"If so, what is he running from?"

"Why don't you call him now that he's back from Crete?" Otus mutters from his huddle position on the couch.

Nodding in agreement, his logic striking through her stress, Clara takes out her phone to call. There's no answer.

"I'm going to go through my spellbooks for any teleportation spells," I say, standing to waddle to my bag.

Arien

If a place can be evil, this place is. The jagged architecture and bland walls attack the eyes, tearing at the will, demanding submission. I cautiously walk the halls of the insane asylum, looking for Emma. My phone buzzes violently; I check it to see a missed call from Clara. Unable to face her yet, I put the phone away and continue on.

I pause briefly, staring down at a large bloodstain marking a death.

A moan makes me turn. A woman's discarded severed head twitches slightly, its flesh mending back with its starved and beaten nude body. It begs, "Please, help me." Deciding to trust this helpless curiosity, I crouch and pull a pebble from her throat, allowing the rejoining to continue. Soon, she sits up, rolling her neck to test it, saying, "Thank you. Who are you?"

"I'm Arien."

"I'm Mnemosyne, the Titan of memory."

I hesitate at helping a Titan, but her wretched appearance is proof enough of her opposition of Atlas. "What happened here?" I ask.

"A goddess carrying the Bolt of Zeus massacred us. Luckily, the Bolt can't permanently kill immortals."

Looking past her into a cell, the scattered corpses of dismembered women catch my attention. "What about them?"

"Unfortunately, they are beyond our help."

"What are they?"

"Prayer spirits. Atlas was using me to read the prayers they heard."

Hope bites at me, realizing the implications. "Are you saying that the Titans can't track our prayers anymore?"

Mnemosyne stares at the corpses with sadness, affirming, "Yes, but at a terrible cost."

I mourn their loss as well but thank the universe that we're free again. Turning back to Mnemosyne, I ask, "Did you hear where the goddess was going?"

"Atlas said something about Ares before she left. I think she's after him now."

"Shit. She'll kill him, or try at least. What about Atlas? Do you know anything about his plans?"

"No, sorry. I didn't hear anything."

I nod slowly, processing this information. "How are you feeling?"

"Better, thank you."

"What are you going to do now? Where will you go?"

"I don't know. I haven't been free for so long. I guess I'll go home to Trophonios and try to restore the oracle. It may even help you in your fight and your search for the goddess."

"Thank you, that would be great."

"Come with me." She extends an arm to me; we both vanish.

***

We appear near the cave mouth entrance to the Oracle of Trophonios. Mnemosyne glares around at the ruins in horror; tourist stairs and walkways weave their way throughout the cave, disturbing the reclusive nature and solemnity of the oracle. "What have they done to you?" She stumbles into the cave in a stupor.

A strange whisper draws me forward toward the inviting stone walls of the cave. The soft rustle of a paintbrush soothes my whirring nerves, exciting a passion long dormant. Reaching out, I stroke the stone.

With a gasp, my eyes glaze over, my mind ripped from me and blasted into the past.

I'm suddenly Victor Van Gogh, raising a knife to my ear and slicing it off. A scream is torn from me, rocketing me back to the present, back to my body.

I stumble back, dazed by the vision's effects still lingering.

"Where are the basins, the monsters? It's all gone?" Mnemosyne's mutter words draw me from my reverie, grounding me in the present. I shake my head, walking to Mnemosyne, who says, "It'll take me a long time to restore this place. I'm afraid I can't help you today."

"It's fine. You've helped more than you know." We nod in farewell, and I retreat into the nearby trees. Once alone, I kneel to pray to Ares:

"Magnanimous, unconquered, boistrous Ares, in darts rejoicing, and in bloody wars fierce and
untam'd, whose mighty pow'r can make the strongest walls from their foundations shake:
Mortal destroying king, defil'd with gore, pleas'd with war's dreadful and tumultuous roar:
Thee, human blood, and swords, and spears delight, and the dire ruin of mad savage fight.
Stay, furious contests, and avenging strife, whose works with woe, embitter human life;
To lovely Aphrodite, and to Dionysus yield, to Demeter give the weapons of the field;
Encourage peace, to gentle works inclin'd, and give abundance, with benignant mind."

I open my eyes and wait for a response, but there is none.

<u>Clara</u>

Charlie looks up from her spellbook in excitement, exclaiming, "I found something."

"Really?" I ask.

"It's from a Norse legend. Ullr had a bone with runes carved in the side that allowed him to travel anywhere. This book has a diagram of the runes, a recipe for the ink, and instructions on how to recreate the bone. Giant's semen, human femur--I have everything we need except . . ."

"What?"

Charlie's eyes lower, the last ingredient defeating her. "This isn't going to work?"

"Why not?"

"The ink needs to be burned into the bone with divine light. We don't have a god."

We sit in silence, thinking. Otus suddenly sits forward with an idea, asking, "Do you think it's literal divine light or more like a god's DNA?"

"I don't know," Charlie answers. "I think DNA might do it."

My eyes widen, realizing what Otus is getting at. "Arien has god's DNA in him."

With a devilish smile, Charlie agrees, "If we could find a hair of his or something, this might work."

"I'll check his room," I cry, leaping to my feet.

<u>Arien</u>

I'm knelt in prayer again:

"... *with forms of ev'ry kind. Hear me, blest pow'r, and in these rites*
rejoice, and save thy mystics with a suppliant voice."

Apollo appears in front of me, exclaiming, "Arien, it's too dangerous to pray right now. What's going on?"

I stand to answer, "The prayer spirits are dead. They can't track us anymore?"

"How'd that happen?"

"Emma, she killed them."

"I see."

"Now she's going after Ares."

"Ares? Why?" he asks with raised brow.

"He forced her to do something a long time ago and she wants revenge for it. Do you have any idea where he is?"

"He's gathering the Macrobi tribe in India. I know where a few of their hideouts are, but I don't know which one he's at. You'll have to check them all."

CHAPTER 112: SECURING FATE

Ares

The god of war should not be the herald of peace, but times have changed; I've changed. Despite my nature, I reach out to accept the Macrobi Chief's hand, sealing my alliance to this secluded, long-living ancient tribe, adverse to modern advancement. The familiar and comforting syllables of ancient Greek roll of my tongue as I say, "Thank you for everything. I'll be waiting for you at Mount Olympus."

A scream on the outskirts of town draws our attention.

We turn to see Aphrodite, baring the Bolt of Zeus, slaughtering the innocent of the Macrobi, with no regard for any within her wrath. Burning the village around her, she cries, "Ares! Face me or let all these people die!"

Horrified by her grim visage, but my warrior nerve and instinct taking over, I turn to the chief and command, "Get everyone out of here." He nods, running off to help his people as I approach Aphrodite, shouting, "I'm here, Aphrodite. Leave these people be." She halts her rampage to stare at me. "What do you want from me?" I ask.

"We shall have the blood we're owed."

"We?"

BOOM!

She fires a massive bolt at me, which I barely sidestep. I conjure my shield and sword just in time to block another bolt.

Roaring a battle cry, I charge.

We weave and flow against each other in an almost beautiful dance, each struggling for the upper hand. Stray bolts continue to level buildings around us, nearly striking the escaping townsmen.

I land a solid spartan kick and send Aphrodite flying through the perimeter wall. She leaps back over, angrier than ever. Barely managing to hold my own, I fight with all my strength just until the locals get away.

Aphrodite and I lock weapons, staring into each other's eyes. I shout, "Why are you hurting these people? They did nothing to you."

"Everyone has wronged us."

I shudder, finally noticing Aphrodite's inverted eyes. "Eris? Is that you? How are you doing this?"

Aphrodite roars, firing a massive bolt into my chest, sending me flying. When I roll to a stop, I look around to ensure that everyone has gotten safely away. I smile slightly, looking back up at the looming Aphrodite.

I feign to block a blow, allowing myself to be disarmed. She smashes my face in before standing back to gloat, breathing heavily. Coughing and spitting up ichor, I whisper, "You're quite impressive."

"The power of 3 gods overcomes all."

"Indeed." Struggling to my knees, I glare up at Aphrodite, defiance in my eyes. "Do it then, Eris. You were once my sister, my best friend, now you're the one who destroys me."

"We don't need your friendship anymore. Not with the power we hold." She grabs me by the hair and presses the Bolt against my throat. "Where's my Mother?"

"Nyx?" I ask, shocked, broken from my preparation of death.

"What did you do to her?"

"As Athena commanded. I imprisoned her because she's needed to fix the fabric of reality itself in the future. If she wasn't contained, the Titans would kill her, leaving our future uncertain. She's happy and comfortable. She agreed to everything."

"Where? Where is she?"

"I can't tell you that." With a growl, Aphrodite presses the Bolt harder into my neck. Still defiant, I affirm, "I'd rather die. Do it. Use that to shred me down so far that I can never reconstitute. That's the only move you have left."

She smiles maliciously. "That's cute, but I know your weaknesses. I was your sister once, remember. Have you spoken to Enyalius recently?"

My warrior spirit finally breaks; I stare up at Aphrodite, horrified by her threat. "You wouldn't hurt my son."

"I already did, and I want to show you. We fought in the Great War. He favored the Russians and I the Germans. So, I destroyed him." She presses the palm of her hand against my head. Darkness creeps down her arm into me, inverting my eyes. I scream and thrash violently, fighting to not see my son's death.

He died with honor protecting the innocent, but he's still gone, left mutilated in the snow. I fall back, released from the vision, breathing heavily. I stare into the dirt, filled with grief, muttering, "She's in a cave under the Sentinel Plain volcanic field in Arizona. The brightest place on Earth to imprison the goddess of night."

Aphrodite smiles softly. "Thank you."

She raises the Bolt for the killing blow, but Arien appears in a dark flash behind her, crying, "Emma, stop this."

Aphrodite hesitates, turning toward Arien to say, "Arien. How did you get out of that cave? Hmm, matters not. Are you here to kill me?"

"No."

"Then what? Fight?"

"If I have to."

"We don't want to fight you. Though Ares was our brother in arms, you are my true brother. I don't want to throw that away. Father would never approve."

Arien stares at Emma in shock, stammering, "Who are you?"

"Eris, the goddess of strife, daughter of Erebus and Nyx. How is Father?"

Quickly recovering, Arien replies, "He's insane."

"Pity. I'd like to see him again."

"You can. I can help you, just please, choose to be good like Emma was. Don't hurt Ares."

Aphrodite smiles, throwing her wrist back to stab me through the chest.

I stare down at the Bolt protruding from me, a drunken stupor deadening the pain and stealing my focus. Arien screams as I topple over.

"He's not dead," I hear Aphrodite say, my mind closing off from everything but the sound. "It'll take a lot more work than that to kill him, but we have something more important to do. Don't appeal to my good side again. I don't have one." She vanishes; I feel Arien's warm embrace a moment later, applying pressure on my wound.

With a moan, I manage to say, "I'm fine. I'll patch myself up again within a few hours. I deserve this after what I did to her. You need to go to the Sentinel Plain volcanic field in Arizona and stop Eris from freeing Nyx. The future depends on it."

"What about you?"

I force my vision to clear enough to see the Macrobi people returning. "They'll take care of me. Go."

Arien nods, standing, and disappearing in a dark flash.

Charlie

My fingers tremble slightly, my nerves and tiredness near stopping me from finishing my final brushstrokes on the runes along Ullr's bone. Clara and Otus hold their breath as I lift one of Arien's hairs and place it against the base of the runes. The runes blaze to life and ignite with fire that sears them into the bone. Once finished, the fire settles into a small ember light that maintains itself on the bone. "Done," I whisper.

"What now?" Clara asks.

I lean over to review my spellbook, reading, "*Whoever shall wield Ullr's bone must be pure of mind and body.* Usually, that means you need to bathe and meditate."

"Alright. Otus, you coming with me?"

"Of course," he answers.

The amulet on the map suddenly slides over to India. We turn to look at it in surprise, Clara asking, "What's he doing in India?"

"I don't know, but I don't like it. We need to hurry. I'll work on the incantation while you guys bathe."

CHAPTER 113: PAIN VS. HATE

Arien

Gaia's bowels long lost to antiquity hold secrets that would baffle scholars for generations, but I am no scholar. The caves under the lava fields hold but a moment's sway over me. In that moment, I relish in the magnificence of the series of mirrors around the cavern, all reflecting the sun's light from small holes in the ceiling. Each reflecting and magnifying the light toward the center of the room, where a column of darkness wells out of the ground. The well is surrounded by stone pillars with runes carved in the side that appear to be containing the darkness.

I'm broken from my wonderment by the sound of sparks.

On the other side of the well, Emma is trying to break into the darkness by throwing lightning at the pillars of stone, to no avail. "Emma!" I shout. She turns to look at me, her inverted eyes filled with anger. Setting aside my fear, I continue, "You have to stop."

"You should not have followed us."

"I can't let you free her."

"Goodbye then, brother." She fires a lightning bolt; I barely block it in time by conjuring the Aegis.

Emma shrieks inhumanly, charging. I try to stave off her attacks, but my injuries from Talos impede my reflexes. She takes advantage of my injured leg, diving to that side and stabbing a solid bolt into my ribs like a knife.

I grunt, barely having time to process the pain before she blasts me back with another bolt. Crashing into the cave wall, my head cracks against the stone.

Emma slowly walks over to me, gloating, "Is that all the hero who's supposed to defeat Kronos can do?"

I spit out blood, looking up at her, fighting the second concussion clouding my view. "I'm not much of a fighter."

"Clearly." She kneels down, cupping my cheek in her hand. "I thought we could be family. I saw the pain inside of you. It's so much like my own. But you chose the side of gods and heroes."

"I might be on the side of heroes, but I sure as hell ain't one." I raise my hand and press my thumb into Emma's head, making her eyes turn fully black.

***

Emma is lying on the cold obsidian ground of the endless darkness. She slowly raises her head, staring around and whispering, "Father?"

My voice disembodied and echoing through the empty, I say, "He's beyond both of us. This is the field of my madness. And now, it's yours." Screaming fills the endless darkness, the sound of every death and harm I've ever inflicted. Emma hunches over as my worst memories wash through her. "You may have pain, but I have agony," I add.

From out of the cacophony of pain, individual voices become clear. "I never want to see you again."

"You killed all those people. They had families and you fucking killed them."

"How soon before you get your due? We should have let you die with that cow of a Mother of yours."

"Not made for bliss."

"Get out! Get out and never come back!"

Emma's tension relaxes, my memories fading from her. I say, "It's my curse to bear, and now it's yours."

She starts to laugh softly before it builds into a demented cackle. "I'm the goddess of strife. You can't drive me mad with your pain. It'll only make me stronger." She stands with confidence and reaches out into the darkness. I'm sucked from the shadows and grabbed by Emma's outstretched hand. She slowly tightens her grip as I struggle. "You know nothing of pain and loss. I've seen things that would make you quiver in fear. You think your pitiful little story means anything to me. You're nothing, nothing but a boy running from his parents. You think your pain is all that you are, there's so much less to you than even that."

My eyes widen an idea birthing within. She's right; I am not just my pain; I have a small seed of hope too. "You're wrong. I'm more than my pain."

The darkness fills with little voices of hope. Emma looks around in surprise and concern, stammering, "What is that? What are you doing?"

"Being loved."

The whispers slowly come into focus. "I think I may even be falling in love with you."

"Hey, Jules. Your mommy and daddy love you so much. We'll never let anyone hurt you, no matter what."

"I missed you. I really did."

"You're my brother."

"I'm always going to be there for you while you're out saving the world."

Emma stumbles back, dropping me and covering her ears in agony. I appear to get brighter as I approach her.

***

A blast of white light explodes from me, blasting Emma away from, the Bolt disconnecting from her and rolling away. She moans and rolls over, freezing when she sees me picking up the Bolt. Another explosion of light fills the cavern, nearly blinding Emma. When the light fades, she stares in awe at me; lightning appears to be flowing through my veins.

I approach Emma, who tries to crawl away, but I grab her hair tight and press the Bolt against her throat.

"Stop!"

I freeze, turning to see Nyx standing at the edge of the well of darkness. Emma whispers, "Mom?" She scrambles to her feet and approaches the well, but she still can't get through to touch her Mother. Tears fill her eyes as she stares at Nyx. "Mom, I miss you. I need you back."

"I miss you too, my dear. But I can't leave this place. I can't do what I need to for the future from out there. Everyone depends on me."

"I don't care about the future. I just care about you."

"I know, which is why this is so hard for me." Nyx reaches out of the well toward Emma. In the sunlight, her hand turns to bone and appears to smoke. She reaches into Emma's chest and pulls Eris from her. Emma collapses unconscious to the ground as Eris screams. Ice expands from Nyx's touch all through her body. She freezes solid for a moment before disintegrating into nothing.

A tear leaks out of the corner of Nyx's eye.

I drop the Bolt and rush to Emma's side, propping her up to check her vitals. Nyx watches, saying, "It's good to see you, brother."

Once I'm sure Emma is safe, I look up and ask, "Brother?"

"Before man knew what incest was, neither did we. Our Father was also Eris's Father." I grimace slightly, but Nyx continues, "I'm proud of you, and I know our Father would be too. You've come a long way. You're making the future. We'll meet again one day when I will take something from you, and I'm sorry, but it will be the end of you." She fades back into the well of darkness, leaving me to think on her words.

Emma's eyes slowly open, and she gasps. I'm relieved to see her eyes are no longer inverted. "Hey, how do you feel?"

"I'm fine." Her eyes widen and fill with tears, remembering what she's done. "Oh, my god. What have I done? All those people . . ."

"None of it was your fault. Eris is the one to blame."

"But it was still my hate that let her in. What will Charlie think? She'll never speak to me again."

"She doesn't need to know. Not until you're ready."

She looks up at me in shock, asking, "You would do that for me?"

"I'd do anything. You're one of us now. You're my family."

"Thank you. Thank you so much." She hugs me tightly. My face hidden by the hug, I stare at the Bolt crackling ominously on the ground.

CHAPTER 114: A NEEDED LIE

Arien

All power in New York shuts off, the electricity sucked into the god Zeus, finally reunited with his Bolt and restored to his power. He slowly floats back to the ground, smiling at Emma and me. He says, "Thank you. It's been far too long."

"What will you do now?" I ask.

"A king needs a throne. It's time to take back Olympus." He turns to look directly at Emma, asking, "Would you come with me?"

Emma thinks for a moment before shaking her head. "No, I'm going to stay with Charlie."

"Very well." Zeus nods in understanding. Walking to his balcony, he looks down at the bustling world of New York City. "I'm going to miss this place. Where anyone could become a god among men. Soon the world will need such people, but not today." A storm cloud forms above the building. "Today, they will stand in awe of a true god, the King of Olympus." A lightning bolt crashes down from the sky, striking Zeus. When the light fades, he's gone.

I smile softly after him, saying, "You were right, total drama queen." Emma nods, unable to smile, so I add, "Are you sure you're OK?"

"I will be."

"What about Ares? How do you feel about him?"

She sighs softly, explaining, "For thousands of years, I've begged people to forgive the crimes done before man's evolution. It's time I became the change I want to see."

I smile at Emma's maturity.

We both turn in surprise as Clara and Otus appear, a human bone in hand. Clara exclaims, "It worked."

"What's going on?" I ask, baffled. "How'd you get here?"

"Charlie found a way. We were worried about you guys. What happened?"

I go to answer but pause, noticing Zeus's secretary staring with shock from around the door, phone out and recording us. "We shouldn't talk here."

We all join hands and disappear in a dark flash.

***

Charlie stumbles back in shock, our sudden appearance frightening her. "You're back."

Emma turns to her, sadness filling her eyes. "I missed you." She hugs Charlie tightly.

"Oh, I missed you too. Babe, what's going on? Where have you been?"

Before Emma confesses, I interrupt, "We were trapped in a maze underneath Crete. It took us forever to find the Bolt."

"I tracked you all over the world."

"Once we found Talos, we fought through dozens of portals that sent us all over the world. He was a really tough bastard." Charlie nods in acceptance, and Emma gives me a grateful look.

"Oh, my god. Honey, you're hurt." Clara starts fussing over me, checking my wounds. "Sit down and I'll take a look." She helps me to sit before inspecting the stab wound in my side.

"I'm fine. It'll be healed by the morning. It's already a lot better."

Emma leans down to whisper in Charlie's ear, "You know what I really missed?"

Charlie blushes and smiles. "What?"

"Weeding. We never finished weeding the flower beds."

"Then we'd better fix that," Charlie replies with a giggle.

"We better had." Emma gives me one last look before leading Charlie out.

Clara grabs a rag to clean my wounds while I look up at Otus, saying, "Thanks for coming for me, Otus. I don't say it enough, but I appreciate everything you do. Things wouldn't be the same without you."

Clara smiles in thanks, and Otus blushes, muttering, "I do what I can."

"Maybe later I could talk to Molly for you."

"You would do that?"

"Of course. You're my brother, man."

He smiles and looks down a little. "Thank you."

"You know what I've been craving, that steak pie that you've been talking about. Do you think you could make it tonight?"

"I'd love to. I just need to go to the store and pick up a few things." Otus hurries away, excitedly planning dinner.

"Thank you for doing that," Clara says. "He's been having a really hard time recently. It'll make him feel better to contribute something."

I think in silence for a moment, just enjoying the sensation of the warm cloth on my wounds. "Clara?"

"Yeah?"

"There's something you said the other night that I've been thinking about."

"Oh, no. What did I say? I didn't tell you the story of when I lost my virginity?"

I laugh softly, asking, "Why? Was it rough?"

"Let's just say that boy had too much to drink and things got messy."

Grimacing slightly, I console, "Luckily, no. . . You said you were falling in love with me."

Clara freezes suddenly, deflecting, "Did I?"

"Yeah. I was just wondering if it was true."

"And if it were?"

I reach down and lift her chin, making her look me in the eye. "I'd say that I'm falling in love with you too."

She smiles, leaning up to kiss me on the cheek. "I love you."

"I love you too."

"Really? You mean it?"

"Yeah. Do you?"

"Of course, I mean it. I just thought since it really hasn't been that long that you wouldn't be ready."

I think for a moment, explaining, "When you know, you know."

"I really want to kiss you right now."

"So do I."

"This'll have to do." She hugs me tightly, adding, "I'm never going to let you go." I smile, holding her tight. Suddenly, I realize that I'm happy; perhaps the first time in my life, I can't bear to give up my future.

Part 14:

HADES

CHAPTER 115: MAKING GODS FEAR

Arien

They scream, exciting my lust. Clara greedily accepts my raging cock into the welcoming embrace of her moist pussy. Anna's tentative fingers explore downward, exciting Clara's clit. Clara leans to take in a mouthful of Anna's nipple in thanks. Their closeness fans the flames of my passion; I thrust into Clara faster and faster, my passion building. With a grunt, I fill her with generations.

Stepping back to recharge, I watch the girls continue without me.

Clara smiles and pushes Anna down onto her back; she climbs on top and kisses her passionately. She kisses down Anna's body in a line from her lips back to her nipple. Anna moans softly in pleasure. As Clara sucks, her hands run up and down Anna's body, getting closer and closer to between her legs.

Anna grabs Clara's chin and forces her to look her in the eyes, commanding, "Get down there."

Clara smiles and nods, kissing in a line from Anna's breast to her warm pussy. My eyes go wide as Clara attacks Anna with a passionate intensity. Anna runs her fingers through Clara's hair, her screams starting to build.

***

TAP-TAP!

I'm ripped from my fantasy by the sound of violent tapping on glass. I open my eyes and stare at Charlie through the car window, my hand frozen on my pulsating cock. Realizing my nudity, I struggle to pull up my pants, stopping when I hear Charlie laughing enthusiastically. I get out of the car and say, "Not cool." She continues to grin, so I add, "Stop. It's not funny."

"It's a little funny. Clara been giving you blue balls?"

I look away in embarrassment. "Sort of."

She stares down at the massive boner still protruding from my pants, saying, "Apollo's here, but I'll leave you to, ah--collect yourself first." With a wink, she returns to the house.

Once I've resolved my erection, I go to the kitchen, where Apollo is leaning against the kitchen counter, eating pop-tarts, and flirting with Emma. He coos, "You're still just as beautiful as you were in ancient times."

Emma grimaces slightly at Apollo's advances. "Mh-hm."

Charlie lowers her pregnant body into a chair, picking up Pluto from the table and saying, "Back off Apollo."

He leans back and raises his hands. "Just being friendly."

"You can be a horn dog later. Focus," I say, sitting with the others.

He winks at me seductively, asking, "Is that a promise?"

I shake my head slightly, deflecting, "What did you want to talk to me about?"

"Right." Brushing the pop-tart crumbs from his hands, he walks around the counter toward me, explaining, "I bring a message from Zeus."

"Isn't that Hermes's job?"

"He refused. Seems he really hates you. I've never seen him act like this."

My face darkens, remembering Hermes's sins. "After he killed that marine, the feelings mutual. What's the message?"

"The siege of Olympus has begun."

Everyone leans forward in surprise and anticipation. I hungrily ask, "Already?"

Apollo nods slightly, adding, "And the mortals have noticed."

"What's Olympus like? How's it work? Is it on the real mountain?"

"Yes, but the peak is a half-dimension off from our own, not unlike Erebus. You need magic to see or find it. All the mortals can see is an army attacking a barren mountain. Kronos's forces are putting up a good fight. The army we gathered isn't going to be enough."

"I don't think I'll be much help," I say, terrified at the thought of open warfare.

"I disagree."

"I've never fought in an all-out battle before."

"Zeus needs something else from you. He needs you to continue your quest and restore Hades."

"Hades? We've been looking for him, but haven't been having any luck."

"He reached out to us. He's in Moscow."

"Not surprising." We all turn to see Otus standing in the doorway. He explains, "The home of villains."

"Just because he's the god of death, doesn't make him evil."

"He abandoned the Underworld and left the souls of humanity to fend against the Titans themselves. That's enough."

"We all did that. We're all to blame."

"Wouldn't it be faster for the gods to help restore Hades?" I ask, confused. "He did reach out to you and not us."

Apollo looks down in embarrassment, drawing a raised brow from Charlie. She deduces, "You're afraid."

Emma looks at Apollo closer to confirm Charlie's suspicion, saying, "You are. But that means . . ." She stumbles back in fear, going pale.

"What is it?"

"Only a few things terrify gods."

We all give Emma a confused look, Charlie asking, "What is it?"

"Hades made a deal with Tartarus," Apollo whispers.

I tense slightly. "And?"

"Typhon is guarding his divinity."

Everyone goes pale, just like Emma. "Oh, god."

"Typhon, Typhon?" Otus exclaims. "The giant that nearly destroyed all the gods and the Earth, Typhon? That Typhon?"

"Hades doesn't do anything partway."

"So, you're afraid of Typhon and are sending us instead?" I say, trying to focus despite my dread. "Why is his divinity so important to the war?"

"He commands an army of the dead. That may be the force we need to finally take Olympus."

"We have a zombie army?"

"Not yet."

Otus grimaces slightly, mumbling, "I hate zombies. World War Z scared me to death." We turn to look at Otus curiously, so he adds, "What? Those zombies were really fast." We shrug off Otus's remarks, turning back to Apollo.

I ask, "How are we supposed to defeat Typhon when all the gods at full power barely did?"

"I don't know," he confesses. "But Hades has what you need to awaken him. You'll need to meet him at the Kremlin. These will get you in." Apollo hands me a stack of Kremlin visitor passes and a set of car keys. "There's a car waiting for you in an alley near the Kremlin."

"Can't we just meet him at home?"

"There's no time to waste. Your appointment's at 5 o'clock, and it's already late afternoon there. These badges will get you in, then just ask for Anton Romanova. You'll need to hurry. We need those soldiers as soon as possible, or the siege might fail. Good luck." Apollo vanishes.

"Doesn't even ask for questions," Charlie mutters.

Turning to Otus, I ask, "There's skiing equipment in the gym, right?"

"I think so."

"Let's go see if we can find some warm clothes. Russian's going to be cold."

"Not this time of year. This isn't an 80's action movie."

"We'll see." Otus and I go to pack, leaving Emma and Charlie alone.

Charlie

"I'd better get ready too," Emma says, standing to leave.

"Wait."

She turns back to me, asking, "What?"

Fighting my better instincts, fighting the love I feel, I force myself to confess my worry, "You're hiding something from me."

Her eyes flash with fear, and she pulls up a chair to sit across from me, stammering, "What? How could you think that?"

"Then why were you flirting with Apollo?"

Her expression changes into one of confusion. "Wait, what? I wasn't."

My fear of losing her explodes out in the form of jealousy fueled tears. "I just couldn't bear to lose you. Not right now."

Her gaze softens, and she pulls me into a hug, consoling, "Oh, honey. You're not going to lose me. I'm right here."

"But why? I can't be there for you like I used to. I can't pleasure you."

"You still do. I could never cheat on you."

"Maybe you should leave me. You'll be better off."

"Not a chance." She strokes my hair, comforting me through the hormone-induced emotional breakdown.

"But I'm just a fat blob now."

She laughs slightly, which makes me pull back and stare at her in anger. She quickly explains, "No, you're not. I love you. All of you, in whatever shape you are. I'm not going anywhere." My anger tempered, we kiss and snuggle closer. She strokes my hair again for a minute before saying, "You know, I could help with the hormones. They're kind of my thing."

I again pull back, this time with a look of hope. "Really?"

"Yeah."

"Ah, OK." With my permission, Emma places her hands on either side of my head. Her hands start to glow, and I feel myself relaxing. "Oh, that's better."

She smiles and lowers her hands. "There you go."

"I'm sorry for what I said. I was really freaking out."

"You're carrying life inside of you. You never need to apologize."

We kiss again as Arien and Otus walk back in. Collecting myself, I ask, "You find what you need?"

"Yeah," Arien replies. "We found some good gear, but Otus was right. We looked it up, and it'll be in the 70's today in Moscow."

"That sounds nice."

Arien lifts the visitor badges Apollo gave him, saying, "There's one for Clara. We could use her if security flags us. I think we should pick her up."

I smile at the mention of Clara, affirming, "Good idea."

Turning to me, Emma asks, "What are you going to do while we're gone?"

"Do more research and hopefully find something that will help you against Typhon."

"Don't have too much fun."

"I never do."

Emma kisses my cheek and stands to walk over to the others. She waves, and they disappear in a dark flash, leaving me alone.

CHAPTER 116: IMPOSSIBLE MISSION

<u>**Arien**</u>

We appear in a dark flash next to the car that Apollo left for us. Our fancy suits and badges create a professional look adverse to the grimy alley around us. I unlock the car, and we start loading our stuff. Glancing at Clara, I notice the shakes of fear racking her. "Hey, are you OK?"

"Yeah, I'm just sneaking into the Kremlin," she stammers, her nerves failing her. "I've never done anything like this before."

"It'll be easier than breaking into NORAD," Otus notes. "At least we're invited this time and don't have to steal anything or stop nuclear war."

"Wait, you guys broke into NORAD," Clara asks, her eyes darting between us in shock.

"It's a long story." I reply.

"Well, you're going to tell it when we get home."

I laugh softly, saying, "Will do."

We all pile into the car, and Otus drives us out of the alley to the nearby kremlin gate. He hands a guard our visitor badges while other guards do a walk around of the car with dogs and mirrors. The guard says something in Russian, motioning to a parking garage. Otus thanks him and follows the guard's directions.

"You speak Russian?" I ask.

"Just *thank you*. I'm just following where he pointed."

I smile and shake my head.

We're soon inside the kremlin lobby; Emma leads the way up to the front desk, where a soldier greets us in Russian. Emma and the soldier talk for a minute until he motions toward the elevator. She thanks him and leads us to the elevator.

Once alone, Otus exclaims, "*You* speak Russian?"

"I'm a god. I speak everything," Emma replies.

"Then why didn't you drive?"

"I'm a god."

We all giggle, riding up the elevator to Hades's office. After a firm knock, Hades answers his door, saying, "You're late."

"You also only gave us an hour's notice," Emma retorts.

Hades smiles slightly, almost creepily. "Aphrodite. It's good to see you again after all this time."

"Good to see you too."

"Please, have a seat." He motions us into his office and to a few chairs in front of his desk. Otus and Clara sit while Emma and I stay standing. Hades smiles again in his weird way before sitting behind the desk.

Emma looks around his office and out his window and the Moscow skyline. "I'm not surprised to find you in a place like this."

"Please, Russia's not so bad. Not anymore. Not after I helped bring down the Soviet Union."

"You did that?"

"No one here knows that, so I'd ask you to keep that to yourself."

"Why? I'd figured you'd be all for the Soviets."

"Just because I'm the god of death doesn't mean I don't care about people and their lives. These people here are good. Their government just isn't always. I do what I can to protect them."

Everyone looks at each other, surprised by Hades's words. "Everyone assumes I'm a villain because I'm the god of death and don't have a throne on Olympus. That's not the case. I don't claim to be perfect or even good. I just try like everyone else does."

"And are you going to try and help Olympus?"

"You can trust my intentions."

"Why?"

"I try to help these people here, but there's only so much I can do. As a god again, I can really make a difference for them. I want to matter again, make a difference. Even as the most hated god, I mattered more than I do now. I want a chance to prove that I'm not the villain that I'm expected to be."

Emma almost smiles, surprised and impressed. "OK."

"Maybe we should get to work now. My divinity resides within the Helm of Darkness at the South Pole."

"Isn't the Helm how you all became mortal?" I ask, trying to remember the story.

"We all gathered after our defeat at Pompeii and took turns wearing it," Emma answers. "It had to be done voluntarily, and some of us wanted to refuse. It took a long time for us all to agree."

Hades nods, adding, "I was the last to use it. My final act of divinity was to scatter the gods around the world with their spirits. I then sent my divinity to the South Pole in the care of Typhon."

"Don't the poles move?" I ask. "How are we going to find it?"

"That's the magnetic pole. I'm talking about the geographic pole."

"Any chance Typhon will just give us the Helm?"

"I'm afraid not. He was instructed not to give the Helm to anyone, including me. In case I was corrupted. Go to the ceremonial pole and pour this onto it." Hades hands me a small vial of liquid, explaining, "It's water from the river Styx. It'll awaken Typhon. Defeat him, and Helm is yours."

Dreed at the fight ahead still near-crippling me, I ask, "How can we defeat something that decimated all the gods?"

"I don't know. He doesn't have any weaknesses." Hades's secretary knocks on the door and opens it. They talk in Russian for a minute until the secretary leaves, and Hades says, "I'm afraid I have an appointment." He stands, shaking all of our hands. "I'll meet you all in Greece once I've wrapped up all of my affairs. Good luck." He walks to the door and leaves us to stare after him.

Her lip curled, Emma says, "I never liked him, not after what he did to Persephone."

"He wasn't so bad, just a little creepy," Clara replies.

"I guess we're going to the South Pole," Otus says, changing the subject.

"Not all of us. Not Clara," I say. "I don't think you should go."

Clara turns her fearsome gaze on me, asking, "And why not?"

"You're not a fighter. You're a straight mortal. . . I'd worry about you. It's not safe."

Her expression softens. "That's sweet, but I'm going." She walks over and grabs my arm, adding, "Now, teleport us out of here so I can get ready." I smile at her a little while the others grab on. We disappear in a dark flash.

CHAPTER 117: CHILDLIKE WANTS

Arien

We appear in the manor kitchen, and someone shouts, "How do you do that?" I turn to see Anna standing beside Charlie, staring dumbfounded.

Horrified and surprised to see her, I ask, "Anna? What are you doing here?"

Before she can answer, Clara steps forward, a little defensive, saying, "Yeah. What are you doing here? Did you invite her, Arien?"

"No, I don't even know how she found us."

"I made Molly tell me," Anna whispers, intimidated by Clara's wrath.

"Molly?"

"I drove all night to come here. We need to talk, Sam--I mean, Arien. Can we go for a walk?"

I glance to Clara for permission, who nods, affirming, "Fine. Do whatever you want."

"Thank you." I lead Anna toward the gardens.

Charlie

Once they're gone, Clara gets out her laptop and hacks into Arien's phone. Otus watches and warns, "You know, if I did that, I'd be a class A creep and probably get a restraining order against me."

"We can talk about sexual inequality later," Clara mutters, turning on Arien's phone audio.

His voice starts to come over the speakers, saying, "How much do you know about what I am and what I'm doing?"

"Charlie and Molly have told me a little," Anna replies. "I know why you tried to sleep with me that time, and why I've always been so awful to you." Clara's face darkens at Anna's words; she fights to not rush out and rip that girl's throat out. Anna adds, "But I want to know everything. I think I've earned that. That's why I'm here. I need to know. I need to understand. I was so horrible to you for so long, and I just need to know how much of that was . . . me."

"OK."

<u>Arien</u>

The manor provides; my tales of heroes, monsters, and gods soon overwhelms Anna, and she requires a strong drink. In the manor bar, we find our refuge. After my tale is done, Anna downs a shot, and I pour her another. "You know I don't believe a word of this, right?" she mutters, drinking the new shot.

I smile a little, replying, "Neither did I at first. It's a lot to take in."

"Did you really fight a dragon?"

"Two, actually."

"This is too much."

Clara steps into the doorway and coughs to get my attention. "I'll be right back," I say, joining Clara in the adjoining gym. "What's up?"

"Why didn't you tell me about her?"

I shrug, lost for the right words. "I don't know. It's hard for me to talk about it. You're not supposed to tell your girlfriend about your exes."

"I thought you couldn't have exes."

My eyes lower in shame, and I stammer, "I can't, not really. She's just the closest thing. We're . . . complicated."

"She's the childhood sweetheart you could never have. Will I always be second fiddle to her?"

"No, of course not. I love you. You're everything to me."

"But I'm not the most important woman to you. I can never be."

I pause for just a second too long, so Clara gasps and turns to walk away. "Wait," I cry after her. "You are the most important person in my life. I'd be dead without you."

She halts and turns back, asking, "What?"

"There was a point in Crete when I got separated from Emma. I was trapped in a cave without my powers, and the air was running out. I'd given up, but it was the thought of you that made me . . . try. I finally had the death I'd always wanted, but I gave it up because I couldn't imagine a second without you and the others. You gave me a reason to live."

Tears fill her eyes as she hugs me. "I'm sorry."

Hiding my face in her shoulder, I let my worry show. I don't know if I told the truth or if Clara is right to worry.

<u>Otus</u>

My senses as a man are dull compared to my owl self; as such, I often make a fool of myself relying on senses that aren't there, coming off as clumsy. Walking back into the mansion, I collide with Anna, nearly knocking her off her feet. Apologizing, I steady her and ask, "Are you leaving?"

"Yeah. I've caused too many problems here. It's better if I just leave."

"Arien will want to say goodbye."

"I don't think he will."

"Let me at least drive you to a hotel, you've been drinking."

"Thank you, but I'll be fine. It was just a couple shots. It was a pleasure to meet you all officially, but you can have your world of monsters and magic. It's too crazy for me." She pauses, struggling with something. "Besides, I don't have a place in his heart. I'll only cause trouble."

"Alright. I'll let him know you left."

"Thank you."

I let her go, watching until she is safely in her car and down the driveway. Returning inside, I see Emma hauling snow gear into the entryway. She asks, "This the snow gear you were talking about, Otus?"

"Ah, yeah."

"I've never been skiing, but I've wanted to try for a long time."

"Me to."

"I'll add it to the rest of the gear." She puts the snow gear into some bags by the door, adding, "Anything else we need?"

"I think that's everything."

Emma pulls some explosives out of a bag, noting, "You really think we'll need explosives?"

"You never know. Typhon's pretty big."

"How do you even have these?"

"Athena gets them for me."

"Oh." She returns the explosives to the bag, turning to greet Charlie waddling in. "Guys, I have an idea that might help against Typhon. Where are the others?"

"Anna just left, and the lovebirds are having a fight somewhere," I answer.

"What did you find, honey?" Emma asks.

"I . . ." Charlie pauses, something through the window catching her eye.

BOOM!

Charlie is cut off as the front door explodes inward, sending us all flying. Emma reaches out and wraps her arms around Charlie to protect her and the baby. We roll to a stop and moan, trying to get up.

Arien and Clara rush into the room and help everyone stand. Arien asks, "What happened?"

"I don't know."

Fear paralyzes us, the sight of the dreaded chimera making our blood run cold. This 12-foot-tall monster with a lion's head, a goat's body, and a serpent's tail prowls through the gaping hole that had been the door.

We stare in disbelief, locking eyes with the beast.

Arien conjures the Aegis, drawing the chimera's gaze. It roars, spitting a fireball at him, sending him flying through the back wall.

The rest of us dive for cover as the chimera advances. I command, "Everyone grab a bag and get to Arien!" We gather the gear Emma'd been gathering, dodging several attacks from the chimera before heading for the back door.

Outside in the garden, Arien moans and rolls over Charlie's flowers, sitting up. We rush toward him; the chimera steps through the hole out into the garden, taking a deep breath, preparing to scorch us off the face of the Earth.

At the last second, Emma raises her hands and creates a magical shield around us, shouting, "Hurry! This won't last long." We all grab Arien and disappear in a dark flash.

CHAPTER 118: THE LAND BELOW

Arien

Ice cold winds bites and tears at our exposed flesh, clawing for warmth. Appearing in the plains of Antarctica, we huddle close together to stave off the cold. Otus passes out the snow gear, and we soon stabilize to spite nature's grasp. Charlie mumbles, "Couldn't have taken us somewhere else first? Anywhere else?"

"Sorry," I reply. "It was the first place that came to mind." Realizing we didn't plan on Charlie coming, so we don't have gear for her, I give her mine, lighting the phoenix to keep myself warm. "I thought the chimera had been killed by Bellerophon?"

"There were twin chimeras," Emma explains. "This was the brother who survived."

"How can we hope to defeat Typhon when we can't even fight a chimera?"

"I have an idea." We all turn to Charlie, expectantly. "Same way we beat Hyperion."

Mine and Otus's eyes widen. I contend, "But that nearly killed me."

"What are you guys talking about?" Clara asks.

Otus explains, "The power of prayer can strengthen a god. Charlie and I prayed to Athena, and it gave Arien the strength to defeat Hyperion, but he was in a coma for nearly 2 days afterward."

"It's the only way," Charlie affirms.

"Just our prayers won't be enough this time."

"I can help. I'll get the whole world to pray," Emma declares.

I look down, overwhelmed by the idea. "If it's the only way, then do it." I look up suddenly, remembering, "What about Anna? We left her behind."

"It's alright," Otus consoles. "She'd already left. She didn't want to make any more problems."

Clara looks away, embarrassed, so Emma turns to the still shivering Charlie to break up the awkward moment, saying, "We got to get you out of here, babe. It's not safe for you."

Charlie nods, taking off her coat and giving it back to me. "Good luck." Charlie and Emma vanish.

A storm starts to build in the distance, and Clara takes out a GPS to check our location. "Looks like you got us pretty close, Arien. It's only a mile or so to the east."

"That storm is to the east, right?" Otus notes.

Clara looks up at the storm with worry. "Yeah. We need to hurry and find shelter before it reaches us."

"Let's go." We all pick up our bags and start heading for the South Pole.

Atlas

Few people strike fear into my soul, but the witch Hecate is so mysterious that even I fear her, but she's my last resort. I drag the strange girl from the mansion through the maze of caves at the entrance of the Underworld, searching for Hecate's abode. I find it and drag the girl inside. She stares around at the sinister cave filled with magical items and herbs growing in strange places, every item capable of killing in untrained hands.

Hecate steps from around the corner and smiles at me, saying, "Thou hast returned to me. May I assume your mission was a failure?"

"Not entirely." I shove the girl to the ground between us.

"Who is she?"

"Leverage."

"Thou shalt need to find them again first."

"I had hoped you could help again."

Hecate smirks, picking up the dagger that I'd stabbed Aphrodite with on the asylum's roof. "A god's ichor is a powerful thing, yet finite. There is none left to perform the trace again. None the less, I completed my part of our bargain. I demand my payment."

"One day you will have to pick a side in this war and stop playing both sides."

She smiles wryly, asking, "Why would I take part in a meaningless war?" It's my turn to smirk, but I concede, handing over the bag of Medea's ashes. She inspects it, saying, "Is this all of her?"

"Every last spec. You intend to resurrect her?"

"Indeed." Hecate steps closer, fire flashing in her eyes. "And thou wilt do good to remember to never cross a witch of mine again. Or my wrath shall be boundless."

I tense slightly, barely managing the fear that courses through me. "It was your potion that killed her."

Her expression darkens even more. "Thou should not lie to me again, either. Tis never a good idea to cross a witch or the goddess of witches."

"And what of the witch Charlie? Is she off limits as well?"

Hecate's fiery eyes fade, and she smiles, stepping away. "She is something extraordinary. A first-life witch with power such as hers is uncommon. And her destiny is not to fall by your hand, for you are incapable of hurting her. I do not fear for her safety."

"We shall see." I turn and grab the girl by her hair, yanking her back, preventing her from crawling away. "Perhaps I could request something from you to cool this one's spirit until her usefulness is fulfilled."

"And what prize may I claim in exchange?"

"Same as the last potion."

"Agreed."

I pick up a needle and prick my thumb, letting a single drop of ichor fall into a vial. "What intentions do you have with my blood?" I ask.

"Many spells call for Titan ichor. It is merely useful to have a small supply of it nearby."

Wiping my thumb clean, I hand her the vial. Accepting it, she exchanges it for a mind control potion.

"Tis not as strong as the last dose. As a mere mortal, it will take less to control her."

"Is this one lethal as well?"

"Not in such a low dose. To revive her mind, simply the smell of a moly herb will do so."

I nod, forcing the girl to drink the potion. She struggles for a moment before her expression goes blank and her body falls still.

"What do you intend for her?" Hecate asks.

"I don't know. An ace in the hole perhaps."

I grunt and fall to my knees, a loud ringing filling my ears. "Atlas!" Kronos's voice commands through the ringing.

"Yes, my lord, Kronos."

"Why is it that I must now descend from my place among the stars to defend the throne of Olympus?"

My face constricts in horror and dread. "You're coming to Earth?"

"Why is it necessary that I do so?"

"The god's army is far too powerful. They're overwhelming our forces."

"How would you know that? From what I hear, you are not leading our army. You're off hunting the goddess of love."

My fear ebbing, I get defensive, "I hunt the boy as well. He is still a great threat to us."

"If we lose the throne, our strength of belief will dissipate completely, and we will be vulnerable. That is our highest concern. It is too late to kill the boy and the goddess. The damage is already done."

"I will leave for Olympus immediately, and I bring a gift of appeasement for my lord." I look at the girl, hopeful.

CHAPTER 119: GARGANTUAN

Arien

A whirlwind of snow swirls around, near blinding us. We trek onward, following the beeping point of Clara's GPS. Suddenly, we reach a ring of flags and a candy cane pole; we've arrived. Her teeth chattering, Clara stammers, "We made it."

"Come here," I say, lighting the phoenix and rubbing her shoulders to warm her.

"Here we go," Otus mutters, pouring Hades's vial of Styx water onto the pole.

"Otus, no!" I shout, leaping to stop him. It's too late. The ground trembles, shockwaves blasting the snow back. We stare at the pole in horror. "We're not ready. We can't see anything in this storm, and Emma hasn't gotten back yet."

Otus's eyes widen in guilt. "I'm sorry."

Time appears to freeze, and the ground stops shaking. Snowflakes hang suspended in the air, no longer falling. We stare around in confusion before I reach out to touch a snowflake. With a whoosh of air, the snowflakes disappear, and the storm dissipates. There is no sound but our breathing, the landscape empty of storm or wind.

BOOM!

A loud booming fills the air as if someone is knocking on the Earth itself. The booming shakes the ground and knocks the feet out from under us. Clara shouts, "Arien! Get us out of here!"

I grab my friends, and we disappear in a dark flash just as the ground beneath us explodes upward.

**

Appearing in the plains miles away, we watch in horror. The great monster Typhon pulls himself from beneath the Earth. This great monster with a man's chest and head, bat-like wings, and standing at a height above 10,000 feet, stares down at the Earth before him. We all pale at the sight, staring at the monstrosity towering above the clouds in the sky. I whisper, "Oh, my god."

A tear leaks out of the corner of Otus's eye.

"What do we do?" Clara stammers.

Taking a moment to collect myself, I let my instincts take over, drowning my fear. "We need to play for time until Emma gets here."

"I've got something for that," Otus says, reaching into his bag and pulling out a large case of C4.

I take it and stare at it in surprise. "C4? How the hell did you get this?"

"Doesn't matter. Can you make a bomb?"

"I have no idea how. Besides, this won't do much damage against that. We're not even ants compared to him." I point at Typhon in defeat.

"Focus, babe," Clara consoles. "We need you."

I shake my head to clear it, nodding. "OK."

Otus turns to Clara, asking, "You think you can do it?"

"I know computers not fucking bombs," Clara exclaims.

"Can you try?"

She shrugs and nods. "If I remember enough from chemistry, maybe."

Typhon lifts a leg and takes several seconds to take a mile-long step. I watch the step, the beginnings of a plan formulating. "He's big but slow. Otus, can you keep his head distracted as best you can?"

"I guess," he affirms.

"Keep an eye out for him breathing fire."

"Him doing what?" Clara asks.

"While you do that, I'll go for the ankles. Try and be as much of a nuisance as I can. While Clara gets the bomb ready."

Typhon takes another step, this one close enough to send a shockwave through the ground and knock us off our feet. Otus gets up and transforms into an owl, flying toward Typhon.

I turn to Clara to make sure she's alright. "Are you good?"

"I'm fine. Go."

I nod, disappearing in a dark flash.

***

The South Pole and the ring of flags are completely destroyed, fallen into the hole from whence Typhon had crawled.

I appear next to the giant's feet and stare up at his ankles, standing over 500 feet above the ground.

Summoning the Aegis and morphing it into a sword, I turn my attention to the base of Typhon's feet. With a roar, I stab at the foot, burying my sword up to its hilt. Even so, the blade barely scratches Typhon's surface, being less than a splinter to him.

Otus

High above the snow, I dive for Typhon's eye, marveling at its magnitude; it must be the size of a building. A gust of wind from his eyelid sends me flying back only to nearly be roasted by a column of fire that he breathes out.

I fly back, unable to get close.

CHAPTER 120: WE BELIEVE

Scientist

How mundane this expedition has become. When I heard of a chance to explore the bottom of the world, my excitement was boundless. I imagined myself as an explorer like Robert Falcon Scott, but all I do is sit in our silo watching a seismograph, a complete waste of my skills. There's no history being made here, no epic tale to be told.

My seismograph whirls to life, surprising me. I stare at the numbers, shocked at their utter magnitude. A moment later, the ground shakes violently. "What is that?" I shout.

Turning to the others, I see them all checking their equipment, each getting insane readings. Realizing our instruments can no longer do justice to this event, we all grab our coats and rush outside.

We pile out of the research base and stare in horror at the gigantic form in the far distance. "My, god." The giant takes another step, creating a shockwave that knocks us off our feet. We all scramble back up to continue staring. "Get on the horn to the mainland. They'll want to hear this."

Technician

The absurdity of the report that I'm receiving mounts, only getting madder and madder. Yet I believe the fear in the voice over my radio. To confirm the report, the voice emails his seismic data and a video file of a giant attached. The sight paralyzes me with fear; how could such a thing exist?

I wave down my boss, stammering, "Sir, we've got--I don't know what it is." My boss and a few over techs gather around the computer to watch the video. Their jaws drop in horror. "What is it?"

"I don't know. I think we should give this to the government," my boss whispers. We're all too shocked to argue.

Steward

I stand, proudly overseeing our rebuilt NORAD NEXUS chamber, relishing in the updates made. Captain Wilson stands and reports, "Sir, I just received word from SecDef. There's a . . ."

I raise an eyebrow, surprised at the fear in Wilson's eyes. "What is it, son?"

He gulps and says, "I'll just show you." He projects a video onto the main screen. My eyes widen in shock, staring at the colossal monster trekking across the plains of Antarctica.

"Dear, god," I hear an airman mutter.

"Is this live?" I ask Wilson.

"No, sir."

"Get me satellite coverage, and scramble the drones. I want a 360 view of this thing."

"The temperature is too low for most of our aircraft, sir."

"We need a plan of how to deal with this thing if it turns hostile. . . I'm taking suggestions."

"We could always go nuclear, sir."

"Under no circumstances will I authorize a nuclear strike. It is the impossible option. Have you got that?" Wilson nods slowly, duly chastened. I continue, "Good. Now, does anyone else have a better idea?" Everyone looks around at each other, lost in the impossible foe this giant presents.

Producer

Missing the excitement of news a mere few years ago, I watch Robin report on the generic news of the day. An intern runs to me, furiously whispering in my ear an impossible story. I ask, "What? Are you sure?" She motions to my tablet. Opening my email, I watch a video from Antarctica, flabbergasted. Turning back to the intern, I say, "Make sure the crew is ready to broadcast this immediately, and get us switched to breaking news." The intern nods and scampers off. I hurry to the teleprompt to change Robin's script.

"All these strange occurrences in Greece have left experts baffled as to their origin," Robin stops, reading over my changes. "Hold on. We're getting some breaking news." Over her Bluetooth, I explain the situation. "What?" Robin asks in confusion.

I nod in earnest, starting the new script.

Robin reads, "We have received a video from the South Pole, and I must warn you, it is quite disturbing." The broadcast cuts to the video of the giant before cutting back to Robin, who's staring in shock. "This footage had been confirmed to be genuine by our experts here. We still have no idea what this thing or creature is or if it's hostile. All we know at this point is that thing is of a height of at least 10,000 feet and has a mass capable of creating earthquakes. All we can do is pray this creature does not mean us harm."

Otus

I dive to the side to avoid another blast of fire breath before flying up into Typhon's massive nostril. Once inside, I transform into a man and cling to the enormous nose hairs dangling all around. Drawing a dagger, I stab him repeatedly. When nothing happens, I sigh, transforming back into an owl and flying higher into the nose. The cavern constricts around me until I get past the giant nose hairs.

Arien

Pausing to catch my breath, I survey the minimal damage I've caused on Typhon's massive feet. A bellowing sucking noise fills the air, and Typhon sneezes, the sound going off like a thunderclap. He bounces slightly as he sneezes, sending me sprawling.

Otus crashes to the ground and turns into a man, covered in snot. "We're not doing anything to him."

"We're just supposed to buy time."

"I feel like if we just left him alone, we'd get the same result."

"Maybe, but I think we have managed to slow him."

"Where's he going, anyway? He can't see Clara."

I turn to stare in the direction Typhon is heading. In the distance, I can see a research base, a massive antenna mounted on top. "He's heading for the only thing he can see."

"Those people are going to die if we can't stop him." Typhon takes another massive step, knocking us off our feet. "Do you think Clara is done?"

"We'd better go find out." We disappear in a dark flash.

***

Once beside Clara, I ask, "How's it coming?"

She shows us her finished bomb, answering, "I have no idea if it works, but yeah. What are we going to do with it?"

I turn to Otus, suggesting, "Maybe you could fly it into his mouth or back up his nose."

Otus grimaces, looking down at the snot still covering his body. "No way. That thing won't hurt him, even in there."

I look into the distance, thinking. Suddenly, an idea comes to me. "Aren't there some mountains in that direction," I say, pointing.

"They're a few hundred miles away, but yeah," Clara confirms.

"That's just a jog for Typhon."

Otus objects, "But not for us. I can't even fly that far."

"He can see about half that distance, though. If I can get his attention, then appear halfway and burn bright enough, he may follow me away from the research base. When we get there, set off the bomb and cause an avalanche to bury him just like Zeus did with Mount Etna."

They think for a moment before nodding. We hold hands, disappearing in a dark flash.

Scientist

Rooted to the spot in fear, we stare up at the giant looming over us. Unable to retreat, we watch him raise his massive foot to level us. Suddenly, a strange young man appears out of nowhere, shouting, "If you want to live, grab hold of me." Without another option, we all obey.

We vanish just as the giant demolishes our life's work.

Arien

Once I've delivered the scientists to safety, I appear in the air above Typhon, falling to latch onto his eyelash. After stabilizing myself, I send a beam of fire into the giant's eye. He roars in annoyance, blinking and knocking me back.

I disappear and reappear 100 miles in the distance, where a burn bright and disappear again. Typhon screams and breaths fire into the sky, following me at a brisk pace.

Appearing on a mountain peak next to Otus and Clara, I burn a pillar of fire high into the sky. Typhon roars again, heading for us. "We've got less than a minute before he gets here. Please tell me you've got that bomb ready."

"Hold your horses," Clara mutters.

Typhon reaches us with surprising speed. He stops and stares at us, his eyes level on top of the mountain. We stare back, waiting for him to do something.

"Arien," Clara whimpers.

"Yeah?"

"Ready."

I grab my friends and disappear in a dark flash. A moment later, Clara's bomb explodes, sending a million tons of combat snow sliding off the mountain and onto Typhon. He roars and is knocked over, buried alive. When the snow settles, we reappear on the peak, staring down at the newly formed pile of snow with hope.

"Did it work?" Otus tentatively asks. The snow shakes suddenly, contending Otus's question.

"It won't last long. I just hope Emma's close."

Producer

Robin shakes her head, struggling to regain control of her fear. "This creature does not come in peace. An American research base was just leveled by this thing. It's hard to believe we have any chance of defeating it. We must now put our faith in the powers that be and hope they can do the impossible." She raises a hand to her earpiece, receiving instructions. "Our agency has just received a video that we're about to show you from a woman claiming to be the Greek goddess of love."

The broadcast changes into a home video of a scarred beauty saying, "Humanity, I am Aphrodite, the Greek goddess of love. So, you'll know my words are true, I will show you my true form. I pray that this recording device will dissipate the image enough to not burn your eyes." Aphrodite turns to a pregnant woman behind her, adding, "Babe, please turn away." She looks away, and Aphrodite begins to glow bright, revealing her godly form in all its majesty.

I stare, transfixed by the emotions the light engenders, such love and hate.

She holds the blinding visage for a moment before fading into her human form and saying, "I am the goddess of love, and I'm here to beg for your help. We gods failed all of you a long time ago. Our arrogance blinded us to what was coming. It took me millennia of living amongst you to realize that you were always the better creatures. Better than us. We don't deserve your worship or your praise. My pride would never have let me admit that before. Now, I have to let all that go and let you save yourselves. That's the only way we'll win the coming war. We gods are nothing without you. You make us better.

"The time to believe in gods is over. The time to believe in yourselves has come. And there is one of you that is fighting right now to save all of us. He needs your help. This man needs you all to believe in him. This man who has been betrayed and set aside by the ones that should have loved him is now fighting for you despite having every reason to give up. To give in. To let himself die. And he might if all of you don't show him that humanity is worth fighting for.

"Now's the time to show your love for him. To give him a reason. To prove we're all worth fighting for. He is standing against a foe that can fell mountains, crush cities, and destroy gods. He needs all of you now. Pray for him. Pray to him that this man may triumph for all of us. Only you can prevent the coming destruction. If you pray to Athena, he'll hear you."

Aphrodite's video ends, switching back over to Robin. "This woman may be a god, or may not be. But we could all use a little faith right now. This monster is coming, and we may not have hope of survival. The moment we accept that is when we really do lose. Pray if you feel the desire. There is no harm in believing."

Steward

Wilson hangs up the phone, turning to report, "NATO has come to a verdict. Our orders will be transmitting presently for authentication, but we are to send out the codes."

I look down in defeat; the impossible option has come. "What do we have in the area?"

"We have a submarine off the coast of Australia on course for Hawaii."

Unable to stave off the end any longer, I take a deep breath and whisper, "Wait for verification, then do it."

"Yes, sir."

Turning to Robin's news broadcast, I whisper, "Praying doesn't sound like such a bad idea right now."

Arien

Emma appears on the peak next to us. I ask, "Emma, is it done."

"I did what I could. Do you feel anything?"

"No, nothing."

Her voice low and haunted, Clara says, "What will humanity do every time they're scared? War over faith." We all turn to her, realizing the horror that she's suggesting.

Sailor

Humanity is at stake, and I hold the power to save it. If there was ever a time to prove the need for man's greatest weapon, it is now. The order to resurface the USS Mars submarine is given. We rise to poke out of the ocean's waves. I press the damning button, and a port opens, firing a nuclear missile into the sky.

Arien

Typhon explodes up out from under the snow, sending it high up onto the mountain and knocking us over. I struggle to my feet first but slip and slide downward, dropping the Aegis to the bottom of the mountain.

Clara shouts, "Arien!"

I slip off a cliff, crashing onto a snow-filled ledge below and smacking my head against a rock.

"Are you alright?"

Shaking my head to clear it, I cradle it and stand. Before I can respond, Typhon turns to us and approaches.

"What do we do?" Otus cries.

Emma looks into the sky and points at a nuclear missile flying through the air towards us. "We have to go, now!"

"Not without Arien," Clara objects.

"He can get out of here on his own. He can help himself."

Accepting her reasoning, they vanish together, leaving me alone. Fighting the ringing in my head, I look up at the missile; it's too late.

BOOM!

Typhon is knocked sprawling by the force of the missile before it explodes. I scream, enveloped by the mushroom cloud that erupts around me, its fire burning away my clothes and flakes of my skin.

I'm dying, and the phoenix responds. Lifted off the ground, I'm spread-eagled, screaming. The wind and fire swirling around tries to tear me apart. The fire is sucked into me and absorbed inside.

As the mushroom fades, I collapse to the now barren ground.

Clara

We appear in the mansion; Charlie rushes to join us, hugging Emma. I wait, expecting Arien to appear. "Where is he?"

"He's still there," Charlie replies, grief welling.

Tears fill my eyes at the horror. I turn to Emma and grab her by the shirt, shouting, "Take me back!"

"I can't," she confesses. "The radiation would kill you."

I start punching her, whispering, "No. Take me back." I fall into her embrace, sobbing into her shoulder.

Producer

Robin raises her hand to her earpiece again to get an update. "We can confirm the military has taken nuclear action against the creature. We're just getting satellite footage back." She turns to her screen as satellite footage of the blast site comes on. We all hold our breath, waiting for the smoke to clear.

To our collected horror, the giant stands in the center of a newly formed crater, utterly barren of snow.

A tear leaks out of the corner of Robin's eye. "The creature lives. Nuclear option ineffective."

Arien

I moan and struggle to sit up despite my charred flesh and nude form. I freeze upon seeing Typhon staring down at me. "You win. Do it."

Producer

Robin stares at her screens in shock. Videos of people all around the world praying together cycle through. "This is incredible. People from all around the world are coming together like never before to pray for this mystery man trying to save us. Muslims, Christians, Buddhists, even Atheists, and Satanists are holding hands in prayer. All four corners of Jerusalem joined at the Wailing Wall. Everyone is choosing to believe."

I join hands with the other producers and crew members. We all have our eyes closed and are whispering to ourselves in prayer. "Athena."

Steward

Knowing who this man trying to save us is, I close my eyes and pray, "Arien." All my soldiers are doing the same.

Arien

I stumble and fall to one knee; images of people praying all around the world flash before my eyes, filling me with power. My skin and eyes start to glow brightly with a godly light as my wounds heal. Rising into the air again, I'm spread-eagled in front of Typhon. He stares in horror at the power flowing through me.

I let out a silent scream as a phantom phoenix appears behind me with wings spread. Typhon roars and bursts into flames. He thrashes, the flame spreading, consuming him.

He stops struggling, turning to ash.

I float down to the base of the mountain where Typhon's ashes begin to be blown away by the breeze, revealing the Helm of Darkness buried within.

The godly power fades from me, and I'm laid to rest on the barren ground, ash swirling around me. I stare up into the ashy sky, letting out my dying breath. My corpse glows with a dark red light; it catches fire and crumbles into ash, joining the remains of Typhon.

Part 15:

ATHENA

CHAPTER 121: UNFORGIVING SAM

Arien

My eyes slowly open; the melancholy spinning of the ceiling fan engrosses me, momentarily becoming my world, setting all pain and grief aside. The fantasy cannot sustain me though; I struggle to sit up, staring around at my manor bedroom; it's just as empty and barren as I am.

Flashes of my death rush through my mind, refusing to give me peace. This death was different, it took more from me. My personality and will had been torn from me and scattered among the very people killing me. They thought they were giving me strength, but they were destroying what it means to be **me**.

"Down in the valley, valley so low. Hang your head over, hear the wind blow." The lilting notes of Charlie's singing echoes through the open window. To distract myself from the emptiness inside, I stumble to the window and watch Charlie weeding her precious flowers, singing, "Hear the wind blow, dear, hear the wind blow. Hang your head over, hear the wind blow. Roses love sunshine, violets love dew, Angels in heaven know I love you."

I purse my lips, my face constricting in an effort to contain my emotions. Shaking my head, I wrap my nakedness in a robe and go downstairs to rejoin civilization.

Shouldering my way past the cyclopes repairing the house after the chimera fight, I go to Otus, who's overseeing the construction. He turns and cries, "Arien, how are you feeling?"

"Good, I guess."

"That's good to hear."

Ducking a large beam carelessly swung by a cyclops, I ask, "These are cyclopes, right?"

"Yeah."

"Huh, never seen one before. . . I'm surprised we came back here after the chimera attack."

"Charlie worked with the gods to reinforce the magical protections. It would take their whole army to get back in."

Nodding in acceptance, I inquire, "Are they still here?"

"They're all waiting for you in the kitchen."

I glance at the kitchen door, sighing. "Give me a minute."

Otus nods and squeezes my arm, heading into the kitchen. I watch after him for a second before slowly sitting on the stairs to just watch the cyclopes work.

<u>Charlie</u>

Returning from my daily chores, I stop at the door; Arien is sitting alone on the stairs, staring. I sigh and grunt, walking over to lower myself down next to him, noting, "You know, I may not be able to stand back up." He snorts slightly without smiling. I purse my lips, sighing again. "You've had a rough couple days, huh?"

"You could say that."

"Yeah. It can't have been easy."

"I died, Charlie. And nothing changed. How am I supposed to get over that?"

Shrugging, I shake my head slowly. "I don't know. Maybe you shouldn't."

He turns to me in surprise, asking, "What do you mean?"

"Do you remember how dark of a place I was in before I met Emma?"

"Yeah."

"I never forgot my pain, never really got over it," I explain, pausing to articulate. "I just accepted that it had a place inside of me. I appease it when I have to, but ignore it otherwise. I don't know if it'll ever go away."

"How do you do that?"

"I found ways to release those emotions in large, controlled, outbursts. It's weird, but sometimes I take a drive and shout Shakespeare lines."

He finally smiles, but only slightly. "Really?"

"Hey, don't judge. It works for me."

Turning to stare off into the distance, he says, "I think I'm done fighting this war. I've done enough."

I nod slowly, accepting him. "I get it. You really have done enough. How many people can say they died for a cause, but still got a chance to live? Whatever you decide, make sure you're happy with it. Don't worry about what anyone else says. Don't sacrifice so much that you're just hollow inside."

"They're not going to take it well."

"Who cares? You defeated a beast that terrifies them. If they're too scared to fight a battle like that with you, they shouldn't get to judge." I watch Arien for a moment in silence before wrapping an arm around him, whispering, "You going to be alright?"

"I don't know."

"Take your time. We can wait." Squeezing him tightly, I stand and waddle toward the kitchen, leaving him to stare in silence.

The sight I'm greeted with reminds me of an awkward family reunion where no one wants to be there. The thought brings a slight smile to my lips as I survey the 13 gods we've met, Pluto, and Otus all gathered around the kitchen table waiting for Arien. Taking my place with Pluto in my lap, I join in the silent patience.

Eventually, Arien mopes into the room, his eyes downcast. He stops in the doorway, waiting for someone to speak; no one does. The gods just stare in a mixture of fear and awe. Accepting their silence, Arien ignores them and pours himself a bowl of cereal, sitting at the head of the table and quietly eating.

All the gods turn to look at each other in confusion, none wanting to interrupt him, except for Hermes, who grimaces and says, "This is . . ." Arien cuts him off with an upraised finger. Hermes shuts up and lets him eat.

A tear leaks out of the corner of Arien's eye, unseen by all except me. I smile in pity at what he has ahead.

He finishes eating, dabbing his mouth with a napkin, placing a clenched fist on the table, and staring into his empty bowl. "What do you want from me? I've already died for you. Can't you just leave me alone? I just want to rest."

"It's almost over," Zeus says. "After that, you can rest forever."

"But why should I help you? I did all this so I'd find a way to die with dignity. A life worth living and a death worth dying. But it's impossible, and I just realized that. I don't have anything left to fight for."

Emma whispers, "You could fight for Clara."

Arien finally lifts his sober gaze to Emma, his eyes clear of emotions. "Is she here?"

"She's in the gym," I answer.

He nods at me, standing. "I want everyone gone before I get back. I can't help you." He just walks out, the gods staring after him, flabbergasted.

Giving him a moment, I follow.

I find him leaning against the gym door, watching Clara training with a punching bag. She's sweating heavily and breathing hard, refusing to stop. Circling the bag, she reigns a storm of blows upon it.

Watching her in silence for a minute, I smile, saying, "She's pretty awesome, isn't she?"

"Yeah, she is," Arien mumbles.

"Do you know why she's training so hard?"

"No."

"I think it's because she never wants to feel useless again. It nearly destroyed her to watch you die and not be able to do anything about it."

"She won't have to be helpless again. I am done fighting."

I again nod in acceptance. "There's one more thing you need to do either way."

"What's that?"

"Athena needs her divinity back."

"I'm done chasing people."

Smiling softly, I motion to Clara, noting, "Except for her. Go, she needs you."

He bites his lip, nodding. "Thank you." Walking to Clara, he stops behind her, saying, "I hope it's not me you're imagining hitting."

Clara freezes and slowly turns. "Arien?" Tear stream down her face, and she runs to embrace him. They hold each other tight for a moment before pulling back and pressing their foreheads together. "I thought I'd lost you."

"I'm not going anywhere." Arien grunts and steps back, wiping his eyes. "Maybe you could teach me some of those moves you've got. Might come in handy."

"Are you sure you're ready? Maybe you should rest."

"I feel great. Come on."

Clara nods, starting to train with Arien.

Otus walks up beside me, taking Arien's place to watch. Turning slightly, I confess, "I'm worried about him. Dying takes a toll."

"He'll be alright. He always is."

"Not this time, I think." We stare in silence for a moment, just watching.

"Athena's on her way," Otus says. "She's driving from Colorado and picking up Molly along the way. She thinks Arien needs her right now."

"She's probably right." I gasp and stumble, pressing my hand against my swollen belly.

"Are you alright?"

"That's a kick. It's his first kick."

"Oh, wow."

I wave down Clara and Arien, shouting, "Guys, he's kicking." Clara squeals and hurries over to feel. They all smile and take turns feeling the kicks. Otus runs off to grab Emma, bringing her to feel.

"Oh, my god. That's amazing," Emma whispers, leaning in to kiss me. The world may be on a knife's edge between chaos and order, but here and now, none of that matters, only the miracle of life itself matters.

CHAPTER 122: COUNCIL OF FIRE

<u>**Arien**</u>

Night is deep and unyielding when I wake with the sudden need for beer. Fighting the clutches of my sleep, I struggle to my feet and stumble to the kitchen. Without turning on the lights, I go to the fridge and choose a drink. "A little early for beer." I slam the fridge shut, turning to Hermes sitting in the dark at the table.

"Why are you still here?" I hiss. "After your antics with the dragon got a marine killed, you shouldn't be around me, or I might snap. I'm not ready to deal with your shit."

His face darkens in anger, and he hisses back, "Summoning my dead wife to manipulate me isn't just my shit."

"I did what I had to."

"I know."

I falter in surprise. "What?'"

"I know you did the right thing, but I don't have to like you for it. And you giving up just makes my pain irrelevant. I can't have that. I want to be able to hate you forever, and I can't do that if we lose."

"I didn't leave the gods empty-handed. I did my part."

"It's not enough. We think that you're the only one who can kill Kronos, for good this time."

"How?" I ask, my anger dissipating.

"Same way you beat Typhon."

"Once you take Athena's divinity from me, I won't be able to use prayers anymore."

"I disagree. Athena's divinity does act like an antenna for you, but the prayers enhanced your powers, not hers."

I raise an eyebrow in confusion. "So?"

"If the world prayed to you, I think the same thing would happen."

Shaking my head, overwhelmed by the idea, I contend, "The world praying to me, I don't how I feel about that. I'd be like a god."

"Not a god. Something new with enormous power." He stands, deciding our conversation is done. "I don't want to see my pain go to waste." He vanishes without another word. I grimace, letting my anger return. Needing time alone to process, I put down my beer and disappear in a dark flash.

***

I'm alone in the endless darkness. Lifting my head, I scream into the empty, falling to my knees. I stare at the cold obsidian ground in defeat.

"Don't hurt her. I'd never hurt her." Erebus's soft whisper from the dark draws my attention. "I don't want to do this. I'm not a monster. Give it to me. Give me more. Eitr, eitr, eitr. I need it. Please let me die."

Standing, I walk through the darkness until I find Erebus huddled on the ground. I whisper, "Hey, Dad."

"Never. You're my daughter, you're my wife, we're supposed to support each other in everything."

I crouch behind Erebus and sigh, confessing, "I could really use some advice right now."

"We all have vices to beat."

I cock my head, wondering if he really responded to me. When he doesn't elaborate, I shrug, continuing, "I'll take that as an OK." Sighing again, I rub my bearded chin and look away. "Everyone wants me to be some sort of savior. Some sort of hero. They think I should still fight, though the death I've fought so hard for can never be had. My whole reason for caring is now immaterial. I have nowhere to go, nothing to do, and nothing to be. What purpose does my life serve if I don't benefit from it?"

"You can't save the girl."

My face darkens; I grunt and stand. "Why did I ever think I should come to you for help? There's nothing left of you. You can't help me." I turn and walk away, heading out into the endless darkness.

Walking in silence for several minutes, a light in the distance catches my attention. I raise an eyebrow and approach it. There's a large glowing portal in the middle of the darkness. I stare at it in confusion because there can be no light in the darkness. Reaching out to touch the portal, I'm sucked in, gasping.

***

I step out of the portal into a wondrous realm, composed of pure light, pure fire. I'm in a sinkhole in a forest filled with trees of silver and gold. The white sky and grass are composed of pure flame. The forest is inhabited by dozens of phoenixes, all living in harmony with one another. This place is impossible in every way; a perfect no place.

A phoenix with a crown of flames upon his head stares at me. He's perched atop a column at the head of a ring of pillars, all surrounding a pool of molten lava. I approach the Phoenix-King and stare at him in confusion. "Welcome."

I stumble back in surprise, exclaiming, "Jesus!" The voice had come from nowhere, from inside of me. I ask, "You can speak?"

The Phoenix-King nods, his disembodied voice replying, "Only in your mind."

"Who are you?"

"You should know. You carry my power."

I look down at my chest before looking up at the Phoenix-King. "You? But I thought it was the spirit of the phoenix that was passed down to me, not just it's power."

He caws almost like a chuckle. "No. We gifted worthy mortals with our power to protect them in the coming wars. But we ourselves transcended beyond the need for physical form. We only appeared to you in this way to put your mind at ease."

I turn to look at the incredible place I'm in, muttering, "I don't think it's working."

"We exist in all time, all space, whispering in the ears of humanity, guiding them. After the death of the Fates, the Council of Fire became the sole purveyors of destiny."

"If you control fate, why have you let so many terrible things happen? Why have you let the Titans rule for so long?"

"There's no true joy without true sadness. No strength without weakness. We whisper in the ear of all and guide them down the path the world requires. We forge the best out of people and foster the worst in them. Both are needed, or nothing has meaning. We keep the balance. And you are the personification of that balance. A man born of fire and night, capable of great love and great madness." I look down in shame, the Phoenix-King's words stirring something inside of me. He continues, "The balance we maintain has been nigh upon perfect for millennia, but that balance is now under attack, threatened. A future is coming where there can be no balance."

Clenching my jaw, I look back up, asking, "And I suppose you want me to fight to prevent it? Is that my destiny?"

"Yes. Or allow us to give your power to one who will." I stare at the Phoenix-King in shock and horror as he adds, "The phoenix fire will come to be the only light in the great imbalances of the future. We need a champion who will ensure the balance remains."

The beautiful scenery around tempts me, but I make up my mind, saying, "Take it. I'm not your guy. I'm done fighting."

The Phoenix-King stares knowingly at me for several seconds. "Your destiny has not been written yet. There are many things in store for you. If, when this week is done, and you still desire to give it up, we will take it."

Nodding, I accept his statement. I go to leave but stop, turning back. "Do the souls of human phoenixes happen to come here as well?"

"The few who die, yes," he affirms.

My body clenches, and I ask the question that will change me, "Is my Mother here?"

"Yes."

My heart skips a beat, hope warming me. "Can I see her?" The Phoenix-King looks up into the sky and caws loudly. From high above, a phoenix soars down to land on one of the pillars of stone. A tear leaks out of the corner of my eye as I reach out to the phoenix, asking, "Mom?"

When I touch it, it glows slightly, transforming into Brittnie. "Jules?" We gasp and pull each other in for a hug, tears flowing freely down both of our faces.

"I missed you so much."

"So did I." She pulls back to look me up and down. "You've gotten so big."

I chuckle softly. "It's what happens."

"What are you doing here? How are you here?"

Grimacing, I glance at the Phoenix-King, explaining, "I don't really know."

"Well, I'm just glad you are."

"What even is this place? Are you happy here?"

"I've been here so long, and I still don't believe it sometimes. It's unreal . . . magical. I'm as happy as I could be without you and your Father."

"What do you do here?"

"I just am," she answers, shrugging.

I look down, preparing to ask a difficult question. "Did I kill you?"

Her expression softens, and she lifts my chin to stare into my eyes. "No, of course not. I gladly gave my life. It's not your fault."

"I don't really see how that's true. I was born, and you died. How is that not my fault?"

"I was already dead. Living a life not worth living. If anything, you freed me. I just regret that you had to take my place in that life. If anything, it's my fault you went through everything you did." I tense, remembering my childhood. She brushes my cheek with her thumb, saying, "And despite all of that, you turned out to be such a great man. A hero. I am so proud of you."

Tears well in my eyes again, and I grab onto my Mother's hand. "But I'm not a good man."

"How can you think that?"

"I can't bring myself to care enough about the war that is destroying the world. I just can't fight anymore. That's why they're letting you talk to me, isn't it? To get me to fight?"

She looks away, nodding. "I suppose, but I won't try and tell you what to do. I just want you to be happy no matter what. The world will keep spinning if you choose yourself and your own happiness."

"But maybe it won't."

"Maybe. But if you dwell on maybes, anything can be impossible or deadly. You need to let the maybes go and hope for the best, or you'll never be able to truly live."

"Our time with you has come to an end," the Phoenix-King declares.

We nod at the Phoenix-King before staring at each other. "I love you, Mom," I whisper.

"I love you too, Jules." We hug tightly. "I don't know if I can let you go again."

"Me either. Perhaps since I know where you are, I can come see you more often."

Brittnie pulls back to look into my eyes. "I don't think they'll let us. They only did this time because they think I could change your mind."

"Then this is probably goodbye again, at least for a while."

"I guess so." Tears well in our eyes again as we hug one last time. "Follow your heart." We pull back and wipe our eyes. I turn and slowly step back through the portal.

CHAPTER 123: MORTAL NIGHTS

<u>**Arien**</u>

Appearing in the kitchen, I let my emotions wash over me. Otus stares at me and stammers, "Arien?"

I turn and put on a brave smile, replying, "Hey."

"Where have you been all day?"

"All day?"

"Yeah."

Shrugging slightly, I shake my head, saying, "Nowhere really. Just needed to work some things out."

"Looks like it helped."

"It did."

"Good. Well, we ordered pizza and are all playing board games in the living room. Want to join?"

"I'd love to."

"Great. Can you help me grab some beer?" We load our arms with booze and head to the living room. Emma, Charlie, and Clara are sitting on the floor around the coffee table, setting up Clue.

Emma coos, "Ah, ah, more booze."

I pass out the drinks and kiss Clara on the forehead, sitting next to her. "Hey."

"Hey. You alright?"

"Never better."

"I'm glad you're feeling better," she says, smiling brightly.

"That fight just took a lot of juice out of me. I'm good now."

"I'm glad. Have you decided what you're going to do?"

My face constricts slightly, and I whisper, "Can we not talk about this now?"

Clara nods slightly, worried. "OK. Sorry."

"It's alright."

"Who wants to do shots?" Emma shouts.

Everyone cheers and starts getting their drinks. Charlie pulls a special bottle from her bag and pours her shot from it. "What's that, Charlie?" I ask.

"Oh, it's a potion of my own making. All the benefits of drinking with none of the side effects, especially pregnancy related."

"Sweet." We all raise our shot glasses together. "Cheers." Downing the glasses, we grimace from the taste.

"Oh, god. What even is that?" Emma mutters.

"I don't know. I found it in the cellar," Otus replies, lifting the bottle to check the label. "It says 1912 Irish whiskey."

"Well, it pacts a wallop, even for a god."

"Wanna do another one?"

"Hell, yeah. Bottoms up."

"I'm going to need a lime this time," Clara stammers, still recovering. We laugh and pass out another shot.

Afterward, I cough, "Wow, that really is awful."

Charlie swipes Emma's lime and eats it before she can. Emma cries, "Hey. That's my lime."

"What are you going to do about it?" Charlie asks with a smile, a piece of lime still sticking out of her mouth.

"Take it back."

"You can try." Emma smiles and kissed Charlie, taking the lime.

Pretending to be grossed out by the PDA, I say, "So, what game are we playing?"

"I thought we'd start with Clue."

"Let's do it." We finish setting up the game and dealing the cards. "Let's see. Otus, you go first."

"OK." He rolls and moves his piece. "I'm going to say it was Colonel Mustard in the conservatory with the pistol."

"Wait," Clara shouts. "I heard of this drinking game version where anyone who shows one of those cards does a shot."

"Sounds fun. So, I will do a shot." I do a shot before showing Otus the card.

"OK, my turn," Emma says, rolling and moving her piece. "I'm going to say it was Miss Peacock in the bathroom with the wrench." Charlie does a shot and shows Emma a card.

The front doorbell rings, interrupting us. "I'll get it," I say, jumping up to answer it. It's the pizza. I quickly pay and take it, stopping when Clara walks up beside me. "Oh, hey. This smells good, doesn't it?" I open the lid and look at the pizza, adding, "Oh, damn. Otus ordered Hawaiian again. Pineapple does not go on pizza."

"I need to talk to you," Clara says, her eyes filled with concern.

"OK."

"Are you sure you're alright? You're acting strange."

I sigh and shrug. "Yeah, I think I am."

"Then where'd you go earlier?"

"I tried to talk to my Father to get advice. He was too far gone to help. Then I saw something amazing. I was pulled into a place that doesn't make any sense, but my Mother was there."

Clara's eyes widen in shock, and she stammers, "Your Mother?"

"Yeah, but it wasn't the Underworld. It was something else. An afterlife for phoenixes. She told me to be happy and choose my happiness. I'm still not going to fight, but I don't know what I'm going to do besides that. I'm just coasting on the high of seeing her again. I think I can be content."

She smiles and nods, conceding, "I'm happy for you." Squeezing my arm for support, she adds, "Why don't you say we take this pizza to the others? You know how a pregnant woman gets when she's hungry."

"Alright." I smile, and we return to the others, greeted by shouts of joy for food.

Charlie asks, "What took so long?"

"I was busy deciding whether or not to throw it away because Otus decided to put pineapples on it again."

"Not cool, man," Emma says, throwing a glare at Otus.

"What?" Otus defends. "It's so good." We laugh and start eating. "So, where were we? It's your turn, Charlie?" We continue playing, all ignoring the impeding cloud of war coming for us.

CHAPTER 124: MOTHER OF MAIDENHOOD

<u>Arien</u>

The night's revels left us all wasted and unconscious on the living room floor. My eyes slowly open, and I moan, the light searing my eyes. Slowly sitting up, I cradle my aching body. I stand and stumble to the kitchen to make coffee. When I go for creamer, I notice a few beers in the fridge left undrunk. I sigh and grab one, greedily drinking.

The sound of the doorbell ringing echoes through the house, making me moan and cover my ears. A moment later, the door opens, and I hear muffled voices. The voices trail toward me, and Otus leads Athena, dressed in Air Force blues, into the kitchen. Her uniform awakens my training, and I go to salute but stop myself, choosing to shake her hand instead, saying, "Ma'am."

She replies, "It's a pleasure to finally meet you officially."

I look up and down Athena's perfect uniform, noting, "I'm impressed you kept your blues looking so good after such a long drive."

"Decades of practice."

I notice Molly standing beside Otus and go to hug her. "Hey, Molly."

"How're you doing?" she asks. "I heard what happened with Anna. I'm sorry I told her where you were. Heard it was rough."

"Everything's alright."

She nods, glancing between Athena and me. "I'd better leave you guys alone then." Otus leads Molly away, leaving Athena and I to sit across from each other.

Breaking the awkward silence, I say, "I was surprised when Otus told me you were in the Air Force. I guess we have more in common than I'd thought."

"Where else would I go?"

"It's just, we could have met before and never have known it."

"I would have known. I've known who you were for a long time. I got you orders to Phoenix to meet Charlie, the most powerful first-life witch alive, and so you'd be near where Apollo kept his divinity. I even had Zephyrus create that tornado to give you my divinity."

Horrified by the revelation, I condemn, "A lot of people died in that tornado."

"I know. Zephyrus wasn't who I thought he was, and needed to be dealt with. I knew to do all of that because of what I saw inside of Erebus before this war even started."

Shaking my head, I stand to get another beer. "Do you want coffee or anything?"

"I think maybe you need the coffee if you're already drinking."

I nod slightly but still grab another beer. "The best hangover cure is more drinking." Sitting back down, I meet her sad look.

"I heard you're finished with us."

"I've done enough."

"I agree. You've given more to the gods than any hero before you."

I scoff softly, contending, "I'm no hero."

"Why do you say that?"

"I can't see myself that way. I'm just a coward who can't manage to die."

"I don't think you're a coward. Pain is a hard thing to outrun. Death may seem like an escape, but it never is. The pain always follows you."

"Not as a phoenix," I whisper.

She falters for the first time, asking, "What do you mean?"

"I've seen where phoenixes go in death. It's not so bad. It's untouched by the ills of the world. I could learn to be happy there."

"And what of the people you love? How will eternity without them be?"

I try to look strong, but that idea scares me. "I still won't fight."

"I don't want you to. I want you to be happy, just living. Maybe living with Clara and having a family."

"I can never have a family," I mutter, looking down.

"Why not?"

"Even if I wasn't forced to remain a virgin, I don't want any child to turn out like me. Who I am or even what I am."

"Once I take my divinity, you won't be a maiden goddess anymore." I look up suddenly, realizing she's right. She adds, "You can have the family that you do secretly want." Tears start to well in my eyes as she finishes, "I want you to stay here and build a life for yourself and Clara. Your fight is over. The one you were destined to create to replace you is almost here. You can rest now."

Clara

Barely awake, I sit with Charlie and Pluto bemoaning our headaches. Suddenly, from the kitchen, Arien yells, "Clara!"

I glance up, listening to the sound of him running through the house looking for me. "Arien!" I stand as Arien rushes into the room. "What is it? Is everything alright?" He doesn't say a word, he just leans in and kisses me for the first time. I pull back in horror and shock, asking, "What about your maidenhood?"

"It's gone."

I smile, filled with lust, and kiss him back fiercely. Charlie grabs Pluto and quietly slips out. I pull back suddenly from the kiss and stare into Arien's eyes. "Take me upstairs." He smiles and picks me up, carrying me up the stairs.

Once within the privacy of his room, I eagerly kneel and pull his pants off. Pausing to appreciate his size, I lean in, taking his entire cock in my mouth, gagging violently but pressing onward. I bob slowly, enjoying the taste and the feeling of his fingers through my hair. He moans at this unknown pleasure taking him.

I pull back, wipe my mouth, and stand to strip naked. He stares at my nude form, speechless and relishing in the sight. Undressing, he pushes me back onto the bed. I giggle softly, letting him climb on top of me. Reaching down, I spread my lips, my pussy already wet, begging for his virgin member. My other hand guiding him, he gently thrusts into me. We both moan softly.

The phoenix ignites inside Arien, warming his skin to a pleasant temperature, making me moan louder and grab his butt to push him deeper.

My moans grow louder and louder until I scream and finish, my heart skipping a beat and my body heat dropping.

He smiles and rolls off to pull the covers up over us. He gently motorboats between my breast, making me laugh. He pulls back to stare deep into my eyes. I whisper, "I love you."

"I love you too."

I lean in for a kiss, but Arien stops me. Raising an eyebrow in confusion, I ask, "What?"

He looks down in embarrassment, confessing, "It's kind of embarrassing, but I don't feel comfortable kissing after oral." I burst out laughing, making him blush and stammer, "Stop it. It's not funny."

"It's a little funny." My laughing slows, and I start staring sexily at him. "So, if I do this, you won't kiss me," I ask, crawling under the covers and down Arien's body. He tenses up as my head bobs slowly again.

CHAPTER 125: THE PRICE OF HEROISM

Molly

Debauchery of those you love is a hard pill to swallow, you can neither condemn them nor guide them; all you can do is love them despite their sin. I love Arien, but the excessive screams of the night make it hard for me; such sin is a stain. Recovering from a sleepless night filled with worry, I sit with Emma and Charlie, all drinking coffee, all equally exhausted.

Clara stumbles into the kitchen, her eyes bleary, hair disheveled, and a large robe her only garment. We watch her greedily inhale a cup of coffee. With a smile, Charlie coyly asks, "Long night, huh?"

Clara grunts, grabbing another cup of coffee. "I didn't get any sleep last night."

"None at all?"

"That guy is a man, let me tell ya. His stamina is insane, and he recharges like it's nothing."

Pretending to be one of the girls but wanting this line of conversation to end, I say, "Ew, that's my cousin you're talking about."

Providing the needed distraction, Arien skips into the kitchen, completely rested, declaring, "Morning, everyone." He gives Clara a quick kiss, grabs a muffin, and whistles as he leaves.

The other girls all turn to smile at Clara. Charlie notes, "He doesn't look so tired."

"I think I hate him. I really do," Clara whines. The others burst out laughing, and I join in without mirth, egging Clara to add, "That's way too much stamina for a virgin. He wiped me out."

"He's not a virgin anymore. Aww, you deflowered him."

"How much stamina are we talking?" Emma asks. "How many rounds did he go?"

Biting her lip, Clara confesses, "Eight." Everyone stares at her in disbelief.

"Nuh-uh."

She smiles and nods. "Yeah."

"Really? I didn't think that was possible for a man."

"Was that eight for you or him?" Emma rationalizes.

Clara's grin widens. "Both."

The girls stare in awe; Charlie mutters, "As a lesbian, even I've rarely experienced that."

"And he had this thing he did with the phoenix, warming me in all the right places. It was . . . magical."

Charlie shakes her head in amazement, saying, "That's incredible. I'm happy for you."

"It was pretty great, but I think I'm gonna need to nap till the sun dies. The only sleep I got last night is when I was knocked out after one of the times." The girls all moan in jealousy, giving Clara time to take a bite out of her muffin.

Not wanting to be a part of this sin any longer, I glance out the window for a reasonable excuse to leave. My discomfort is replaced with guilt upon seeing Otus outside hauling a bag of birdseed. Deciding resolution is necessary, I sigh and stand, announcing, "I'll be right back, guys." I feel their curious eyes behind me as I go to join Otus.

He's walking around the garden and refilling several bird feeders when I approach him, whispering, "Hey."

Unable to meet my gaze, he mutters, "Hey."

We both stand around awkwardly for a moment until I ask, "So, ah, what are you doing?"

"Oh, I'm refilling the bird feeders. I try to get out here every morning to refill them."

"That's sweet."

"I guess so."

"Why do you do it?"

"They're not so different from me."

"Right, you turn into an owl. Make sense."

"Yeah."

The awkward silence restored, we look away from each other, my foot brushing through the dirt. "Hey, I just wanted to say, I'm sorry for brushing you off back at the diner. It wasn't cool of me."

"You don't need to apologize. You get used to it."

"Well, you shouldn't. You're a great guy. A little weird sometimes, but in a lovable way."

"I guess."

"I just can't think about being with anyone right now. My whole life perspective just got shattered. I need some time to think about myself. Redefine myself without Christianity. Think about what I believe in. It may take years."

He nods in understanding, affirming, "I get it. You don't need to feel bad about it. We can just be friends."

"I'd like that," I say with a soft smile.

We hug briefly but are interrupted by Arien sticking his head out a window and shouting, "Hey, Otus. You busy?"

We pull back suddenly, and Otus replies, "No, why?"

"I was hoping we could train a little."

He turns back to me, asking, "Do you mind?"

"Of course not."

"Thanks. I'm glad we can be friends."

"Me to."

He smiles, walking back toward the house.

Arien

Otus and I prep to work out, me excitedly divulging all events of the previous night. "I think I'm officially a boob guy. I've been on the fence between ass and tits, but after last night. Wow. I love boobs so much."

He turns away to hide his jealousy, muttering, "I'm happy for you."

Noticing his discomfort, I change the subject, "Did Athena leave?"

"She was going to say goodbye, but you were busy, so she left for Olympus."

"They still haven't taken it even with the army of the dead?"

"Well, Kronos finally came down from the moon to join the fray. He's decimating our forces. But I thought you don't care anymore."

I look down in embarrassment, mumbling, "I don't. I'm just curious."

"Right. Well, Athena asked all of us if anyone wanted to go with her."

"And you didn't want to go, with her being your patron goddess and all?"

"She's not anymore."

"Oh?" I ask with raised brow.

"I follow you now."

Unsettled by this revelation, I turn away, saying, "I'm not a god, though."

"But you're a good person, and that's more important."

I cough, shaking my head to change the subject. "What about the others? Emma?"

"Well, she wasn't going to leave Charlie, and she's not much of a fighter anyway."

Going to pick up a weight, I stumble, leaning against a padded column. A pounding headache slices through my consciousness, blurry my vision. I press my hand against my head, trying to stave it off, to no avail.

"Hey, are you alright?"

"I'm fine, it's just . . ." I grunt, the pain increasing.

Molly rushes into the room and stares at me, horror all over her face. "Sam!" I turn to her, but time seems to freeze. I look around in confusion at the frozen Otus and Molly.

***

Without my notice, I am no longer in the gym, I am in what must be the throne room of Olympus. The great hall of the gods is lined with ornate pillars stretching high above any human structure. From the doors the size of skyscrapers, the pillars guide the way to a ring of 12 thrones, all too large for any man to sit in. I turn and stare in awe at the sights, all beyond human sight or understanding.

I'm torn from my reverie when I see Kronos standing by Zeus's massive throne. Without turning to face me, he greets, "Hello, Arien."

My instincts taking over, I scream and summon the Aegis, attacking. Kronos doesn't even flinch as the Aegis-sword passes right through him. I freeze and stare at Kronos in anger, muttering, "Parley spell again?"

"Indeed."

Returning the Aegis to Erebus, I step back, saying, "I still didn't agree to this."

"A bridge once built can be crossed again."

I nod, turning again to look at the grand throne room. "So, this is Olympus?"

He smiles, amused. "Indeed."

"I suppose you just want to talk."

"I do."

"I don't want you to hear your bullshit about defending the Earth from Chaos. I've seen what you've been doing. Taking souls for god knows why."

Nodding, he concedes, "I apologize. That story was, as you put it, bullshit. This isn't about the lives of humans, gods, or even Titans. This is about reality itself. Chaos *is* coming, but not to destroy. To sanctify. It's one of the reasons that I fell in love with her."

"You're in love with Chaos?" I ask, giving him a curious look.

"I have been for a long time. She just wants to fix things. Fix everything that's ever gone wrong. She cares about humanity. They're her children too. She wants to end all their pain and suffering. But we must defeat the gods first. That's why I'm doing this. To make a better world for humanity."

"Just so you can rule it."

"Yes. Chaos and I will rule, but only to keep order." He turns, stroking his chin before looking back at me to add, *"The history of all hitherto existing society is the history of class struggles. Freeman and slave, patrician and plebeian, lord and serf, guildmaster and journeyman, in a word, oppressor and oppressed, stood in constant opposition to one another, carried on an uninterrupted, now hidden, now open fight, that each time ended, either in the revolutionary reconstitution of society at large, or in the common ruin of the contending classes.* I wrote those words. The gods created a system where pain was the only reward, and I will break that system. There will be no classes, no hierarchy, only equality in everything because everyone will be the same. The world will have peace. It will be a Utopia."

"But you'll still rule."

"Only to maintain the new world order."

Recognizing this as the age-old debate of communism versus freedom, society versus the individual, free-will versus uniform indenticalism, I contend, "All this will do is take away people's individuality, their will to excel, and no effort will be made to become better than we are. We'll regress as a species into laziness. Nothing will ever be accomplished, leading to starvation and the eventual destruction of everything."

"I won't let that happen. Chaos and I will ensure humanity will do what work is needed for their own survival."

"That sounds like slavery. You'll have just turned humanity into cogs in a wheel."

"Perhaps, but by taking away their individuality, we'll also take their pain." I falter slightly at the thought. Smiling, Kronos continues, "I've been using politics and media to make people war with each other, but also make them apathetic and weak. I'm slowly taking away free will as a gift to Chaos. I'm just trying to reset everything to before the gods turned everything sour. Chaos will reclaim everything and start over. But I can't give humanity to her until all the gods are dead. I need their spirits to free the souls of humanity trapped in the last vestiges of the old system, so I can give them all to her." He smiles again, shaking his head. "I can't deceive you anymore. I know you can never fight for this perfect world. I brought you here in hopes that you would, but I see it's impossible. Despite what you tell the world, you need your pain. You're defined by it and will always fight against those who try and take it away.

A tear leaks out of the corner of my eye, and I nod. "You're right. I want to let go of my pain more than anything, but you are right. I need it. There's no true joy without true sadness. You'd take my sadness, but then also my happiness, and I have to hold onto that. It's all I have."

"I'm sorry to hear that. I'll need to rely upon my insurance then."

"What?"

"I'm sorry, but I have your friend Anna."

"Anna?" Horror fills me, my mind filling with dozens of questions on how this could have happened. A scuffle behind me makes me turn and see Atlas dragging Anna behind him, her eyes blank of expression or life.

Kronos explains, "I know you want to let your pain go, but you can't make the decision to do it on your own. So, I'll make it for you, as I will for all of humanity in Utopia. Her life depends on your inaction. I don't want to hurt her, she's a beloved child of Chaos, but I will if I have to. I just want you to choose what you need, not what you want. You both can be together in Utopia if you wish."

My face constricts as I wrestle with the deal. I gaze into Anna's expressionless eyes, deciding.

Sighing and shaking my head, I turn back to Kronos, declaring, "I know what happens in situations like this well enough to know you're going to kill her no matter what."

"I don't want to hurt her, but I will if you come here. I know how much she means to you. Think about it."

I close my eyes, a loud ringing filling my ears.

CHAPTER 126: STILL VICTIM

<u>Arien</u>

I'm suddenly back in the gym, no time having passed. Time resumes, and Molly rushes over to Otus and I. Her terror-stricken face gives me pause; I forget about my recent order to ask, "What is it, Molly?"

"It's Charlie."

"What?" My question is answered by the sound of Charlie screaming violently. Without hesitation, I race through the manor until I find Charlie in the kitchen. She's sprawled on the floor, screaming and thrashing, blood coating her and the ground. I grab her hand and look up at Emma, who's cradling Charlie's head, to ask, "Is she going into labor?"

"It's too soon," Emma cries. "She's not due for weeks. I'm trying to stabilize her with magic, but nothing's working." We look down in horror at the expanding pool of blood, realizing at the same time that Charlie is losing the baby. A tear leaks out of my eye at the sight. Emma stares at the tear with hope, exclaiming, "You're crying."

"What? Yeah, I guess. What are we going to do?"

Without another word, Emma reaches out and takes my tear, dropping it onto Charlie's cheek. The tear glows and sinks into her skin, making it glow with a fiery light. The light fades, but Charlie continues to scream in pain. "It didn't work."

None of us know what to do; I shake my head to clear it, but I'm having a hard time thinking. Molly shouts, "Sam, we need to get her to a hospital. Maybe they can do something for her."

"OK. Everyone grab on," I reply with a nod. Everyone grabs hold and we disappear in a dark flash.

***

We appear in the bustling E.R. in the center of the floor. Nurses and other patients scream and stumble back in fear at our sudden appearance. Charlie's face appears to melt and shift as if it's changing. Her eyes turn to gold, and she screams in a deep-pitched voice, "I shall walk in starlight. The endless nothing will fear my name. I am the savior, the bringer of death. I must never die." She turns her golden gaze on Clara, cackling, "The empty will claim your soul and burn you to his core."

Clara stares at Charlie in horror as I ask, "What's happening?"

"It's the baby, Emma explains. "Fighting to stay alive."

Charlie's eyes clear, and her face reforms at the sound of Emma's voice. "Emma?"

"I'm here, baby."

Charlie smiles, reaching up to cup Emma's cheek with a blood-soaked hand. "Make it stop," she begs.

Tears stream down both Emma and Charlie's faces as they hold each other. Emma coos, "Hang in there."

She holds Charlie tight, leaving me to stand and rush to the front desk, where a nurse stares at me. I shout, "We need a doctor. She's losing her baby."

The nurse picks up her phone to connect to the P.A. systems, saying, "I need a gurney in the E.R. immediately."

I nod my thanks, returning to Charlie. "It's going to be alright, Charlie." She smiles at me before her body is racked with a seizure. Several nurses rush over with a gurney and help Charlie onto it, wheeling her away.

We try and follow, but a nurse holds us back, saying, "Sorry, no one beyond this point." We watch in horror, getting what may be our final glimpses of Charlie.

CHAPTER 127: DEALS MADE

<u>Charlie</u>

There's nothing, nothing except a wide white expanse, pure of smudge or stain. I stand alone in this whiteness. "Hello." I slowly turn to see my son Adonis full-grown and standing before me.

"Adonis?" I ask, barely able to believe it.

He smiles sadly at his Mother, replying, "Hi, Mom."

"What's going on?"

"I need to say goodbye."

"Goodbye? We haven't even met, not yet."

"And we won't. I wanted to see your face before I leave you."

Tears stream down my face; I reach out to cup his face, demanding, "That's not going to happen. I won't let it."

"You won't have much of a choice."

"I'll find a way."

"We'll both die if you try."

"At least we'll be together."

"You have work yet to do. My work is done."

"You're needed too, and not just by me," I say, setting aside my selfish wants and thinking of humanity. "Apollo said you're the key to the future. Only you can save us all. Without you I'm . . . we're doomed."

"You'll have to be the key now. I can't be."

"No. There must be a way."

"Not for my body."

I give Adonis a curious look, an idea coming to me.

<u>Doctor</u>

My patient is sound asleep on the operating table, attached to a dozen machines measuring her vitals while I perform an emergency C-section. Her body tenses suddenly, and she thrashes in the throes of a seizure, her heartbeat skyrocketing. "Hold her down," I shout. The nurses help me keep her still. "What's going on? Are her anesthesia levels wrong?"

A tech checks the levels, shaking her head. "No, doctor."

"Then what, the hell, is wrong?" The girl's seizure slows to a stop. I tentatively let go of her, lifting my tools again. "Increase the anesthesia a little. Can't have that happening again."

Arien

Molly, Clara, Otus, and I wait in the hospital lobby, our patience gone. I pace back-and-forth, breathing heavily while the others sleep in the lobby chairs. Clara slowly opens her eyes and watches me pace. She sighs, standing and walking to me to say, "Come here."

She pulls me in for a hug, letting me release my pent-up tears. "I can't lose her, Clara."

"I know."

"Why isn't there anything I can do? I need to help her."

She pulls back to look into my eyes, saying, "The only thing you can do for her is sleep. When she wakes up, she'll want you to be there, rested, and by her side."

"What if she wakes up while I'm asleep?"

"She's still in surgery. The doctors will let us know when they're done. At least sleep until then. There's nothing else you can do for now."

"Are you sure?"

"Yeah, I'm sure."

I think for a moment, eventually nodding. "OK."

"Come on." She leads me to sit down, letting me lay my head in her lap. She runs her fingers through my hair as I stare into the distance.

I slowly close my eyes, letting sleep take me.

***

I step through the portal and into the Perfect No Place. My face set in determination, I approach the Phoenix-King. He asks, "Have you come to a decision?"

"That depends on you."

"What do you require?"

"You said you exist in all time and space, right? My friend Charlie, you're going to go back and save her baby."

"We cannot. It would create a paradox that would destroy your world."

Tears stream down my cheeks, and I scream, "I don't care! You're going to do it, do anything to save them. Neither will have to feel this way. To feel this pain. You will make sure of that."

"We cannot."

I fall to my knees in despair, whimpering, "There must be something you can do."

"There is one way that I can help."

I look up at the Phoenix-king with hope, asking, "How?"

"The child's impending death is not an accident."

I stand and approach him, hissing, "Who could have done this?"

"That has been hidden from us. All we know is that it was an unnatural event that changed the future in ways no oracle can foresee. Behold what little we can see."

I step forward to gaze into the lava. The surface of the pool of lava clears to reveal an image of London in ruin, long since destroyed. "What happened?"

"An imbalance of untold size. There will be so little left of humanity to keep the balance for. This future will happen no matter what, but you can undo it."

"How do I do that?"

"You know how." My face sets in determination, so he asks, "Will you give your power to one who will fight for the balance?"

"No."

The Phoenix-King almost appears to smile before spreading his wings and cawing.

I stumble back in surprise as the Council of Fire soars down to each land on the pillars surrounding the lava pool. The Phoenix-King looks at me and nods, commanding, "Go and bring balance to the world."

I nod in reply, returning through the portal.

***

To my surprise, I do not return to the hospital but to the Israeli hill with Timorian. He greets, "Tis good to see thee."

I tense with anger, attempting to contain it. "I have nothing to say to you. I'm done with this debate of you versus Kronos. You let him kill my friend's child. If you can't even stop that, then there's no point in caring about a difference."

"Mine Father hast killed a child?"

"A babe not yet born." Tears fill my eyes, and I'm forced to turn away, adding, "He didn't get a chance to even see his Mother's face. To feel loved. To be held."

"Thou saw him do it?"

I turn and shrug, answering, "No, but who else would have or could have done this? My tears couldn't even heal her."

"I did not see this act of which you speak, by I hast seen such things before. Mine Father is more than monster enough."

I clench my fist, declaring, "I'm going to kill him."

Timorian looks down and nods. "I knoweth that thou must do what is needed."

"I'll be killing you too."

"I hath been dead for millennia. The time has come to make it official."

"Where are you? Olympus?"

"I am in the throne room waiting for thee. Thou shouldest know that a plot is afoot to steal thy powers from thee."

"They can try."

CHAPTER 128: MESSIAH LOST

<u>**Arien**</u>

I slowly open my eyes to see Otus and Clara awake and sitting next to me. Clara asks, "Hey. How are you feeling?"

Rubbing my eyes, I sit up, replying, "Better. Have we heard anything?"

"No. Nothing's changed."

Moly returns and passes out coffee, saying, "Morning. I can't attest to the quality of this coffee, but it's the best they've got."

I greedily drink it. "It's great, thanks." I look up and see a nurse typing at the front desk, so I squeeze Clara's knee and stand to approach the nurse.

She asks, "How can I help you?"

"Hi, I was wondering if you could tell me the status of Charlie Bills."

She searches her computer for Charlie's file, saying, "Let's see, Charlie Bills. Here we go. Looks like she's still in surgery."

"Have they found anything? Do they know what caused this?"

"There's nothing in the file. I'm sure they just haven't updated it. The doctor will come and tell you if anything changes."

"Thank you."

"Arien, where is she?" I turn to see Apollo behind me, frantically shouting.

"She's still in surgery."

"What happened?"

"We don't know yet. She just started screaming and bleeding. None of us could heal her, and her voice went all deep and her face--I don't know. Melted for a second."

He turns away, muttering, "No, no, no. This isn't how it's supposed to happen."

"What do you mean?"

"The child is supposed to do something essential for the future."

Utterly confused, I ask, "What are you talking about?"

"I had a vision. The child is key to proving to the world the gods' capacity for good. He needs to be the best of us."

"He'd become a god?"

"Yes. But without him, all that I can see in store for us is blood. You were never meant to be the hero of this story. You were what was needed to create him. That's what Athena saw in Erebus. You made the future possible, you were our tool to make it. But now there's no hope. You were never meant to carry the burden of our salvation. It's not your destiny."

"Does that mean I'd lose?" I whisper, not wanting the answer. He gives me a strained look but is interrupted by Emma rushing into the room, a horrified expression on her face. I run to her and ask, "Emma, what's wrong?"

Tears stream down her face as she mumbles, "She lost the baby."

I collapse into a chair, and the girls gather around Emma to comfort her. Clara says, "I'm so sorry."

Apollo reaches down and squeezes my shoulder before leaving, tears welling in his eyes. I stare into the distance, ignoring everyone around me. I suddenly clutch my fist in anger.

***

Eventually, we're allowed to see Charlie. We spend the day with her, Emma holding one hand and me the other. Despite that and Pluto's warmth on her chest, Charlie refuses to wake, life-support barely keeping her alive.

Her hand squeezes suddenly; my eyes go wide and glaze over.

I see a memory, not mine or Charlie's but from the Odyssey. Odysseus and Calypso walk hand in hand down the beach. She smiles up at him, not a care in the world on her face, just love.

I'm pulled back to the present; I shake my head to clear it, staring at Charlie in surprise. The vision must have come through her somehow. Reaching out to brush a lock of hair out of her face, I whisper, "There you go. All better now." Tears overwhelm me again; I press Charlie's hand against my face, trying to feel a connection. Molly touches Clara and Otus on the arm, herding them out of the room. I wipe my eyes, coughing softly. "I can't do this without you. I can't lose you too."

"Please," Emma begs. "She's not gone yet."

I look up at Emma to see tears filling her eyes too. "Why can't we help her?"

"I don't know. This is beyond me."

"I think it was Kronos."

She stares at me in shock. "Why?"

"My gut. There's something supernatural going on here."

"But why would the Titans do this?"

"To warn me that there's no line they won't cross. They have Anna."

"Oh, god," she whispers, tensing softly.

I turn to stroke Charlie's cheek, fire burning in my eyes. "I'm going to kill them all. I'm not going to rest until they burn. For you, Charlie." I stand and walk out, leaving Emma alone.

Outside in the hall, I walk with purpose past the others, but Clara chases me down, crying, "Arien." I slowly turn to her but don't reply. She asks, "What's going on?"

"Kronos has Anna, and I think he did this to Charlie."

"Oh, my god. What are you going to do?"

"Save Anna and kill them all."

"I'm coming with you."

"No. I need you to stay here. Please. I have to do this alone."

She thinks for a moment before nodding. "OK. Good luck." She kisses me gently before I turn and walk away, leaving her alone in the bustling hallway.

CHAPTER 129: ENGINES OF WAR

Atlas

Humbling myself, I kneel before my lord upon his throne, I proffer, "My lord."

"Did you find the Father?"

Standing, I shake my head. "Not yet. I'm setting a trap for him reliant to his madness."

A shapeshifter wearing the girl Brittnie's face walks up behind me and bows before Kronos. "My lord, Kronos."

A faint smile cracks Kronos's face.

Arien

All the gods save Emma are gathered together in the Dion Museum, preparing for the assault. Their robes are those of their classic era, their classic weapons held close, though Poseidon's Trident is noticeably missing its center spike. I storm in, and everyone falls silent, showing deference to me. "I'm in, but I'm in command." They all look at each other, eventually nodding. I continue, "Good. Now, is there a way to pull Olympus out of its half-dimension to boost our prayer intake?"

"I designed the machine that conceals it," Hephaestus answers. "I can send a signal to disable it."

"Good. The plan is simple. I'm going for Kronos. The rest is on you." I turn and walk out without another word, feeling their fear-filled gazes following me.

Soon I'm standing on the slopes of Olympus at the head of an army consisting of 12-foot gods, all matter of magical creatures, and the bodies of the dead. The gods are all standing in their classic chariots, each reliving the war of Pompeii in their minds, unwilling to repeat that day.

I turn and nod at Hephaestus, who activates a device. A shockwave bursts out of the device and toward the empty peak of Olympus. It crashes into a magical barrier and expands to encompass it. As the shockwave expands, it reveals the city of Olympus mounted in the crater on top of the barren mountain. The awe-inspiring sight doesn't even phase me as I stare at it.

Producer

After the giant, I never assumed we'd get a bigger or crazier story, but the helicopter footage coming in seems to disprove that assumption. Robin stares at the footage of a great city getting pulled into focus atop Mount Olympus. Her jaw drops before she shakes her head to clear it, reporting, "That's impossible. For those of you at home, witness final proof that gods walk among us. I only pray that they emerge victorious, and I ask that you all do the same. We now go to our foreign correspondent, April Kent, for local coverage of the event."

The broadcast switches to a reporter in Greece talking about Olympus while Robin slumps, a tear leaking out of the corner of her eye. She takes off her glasses to clean them, relishing in the routine. I approach her and say, "Robin."

"What is it?"

"An anonymous source just reached out to us with the name of the fighter in Antarctica."

"What?" Robin takes my iPad to look at a picture of the boy Arien. "Are we sure?"

"He was there for every strange occurrence in the last few weeks, including Sydney. According to this source, he's leading the charge in Greece, and he needs our help."

Arien

The time of war has come, the time of reckoning; none shall escape my wrath.

I raise my arm to call for a charge but stop when I see Atlas on the battlements of Olympus. A ringing fills my ears, making me tense up. I'm suddenly on the battlements of Olympus with Atlas and the blank Anna. I glare up at Atlas and growl, "Parley?"

"Yes."

"What do you want?"

"I think you know." Atlas forces Anna to eat a handful of moly herb, awakening her mind. She stares around in horror, bursting into tears, and asking, "Sam, what's going on?"

"It's going to be alright."

"It will, if you back off," Atlas demands.

I give Anna a strained look and turn back to Atlas, saying, "Why'd you have to kill the baby too? You already had the leverage you needed."

He raises an eyebrow, smiling. "I don't know. If I did do something like that, it might be because I want you here. That might also be a good reason for me to do this." He slits Anna's throat, and I scream. Anna goes limp and topples toward the edge of the battlements. I try to catch her, but she passes right through me and tumbles to the ground, far below.

I stare at Atlas in horror, crying, "You didn't have to kill her."

"You knew the deal, and you broke it."

I clench my jaw and leap at Atlas; he smiles as I vanish, returned to my place at the head of my army. Anna's body hits the ground far below the massive walls, rolling hundreds of yards down the hill, stopping at my feet, her empty eyes staring up at me in reproach.

The sight of her corpse makes my rage build, lighting the phoenix on its own.

All sound dies away; I stare up at Atlas, whispering, *Once more into the breach.*" Clenching my jaw, I summon the Aegis and whisper again, "Charge."

The army behind me roars and charges. News helicopters circle high above as I lead the charging army toward the gates of Olympus.

CHAPTER 130: THE SIEGE OF OLYMPUS

Atlas

Smiling down at the charging army, I grow to my full height and heft my new battle-ax. I look up into the air, watching several gods launch their chariots into the sky. Apollo and Artemis swing the sun and moon chariots toward me, firing blasts of sun and moonlight at me. I just smile as they bounce off of the magical barriers around the city.

Arien

The gods all swell in size, and my eyes turn black filled with white-hot flames, the prayers of humanity strengthening us. My anger and grief open my connection to Erebus more than ever before, creating a cloud of darkness that expand out of me. The darkness envelopes Olympus, darkening the sky. Cyclopes start to try and beat the gates down with massive clubs, but they bounce off harmlessly.

The darkness deepens, and my phoenix fire grows brighter. My hair ignites into flames and grows to become a full mane of fire, my fiery eyes piercing through the darkness. Only the phoenix, a few torches, and the gods' chariots illuminate the city now.

The cyclopes cannot break down the magical gates, so I step forward, reaching out and placing a hand upon the metal of the gates, lighting it on fire. The fire expands, melting the metal and breaking the enchantments. I step aside for the cyclopes, who finally beat the gates down and break the magical barrier around the city.

BOOM!

I walk into the city to be greeted by an army of tall Titans, giants, monsters, and men. Both armies roar and break against each other like the tides of the sea. Swinging the Aegis, I cut down enemies like wheat, seamlessly changing the Aegis into different shapes to combat my many foes.

A dragon slithers out of an alley and spits poison at me, which I barely block with the Aegis. I manage to dodge a dragon bite, leaping into the air and impaling the Aegis-spear deep into the bottom of the dragon's mouth. The dragon struggles to get free, to no avail. I reach up and touch its flaming nostril; it bursts into flames and melts away.

Lifting the Aegis-spear off of the ground, I rejoin the fray.

A flash of light in the darkness makes me turn; my phoenix is no longer the main beacon of light. Out of the ranks of the enemy, Hyperion saunters, using a beam of light to impale a satyr. He drops the satyr's corpse and approaches me, smiling. "Been a long time." I remain silent, just staring back, so he adds, "I've been waiting for this."

Hyperion roars and throws a beam of sunlight toward me; I don't even attempt to block it. He smiles at the sight of the beam impaling my chest. I just reach down and pull it out, my skin healing on its own.

Hyperion's smile fades as I launch the beam back at him.

He ducks just in time, and I charge. Blocking an incoming blow from the Aegis with a new beam, he tries to stab me with a second one. We exchange several blows with each other, but I'm merely playing with him. Hyperion manages to stab me in the eye with a small dagger-like beam.

I turn a venomous glare upon Hyperion, done playing around.

Quickly knocking Hyperion's beam aside, I impale him through the chest, returning the favor. He falls to his knees and grunts. The skin around the wound begins to burn and flake away. Staring down at the wounded Titan, I pull the beam from my eye, the eye healing immediately.

Hyperion stares up at me before spitting blood at my shoes. "Do it."

Complying, I yank the Aegis-sword out of his chest. As soon as I do, the flames expand faster over Hyperion's skin, crawling up his neck. I kick him in the chest, sending him flying back to disappear in a dark flash.

Turning away, I wade through a literal river of blood, cutting down enemies left and right on my way toward the palace at the top of the mountain.

Ares

Seeing Arien's rampage, I go to follow, but a maniai, a madness daemon, steps between us. The maniai smiles and rushes me. I try to stab it, but my blade passes through it, and the maniai passes into me.

I grunt and fall to the ground, convulsing. My eyes turn bloodshot, and I growl like an animal. Blood pours from my eyes, the sign of berserker rage.

I stand and roar, challenging the world itself to stand against me, to stand against my utter rage. Turning to my once allies, I cut them down without remorse. A group of the dead charge me and attempt to subdue me, but they're no match.

I cut down any in my path, filled with a crazed frenzy.

Artemis

With the barrier gone, I'm able to swoop the moon chariot in close to the battlements and rain a storm of arrows down upon the defenders.

But my glowing chariot becomes an easy target for enemy archers. A lone arrow soars from the dark, striking my lead mare through the heart. The chariot dives down toward the ground; I grab my weapons and leap over onto the battlements. I duck and roll, avoiding the chariot that swings over and nearly crushing me.

The chariot crashes down and rolls to a stop down the battlements from me. I get to my feet and rush to help my horses, but stop as the starry form of Orion steps over my mares. He's now framed by the moonlight of the crashed chariot, staring at me. Without remorse, he steps on the neck of the only surviving horse, crushing her throat. I scream, "No!" To finish the job, he impales her with his spear. I scream again in rage and charge.

Rolling to avoid several arrows that Orion fires at me, I return an arrow of my own. He multiplies into 3 smaller forms to avoid the shot. I switch to spear and stab at the Orions charging me.

They dodge several blows and land a few of their own before I impale one through the chest. It yells a silent scream and explodes, returning to the sky. The other Orions stare at me in horror, and I gloat, "Moonstone blade." I swing my spear around at another Orion, but a boulder crashes into the battlements, nearly crushing us before crashing into a group of the dead in the city below. I turn to see the 500-foot giant Porphyrion standing on the slopes of the mountain and throwing stones at our army. Apollo, in the sun chariot, turns to face the giant, flying toward him.

Apollo

Soaring high above the mountain, I pilot the sun chariot toward the giant Porphyrion, shouting, "Porphyrion, I thought you dead. My fault. I forgot that you're basically a giant cockroach. A total bitch to kill." Porphyrion roars and launches a boulder at me; I barely pull the chariot out of the way in time, again shouting, "Whoa there, big guy. No need to be so aggressive." I return fire with a volley of flaming arrows at his face. He roars in pain, the arrows burying themselves in his cheek. "Oh, I'm sorry. I'm out of practice. That was supposed to hit your eye and kill you. I never meant for it to hurt." I continue firing, circling his massive head, taunting him the whole while.

Artemis

I stab another Orion, leaving only one left. "You can stop, Orion. We were friends once."

Orion's jaw goes slack, and a raspy voice echoes out of him, stammering, "You--had me killed."

"I know, and I'm sorry."

"Look at . . . me. What I am. You did this to me."

"I'm sorry." I throw my spear and impale him, sending him back to the stars.

Emma

The hospital is silent, a tense dread tangible in the air. I try my best to ignore it, focusing on stroking Charlie's hand while she sleeps. "Wake up for me, honey. Please. I can't lose you too, not after everything else." A tear leaks out of the corner of my eye, and I smile slightly. "I was such a bitch before we met. For real. A total bitch. But you changed me. You gave me a reason to live again. To leave that little cabin in the middle of nowhere. To feel beautiful because of these scars." I unconsciously stroke the scars traversing my face, remembering their cause.

Charlie slowly opens her eyes and blinks slowly.

I gasp and lean closer to stroke her cheek. "Hey, honey. How are you feeling?"

She grimaces and presses a hand against her head, saying, "I'm alright. Just a little foggy. What . . . what happened?"

I look down, another tear sliding down my cheek. "Maybe it would be better if the doctor told you."

Her eyes fill with fear, and she demands, "Emma, tell me."

"You lost the baby," I confess with a sigh of defeat.

"Adonis is gone?" She breathes in deep, tears welling in her eyes.

"There's nothing you could have done."

"What happened?"

"No one knows. The doctors are running tests now, but they don't have any ideas. It looks like your body just rejected him."

"So, it's my fault?" she whispers, turning away.

"No, of course not. It might have been the . . ." I trail off, deciding not to add to her pain.

"What? It might have been what?"

I take a deep breath, continuing, "Arien thinks the Titans caused it."

She gasps and tenses up. "No, no."

"I'm sorry."

"Where is Arien?"

"He's gone to fight."

"No, he was done. He was finally going to have a happily ever after."

"He thought he was going to lose you, and he'll never have a happily ever after without you."

Poseidon

Oceanus towers over a group of satyrs, summoning a flood to drown them. I leap from my chariot to the street in front of the satyrs, slamming my broken Trident into the ground.

The flood crashes into a magical barrier made by the Trident and dissipates into the adjoining alleys. I turn to the terrified satyrs, commanding, "Go!" They flee, leaving me to turn to Oceanus, my old mentor and friend. Without a word, we send volleys of waves at each other, weaving against each other, each trying to find an opening.

Hades

Arien barely dodges a blast of water from Poseidon's water-bending duel, halting his carnage. Taking advantage of his distraction, the 3 furies dive from the sky and latch onto Arien, throwing him against the side of a building.

Before he can stand, they're on him again, tearing at his flesh.

From my Helm, I blast the furies back with a wave of darkness, freeing Arien from their clutches. He nods his thanks and continues his quest to the palace.

My black sword in hand and a group of the dead behind me, I approach the furies. One hisses, "Our master has come home. Should we kill him? Yes, I think we shall."

The furies screech and rush me. I just barely keep them back using my sword and the dead as shields. The furies all flick their fiery whips at me, wrapping them around my arms and neck, pulling me down. I grunt, the whips searing my flesh. With a roar, I send another wave of darkness out of the Helm, knocking the furies back. I yank on one of the whips, pulling a fury close enough to be impaled by my blade. The fury screeches and falls to the ground, dead. Slowly standing, I turn to the other furies, their sister's blood covering my face. I roar and attack.

Athena

Ares is swinging his blades wildly, trying to beat down my defenses. I use my shield to hold the manic god at bay, shouting, "Snap out of it, Ares." He just cackles, blood still filling his eyes.

I manage to graze him with a blow from my spear, which only makes him angrier. He roars and presses forward harder.

Artemis

Decapitating a monster, I turn to see Apollo still fighting Porphyrion in the distance with little success. Unable to help, I turn my attention down toward the gate where Athena is barely holding back the crazed Ares. Leaping down, I join Athena, but manic Ares is too strong even for both of us.

On the other side of the gate, Hephaestus is in a battle against a group of evil cyclopes, crushing their skulls with his massive hammer. He bashes several of them aside, rushing to help us in our fight against Ares. Even all together, Ares manages to keep us at bay.

Arien

I cut my way through griffins, harpies, giants, and all manner of monsters indiscriminately on my way to the palace. The only thing that stops me is a keres, a death spirit with flowing black robes and furled bat wings. She hisses, "Uncle." Not responding, I roar and charge. The keres dodges my first blow and reaches out to grab my head with a gauntleted hand. "Feel death." Phantom versions of me appear all around us, all dying in horrific ways, and I feel each death as if I were dying them all at once.

The keres's face turns to horror when the phantom Ariens all regenerate. Her gantlet begins to melt as I smile, whispering, "Death is an old friend." I stand and impale her with the Aegis-sword. She screams and turns to dust. Breathing heavily, I continue toward the palace.

Demeter

After stabbing a Gargarean with my sickle, I turn to see another fleeing down the alley.

I give pursuit, stopping when the Gargarean halts in front of a massive cage. He smiles and opens it. A catoblepas buffalo tentatively steps out. I lower my weapon and raise my hand in a sign of friendship to the catoblepas. "I don't want to hurt you. You're innocent." The Gargarean smiles wider, zapping the back of the cage with a cattle prod. A herd of catoblepi roar and stampede. Before I can react, I'm plowed down by the stampede. I huddle up to protect myself from the storm of hooves that crash down upon me.

When the herd has passed, I stumble to my feet and grab my sickle. The Gargarean's smile fades as I throw the sickle to impale him. I slowly lower myself to the ground to nurse my many injuries.

Zeus

Riding down on a lightning bolt, I crash into the streets of my old city with a bellow. Slowly standing straight, I turn my venomous eyes on the monsters all round me. A herd of manticores all send a volley of their spikes at me. I bellow again as the spikes bounce off me. The manticores try to retreat in terror, but I'm too fast. I zap one with a lightning bolt before proceeding to tear the rest apart.

Hephaestus

I manage to land a blow on Ares that disorientates him and gives the females a chance to drop their weapons and leap for his arms, pinning him to the ground. Athena shouts, "We've got to get this thing out of him."

"No. We could use him," Artemis contends. Athena and I look at her in surprise, and she affirms, "Trust me."

"What do you have in mind?"

Hades

I smile and stab the last fury, turning in time to see Oceanus raising his sword to kill Poseidon. Roaring, I send a wave of darkness at Oceanus, allowing Poseidon to lift his Trident and stab Oceanus in the chest. Oceanus falls to the ground and convulses, not dead but incapacitated for now. Poseidon hurries over to say, "Thanks for that. How are things going?"

"Our forces are crumbling. They won't hold for much longer."

"Hopefully, they hold long enough for Arien to get to Kronos."

Hermes cuts down a monster, rushing up to join us. "I have a plan of how we can help him."

"How?" my bother asks.

Hermes turns to me, explaining, "I'll need your Helm."

Dionysus

I'm thrown by a giant into a building; I crash through it and roll to a stop in an alley. Moaning, I sit up, grunting in surprise at the pack of cerastes serpents crawling all over me. I summon a swarm of vines to latch onto the snakes, but their spineless bodies easily free themselves. The snakes bite me over and over, their poison making me sluggish. Demeter rushes in and starts slashing at the snakes with her sickle, giving me time to pull myself out of the nest.

Hera

I stab at a giant's leg with my spear but miss. The giant turns and grabs me by the throat, lifting me up and choking me. I struggle against the giant until a lightning bolt erupts in his chest. He goes slack and falls to the ground. Coughing violently, I pull myself to my feet before seeing Zeus standing over the giant, Bolt in hand.

I smile and rush to kiss him in thanks. As we kiss, a centaur attempts to impale us with a spear, but it only bounces off my husband's back. Zeus glares at the centaur, who turns and flees, escaping Zeus's wrath.

"I missed seeing you like this," I say, stroking his exposed peck. "I missed you all of you."

"Does that mean we're still together?"

"I definitely think so."

He smiles broadly, whispering, "I wish we were alone right now."

"So do I."

"When this is over, we're going to have a long, *long* talk about this."

I chuckle softly, saying, "I look forward to it." We kiss again, returning to the fray.

Apollo

Landing the sun chariot in the courtyard, I help Hephaestus and Athena struggle to drag Ares into it. "What's the plan? We can't control Ares like this."

"We don't need to control him. Just aim him," Artemis answers.

I shake my head, conceding, "Your call, sis." The others hold Ares down as we take off, flying toward Porphyrion. Ares's thrashing becomes stronger, and he manages to free a leg, using it to kick Artemis off the chariot and down to the ground below. Hephaestus and Athena try to contain him, but he manages to knock them both out of the chariot as well. He stands and grabs me. "Fuck." I'm hurled from the chariot as well, just as Porphyrion tosses a boulder at the chariot, crashing it.

Ares leaps out of the wrecked chariot, two swords in hand, and charges Porphyrion. Porphyrion tries to kick Ares, but he rolls clear. Ares leaps up and uses his swords to climb the screaming Porphyrion. He reaches the giant's head and stabs him in the eye. Porphyrion roars in pain and stumbles back. Ares screams in bloodlust and repeatedly stabs the eye until Porphyrion goes limp. Porphyrion sways, falling face-first into the side of the mountain, smashing Ares underneath him.

We rush to the giant's corpse to search for Ares, finding him unconscious by the giant's head.

Hestia

Struck by a blow from a centaur, I crumple back against a building. I slowly sit up and shake my head to clear it. Before I can get up, a herd of centaurs rush me, each grabbing a limb to hold me down while the leader lowers his erect horse penis toward me. I grunt and struggle, fighting back, but the enormous rod enters me, making me scream and thrash, blood flying. Arien rushes into the square and roars when he sees the centaurs. He throws a beam of fire at the rapist, allowing me to free an arm and touch the rapist's forehead. He turns and screams, the sound of his family getting murdered echoing through his head.

Taking a centaur's sword, I kill the entire herd except for the rapist, who is still experiencing a vision. I walk around to stand in front of him, waiting for the vision to end. When it does, he stares up at me in horror. I smile and reach out to touch his cheek. The fire of the hearth flows through my body and turns the centaur to ash.

Arien

Continuing to cut down enemies in my trek toward the palace, I stop when I see Atlas standing upon the steps leading to the palace. I approach him but am interrupted by a giant attacking me. I slice the giant's knee, making him kneel before cutting off his head.

I continue toward Atlas, shouting, "I would have walked away, but you couldn't leave it alone."

"It's good you're here," he replies. "I need to be the one to kill you."

"I don't die."

"We'll see."

I roar and charge. We fight back-and-forth, neither getting the upper hand. Atlas is being smarter than our previous fights, keeping his distance. He swings a massive blow at me with his battle-ax, which I dodge, but as the ax swings by, it slices the top of my ear, making me stumble. I stare at the ax in shock, a large part of my power seems to fade.

Atlas coos, "You like it. Bit of an upgrade. I bathed it in the blood of the prayer spirits to absorb the prayers coming to you. I had a lot of it just lying around thanks to your friend. The humans can't help you now."

"I don't need them."

We re-engage, my anger overwhelming me and helping him push Atlas back. I scream and fire a blast of darkness at Atlas, knocking him to the ground. Seizing upon my advantage, I rush in for the killing blow but stumble at the last moment. I clutch my head, filled with pain. "What did you do to me?" I ask.

I suddenly see Erebus strapped down to an operating table by golden ropes. A creature with Brittnie's face pours eitr onto a knife and stabs Erebus, making him scream and thrash.

My sight returned to Olympus, I stumble again and fall to my knees, shaking my head. My eyes return to their normal blueness, and the cloud of darkness surrounding Olympus dissipates, allowing sunlight to stream in. "You have my Father?" I mutter.

Atlas slowly stands and smiles down at me, saying, "It's far too dangerous to connect with him while he's like this."

Struggling to my feet, I reply, "I still have the phoenix."

"Right." He stabs me in the stomach with a strange looking dagger. I step back and gasp. Ocean water starts streaming from all of my pores, putting out the phoenix.

Coughing up water, I stare up at Atlas, stammering, "What is this?"

He hefts his dagger, explaining, "This is a prong of Poseidon's Trident. I've shoved the ocean into you, making it impossible to light the phoenix. I've effectively taken all of your power, now you're just a man."

I stare up at Atlas in horror.

CHAPTER 131: THE FINAL YARD

<u>Clara</u>

Rushing into Charlie's room, I cry, "Emma, you've got to see . . ." I stop and gasp, seeing Charlie. "Charlie! You're awake." Otus and I hurry to her bedside.

She whispers, "Hey, guys."

"How are you feeling?"

"I'm alright. What's going on? What were you going to show Emma?"

"Oh, right." I grab the TV remote, turning it on. News coverage of the battle of Olympus is playing. Helicopter footage of Arien and Atlas fighting at the base of a palace plays over the screen, and Robin narrates, "We can't be certain, but it appears to be Arien Vlahos battling a giant in the square there."

"How do they know about him?" Charlie asks.

I explain, "We leaked his name so they could pray directly to him."

Charlie turns to look up at Emma, saying, "Go. He needs all of you."

"I can't leave you. Not now," Emma objects.

"I'll be alright. I'm on enough drugs that I probably won't remember this."

Emma chuckles softly through her tears and gently kisses Charlie, conceding, "I'll come back."

"I know you will."

I reach down and squeeze Charlie's shoulder, consoling, "We'll take care of her."

"Clara, I have something for you in my bag. Where is it?" Otus picks her bag up off the back of a chair and hands it to her. She starts digging through it, looking for something. "This stuff is hard to make, phoenix semen is impossible to come by. So, I wanted to save it for a special occasion. This seems as good as any." She pulls a potion from her bag and hands it to me.

"Did you say phoenix semen?" I ask.

"Well, you'd know all about that. Besides, only the real bird's stuff can be used for this potion. It's just basic strength."

"Alright, whatever." I down the potion and grimace.

Charlie pulls out two roman short swords from her bag and extends them to me, adding, "You'll need these too."

Arien

I fly off the stairs and slam into a building. Moaning, I roll to my knees, starting to choke on seawater. Atlas approaches and raises his ax to beat it down on me; I barely manage to block with the Aegis, still choking. I've always relied on brute strength to win fights and am now paying for it. Atlas continues to swing down at me, pushing him back. Without the phoenix to reforge the Aegis, chunks of it break off and fall to the ground. I grunt, and the final piece of the Aegis breaks away, leaving me defenseless. He smiles and lifts his ax for the killing blow.

BANG!

Atlas stumbles back, an alchemy bomb exploding against his chest. He looks up to see Emma, Otus, and Clara standing behind me. Emma walks around me to confront him. Atlas shouts, "You? Are you here to take everything else I have?"

Behind Emma, Clara helps me sit up, fighting the water pouring from my lungs. Otus says, "I'll find Poseidon," running off to find the god.

Emma shouts, "I'm sorry about Calypso. I really am. I loved her."

"Yet you killed her," Atlas replies.

"There's more to that story."

"Nothing I need to know. You killed her, and I'll kill you for it."

Otus brings Poseidon over, and he starts to draw the water from me. "No!" Atlas cries, trying to leap past Emma, but she swings her sword at him, forcing him back. He swings at her, and she barely blocks in time.

I gasp loudly, the last of the water is pulled from his body. I relight the phoenix, reforge the Aegis, and stand. Atlas grunts, backing away behind a horde of monsters, the chimera at its head.

We all heft our weapons and stare down the monsters. Emma cries, "Arien, you need to end this. We got them."

I nod as Atlas roars the command to charge. The two groups slam into each other, weapons flying everywhere. Atlas swings at me and is blocked by the Aegis, but before either of us can act, Emma tackles Atlas away from me. I continue up the stairs toward the palace but stop when I see the chimera standing in my way. It sends a blast of fire at me, which knocks me off my feet and knocks the Aegis from me.

It roars and bites down at me. I grunt and grab the chimera's jaws, forcing them apart and away from my neck. It growls, the fire building in its throat. My eyes widen just as I'm blasted by a wave of fire to the face, which sends me flying.

I roll to a stop at the bottom of the stairs. The chimera roars again, leaping at me. I grab a spear from a dead soldier, bracing it into the air and closing my eyes.

THUD!

I'm knocked to the ground by the force of the beast's attack. When no further attacks come, I open my eyes to see the spear impaled deep into the chimera's throat. Pushing the beast off me, I stand and grab the Aegis. Briefly looking back to see how my friends are doing, I head up the many flights of stairs toward the Palace of Olympus.

Atlas

I wholly decimate Aphrodite. I'm a far better fighter than she, but I keep wounding her to drag this out and enjoy my revenge. Once I've had enough, I swipe her feet out from under her and press my ax down toward her chest, which she only just holds back. "She was so beautiful, and you killed her," I hiss, tears welling in my eyes.

"I know she was," she whispers.

Grunting and falling to one knee, I allow her to slip out from under me. I shake my head to clear it, but the sound of the battle fades around me. The battle's gone and I'm in Hecate's cave, staring widely. "What are you doing to me?" I ask.

With a smile, Hecate lilts, "I warned you not to hurt one of my witches. I never thought even you were capable of killing an infant." Her lip rises in disgust despite my confused expression.

"What infant?"

"You should not have given up your ichor so easily because this is going to hurt." She pours a drop of my ichor into a fire, causing the flames to turn blue. I grunt, collapsing into a seizure.

I'm back on the battlefield, staring up at Aphrodite, pain transfixing my face. She screams, and she swings her sword, decapitating me. Everything goes black.

CHAPTER 132: DOWN IN FLAMES

The great doors of the throne room slowly open, granting entrance to a shadowy figure. Kronos doesn't turn from his place at the foot of Zeus's throne; he just smiles, whispering, "I was beginning to worry that you weren't coming." He turns to see not Arien but Hermes standing in the doorway, Helm of Darkness in hand. "You? What are you doing here?"

Hermes drops the Helm and hefts his Caduceus, saying, "I'm here to kill you."

"You'll never defeat me."

"I know."

"Then why are you doing this?" Hermes doesn't respond; he just tenses and charges. Kronos easily avoids all of Hermes's attacks, not even drawing the Scythe until a single cut draws blood from his cheek. Kronos checks the wound, glaring at Hermes and hissing, "Enough." He draws the Scythe and attacks, driving Hermes back toward the door. Hermes holds his own for a moment before Kronos runs him through. He grunts as Kronos pulls out the Scythe and looks down in surprise at it, expecting it to glow. "Where's your divinity?" Kronos frantically asks.

Hermes smiles, blood pouring from his mouth.

Arien

Rushing into the throne room, I'm greeted by the sight of Hermes's falling to his knees, Kronos standing above him with the bloody Scythe. "No!"

Kronos kicks Hermes toward the door and walks back to his place beneath the throne of Zeus. I kneel beside Hermes and lay his head in my lap, whispering, "Why did you have to do that?"

"I . . . I forgive you for what you did." Tears well in his eyes, and he coughs up blood. "I forgive you."

I shake my head, defiant against his forgiveness. "You don't need to. You get to hate me forever, remember?"

"No. You gave me a chance at an honorable death. At a chance to become a good man again. I have a lot of mistakes to make up for, like killing the marine. This might help me do that. We gods say we evolve with humanity as an excuse. The truth is some of us are just dicks. I was a dick. I'm going to see Nancy again."

"But you said without a mortal soul, you can't."

He points at where he'd dropped the Helm of Darkness, explaining, "I made a new one. I did what you never could. I chose to die." Lifting his Caduceus, he hands it to me. "It's in here. Do whatever you please with it. Just don't bring me back. Give it to someone worthy of it, like I never was." His body tenses suddenly as he adds, "Thank you." He grows cold, falling still, his life leaving him.

Kronos smirks slightly and caws, "He has no idea what he's getting himself into. But he will benefit from Utopia, none the less. You could have made Utopia better for him, but you chose the gods. Why?"

I slowly stand and turn to him, shouting, "Because they're willing to do things like this for love." I motion at Hermes's corpse, adding, "And you never will be."

Kronos nods in acceptance. "You're probably right because a death like that is pointless."

I heft the Caduceus and stare at it, declaring, "It wasn't pointless."

"Give that to me. His divinity has one last purpose to serve."

Cocking my head, I send the Caduceus away in a dark flash. Kronos smiles at my defiance as I say, "You won't defile him."

Without anger or hatred, completely at peace, I attack. We cross blades, weaving around the room in fierce conflict. Without the power of the darkness or prayer, I'm no match for him. He effortlessly weaves through different speeds of time during the fight, sometimes slowing me enough to land a blow. It's clear he doesn't want to kill me, though. He kicks me and sends me flying into a throne, where I collapse to the ground. "You can stop fighting me. It's not too late," he offers.

I spit out blood, slowly standing. "Shut the fuck up.

Kronos shakes his head, accepting my fate. He's done playing, so he quickly disarms and impales me.

"Arien!"

I grunt and fall to my knees, horrified to see Clara rushing into the room. Kronos gives her a curious look and locks me inside a time bubble which holds me suspended in the air. He starts walking toward Clara; she tries to flee, but he freezes her in time and grabs her.

Kronos looks up at me in disappointment, asking, "Is she why? Why you won't let Utopia save humanity?" He pauses for a second and sighs. "Pity."

He stabs her in the gut with the Scythe. I try to scream, but my body won't move or react. All I can do is let a single tear slip free. Clara collapses to the ground and attempts to drag herself away from Kronos, despite the blood she leaves behind.

My eyes turn black as anger overwhelms sadness.

***

I appear in the endless darkness and collapse to the ground, sobbing. Erebus's screams echo through my head; I struggle to focus through the noise.

Suddenly, I'm back on the Israeli hill with Timorian. He stares around in awe before turning to me to ask, "How art thou doing this?"

"A bridge once built. I need your help now. He's going to kill Clara."

"I cannot. Tis hard enough to think on mine own."

"I need you to do this. Please." Tears stream down my cheeks as I beg.

"I am sorry."

"No. I . . ." I trail off and collapse, the sound of Erebus screaming echoing through my head. "I can't." A shockwave explodes out of me, hitting Timorian and sending him flying, the darkness absorbing into him.

I'm in the insane asylum, strapped down to an operating table by golden ropes. The shapeshifter with Brittnie's face pours more Eitr on a knife and stabs me, making me scream and thrash.

My eyes turn black, and I start chattering like a mad man.

***

Kronos looks down and smiles slightly at Clara as she leans against a pillar. He crouches in front of her and strokes her cheek, whispering, "You've got heart. You shouldn't fight. You're going to a better place. Utopia is waiting." She spits out blood all over Kronos's face. He sighs, raising the Scythe to finish her.

His arm freezes, suddenly not his own.

Kronos attempts to end Clara again and again, with no success. He turns to look at his arm in shock; the darkness of Erebus runs through its veins, turning the skin black and making him drop the Scythe.

I'm released from the time bubble, dropping him to the ground. Kronos stands and turns to stare at me, crying, "What have you done to me?"

Clara passes out from blood loss as I charge for the last time, my eyes black and full of insanity.

JED MORGAN

Drawing the bear-bone-knife, I try to stab Kronos, but he avoids the blow. I light the knife with the phoenix, making it glow before attacking again. I manage to knock him to the ground and stab him in the chest.

Kronos screams, the phoenix fire burning through him. I reach up to touch his face, the darkness flows down my arm and into him. He moans and thrashes, the insanity taking him. He gnashes his teeth and screams, "No!" With a quick jab to my gut, he sends me flying back.

632

EPILOGUE

<u>Arien</u>

Blackness fades from my eyes; I slowly sit up, rubbing my aching muscles and swore head. Freezing, I stare around at my surroundings in surprise. I'm laying atop a pile of rubble at the base of the massive wreck of a Ferris Wheel that's crushed half of the building I'm in, vines growing through the wreckage.

I pull myself to my feet and start to climb up the wreckage toward the roof. Climbing into the ruddy sunlight, I stare in shock at the long-destroyed city of London, the same scene that I'd seen in the Council of Fire's pool of lava. I fall to my knees, tears filling my eyes.

THE END

Arien will return in:

Odyssey of a Phoenix:

APOCALYPSE THEN

Coming Soon

CPSIA information can be obtained
at www.ICGtesting.com
Printed in the USA
LVHW092028120621
690064LV00005B/798

9 781637 285053